Caged Between the Beta & Alpha

Book 4 of The Alpha Series

MOONLIGHT MUSE

Caged Between the Beta & Alpha

To all those who believed in me.

Acknowledgement

I WOULD LIKE TO THANK Monroe Thirty for her advice and support with the couple Taylor and Zack, and for helping write the chapter "Getting Closer". Thank you.

Prologue

TWO YEARS AGO...

LIAM

*A*NOTHER BLOOD MOON, ANOTHER mating ball, another goddamn reminder that I had a mate, yet she wasn't mine. How the hell do you come to terms with that?

Dad was adamant that I come to this mating ball as we were off from the Alpha training regime for a week. No one really knew that I had found my mate already, and I intended to keep it that way. What kind of Alpha had to share his mate? What Alpha would accept that? I couldn't.

That night was still raw in my mind. I wouldn't ever forget that both Damon and I wished each other luck before stepping into the hall, hoping that we would find our mate. The Blood Moon occurred twice a year, and it was only on that night that one could find their mate if they were of age. I still remember walking in, seeking out the woman I had loved for years, praying that she was my mate, and she was.

My heart raced when I laid eyes on her in that sexy black dress, only for my best friend to also claim her as his. 'Mate,' we had both said in unison. I couldn't handle it, so I had turned and left.

I sucked in a sharp breath, glaring at the glittering lights, unable to ignore the smell of expensive fragrances, wine, and food that hung in the air, laced with a hint of sex and sweat. It all made me sick. I didn't want to be here; I wasn't meant to be here. It just brought back the painful memories of that night. I downed my twentieth-odd glass of vodka. It wasn't enough. I needed something stronger.

Fuck this. I had shown my face, I wasn't going to stick around any longer. I pushed through the crowds, not caring for anyone here. Right now, I felt like I was in a place I didn't belong. I grabbed a glass of wine from a passing waiter, feeling detached.

The flashbacks of that night and the familiar pain in my chest returned with renewed vengeance. I hated the entire fucked up situation. Overnight, I lost the woman I loved and my best friend. Wallowing in self-pity wasn't going to change shit, though. It was what it was. I made the decision.

I felt relieved when I stepped out into the bitter cold. It was raining, and the moon was hidden behind a layer of thick clouds. Sounds of snickering and swearing made me glance up to see a group of young werewolves gathered in the corner, popping some pills. They tensed when they saw me. I knew they knew who I was.

"H-hey, Alpha…" one of them muttered, shoving something into his back pocket. I walked over, grabbing two of the bottles of alcohol from their stash.

"Give me a couple," I said. They looked surprised at that.

"Umm, you sure? You will get super…" he trailed off the moment my eyes flashed a dark magnetic blue, and he quickly took the packet out of his pocket. I could sense their fear and nervousness, but I didn't care what they were up to. I just needed a fucking break from my own head.

"One or two?" The teen asked.

"Make it three."

They exchanged looks, and I held my glass out. He dropped three in. I turned and walked off, watching the pills fizz in my glass. Taking a deep breath, I knocked it down in one go, enjoying the exhilarating rush that travelled through me as I tossed my glass to the ground. The sound of it shattering was pleasant in my ears. I bit the cap off one of the cheap bottles of beer and downed it, not caring that half of it splashed all over me.

Memories of long ago seeped into my mind like a poison spreading through every vein in my body, unable to shut them out.

"Mates…. You're my mate… Liam…"

"Please, man, don't do this…. Don't hurt her… give her a chance…"

"Liam, the moon goddess paired you three for a reason…"

"Don't tell me what I should or shouldn't do!"

"Liam, please…"

My eyes blazed, and I threw the bottles to the ground. Shards of glass hit my face, but it didn't bother me. My chest was heaving with anger.

Unable to ignore the voices in my head, I frowned, walking without any aim towards the woods, the voices only getting louder in my mind.

No, it wasn't my fault. I gave her a chance… that night, after talking to Kia, I thought I'd give it one shot… one fucking shot to talk to her… because, in the end, I'd fucking loved her since I first started noticing the opposite sex. But I couldn't get through the mind link. I thought she might have fallen asleep, so I left her three messages… I confessed my love for her. She was all I fucking wanted. Was it that fucking much to ask for?

Those three messages had been read, but she didn't bother replying, so what was the point? Clearly, I wasn't fucking enough.

My vision swayed as the drugs took effect. It felt good. The pain in my chest had eased, and I felt like I was floating. Wouldn't it be ideal to stay like this forever?

Was that the sound of water? I kept walking, the floor becoming uneven. The rain began pouring down faster, and my tux was fully drenched. I took my jacket off, staring up at the sky as rain poured down on me. Where was my reprieve?

That was when I saw her sitting against a tree, staring up at the moon that was masked. My heart beat like a thousand drums, my head ringing, and the distant, vague thought of whether this was real or not crept into my mind. Tears streamed down her cheeks as she gulped down some beer. Her black and pink bob looked longer, and she looked even smaller than I remembered, her hand shaking as she tossed the empty bottle aside and grabbed another.

Raven.

Was this real? Was she really here? That didn't make sense… this pack was at least a thirty-minute run from the Dark River Pack, wasn't it? It's a dream… a perfect hallucination.

I stepped closer; her delicious scent hit my nose, only adding to the high that I felt. She suddenly froze, staring up at me, looking shocked, before she clambered to her feet.

"Raven?" I whispered.

Was it really her, or had I imagined her up? She looked even more beautiful than I remembered. There was something in those unique coloured eyes of hers. Something that called me to her. I closed the gap between us. Was that her heart thudding wildly?

She opened her mouth to speak, and I felt the fear knot in the pit of my stomach. *Don't reject me, fuck, don't do it...* A fucking nightmare that I woke up to so fucking often. I reached over and placed a finger on her lips, shaking my head. My vision blurred. I didn't care if this was a dream or if I was mistaking someone else for her... I needed it, needed her.

She tugged my hand away.

"... with you?... okay?"

What was she saying? I wasn't sure. All I could focus on were those wet, plump lips of hers that moved silently. This was a dream that wasn't going to happen in reality. I brushed her soaking hair off her forehead, cupping her face.

"You're beautiful," I whispered.

Before she could even reply, I leaned down and pressed my lips to hers in a passionate kiss that sent sparks rushing through me. The sweet taste of her mouth mixed with alcohol was perfect. Goddess, she tasted perfect. Yeah, those pills worked... this felt good...

A soft whimper escaped her as I relished the pleasure that wrapped around me like a blanket. Fuck, this felt so good.

The moment she began to kiss me back, her intoxicating scent enveloping me, all control I had was gone. I wrapped my arms around her tightly, kissing her like there was no tomorrow, and maybe there wasn't. Whatever this was... would be gone...

A soft, tantalising moan left her lips, and I groaned. Fuck, *fuck*, she tasted so good. Everything darkened for a moment, and I staggered but held on to her tightly, pinning her against the nearest tree. She gasped when her back hit the bark, and I took the chance to plunge my tongue into her mouth, but that just caused her to free herself and move her head away.

My stomach knotted, and I realised this was it... she was denying me once more. Her heart was pounding, but... I forced myself to look into her face. Was that rain or tears?

I ran my hand over her body, grabbing her breast, wanting to kiss her again when she tensed, suddenly grabbing hold of my hands and moving them off of her. The pain of rejection fucking stung. My mate did not want me.

"You're not yourself. Listen to me," she whispered, cupping my face. Sympathy and sadness shone in her eyes, and I frowned. I didn't need sympathy. I hated pity.

It's not Raven… fuck, there's no way she could even be here. It's just the effect of the pills. I jerked away from her, stumbling slightly. She moved towards me, but I raised my hand.

"Don't come near me. I don't fucking need you," I hissed. It hurt so fucking much. I turned away, ready to walk, when she grabbed hold of my shirt from behind. My eyes flashed, and I pulled free. "I said leave me the fuck alone!" I growled, shoving her off roughly.

I heard a thud, making me pause and turn back to her. In my dark haze, I looked at the woman I had knocked to the ground. Yeah, my mind was playing tricks on me… she couldn't be Raven, no matter how much I thought it was. I turned away, forcing myself to shift before breaking into an unsteady run and vanishing into darkness…

Returning Home

RAVEN

THE SUN BEAT DOWN on my skin, a thin layer of sweat coating it. I jumped back as the two men attacked simultaneously.

Three…

I twisted around, elbowing one of them in the neck and hearing a satisfying crunch.

Two…

I flipped backwards, grabbing onto the other one, and slammed his face forward into the ground.

One…

With a final spin, I slammed my fist into the first man's nose. He grunted as he staggered backwards before falling to his knees. I smiled slightly, breathing hard as I stepped back.

"And that is how you do it," I said, looking at the group of teens who had been watching. They didn't say anything, just stared in awe at the two giants who were flat on the floor.

"That's amazing," one of the boys muttered.

I crouched down and took off the weights I had tied around my ankles. I heard a clap and turned to see Aunt Angela walking over. Her long hair was in a high ponytail, and she was dressed in jeans and an oversized top.

"Once again, impressively done, Raven," she said, passing me a water bottle.

"Thanks. I think everyone is getting too predictable," I said, standing up and taking it.

"Or you're just incredible. You got an email from Elijah," she said quietly. My heart skipped a beat, and my nerves began to brew in my stomach.

"Really?"

"Yes, he has officially asked for you to come home and take the position as Head Warrior."

Return home… my stomach twisted as the memory of that night returned to me… the night the moon goddess led me to my mate but made me lose everything.

I walked hand in hand with my friend, Kiara. My nerves were kicking in big time. The mating ball was being held out in the open, lit up brightly with dazzling lights. My eyes were looking for two familiar faces, our other two friends, Liam and Damon. Would one of them be my mate?

When I started searching for them, the most delicious mix of scents hit me, and I froze. My chest pounded as I inhaled deeply.

Roasted walnuts, fresh rain, spiced cinnamon, and honey… scents that drowned me… scents that were faintly familiar…

"Oh, hey, boys," Kiara said with a smile.

I turned slowly, my mouth still full of the chocolate that I had been eating, as I stared at the duo before me. My heart was thumping wildly.

Liam looked mesmerising in a grey suit, and Damon looked just as hot in black. Both oozed sexiness, and if I thought they were handsome before, Goddess, they were complete invites now! Both of their eyes were glowing and fixed on me with a possessive look that made my core knot and my wolf howl in happiness.

"Mate," they both said in unison.

Mates. My mates… I have two mates…Goddess…

The boys' gazes snapped to each other. I couldn't speak as I gauged their reaction. Damon looked stunned, and Liam… Liam's reaction pulled at my chest; accusatory, hurt, and disappointed. He stepped back, running a hand through his locks, which had been styled in a quiff moments earlier.

"I… how can she be both of our mates?" He asked in his husky voice.

"It happens," Damon's deeper voice answered.

My heart was pounding as I looked at Liam. No… he would not reject me, would he? He shook his head, stepping back.

"I can't do this."

His words cut me like a knife, and I felt the pain of his indirect rejection destroy me. He turned and walked off, not even giving me a chance to say anything.

"Liam!" Damon called after him. He looked at me for a second, his blue eyes softening before he ran after his friend.

No matter what I said or thought, the pain of Liam's rejection stung worse than being doused in wolfsbane. I realised at that moment that I wouldn't be happy with one... I needed them both... they were both a part of me...

"Raven?"

I snapped out of my thoughts as the wind blew through my deep purple and blue ombre hair as I stared at my aunt.

"Sorry, I spaced out." I gave her a wry smile and turned to the kids. "Lessons out for today!"

"Yes, ma'am!" They hurried off, chattering amongst themselves, discussing the match or certain moves, and I smiled at the two men who were picking themselves up.

Both Aunty and I fell in step as we walked towards the packhouse. Despite being an outsider, I had been welcomed here with open arms. For the last three years, this had been my home.

"Are you going to tell your parents about the position?"

"No, I'll tell them when I return if Uncle El hasn't already done that," I said, drinking the water.

Aunt Angela nodded, and I knew her strained relationship with Dad only got worse with each passing year. They barely talked, and when they did, they clashed.

In the beginning, Aunt and her mate, Cassandra, had moved to the Blood Moon Pack, but when Cassandra's mom became ill, they moved back to the Dark River Pack and decided to stay on. I knew Dad was the reason for that, but I never really asked what the final push had been because I, too, had my secrets, and I didn't want anyone prying in my life either.

"You earned this, Raven. I have watched you train endlessly, push yourself further and harder. If anyone does, you are the one who deserves this. I am proud of you. So, when you go back, I want you to keep your chin up and face them all."

Our eyes met, and I wondered how much she knew or assumed, but I simply gave her a faint smile. I would do exactly that because I wasn't weak.

Two days later, I arrived home. Dressed in a pair of black jeans, a purple halter top, a leather jacket, and boots, I stared up at the huge wall that surrounded the pack grounds. When did they build this?

I approached the gate, driving slowly, and lowered my car window as the guard looked me over. A small smile crossed his lips, and I gave him a bright one in return.

"Raven Jacobs!"

"The one and only," I said, flicking my hair dramatically.

"Damn, girl! I never knew you were coming! We were only expecting the new Head Warrior… holy shit, it's you?"

"I guess so."

"I won't keep you waiting then, the Alphas are waiting."

"Nice seeing you again."

I drove through, trying to keep a cap on my emotions. I wasn't ready for this. Goddess, I didn't think I'd ever been ready for this, but I had to do it. I parked up outside the packhouse, and, to my relief, it was only Uncle El and Aunty Red.

"Raven. Welcome home," Aunty Red said, coming over the moment I got out of the car and hugging me tightly. I hugged her back, inhaling her familiar, comforting scent.

"Thanks, Aunty Red," I said before Uncle El gave me a tight hug.

I felt a wave of sadness wash over me. He had lost the last of his closest friends two months ago, and I knew it must be affecting him greatly. I looked up at him, my heart skipping a beat as I looked into those cerulean blue eyes, eyes that reminded me of Liam's.

"I haven't actually told the boys your back," Uncle El said, smirking. "Think they'll be happy."

"I'm sure," I said, faking a smile, very aware of Aunty Red watching me keenly. "But I think I'll see them tomorrow; I need to go home first."

"Ah, yes, I did tell Haru and Kimberly you were back," Aunty Red said.

"Great."

Later that night, I was back home. I didn't unpack because I wanted to ask Alpha El if I could relocate to the packhouse, and, boy, I think I was making the right decision to do so. The tension was suffocating. I stirred my food on the plate, not even wanting to eat the orgasm-inducing dishes my mom had cooked with the tension.

"So, Alpha Elijah told me you applied for the Head Warrior position," Dad remarked, his jaw clenched and his sharp brown eyes looking at me calculatingly.

"Yeah, I did," I said blandly.

"You didn't once consider to, I don't know, ask my opinion?"

"Umm, why would I?" I raised my eyebrows. Was he seriously going to still do this?

"Raven, don't speak to your dad like that," Mom said quietly. I pursed my lips, taking a deep breath to calm myself down.

"Too much time spent around Angela. It was bound to happen," Dad added, drinking some of his fresh orange juice. Oh, for real?

"Dad, how can you blame Aunty for this? Like, for real, she has nothing to do with my decision!"

"That attitude is a mirror of hers," Dad hissed.

"I'm not even arguing!" I exclaimed, trying to keep my voice calm. "I'm just saying you can't blame Aunty for my decision or anything. This is all me."

"Well, it doesn't really look good. So, you chose a position where you are going to prance around amongst men. Befitting." That stung.

"Dad… it's training. I am not going to go put on a strip show for them, and even if I did want to become a stripper, you really shouldn't be putting me down like that."

"Wow, see that, Kim? Your daughter wants to be a hooker or stripper or whatever."

"Dad! I…"

I shook my head. I couldn't believe he was so backward. I stood up, placing my knife and fork down slowly, not wanting him to lash out at me for being loud.

"I worked my ass off to become something, to be accepted to such a position… Dad, it's no small feat. Head Warrior means I am one of the strongest fighters of this pack. I worked day and night to prove that I'm good at something. Aren't you at least a little proud of me?" I asked, glancing at Mom only for her to look away. That hurt, even when my mates abandoned me, I wished that I at least had my mom's arms to cry in, but I didn't…

"Proud? What's there to be proud of? You're just another Angela, another disappointment." He stood up, slamming his fork onto the table and stormed out of the room.

"Haru…" Mom said, rushing from the room. I stared at the table, swallowing hard.

A disappointment… a failure… unwanted… useless…

I took a deep breath, smiling faintly. It was okay. I was used to it all.

☙❦❧

The following day, I went for a run before showering and getting ready in black flared pants and a black high-neck top, and applying my signature dramatic eyeliner with some mauve lipstick.

Opening my window, I climbed out, not wanting another run-in with my parents. Making my way to the packhouse with the memory drive of some training regime and ideas I had, I headed towards the Alpha's office. I slowed down when a familiar scent hit my nose. Roasted walnuts and honey. A scent that enveloped my entire body and made every nerve stand on edge.

Goddess, please don't be around.

With each step closer to the office, my heart was fluttering with nerves. The last memory I had of Liam tugged painfully at my chest, and it was pretty difficult to breathe. Raising my hand, I knocked on the door lightly before I opened it and stepped inside, stopping dead in my tracks when my gaze fell on the man in the leather chair. His legs were crossed at the ankles as they stretched out in front of him, his elbow resting on the armrest. He was flicking through a file when his eyes snapped upwards, piercing into mine.

He was so much more handsome than I remembered him. He was dressed in a fitted black tee that did nothing to hide his bulging arms. Goddess, he was even bigger than before. A tattoo covered his upper left arm, peeking out from his sleeve. His hair was styled in a quiff with a short back and sides, and a scar went down his right eye. How did he get hurt?

But the thing that was most different about him was the coldness in those cerulean eyes. Gone was the warmth that one would have associated with Liam years ago. He cast one glance over me, sending another gutting stab of pain through me. Unwanted, but I didn't care. I would live for me, mates or not.

When it was clear he wasn't going to speak, I stepped up to the desk.

"I'm sorry, I thought Alpha El would be here. I have some training regimes I put together," I said as his eyes were back on his file.

"Why were you looking for him? As your Alpha, shouldn't you be running it past me?" He asked coldly. My Alpha?

"I…" He cocked a brow, leaning back.

"Don't tell me you took this position without even knowing who the Alpha is… nice." His sarcasm irked me, but I said nothing. No one had told me. Surely Kia and Aunt Angela knew…

"Sorry, I guess I'm a bit behind on the latest news. Congratulations on becoming Alpha. I will pray that you can be half the Alpha your dad was," I said, trying to hide the sarcasm in my voice and displaying a fake smile. His eyes flashed a deep magnetic blue, and I felt his anger rising.

"You will remember whom you're talking to," he said icily. "Besides, I don't have time for some stupid training plans. Discuss them with the Beta." My heart skipped a beat at the resentment in his voice when he said Beta.

"Okay… sorry for wasting your precious time, Alpha Liam." I didn't care that my voice sounded bitter.

I didn't wait for a reply. Turning and leaving the office before he could even reply, I slammed the door shut behind me. I stormed down the hall, feeling my irritation growing. *Great, now I have to face Damon…*

Although he hadn't been as bad as Liam, he didn't really make an effort with me either. On my birthday and on Christmas, he would send a message, and when I got injured pretty badly last year, he had sent a small message, but that was it...

That night, not only had I lost my mates before I even got them, I had also lost two of my best friends. I wish I hadn't gone to the ball; if I didn't nothing would have changed between us.

I was so lost in thought that I didn't realise where I was going when the sound of a woman's breathless giggle made me stop in my tracks. I looked ahead to see a gorgeous woman. I vaguely recognised her. She was leaning against the wall, her hand on a man's chest as he leaned over her slightly, speaking quietly; a man whose scent of spiced cinnamon and fresh rain hit me like a storm, and with it, the gutting feeling of pain twisted in my stomach.

His head snapped towards me, and I stared into the deep, powdery blue eyes of Damon. He quickly moved away from the woman, and that stung. Why would you do that unless your intentions weren't innocent?

"Raven… I didn't know you were back…" he said quietly, his voice sending a rush of tingles through me.

"Yeah, I came last night. I, uh, Liam told me to discuss the training regime with you. Umm, take a look at them when you have time and see what you think," I said. Walking over to him, I held out the memory stick.

He looked down at me, and I saw the concern in his eyes. His heart was racing a little as he took it. I let go quickly, not wanting to touch him. Despite it all, I felt a sliver of guilt go through me for what happened two years ago. I looked away, giving the woman a small smile. She really was gorgeous…

"Hey," she said.

"Hi."

"Robyn," she introduced herself, holding her hand out.

"Raven." I took her hand, and she gave Damon a smile.

"Nice to meet you, girl."

"You, too." I turned and walked off, not wanting to spend another minute here. With each step I took, my smile faded away. Crap, I was meant to talk to Liam about the packhouse… I didn't want to ask him again. *Maybe I'll go visit Azura and ask Aunty Red…* That sounded like a better plan!

I quickly left the packhouse, feeling a lot better as I hurried through the woods towards the house that stood a little away from the rest of the pack, a home where I had most of my childhood memories. An escape from the tension and gloom of my own house.

My heart skipped a beat as I looked around, remembering how I would sit with Kiara under that tree near the river… remembering Liam smacking my ass and calling me bitesize… Damon's smile when he got everyone some fresh doughnuts or something.

Don't think about them.

The saddest thing was, with time, my wolf became disconnected from me too.

I rang the doorbell, and I heard the sound of laughing.

"Mama! Someone door!"

I smiled, hearing Azura's voice. Damn, I shouldn't have come empty-handed! I even got her a gift from up north. Goddess, my memory was ridiculous!

"Raven, come on in," Aunty Red said the moment she opened the door.

"Don't mind if I do," I replied stepping inside and closing the door behind me. "Azura!" She moved away, looking at me wearily. "I'm Raven."

"Waven?" She said. I smiled and nodded.

"Want me to give you a piggyback ride? Or I can be a horsy?"

"Ooo, piggyback!"

I smiled, *Atta girl*. I picked her up, spinning her around and making her giggle. She looked a lot like Indigo, and I wondered how Aunty Red coped with that. I kissed her forehead gently before I placed her down on the worktop. Aunty Red seemed to have been busy cooking.

"Did you end up seeing the boys?" She asked. My heart skipped a beat, and I swore she knew something.

"Yes, I did," I said smoothly, pulling faces at Azura, who burst out laughing.

"That's great. You'll stay for lunch? I'm making Sheppard's pie."

"I don't mind." I hadn't eaten and I couldn't cook... "Umm, I came because I wanted to ask for something," I said, perching on one of the bar stools.

"Sure, what is it?"

"I wanted to ask if I could put in a request for a room at the packhouse," I said, hiding the nervousness I felt inside. She frowned, looking at me, concerned.

"Angela told me you would probably ask for that. Is everything okay?"

"Yeah, I just think I'm old enough to have my own place," I said, shrugging lightly.

"Sure, I'll get someone to set up a room for you there. Liam stays there, too, since he's come back..." She frowned, and I tried not to react to the mention of Liam. "He's changed a lot, hasn't he?"

"Yeah..."

"Surely there must be a reason behind that," Aunty Red said lightly, popping the tray into the oven before she turned to me, her sharp eyes fixed on me. "Would you have any idea what that reason might be?"

Down by the River

RAVEN

*H*ER QUESTION TOOK ME by surprise, but I simply shrugged. "I haven't been around for ages, Aunty." She smirked.

"You girls do know, you and Kia," she stated. "But if you don't want to tell me right now… that's fine, but nothing stays hidden. Besides, I have my assumptions." Trust Aunty Red to say that. She wasn't dumb, I had to give her that. I really didn't want to ask her what she assumed because I might give something away…

"Aww, well, I hope you do get to figure it out. Aunty, if you ever need this little gummy bear babysat, I will do it willingly. She is so adorable!" I smiled at Azura, who was playing with my hair, and I wouldn't deny that I liked it. She was so cute.

"Oh, I'll definitely hold you to that," Aunty said, smiling.

"Good," I replied, thinking this place felt so much better to spend time at.

⟡

Night had fallen and I was in my room. My stuff hadn't really been touched since I had gone and I was doing a clear out. I would bin what I didn't want, and what I did, I'd pack it up. I needed to tell Mom and Dad about me moving, too… but the moody look on Dad's face had put me off. I didn't want more drama.

I put on some Disney classic songs, singling along to 'Colours of the Wind' as I began on my wardrobe. Some of this stuff was way too childish.

My phone rang and I hurried over to it, smiling when I saw Kia's name pop up on the incoming video call.

"Kiki!" I said, answering it. "Ahh, and my babies!"

Kiara laughed as she sat there, feeding one of them. Goddess, those two were gorgeous. They were about three months now and were like two little dolls.

"I thought I'd video call whilst I'm feeding. How are you?" She asked. I plopped onto my bed and smiled.

"I'm great, I am going to start training tomorrow. I saw Liam and Damon, both are doing great, and I asked your mom about moving to the packhouse," I ended with a whisper. She smiled gently, but from the knowing look in her eyes, I knew she saw past my façade. Over the years, Kiara had become so much more observant. She didn't fall for my fake smiles.

"You are brave," she said softly. "You got this."

"Thanks, hun," I whispered.

"I'm going to try to visit in a few weeks' time," she said.

"Really? I can't wait to meet these two munchkins." I had only seen them when I visited her pack with Aunt Angela.

"I'm sure they want to see their aunty, too," Kiara replied with a small laugh.

We sat there, chatting and talking like we did often enough. Although Kiara had an entire pack to run, and as queen it was more than just a pack, we still found time to talk to each other and it felt good. After a good half hour, we said goodbye and I returned to clearing out my wardrobe. I had just finished when a panicked voice came through the link.

Someone's been killed down by the west side of the river! The man sounded fearful, and my own heart was thudding at his words.

An influx of voices came through the link as I rushed to my window. Opening it, I jumped out, not even realising I was barefoot until the stones beneath my window poked into my feet, but I was too worried to care as I rushed down towards the river.

It's covered. No one panic and stay in your homes, Liam's cold voice came through the link, sending a rush of warmth through me. I missed it… missed the mind link with them…

I ignored his command as I approached the spot, slowing down to see several men standing around looking at something on the ground. My heart thumped as I stepped closer. Damon was there, and when I approached, he looked up. I didn't miss the way he looked me over. It was then that I realised I was only in my leggings and a crop top. My heart thudded, but I tried not to focus on him as I stepped closer.

"Don't come closer, Raven." His deep seductive voice made me stop. "It's not pleasant."

"I can handle a lot more than you think," I said, quietly stepping forward.

But maybe not. The face of the body had been cut from ear to ear and the eyes had been removed. My stomach churned and I clamped a hand over my mouth feeling sick.

"The teeth have all been taken too," the Delta, Zack, said quietly. I knew him as he was only slightly younger than I was.

"What the fuck happened?" Liam's voice came from behind us. I turned to see him shirtless, and clearly, he had been in the middle of a shower.

He glanced at me, his frown deepening when he looked at Damon before he brushed past us both. Sparks flew through me at his touch and my breath hitched. Fuck...

"Scour the area. Did anyone witness anything? Who found the body?" He asked, his Alpha aura whirling around him.

"Ralf... his brother," Zack said, motioning to the side with a jerk of his head.

I turned to see a boy around twelve or thirteen sitting under a tree, shaking, and rocking himself. An Omega child. Shit, why the hell was no one comforting him? I hurried over to him and sat down, wrapping my arms around him.

"Hey, it's okay, I got you," I whispered, seeing his hands tangled tightly into his hair.

"It's not true. It's not true," he muttered repeatedly. Liam approached, looking down at him.

"When did you find him?" He asked. The boy continued to mutter, not even hearing Liam, who frowned.

"Can't you see it has affected him greatly and you're asking questions?" I asked icily. His gaze snapped to me, and his eyes flashed.

"And didn't I say to everyone to stay inside?" He growled.

"You did." *But that doesn't mean I would listen!*

I looked away from him, feeling two pairs of eyes on me, but they could look and get as mad as they wanted because right then, I was more concerned about the kid who had seen his brother in that horrifying state. I knew his face would haunt my dreams too.

"Scour the area, track any scent that lingers here, and I want anyone whose scent is here to be brought in for questioning. Maybe they saw something... this doesn't look like a normal killing."

"What was the cause of death?"

"No fucking idea..."

"Maybe poison. Request an autopsy," Liam muttered.

"There's no strange scent from him..."

"Wait, what is that?" Damon said suddenly, making me look up sharply as he bent down and took a piece of paper from the man's hand. The group of men fell silent, and I looked at them curiously.

"What does it say?" I asked. No one spoke, and I frowned. "Tell me." Damon turned, his eyes meeting mine, and he frowned, holding it up.

"Who's next?"

❧❡❧

Last night, the image of the Omega Ryan kept replaying in my mind. I couldn't sleep or anything. The way his mouth had been cut open, his teeth ripped out, and no lingering scent? It was creepy. I shuddered, unable to remove that image from my head as I got dressed for training in a sports bra, leggings, and an oversized hoodie before grabbing my portable music player and jumping out the window. It had always been my way out, and although my parents hated it, if Dad wasn't so controlling, I wouldn't have to. Okay, maybe I still would.

I walked to the training fields, and, to my dismay, Damon was standing there, dressed in baggy bottoms, a black vest, and sneakers. He was leaning against the wall and looking at the throng of people who were training. My heart skipped a beat as I looked him over. He really had gotten even more handsome over the years, if that was even possible. He had lost the boyish looks he once supported; his face was more angled and rugged. His eyes snapped towards me, and my heart skipped a beat when I thought I saw them flash pale green as he looked me over. He gave me a small smile and pushed himself away from the wall.

"Hey," he said, looking down at me.

"Hi, are you here for the training session?" I asked, taking out the bandages for my hands and beginning to wrap them up. I didn't want to just stare into those eyes of his.

"Partially… we didn't get to talk properly yesterday. I, uh, congratulations on the new rank."

I glanced up at him. Had he been thrown off by seeing me yesterday? I wasn't sure if it was that or that I saw him step away from Robyn a little too quickly.

"Thanks."

"I checked out the training plans. I liked them, a lot. Especially the wolf vs human sparring. That's something we haven't actually done, and your points were pretty neat." I nodded and began doing my stretches. We hadn't spoken much in three years, so why should that change now? "Welcome home, Raven." His voice was soft, and I didn't miss the sadness in it.

I looked up at him sharply. My chest felt painfully tight. As much as I felt his sadness was genuine, we both knew his duty to his Alpha and the bond he had with Liam clearly outdid what we had. That did hurt, but I couldn't blame him. Was that why the moon goddess gave me two mates? In hopes that perhaps one might just accept me? Or her having sympathy for someone like me? All I had wanted was someone who would love and cherish me.

"Thanks," I said, giving him one of my fake smiles. He smiled back, and I turned towards the group. They were all young adults, and I knew they were all full-fledged warriors.

"Alright, everyone, those butts should be warmed up, and you all should be standing to attention!" I called loudly, my eyes skimming them all; taking note of those who were already standing, those who were clambering to their feet, and those who were distracted. I would target them at their weakest point and see who did best.

"As you all know, I'm Raven, the annoying girl who was a little too loud. If you have forgotten me, then I'm Raven Jacobs, the new Head Warrior, which means it's my job to make sure you are all at your best. The Blood Moon Pack is one of the strongest packs in the country, and with it, we are always in everyone's line of sight. Things may have calmed down since the battle that occurred three years ago, but there is always the chance of danger. So, we need to be in the best shape possible."

Last night came back to me, and I frowned, wondering how anyone had gotten into the pack grounds in the first place.

"We've never had a female lead warrior... like ever," some guy murmured, and a few nodded.

"Hey, she's -" Damon began, but I raised my hand. *I got this.*

I raised an eyebrow.

"I don't think my capabilities should be defined by whether I have a penis or not. If anyone has doubts about my capabilities, you are welcome to come and face me one on one," I said clearly.

"Make sure you treat her with respect," Damon added, a warning clear in his voice. I looked at him, my eyes flashing.

"Thank you, Beta Damon, but I do not need anyone to defend me." Guilt flashed in those eyes before he nodded.

"I will leave you to it," he said quietly.

I moved away, turning on some music on my portable player and letting the upbeat music travel around the area. I was serious about training, but that did not mean we couldn't have a little fun.

"Okay, I want everyone paired with the person behind them!" I clapped my hands. I could feel his eyes on me, but I ignored him. I needed to focus on my job. "Name?" I asked, pointing to a young man who was loitering along the side.

"Owen," he replied, sounding bored.

"Pair up with... Taylor, isn't it?" I said, looking at a well-built man who stood to the side. He smirked and nodded.

"Surprised you remembered my name, babe." I smiled at him. Oh, I remembered Taylor; he used to live right next door to us.

"You were an annoying neighbour," I said. He grinned.

"I am not pairing up with the loser," Owen spat, making both of us look at him.

"Hey! That was an order, and I won't tolerate you calling your teammates names!" I snapped, walking over to the six-foot-tall guy. I didn't know what issue the two had, but I was not going to tolerate it in my sessions.

"You may be the Head Warrior, but you don't have control over what leaves my mouth," Owen said, smirking cockily.

"Well, Owen, I'm the boss here, and unless you want me to put on Disney songs for the rest of the session, I would listen because I swear, everyone will want to kill you after listening to Let it Go on repeat for the next hour or so."

"It would make this training what it is, a joke," he muttered.

"Want to spar against me, Owen? Maybe I'll show you I am not here to play," I said coldly, my eyes flashing.

He clenched his jaw, but it was clear he wasn't stupid enough to challenge me. Everyone knew this position didn't come easily. I had gone through my training and proved myself for this post. Taylor stepped forward, and I gave him a curt nod.

"Let's see what you got, you fucking wuss," Owen muttered tauntingly.

I got this, Raven, Taylor's voice came through the link just when I paused.

Well, break his damn nose before I do it, I said. Regardless of the outcome of the sparring, he was going to get punished for his attitude.

I walked through the ranks, making small changes to posture and giving some input and advice as I went. I had just reached the front when Owen's irritating voice reached me.

"Come on, faggot, show me what you got."

That was my fucking snapping point. I spun around, breaking into a run, my eyes blazing as I raised my fist, punching him across the face, not caring when he hit the ground and rolled over several times before he came to a stop. Everyone was staring at me. Blood dripped from my fist, and my eyes blazed. My chest was thumping wildly, and my anger was raging around me as I stormed towards the man who was coughing up blood.

"I will *not* tolerate homophobic shits," I growled, raising my fist, ready to punch him once more, when Taylor walked over.

"Hey… it's fine," he said.

It's nothing new for him.

"It isn't fine," I hissed, shoving Owen back to the ground.

It is. He just has issues, Taylor said through the link.

It may not have bothered him, but it sure bothered me. Taylor was one of the nicest guys I knew growing up, and I could not believe him being gay was the issue here.

"I want fifty laps around the pack grounds, and if I see you flunking, I swear I will take this to the Alpha," I said coldly, turning away just when he spoke.

"Wow, it seems like someone can't control their temper tantrums," he muttered.

Oh boy, you asked for it now.

Spinning around, I was about to punch him when someone grabbed my arm and yanked me back. The rush of sparks that coursed through me told me who it was before their scent even registered. He pulled me back, punching Owen across the face and knocking him out cold.

"Whoa..." Taylor muttered.

The group fell silent, and, oh, I was so mad.

"I will not tolerate disrespect," Liam growled, glaring at the mass of warriors.

"I was handling that," I said quietly, doing my best not to lose my shit because I swear by Selene and the power of her moon that I was this close to snapping! He looked at me sharply, as if he was not expecting me to say that. What did he want? Me to thank him and gush over his heroic move? No, I don't think so. "If you are done, Alpha. Can I carry on?"

He frowned, turning to me. I glared at him before his gaze dipped to my lips. Not bothering to say anything, he stormed off. I shook my head. This was not over because as much as I didn't want to see him more than necessary, I needed to make it clear that I was not going to allow him to get up in my business.

Oh, blue eyes, you are so done for!

Fire & Ice

LIAM

*I*RETURNED TO MY OFFICE, trying not to let her anger get to me. I don't know what I was expecting... seeing her again, those gorgeous eyes of hers. Was this mate bond only affecting me? Damon seemed to be doing fucking fine too. Was it just me suffering like this?

Jealousy reared its ugly head at that thought. *Don't fucking let shit get to you, Liam.*

I sat back. With the killing that happened last night, the pack was a little restless, and everyone had heard about it. Although I made sure everything carried on as usual as best as possible, the tension was clear in the air. The uneasiness of what happened the night before still lingered on everyone's minds. It wasn't something we were just going to forget overnight. The darkness that had settled over the pack was palpable, and I could sense the unease and fear clawing its way through the pack link.

I really wanted Dad and Mom to go away for a week or so. Dad needed it, and with all of this crap, I think it was time for him to just relax. Even if he didn't let on, he was going through a lot, and I wanted him to know he could count on me. They needed a break. I would offer to babysit Azura... but I wasn't sure I'd manage that, considering it would be an entire week or two.

On top of that, I needed to get to the bottom of the murder. We had no leads at all. Last night, I had tried to track and trace any scent that lingered, but there was nothing. I frowned and was trying to figure out what I needed to do next when there was a knock on the door. My eyes flashed, and my mood just got darker when a familiar scent hit my nose.

Enter, I said coldly.

The door opened to reveal none other than Damon. Now, why the fuck did I need to see him?

"Hey." I raised an eyebrow.

"What do you want?"

"I thought I'd just come to see if there's anything I could do. What happened last night, it's damn shocking, and I know -"

"If you have nothing useful to say, leave. I have things to do," I said coldly.

"Liam, can we just talk about this?"

"Didn't I just say take a fucking hike?" I said, my eyes flashing.

He only frowned deeply. Well, if he wanted to be fucking stubborn, I didn't have time for his shit. Flipping open my laptop, I decided to ignore him instead, but he didn't take the fucking hint.

"Liam… I am your Beta. We need to work together and at least try to get on. We can't carry on like this," Damon said quietly.

"Yeah, well, shame that it is what it is. Unless, of course, you want to step down from your position?" I said, knowing I was being a fucking jerk. I didn't really care though; thanks to him, I couldn't even call Raven mine.

"I am not going to step down, especially when there is stuff going on. We need to just stop ignoring each other, man," he said exasperatedly.

"There's a difference between ignoring and just not wanting to see your fucking face," I shot back, standing up. He was getting pissed off, but he was staying calm. I wondered what it'd take for him to get the fuck out of my face.

"It's been three years, Liam… can't we set our differences aside and -"

"Are you for real, Nicholson? Differences? She may just have been a passing thing for you, since we all know you jump from one infatuation to the fucking next, but for me, she was the one I wanted from day fucking one, so don't think three or ten years will change that," I growled, walking up to him and looking him in the eye. "Understood?"

"Understood," he said, clenching his jaw. "One question though, why aren't you going and getting her? This is about her, right? Then why not go after her?"

"Why don't *you* reject her?" I shot back.

"I wanted us to work something out. You ran away from her, Liam, you hurt her." I smirked coldly. I knew I did, but I didn't trust myself or my mental state back then.

"There was a lot worse I could have done. Walking away before I said or did something I regretted was the smartest choice. The only disappointing thing is now that I'm back, I'm stuck having to see your damn face," I said coldly, my eyes burning with anger. He clenched his fists, and I knew I had pushed him enough. "What's wrong? Finding it hard to control your temper?"

"Fuck off, Liam, this isn't a fucking joke. I get it! I get that you fucking loved her since day one! But the moon goddess made this decision! Don't you think either of us rejecting her would hurt her?" He snapped, shoving me back a little.

"I don't think hurting her is something you really care about, right? I mean, you had no issue -"

"Stop it, man!"

"I'm fucking stating facts. You wanted me to talk to you, I'm fucking talking," I said coldly, shoving him back.

His eyes flashed, and I don't even fucking know who jumped forward first. I aimed a punch at his jaw, only for him to block and throw in his own. I slammed it away and was about to grab his collar when her delicious fresh, floral scent hit my nose. I felt her small hand on my chest, pushing me away from him as she forced herself between us.

"What are you two doing?" She growled, flinching when I refused to let go of Damon, crushing her between us. I slammed him against the desk, my hand tightening on his neck with Raven still caught between us.

Suddenly, I was fucking aware of her stomach against my dick and those fucking sparks. All three of our hearts were fucking racing. The storm of emotions that surrounded us, anger, rage, irritation, confusion, and so much fucking more, spread like a toxic poison.

I was the first to pull away, tugging Raven away from Damon. I didn't want him anywhere near her, only for her to yank away from me, her eyes filled with rage as she glared at both of us.

"You both need to get your shit together. Neither of you is fucking man enough to do anything but whine? Seriously? We lost someone yesterday, and today you two are acting like goddamn high-school-aged pigs!" She snapped.

"I came here trying to sort this shit out," Damon said, frowning. He didn't look at me, and I knew I had really pissed him off. Good.

"Well then, sort this shit out! Liam, for your dad, show you can be a responsible Alpha. If you two are still hung up over the mating ball, well, then get over it and move the hell on. It's been three years. What happened back then is in the past. I'm enjoying my life, you should enjoy yours! Reject me, or if you want, I can do it …"

The very thought made my stomach churn. *Don't fucking say that.*

She shook her head, looking between us. I thought I saw a glimmer of sadness there, but I wasn't sure. She was about to leave the room when she paused at the door, turning and looking at me.

"As for Owen, I can handle him myself. I don't need a man to fight my battles. Let alone either of you two," she said coldly.

I didn't have any fucking right to feel like shit over her words, but I sure as fuck did. Her parting left a heavy silence in the room. I glared at Damon.

"Get out," I told him coldly. He shook his head in defeat, stopping at the door and glancing back at me.

"Well, if you ever decide to get your head out of your ass, you know where I am," he said, slamming the door shut behind him.

I frowned. Despite him fucking disrespecting me... we went way back. He had been my best friend, like a fucking brother to me, until that night. Fuck, why did it have to happen? I dropped onto my seat, placing my feet on my desk and running a hand through my hair.

He had lost his father in that final battle, he had been through a lot, but I had shut everyone out. Now that I was back, I knew, deep down, I did need to tolerate him, but that meant I needed to do something about us, about Raven, about everything. I couldn't keep shutting it all out because it wasn't helping anyone.

I had a pack to run. He was my Beta, and she... she was meant to be my Luna. My wolf stirred, and I pondered on their words. Do something about it... what I wanted to do was take her and claim her as my mate. I was an Alpha, and I was done stepping down. I had given them a chance... and now that we were back to square one, it was high time I took what was mine for the claiming.

It was evening. Mom had mind-linked me to stop by, only for me to realise she had tricked me.

"Me alone with her?" I asked, looking at the little pumpkin.

"She's a good girl, Liam," Mom said dismissively. Dad smirked.

"Yup, a real angel," he added, not sounding very convincing. "We could do this tomorrow?"

"No, baby, we are going," Mom said firmly.

They were going to visit some lone wolves who lived near our pack territory. Considering the murder, Mom and Dad decided to check in on them, and here I was stuck with my little sister, Azura - Aunty Indy's girl that Mom carried.

"Wiyam, I be good." She blinked those large blue eyes as she assured me.

No, that was an alarm bell right there. No kid who says they will be good will be good... and I had seen the devil, Dante. Kids were scary... don't mess with them.

"So, since you're visiting a few elderly wolves... you should be home by eleven?" I asked. Mom smirked.

"Yes, hopefully. Relax, Liam, but I do think we will be back before eleven. It's only six pm now," she said, glancing at the clock on the wall.

"Anything I need to know..."

"No, just keep her away from the sugary stuff. There's pizza in the oven. It should be done in twenty minutes. Eat, get her ready for bed, tell her a story, then she should knock off," Mom said, grabbing her jacket before meeting Azura with a hug and kisses.

The fact that it had been just me and my twin, Kiara, growing up, we didn't have younger siblings, so seeing Mom like this was strange. Not to mention, I wasn't here for Azura's entire three years of life. Was she really going to sleep? Didn't look like it...

"Oh, yeah, Liam, Raven was saying she wanted to move to the packhouse, get something sorted for her. I was going to tell you earlier, but then with everything that happened last night, I wasn't in the right headspace," Mom said just when she was about to step outside.

"Sure," I said emotionlessly.

Raven at the packhouse? Fuck, that's where I was staying... I couldn't deal with this, not when just looking at her made me want to go over to her and claim her as mine.

Once the door shut after Mom and Dad, I looked at the little girl who had her finger shoved up her nose.

"Don't do that. It's gross," I said, crouching down in front of her.

"Do what?" She said, taking her finger out of her nose and... fuck! She ate it!

"Azura, pumpkin, you don't eat that."

"Eat what?" She asked. Did she not realise what she had just done?

"Okay, let's wash your hands..." She frowned as I tugged her into the kitchen. Goddess, kids were gross.

"I washed my hands after I went to the toilet, Wiyam."

"Yeah, but you were picking your bogeys," I said, lifting her onto the worktop.

"Oh, they're tasty," she giggled. I cringed. Were we this disgusting as kids?

"Alright, how about we get the pizza and watch a movie while you eat?" I suggested. *Hopefully, she'll fall asleep in the process.* I took a tray out, grabbing what we needed before taking the pizza out.

"Wiyam, can I have Coca-Cola?" She asked as I took a can from the fridge for myself. *I'm sure Mom said no sugar...*

"Aren't you too little?"

"No, I'm allowed half a can," she said, looking up at me with those large eyes of hers. That's true. We were werewolves. I guess pups were more tolerant to caffeine how adults would be to alcohol and stuff.

"Ah. Okay." I shrugged, grabbing another one and placing it on the tray before carrying it to the living room. Placing the food down, I put a slice on her plate and asked what she wanted to watch on TV.

"I watch... that!" She pointed at a show and I put it on for her. Sitting back, we began eating and my mind wandered to Raven and what she had said earlier. It was hard seeing her, yet all I wanted was to see her all the fucking time. The urge to just pull her into my arms and tell her to fucking accept me and me alone was so damn strong, but I didn't really deserve that, not after how I shut her out for the last three years.

What are the autopsy results? Anything yet? I asked Zack through the link.

Poison, but the traces are so light we barely picked them up.

"Wiyam, coke!" I opened the can, putting a straw into it for her as I held it out to her distractedly.

Of? What did it include?

They still working on that, but there were traces of silver and wolfsbane mixed in too.

Get pictures of the mutilation, exact time of death, and whatever else you can before returning the body to the family...

So soon? Zack sounded surprised.

His parents wanted him back... if we can't get any more information from him, then it's best we accept their wishes. There were a few scents around him, I'll question those wolves tomorrow.

Okay, Alpha.

I closed the link to see Azura sucking on the straw-like there was no tomorrow. Shit, how much did she have? I pulled the can out of her iron grip to see it was practically empty. Well, fuck.

"That was tasty," she said in awe, shivering from the fizziness before she gave me a big smile. "I love coke."

A sliver of doubt entered my mind, and I wondered, *Was she really allowed it?* I got the answer to that ten minutes later...

"I want to go out! Let's go for a walk, Wiyam!" She was hyper and acting like a rabid dog right now. "Wiyam!" She pulled at my sleeve before biting it and pulling my arm. "Out!"

"Mom said bed, Azura," I said, about to pick her up when she tensed, and I could hear her pounding heart. Shit, she was going to cry! "Okay, fine, let's go for a walk."

Seriously, I hoped this wore her out. I guess I couldn't really complain. What idiot gives a kid coke just because they said they are allowed it...? Me. That's who.

Two hours later, Azura still had not settled down. She was beyond upset, crying and asking for Mom. I did text Mom, who said they had a little ways to go, but, thanks to an accident, they were in the midst of a traffic jam, and they couldn't really abandon the car.

At first, Azura had been happy and running around, but then she started getting upset, and now she was out of control.

"I want Mama!" She was screaming in my arms. Damn, kids were loud.

"Look, Azura, how about we go back home -"

"MAMA!!!"

Fuck! My ears were going to burst. She was trying to escape my hold, hitting my shoulder as she cried. If Mom saw the state she was in, she was going to castrate me.

"Need help?" Raven's sexy voice came from behind me.

My heart skipped a fucking beat as I turned towards her. As much as I wanted to refuse her help, I couldn't handle the pup in my arms. I didn't reply, watching her. Her eyes weren't on me but on Azura, giving her a gentle smile, although she was crying too much to even pay attention. With Raven, she always had that smile on her face. You wouldn't think she had snapped at me in my office earlier by the look of her now, but it was one of the things I loved about her most growing up.

She had been a lot smaller than Kiara, but she always held her hand, taking care of her, making sure she never stumbled or hurt herself. Raven had always been tiny, but the size of her heart was fucking huge. She always held such a positive and loving energy around herself that even when I sensed her sadness, it would be accompanied by the biggest smile.

She began walking over to us and I looked her over appreciatively. She looked good in an oversize off-shoulder knitted jumper dress that draped off one shoulder, and she wore thigh-high boots underneath.

I couldn't fucking speak, trying not to look at her thighs that were drawing my attention.

"Eyes up here, Westwood."

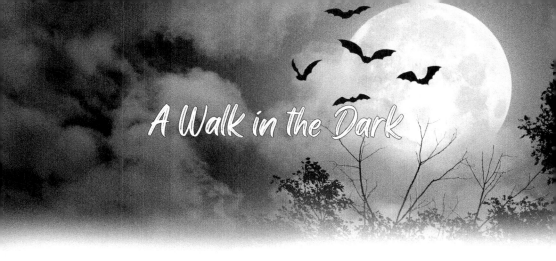

A Walk in the Dark

RAVEN

STAYING IN WAS SUFFOCATING, so I did what I did best: I jumped out of the window and left. I was enjoying the fresh air; it was slightly chilly, but nothing that would affect us werewolves. I wrapped my arms around myself while walking along, glad I wore my suede thigh-high boots. I was just walking around the edge of the trees when I heard someone crying hysterically. A child at that.

Concerned, I followed the sound only to find Liam wrestling a very upset Azura. Her face was a dark pink and she looked distraught.

"Need help?" I asked without thinking.

He stiffened before turning to me sharply. Goddess, he was so annoyingly handsome… even while wrestling an angry, red-faced, cute little chibi. My stomach fluttered nervously, feeling undressed under his intense, sharp gaze that still threw me off. It was like he was a stranger I didn't recognise. His eyes were burning into me. I saw them darken when they fell on my bare thighs. This stupid oversize top was ridiculously short, but I wasn't expecting to run into him… I resisted the urge to tug it down and instead remained smooth.

"Eyes up here, Westwood," I remarked.

I walked over. Reaching up, I took Azura from his arms. I hated this… the way my heart pounded when he was near. Oh, how I wished I could turn back time to when I had him as a friend without this bond. My heart clenched painfully, and I instead focused on Azura, who began to fight me, screaming.

"I want Mama!"

"Mom and Dad have gone out and won't be back for a while," Liam added, only making her cry louder.

"Awe, Zuzu. Look, Mama will come back soon!" I said, wrapping my arms around her tightly, only for her to scream harder. I ignored the big broody boy behind me, turning and carrying her towards the playground.

"*Mama!*" She screamed.

"What did you do?" I asked Liam, not even bothering to turn, knowing his eyes were fixed on me.

"Nothing. She had some fizzy drink, and then she wanted to come out, so I brought her... then she just got upset," he said in a broody tone. "It was probably the caffeine."

"I doubt it," I said, sitting down on the swing. I placed her on my lap, wrapping my arms around her, her head on my shoulders as I began rocking her gently. "She was probably overtired. I'm sure it must have been her bedtime."

"Yeah."

The hinges of the swing next to me creaked when Liam sat down gingerly. I had never seen him sit on it before. When we were younger, he used to say he was Alpha and was too big for it. As I got older, I realised he used to just do it to let Kia and me take all the turns whilst Damon would push us... memories that pained me.

I stroked Azura's back, rocking her gently, her crying decreasing despite the fact that she was still sniffling. The last time I had come here was that fateful night...

His beating heart, his scent, and his long legs were unmissable even when I tried to ignore him.

"Shall I take her?" He asked after a moment.

"Let her settle down," I said, kissing the top of her head.

"She's falling asleep," he murmured.

I looked up at him, our eyes meeting, and that same crushing feeling tightened inside. The distant whimper of my wolf rang in my head. This bond between us... I knew I needed to end it, but rejection would hurt both parties. If we were to do it, we needed to do it discreetly and then make sure we had time to recover. There had been one promise I made to myself that when I came home, I would reject them both, but with the scary murder and all the other stuff that had been going on, the timing just didn't feel right.

I sighed heavily, hearing Azura's heartbeat become steady.

"You actually got her to sleep."

"All she needed was a little comfort," I said, standing up and holding the child close to me.

"Guess so…" He reached over, trying to untangle her from me, when she sobbed in her sleep and tightened her hold on me.

"I'll put her in her bed."

He didn't argue, I had a feeling he was glad to have her off his hands.

"With what happened last night, you shouldn't be out alone."

"I'm strong enough to handle myself," I replied. I did not need any of that. I was not a baby.

"Yeah, but with the killer still out there –"

"I'm a big girl, Liam," I cut in.

"Yeah? From what angle?" My eyes flashed and I turned, glaring up at the giant.

"Just because we are not all overgrown turnips doesn't mean we aren't strong enough to take care of ourselves," I said, shaking my head in irritation.

He cocked his brow but said nothing as we reached the large house in the woods. The lights were glowing welcomingly as we approached. He unlocked the door, and I stepped inside, not even realising how cold it had been out there. I led the way up the stairs. I had no idea which one her room was…

Seeming to understand my hesitation, Liam brushed past me, making my stomach flutter, and opened the door opposite Aunty Red's room. I entered, and I had to admit her room was so cute, decorated in a unicorn theme with pinks, rose gold, and white. The wallpaper had clouds on it set against a glittering pink background. The bedding and curtains were covered in unicorns, and the pink fairy lights that made the room glow made me want to just jump onto the bed and sleep in the cutesy room.

I carried her to the low bed; it was small, yet big enough for my five-foot frame if I had wanted to fit. *See, I could totally sleep here.*

Liam moved the covers back, and I slowly lowered her to the bed. She began crying, and I winced. Oh, crap.

"Shh, I got you," I whispered, slowly lowering myself onto the bed and patting her back.

"Damn…" Liam muttered, "Kids are so hard."

He reached over, taking Azura's shoes off. Her leg was draped over my waist. His arm brushed my thigh, sending a shock of sparks through me, and I couldn't stop the gasp that escaped me. His eyes snapped to mine, changing to a dark magnetic blue. My heart was thundering but I looked away quickly, trying to de-tangle Azura from my neck.

"I'll get her," Liam said, slowly taking her hands from around my neck, only for her eyes to flutter open, and the start of a new wave of tears threatened to spill.

"It's okay, I'll hold her," I said, not looking at him. "It's near ten anyway; Aunty should be back soon."

"You sure?"

"Yeah," I said, not missing how his gaze fell on my bare legs.

Goddess, please tell me my ass is not peeking out cheekily. He looked away smoothly, and I was glad because otherwise, I was going to give him an earful. I reached down and unzipped my boot, pulling it off before reaching for the other. I was about to remove it, trying not to disturb Azura when Liam reached over, unzipping and tugging it off for me, making my heart thump louder. His piercing eyes met mine as he dropped the boot on the floor and leaned closer.

I clung to Azura tightly, despite trying my best to remain indifferent. However, I was not able to stop the fear from consuming me when I realised that I was still vulnerable to the bond. His closeness, his scent, and those dangerously sexy eyes were a thirst trap I couldn't deny. I turned my head away, closing my eyes.

I can't see you. Go away.

I thought I heard a small chuckle, but I wasn't sure, when I felt the blanket cover us both, and then I felt him move away. I was not able to breathe until he left.

"I'll be downstairs," he said quietly before he shut the door after him.

My eyes flew open, and I let out the breath I didn't know I was holding. I had always wished Liam was my mate, but the older I got, I had that connection with both Liam and Damon. Like there was just that chemistry there. I know someone would say choose one and reject the other, but it hurts to think of doing that to either of them. Just the thought made my wolf whimper and my chest tighten. It wasn't even my own fear; it was the fact that I would have to hurt one of them, and because of me, I might destroy their friendship completely. I didn't want to be that woman, not now, not ever.

That was why I never approached them, not wanting to be the reason for their bond to break. Deep down, in the beginning, I hoped they'd accept it and we could be happy no matter how unique our situation was. Yet, as time passed, I stopped thinking about that and made it clear to my wolf and to myself that I didn't need a mate.

I eased out of Azura's hold, quickly replacing a large plushie in my spot. She hugged it loosely, but she was in a deep sleep, and I was sure she would stay that way now. Yay!

I picked up my boots slowly and padded to the door, exiting silently. I shut the door as quietly as possible behind me, stepping back when I suddenly knocked into someone. I gasped as a hand clamped over my mouth. Before I could even register the shock of sparks that coursed through me, I had flipped him over my shoulder, slamming him to the ground, one hand going to his neck as I pinned him down with a knee to his chest. For the first time since my return, a small smirk of amusement crossed his lips.

"Nice move, bitesize," Liam said, making my heart race at that old nickname. His eyes roamed down my body until they lingered on my bare legs, but it was his next words that made my eyes fly open. "And an even nicer view," he whispered seductively, the back of his fingers ghosting down my left thigh. The moment those sparks rushed through me; my eyes blazed as I looked at the man beneath me.

"And this is an even nicer punch!" I growled quietly before punching him square in the nose. The sickening crunch as I broke it satisfied me. How dare he!

I jumped off of him, resisting the urge to kick him in the balls, and instead kicked his knee, hard! How dare he!

Grabbing my boots, I turned and stormed down the stairs. My heart was thundering with a hundred emotions, but above all, I felt angry. How could he ignore me for three years and think he could just start flirting with me?

Nope, not happening. I am not a pushover. I will not–

"Raven!" He grabbed my arm just as I reached the front door, and I was annoyed to see he had put his nose back in place.

"Don't touch me, Liam," I hissed, yanking free.

"I'm fucking sorry," he said, raising his hands in surrender. "That was out of line." He looked away, and I shook my head. He didn't get it. What was out of line was being out of my life for three years and then pretending it never happened, that he never left or hurt me.

"Good night, Liam."

"It's not safe -"

"I said good night," I said coldly, glaring at him, daring him to argue with me. He frowned, clenching his jaw.

"Night," he replied coldly, and his walls were up once more.

I turned away, walking out of the house, not bothering to put my shoes on. I knew he couldn't follow me with Azura sleeping upstairs, and I was glad. I made my way back towards my parents' house, not bothered by the wet floor or the dirt that was sticking to my feet. The rain was still falling lightly, and the sound of distant animals could be heard.

That night, two years ago, I went with Cassandra and Aunty Angela to a neighbouring town. They had been on pack business with the pack that was hosting the mating ball. Aunty had asked me if I wanted to attend, but I told her no. As per the rules, one ball per year was hosted by King Al and the other by a different pack. The memory of me finding my own mates had been too damn painful. I had left my hotel room and gone to get some drinks.

Then, to my surprise, Liam had shown up. I was beyond shocked. I had never expected to see him like that. He had been so drunk. For someone who didn't want me and had left me on the mating ball, he had stolen my first kiss that night. Although my entire body had wanted to give in to him, I couldn't, not when he was in that state and not when I was tied to not one but two mates. I couldn't do that to Damon. I had wanted to help Liam that night, but he had just pushed me away...

It made me wonder how many women those two had been with - my so-called mates. I smiled gently; life truly sucked at times.

I reached home and decided to climb through my bedroom rather than face my parents. Once inside, I pulled my dress off and wiped my feet on it before shutting and locking the window. I walked over to my wardrobe, taking down one of the suitcases that I hadn't unpacked knowing I was going to leave this place anyway.

Opening it up, I rummaged around until I pulled out Liam's suit jacket from that night. I caressed the fabric, my heart clenching at the way he told me to leave him alone. I sighed heavily, shoving it back into my suitcase and replacing it on top of my wardrobe before deciding to take a shower.

I had just showered, pulling on my high-waisted panties, a sports bra, and some baggy pyjama bottoms before I returned to my room, towelling my hair. I shut the door behind me when a sudden scent hit my nose, and I froze. Yanking the towel from my hair, my eyes snapped to the bed where none other than Damon was sitting, flicking through one of my books. He looked up, giving me a small smile.

"Hey."

My heart thundered, and I glanced at the shut door behind me. Why was this happening today? I didn't want to see my mates, yet I ended up seeing both of them.

His eyes trailed over me, and I realised my trousers hung low, showing off the band of my knickers. His eyes flashed for a moment before he looked away smoothly. I hated how these two pigs were looking at me like I was a piece of meat, yet neither had the audacity to even care about how I had felt years ago, the way they left me feeling broken and unwanted. Now that I had pulled myself together and became strong, they decide to come back into my life? *No, I don't think so.*

"Hey, so, can I ask why you are in my room?" I asked, raising an eyebrow, trying to ignore how hot he looked. I had broken one pretty nose tonight; I wouldn't mind adding another to that list.

"I thought we could talk… without anyone interrupting us," he said quietly. Reaching behind him, he held up two packets of fizzy sweets and a bag of doughnuts. "I brought a bribe?" My heart skipped a beat, but I tried not to let it get to me. Walking over to my wardrobe, I took out a black vest and pulled it on.

"Who let you in?" I asked. Deciding to keep myself busy, I began to clean my room up a little.

"Your mom. I was going to come through the window, but it was locked. Your dad left, too, so I decided to just come through the front door." He said, laying back on the bed.

"Hmm." Thank Goddess, Dad wasn't around. I didn't need more drama. "Raven, can we talk?"

"You want to talk now? Go ahead, I'm all ears," I said, picking up my wet dress that I had left near the window.

"First of all, I want to apologise for everything. Nothing I say is going to justify that night, but you have got to remember Liam is my Alpha. I fucking see him as my brother. I needed him to be okay with this, with us."

"I get that, Damon, but it doesn't excuse that you both were so caught up in how you both felt that you didn't even once consider how I was probably feeling. I never wanted two mates, but I was given them, yet you both cut me off without a second thought," I said. My voice was emotionless, and I made sure to hide every emotion that I was feeling. Emotions that were eating up at me every time I thought of them…

I glanced up at him, feeling his intense gaze on me. I hated seeing the guilt in his soft blue eyes.

"I know… I just didn't know how the fuck to react," he muttered.

"Tell me, Damon, why now, then? Why are you talking about it now?"

"I tried to talk to Liam again. That didn't go well, you saw that. I wanted to know what you wanted…"

I almost laughed. What I wanted? Did what I want even count?

"Care to explain?" I asked.

He stood up. After taking a doughnut out of the packet, he walked over to me and held it out. I took it, not wanting to be a diva, but it did not mean he was forgiven.

"We both want you, but clearly, Liam doesn't want to share… what're your thoughts on this?"

Three years too late, Damon. Three fucking years too late.

"I don't want either of you anymore," I said quietly.

"Don't say that. Liam's stubbornness -"

"Tell me something, Damon, who is Robyn to you?" I asked suddenly.

He seemed to have been struck. His face drained of colour, and he looked shocked. It was clear he wasn't expecting that, and I felt a stabbing pain in my chest, as if something was squeezing my heart painfully. He looked away, and I saw the guilt in his eyes. I got my answer and as much as I wanted to say it didn't hurt, it did.

"She's…"

The urge to smile and tell him he didn't need to explain almost overtook me, but, no, I needed to know, and I didn't need to make things easier for either. They were big boys.

He ran a hand through his gorgeous curls and exhaled. My chest constricted painfully. I knew whatever it was, and I was not going to like it.

"I didn't think you'd come back like this or…"

"You don't need to justify anything, Damon, just answer the question," I said, biting into the doughnut, trying my best to act normal, trying to prepare myself for his words as I tossed a few items of clothing into the washing hamper.

"We have been kinda dating for the last year or so."

My heart thudded. The whimper of my wolf in the back of my mind stung as sudden pain and betrayal overwhelmed me.

"I'm sorry, Raven… I just… I don't know how it happened, we just had a connection…"

Don't, Raven… he was never yours… fuck, he was never yours.

"I am sorry," his whispered apology came, but I couldn't comprehend anything anymore.

This pain… I thought I could handle it, but… fuck, it hurt so much.

Fuck. Fuck. Fuck.

Trying my Best

DAMON

I SAID IT. THE REASON behind the guilt that had been fucking consuming me since she returned... I needed to tell her anyway.

Her porcelain doll-like face stayed in its perfect mask, yet I could feel her pain, hear her racing heart, and see the way her fingers trembled ever so slightly on that doughnut. Her eyes, which were so fucking unique and perfect, looked at me, but there was no hatred there.

Dammit, I fucking hurt her... I'm fucking sorry, Raven.

"Raven?" I whispered closing the gap between us, but she suddenly snapped out of it, despite her erratic heartbeat.

"Thanks for telling me. Do you have anything else to say?" She asked with a blank face. I frowned, slightly concerned. Shit, I didn't know what to say... fuck it.

I stepped closer, pulling her tightly into my arms. I didn't care if the doughnut went everywhere; I just needed to tell her I was fucking sorry. Her fresh floral scent and the beating of her heart soothed me. That emptiness I felt inside seemed to lift, and I inhaled her scent for a split second before she pulled away roughly.

"Don't touch me without my permission," she growled. "Now get out."

I fucking felt like shit, but it was a little late for that. If anything, I needed to fix things with her, with Liam...

"Sure, I'll leave, but I am sorry, Raven," I said softly, reaching for her face only for her to move away from my touch.

"Out," she said icily.

I looked into her gorgeous face; her pouty lips with that cupid's bow... her slender frame with those small round breasts of hers and curved hips. She was fucking perfect...

I turned away, wishing things could have been different. There was one more visit I needed to make tonight, and I wanted to get it over with. I left her room, shutting the door behind me, walking down the stairs to see Raven's dad just step inside.

"Oh, hey, Mr Jacobs," I said, giving the man a smile. He gave me a small smile.

"Damon, it's nice to see you here. Catching up?"

"Yeah," I replied with a small smile. He nodded in approval.

"What's that?" He asked, looking at the jam on my T-shirt. I smirked.

"Raven being Raven," I said. He shook his head, chuckling.

"She never changes."

"It's what's great about her," I said, giving her mom a small wave. I glanced back up the stairs, but she hadn't followed. Well, could I blame her? I had fucking hurt her...

I left the Jacobs home and headed towards the packhouse where Robyn lived. I did need to tell her about Raven, and I knew even this was going to fucking hurt.

I entered. It was pretty silent. I could hear a few of the teens in the game room, and I first went to the laundry room to grab a random clean shirt. I didn't really care who the hell it belonged to. I then made my way upstairs to her room, knocking lightly on the door.

"Who is it?"

"The big bad wolf," I replied.

Her soft laughter followed before the door was pulled open and she pulled me inside, kissing my lips softly. Instead of pulling her into my arms and kissing her back, I moved back, casting her a small smirk. I shut the door, not missing how she was observing me.

She was gorgeous, with warm brown skin, dark brown eyes, and her black hair, which was currently open. She was so different from Raven, yet still beautiful. She wore a crop top and tiny shorts that left her thick thighs and sexy booty on display.

"Okay, I know that face. What's up?" She asked, concerned, before she tugged me to the bed.

I looked at her calculatingly. *How the fuck do I do this?* I needed to end it. For a moment, I remembered how I felt when Kiara ended it with me. Although we had just been sex partners, it had fucking hurt…

"I, uh…" I ran my hand through my hair as she sat next to me, crossing her legs and placing a hand on my arm, concern clear in her face.

"Damon, you're scaring me, babe." I stared ahead, my hands folded in front of my mouth.

"You know Raven?" I began glancing at her. She frowned, a pout on her plump, lush lips.

"Yeah?"

"Well, it's just that… we need to end this," I muttered.

She looked confused for a moment before her heart thudded in her chest, and I knew she understood what I had just said. I stared into those chocolate eyes of hers, seeing the hurt in them.

"I… I never knew you and Raven were ever… something… I know you talked about her, but I thought you were just friends…" she whispered, staring at her hands and examining her painted nails. I reached over and took her hand.

"She's my mate," I said quietly. Robyn's eyes closed, and I heard her suck her breath in.

Shit. Thanks to my selfish reasons, I had hurt two women…

She slowly pulled out of my hold, moving away from me on the bed. Her chest was rising and falling heavily, but despite that, she was trying to hold herself together.

"Shit, Damon… she's your mate? How long have you two known?"

"Three years," I said quietly. Her eyes flashed and a frown creased her forehead.

"So then why did you even get involved with me?" She asked, unable to hide the hurt in her voice.

"I fucking don't know… I just… you fucking made me feel better," I said, feeling like shit. She nodded, placing her forehead in her hand.

"Fuck… that day she returned, no wonder you pulled away; I thought for a moment it was strange. Then I thought maybe you two had dated, but then I thought no… I thought you had shared stuff with me… but I never thought she was your mate. What must she have fucking been thinking?" She snapped, jumping off the bed. She grabbed a pillow and whacked me across the head. "You are such a fucking dickhead!"

Okay, maybe I deserved that.

"I'm sorry, Robyn," I said softly.

"You should be apologising to your mate, not me!" She shook her head. "Get the fuck out, Damon, we are fucking done."

"Yeah, that's why I came -"

"*Out*!" She snapped, and I got up. I was literally losing someone else important to me.

I didn't say anything. Casting one last glance at her, she had her back to me, but her heart was racing erratically. I left, closing the door behind me but I didn't move, leaning against the wall and closing my eyes.

Silence. For a few minutes, there was nothing until I heard the stifled sobs coming from inside the room. I closed my eyes. She had waited for me to leave...

Dammit... tonight, I had hurt two women I cared for. I really need to talk to Liam, like fucking for real. We needed to sort our shit out, one way or another.

I headed home, unlocking the front door. I stepped inside; the television was on, which meant Mom was still downstairs. I walked through to the living room, sighing inwardly when I saw the empty beer bottles that were strewn across the floor. As for my mom, she was sitting on the couch, her arms wrapped around her legs. *Fuck, another bad day.* I should have come home sooner.

"Hey, Momma," I said brightly, picking up a few bottles when I entered the room. She looked up, her heart thundering as she looked around, as if searching for something. A shaky, hopeful smile crossed her face before it vanished.

"Damon, where's your dad?" She asked. I placed the bottles down and dropped onto the couch next to her. The smell of alcohol was strong in the air and Mom was a mess.

"Momma... Dad ain't -"

"He must have gone to Elijah. He called him, right? Is he coming home soon? You know, as Beta, he has a lot going on," she said to me, her voice shaky, her eyes blurring with tears.

It fucking hurt. Nearly three and a half years had passed since Dad was killed, but Mom had never overcome it. She lived in the past, and with each passing year, I was losing her a little more. Sometimes she was numb, sometimes she thought he would return, sometimes she completely refused to believe he was gone, sometimes she'd just relapse into breaking down and sobbing over his loss all over again.

"He'd want you to go to bed on time and get your rest," I said quietly, smiling at her. She shook her head.

"No... no, Aaron prefers me waiting for him. Why are you lying?"

"Okay, I'm sorry. Come on, how about you wait upstairs for Dad so I can get this place cleaned?"

"Wait, is that him?" She suddenly perked up, staring into the corner, unseeing.

The loss of a mate... some people recovered, but many weren't able to survive it. As for Mom, she was a shell of the person I once knew. Losing Dad that night, having to take up that position as Beta, being here for Mom, trying to hold it all together - it wasn't fucking easy... I know I'm not doing a good job at it.

Then everything with Liam and Raven, losing the last of my closest friends in one go had been another hit, and the fear of losing either forever had messed me up. The fear that if I went after my mate and Liam did something in anger scared me. I kept away from her. I didn't make the right choices, I know that, but what was I meant to do?

Uncle El had lost his dad, sister, and best friend, then Liam wanted to leave, and he hadn't wanted anyone to know about our situation. I couldn't stress his parents out anymore by telling them the truth, so I stayed fucking silent, hoping things would get better. But every message I sent, he refused to acknowledge. Every email, every social media DM, he blocked me from everywhere.

That's when Robyn had entered my life and we began to connect, soon she became that happy place for me. Even if it didn't complete me, it took the edge off the gaping hole in my fucking chest.

Mom began sobbing, bringing me out of my thoughts as I pulled her into my arms, rocking her gently.

"Your dad's not talking to me, he's not replying, he blocked me from the link!" She sobbed, clinging to me.

"I know... it's going to be okay," I whispered, stroking her hair.

When would things become easier?

Party at Night

RAVEN

*S*HIT, I WAS RUNNING late!

Last night I hadn't been able to sleep properly, and I was paying for it! I ran down the stairs three at a time, jumping down the final six, and was about to rush to the door when Dad stepped out of the living room.

"This is a house, and I would appreciate you treating it like one," he said curtly.

"I'm getting late, sorry!" I said, hurrying to the kitchen and going to the fridge to grab a water bottle.

I was about to reach for one when Dad snapped the fridge shut, missing my fingers by inches. I moved back, my heart skipping a beat as I looked at Dad, who was staring at me with a cold glare on his face. I glanced at Mom who turned her back on me and busied herself with making breakfast.

"This is my house and as long as you are living under my roof, you will obey my rules and that includes letting boys into your room."

"Okay." I didn't have time for this. I needed to ask Liam or Uncle El when I could move out… I needed out.

"Raven!"

"What?"

"Are you showing me attitude?" Dad said, frowning coldly.

"I said okay, that I agree, no boys in my room." I shook my head, leaving the kitchen empty-handed.

"Useless," Dad muttered, and I glanced back over my shoulder. How was I useless?

I left the house, just glad to be out of there.

"Hey, Raven!" I looked up to see Taylor strolling over to me from the house next door. I smiled brightly.

"Hey."

We fell into step. It was clear he was ready for training. As the elite group, I would train them, but there were other top warriors who headed the other training sessions. From what I could see, Taylor was one of those who taught some of the other lower groups.

"You know, it's impressive to see you in this position," he said.

"Thanks, I guess? Was it so hard to imagine? I've always been a tough one!" I said, showing him my biceps. He whistled.

"Damn, now those are some perfect muscles. I'm envious," he said, tapping my arm as he grinned.

"Of course," I said, glancing at his muscular arms. "You hold nothing in comparison."

"Oh, absolutely not." We both started laughing, just as someone called out to me.

"Raven!"

We stopped, turning to see Zack, the Delta, come jogging over. He was shirtless. His earring glinted in his left ear and his black hair tumbled over his forehead.

"Hey, guys…" he said, trailing off when he glanced at Taylor. Taylor's heart was racing, and I could sense the tension between them.

"Hi…" I said, wondering what that was about.

"I'll see you two around," Taylor said suddenly, running off towards the training grounds. Weird.

"What is it?" I asked Zack, who was frowning slightly.

"Ah, yeah, sorry, we're throwing a welcoming home bash for Liam. I mean, we didn't really get to with everything that had happened," Zack said, running his hands through his black hair.

"Oh, okay, and?" I asked.

"Well… can you get him there? I mean, it's supposed to be a surprise." He flashed me a small smirk, and I really wanted to refuse…

"I don't really know. I mean, I might be busy -"

"Raven, you have got to come, too. Come on, it's tonight at nine, down by the river on the east side." The east side… opposite to where the killing had happened. I didn't really blame them for choosing that. I sighed,

"I don't know, Zack, I have –"

"Come on, please? Damon said he couldn't, and I don't know who else to ask. You two are his best friends." *Correction; were his best friends.*

"Fine," I said in defeat.

"Thanks." He flashed me a grin before running off.

Great. Liam better not get any ideas.

Shaking my head, I ran towards the training grounds. I couldn't be late; I was the one that needed to set an example.

Training was over, and I was trying to figure out if I should go find him or if I could just mind-link him... actually, that would be easier.

Liam?

Raven... hey.

I was wondering if you know anything about what's happening with my place. I requested to see if there was a room in the packhouse...

Yeah, about that, there's room three on the third floor, you can take it. Just pop down later to my office, and you can grab the key.

Oh, okay, great.

Anything else?

No.

I didn't know how to continue, so I left it. Maybe later, when it was time, I could just call him. Yeah, that sounded better.

❧❀❧

I had spent the day packing the last of my stuff. I was so ready to get out of there. I only had a few items left when I quickly decided to get dressed for the evening. I took out a black strapless bodysuit, black shorts, lace net tights, and some leather slouch-heeled boots that reached just below my knees.

I sat down and applied my makeup. Finishing off with a dusting of highlighter, I looked in the mirror. My smoky black eyes and dark purple matte lipstick complimented my full look. Satisfied, I put on some black lace earrings and a choker necklace then finally painted my nails purple.

Okay, all done. I'm here to show everyone I am living my life to the best. I am not going to mope around.

I exited my bedroom, making sure to lock my bedroom behind me before Dad and Mom saw the packed bags. Slowly, I crept down the steps. Only when I reached the front door did I call out,

"I'm off to Liam's homecoming party!" before slamming the door shut behind me.

I was not going to deal with them right now. I walked down towards the river and took a deep breath.

Liam?

Raven. I was expecting you to come to get the key.

Yeah, I'm still packing. Maybe tomorrow or the day after? Look, there's something I need to show you down by the east side of the river. Could you come here?

Is everything okay? His voice was cold, yet I could hear the touch of worry in it.

Yeah, please come quick.

On my way.

There, my job was done. I continued walking along. Soon the smell of pizza filled my nose, and I smiled. *Oo, they got pizza!* Now that was more like it. I walked through the clearing just as Zack appeared.

"Liam with you?"

"He's on his way. What pizza you got?" I asked. He smirked.

"No pizza until you bring the Alpha," he said with a wink. I pouted.

"Meanie, don't bribe me," I said unhappily.

Raven, where are you?

"Shit, he's here," I whispered.

"Go get him and give me a heads up," Zack whispered. I sighed and nodded, turning back the way I had come.

Where about are you?

Near the largest oak tree? What is this about? Liam's voice came.

I'm coming, I said, walking towards him. Soon his scent filled my nose, and I followed it until I saw him.

"There you are, what is…" Liam trailed off, his eyes flashing a magnetic blue as his gaze raked over me.

Shit, don't get the wrong idea.

His heart was racing, but when he stepped closer to me, I stepped back.

"Come with me," I said curtly.

I didn't want to be alone with him. Turning quickly, I led the way, power walking towards the location Zack had told me, but sadly my short legs had nothing on his.

On our way, I mind-linked him.

"Raven," Liam said, grabbing my arm. Sparks shot up my arm at his touch, my stomach fluttering and my heart pounding as he spun me around to face him, grabbing my other arm too. "What are you doing?"

His cerulean eyes were fixed on me, his sexy jaw clenched as he looked down at me. Goddess, did she have to make these men so handsome? Stupid oafs… I frowned when I saw his gaze dip to my cleavage and pulled free.

"Just follow me, Liam."

Luckily, this time he followed silently. Soon the scent of pizza filled my nose again, and I knew Liam could smell it too. I glanced at him, and he was frowning, his hands shoved into the pockets of his leather jacket. I thought I heard him mutter.

"Great." He didn't sound impressed. Suddenly, the lights came on, and everyone jumped out.

"*Surprise!*" Liam cocked a brow, unphased.

"You do know I could sense most of your heartbeats…" he said, frowning as he looked around at the crowd.

"Well, we masked ourselves the best we could," Zack said, grinning. "Come on, this is a small welcoming home party for our Alpha."

"Yeah, well, I told you not to do this shit," Liam said coldly as someone put some music on. I frowned.

Don't be so bitter. This is your pack. Treat it with love and respect, I said through the link.

We just lost a pack member, his reply came. He turned sharply towards me. Our eyes met, and I glared back at him.

I know, but sometimes when something like that happens, people need more of a distraction. He frowned and broke our eye lock. I didn't miss his eyes roaming over me once again, but I ignored him, turning and scanning the area.

It looked good. There were a few tables set up with a huge pile of pizzas. Damn, I wonder how many guys went to get those. There were a few tanks of beer, plenty of cans and some cocktail drinks ready to pour. A table of shop-bought cakes and doughnuts, along with a variety of chocolates and dessert shots, sat to one side. Lights were set up around the entire area.

Most of the girls were dressed sexily and the majority of the unmated ones had their eyes fixed on Liam. I glanced at him. He was standing there, frowning moodily as Zack said something to him. I looked around, seeing Damon sitting in the corner, already holding a bottle of beer. Our eyes met, and I looked away. I didn't need to see his guilt.

The music was blaring loudly. Everyone was beginning to talk or help themselves to the food. Well, this was the perfect time to help myself to pizza. Oo, they had my favourite chicken one! I had just about grabbed myself a large slice when someone tapped my shoulder.

I spun around like a thief caught stealing and stared at the taller woman, one who I wasn't expecting to see. A sharp stabbing pain rushed through me, and I wouldn't lie, it really hurt.

"Hey…" Robyn said. She looked gorgeous in a fitted black dress that hugged her curves perfectly.

"Hi," I replied, my heart aching when I remembered Damon's words from last night.

"Can I have a word?" She asked softly, and I wondered why she was keeping her voice low.

"Sure," I said, wondering what this was going to be about. I closed the pizza box, biting into my pizza slice as we both walked away from the crowd. "What is it?" I asked once we were out of hearing range. She brushed her hair back, licking her nude-coloured lips.

"Umm… I'm sorry," she said quietly. My heart thudded as I stared at her. What did she mean? She looked down as if ashamed before she looked up at me with guilt in her eyes. "I'm really sorry. If I knew he had a mate, I would never have gotten involved. I'm really fucking sorry."

An Apology & a Secret

RAVEN

*I*WASN'T EXPECTING THAT. NO matter if she did know, I still wasn't expecting her to apologise to me. More than that, did that mean Damon had told her?

"I just want you to know we have ended things," she said, twisting one of the several delicate rings she wore on her fingers. I didn't know what to say. Our situation, as a whole, was a mess. "I don't know why you two aren't together, but he is a really selfless, caring person. He'll treat you great." She smiled.

Come on, I was the queen of fake smiles and I could see right through hers. She was in pain thanks to that dimwit, and here she was telling me that Damon was good enough for me. I felt sad for her. I know the mate bond played a part for me, but I also knew that love without the bond existed. It was what I had felt for Liam for years. I was scared he'd find his mate.

"One bird to another, men are idiots," I said with a crooked smile. She frowned for a second before smiling genuinely.

"Oh! Robyn - Raven! I never even realised that!" I nodded, biting into my pizza as she laughed. "I guess they are idiots," she said wistfully. I looked at her. No matter how much it hurt, I was not going to be a bitch about this.

"Don't feel guilty, you didn't know... besides, he had a lot going on," I said quietly. "Thank you for being there for him." She nodded.

"Although it doesn't make it right, it has been hard for him, especially with his mom's deteriorating health." What?

"What do you mean?"

"Monica's mental state…" she said, clearly seeming unsure if she should say more.

Fuck… I know Kiara had mentioned that she was getting more and more depressed. Suddenly, I realised that I wasn't completely in the right either. Sure; Liam left, Damon distanced himself, but when did I try? Did I try to talk to either of them? No, I didn't…

Shit.

I turned away, barely hearing her ask me if I was okay. I nodded, walking off into the woods. My mind was spinning.

Shit, shit, shit.

I know it hurt, seeing them both just pull away, but had I tried? No, I hadn't. I didn't really give Damon much time either; he had been going through a lot back then. Suddenly, the pizza slice in my hand wasn't so appetising anymore.

I walked away until the music was a faint hum, my mind spinning with so many unanswered questions. Sighing I walked over to one of the large trees and sat down at its base, staring up through the branches at the crescent moon, slowly eating my pizza slice. *What do I do?*

What should I do?

We did need to talk because if I was to reject them, we really needed to discuss this first.

"Can we talk?"

Taylor? The sound of two pairs of heavy footsteps followed. I quickly calmed my heart rate the best I could, hoping no one spotted me. Right then, I didn't think I could just smile and pretend I was okay.

"I don't want to do this right now, Tay," Zack's voice came. Tay? Since when had they been close?

"You never do," Taylor's soft voice came.

"Let's head back."

"No…" Taylor murmured. Wow, he was answering back to the Delta? That wasn't like him. Don't tell me he was drunk already? Did they lace the damn drinks? Idiots.

"Taylor…"

I frowned. Their hearts were racing, and I knew they were very close. I was praying they wouldn't discover me.

"I need you, Zack. Fuck, how long will you hurt me?" Taylor's voice sounded so broken that my own heart clenched.

"I –"

Zack was cut off, and I heard a low moan. My eyes widened when I realised Taylor had kissed him. Wow...

The rustle of clothes and a slight grunt as someone was pushed up against the tree was heard. Damn, I never knew Zack was... I frowned. What was going on between them? Well, it wasn't my place to be nosy. I just hoped Zack didn't hurt Taylor. He sounded so vulnerable...

"Fuck, Tay... stop it..." Zack groaned, and my own cheeks burned.

Goddess, I need to get out of here! Now! I was about to creep away when Taylor's next words made me freeze.

"You're my mate, Zack. I fucking want you." The pain and desperation in his voice tugged at my own heart. That pain... it was far more familiar than anyone would ever know... but unlike Taylor, who went after his mate, I wasn't that brave, nor did I have that confidence.

Oh, why was this pack full of dickheads? I silently made my way away from them. It was clear they were keeping that a secret. Well, stupid Alpha, stupid Beta, and now we have a stupid Delta. The dumb idiots...

I needed to decide what to do about my stupid mates, and it seemed Taylor had his own problems... I wished I could help him. Maybe I needed to talk to Zack? I suddenly felt really disappointed in him. How could he treat Taylor like that? I mean growing up, I had no idea if Zack was bi or what, but he did have a girlfriend here or there. But seriously, it was clear he had feelings for Taylor since he loved that kiss.

My cheeks burned. I immediately pushed the thought of the two of them getting dirty in the woods out of my head. Naughty, naughty...

I was brought out of my thoughts when I thought I heard something in the trees to the left. *Strange...* I stopped, trying to hear, but there was nothing. I heard a branch snap in the tree above me. My eyes flashed as I stared into the tree. I couldn't hear a heartbeat...

I moved closer, sniffing out if anyone was there, when the smell of blood filled my nose. I approached the tree, my heart racing.

"Who's there?"

I was about to reach for the lowest branch, ready to climb up, when I heard another branch snap and something heavy fall through the branches. I jumped back just as a body fell to the ground, making me scream.

"Fuck!" I swore, my heart thundering as I stared at the body that had fallen out of the tree.

The mouth was cut from ear to ear and the teeth were once again missing. My stomach was twisting, and I could barely comprehend what I saw as I looked over the woman's body. I didn't know who she was, but... I backed away, looking into her empty eye sockets.

Another murder.

Despite my racing heart and the worry and fear that rushed through my veins, I hurried over to the body, but made sure not to touch it. Shit, this was not good. I saw a note in her hand and was about to reach for it.

"What the fuck?"

My head snapped to the side, and I saw both Taylor and Zack standing there. Zack's gaze went from the body to me instantly, and my heart thundered when I saw the suspicious look in his eyes.

"The body fell out of the tree," I said, quickly moving away.

"I'll tell the Alpha and Beta..." Taylor said, looking unnerved.

"What were you doing out here?" Zack asked me. Despite the fact that I knew it looked strange. I hadn't done anything wrong.

"I... I walked away when I saw you two kiss," I stated, crossing my arms.

That was my damn alibi! If Zack even thought I was behind this, then he needed to know I just got here! Both men froze. If the situation wasn't so dire, I would have laughed. Taylor blushed whilst Zack paled, frowning slightly.

The sound of footsteps running and two familiar scents filled my senses. My heart was thudding and, although I was innocent, I felt as if I had something to prove - I suddenly felt like I was the culprit here.

"What happened?" Liam asked, assessing the situation quickly.

The moment he and Damon saw me, they were both before me in a flash. Liam took my wrists as he looked me over, his heart racing, and Damon's hand went to my lower back, checking me over. I gasped at the surge of sparks that rushed through me at both of their touches. Fuck.

My own heart was thumping. Liam's eyes blazed with anger, but that hurt, too, as he looked at Damon. I pulled away from them both and moved away.

"I was walking through the woods. I thought I smelt blood, and then that body fell out of that tree," I said quietly.

"And we showed up when she was leaning over the body," Zack said.

"I was just going to look at the note."

"Raven didn't fucking do this," Damon said, frowning. "If that's what you're insinuating."

"I didn't say that," Zack said.

"The first thing you should have done was notify someone," Liam told me, scanning the area before crouching down by the body. "The teeth and eyes are removed already. This wasn't done just now. Raven was at the party fifteen minutes ago," he said.

"We need to see if there's a trail of blood. Surely something must have been left behind," Damon added.

"This is getting fucking worrying. Don't let anyone at the party know for now," Liam ordered, standing up as he took the note.

"What does it say?" Zack added quietly.

"Two down, I wonder how many more to go…" Liam read quietly. I could feel his anger and worry as we all fell silent.

"That's two deaths," Taylor muttered as he walked over to me and pulled me into his arms, giving me a hug I really needed.

"Two deaths and no break-ins," Liam said quietly.

I knew security had been doubled. I also knew he had gone over everything; the cameras and the sensors around the borders, everything was at its best.

"Which means…" Damon began.

We were all thinking the same thing, but no one spoke, as if admitting it made it a reality.

"It's an inside job, isn't it?" I asked quietly.

A sharp wind blew through the trees as we all exchanged looks, and I felt a shiver run down my spine.

The killer was walking amongst us, and we had no idea who they were.

Always Been You

RAVEN

*L*IAM HAD TOLD TAYLOR and me to return to the party whilst he and Zack dealt with the body. Damon had gone off to see if there were any traces or anything left behind. Although we returned to the lively party with upbeat songs playing, I still felt glum.

So... you know about Zack and me, Taylor said through the link as he passed me a beer bottle. I looked at him and nodded.

Why haven't you gone public or accepted the bond? I asked, unable to resist. Taylor looked pained; his eyes were fixed on a spot in the distance.

Zack doesn't want anyone to know yet, he said he needs time.

Well, even I was surprised that they were mates, but now that I knew, I could just see how perfect they could be. I stepped up to Taylor and hugged him tightly.

I'm here if you need to talk. I know you have a lot going on, yet you're still smiling.

Isn't that what you do, too? He asked softly, looking down at me, concern clear in his eyes. My heart skipped a beat. I knew this was my chance to share my own problem, even if I usually kept it inside.

I do... but I don't want to bother anyone. Besides, it's nothing new, the same as you I guess... I found my mate, but thanks to certain issues, we can't be together.

There I said it.

Oh, damn girl, I'm sorry, Taylor said apologetically. I shrugged.

It happened three years ago; I'm just thinking of rejecting them now.

Rejection will hurt, Taylor said, sounding pained.

But is staying in this deadlock any better?

Have you tried to work it out with them? Like, have you asked why he or she can't accept it? Taylor asked gently.

I looked down at the bottle I held. *Have I tried?*

No, not even once... all I did was just run away and act like the victim. If those two idiots couldn't talk, then wasn't it my job to make them sit down?

I'll take that as a no... Taylor said wryly.

Yeah...

I needed to sit down with them... I really had to do this, but how would I get them to? I guess that was a problem for another day.

"Well thanks, Taylor. Honestly, just that one question has got me thinking," I said, giving him a small smile.

"I'm sorry, I didn't mean it like that."

"I know, but you're right. Well, I'm heading home. I'm moving to the packhouse tomorrow, so I want to finish my packing."

"Damn, you're moving? I never knew..."

"Yeah, I think I need my own place,"

"Well, I'll help you with moving your stuff."

"I will actually take you up on that offer," I replied brightly. "Thanks!"

"I think I'll head home too," Taylor said. We looked around, everyone seemed to be having fun but since the murder, our hearts weren't into it.

"When do you think they'll announce it?" I asked quietly as we walked out into the woods.

"My guess is as good as yours," he sighed deeply.

"Who can it be? Like, why would someone do something so twisted?" I mused.

"I know, I don't get it. It's weird."

We fell silent, trudging through the pack grounds until we reached our homes. Or in my case, Dad's house...

"What time tomorrow?" Taylor asked.

"After training?"

"Perfect, see you then."

He gave me a salute before going over to his own house and I slowly went to the front door. Sadly, I didn't have a key, but it wasn't that late; it wasn't even twelve yet. I did the door; I could see the living room light on, so hopefully, they'll be in.

Mom, can you open the door?

No response. I knocked on the door. Still nothing.

Dad? I called through the link.

You found your way home, I'm surprised, his curt reply came.

That was the plan, nice and early, I chirped lightly. He didn't reply but the door was pulled open. He stood there, clenching his jaw. I stepped inside, stopping when I saw the pile of luggage thrown at the bottom of the stairs.

"What is this…?"

That was my stuff.

"What does it look like? I saw you were planning on leaving, so I just thought I'd bring your stuff down… since you are in a rush to leave. Not once did you think to tell us?" He spat. I shut the door slowly, frowning deeply.

"Still, to go into my room and just take my stuff out?" I asked, looking at the suitcases, some that I hadn't even packed, and a few extra black bags that had my stuff in them. My anger only began to rise when I saw my teddy bears and plushies just tossed in a pile at the bottom of the steps.

"My house, that bedroom that belongs to me. So, where are you going?" Dad asked, crossing his arms. I looked up at him and shook my head.

"I never should have even stepped into this house, that was my mistake. I don't need to tell you where I'm going," I said, about to go upstairs when Mom stopped me, placing a hand on my arm.

"I brought everything down. There's nothing up there," she said, pursing her lips. I frowned. So basically, they wanted me to leave asap?

Fine.

"Raven, are you going to tell me where you are moving to? Or should I say with whom?"

"Piss off," I muttered, trying my best to stay calm, but the anger that was blazing within me was taking over.

"Excuse me? What the fuck did you just say?" Dad growled.

"I said, piss off! Or are you deaf? I have done nothing, Dad! Nothing but try my best to be a good daughter! I don't even get why you hate me so fucking much!"

"Raven, don't talk to your father like that," Mom scolded lightly.

"Really, Mom? The one time I'm flipping speaking up for myself and you're telling me to stop? If you even told Dad once to stop this behaviour of his, even once, I'd think you at least cared for me. But you never have, you always side him!"

"He's my mate -"

"And I am your daughter!" I cried in frustration. How the hell can they be like this?"

"This is her appreciation for us, Kim, after everything we have fucking done for her."

"Done for me? What have you done for me? Apart from telling me since I was a child how useless, annoying, and irritating I am," I said. No matter how used to it I had become, it still hurt…

"You're ungrateful! Despite being a disappointment, I kept you under this roof!"

"How am I a disappointment? Tell me!" I shouted, no longer caring to keep my voice down.

"If it wasn't for you, my son would still be alive!" Dad hissed, making my blood run cold. What brother? "You are the harbinger of bad luck! Since you cast your shadow on this house, I have not seen one happy day!"

Brother? I couldn't focus on Dad. I was confused, what brother?

"…useless, unwanted…. Just leave, I don't want to see you here…"

I looked at Mom, who looked upset but I didn't know what to make of it.

"What brother?" I asked.

"Like you need to know," Dad spat.

So, he wasn't going to discuss it, fine.

"Okay… don't tell me. I'm out," I said, grabbing the first of my two suitcases and carrying them out.

Dad picked up the next two and tossed them out. I heard something break, and with it, it felt like something inside of me was breaking. Mom just stood there whilst Dad was just raging with anger.

"I never knew I had a brother… and clearly you guys don't want to tell me, so fine. But I do want to say one thing before I go. You said you lost your son because of me… I'm sorry for that, even though I have no idea what I have done, but I hope you realise you are also losing the only child you do have," I said quietly. They were my parents at the end of the day, but I wondered, was there really not even one ounce of love in them for me?

"That won't be much of a loss," Dad spat, grabbing a few more of my items and throwing them out of the door. I moved out of the way just in time or I would have been hit by one of the suitcases.

"What the fuck?" A cold, dangerous voice spoke.

My heart thudded when I felt the huge aura behind me. His scent hit me hard, but more than that, the anger in his voice terrified me. Clearly not only me; Dad looked like he had just seen a ghost.

"A-Alpha Liam…"

"What the hell is happening?" Liam asked, his voice menacing, stepping forward as he looked at the bags strewn across the front yard.

"Raven's apparently leaving, aren't you?" Dad said, his voice not even holding an ounce of venom.

"Tomorrow. I was going to leave tomorrow but Dad decided to throw me out a day early," I shot back icily. I didn't care if his stupid reputation was ruined, I was so done with his fake ass.

"Care to explain, Mr Jacobs?" Liam asked. His voice was so cold that I shivered. His anger was something I was still not used to.

"It's late, I am going to bed." Dad started to turn away until a menacing growl ripped through Liam's chest.

"I am your Alpha. Don't you dare turn your back on me."

Before I could even comprehend, he was before Dad in a flash, one hand around his throat as he slammed him up against the wall. Mom screamed and my hand clamped over my mouth.

"I… I'm sorry, but this was between my daughter and -" Funny he should call me daughter now…

"Liam, leave him," I said quietly. He wasn't worth it. Neither was this entire thing. I didn't want others to come out of their houses for the drama. Liam's hold tightened until I walked over to him, tugging at his jacket. "Leave him. Help me?" I asked quietly, motioning to the luggage.

His eyes, that were burning a deep magnetic blue, glared at Dad one final time before he shoved him to the ground roughly.

"This isn't over," he said, and something told me he wouldn't drop it, not until he had gotten to the bottom of it.

He turned to me, his eyes dipping to my legs, before he looked away and grabbed a few of the bags. Wow, how much can he carry? Okay, I think we'd be able to manage alone. I grabbed what I could as Liam picked up the final one, walking off towards the packhouse without another word.

Go be a whore, Dad's final words came through the link.

I won't react. I'll just walk away, like I always do…

When will I stop and actually speak up?

"Here's the room… I'm next door," Liam said curtly, making my heart hammer. He looked down at me, raising an eyebrow. "It wasn't planned."

"I didn't say it was," I said when he unlocked the door and picked up the bags. A few were in the hall downstairs as we hadn't managed to carry them all up the stairs in one go. The packhouse was empty, as everyone still seemed to be out partying. "Good," I said, looking inside the room.

Boy, did this room need a personal touch. Well, fear not; I had plenty of stickers, plushies, and posters to decorate the place!

"If you want anything done, I'll get the boys to do it tomorrow," Liam said, his husky, sexy voice making my stomach flutter. I glanced at him to see him leaning against the doorframe, his arms crossed over his chest, his jacket straining against his huge, bulky muscles, and his intense gaze burning into me.

"I can do everything myself," I said, slipping my hands into the back pockets of my shorts as I swivelled around on my heel and stared around at the white wall.

"I'll get someone to get some black paint…"

"Who said I like black?" I asked lightly, despite how my heart was thumping. He raised an eyebrow.

"Don't you? Black and purple are your favourite colours, aren't they?"

"Mmm…" I said, trying not to look at him. Why was it so stuffy in here? His eyes were burning into me.

"I'll go get your bags," he said, turning and walking out.

I sighed, looking around the room. This was it, my new home… a home that meant having Liam around often… we needed to talk. All three of us…

His footsteps and his intoxicating scent returned as he placed the stuff down just as I drew the blinds, scanning the room. It was a good size, bigger than my room at Mom and Dad's house.

"What is up with you and your dad? Did something happen?" He asked, and I could sense the anger in his voice…

"No, nothing at all. Dad was just being Dad," I said lightly. The same way he's been for the last twenty years of my life. "Liam… can I ask a favour?" I asked quietly, turning back to him.

"Sure," he said, shoving his hands into his pockets.

I walked over to him, my heart thumping as his eyes trailed over me. *Don't look at me like that… like I mean so much to you when I don't…*

I hated how my core throbbed under his gaze, the way my heart was pounding and the urge to be in his arms consumed me.

"Can we talk? Like a proper talk. You, Damon, and me? Please?" I asked softly, stopping a foot away from him. As predicted, his eyes darkened, and he clenched his jaw. "Please?" I said softly, stepping closer.

I placed a hand on his chest, my stomach knotting at the sparks that coursed through me. I had heard of the power of a touch… I had also seen it first-hand with Uncle El and Aunty Red, then again with Kia and her Al.

"What's there to talk about?" He asked quietly.

"Us. We can't carry on like this. I can't deal with this forever. We need to talk, tell each other what our issues are and find a solution," I said quietly. I wasn't sure if it was the alcohol in my system or what Taylor had said, but I needed to do this.

"My issue? My issue is that I am not fucking enough! I would love you so fucking much that you wouldn't need another… is Selene trying to say I alone am not enough?"

Sadness and pain washed through me. I could see the pain in his eyes. He removed his hands from his pockets and gripped my waist, making me gasp. My heart thudded as I placed my hands over his, but it was his next words that threw me off completely.

"Tell me, bitesize, wouldn't my love be enough? I know I've done nothing to prove myself for the last three years, but I've always loved you. Even now, no matter how much I fucking hate our situation, I do love you. I left before I did something I regretted. This is not my fucking justification, but I loved you before I even knew what the fucking feeling was… I've always wanted you, Raven, no one else, just you. It has always been you."

Assumptions

RAVEN

M Y HEART POUNDED AS I stared up at him, his words ringing in my ears. Liam loved me...

Yes, although I had a connection with both him and Damon even before the bond, I had loved Liam for far longer. Then Damon's father passed away and I began to spend that time with him, and I realised he, too, was special. But now that the bond was there, I needed to do this the right way. Even if Damon had been able to move on in my absence, I wasn't him, I needed to discuss stuff first...

It stung painfully.

"Liam... can I ask you something?" I asked, pulling out of his hold. He didn't reply, but I knew I had his attention. "In the three years we were apart... have you...I mean, I know we weren't together, but was there anyone?" I asked quietly.

I didn't know why I asked. The fear that he may have would crush me. I needed something, some sign that at least someone wanted me. My parents clearly regretted having me, my mates didn't seem to care, and Damon... well, he had moved on in my absence. I just needed something...

"No..." Liam said, but I saw the guilt in his eyes.

My heart clenched painfully. The room was suddenly lacking air ,and I knew I didn't want to hear it.

"But?" I still asked, trying to remain calm.

He looked away, swallowing hard and my gaze went to his Adam's apple. Goddess, he was so handsome. But instantly, I remembered the guilt he was feeling, and I turned away.

"I… two years ago, a year after the time we found out we are mates, I got drunk at a mating ball that Dad wanted me to attend…"

My heart thudded. He was on about that night, that night he saw me. What did he do? My chest squeezed painfully but I still wanted to hear this. He walked over to me, cupping my face in his large hands.

"I took some pills to take the edge off the fucking pain, and I know that isn't a fucking excuse, but… I saw a girl. I swear, I fucking thought it was you. She was just sitting there. I don't know what overtook me. I kissed her… but I promise you, nothing more happened. When I realised it wasn't you and just the fucking drugs in my system, I walked away."

I was stunned, unable to move or speak. That night… fuck, that night, Liam thought I was someone else… I felt a surge of relief. He pushed me away because he thought it was someone else! The urge to tell him that it was me was on the tip of my tongue, but I held back. No, we needed to do this together, all three of us…

"Thank you for telling me. Good night, Liam, it's been a long night," I said softly tugging out of his hold.

"Night," he said quietly, a frown on his face and that coldness surrounding him once more. He left the room, shutting the door behind him. I went over and locked it. *Liam doesn't even know he kissed me that night…*

Goddess, why was this all such a mess?

❧✦❧

The following day, training went by without a hitch. Taylor asked if everything was okay; apparently his mom had heard some noises, and I assumed she saw what took place. I told him I left early, having a little argument with my dad, but what kept niggling my mind was this 'brother' of mine that I had never ever heard of. Surely Aunty Red or Aunt Angela must know something?

I had come home to find three of the pack warriors in my room, painting the walls. Three walls were a grey-lilac, with one wall a deeper purple. This was totally Liam's doing, but did I find it cute? Yes, yes, I did, but it didn't mean everything was forgotten.

Knowing that my room was being hogged by those decorating, I decided to sit in the lounge and order some items for my room. I needed bedding, curtains, and a few other bits and bobs.

The lounge was huge. The walls were painted a pale grey, the floor had grey floorboards, and there were three sets of black leather sofas. A huge TV was on one wall with a choice of several movie apps already there for anyone to watch what they wanted. To one side were a few bookshelves with many books on them, and where I was sitting, there was a coffee table in the middle. Soft teal rugs were in front of the sofas and under the table. A mix of coloured cushions scattered across the sofas in ochre, teal, and navy. The curtains were navy, and the windows were open, letting in a pleasant breeze. A few she-wolves were sitting in the corner near the bookshelf, chatting and doing something with their hair. I was busy browsing when Aunty Red mind-linked me.

Raven, I hope I'm not disturbing you.

Oh, not at all, I replied cheerily.

Well, we are having dinner tonight, and I want you to come.

Dinner? Who else is going to be there?

Oh, just family, she replied.

Okay, want any help with cooking? Not that I can cook… Aunty Red laughed.

No, just bring yourself, say six o'clock?

Perfect, see you then.

My fingers paused on the iPad screen. Liam would be there. I didn't think I was ready to be in the same room as him with Aunty Red and Uncle El around… but there was no reason to refuse. Growing up, that had been my home, where I felt happy, so why should I shut them out? At least Aunty Red actually cared enough to text me and phone me often enough, despite how much she had going on.

"…Believe it."

I looked up as Owen and another guy whose name I couldn't remember entered.

"This is getting fucked up," Owen muttered, shaking his head. Both stopped talking, noticing me.

"Hi," I said, flashing them a grin. Was it bad that I knew my bright grins irritated people, yet I still used them?

Owen clenched his jaw. He didn't cause a scene in training anymore, but he still had a mood on. Not that I cared if he was going to have issues, as long as he wasn't a dick towards others.

"Hi…" the other guy said.

"Hmm, don't you think it's weird, Chayce, that these killings only started recently?"

"Owen…" Chayce muttered, but I did see that flicker of uncertainty in his eyes. I smirked. Really? Was he going to insinuate that this was my doing?

"If I wanted to kill someone, I think I'd start with assholes," I remarked, shaking my head and returning to my tablet.

"Yeah? Well, it's weird… why now? Like too strange, huh?" Owen said, walking over to one of the sofas and dropping down.

"I don't know but I'm sure you will have your damn assumptions," I said, glaring at him.

"I'm just saying it… but everyone is thinking it." He shrugged.

My stomach twisted at those words. That was true… this did start after I came back, and although I wasn't the one behind it, how many people would be suspicious of me?

Dinner for seven

LIAM

*S*ERIOUSLY?

"Don't look at me like that, is there a problem?" Mom asked, cocking a brow. I swear she had that attitude of a feisty lioness and if you get on her bad side…

"No, I just thought it's a fucking family day?"

"Yeah family, and they are our family," Mom said. For a moment she looked concerned. "Liam… talk to me."

"Isn't that what I'm doing?" I asked glancing out the kitchen window, where dad was pushing Azura on the swing. It fucking hurt seeing him so much quieter. Losing Uncle Raf really did fucking do a number on him.

"You know what I mean," Mom said shoving an electric whisk into my hand and a bowl full of powder and milk.

"Yeah, well time changes people."

"Yes, but you never said what happened," she said as she sliced the puff pastry before she began spooning in the tuna and cheese filling. Mom was an incredible cook, her and Kiara both were…

"Nothing happened," I lied.

"Sooner or later, you will need to talk about it," Mom said, stubbornly.

"Yeah… maybe."

"After you have whisked the cream, go set the table for seven." *Seven?*

"Who's the seventh?"

"Raven."

Fuck, just fucking great… this was going to be so fucking stressful…

An hour later, the scent of delicious dishes, mixed with Raven's scent, filled the dining room. I had just set the table, and everyone had just arrived.

Raven looked fucking fine, dressed in a black halter dress that left most of her back on show, paired with net tights and boots. The only colour in her look was her deep blue earrings that matched her hair and the same colour that touched her smoky eyes. Her lips were painted a gorgeous nude that made them look oh so fucking tempting.

I looked away from her, just as Aunty Monica and Damon had just entered. Shit, thanks to my own fucking ego, I never bothered finding out how Aunty Monica was doing and by the fucking looks of it, not good…

She had lost weight, and that vibrant, gorgeous smile that once used to light up her face was gone. I couldn't help but notice how Damon was holding her hand. Losing a mate wasn't easy for most…

"Monica," Mom said pulling her into her arms.

"Scarlett, you shouldn't have," Aunty Monica murmured, giving mom a weak smile.

"Hey," Dad said before hugging her.

"Hey guys," Damon said with a small smile glancing at me and Raven. "You look great," he added to Raven which only made jealousy flare up inside of me.

"Thanks," Raven said smoothly, but I didn't miss the way her heart was fucking racing.

We all sat down with Dad at the head of the table, mom on his right, and Azura between Mom and Aunty Monica. To my irritation, Damon took the seat opposite his mom, and Raven sat next to him, which fucking annoyed me, and I got the last seat next to her, with dad on my other side.

Well, fuck.

"Did you ladies have anything planned for the weekend?" Dad asked, his gaze on Aunty Monica, who sat silently.

"Me and Monica are going for a manicure," Mom said.

"I can't, Aaron said we're going out," Aunty Monica said quickly.

I looked down, thinking she lost her mate and was suffering, and there I was not even able to have mine who was right by my side…

"I think he'd like you going out, M," Dad said, giving her a small smirk. He glanced over at Mom and I saw the love in his eyes, yet there was also the fear of losing her, or her losing him.

"I want manicaw too," Azura added staring at her hand.

Speaking off the little pumpkin, I had got a proper fucking telling off from mum about her having coke. Like it was my fault. When I had asked, she had said that she was allowed to have it. Mom and dad had looked at me like I was fucking stupid. Guess I was, for listening to a little monster.

"My baby can come too," Mom said, kissing her head as she placed a pastry on her plate.

"I heard you moved to the packhouse, Raven, how is it so far?" Dad asked her.

I glanced at her. She was so fucking tiny that I really fucking wondered how she had been paired to Damon and me. Like, how did that shit even work? I think one man was more than enough for her…

"It's good. My room was painted today, and I ordered some curtains and stuff, so it's going to feel like home super soon," she said brightly, crossing her legs. My gaze dipped to her thighs and, really, was it so fucking wrong to admit that I wanted to run my hand up those sexy thighs? She may be tiny, but she had meat in the right places…

"Sorry to change the topic, but with everything that's going on, what's your take on it, Uncle?" Damon asked, glancing at Azura, who was eating a potato croquette like there was nothing more fascinating in life then food. Dad sighed.

"I don't actually know, it's rather baffling. The notes, the way it's done, no scent… I mean, if we think it's internal, as Liam suggested, we could go down that path, but it might rile the pack," he said clearly reluctant about my proposal.

Damon glanced at me. Okay, so I hadn't told my fucking beta my idea. Who cares?

What idea? Damon asked through the link.

To fucking put everyone under Alpha command and question them.

"What do you think of his idea anyway?" Dad asked.

"What is the idea?" Raven asked.

"To question everyone under Alpha command," Mom said, frowning with concern. Raven's heart skipped a beat as she looked at me.

"Liam would have to be the one to do that... if you put your pack through that... it would be..."

"Damaging," Damon said quietly. "Putting everyone to trial would really hurt them, not to mention they would feel betrayed and that they are being accused." I clenched my jaw.

"And you just recently took that position," Dad added.

"Exactly..." Damon murmured.

"Yeah, well then how about we let them carry on and let another few get killed?" I glared at him.

"Liam," Mom said warningly, looking between me and Damon.

The tension in the room was fucking thick, and Dad glanced between the two of us as well.

"What is wrong with you two?" He asked frowning deeply.

"Nothing," we both replied in unison. Mom cocked a brow and Aunty Monica looked at me suddenly.

"Damon will be a good Beta. He is a good Beta just like his father," she whispered before looking away. Guilt rushed through me. *Fuck, I don't want to hurt her...* Mom reached over, giving her hand a gentle squeeze.

"He is a good Beta," Dad said firmly, now turning to me. "And I would expect you to work alongside him. I don't know what happened between you two, but I want it fucking fixed." The table fell silent and Azura gasped.

"Daddy said a bad word! Daddy needs a spanking, Mama! Just the way he said he's going to spank you the other day!"

Kill me fucking now. I did not need to know that shit.

DAMON

The tension that had built vanished the moment Azura spoke, replaced by shock. Everyone had frozen, Aunty Red's cheeks burned, a rare sight actually, but Uncle El simply smirked. A small giggle from Raven made me glance at her. Although her cheeks were flushed, she was finding this amusing.

"Yeah, it doesn't work like that," Uncle El said pointedly to a very confused Azura.

"And you two need to be careful, there's a kid in the damn house," Liam muttered.

"I'll remind you of that when your time comes," Aunty Red shot back. That made Liam tense and Raven's heart skip a beat.

I mean it. I want you both to sort your shit out. This pack needs their leadership united, his voice came through the link. I knew we both could hear him.

Understood, I said, making sure Liam could hear too. I wanted to sort this shit out, I really fucking did.

I glanced at Raven. She looked hot. There was something about her. Although she was twenty-one, she was a tiny thing. I wouldn't lie, there were definitely things that I wanted to do to her, but I knew I had no fucking right to even think that right now.

"When I grow up, I'm going to be were-koala!" Azura stated.

"You can be anything you want, baby girl," Aunty Red said, smiling down at her.

"Oo, I want to be a were-panda!" Raven added excitedly. Azura's eyes sparkled with excitement.

"Really?" She said with awe.

"Yeah, you just need to gain about 150 pounds or so..." Liam remarked, smirking slightly as he looked at Raven. I felt envious at that, wishing that we could have that old bond again with Raven. Every time I felt like speaking to her, the fear that Liam was going to lash out only grew. But we did need to get our shit together, if not for each other, then for the pack at least.

Dinner finished, and Raven offered to clean up. Aunty Scarlett agreed and took Mom to the living room with Azura. I had offered to help and even Liam stayed behind. The tension that settled the moment the adults left was fucking palpable. Raven quickly began gathering the dishes, leaning over to reach the plates from across the table, leaning on one leg with her other one raised, only making her perky ass a little too tempting.

If you are done fucking perving at her, Liam's cold voice came in my head.

She's my mate too.

Funny you remember her now, he shot back.

I didn't reply, not wanting to cause even more fucking drama.

We headed back to the kitchen, and Raven began emptying the dishes into the bin.

"Who's washing?" She asked.

"Didn't you offer?" Liam asked, cocking a brow. She frowned.

"Yeah, and so did you two. So, Liam, you wash, Damon, you dry, and then when we're done... let's talk," she said.

Damn. The dreaded words: Let's talk. That shit ain't good.

"Not that there's much to talk about," Liam muttered.

Raven shot him a glare, and I hid my smirk. She was a tough one. Like Grandma Amy used to say - she was a 'tough cookie'. She really was; small and sweet but a tough one.

"You heard the woman, get washing," I said lightly, smiling ever so slightly.

"Shut it, or I'll fucking shove your face in the sink."

"Want to try it?" I shot back. He was seriously being a dick now.

"Can you two not do this?" Raven said suddenly. We both looked at her, and the hurt was clear in her eyes as she held the dishcloth and spray to clean the table. "You keep acting this way, but it just makes me feel like shit, knowing I'm the reason for you two being at each other's throats. Fix up, boys, because I swear, I'm so close to being done." She shook her head and stormed out of the room, leaving us both feeling fucking guilty.

"She isn't wrong. We do need to sort this out. Now that we're all back, we need to come to an agreement."

"So, what? Tell me, how will we decide what's going to happen? I want her, for myself. I don't share," he said coldly, his eyes flashing with anger.

"I know, but what about what she wants?" I asked quietly. It fucking hurt knowing I was the inferior one...

"She can choose. The bond will hurt for a short while, but she'll get over it," he said quietly. My stomach twisted, and I looked at him as he began washing up.

"So, you are okay with her experiencing pain? Liam... do you fucking hate me that much?" He paused, clenching his jaw, before continuing to scrub the dishes.

"No. I don't hate you; I hate this fucking situation. She is the one girl I always fucking wanted, Damon. You got your shit on with Kia, then Robyn, and Goddess knows who the fuck else, but I want just her. I am an Alpha. Sharing isn't in my fucking nature. It's almost as if Selene's fucking making a mockery out of me. Yeah, share your fucking Luna with your Beta; that's some messed up shit. The mate bond is meant to be between two souls. There's no space for a third." His voice was cold, and if I already felt like the third wheel, then I felt even worse now.

Yes, there had been a connection between Raven and me, but what Liam felt for her had probably been fucking more. However, now that the bond was there...

I couldn't even reply. I felt like shit. I suddenly didn't even feel worthy of anything. I kept my gaze down, drying the dishes silently and thinking of all the crap that was going on.

I heard footsteps. Raven was back, glaring at us both. She went to the fridge and took the milk bottle out.

"Do either of you want a drink?" She asked coldly, or what was her best version of a cold tone.

"I'll have a latte," Liam replied.

"No, thanks," I added quietly.

"Can you even make hot drinks?" Liam asked. She shot him a frosty glare.

"Yes, I can."

"Okay... good luck." Liam definitely did not sound reassured.

She got about to making the drinks. The kitchen had just been cleaned, and I wondered if we were actually going to talk. She was about to carry the tray of hot drinks to the lounge when the doorbell rang.

"Who could that be?" Raven asked.

"I'll go check," Liam muttered, leaving the room.

Raven placed the tray down, walking over to the door. I followed. Her scent and the way her bare back looked... I turned away, feeling that hole inside only grow.

The front door opened to reveal none other than Alejandro carrying two car seats. Behind him was Kiara holding Dante's hand. The king smirked coldly as he looked at us.

"Well, well, well, looks like we have a fucking house full."

"Surprise!" Kiara said, her eyes on Raven, who had gasped.

Just when I thought we were going to actually get to talk. Damn.

A Surprise

RAVEN

"Kia!" I EXCLAIMED, RUNNING over to her. She rushed forward, and we both hugged each other tightly.

"We weren't expecting you," Liam said, lifting Dante up.

"It's a surprise," he said as if that wasn't obvious. I smiled. Oh, Goddess, that kid was cute. Al shook hands with Liam whilst giving Damon a curt nod.

I had video-called Al after his brother had passed away, but I didn't go, knowing they needed time with both their own families. I didn't want to go and make Liam stay away.

I bent over, looking at the two adorable dumplings that I just wanted to gobble up completely. They were soo cute!

"Kia, you make cute babies! Ah, they are even cuter than the last time I saw them."

"Hun, I sent you a picture of them just two days ago," Kiara said, hugging Liam tightly.

"Hmm, nope, still cuter than ever," I whispered, caressing Skyla's cheek.

"Alpha Alejandro, Kia," Damon said.

"Hey, Damon," Kiara said with a small smile, giving him a quick hug as Al looked at him coldly. I felt sorry for him, what with Liam's treatment of him and now Al's.

"I never can get away from you," Al said to him, but compared to how much he hated him years ago, I could tell it had calmed down. I knew his reason… Damon and Kia had been in a sexual relationship for a while.

"Kiara," Uncle El said, smirking as he came over, meeting his daughter first, then the rest. "How are you all doing? It's a nice surprise to see you all come down."

"Yeah, I thought we'd stop by, not that we'll be here for too long," King Al said. Uncle El nodded.

"How are they doing?" He asked quietly.

My heart squeezed seeing the wave of sadness that washed over Kiara, Al, and Uncle El. I knew he was asking about Alpha Rafael's family.

"As best as they fucking can in this situation," Al said with a smirk that held no light.

Kiara looked up at him, her eyes filled with emotions, the love she felt for him strongly showing. She stepped closer, cupping his face as she tugged him down and kissed him softly. Gosh, if you wanted a perfect hot couple, it was those two.

"Don't just stand out there, come on in! Monica and I want to see the kiddies!" Aunty Red called.

I smiled. I loved how Aunty Red was so considerate of Aunty Monica. It was heartbreaking to see her like this. *I promise I will do more. I will, I don't care what happens with me, Damon, or Liam, but I will try to do more for her...*

I headed back to the kitchen to make some more hot drinks. Kia followed me after meeting her mom and Aunty Monica.

"So, how is it being back here?" She asked.

"Okay, I guess..." I said. I wasn't sure if they knew about the murders. They had enough going on, so unless Uncle El or someone told them, I wouldn't mention it.

"Still nothing?" She asked softly as I poured some more milk in to make something for them.

"Nope, nothing. So, do you guys want food first?" I didn't want to talk about my issue.

"No, we ate on the way. A hot drink is fine," Kiara said as she took out two mugs. "Things will get better."

"I'm sure they will..." I said, smiling at her.

I still wanted to ask someone about my brother, but I guess it was going to have to wait. The evening passed by with everyone just sitting and chatting.

Dante and Azura played together, although Dante was a little bossy, and when Azura refused to listen, he just got angry. He also told Azura he was a big boy and she was a baby, which only angered her even more. What could I say about these two Alpha-blooded children?

The twinsies were happy. Although Kataleya cried a lot, Skyla was a little calmer. They both settled down and enjoyed the constant being carried. They were passed around, and even Aunty Monica looked a little more cheerful.

No one mentioned the murders, and when Kiara got up to put the kids to bed, Damon also said he and Monica would be heading home. Uncle El gave him a small nod before telling him to be careful.

If you need anything when it comes to Aunty M, I'm here, even if it's just to spend some time with her if you're busy, I said through the link, glancing at him. He wasn't alone; he had us all. I wanted to make sure he knew that I would be there for him, too, even if I was three years too late...

Thanks, Raven, his reply came. Was it me, or did he sound sad?

"I better head home, too," I said, standing up and picking up the dishes. I had no idea the state my room was going to be in, but I'd see when I got home.

"Okay, take care of yourself," Aunty Red said, giving me a smile as she picked up Azura.

"Finally," Al muttered, taking out a cigarette.

I knew he tried to hold off on smoking inside when kids were around, even if the smoke still travelled, but hey, at least he tried.

"I'm going to head out, too. See you all tomorrow," Liam said with a small nod. I knew it was because I got up.

Al looked between both of us but said nothing, turning back to Uncle El. The two of them were friends, a bond that was first forged by their link to Alpha Rafael... a bond that was still in existence. My heart ached as I looked at them, and I suddenly felt very upset. Life was short; what were we doing?

I didn't speak to Liam, even when he reached over and opened the door for me. We both silently made our way back to the packhouse.

"We still need to talk," I said the moment we were inside.

"Hmm," he said emotionlessly. I frowned, looking up into those cerulean eyes of his.

"Liam, you've changed," I said quietly. He looked away, and my heart ached a little more. Where was that compassionate, loving Liam?

"Good night, Raven," he said quietly, walking off towards the stairs.

I sighed, deciding to grab a water bottle before I headed upstairs. I could hear some of the guys in the game room and someone watching TV, but the kitchen was dark. The smell of freshly mopped floors and detergent filled my nose. I liked the smell. It was so clean.

I tiptoed to the fridge, hoping I didn't ruin the floor that the Omegas must have just cleaned and grabbed a bottle from the fridge. I was about to close it when I saw a shadow of someone walking past behind me. My heart leapt, and I jumped, spinning around only to see a young Omega girl holding a mop.

"Goddess!" I muttered, placing my hand on my chest.

"Sorry, Miss," she said nervously. She looked startled too. She was slim and of average height, her hair up in a messy bun.

"Hey, it's cool. Damn, I just didn't hear you," I said, flashing her a smile. She smiled, looking relieved.

"Oh, sorry, I was just going to put the mop away," she said, holding it up and brushing back a strand of her straw-coloured locks.

"Sure, carry on. I'm sorry if I messed your floor up," I said apologetically. She smiled and shook her head.

"It's fine, it gets dirty quickly anyway."

I left the kitchen thinking that since the murders, I felt on edge. Even then, I couldn't get the images out of my head. I knew, just like yesterday, those eyeless corpses would haunt my dreams…

❧❧❧

I stepped into my bedroom with a small towel wrapped around me, towelling my hair with a second towel when I froze, seeing both Damon and Liam standing there. Arms crossed, both shirtless, their gazes fixed on me. My heart was racing as I stared at them. What the hell was going on?

"What…" My words died on my lips when they both approached me.

Liam pulled me close, sending sparks rushing through me. Those were only heightened when I felt the heat of Damon's body behind me. His fingers grazed up my thigh, sending off rivets of pleasure. I gasped. What was happening?

"Don't think so hard, beautiful. Relax…" Liam murmured. Reaching down, he threaded his fingers into my hair, tugging my head up. With his other hand, he ripped my towel off, making my eyes fly open, but before I could even say anything, his lips met mine in a delicious kiss.

I sighed softly against his lips, feeling Damon's hands cup my breasts. My cheeks heated up, unable to comprehend both men closing in on me and caging me between their muscular bodies. Fuck…

My core throbbed, my lips moving against Liam's hungrily, his touch dominating, hungry, possessive…. Damon flicked my hardened nipples, his lips meeting my neck and sucking hard just as Liam's hand slipped between my legs. Goddess! The pleasure that was coursing through me was dizzying when suddenly, someone was knocking on my door.

Go away…

Liam's tongue slipped into my mouth as Damon squeezed my breasts, biting into -

"Raven?"

My eyes snapped open, and I jolted upright in bed, my heart pounding. I looked around my room. My cheeks were burning, my entire body was tingling, and my core was throbbing.

"Oh, goddess…" I groaned, burying my face in my hands, mortified. I just had such a naughty dream. Dammit! I mean, I don't even have a bathroom in here! Urgh, why hadn't I realised it was a dream?

"Raven?" Wasn't that Taylor?

"W-what?" I called out, still sounding breathless. There was no training today, what did he want?

"There are a few items that have arrived. I picked them up from the collection point. It's nearly eleven, I'm sorry if I disturbed you…"

"Oh, umm, no, you didn't… it's just on my day off, I like to sleep in. Just leave them outside…" I mumbled.

"Okay, if you're sure, girl!"

"Thanks!"

The smell of my arousal was in the air, so I was not going to let him in! This was mortifying! I jumped off my bed, running to the window and opening it fully. The smell of paint was still strong, but still, I wasn't going to risk it!

The room was fully painted, and my luggage still lay in the middle of the room. Opening one of my bags, I pulled out one of my perfumes and sprayed the room strongly. Taking a whiff, I felt satisfied and quickly went to the door, opening it. I looked around the hall and quickly tried to grab my parcels, only for a few to slip from my grasp. I flinched, quickly picking them up and throwing them over my shoulder before slamming the door shut behind me as if someone seeing me might result in them learning what I had dreamt of.

"Yikes!"

I breathed a sigh of relief, looking down at my parcels. *Ooo, this is going to be fun!* But before I could even open them, my phone rang. Going over, I looked at it to see it was from Kia.

"Hey, baby girl!" I answered.

"Hey, hun, hope I didn't disturb you."

"No, not at all. I just woke up," I said, my cheeks burning from the reminder of my dream. What would have happened if I hadn't woken up?

"Great! Well, I have told Mom and Dad to take some time off and that I'll manage Azura for the night, soo I was wondering if you want to come spend the day with us?"

"Is that even a question? Of course, I will! You can't get rid of me when you come to our pack!" I said, smiling.

"Well, pop down whenever you can. I'm making brownies, too!"

"Ooo, chocolate brownies…" I loved chocolate, and Kiara's cooking was to die for.

Hanging up, I looked at my parcels. *I guess I'll open them tonight.* Bending down, I opened my suitcase and chose an outfit before rushing to the bathroom.

An hour later, I was carrying three plushies and a Batman action figure as I made my way downstairs, planning to head to the Westwoods' home. *I hope they like these…* I smiled at the alien plushies I was holding. They were so unique and cute!

I was dressed in blue jeans, an oversize black top, and boots; my hair was pulled up in a messy bun. I was excited to spend the day with Kia.

I stopped on the stairs, spotting Liam making his way upstairs. He stopped, too, and our eyes met. My dream from earlier rushed to the forefront of my mind, and my cheeks burned once again. I quickly looked away. *Oh, Goddess, send him away...*

"Are those for the bin?" I frowned at that, looking at the plushies that I had chosen with such thought!

"What does that mean?" I asked unhappily.

"They're ugly."

"Hey, they are so ugly they're cute!" I said, glaring at him. He simply gave me a small smirk.

"You really are a unique one, bitesize."

He brushed past me on purpose, making sure his arm lightly knocked mine and sending a flurry of tingles through me. His scent filled my head, and I felt dizzy for a moment until he was gone. Taking a deep breath, I continued on my way.

Knocking on the door to the Westwoods' home as I held the three large plushies and the action figure, I waited for someone to open it. Just then, Al pulled open the door, cocking his brow arrogantly as he stared down at me.

"Why the fuck are you here so early, brat?" I frowned up at him.

"Listen to me, big boy, Kia invited me, and besides, I don't need an invitation to come here." I tried to push past him, only for him to clamp one of his hands on top of my head and actually lift me off the ground, dropping me back outside again. He smirked coldly.

"Don't test me. Now, how about you ask fucking nicely?" He folded his arms, and I glared at him.

"Kia! Al is being a bully!"

"Baby..." Kiara's soft voice came, and I heard her approach.

I cast Al a dirty look, but he simply turned when Kiara reached us and pulled her into his arms, kissing her passionately. *I hope Kia remembers what he did after he's used his charm to seduce her...*

I pouted unhappily before smiling brightly and snuck past them, rushing into the lounge where the two babies were sleeping on the sofa while Azura and Dante were sitting on the floor playing with blocks.

"Babies!" I exclaimed, "Look what I brought!" Azura looked up curiously whilst Dante simply rolled his eyes, ignoring me. I pouted, *A Rossi to the core...* "Zuzu, look, which one do you want?" I asked, holding out the three plushies as I crouched down.

"Hmm…" She came over, pouting thoughtfully as she stared at the three before taking one and examining it. I smiled, watching her as she placed that one back in my arms and took a blue one. "This one," she said happily, "Thank you, Waven."

"Aww, you are welcome, my baby."

"Yes, Azura baby," Dante snickered, making me shake my head.

"I no baby!" Azura retorted, walking back to the blocks. She purposely stepped on Dante's tower of blocks.

"Azura!" He shouted, picking up a block. He was about to throw it when Kiara grabbed his wrist.

"Dante, no hitting," she said firmly.

"Azura destroy my tower!"

Oh, dear… I walked over, silently placing the action figure next to him before placing the other two plushies next to Kataleya and Skyla, giving them both a tender kiss. *I love babies, I can just eat them!*

"He is his father's son," I said, smiling slightly when Kiara managed to calm him down.

"I hate girls!" Dante said, pouting before standing up and storming out of the room. Kia paused; I knew she probably mind-linked Al. She then turned to me and smiled slightly as she caressed Azura's hair.

"Thanks for the toys, you really didn't need to."

"Oh, it was nothing much."

"So, I heard you're at the packhouse now."

"Yeah, I moved. Think it was high time I did."

"That's good. Your parents may have been upset that you left," Kia said.

"They're okay, actually." Neither cared to mind-link. Well, I actually had no hope for Dad anyway, and, after all that, I didn't really want to talk to him.

A short while later, I was telling Kiara how I told the boys we needed to talk. Just then, Al came walking in with a moody Dante, who stormed back to the blocks and began playing very unhappily. Al took a seat behind Kiara, who was on the floor next to Azura, threading his fingers together as he leaned forward, his elbows on his thighs.

"So, now that you're back, any of the fuckers made their move?" Al asked, glancing at me. I knew he probably heard the conversation anyway, considering his hearing.

"It's complicated," I said, sighing.

"I still don't get how this shit will work," Al remarked.

"Alejandro…" Kiara said softly, looking up at him with a frown. He shrugged.

"I'm just saying, a fucking Alpha having to share is fucking degrading. That's my fucking take on it."

"Or it just means Damon is equally worthy," Kiara added firmly. I simply stayed silent; it was a constant tug of war either way.

"You should be prepared for the worst-case scenario," he said, turning his cold gaze upon me.

"Baby… that's not fair," Kiara replied, displeased.

"Life fucking isn't." Kiara frowned. I really didn't want them to have a disagreement because of me. "I'm not going to sugarcoat shit; if this doesn't work, you will have to choose one over the other. If you three can't work this shit out, then ultimately, a rejection will have to happen. It seems they both fucking want you, so you may have to choose one over the other, or neither. So, the million-dollar question is, who will you fucking choose?"

A Late Night Visit

RAVEN

NIGHT HAD FALLEN, AND I had returned home to the packhouse an hour ago. I had decided to get my stuff unpacked. I was opening my parcels, admiring my new bedding and curtains, when I paused, remembering part of the conversation that I had with Al and Kia as it replayed in my mind. My stomach twisted, and I dropped onto my bed, sighing heavily.

I was so scared of this talk that I knew we needed to have, but it needed to be done. I picked up one of my parcels before sighing and tossing it on the bed again.

Rejection… Al was so adamant that it would need to happen. Why did Selena pair us together if all she wanted was to hurt us and tear us apart? I sighed, standing up and grabbing a plastic tub from the bedside table.

I think I needed to talk to Damon about this, and I wouldn't lie, I needed to see Aunty M. I walked downstairs; the warm bustle of the other young adults around the packhouse was pleasant. I snuck out and headed towards Damon's place.

I wondered if they had found any lead on the killings. I knew for a fact that Kiara didn't know, but I had seen the guards posted around their house too. Well, I guess with everything they had going on, they didn't need any more stress and they weren't here for long anyway.

I looked around. The entire place was like a small town. Lights glittered in the windows of the houses and the few shops that lined the streets. There was the odd person walking around, but one huge difference that

I noticed was that there were no children out and about. I guess it made sense. I stopped outside the Nicholson home and rang the doorbell.

"Is that your dad, Damon?" Monica's voice came. I closed my eyes, feeling so broken at the hope in her voice.

"No, Momma, I'll get it," Damon's voice came before the door was opened. His eyes widened slightly, clearly surprised to see me. "Raven…" he said softly.

"Sorry for intruding. I got brownies that Kia baked?" I offered, holding out the small tub and smiling gently. My heart was racing under his gaze, but when he smiled, stepping back, I felt relieved.

"Well, I can't turn down an offering," he said, shutting the door behind me. "I won't lie, though; I'm surprised to see you here."

"I know, I just… why didn't you ever tell me Aunty M's health was getting worse?" I asked quietly. He paused, his dusky blue eyes meeting mine before he looked away.

"I didn't want to worry you. You left and -"

"I made a mistake; I should never have left," I said quietly as we entered the living room, ending the conversation.

Aunty Monica was sitting on the sofa, holding a book limply in her hand. She looked at me and smiled slightly.

"Oh, Raven. Welcome, I'll put on some tea…"

"I'll do it, Momma."

"No, you two sit and talk…"

A better day? I asked through the link.

One of those where she thinks Dad will be home soon, he said quietly as Aunty M left the room.

"The usual? Hot chocolate for both?" She called out.

"Sure, thanks," Damon replied. I frowned at him, taking a seat on one of the sofas.

"You know, you should have still told me. Then again, I knew you had just lost your dad, but I still left," I said quietly. Sure, I had stayed around for two months, but it clearly wasn't enough. We had become closer at that time, but then everything went out of control after that Blood Moon.

Damon sat down on the opposite sofa, and I looked at him. He was playing with a ring on his finger, his head down. It was almost as if he was keeping that distance between us.

"Damon…" His head shot up, his heart thumping.

"Hmm? Sorry I spaced."

Yeah, I could see that... It was almost as if he was worried about something.

"Mind sharing what was on your mind?"

"Not much, I guess." He flashed me a smile, but I wasn't blind or stupid. Like I said, I was a pro at those fake smiles.

Aunty Monica returned with the hot drinks and a Victoria sponge cake.

"There you go. I'm going to head to bed, I'm so tired. Have fun, you two," she said, smiling brightly.

"Sure, Momma, goodnight," Damon said. Standing up, he gave her a tight hug and kissed the top of her head. I smiled, watching them.

"Thank you, Aunty M, I love your hot chocolate!"

"You love anything with chocolate," Damon added with a small smirk. I smiled sheepishly.

"Well, yes, but still…" I pouted.

Aunty Monica laughed. I just wished she would always remain like this: happy and herself... but it was just thanks to the illusion that her mate was alive...

She left the room, closing the door behind her as Damon sat on the sofa a few feet away from me. Picking up the TV remote, he put a random movie on. I knew it was so a tense silence didn't fall between us. A typical Damon move.

"So, want to share exactly what's going through that mind of yours?" I asked. He glanced at me before placing a slice of cake on a plate for me. He held it out, but I simply smiled, taking the icing-coated slice in my hand. He grinned at that.

"You never change."

"Nope, and you shouldn't either. So, how about for one evening, you forget I'm your mate and talk to me like a friend?" I said, biting into the cream-filled cake and licking my lips to remove the layer of icing powder that coated them. I didn't miss how he swallowed at that, and I looked away.

"I thought we are doing that already?" He sidestepped. I raised a brow, tilting my head,

"Really, Damon?" I replied, kicking my boots off, and turned towards him on the sofa, crossing my legs. Damon smirked, spotting my Little Miss Naughty socks.

"Nice socks."

"Why thank you, I got them in a pack of six," I replied proudly.

"Are they for adults?" He asked teasingly.

"Hey, I have a small foot… and maybe they were from the kids' section…" How the hell did he figure that out? They weren't that childish! He chuckled.

"So you."

"I like my socks and tights," I protested, sticking my tongue out.

He reached over, taking one of the mugs, making my attention fall to those bulging biceps of his. Damn these boys for having mighty fine sexy bodies. I quickly looked away, blushing when I remembered the dream that I had this morning. He leaned back against the sofa, relaxing visibly, and I smiled internally.

"So… can I ask you something, and will you answer me honestly?" I asked, finishing off my cake.

"Do I even have an option?"

"Not at all, or my socks might come to haunt you in your dreams," I said, sticking my foot out and wiggling my toes. Damon chuckled, reaching over. He grabbed my foot, making my stomach flutter.

"These tiny feet can't scare me," he teased.

My stomach jumped when he smiled. His eyes met mine, and his smile faded. I couldn't bring myself to look away from those eyes that always held warmth.

"Talk to me, Damon," I whispered.

"What do you want to know?" He asked quietly, letting go of my foot, but only after brushing his thumb across it gently.

"Everything."

I reached over and took his hand. I didn't care what anyone thought, I didn't feel guilty about Liam right then either; this was one friend to another. I needed to know. Before we had this sit down, I wanted to know what was inside Damon's head because I knew he wouldn't be able to be completely honest in front of Liam.

Damon stared down at our hands, before turning towards me and placing his mug down. He blew out a breath before nodding.

"I messed up. Unlike Liam, who stayed true to you, I didn't… I feel fucking guilty for that, and it's no excuse…"

"But?" I asked softly, sensing his turmoil. He was struggling to say what was deep in his heart.

Speak to me however you find easier, I mind-linked. He looked into my eyes before looking down at his hands.

That night of the blood moon… I was scared I would lose my best friend, someone I considered a brother, my Alpha, whom it was my duty to serve. I respect him, and I would die for him… The pain in his words squeezed at my own heart painfully. Why did Selene do this?

I've always loved you; you were always the warmth of our group. Kiara was the heart, but you were that bright flame that wrapped us all in your warmth. I always thought… you know, maybe Kiara might be my mate and you would be Liam's. He's always loved you, after all. He looked into my eyes. I gave him an encouraging nod to continue. He sighed heavily, looking down at our hands once more. **But after Dad died, I started seeing you fucking differently, and with it, it became more… there was a small part of me that was greedy and hoped that maybe you might be mine. I know I was fucking wrong to wish that when Liam has -**

Don't. Don't put yourself down like that, I whispered His words had sent a storm of emotions through me, and with it, his pain was so obvious. He nodded and continued,

But then you were mated to us both. I didn't know what to think but I was ready to accept it instantly. Then, when Liam walked away, I felt like my worst fucking nightmare had just come true. Everything went out of control, and I felt like I just didn't fit into the equation. You are Luna material. Liam is an Alpha who obviously doesn't want to share… and with his Beta? Why should he? I'm like the third wheel in this entire equation that shouldn't be here. He swallowed, and his grip on my hand tightened. **But still… I wish we could make it work,** he said quietly, looking straight into my eyes.

"Me too… you are not a third wheel. Don't ever feel like you are not enough or that you are below someone else," I replied firmly, so happy that he had opened up to me. Al's words rang in my mind once again, making my heart skip a beat.

"What is it?" He asked softly. I shook my head, and he tilted his. "Now, you can't go around having double standards, beautiful. I shared; your turn…"

"I'm just… scared… what if Liam doesn't want to listen?" I asked, the fear I had been trying to suppress for so long coming to the surface. He raised my hand to his lips, kissing it gently, sending tingles of pleasure through me.

"I promise you, you won't have to ever choose between us. No matter what," he said with a soft smile, yet there was a confidence in those words, although I couldn't understand the emotions in his eyes. Despite that smile, despite the love and warmth on his face, I felt a sliver of doubt. Why did those words of his scare me? "Now, shall we drink that hot chocolate and actually watch this movie?" He asked. I smiled, pushing my doubts away and feeling a lot better.

"Sounds like a plan, but I get to choose the movie!" I said, grabbing the remote.

"That isn't fair!"

"Life isn't fair, dear boy," I said, smiling as he chuckled.

Please, Selene, let stuff work out… please…

෨ඏඏ෧

Training was over, and I felt exhausted. I had ended up falling asleep at Damon's, waking up to find that I was in his bed, but he wasn't there. I came downstairs to see he had slept on the sofa. I thanked him before rushing from the house to get to training on time. I had just returned to the packhouse when I saw Liam leaning against the wall near my door.

"Hey. You didn't come home last night, everything okay?" My heart skipped a beat, and although I shouldn't feel bad, something about those sharp cerulean eyes watching me made my heart thump.

"Yeah, I was at a friend's and ended up falling asleep watching a movie," I said, praying that Damon's scent wasn't all over me.

A prayer that was in vain. The moment I opened the door to my room and moved past him, I heard him inhale and knew he had caught the scent. His eyes blazed a deep magnetic blue, and the surge of power that rolled off of him made my heart thump.

"Damon's," he stated, his voice full of such anger that I wasn't sure if it was smart to speak.

"Yes," I answered, about to close the door behind me when his hand shot out, forcing it open. "What are you doing, Liam?"

"Tell me, Raven, do you want Damon?"

What the hell? I moved back, wanting to put space between us.

"You are both my mates, Liam, and I love you both. Don't do this," I said firmly yet quietly.

"Love us both? You don't love two people at once, it's not possible."

"It is."

"Not in the same way," he said quietly, his eyes raking over me. For training, I had borrowed Aunty Monica's leggings and one of Damon's oversized shirts to put on top, but it had clearly been a bad, bad idea. His fury was only heightening as he glared at me. "You *are* mine, Raven, and only mine. I swear, I'll destroy anything that stands in my way," he hissed, his hand wrapping around my throat. His grip was tight yet not painful. My chest was pounding as I stared up at him. Never had I seen him so angry. How much pain was he keeping inside that it had birthed such deep embedded rage and hatred?

"Liam, please... calm down, nothing happened."

"It better not have because I assure you, if he touches you again, I will kill him."

"Liam!" I cried out in shock, shoving him back. "He is your friend! How can you be so cruel?"

"Oh, darling, you haven't seen cruel," he said. His voice was so dangerously calm and cold that it sent a shiver of fear through me.

His eyes darkened, and my stomach twisted. The burning dark navy shade of his eyes was something I had never seen before. I backed away, my heart thundering loudly.

He reached over suddenly, grabbing my shirt and yanking me roughly towards himself. In one swift moment, he ripped it right off of me and tossed it to the ground. Although not once did his gaze dip down as I crossed my arms over my chest, which was clad only in a black bra, I still felt humiliated. A surge of pain and hurt rushed through me, but he simply glared coldly into my eyes. Reaching over, he grabbed my chin, jerking my head upwards.

"Let me make this clear to you one final time... you are mine and only fucking mine."

The Cottage

LIAM

I TURNED, LEAVING HER STANDING there, looking fucking devastated. The anger that was burning through me was out of my control. No matter how much I tried to calm the storm within me, I couldn't. I needed to get away before I did any damage.

I rushed down the stairs. The anger of my wolf was out of my hands now. My claws and teeth were already out, and I was just trying to make it to the fucking door. My feet hit the bottom step just as one of the Omegas stepped out,

"A-Alpha, your..."

I snapped my gaze towards her, my heart thumping dangerously. Her eyes widened, dropping the Tupperware box she had been holding out to me and backing away slowly before scampering away. Smart move.

Ripping the door open and almost off the hinges, I rushed out, shifting and running into the woods. I needed a fucking break from everything. Deep down, I knew the jealousy and anger that was festering inside of me was only growing with each passing day. Returning home, I thought I'd be able to reign in the anger and hatred that had built inside of me, but now... I wasn't able to. I was fucking losing control.

The dark thoughts that consumed my mind, the words that I spoke, and the way I reacted were all foreign to me, too. I felt like shutting off and unleashing my wrath upon everything around me, but I couldn't. I was the Alpha, and it was my job to protect, not fucking destroy.

I don't know how long I ran, but when the sun began to set, I headed back towards pack grounds. I was a lot calmer and after my initial surge of anger, I felt like fucking crap for ripping her top off. I just… seeing it fucking pissed me off, not to mention she spent the night there. I needed to apologise to her.

There was so much fucking crap that was going on. If Dad, Mom, and Damon weren't so fucking against it, I would have questioned everyone in this pack until I got to the bottom of it. It would make things so much fucking easier.

I stopped outside a small cottage that stood at the edge of the woods. Shifting back, I grabbed the key from beneath the step where I stored it and unlocked the door. It was the cottage that once belonged to someone very important to us, Grandma Amelia. In her will, she left this place and its contents to me, apart from the medicinal books that belonged to our grandfather's brother, her mate. Those went to Kiara.

Stepping inside, I locked the door behind me and went over to the shelf, pulling off one of the pairs of joggers that I kept here. Since coming back, I had begun to clean it up. Somehow it was the only place I actually felt at ease. No matter how much time passed, or the fact that her scent had faded, this place still pulled me to it just like it did as a child. I loved to bring Kiara here, sneaking away from home. Sometimes she would suggest it, and I would happily accompany her. The smell of cinnamon hung faintly in the air, and, closing the curtains, I switched the light on.

I walked over to the sofa and dropped onto it, the springs creaking under my weight. This place had been kept just as it was when Grandma Amelia died. This was the place where she had breathed her last breath, casting one last miracle before she went. Something she kept hidden was that she was actually of witch heritage. Although she was more wolf, she still had the abilities of a witch, and with her last breath, she had used her powers to save Azura's life.

Mom couldn't bear to come here; the pain and memory of this place were too much for her. Dad had said he would come in to check that the pipes didn't freeze over or anything in winters, but it had been empty since

I had left. Looking around, I scanned the shelves of books and other bits and bobs. Grandma Amelia's voice rang in my head like a distant song,

"Come on, Liam…. Now don't be a silly oaf.... Sit down… I'll put on some tea…. Boys! Can't do one thing right…"

No, I can't. I fucking can't, and even when I try… I can't accept this fucked up situation… *Weren't you the one who had the solution to everything? Weren't you the one who knew what to do?* I looked out at the room, almost as if I was hoping she'd give me an answer.

I was always the silent one. I never wanted to cause trouble because I knew Mom and Dad were worried about Kiara due to her injury and night blindness. I didn't want to be a burden on them.

Standing up, I walked over to the shelf, remembering how she'd play games with us, read us stories… read her cards. I always felt there was more to her stories… to everything. Grandma Amelia always seemed to know stuff. She always held a mystery about her that we would never truly ever know the extent of, but that was just the type of person she was.

I took out a book, remembering her reading this very book to us on Halloween when we were ten. I smiled slightly, placed it back on the shelf, and walked along the rows slowly. I frowned, spotting a black box, *I remember this.* They were her cards.

I took the box down and, opening it, took out the deck of cards. Walking over to the small table, I tossed the empty box onto it and turned the cards over, spreading them across the table. I remembered her reading these for Kia and me. No matter what cards I picked, there was one card that I always drew last, each of the three times she ever read them. After that, she refused to play this 'game' with us.

I moved the cards around, searching for that one card. Frowning, I realised it wasn't there. That was odd. I picked up the box, but it was empty. It wasn't like Grandma to misplace things. I stood up, staring at the shelf. It had to be here…

I began to search around everywhere, the strong urge to find it over-coming me. Soon I had begun to take every book off the shelf, shaking the pages, just in case it was in there. An hour passed and I was almost done with the entire bookshelf, but no sign of the damn card. Where the fuck was it?

Another few books, and I was on the last one, but the card was nowhere to be found. *Did it maybe slip under?* I placed another book down before looking at the shelf. It was large and made of solid oak. You could see that the bottom shelf was at least five inches off the ground, but there was no panel I could take off. Slowly I tried to move the shelf, cursing when I realised it was bolted to the wall. *Fucking great.*

Going over to the kitchen, I searched around until I found the toolbox Grandma Amy kept. Taking out what I needed, I returned to the shelf and began to undo the bolts that held it to the wall. Twenty minutes later, I was able to move it away from the wall. Nothing. Fuck, that was a waste of time!

I was about to turn away when my gaze fell on a slightly uneven floorboard that looked loose. Crouching down, I used the screwdriver to pry it up. Looking inside, my gaze instantly fell on an old, cracked, leather-bound book that lay inside. It was extremely old. What the heck was it? It held far too much dust as well. How long had it been in there? Picking it up, I blew away the layer of dust that had settled upon it, coughing as dust erupted around me. Moving away from the cloud, I wiped my arm over the book, trying to read the words on the cover. They were too faded to make out, even with my sharp eyes.

Sighing, I unwrapped the strap and flipped it open; an old manila envelope fell out. I picked it up and frowned when I recognised Grandma Amelia's cursive writing, but what made my heart race was the words upon it:

To my dearest Liam,

I placed the book down and ripped the envelope open. What the hell was this? And why was it hidden? It was clear that it had been written and sealed many years ago. There were two things inside: one was a small square of paper with the words, *The future is still undecided; you are in control of your destiny,* written by Grandma Amelia, but it was the second item that made my heart beat even faster.

It was a card, nothing special in appearance. The image upon it was of a man standing alone, looking towards the darkness. Above him was a shadow of a deformed humanoid being with long claws where hands would usually be. They were digging into the man's back as it leaned over him, casting him in darkness. Now that I looked closer, I could see there were people on the ground grasping onto man's legs in desperation. Each face that you could make out looked anguished, and in pain, but from his posture, you could tell he was disgusted by them.

The card that I would always draw on all three occasions, but she refused to tell me what it truly meant...

My heart was thudding as I stared at both items. What was the meaning of this? Frowning I placed both items down, I needed to find out what that card was depicting.

I looked down at the book, my brows furrowing at the words that were written in calligraphy that was clearly from long ago. The heading glaring back at me filled me with unease and curiosity.

The Anthology of The Deimos Curse & The Prophecy of Light and Darkness.

Pictures

RAVEN

*T*HE MOMENT HE STORMED out, I took a deep breath; my heart was fucking hurting. The Liam that I knew was so far gone; that fucking hurt, too.

I walked over to the door, locking it before picking up Damon's torn shirt. I dropped to my knees, letting out a shuddering breath. Why were things so shit? When one wanted to make it work, the other wanted to destroy it. Even then, I knew Liam was hurting. No, I couldn't excuse his behaviour, but he was just the type of person who loved deeply. I understood that. Where Damon was able to cope and even move on with Robyn, Liam hadn't been able to, letting his emotions and pain eat him up inside. I couldn't blame him for his stance.

Liam… I placed my head in my hands. What do I do? And what was with the colour of his eyes? That anger and darkness…

Closing my eyes, I inhaled deeply, still clinging to the torn shirt. Damon's scent was soothing, but even then, I couldn't get rid of the unease and worry I felt for Liam. I needed to talk to him, too. I needed to reach him and pull him from whatever dark place he had pushed himself into. We needed to do this so fucking soon. *No matter what, tomorrow, right after Kiara and Al leave, we'll do this.* Damon would listen, but it was Liam I needed to get on board. Remembering the way he had ripped my shirt off, a pang of pain shot through me. No matter how much I just wanted to curl up and cry, that wasn't who I was. Crying never solved anything.

Standing up, I decided to shower and get all this sweat off. Once I had showered, I returned to my room. Pulling on a pair of pants and an oversized hoodie, I walked over to my bed and picked up my remaining parcels from yesterday. I began to open them. A gorgeous crystal lamp… it was pretty, but the excitement I would usually have was absent. I placed the lamp down carefully before opening the final package. It was flat, *I don't actually remember ordering anything else.*

A pile of photographs fell out. My heart skipped a beat as my eyes landed on the very top one. It hurt… it felt like an entire hurricane of pain was unleashed within me. I clutched my chest, feeling the crushing emotions cripple me. My heart was ringing in my ears, and tears prickled my eyes. Even knowing it would only hurt me more, I spread the pictures slightly with my shaking fingers, looking at the dozens of pictures of Robyn with Damon. Him holding her hand as he kissed her cheek. Him kissing her lips… hugging her… With each image, I couldn't breathe. Hearing, knowing, and seeing are three very different things.

Goddess, please… My eyes landed on the final four pictures, and I felt as if someone had just ripped my heart out completely. Despite the edge being blurred by what could be a curtain, they were images of them in bed, clearly in the throes of passion and both utterly enjoying it.

My worth was nothing. Was I so easily forgotten? It was my fault, though, right? I left… who would remember me? *I won't cry… I won't…*

I wiped my eyes with shaking hands, a sob escaping my lips as I backed away from my bed. I clamped my hand over my mouth, trying to stifle the sobs that were begging to escape. The pain I felt needed an outlet, but I couldn't cry. I would always keep smiling, keep going, keep strong…

Tears trickled down my cheeks as I stared at my bed. Although I was now across the room, I still backed away further, as if being near them would harm me… but the damage had already been done. I knew he needed that support… but looking at those pictures, was there even any need for me? He said he wanted me. He said he missed me, and he broke it off but was I really what he wanted? Was I really worth either of them?

Why couldn't I turn back time?

I just wished the moon goddess left me mate-less. That would have been better than this torture. *I hate life.*

I slid down the wall, resting my head against the smooth, painted wall, and closed my eyes, my lip quivering as I tried to control my emotions. *Come on, Raven, you are stronger than this!*

I stayed there, trying to contain my emotions. After a good twenty minutes, I got up and went over to the bed, quickly gathering the pictures up and trying not to even look at them. Who took these and sent them to me, why would they? Did someone else know he was my mate? We hadn't really told anyone. Shoving the pictures into the bottom drawer, I left the room. I needed to get something to eat, that would make me feel better.

An hour later, I was sitting in the large black and grey kitchen at the counter on one of the bar stools with a large plate of steaming chicken pasta in front of me when Zack entered the kitchen, frowning. He went to the coffee machine and began making himself a cup. He glanced up, seeming to have just noticed me there.

"Oh, hey Raven, didn't see you there. Have you seen Liam?"

"No," I replied icily, remembering how he was refusing and hurting Taylor. He seemed taken aback by the hostility in my voice.

"Everything okay?" He asked, coming over.

"Yes," I said haughtily. He raised his eyebrows.

"We both know that ain't true," he replied.

"I just hate men," I said, making him smile slightly, but he was wise to hide it quickly.

"What did they do? Or should I ask who?"

The door opened, and none other than Taylor entered. I hid a smirk, seeing the way Zack tensed.

"Actually, I take it back. Some men are perfect. Hey, Taylor!" I said, swivelling around in my seat.

"Hey, girl," he said, coming over and giving me a hug. I hugged him back before we both turned towards Zack.

"Hey," Taylor said, looking at Zack.

"Hey…" The sexual tension between them was so obvious that I was surprised I didn't notice it before.

"You know… you two really need to just give in. The sexual tension is suffocating me," I said, pretending to gasp for air. Taylor gave a small smile, but Zack seemed conflicted. His eyes met Taylor's, and I didn't miss the way they softened. I wondered what exactly was going through his mind.

"Zack… can I ask a favour of you?" I asked, making him drag his gaze away from Taylor.

"Sure," he said, going over and finishing off making his coffee.

"As you probably noticed, things with Damon and Liam haven't been great…" I began, glancing at the door in hopes no one heard.

"Yeah, I think we all have," Taylor added, grabbing two cans of Coke from the fridge before opening one for me and sitting down on the seat next to me. I smiled appreciatively at him as Zack frowned, nodding.

"Yeah… I noticed that. Being stuck as Delta with a Beta and Alpha who don't get on fucking sucks." He came over, resting his elbows on the worktop as he leant over. "You got a plan?"

"Of course, I do… I just need you to get Liam there. The rest is on me…"

"I'm all ears," Zack said, his gaze once again going to Taylor. I smiled internally. It was only a matter of time before those two got it on, I was confident of that.

"So, what's the plan?" Taylor said, gulping down his coke.

"The plan…" I leaned forward as I began telling them exactly what I had in mind…

LIAM

Everything else was gone from my mind. I didn't know how many hours had passed since I had begun to read the book. Some of it was far too worn to read, yet it was preserved well even then.

Some of it was what we already knew; how the Deimos was one of the first four werewolf lines, alongside the Asheton and Solaris, and the new piece of knowledge was the name of the fourth line - the Volkov. This was the line that the very first Lycan was born into, but unlike the other three who were like royalty, the Lycan was shunned and ousted from the inner circle of the other three lines, as it was feared by the werewolves. It was interesting, considering it was the Lycans who were destined to be the kings who would rule over us whenever born.

The story was otherwise the same as what the witch Janaina had once told Kiara and Alejandro, with perhaps a few minor additional details. The book was mostly about the Deimos line: how our line had moved away first and been one of the strongest, conquering many lands and spreading our territory far and fast. The Deimos line was gifted with the ability of speed, to see the future, a sixth sense, and the ability to foresee disaster, traits that Kiara held, being a blessed wolf. Along with the Deimos traits and abilities, Kiara also had the Asheton ability, the gift of healing.

When it came to light about Kiara being a blessed wolf, I had a lot of judgement from the pack ~ how the Alpha should have been gifted something, not the secondborn daughter. It annoyed me, considering Kiara was no less competent than I was. She was my twin and equal. Obviously, the pack didn't see it like that. Although they tried to be subtle, not daring to say anything in front of Dad, I heard it enough.

"The future Alpha is ordinary, but the blessed princess has found a mate who is already so strong, making his pack even more powerful."

Yeah, apart from being one of the fastest and having a stronger sense of auras... I was just a strong Alpha. I just didn't get why Grandma Amelia didn't leave the book to Kiara. Why me? I was ordinary. She was the blessed wolf of two strong bloodlines, that all skipped me.

I was halfway through it, or what I could read anyway, when the next section piqued my interest, and I sat up straighter. *The Prophecy of Light and Darkness.*

I'm so fucking tired, though. I'll continue reading this tomorrow. Sighing, I snapped it shut, coughing as another puff of dust hit my face. Groaning, I shoved the book and card under the sofa before resting my head on the seat, my legs sprawled on the ground in front of me. The image of me ripping Raven's shirt off flashed in my head. I fucked up... I owed her a fucking apology, but it wasn't enough. What the fuck was I thinking? I can't treat her like fucking shit. I needed to control myself, I closed my eyes.

Have I ever considered making it work? The three of us? Yeah, and the entire fucking idea doesn't sit right with me. But we are stuck in this fucking deadlock... Maybe this fucking talk is needed because I sure as fuck am not going to let him have her. The same anger began rising within me and I exhaled sharply.

Breathe, Liam, and don't fucking think of it...

I glanced at the clock on the wall, but it no longer worked. It was almost as if everything in the cottage had stopped in time along with its original owner.

"The future is still undecided; you are in control of your destiny."

I don't know what Grandma Amelia was referring to when she wrote that, but I would decide my own destiny. *Raven is mine...*

Deep inside, the doubt that perhaps I wasn't what she wanted clawed at my chest, but I pushed it away. I couldn't go on like this, I fucking couldn't...

I need her.

✎✲✎

The following morning dawned grey and cloudy, just like my mood. I left Grandma Amelia's home with the book and card in hand. I'd look more into it at another time.

Locking up after me, I replaced the key where I usually hid it and returned to the packhouse, making sure to avoid everyone, then placed the card and book into the safe in my room. Showering, I got dressed quickly as I needed to go see Kia and Alejandro off. I knew Raven would definitely go to see them off, too, and I didn't want to run into her there, not after last night...

After I had visited them, I headed straight to the pack security building. It had everything, including the surveillance centre. The cells were beneath this very building, too, along with the morgue and the rest of the labs or holding rooms. Let's just say it was the headquarters of our pack, and it was the only place that not all members of the pack had access to.

I made my way inside after scanning my hand and keying in the security code. The metal doors slid open, and I walked past the entrance guards, making my way upstairs to one of the labs and wondering if Esteban, one of our forensics, had found anything on the new body. Scanning my hand once again, I entered the room. Luckily he was there, coat, mask, and gloves on, despite the body being covered with a sheet.

"Anything?" I asked.

"Alpha." He lowered his head to me respectfully before looking at the covered body. "Well, like the first, when we ran the blood tests, there were slight traces of wolfsbane, silver, and ricin. Ricin, as you know, is not something that can really do too much harm to a werewolf; however, it seems when it's added alongside wolfsbane and silver, which slow down the healing capability of a werewolf, it does wonders, but it's very faint, whoever has done this thought it out. Like the first, the body shut down due to organ failure." I crossed my arms, thinking how well-planned it all was. Who was doing it, and why?

"Any idea on how the teeth were removed? Or the eyes?"

He frowned, his brown curls falling into his eyes as he placed the clipboard down. He passed me gloves and a mask before moving the sheet back.

"See these cutting marks? There's bruising on the gums where the teeth were pulled out. By the looks of it, I would say garden pliers," Esteban said, glancing up at me, his sharp hazel eyes turning back to the body after a moment.

"Some sicko..." I muttered. "And the eyes?"

"Going by the striation marks, or lack of them in this case, I would say a spoon," he said, making me glance away disgusted.

"Right..."

"We didn't find any residue or DNA, so the killer was probably wearing gloves," he continued, moving back. "As for the incision along the mouth corners, I would go with a small kitchen knife." Covering the body once again, he took his gloves off, shaking his head. "Whoever did this knew what they wanted to do prior."

I nodded, thanking him and removing my gloves and mask before I headed to the IT quarters. From the temperature of the body at the time of discovery, it was clear the person had been dead for at least two hours before being discovered. It was all so planned out.

Entering the IT department, I walked over to Zoe, who was our pack hacker and the smartest wolf I had met, when it came to computers anyway.

"Did you manage to get the data?" I asked her. She looked up at me, pushing back her bright red curls.

"Yes, Alpha, most of it, but gathering data from hundreds of people using the internet is going to take time. I'm getting there. Apart from having to wash my eyes out thanks to the amount of porn that is being accessed, I haven't come across anything disturbing," she said, blushing almost the same bright shade of red as her hair.

"Filter out the trash and send me the rest. I'll take a look myself and see if anything has been missed."

"Yes, Alpha," she replied, glancing up at me. I gave her a curt nod.

The thing was, I didn't trust anyone. Leaving the room, I looked around, observing my men doing their jobs through the glass partitions of separate quarters. From watching the cameras to discussing something to those standing around… the killer could be anywhere, at any rank and position in this pack. They could be on the inside, with a good chance of avoiding detection and covering their tracks.

I didn't care if I was hated… I really wanted to put everyone under Alpha Command, but the only thing that made me truly hesitate was what happened with the Sangue Pack when Rayhan had visited them. His actions had only caused unrest within that pack.

I cast a final glance around at my people. Those who caught me watching lowered their heads in respect, and I gave them a small nod of acknowledgement.

Who knows who the killer is and, above all, where and when will they strike next?

Let's Do This

RAVEN

I HAD TOLD ZACK THE plan and filled Damon in yesterday. We were
going to do this at eleven pm tonight. However, I was feeling extremely
confused. There were so many things that were eating me up inside, from
the pain I felt in my chest when I remembered Damon's pictures to the
way Liam had treated me.

When I had gone to bid Kia farewell, the way Aunty Red had remarked
that I had just missed Liam was almost as if she suspected something was
up. I just remained smooth and blew it off.

I was adjusting my dark pink ribbed top when there was a knock on
the door. Who was that?

I walked over to it, pulling it open. My smile vanished the moment I
saw Liam standing there. Like always, he looked like a Greek god in grey
pants and a black and white graphic tee that stuck to his body like it was
painted on, along with black boots. Why did he look so damn good? He
had his hands in his pockets. His intense cerulean eyes trailed over me
slowly. I suddenly felt very self-conscious about my fitted, clingy top, with
a V-neck that I knew showed off a hint of cleavage, and my black fitted
jeggings. I saw his eyes darken with desire, lingering on my neck before
they slowly met mine.

My heart thundered, and I clenched my jaw, trying not to fall for the
hold he had upon me. If he thought I was going to let him do that again,
then he was in for a reality wake-up call. Last time he took me by surprise,
but not this time.

"Can I help you?" I asked. I wouldn't lie, it hurt remembering what he did yesterday. I hadn't been able to sleep properly last night, thanks to that and the damn photos. For a moment, I wondered if he had sent me them, but I pushed the thought away. It wasn't something Liam would do.

"Can we talk?" Came his sexy husky voice.

"Isn't that what we are doing?" I asked, raising an eyebrow, trying to act like he had no effect on me. He clenched his jaw, looking away and frowning. I tried not to let his scent, or his very appearance, get to me.

"What I did yesterday… I'm sorry. I lost control, and I know I fucking shouldn't have done what I did. It was a dick move," he said quietly. I looked up at him. *Really, blue eyes? Do you realise that now?*

"It was, but you are literally making a lot of dick moves. Liam, I get…" I glanced down the hallway. After those images, I didn't trust anyone who may be listening. I jerked my head towards my room, brushing back my bangs that fell in my eyes. Stepping back, I allowed him in and shut the door. I looked up at him. Once again, I wondered who had sent those pictures. It couldn't be Robyn either, as she was in the pictures…

"You were saying?" His husky voice brought me back to the present.

"I get that you care for me, but you can't go around doing things you're going to regret later. Liam, do you know Damon is worried about you? He's trying to be the patient one for you. Don't you get it? You are the one -"

"Tell me, Raven, if, say, the roles were reversed… and not you but your mate was mated to another, would you have accepted it?"

The image of Robyn and Damon together made my heart ache, but… if it meant his happiness, yes, I could accept it. I looked up at Liam and smiled sadly.

"Yeah. It would hurt, but I'd understand because I wouldn't want to hurt him," I whispered. I had been through so much pain in life, and it seemed Selene wasn't done.

"We are going in fucking circles," he muttered, shaking his head. "Maybe you can accept it, but I won't." He reached over, running his fingers through my hair, making my heart thunder. I moved back, only for his eyes to flash a magnetic blue as he backed me against the wall.

"Liam, you need to stop doing this," I said firmly, but my voice just came out pitchy and breathy. I didn't want to touch him, knowing those dreaded sparks would throw me off.

"I won't ever stop because I've staked my claim on you."

"I am not yours to claim, I don't belong -" His eyes flashed as he pressed a finger to my lips, making my breath hitch.

"Oh, I wouldn't say those words. You are mine," he added dangerously, his finger running over my lips, making my heart thud violently. My stomach was fluttering with nerves, and, when he placed his other hand on the wall, that sexy smirk crossed his face. I knew if I let him continue, he'd make me forget everything.

"I am yours, Liam… but I'm also someone else's. Can we not just be happy?" I asked, taking hold of his wrist, slowly tugging his hand away from my lips and holding it to my chest. My heart was pounding loudly, and I knew he could hear it.

I could tell he was getting irritated again. I took a deep breath, raising his hand to my lips and kissing it softly, hoping it calmed him. Something told me I needed to approach him lovingly. There was something about him that seemed to snap at times, like he went from calm to suddenly angry and aggressive. That seemed to work; his eyes softened, and, for the first time, I saw the storm of pain in those bright, dazzling blue orbs of his, but it was gone in seconds, his walls raised once again. It had been enough, enough to show he was struggling…

"Two mates means another man would get to fuck you," he said dangerously, but the embarrassment that hit me at those words made me forget everything. *Don't go there! Oh my god! My dream was bad enough!*

"Did you need to mention that?" I hissed, mortified. He cocked a brow.

"What? Sex is sex, darling, and I am not okay with my mate being with anyone else." Thinking of sex with Liam was making my head feel light. *Oh my god, let's not talk about this.* He took hold of my chin once again, tilting my head upwards. "I can't share you." His hand left the wall, slowly running his fingers up my thigh and onto my hip and waist, making my heart pound like crazy. My core throbbed, and I swallowed hard.

"Let's figure this out together," I whispered softly.

"Do you think one sit down is going to solve things?" His husky reply came, his gaze dipping to my chest.

"No, but at least we can talk without our anger and ego getting in the way," I replied. I couldn't breathe…

"Fine," he said, taking me by surprise before he moved away.

"What?" I asked, shocked. He raised an eyebrow, drawing my attention to his scar, wondering how he got it. We might all be together… but Liam and I hadn't even talked properly yet. After this talk, I promised I would give him some time, too. I wanted to break down that wall of hatred he had built around himself.

"I said fine. Call him. Let's get this talk over and done with," he said icily.

Damn... I was glad that he suggested it, but now my plan to get Zack to lock us in the cells was gone - which meant if Liam wanted to run off, he easily could.

"What's wrong bitesize? Isn't this what you wanted?" He asked coldly.

I nodded, mind-linking Damon to come to the packhouse and telling Zack there'd been a change of plans. His 'Good luck, you got this' didn't give me any consolation.

"Let's go to my office," Liam said coldly before walking out.

I sighed, leaning my head back against the wall. This was about to happen... but what about me? What did I want to say? Was I going to be able to even speak?

It didn't matter. Tonight, we needed to at least try to talk this out...

Ten minutes later, Damon arrived and entered Liam's office, shutting the door behind him.

"Hey."

"Hi," I said. Our eyes met as Liam took a seat at his desk, placing his legs on the table and crossing them at the ankle. The arrogance and power that exuded from him were dizzying, yet at the same time, he looked incredibly handsome.

Damon dropped onto one of the seats opposite, one leg stretched out, resting his elbow on the arm rest. I could feel his aura too, and although it was nowhere near as strong as Liam's, it was powerful. Yet there was something warm and welcoming about it. He was dressed in black Nike jogging bottoms, a matching hoodie, and Nike sneakers. So different...

Both were gorgeous... they both pulled at me, and once again, Al's words rang in my head. The fear that there was no way for all three of us to work ate up at me. Both of them were watching me. I wished I had grabbed the largest hoodie I could find to hide in. Their gazes were intense. I felt so damn small and bare.

"For two people who wanted to fucking talk, you're pretty silent," Liam remarked, reaching into his desk drawer and taking out a small knife that he began playing with.

"I'll start..." I said, smiling brightly.

I was standing at the end of the desk, looking at both men. Liam simply raised an eyebrow as if he was bored already. *Argh, he is such an asshat!*

You got this, Damon said through the link.

Thanks, I replied.

"Okay... first, let's put how we feel on the table. No anger, no judgement, let's not even think we're mates, just how you feel on the topic... please..." I said.

"Ladies first," Liam said, spinning the knife and throwing it up before catching the blade between his teeth, making my heart pound at how dangerous that was. Goddess!

"Okay, you're distracting me, Liam," I said pointedly. He simply gave me a sexy, arrogant smirk.

"Good." I shook my head and looked at the table instead.

"I get that this is hard for both of you. In this scenario, you are both connected to me, not each other," I said softly. "I... I want this to work... but I won't lie, I don't know how. Damon is willing to make it work, but Liam, you don't want to. I, myself, know how confusing this is... if it was a three-way mate -"

"Fuck gross," Damon cringed.

"No fucking way," Liam shuddered.

"There is nothing wrong with two men being mated," I said, displeased.

"No, there isn't unless you consider the other your brother," Damon said sheepishly.

"And I'm straight," Liam said very adamantly. Yeah, the world knew that. From those two, I could see Damon as the one who could be bi... I shook my head, clearing another naughty image from my head. I blushed lightly and Liam glared at me. "You better not be fucking imagining anything."

"I was not!" I denied vehemently. *It's not my fault that my imagination runs wild!* Damon snickered, earning himself a dangerous glare from Liam. Ever the Alpha...

"Anyway, I don't want to hurt either of you. I love you both... I always have loved you both, even if that love changed to something else. Growing up, I loved Liam and hoped that he'd be my mate... that maybe I was worthy of him, hoping that if I was a good girl, the moon goddess would bless me with you. Damon always had eyes for Kiara, and I didn't mind that, I loved him as a friend, but when Uncle A passed away, that changed into something more. Then I was confused. All my life, I thought

I wanted Liam, and then this happened. I know it's selfish, and both of you deserved your individual mates... not just me, who is just... nothing special." I looked down at my hands before my eyes blazed as I stared at them both with reborn confidence.

"But I have an ultimatum. I swear on my life that I won't accept either of you unless you make amends with one another. If your bond, that bond you had as brothers, as best friends, is gone, then this mate bond is gone, too. I will not let a newly forged bond destroy one that is years old. Stop hurting one another because it's killing me inside, knowing that I am the reason you two are like this. That I destroyed that friendship and brotherhood."

I looked at them both, though my eyes lingered on Liam. That cold exterior had a crack on it and the guilt he felt was clear in his eyes. He stood up suddenly, walking over to me. Despite moving back, he pulled me roughly against his chest, wrapping his arms tightly around me, making me gasp and very aware of a certain something pressed against my stomach. Damon... I didn't want to hurt him either. I looked at him; he gave me a small smile and a wink that made me feel better. For a moment, I let myself relax into Liam's embrace, inhaling his intoxicating scent.

Someone's going to have to build bridges, Raven, and if that means you two working on your relationship, I'm all for it. His voice came through the link. My heart skipped a beat, and for a moment I relished in the embrace, trying not to focus on certain body parts touching me before looking up at him.

Please hear him out, I mind-linked him. I felt him tense slightly before he moved back, leaving me feeling lightheaded and my heart pounding loudly in my chest.

"Your turn," Liam told Damon coldly before taking my hand and making me sit in his seat. I looked up at him, only to see him sit at the edge of his desk, one knee bent on the desk and his other leg on the floor next to mine as he looked at Damon. Despite the hostility I could sense from Liam, he at least was willing to listen.

Damon glanced between us both before blowing out a sharp breath. Threading his fingers together, he placed two fingers on his gorgeous plump lips.

"When you left, it fucking hurt. Everything seemed to have fallen apart and I felt guilty... I knew that you always loved Raven, and then I was thrown into the mix. I know you hate the fucking idea, but if you did agree... I promise that I will take it at your pace. I won't take her from you or expect more than you are ready for her to give me." He looked down. It hurt that he was yielding to Liam, but it also warmed me. Obviously, there had to be a way the moon goddess wanted this to work, right? They needed to be opposites.

I stood up and walked around. Placing my hand on his shoulder, I gave it a gentle squeeze. I looked at Liam, who was watching him coldly. His jaw ticked but he didn't speak, allowing Damon to carry on.

"I do love her, regardless of Robyn. I needed to cope, and that was the easiest distraction," Damon said. I could sense his guilt. Those images returned to me, and I felt a pang of pain.

"Anything else?" Liam asked calmly, but his calmness made me uncertain too. Right then, I couldn't read him, but his eyes seemed to look darker than his wolf eyes. That same dark navy I saw yesterday...

My heart was thundering. Damon looked up at me sharply, then at Liam, who was once again playing with the knife, his eyes hidden from my view. What was that?

"I love you as a brother, as well as my Alpha and best friend, Liam. I don't want to ruin that. I'm holding out hope that you'll remember that this brother of yours never wanted to hurt you," Damon finished looking at Liam, who didn't even bother looking over. He simply nodded, licking his lips.

"Fine, so you messed around as you needed a distraction? When I left, I told you to do what the fuck you wanted. Why didn't you two mate and mark each other? You had that chance," he asked us both. Despite the hatred in his tone, his voice was steady.

"I couldn't betray you. I wanted you to be okay with this," Damon said quietly.

"And you, darling?" Liam asked, yet the mocking tone in his voice made me frown.

"Neither of you bothered to pursue me, and I didn't know what to do. I felt shocked, numb, confused - neither of my mates wanted me. Back then, I felt I was the extra in your relationship, so I ran away... after you left, Damon avoided me because he couldn't just forget you. Neither of you bothered to even try to talk to me -"

"Hold up, let's not play victim, love," Liam said dangerously. A frown creased his brow as he pointed the knife at me. "I tried to mind-link you that night, and you didn't answer."

"I had drunk a lot that night, I was completely knocked out!" I said, my heart aching. "It was night. You could have tried to -"

"Really? Then how about when I came to your house and your dad said you didn't want to see me?"

Did Dad say that? My heart was thundering. What was going on? Why would Dad do that?

"And what about those texts? Those fucking messages that you read but never replied to," he growled, his eyes blazing. I frowned, my heart skipping a beat.

"What messages Liam?"

He reached into his pocket, pulled out his phone, and unlocked it. After a moment, he held it up to me. I stared at the three messages that were clear on the screen and, sure enough… the word 'SEEN' was as clear as day under the final text…

Ultimatum

RAVEN

I STARED AT HIS PHONE, unable to focus on anything else but the words on his screen.

Raven, can we talk? Please, I really need to see you. I get that you are hurt that I walked off, but please give me one fucking chance.

Please, bitesize, don't ignore me. We're mated for a reason. You're meant for me. Please, talk to me.

Just one chance? Five minutes of your time. I'll show you what you mean to me, please. That's all I'm asking for. I don't want to do something I regret. If after this you want me to leave, I will.

I never got those messages… fuck, I never got those messages…

I ran my hand through my hair, barely registering Damon's hand on my shoulder. I looked between them, trying to focus, before turning to Liam.

"I didn't get them. I swear, I never received them," I said truthfully. He seemed uncertain, but he should know that I was not a liar. Well, in serious matters, anyway.

"Is there a possibility someone else got onto your phone and deleted them?" Damon asked, instantly raising his hands in surrender the moment Liam's eyes fell on him. "I swear it wasn't me." My stomach twisted even when Liam scoffed,

"You're the only one that would benefit from it."

"Come on, man, I wouldn't do that shit. If you didn't manage to see her, how could I have managed that? When I went the following day -"

"Did my dad also tell you I didn't want to see you?" I asked softly. He nodded. I knew that realisation had dawned on all three of us. Both of their eyes flashed dangerously.

"Your father's got an issue with me?" Liam asked dangerously. I could feel his aura surge around him.

"I thought he liked me," Damon murmured, confused.

How do I tell you both that my father is a twisted, mentally abusive misogynist and a class A asshole?

"So, if Mr Jacobs hadn't interfered, things could have been different?" Damon murmured, frowning.

"Forget Dad for now. Liam, it's your turn," I said, thinking I would deal with Dad myself.

"This conversation isn't over," Liam said, and I knew it wasn't. He had already been pissed with Dad last time, and this was even more personal. His eyes seemed to turn even colder as he turned his gaze to Damon.

"You already know my standpoint on this, so why should I repeat myself? What more do you want me to say?" He asked arrogantly before looking at me. "I know you say you can't pick one, but I don't see how else this will work. I want you. I intend to make you fall so hard for me that you'll forget him." I felt a stab of pain in my chest. Damon ran his hand through his curls.

It isn't that easy, Liam. If it meant just me getting hurt, I'd easily do as he wanted, but this meant hurting Damon too.

"Like I said, why don't you and Raven try working things out? Pretend I'm not even a part of this. If you think you can let me in, then I'll wait. I'll be fine." He looked at me as he said the last part, and even though I could sense the pain he was trying to cover up, he still smiled at me. I shook my head, glancing at Liam for a moment. He looked thoughtful before he frowned and shook his head.

"Don't hold your hopes out. I won't change my mind."

"And what about what I asked for? You two to be okay again? Because I might plan on keeping a twenty-metre distance from you guys until you are best friends again," I said, glaring at Liam.

"Things take time, so you can't expect it to happen overnight," he replied coldly.

"Well, start now," I replied, crossing my arms.

"We'll try. This is a start," Damon said, giving me a wry smile.

I sighed and nodded, looking at the two men that I had a connection to. These bonds, the feelings, everything between them was different. They were solar opposites, each one so different, yet so perfect.

The spark with Liam was like a live wire that shocked me to the core and made every inch of me feel alive. Around him, I felt like anything could happen. I was unable to predict his next move and he took away the very air I needed to breathe. Promising me unconditional love, passion, and desire, knowing he'd protect me from anything and everything, but at the same time, he'd devour and consume me completely.

Then there was Damon. He was that soothing warmth that tingled like an embrace on a cold winter's night. One that promised security, happiness, and contentment. One who would always be patient and listen to me, the one who would put up with all my mistakes and never get angry at me. The safe warmth of his aura was like a protective blanket.

"Please, for this pack, for your parents, and for me," I said softly.

Suddenly, remembering the photographs, I frowned slightly, tucking my hair behind my ear in a failed attempt as the silky strand just slid out again.

"What is it?" Liam asked.

Did they need to know right then? No, this talk didn't really get us far in some manners, but in others, I felt we had made a little progress.

"You can't get angry if I meet Damon, or talk to him…" I said quietly. He frowned calculatingly, but to my surprise simply nodded.

"Fine," he said, casting a withering glare at Damon, who simply gave him a half-smile. "But also know that I will do as I want. I assure you I will win you over."

"Good. I doubt that will happen unless you start treating others nicely," I said, glaring at Liam. "Well, I'm going to head to bed. Goodnight both of you."

"Night, Raven," Damon said. Liam didn't speak, although I could feel his intense gaze burning into me. "Night, Liam," Damon said, standing up. "If you need me to do anything regarding the case, you know that's what I'm here for."

"Hmm, I might have a job for you." I heard Liam reply coldly.

"Great," Damon's reply came. I smiled gently. More than anything, I wanted them to restore their bond, a bond that was just as sacred.

I heard Liam reply but I couldn't make it out. Entering my bedroom, I was about to rush over to grab my phone and tell Kia how it went when there was a light knock on the door. Now, who was that?

"Yeah?"

No reply. Frowning, I ignored it, dropping onto my stomach on the bed and began to type my text. *Hey babe-*

Another knock. What the hell?

"Yeah?"

Another knock. What the actual fuck!

I jumped off the bed, yanking the door open, my eyes blazing as I stared at a very muscular chest. My eyes shot up to see Liam standing there, a cocky smirk on his face.

"Can I help you?" I asked extremely sweetly.

"Actually, yeah." I frowned, trying to ignore how good he smelt.

"Well, I don't want to help you. First of all, when I said 'yeah,' it meant answer. You made me get up," I growled. He smirked.

"If you're angry about getting up, I can carry you back to the bed," he suggested, his gaze dipping to my breasts.

My heart thundered, but before I could even reply, he rubbed the back of his neck, making my attention fall to the tattoo that peeked out of his shirt. I wonder what tattoo he had...

"I actually came to ask if we could actually talk, and I don't mean the shit that we just talked about," he said. I looked up at him. Just a small, light conversation. Even though I wanted that...

"Sounds good, but only if you have something to bribe me with," I said, crossing my arm.

"Apart from my sexy good looks? Isn't that enough?"

"Since when have you gotten so cocky?"

"Time changes a person, bitesize. Come to my room in ten, I'll have something to bribe you with."

"Why your room?" I asked suspiciously. He cocked his right brow. The urge to touch the scar was tempting, but I didn't. *Tonight I'll ask him how he got that.*

"My room because you were okay to sleep over at Damon's." I rolled my eyes,

"Seriously, that again?"

"Yeah, and I don't care if it sounds pathetic or petty as fuck. I want you in my room in ten minutes, and that's an order," he said as his eyes glinted. Although I knew he said just to talk, my stomach knotted under those burning cerulean eyes of his. One day, regardless of everything, I hoped the three of us could actually have fun and hang together like old times.

Well, I disobeyed him and took twenty minutes since I decided to shower and change into something a little less body-shaping. I pulled on some tan-coloured leggings, a sports bra, and an oversized, tan, off-shoulder top. *There, now I look like a Raven Potato. This is good; no intense stares from guys trying to look at my smaller potatoes...* I cupped my boobies. Yes, they were small, yet they were nice and rounded. They weren't flat either. Maybe they weren't anything like Aunty Red's or Kiara's, but they would do. My little cutesy boobies...

I quickly applied some moisturiser to my face and left my wet hair open, making my way out of my room. I locked my door behind me and knocked on Liam's. He didn't answer, so I tried the handle.

It opened, and I stepped inside, instantly hit by Liam's seductive scent of roasted walnuts, honey, and that intoxicating underlying note mixed with expensive cologne and leather. Trying not to focus on the fact that I was in Liam's room, I looked around. It was completely dark, save for the red LED light that ran along the black TV stand. A huge 65-inch TV stood upon it. The curtains were drawn next to a huge king-sized bed covered in black sheets. The cushions were a dark red, and the floor was covered in black carpet. A drinks bar stood to one side, a fridge stood in the corner near the desk, and he had a two-seater near the window with a small table before it. From the open door on the other side, I could see he had his own en-suite dressing room and bathroom. I was tempted to go have a peek in the fridge as I was sure it would be full of snacks and drinks, but I kept my nosy ass in one place.

There were other touches of red in the room, from the lampshade to the abstract art on the wall. The walls themselves were a pale shade of grey. Just then, the light came on, and I saw Liam standing there with a tray of snacks.

"Did you just get here?" He asked.

"Ten minutes ago," I lied smoothly. He didn't look convinced but didn't push it.

He shut the door with his foot, locking it and making my heart race. Did I just agree to enter the wolf's lair, especially when I knew he was rather unpredictable? He placed the tray down next to the bed and walked over to me. I backed away, and he simply smirked.

"I won't bite," he said, his gaze dipping to my neck. "For now…" His words sent a shiver down my spine. I swallowed as I watched him walk to his bed and sit down, crossing his legs at the ankle as he leaned against the headboard. "So, will you just stand there all night? Are you scared of what might happen, or is it that you just don't trust yourself?"

"Oh, please, I am not that easy."

"I never said you were," he said, leaning over and taking a chocolate bar from the tray. My gaze instantly fell on those delicious arms of his. "Want one?"

I pouted, narrowing my eyes as I watched him bite into the chocolate, his eyes locked on me. Fuck, how could a guy look so sexy eating chocolate? That familiar ache settled in my core. I swallowed, looking away.

"Shall I put a movie on?" I asked.

"If you want to," his reply came. Was that a hint of amusement in it? I thought so… he knew he was getting to me.

I went over to the TV, grabbed the remote and switched it on. I selected one of the movie apps and chose a comedy. I then walked over to the tray, looking at the array of chocolates and sweets he had brought, smiling when I saw the gummy bears. Grabbing a packet, I walked around the bed and sat right on the other end. Liam cocked a bow.

"So, tell me… what have you been up to in the time we've been apart?" He turned towards me, raising one leg and resting his arm on his knee. His eyes fixed on me.

"Training. I put everything into keeping busy," I said, looking into his blue eyes as I opened the gummy bear packet.

"Can I ask you something?" I nodded, watching him frown. "You said earlier that you started falling for Damon after his dad's death and that before that, you had feelings for me. How could that change? I know what I'm asking doesn't make sense, but -" I saw how he was trying to hide the hurt and even insecurity that he felt.

"It makes sense," I interrupted. "You never made a move, Liam. You were always so reserved. I knew you were waiting for your mate… and I knew you were the type who would go after your mate because you wanted your mate. So, I never held out hope."

"No, that's not why I kept my distance, Raven. Yes, I was waiting for my mate, but the reason I never pursued you was because I was fucking scared that you'd find yours, and it would ruin everything. I loved you, but you were so unpredictable… so carefree that something told me without that bond, I would never be enough for you. But obviously, even with the bond, I'm not enough, so you were given two mates." With each word, I could see that anger building. Without thinking, I scooted closer, placing my hand on his leg.

"Liam, stop that. I honestly wish I had just been given one, not two. All this heartache would have been avoided," I said bitterly. It sucked that both of them thought they weren't good enough in their own ways.

"Me being reserved was the reason I lost you… I don't intend to make that mistake again," he said huskily, making my heart thud when he suddenly pulled me towards him by my arm. I gasped when I tumbled forward, my head hitting his shoulder.

"Liam!" I exclaimed, my heart thundering. He wrapped an arm around my waist, crushing me flush against him, making my core clench once again. *Oh, please don't…*

"I told you before… I will make it so fucking hard for you to ever refuse me… I intend to make you mine and mine alone, darling," he said, his eyes darkening as his gaze dipped to my lips. The way he said 'darling' or 'love', really got to me, there was just something so different about it.

"Liam…"

I couldn't do this… Goddess…

My breath hitched when his hand caressed my waist before stroking my ass. A small whimper escaped me when he squeezed it, sending another jolt straight to my pussy.

"Stop feeling fucking guilty or torn, love. Damon didn't seem to care when he messed around, so why do you? Not to mention, I am your mate, not just a random man," he murmured seductively. I felt him throb against me, which only made that fire within me grow.

Pull away…

But… why should I? Damon, himself, said we needed to work on this… and although there was so much to talk about, so much to discuss, that desire deep within me wanted something more… *Just a little…*

There was just something about Liam that threw me off completely since my return. This Liam took what he wanted. That dangerous, dominating possessiveness surrounding him was so strong I couldn't escape him.

I sighed when his fingers brushed my inner thighs, making my eyes burn into his. I almost stopped breathing, seeing the raw, unmasked hunger in his magnetic blue ones. I licked my now dry lips, my heart thumping even louder when his gaze dipped to my lips once more.

Before I could even comprehend what was happening, his lips crashed against mine in a sizzling kiss. Sparks erupted inside, coursing through me like a storm that saw no end. Right down to the tips of my toes and the pit of my stomach, all I could feel was the delicious feeling of an ecstatic high. His lips moved against mine sensually, and any logical thought was gone from my head. I didn't care... I just wanted this...

Moments

RAVEN

*S*LOWLY, I KISSED HIM back. My heart was pounding as my body invol-untarily arched into him. A deliciously sexy groan escaped his lips, sending another shiver of pleasure through me. My arm snaked around his neck, my fingers brushing the short hair at the back of his head.

The feel of his lips, the taste of his mouth, everything was just perfect. Suddenly, I was flipped onto my back, and he was straddling me. My heart thumped, yet I couldn't stop kissing him. Kissing Liam was something I had wanted since I was a teen and goddess… a drunk Liam's kiss was good, but this one…

This was where I belonged. It felt so right. We felt so right.

I moaned softly into his lips. His caress became more dominating and rougher as he plunged his tongue into my mouth, exploring every inch. I played with the tip of his tongue with mine, both moving in perfect sync, gasping as the pleasure coursed through me when he sucked on it.

His hands slipped under my top. My heart thumped, and I froze, making him tense, slowly breaking the kiss as he stared into my eyes. His hands were still running up and down my waist, sending explosions of tingles through my entire body, but even then, they stayed away from my breasts.

"I won't rush you, love," he murmured before placing a final kiss on my lips, moving back and laying on the bed next to me before pulling me into his arms as if I weighed nothing.

My heart thundered and I clutched onto his shirt, tightly curling into him. He was huge, and I felt tiny in his arms, but it felt so right. The prickle of tears stung my eyes, and I fought them away.

What the hell? I don't cry! Why did this have to be so complicated? Why did someone have to be hurt regardless of the outcome? I didn't even know how two mates would work. *I don't know what to do.*

Why couldn't it have all been simple?

As if sensing my turmoil, he rubbed my back comfortingly. I placed my leg between both of his, blushing when his package pressed against my thigh. His scent and warmth were so comforting, and that emptiness that had accompanied me every night in bed for the last three years was somewhat lifted. I wanted to talk to him. I wanted to ask him so many things, but the fear that if I opened my mouth, I'd start crying kept me silent.

Talk to me, bitesize, his voice came through the link. My lip quivered.

"Tell me what's on your mind." He asked softly.

"I wish things could be simple. I understand your point, too. I just don't want anyone hurt, but I realised that even together, someone will feel hurt often," I whispered.

"Don't think about it. Damon and I will figure this shit out," he said coldly, and although he said that, I knew the meaning was not the same as what Damon had meant. "Tell me, bitesize, do you feel the exact same way about both of us?" I shook my head.

"You both are opposites; Damon is like that soothing warmth of security, happiness, and safety," I said, finally looking up at him. "I know he'll always be that friend I can just be myself around." His jaw ticked and he raised an eyebrow. "And you... you consume me. I can't think straight when I am around you. You are the promise of unconditional love and passion..." I blushed, looking down once more.

"I'm waiting, love."

"I lose my mind around you. You're that electricity that keeps me on edge, fulfils me, and I know that you will always protect me from anything and everything." I looked up slowly, and he smirked.

"So basically, Damon's a friend, and I'm the mate material," he said, and I could sense his satisfaction.

I frowned, looking away. Did I think about kissing them both when awake? Maybe a few times here and there, but it was the emotional connection that I yearned for. Yes, maybe sexually, I thought of Liam more, a lot more... but that was because our dynamic had always been different, I always saw him as someone I loved sexually, whilst I saw Damon as a friend first.

"The bond is there."

"But without it, if you had to choose -"

"Liam... let's not do this," I pleaded.

"Fine, as I said, we'll figure it out," he said coldly.

I love you, Liam. I want to help you. He was going through so much...

I hugged him tighter, feeling him throb against my leg but I still didn't let go of him. His scent, the way his body moulded so perfectly with mine...

A silence fell between us, and I could sense his irritation lessening.

"Tell me how you got your scar," I whispered, not daring to look up. He let out a slow breath, as if pondering where to start.

"It was on one of our training visits up North. Some of the boys and I were out for some drinks, and there was this Alpha who was being a fucking dickhead towards us. He was from another country, so obviously, British pack laws under Alejandro didn't apply to him, and he was acting like a fucking entitled dipshit. He was too fucking full of himself, and I needed to vent... I may have underestimated him a little as he was carrying a blade laced with poison and was trying to gouge my eye out. I managed to do a number on him with his own fucking knife, too, until Rayhan pulled me off him," he said, not sounding very impressed. I jerked back, staring up at him shocked.

"Liam... you have never been so impulsive." I was shocked.

"Yeah... well, things change," he said, his voice cold once more. Even then, despite the coldness in his voice, his embrace was warm. He looked down at me. Raising one hand, he brushed my hair back, sending tingles of pleasure through me.

"I like this colour better," he said quietly, "and the length."

My heart skipped a beat, my stomach fluttering at his compliment as he pushed my bangs back off my forehead, looking into my eyes. I always kept them long so I could hide behind them if needed. Our heart's raced and as much as I wanted to kiss him, I wasn't ready for more.

"Thanks... so I see you got a tattoo. What's it of?" I asked curiously.

"Is that your way of asking me to strip?" He asked, caressing my leg.

"No," I said, trying to ignore his tantalising touch.

"I'll show it to you sometime," he said, his gaze falling on my lips once again.

"Liam... have you noticed your eyes sometimes darken? Like, not your wolf's eyes, I mean, they go really dark, like navy?" I asked hesitantly. The slight softness that had been in his eyes vanished and he looked at me sharply, frowning.

"No, what do you mean?"

"When you tore my shirt... your eyes weren't normal," I said softly. Reaching up, I caressed his jaw. The prickle of his stubble felt good against my fingertips. I didn't want him to get angry, but it was eating up at me. His brows knitted together, and he clenched his jaw.

"Are you sure you weren't just fucking imagining that?" He asked, tapping my ass. I gasped, jerking away, my cheeks burning as I glared at him.

"Hey!"

"Nice ass," he remarked as I scooted away, grabbing the gummy bears.

"Of course it's nice and cute. I've worked out a lot," I grumbled, frowning as I looked at him. Was he trying to change the topic? "Liam... I'm serious, I didn't imagine those eyes. Even earlier in your office, when you were playing with that knife, your eyes changed... and it didn't seem normal..."

I felt like an idiot. I shouldn't have mentioned it. He clearly didn't believe me, and I knew it didn't really make sense either...

"Never mind. Maybe you're right, and it's just me," I said, brushing my hair back.

"You don't actually believe that," he said, seemingly thinking about something. "There's something I wouldn't mind a second opinion on."

He got off the bed and walked into his closet. I wondered what he meant, glancing at the TV that no one was paying attention to. He returned after a short while holding an old book.

"What's that?" I asked curiously as he picked up the remote and put some music on instead. *Not a wise move, blue eyes...*

He walked to the bed, my heart skipping a beat at just the thought of one day this being permanent. I pushed the thought away when he sat down on the bed, frowning deeply.

"Grandma Amelia left me this book. Inside it was this note and a card I used to always draw when she did our readings. I don't have any fucking idea what it means," he said hesitantly. I knew he wasn't sure if he should share. I took the card and note, frowning as I stared down at it. I knew a little about readings, and this card definitely depicted darkness.

"You drew this card?" I asked, feeling my stomach knot uncomfortably.

"Yeah, three times. After that, she refused to read our cards," he said, settling back on the bed. His shirt rode up slightly as he flipped the book open, showing off his defined V. I looked away quickly and down at the card, frowning.

"Why not ask Rayhan to ask his mate? I'm sure they'll know what it means," I said. "His mate's powerful, Kia said so."

"That's an idea, actually. I looked online and didn't find shit. This card doesn't exist in normal tarot cards."

"That's because I doubt these are just any cards. We all know of Grandma Amy's lineage," I said, staring at the card. "And if you don't want to share why you want to have this card read, I'm sure they won't question you."

"Hmm, it's not that late... let me see if he's awake." He grabbed his phone, typing a quick text before dropping the phone on the bed.

"What's that book about?" I asked.

"She left it to me. It's about a curse on the Deimos line and the prophecy of light and darkness," he said.

That piqued my interest, but before I could even ask if I could have a look, his phone started ringing - an incoming video call from Rayhan.

"Let's hope she has answers," Liam muttered.

A Dark Explanation

RAVEN

I HADN'T SEEN RAYHAN IN a while, and I was super curious to see Delsanra. Everyone said she was really gorgeous, not to mention Dante was crazy over her. Liam sat up, answering it as he held his phone in front of him to reveal a shirtless Rayhan. From the look of his wet hair, it was clear he had just showered.

"Liam, hey, Raven," he said, giving me a small smile.

"Rayhan," Liam said emotionlessly. That mask that had lowered a little was back up. I had a feeling Rayhan knew we were mates because that knowing smirk he was giving Liam kind of gave that away.

"How are you and your family?" Liam asked.

"Good," Rayhan said, but despite that smile, the sadness in his eyes pulled at my own heartstrings. Alpha Rafael…

"Kitten… come here," Rayhan said, turning away. Oo, I wanted to see his pretty kitten!

I waited for Delsanra to come into view, and soon, she did. She was gorgeous. Her skin was pale yet glowing, or that might just be an after-sex glow. She was dressed in a red satin dressing gown, from what I could see.

"Hi, Alpha Liam," she said, her startling blue eyes meeting mine.

"That's Raven," Rayhan said.

"Raven…" she repeated. Curiosity flitted in her eyes. I saw her gaze flicker to Liam before a knowing smile that I swear reminded me of Grandma Amy crossed her face.

"Nice to meet you. I'm Raven, Kia's friend…" I trailed off, suddenly feeling awkward.

"Delsanra. Nice to meet you too, Raven."

"So, I'll get to the reason I called. I won't take up too much of your time," Liam said as Rayhan situated Delsanra in his lap, the phone angled on their faces. Another perfect couple. I smiled gently, loving the way Delsanra was snuggled into Rayhan's chest.

"Sure, what is it?" Rayhan asked, kissing her neck.

I watched as Delsanra whispered a spell and, before my very eyes, his hair dried back into its natural loose curls. Damn… I wanted that! She smiled as she saw me staring.

"Saves us from using the hairdryer," she said with a small smile. "Right, yum yum?"

"It's so cool!" I said with admiration. "And that nickname is the best."

"It is, isn't it? I love yum yums!"

"I love them too," I added. Liam gave us both a pointed look, whilst Rayhan chuckled.

"If you two want to talk, I'm sure you can exchange numbers. Lunas should keep good bonds," he said with a wink. My heart skipped a beat… Luna… Liam's Luna…

Our eyes met for a moment before he looked away, flipping the camera so that it wasn't on us and instead pointed at the card he held behind the phone.

"I was curious as to what this card meant. I found it down at Grandma Amelia's. She had some witch heritage," he explained curtly.

I watched the screen, seeing Delsanra's smile vanish. A frown creased her gorgeous brows and a flash of emotions I couldn't read crossed her face. Rayhan's arms tightened around her as he whispered something to her, kissing her neck. She shook her head before giving him a small smile.

"If it's hard for you -" Liam began.

"No, it's okay… that's a dark card. Of all cards, why ask about this one?" She asked.

"Just answer, please," Liam said curtly. Delsanra sighed.

"That card shows the darkness in one's life. See the shadow behind it? It's showing that it's taking over the man. On the floor, each body stands for different things. They are begging for forgiveness, help, hope, love, compassion. But the man, he doesn't care. He has become darkness itself.

The card can have three meanings depending on where it is drawn in a reading," Delsanra explained. My heart was racing as I listened.

"If it's the first card that is drawn, it means there is a darkness that is trying to destroy your life or bring ill will your way. If it's drawn second, it means you are going through a dark time, and you are in inner turmoil, that your demons are trying to win you over, but the fact that it's drawn second means there's hope, and it doesn't mean it's your end," she continued.

"And if it's drawn third?" I asked, my stomach a mess of nerves.

"It usually won't be drawn third," Delsanra said, shaking her head.

"Why not?" Liam asked.

"Because it would mean that the person is darkness themselves. They have embraced the darkness and lost any ounce of humanity that they once had. That the darkness within them will be their end, so that isn't something that is often possible." Her words seemed to swirl around in my head. Darkness… lost humanity…

No… Grandma Amy was right… his destiny is not set in stone!

"There was one Alpha years ago who had this card drawn on the third, and he was a monster through and through," she said quietly.

"So, it means doom," Liam said emotionlessly.

"More like the birth of a monster," Delsanra said quietly. "That card shows the person has submitted to the darkness within them and embraced it. With it, they will destroy everything in their path, wreaking havoc and carnage… and they'll relish in it." If this had affected Liam, he was doing a good job of hiding it.

"Who was that Alpha?" Rayhan asked, frowning slightly.

"Zidane Malone," Delsanra said, "Endora regretted losing him, saying he was the perfect depiction of darkness." Shit. Liam's granddad…

Liam was looking down. I didn't miss the way he swallowed before looking at them smoothly.

"Night. Thanks for your time."

"Goodnight, nice seeing you, Raven," Rayhan said.

"You, too. Night guys," I said as Delsanra gave me a small wave before Liam cut the call.

"Liam…"

"Don't," he said, standing up and running his fingers through his hair. "I don't fucking get it… Zidane was from the Asheton line… but he was still my blood. The book she gave me is about the Deimos line… is it a coincidence that we both drew the same card? Because I wouldn't ever want to be referred to as similar to him. That bastard was sick."

"You are not him, Liam," I said, standing up and walking over to him. He looked at me, his eyes flashing magnetic blue.

"How can you be so sure, Raven?" The uncertainty in his eyes that he tried to hide made my heart clench. I shook my head. I believed that Liam could never be darkness.

"I won't believe that, Liam. You have always been so caring, loving, and -"

"Used to be. I no longer am," he said coldly, turning away from me. "That book mentioned the prophecy of light and dark and a curse... I guess it could have the answers." He grabbed the book, but I could feel his anger and irritation rise.

"Hey, we'll look together. Relax," I said softly. There was something else worrying him, I could see it in his eyes. "Liam... What is it? There's something else that's eating up at you," I asked, cupping his face. He wouldn't look in my eyes. His heart was racing, and his aura was swirling around him.

"She wasn't wrong, Raven... there is something dark inside of me. There are times I just want to destroy everything, an anger that I want to unleash upon everything and everyone." His words were quiet and icy, sending worry coursing through me. "There is a darkness inside of me, Raven, and I can't deny that because I feel like I'm always battling to reign it in," he said, his voice so hushed and icy that it sent a chill through me, yet it wasn't his sentence that made my blood run cold... it was the dark navy of his eyes that bore into mine...

Despite my beating heart, I cupped his face, feeling those sparks course through me at our touch.

"Then, I'm going to be right by your side. We are going to figure this out. I'm sure Grandma Amelia gave you that book for a reason," I said softly yet firmly, biting my lip when he grabbed my hips and yanked me against him. His eyes returned to normal as he frowned deeply.

"You're probably right," he said quietly. Letting go of me, he grabbed the book and was about to read it when he swore. "Fuck, I got to go..." he said, standing up.

"What is it?" I asked nervously. Was it another killing?

"Zack may have found something. Stay here; I'll be back."

"Okay, I'll read the book until you come back. See if I can figure something out," I replied.

"Sure." He leaned down, placing a chaste kiss on my forehead, just the way he used to years ago. Our eyes met, and my heart skipped a beat as he gave me a smirk. "You're gorgeous. Have I ever told you that?" My mind was blank, not expecting that. My stomach was a mess of butterflies. He chuckled before walking to the window. "And fucking cute."

With that, he was gone. I pouted. I hated it when I got tongue-tied. I huffed, scooting back on the bed and resting my back against the headboard. I flipped the book open, becoming serious.

Grandma Amelia never did something without reason. This book had to be the answer. I flipped through it, skimming through it to start with, refreshing my mind on the different wolves' heritages and the original families. Of course, we all kind of come from these lines, but as time passed, many were mated to humans. Hence how the lines expanded and became weaker, and only certain wolf lines came from the original lineages. Each of the four lines had special abilities; the Volkovs were the most different. They were the first of the Lycans. It is said a Lycan is born every few centuries, and only one at a time would ever exist. Then we had the Asheton line, which had the gift of healing that sometimes popped up throughout history, but they were rare. Then there was the Solaris, who could control nature, creating more fertile lands and, at times, even command nature; they were the least known. The final one was the Deimos, who had the ability of speed, a sixth sense and the ability to foresee the future, abilities that both Kiara and Dante had inherited. The Deimos curse...

I slipped into the sheets as I began reading the origin of the curse. The original Deimos wolves, like the Solaris and Asheton, were arrogant, powerful, and gifted. They were seen as gods by the werewolf kind. Back when the gods walked the earth, there was a certain Deimos prince who upset Helios, the god of the sun, after challenging him to a match, not knowing that he was talking to a god. After being made a mockery of, Helios told the Deimos wolf, Andronikos, that he would make sure that the Deimos line perished and yielded to the darkness that would one day destroy them. Andronikos simply laughed at him, saying they were far too strong to ever be destroyed completely. However, Helios stayed true to his word, and the Deimos powers began to diminish.

Andronikos' sons and grandsons did not hold anything special in comparison to him. However, of course, Selene, too, held power, and so she countered Helios' curse with her own decree. She declared that when one of the original lines was mated with a Deimos, their offspring would be able to channel their Deimos blood and, in this way, preserve the Deimos' power. I looked up, mulling over what I had read. Kiara. This all pointed to Kiara. What I didn't get was how this came to Liam. How did it involve him?

I took a handful of gummy bears, eating them slowly as I continued to read. Helios vowed to Selene that his curse was not so easily broken, that there would be repercussions for such an act. Selene loved her wolves dearly, and so she sought a way to break the curse. That leads us to the birth of the prophecy of light and darkness.

I rubbed my head. It was a lot to take in, and the worst thing was that some of the words and story were missing. I was getting a headache from scrutinising the faded pages. Liam wasn't even back yet... two hours had passed, and it was pouring down outside. Turning the page, I looked at the paragraph before me – the prophecy itself.

When the promise of the sun and the wish of the moon clash,
As different as day and night itself, the birth of the two shall weaken the curse,
From light and darkness itself,
The blessed wolf and the royal prince.
Only then, giveth the gift of breaking the curse.
Alas, if failed, the curse shall end the Deimos for eternity.
Remember when the light gives birth to a....

I frowned, trying to read the word, but I couldn't. Shaking my head, I continued,

The darkness will reign through the veins of the Deimos prince.
Find the key within the darkness to break the curse.
Before the seventh blood moon, end the curse or yield to the darkness.
If all fails, under the blood moon, you shall take your final breath.
Will the Deimos line end or will it survive?
The answer lies within.

Urgh, that was so complicated. Flipping the page over, I searched in his bedside drawer, taking out a notebook and a pen, and began to look at the explanation and jot down key points.

Okay, this makes more sense... With each sentence and cross-referencing it back to the Deimos curse, I felt like I was on to something, even if it didn't give any answer on how to break the curse. As I continued to delve deeper, my stomach was a knot of nerves, and the fear that this could become Liam's reality hurt me deeply.

Another hour had passed before the window opened, and Liam entered, clad only in a pair of joggers, something that told me he had shifted. Water trickled down his chiselled abs and into the band of his pants, making my heart beat wildly. My gaze ran over his body, but it was the tattoo on his left breast that caught my eye. Along with the compass and symbols, there was a bird – a raven.

My heart thundered as Liam turned away quickly, as if realising what I was looking at. He walked into his closet, reappearing in a T-shirt.

"Liam… that tattoo -"

"It's nothing," he said coldly.

I frowned but didn't push it. I didn't know what happened, but I could tell he wasn't in the best of moods.

"Is everything okay?"

"Yeah," he said, running a hand through his wet locks, making the usually strawberry blond locks look a lot darker. "Find anything?"

"Actually yes. How much of this book have you read?

"Up until the light and darkness part," he said, grabbing a towel and beginning to dry his wet hair.

"Okay, so basically, the prophecy talks about how Selene and Helios tried to counter each other, and in the end, Selene's final attempt was that a pair of twins would be born, and only then would there be a chance to break the curse. The birth of the Deimos prince, you, and the blessed wolf, Kiara. It also says how a blessed wolf has no darkness in them, but there can't be light without darkness. So, where there is only goodness and light in Kiara, you inherited the darkness. Your birth was said to have weakened the curse, and then there's something about when Kiara gave birth - possibly to Dante, I'm assuming - that is when your darkness will reign. Do you think that's around the time you felt this darkness within you, or would you say it was when the twins were born?" I asked, looking at him. He was silent, listening with a frown on his face.

"Possibly when Dante was born… although I was angry with the entire mate situation at that time," he muttered.

"So, our mate situation only fuelled it. It's almost like a catalyst that made that darkness come out..." I murmured thoughtfully.

"Maybe," he said, frowning. "Anything else?" I looked down at the notebook.

"It says you will either relinquish yourself to the darkness and thus meet your end and, with it, the end of the Deimos line, or you will find the key to breaking the curse within, hence releasing your true potential and destroying the darkness that is trying to consume you, along with it, the curse forever."

"I would say it's all fucking bullshit if I didn't know better," he muttered. "That card says I am darkness, so we got our answer. End of fucking story. This darkness will be the end of me."

"It won't be," I said coldly, my eyes flashing. "You will not be the end of this line. It says within seven blood moons. How many blood moons have we seen since Dante's birth..." I trailed off, counting off in my head. He was born right after that fateful day when I found my mates. We have had six, which means we have less than three months until the next one...

"I have three months," he said in a flat voice that held no emotion. Three months before we might lose Liam... just the thought terrified me. No, never.

"Grandma Amelia said you can decide your own destiny," I said firmly.

"Trust me, Raven, this darkness isn't going anywhere," he muttered coldly, tossing the towel aside. "So, what? I have three months or so before I fucking die and this darkness consumes me? Great, then let's find this fucking killer. It's the least I can do in my short term as the worst fucking Alpha of the Blood Moon Pack. Once I'm gone, it will do everyone good," he said icily. He was on edge, and he was angry. I could sense his emotions despite his trying to keep them hidden.

"There've got to be answers, there's got to be a way. I will find the answer. This book must have something more to it," I said desperately, getting out of the warm bed. His back was to me, and I was worried.

"I don't have time to waste on a stupid book and a fucking curse. I have a pack to run, and things to do." I reached out, placing a hand on his back.

"Liam, this is about your –"

"I'm nothing special, Raven! Maybe me fucking dying is best for every-one!" He snapped, spinning around and making me flinch at the anger that whirled around him. His eyes blazed magnetic blue.

"How can you say that? Liam, you dying doesn't solve anything!" I exclaimed.

"Doesn't it? Maybe that's why you were given two fucking mates because if I died, you'd have a backup mate. At least dying means I'll catch a break from all this fucking shit that goes on in my head."

Those words stung. It hurt knowing Liam kept questioning why. The fact that he was tired of his own mind…

"This pack needs an Alpha!" I pleaded, frustrated.

"Kiara's kids hold our blood; they can take over," he growled.

I knew the bloodline continued through the Alpha heirs. Kiara's kids didn't count in this equation, even if they contained the Deimos abilities. They were Alejandro's legacy of the Night Walker Pack, not the Blood Moon Pack. I pursed my lips; Liam was far too angry to reason with right now.

I walked over to the bed, gathering up the card, notebook, and book.

"You do whatever you think is right. I'm going to find an answer, with or without you, because I am not going to see you just give up without a fight," I said quietly. "Goodnight, Liam."

"Why are you fucking trying so hard?" He asked when I unlocked the door. I paused, looking back at him.

"Because I will never give up on someone I love," I said softly.

I remembered the little blue-eyed boy who would always take care of me as a child. The first person to look out for me and show me that there were people who cared for me. It was high time I paid that pure-hearted boy back. One who was hidden deep within himself…

I didn't wait for a reply, shutting the door behind me.

A Scuffle

LIAM

W E THOUGHT WE HAD a fucking lead, but the rain fucking washed it away. By the way the marks were left along the far side, it was clear a body had been dragged along the northern side of the forest. What fucking confused me was that it was almost as if the person knew exactly what angles the cameras were positioned at, which made me even more pissed off. It meant there was a high chance that the killer was on the inside of the IT or surveillance department.

I had told Zack and Damon that I wanted to question every fucking person again, but they had been against it. I was fucking tired of being told how to run my pack. Coming back to my room, seeing Raven sitting there in my bed telling me how I might not even live past the next fucking blood moon was the fucking icing on the damn cake. If that were the fucking case, then what was the point of all this? What was the point of hurting her by keeping her around me? What was the point of keeping a good reputation within the eyes of my pack? I should just do this shit and make sure I found the culprit before the blood moon. If I was to die, then at least I could do one thing right before I go.

I dropped onto the bed, her scent still clinging to the pillow, and closed my eyes, my heart fucking clenching painfully. The selfish side of me told me to make the most of the time I had… to love her and spend it with her before it was too late. The bitter truth that I had wasted three years of my life left a sour taste in my mouth.

I stared at the ceiling, hating how I had just treated her so coldly. This shit was not something I wanted to worry anyone about, especially not Mom and Dad… and I shouldn't have told her. It wasn't fair to her.

If I only had a few months, then I promised I'd spend it well…

❧❧❧

I didn't know how long it had been, but I couldn't sleep. I got out of bed and left my room. I locked the door behind me and stared down at the keys in my hands, taking a second before I unlocked Raven's and silently slipped into her room. She was fast asleep. I closed the door quietly behind me. Yeah, I kept a key to her room. Who fucking cared?

I stared at her. She was holding one of her ugly plushies to her chest. Raven was the type of girl who would look past all the cute plushies in a shop and choose the ugliest, weirdest one she could find. She was the type of person who thought the neglected ugly animal in the zoo was cute, who would buy a used item to make someone happy even if she could afford something better. She was different. People hated her energetic attitude growing up, but I loved it; I loved her quirky nature, her warmth, and her fucking smiles. But I was hurting her too…

She turned over, her arms loosening around the ugly goddamn plushie as she pushed the blanket half off her. I realised she had ditched her over-sized top, only wearing her sports bra and leggings. I found myself quickly admiring her body. She was fucking gorgeous, from her rounded breasts, curvy hips and thighs, right down to that pierced navel of hers.

Leaning down, I tugged the plushie from her arms and tossed it to the ground before sliding into her bed. I knew I was a dick to her earlier, but I just needed something calming to let me fucking sleep.

I was hot and cold, angry and calm, but right then, I just needed her, wanted her. I was about to slip my hand under her head when she wrapped her arms around my head, pulling me to her chest and snuggling against me. Well, fuck…

Her breasts did feel fucking good…

Smirking, I slipped my arms around her waist instead, pulling her against me. Even if we couldn't be together for long, I would treasure the time that I did have, even if it wasn't long.

I awoke to a piercing scream. The next thing I knew, I was kicked with full force in the chest. It knocked me off the bed and straight into the shelf beside the window, sending shooting pain through my neck and back.

"Fucking hell, what was that for?" I growled, seeing Raven sit up and cross her arms over her breasts, her cheeks flushed.

"Why were you squashed against my boobies?" She shrieked.

"The fuck? You pulled me into your arms," I groaned, standing up. *At this rate, I won't even live until the fucking blood moon.*

"I didn't! You came into my room and molested my poor little potatoes." She looked down at her breasts as if sharing sympathy with them.

"First of all, they are nothing like potatoes, way too fucking soft," I said with an arrogant smirk, only resulting in her cheeks darkening. I didn't think she could get even more embarrassed. "Secondly, if I wanted to molest them or whatever shit you just came out with, I would have at least gotten a feel of your nips." Okay, I was wrong. Her entire face and neck now looked an even darker shade of red as she glared at me, absolutely mortified.

"Leave!"

"Good morning to you, too," I growled, walking over to the bed. I dropped onto the bed on my knees, leaning towards her. She jumped like I had just electrocuted her. Seriously, didn't she realise that just made it a whole lot fucking more fun to tease her?

"What's wrong? Never had a man touch your breasts?" I taunted, smirking when I glanced down at them.

"Liam, this isn't funny!" She growled, about to kick me again, but I yanked her by the ankle and dragged her flat onto her back. A squeak escaped her, and I wouldn't deny that it was pretty amusing.

"I'm actually finding it fucking fun," I growled huskily, about to straddle her when she tried to kick me again. "Seriously, love, you really need to learn to behave."

"Well, news flash, I don't like to behave!"

In a flash, she flipped us over, about to punch me, but I was ready. Grabbing her wrists, I rolled us over, but she pulled to the left. I was not expecting the force, and we both fell off the bed and hit the floor, tangled with the duvet. I kicked it off, pinning her wrists to the floor, straddling her hips with both of us glaring into the other's eyes. I was very fucking aware of my morning wood, and the way she wriggled under me only made me fucking throb harder.

"Let go of me," she pouted, trying to jerk free only for my arm to hit the bedside table, knocking it against the bed frame.

"Raven, are you okay? I heard something…" Followed by a gasp.

Both of our heads snapped up to the now open door to reveal none other than Mom standing there looking completely stunned as she took in the scene before her. I glanced down at the way this probably looked; me shirtless with a fucking hard-on, Raven a flushed mess… my eyes widened as I stared into Raven's unique, alarmed ones.

Well, fuck…

A Luna's Opinion

RAVEN

"THIS ISN'T WHAT IT looks like!" I squeaked, pushing Liam off roughly, my eyes falling to his hard-on. *Goddess, kill me now! Let the earth open up and swallow me whole! Is this karma for all the times I've seen Uncle El and Aunty Red making out and made fun of them?*

We both got to our feet, and Liam quickly sat down on the bed, grabbing the duvet and pulling it onto the bed before very smoothly draping it over his lap. I stood there staring at Aunty Red, who was smirking despite the clear confusion in her eyes. She crossed her arms under her big plushies and looked between us. I knew she could smell Liam in my room, which meant she knew he had been there for a while…

"So… I guess I disturbed you guys," she said, clearing her throat.

No matter how smoothly she was behaving, she was clearly surprised. She looked at her son, who was running his fingers through his messy locks. That just made him look so sexy… his chiselled body was drool-worthy, but now was not the time. He hadn't spoken a word, so I nudged his ankle sharply.

"Not really. We were just messing around," Liam said with a shrug. Aunty Red cocked a brow, and I felt my cheeks burn.

"Not in that way, we were just… Liam was being annoying," I stated lamely. Aunty Red nodded. Her lips pressed together in a pout, and I noticed she was staring at Liam's tattoo.

"Alright. Now, how about you tell me exactly what's happening? I know there was something going on between you two… and Damon. And if this is what I think it is, then -"

"What do you think it is?" Liam asked coldly. Aunty Red entered the room, shutting the door behind her.

"My assumption from the start was that Raven and Damon ended up as mates, and since you always loved her… you couldn't take it and left."

Okay, I was not expecting that! Liam frowned, glaring at the floor.

"But then Raven left, and I wondered if she couldn't choose between you or her mate." My heart skipped a beat thinking Aunty Red was wrong, yet she had the gist of it…

"Clearly, I wasn't enough, with or without the bond. You're wrong about whatever's going on, Mom. We aren't kids, so whether we were messing around or not, it really should have nothing to do with you," Liam said, standing up.

"No, it shouldn't, but when I know it's affecting you and your friends -"

"It's still none of your business," Liam cut in, curtly brushing past her and leaving the room, slamming the door behind himself.

Nice move. Leave me alone to deal with this. I felt a little hurt until his voice rang in my head,

I don't want to share anything. If you want to, then go for it, but tell her I don't want her harassing me. I'm sorry for coming to your room like that to begin with, I shouldn't have. I just couldn't sleep last night. My heart skipped a beat, and I hid my smile.

That's okay, but next time at least wake me up and let me know you're sneaking in. Waking up to see someone in my bed nearly gave me a heart attack.

Sure. Expect me tonight, then.

I rolled my eyes. Was he always so cocky?

I looked at Aunty Red, who was looking around the room. I saw her examining the edge of the door frame.

"They did a decent job with the paint," she said, turning her sage green eyes on me.

"Yeah," I said, brushing my hair back awkwardly.

"Want to tell me what's going on with you all?" She asked.

I looked at her. With everything going on, I could use a proper adult's advice. I fixed the bedding, my stomach fluttering as I realised I had spent the night with Liam. It had felt good, and I had slept well, too.

"It's a long story," I said.

"Well then, how about you go get dressed, and I'll go grab us some breakfast?"

I didn't get to reply when Aunty Red turned, leaving me alone in my room. I quickly grabbed some clothes and left my room to use one of the bathrooms, mind-linking Damon in the process.

Morning!

Good morning, you alright? His deep, sexy voice asked. A sliver of guilt filled me, thinking of how I seemed to forget him when Liam was around. Knowing that he was fighting his own emotions just so this could work…

I am. Can we meet later? I want to talk to you about something.

Sure, I'd like that.

Me too, I replied softly.

I finished showering, pulling on my purple lingerie, grey denim shorts, and oversized black hoodie. I returned to my room to see Aunty Red sitting on the edge of the bed with a tray of toast, croissants, pastries, and two steaming mugs of hot chocolate sitting next to her. I went over and sat on the bed cross-legged.

"So, shoot." I looked at her, thinking this was more awkward than I thought it would be.

"Okay, so three years ago, Liam and Damon both found their mate," I said quietly. Aunty Red frowned deeply but said nothing. "Both of them were mated to me," I continued, not missing the way her eyes widened. Yep, she was not expecting that, but she didn't speak, and I appreciated it. "Liam couldn't accept it, saying an Alpha doesn't share… and I get that. Damon wanted to make it work, but he didn't want to make a move with me until Liam was okay with it. I get that too…" I stared at the plate, picking up a toast slice.

"And what did you want?"

"I don't know. I just wanted everyone to be happy."

"Understandable, but I mean, what did you want?"

"I don't understand," I admitted, confused. Aunty Red picked up a cinnamon bun and crossed her legs.

"I'm asking what you want without even thinking of anyone else's feelings. Forget the boys; what do you want?"

"I…" I fell silent, pondering it. In an ideal world, I'd just want a mate who would love me unconditionally. I didn't want anyone to be in pain.

I didn't want a complicated dynamic. "I want to be happy; I didn't want such a complicated relationship," I said, shrugging.

"What about the two mates? Not considering their emotions, what was your take on it?" I never really thought of that in that way.

"Honestly, it threw me off. I don't get how you can have feelings for two people. A mate bond is ideally between two people, and here I'm paired with two separate people. It's not even a three-way bond, it's them two tied to me, but I've always liked Liam..."

"I know." I blushed. Was I that obvious?

"But after Uncle Aaron died and I was there for Damon, things changed. Before that, he always seemed to have eyes for Kiara, so I don't know..."

I carried on, telling her a little bit more about the situation and what we had discussed last night. She sighed, leaning back on one hand.

"I can't believe none of you even talked this out. Three years of absolutely wasting time. A complete waste of time, and still stuck with clearly nothing sorted out. It didn't do any good for anyone," she said. "I am going to give my honest opinion."

"Please do," I said, ready to hear it. Aunty Red did not sugar-coat anything, and I knew I needed this.

"Well, first of all, you all acted stupidly. I'll start with that idiot of mine." She shook her head. "I get that he doesn't want to share. Then, instead of running away, he should have stayed here and come up with a solution, but he's always been the passive one… even when they were younger, and both he and Kiara wanted something, he'd let her have it. I guess in this situation, he couldn't really just give you up but also didn't want to cause damage, so he left. I personally think seeing that you two didn't even move on probably just confused him even more, and he now thinks Damon has lost his chance, so he has decided he will take what he wants. What irritates me is that you aren't an item."

I remembered Liam saying, "You two can do whatever you want". That was a good point. He did give us a chance in a way… even if it was in anger and bitterness.

"Damon, his heart is in the right place, but by playing the lenient passive one, he's giving both you and Liam the impression that you aren't that special to him, and I won't deny that his relationship with Robyn doesn't help his case. He told Liam that he'd wait, but what if Liam never changes his mind? Then what? I know Liam is calmer than Elijah, but he is still his father's son. They are possessive and stubborn; they won't budge from their decision."

That was true too. Liam is fighting for me now, but Damon is still taking the back seat, and that did hurt deep down. Aunty Red was right. I did feel it inside, even though I knew his reason. He was trying to diffuse a bigger problem.

"And you, Raven, just waiting for men who lack brain cells and think with their dicks rather than their minds? This isn't the fifteenth century. We women take what we want, know what we want, and own it. You can't string them both along without being clear about it. I understand you want it to work, but how? How will it work? It's not only the emotional aspect, it's the sexual aspect. Will you give them a day each? Will you all be together? I don't personally see that happening, considering Liam can't even deal with the fact that you're mated to Damon. But things could change. What is your plan? *How* were you going to make this work?"

Her words rang in my mind, and I realised how true they were. I kept thinking, 'poor me' and feeling sorry for myself. Talking about making it work, but never about how it was going to work... *Urgh! I feel so stupid right now.*

"You're right... I never really thought of it. I just wanted everyone to be happy without even thinking how."

"This is reality, and as much as having two mates sounds hot or great, I don't think we realise that there's so much more to it mentally. We are beings with complex emotions. Ultimately, in a two-mates-to-one-woman situation, there will be jealousy and issues throughout. Even if it works out, you have to remember that there will be issues that will pop up, and you have to be ready to diffuse them because you are mated to them both. Just because Liam might be acting entitled, it does not mean you should be giving him more. What if when things work out, if they do, he always expects you to be his first? At his beck and call whenever he wants?"

Damn, I didn't even think of that... this was hard...

Aunty Red sipped her hot chocolate and paced my room.

"And what if it doesn't work? Who will you choose? And if you can't choose, ultimately, will you reject them both? You can't let them fight over you, you will have to be the one to make that decision then. We both know they can't be strung along forever. This pack needs its Alpha, its Beta, and it needs you. I want you all happy, and regardless of what decision you three make, you have to make sure that everyone is treated equally. You cannot favour Liam over Damon, even if he is an Alpha. Both are men who deserve equal respect and love. If you want it to work with both, then I'm hoping tonight you were planning on having Damon in here." She winked, smirking at me. I blushed, embarrassed.

"Tha- that wasn't the plan! I didn't even realise Liam was here. He snuck in!" I protested. She frowned at that. Any amusement she had was gone.

"Raven, you need to make sure you know what you want and don't let anyone push themselves on you, Liam included. If you have boundaries, make them clear. But also, I think you being uncertain about what you want doesn't help. Take the reins; they are your mates."

"I understand. Thanks for your insight, Aunty Red... I'm glad you gave me your opinion. It's really given me a different viewpoint on it."

"That's what I'm here for," she said with a small smirk. I glanced at her, thinking this was my chance to ask her about something else that had been on my mind.

"Aunty Red, there's something I wanted to ask."

"Shoot," she said, sitting down again.

"Dad said I had a brother, that..." *How do I say he died because of me?* "Do you know how he died? Sadness washed over her, and she looked at me sympathetically.

"Your parents never liked talking about it. I'm surprised they even told you," she replied, looking out the window. The sun shone on her vibrant red hair. She looked stunning, and she seemed to be lost in a memory from long ago. "Your brother was two years senior to you, but he was extremely ill. He had leukaemia, and even his werewolf healing ability wasn't enough to heal him. The doctors advised having another child, that the chances of a sibling being a bone marrow match would be potentially higher. However, his health deteriorated fast, and even when you were born prematurely..." She hesitated, looking at me keenly. "What else do you know?"

"Nothing, but I would appreciate it if you told me the full story. Mom and Dad won't ever tell me," I said quietly.

"Your father -"

"He blamed me for his death, so I think I deserve to know, Aunty," I said softly, hoping she listened. She frowned at that, clenching her jaw.

"You were not responsible! I thought Haru was delusional at the time due to two children on their deathbeds. How can he blame you?" She hissed coldly.

"Please, forget Dad; just tell me the full story," I pleaded. She ran her hand through her hair.

"You were born at four months rather than the usual six months. They already said Renji wouldn't make it by then, and it caused your mom to go into early labour. When you were born, you were far too weak, and they weren't sure you would make it either. Your father wanted you to get better and stronger, but it was far too early to even consider you for the bone marrow transplant or even check for a match. I can't believe Haru is actually blaming you for his death." She sounded angry, and her eyes flashed silver.

"It doesn't matter," I sighed softly. "So, he died because I was too weak to give him the bone marrow he needed?"

"Even then, the chances of him surviving were slim. You can't blame yourself for something that was not in your control. You were blind in one eye as well..."

"What?" I asked, surprised.

"That blue eye of yours, that was Renji's. When he passed away, the doctor offered to transplant it into you. Haru refused, but your mother said it would be a way for Renji to see the world he never had a chance to explore. When you were little, she used to say that you were so adventurous because you wanted to see the world and explore it for both of you," she said, smiling softly.

I swallowed hard. The emotions that rushed through me were inexplicable. So, I had an eye from my brother and had never been told? To think Mom had agreed.... Where was that mom of mine? She seemed so far gone under Dad's opinions. Renji...

"Where is he buried?" I asked. How could you feel sadness for someone you have never met?

"The children's graveyard down by the blossom trees," she said softly.

I nodded. I thought it was high time I paid my brother a long overdue visit...

Hope & Determination

RAVEN

I PUSHED OPEN THE LOW white fence that surrounded the graveyard. Not all children were buried here, as some would be buried with their parents, but there were still many graves. It was strange to know that I had a brother that I had never gotten to meet.

I looked down at the grass that was sprinkled with daisies and buttercups. Scattered between the small graves were several cherry blossoms. I walked through the graves, scanning the names for my brother's, and stopped when I saw a young woman bending over, placing an orchid on each grave. She turned, sensing me watching her, and gave me a small smile. It took me a moment to realise she was the Omega who I had seen in the kitchen the other night.

"Sorry…" she said, stepping away from the grave. I waved my hand.

"Oh, don't apologise! I'm just searching for a grave…" I said, giving her a small smile.

"Whose?" She asked. "I might know, I visit often."

"Oh… Renji Jacobs." She frowned, paused, then turned and pointed to the far side.

"It's under that cherry blossom tree," she said.

"Thanks…" Goddess, I didn't even know her name.

"Nina," she said with a smile.

"Thanks, Nina," I said before walking through the trees.

I stopped and stared at the marble tombstone. I could just about make the name out. It was so small that if I had never been told, I would never have realised that my brother was here. I dropped to my knees, feeling my eyes sting. I felt as if I had been robbed of something. This was my brother, someone who I had a part of inside of me, someone who had died but left me a gift, and I couldn't even spend a moment of my time to thank him or to remember him? I didn't even know of his existence. Some sister I was.

I looked at the date on the tombstone. He had barely been three years old. I placed my hand on top of the grave.

"Hi. I'm Raven, your sister," I whispered, fighting back my tears. I wanted to say so much more... but where do I start? I sniffed, reaching into the pocket of my hoodie and taking out a small octopus plushie.

"And this is Sparks." I said, "He's for you." I placed him against the tombstone near the flower Nina had left. "Where do I start... well, I'm sure you are watching down on us wherever you are, but I still want to tell you about myself..."

❧

Evening had fallen. My morning at the grave had felt like I had a burden lifted, and I promised to visit often. I had just rung Damon's doorbell. I had the journal and stuff in my backpack; even if Liam wasn't going to tell anyone, it wasn't something we could just deny. If Damon had no answers, then we needed to tell someone like Aunty Red.

Liam had asked what I had told her, and I told him she knew about us. He didn't ask me anything further after that, but I could sense his irritation. I knew he had been busy with other stuff today. I wondered if he planned to come to my room tonight, although Aunty Red's words rang in my head. Treat them equally... but I also knew she didn't know about Liam's curse. Hence I needed to tell Damon that. I rang the doorbell again, frowning when no one answered. He knew I was coming...

Damon?

Yeah?

I'm at the door?

Oh, shit, sorry! Mom's asleep, I'm coming!

Sure enough, the door was pulled open by a very wet Damon, a towel around his waist and water trickling down his body. My heart thudded as my eyes trailed over his sexy body before I blushed, looking away.

"Umm, sorry, didn't realise you were in the shower…" I said, unsure if I should hug him or not.

Oh, who cares? I hugged Liam shirtless. I moved closer, giving him a quick squeeze around the waist, much to his surprise. His arms wrapped around me, pressing me into his chest. My cheeks were burning when I moved back, my stomach fluttering, and he cocked a brow.

"I wasn't expecting that."

"Why not? I am a very huggy person," I said, closing the door behind me.

"Mhmm…" Damon replied with a smirk. "You had something serious to talk about, right?"

"Yes…" I replied, sighing.

"Alright, let me go get dressed and I'll be down in five. Actually, better come on up. You can wait in my room."

"Okay," I said, following him upstairs.

I entered his bedroom, watching him grab some boxers and pants. I turned my back, allowing him to get dressed, my stomach fluttering nervously.

"Alright, all done," he said, coming over to the bed. He pulled the duvet up and made some space for me to sit. His room was a mess, I wouldn't deny that… "Take a seat," he said, running his fingers through his wet locks.

"Thanks. Okay, I need you to pay attention. This is serious," I said, unzipping the bag and taking out the book, notebook, and card. Taking a deep breath, I told him everything I had learned.

Thirty minutes later, Damon was frowning. He had asked a few questions, but for the most part, he had listened and skimmed through the book towards the end. He now stood there, his emotions a mess.

"There has to be more. What did Liam say?" He asked, concern clear in his powder-blue eyes.

"Liam? He said whatever is meant to be will happen. He seems to have just given in," I said. Sighing, I placed my head in my hands for a moment. Damon crouched down before me, placing his hands on my knees.

"He's going to be okay. We aren't going to let anything happen to him," he said firmly, his scent clouding my senses. I looked up at him.

"Of all the Deimos princes, why Liam? Why someone who was so sweet and giving? Why did he deserve all this?"

"He didn't, but he is probably the one capable of doing this, of ending this curse. Even if he is the darkness, he has good in him. Darkness doesn't mean evil," Damon said, taking my hands in his. I nodded and took a deep breath.

"I also told Aunty Red about us…" I said, feeling a sliver of guilt at what I was about to say next. "This morning… she walked into my room when Liam was there." There it was the flash of pain, but it was gone as quickly as it came.

"Oh, so how did she take it?" He asked with a small smile.

"She said I need to know what I want and to not favour one of you over the other… and ultimately, if things don't work, I will have to choose one," I said, feeling my chest squeeze painfully.

"Well, don't think you need to treat us equally. We both know Liam is going through a lot. Right now, he needs his mate and friend. We need to be there for him, not make him become even angrier and more bitter," Damon said. *Oh, Liam, if you knew how much your friend cared for you…*

I stood up, feeling even more confident, knowing that I wasn't alone.

"So, what do we do?"

"The answer lays within…" Damon murmured. "Within the prophecy or within Liam? I swear we need to rip this thing apart like a damn Shakespeare play."

"English was Liam's forte," I grumbled. Damon chuckled.

"Yeah, well, guess we need to pull our socks up," Damon said.

"Hey, I did good, okay? I got a B…" I grumbled. "You barely passed!"

"That's because I hated reading. I only passed because Liam did my coursework." He grinned and I smiled. Oh, how I missed those days.

"There is someone who's a pro in literature…" Damon said hesitantly. "Someone who might see something we didn't."

"Who?" I asked.

"Robyn. She's still studying literature and history, and she's smart." I felt a pang of pain, but I nodded. If Damon could be selfless, then why couldn't I?

"Perfect, then we should ask her. She can be trusted, right?"

"Yeah," Damon said. He walked over to me and cupped my face, making my heart thunder. "This will be nothing more than her helping us." I smiled, looking up at him.

"Do I even have any right to act so selfish?" I asked, smiling softly. Damon smiled back.

"Of course you do, and I like it," he whispered huskily. "I do care for you, Raven."

"I know," I said, staring into his eyes.

His smile faded, his gaze dipping to my lips. He slowly looked back into my eyes as if seeking permission, his heart thudding as fast as mine was.

"Can I kiss you, gorgeous?" He asked quietly.

I nodded slowly, and Damon leaned down, claiming my lips in a soft, tender kiss. A wave of tingles rushed through me, the sweet taste of his mouth and the softness of his lips making my heart race like a galloping horse. I slowly placed my hand on his chest, kissing him back, but before we could deepen the kiss, Dad's voice erupted in my head.

How dare you? Where are you?

I flinched, pulling away.

"Hey, are you okay?" Damon asked, worried. I nodded.

"Yeah... Dad's just..."

"Raven!"

Both of our heads snapped to the window. Dad was there, and his anger was clear. I had no idea what I had done this time.

Damon and I quickly rushed downstairs, not wanting to disturb Aunty M with Dad's shouting. I pulled open the front door to see Dad standing there, his eyes blazing as he glared at me with such hatred that my heart skipped a beat.

"Who told you about him?" He hissed, advancing towards me. I stepped back, flinching, a vague memory of long ago flitting through my head. Dad had never hit me, had he? Subconsciously, something didn't feel right. He stopped a few feet away, holding out Sparks.

"I said, who told you?" He thundered.

"What the... calm down," Damon said warningly, placing his hand on my back comfortingly.

"I'm talking to her," Dad hissed back, shaking Sparks in front of me.

My breath hitched, my chest aching as I stared at Sparks, a plushie that meant a lot to me. I had made him when I was a child all by myself, with a needle and thread. I had pricked myself a hundred times that day, but I wanted a plushie. Dad and Mom didn't want to get me one, so I made Sparks. I remembered everyone asking why it was so ugly, but I told them I liked it, and I didn't want it to be one of those perfect, pretty teddies you can get from the shop. Since then, I had always picked the most eccentric, oddest plushies I could find because they were just like me; lonely, neglected, and alone.

Dad was shouting, shaking Sparks wildly as he said something I could no longer hear. My eyes were fixed on Sparks. *Please don't hurt it.*

"Mr Jacobs, calm down," Damon said, his voice quiet, yet a dangerous finality was in it.

"Oh, did I disturb you both?" Dad spat, taking in Damon's shirtless torso.

"This isn't what it looks like," Damon said curtly.

"I'm sure it isn't. She's always had a habit of playing people," Dad said hurtfully.

I wished I'd stop being so quiet, but I knew if I opened my mouth, I would end up saying everything and anything that came to mind. Perhaps that was what I needed to do, but I wouldn't do that when Aunty M was sleeping upstairs.

I felt the hair at the back of my neck prickle, almost as if someone was watching me from inside the house. I turned back, staring over my shoulder into the dark hallway, but there was no one there. Shaking my head, I turned back to Dad and Damon.

"Stay out of this, Damon. This is between me and her. Let's go," Dad hissed, trying to grab my arm.

"No, if you want to say something to me, you can say it right here," I said, trying to grab Sparks. He stared at me hatefully, his claws digging into Sparks.

Don't cry, Raven.

"You had no right to visit him! What did you think? That you could go there and cast your shadow of darkness upon him? Don't you get that you are nothing but an omen!" Dad spat.

"Mr Jacobs, stop it!" Damon growled, moving protectively in front of me.

"I told you to step aside!" Dad growled, trying to push Damon aside.

"Dad, stop it," I warned quietly, my eyes fixed on Sparks. His claws were already tearing through it. I felt as if a part of my soul was being stabbed and shredded.

"You know, there are already several questionable things on your head. Mr Jacobs, the Alpha wishes to see you. Now," Damon growled venomously.

"So, you will protect the whore!" Dad hissed.

"That's it, I'm done being nice," Damon growled, grabbing Dad by his cuff and glaring at him. "Yes, I'll protect Raven, and I'd appreciate it if you didn't call her that shit. I'll accompany you to the Alpha."

Do as you want! Raven! If you visit there again, I swear I will disown you and have Renji moved! You don't deserve to speak to him or see him! You should have been the one to be lying there, not him! I don't know why Selene didn't do just that! His words rang through the mind link.

With every word, I felt a stab of pain through me, but I remained silent, fighting back the tears that I refused to let fall. My face remained stoic and indifferent. Damon looked at me, concerned, but I simply gave him a small nod, telling him I was fine.

Sparks' head suddenly rolled to the ground before Dad's claws ripped his body apart.

I hate you!

I know, I replied emotionlessly.

"I'll be back," Damon growled, dragging Dad away.

I didn't reply, staring at Sparks' remnants…

".… And then Kia and I hid away. When Liam and Damon came out in their teeny, little shorts and started looking for their clothes, well, let's just say they never found them." I laughed, resting my weight back on my hands as I crossed my stretched legs at the ankles and smiled at the grave.

"You know, if you were here, you would have made a great addition to our little group. We could have had just one more person to tease. Boys are so much fun to tease," I said, smiling down at the grave. "Anyway, Renji… I want to apologise for not visiting before. I'm sorry that I've been a horrible sister and, you know… I want to thank you for the gift of sight. For this eye. Do you know what I'm super lucky about? That, despite it all, there is a part of you beside me forever. No matter how long Dad kept me from you, he could never keep you away fully because even though I didn't know, you were always by my side."

I looked at the grave, my heart clenching painfully. I didn't know it was possible, but I felt such strong emotions for someone I never even knew existed.

"Lastly, I am sorry I spent the last three hours boring you with my silly stories! But don't worry, I'm going to go for now, give you a break, but I'll be back another day to tell you about my life at Aunty A's pack. In my absence, Sparks will keep you company. He doesn't talk as much as I do, but he's great. As long as he's by your side, you won't feel alone, Renji… I… love you."

I stared down at the grave, a few tears escaping my eyes. Wasn't I worth anything? Is that why I was never told about my brother? He was easy to talk to. I felt at peace here… I wished he hadn't had to die. I wished we could have grown up as brother and sister. I wished I had been strong enough to give him my bone marrow… but we often wish for things that will never be. Wishing will never get us what we want. We just learn to live with life as it is.

I stood up, waving at the grave before I walked away, my heart aching painfully…

I fell to my knees by Sparks' remains, picking up his head. What had I done to be hated so much?

I needed to talk to my parents, just once, to put my feelings on the table and then end it with them. I was done with this toxic relationship. I had no time for fake relationships anymore.

As for Renji, I would find a picture of him, and I would keep him close. I didn't need to go to the graveyard to be close to him. Gathering up the wool and the bits of remains left of Sparks, I walked back inside, feeling down.

I was about to head upstairs when I heard the backdoor shut quietly in the kitchen. My head snapped towards the sound, and I calmed my heartbeat, slowly making my way down the hall and towards the kitchen, trying to catch a scent, but there was nothing out of the ordinary there. Had I imagined it?

Silently, I padded towards the kitchen and entered. Darkness bathed the entire room, but my eyes snapped to the back door. It was shut and nothing seemed out of place. How strange…

I was about to turn away when I saw the string of the blinds on the back door moving ever so slightly, a clear signal that I hadn't imagined I had heard it. I rushed to the door, yanking it open and frowning. It was unlocked. I scanned the area outside, my heart pounding, but everything looked to be in place. Slowly, I closed the door and locked it, staring around the kitchen.

Someone had been here, regardless of the fact that there wasn't a scent. There were certain sprays and things to disguise a scent, but who was it? I was about to leave the kitchen when my stomach plummeted with dread.

Was it the killer? If so, why were they… My thoughts died and my eyes went to the ceiling, my heart thumping. I ran from the kitchen straight up the stairs, fear consuming me as I rushed to Aunty Monica's room.

Please be okay…

His Ugly Reality

DAMON

"*L*ET GO OF ME, Nicholson!" Raven's dad hissed.

Yeah, I don't think so. Not when he gave shit like that to Raven. I had mind-linked Liam, who told me to bring him in. He fucking needed this.

Entering the headquarters, I dragged the growling and shouting Haru Jacobs to the room Liam was waiting in. I didn't think addressing him as Mr Jacobs felt right anymore, especially after all the shit he's clearly given Raven.

"If I were you, I'd stay quiet. I'm sure your reputation matters, and if you continue like this, the entire pack will know you're here," I growled icily, pushing open the door.

Liam was sitting on one of the two chairs, his legs up on the table, crossed at the ankles, playing with a small knife in his hand. He looked at us, his glare on Raven's dad with a glint in his cold blue eyes.

"Nice of you to drop by. Do take a seat," he said with a cold, mocking smirk.

"I wish to speak to Alpha Elijah! I am not going to let two boys make a mockery of me!" Jacobs growled.

Liam's eyes flashed, and he motioned for me to put him in the chair. I shoved him into the seat, trying my best to remain calm. The way he made Raven feel, although she hid it well, was not fucking fair.

"The thing is, Haru, I'm the fucking Alpha, not Dad. So, before you try to act like an entitled dipshit, show respect," Liam growled, suddenly flicking the knife across the table.

My eyes widened, and Mr Jacobs froze. The knife whizzed past his face, slicing his cheek in the process. He gasped. I saw a few strands of hair that fell to the ground before the knife impaled the far wall.

"Damn… I missed. So anyway, to what do I owe the fucking pleasure?" Liam remarked mockingly. We all knew he missed on purpose… sometimes I swear I didn't recognise the man he had become.

Will you grab my knife? His voice came through the link, making me nod and go to grab it, frowning at how deeply it was lodged into the wall. I returned to the table and placed it down on the table. Our eyes met and I saw him frown slightly. He knew Raven had been with me… and I suddenly remembered our kiss.

Goddess, that kiss… it was sweet, innocent, and beautiful, just like Raven. My heart skipped a beat when Liam looked at me, almost as if he knew what we had done. He took the knife and looked away, sneering. He scoffed and shook his head as if he wasn't surprised. Did he know? Fuck, I hoped not. Shit, this was fucking messed up. We shouldn't have to hide. I told her to pursue Liam. I needed to keep control of my emotions.

He turned back to Mr Jacobs, who I hoped knew that Liam was not someone to mess with.

"How about we start from the fucking top?" Liam suggested coldly.

Reaching into his pocket, he took out his phone and, after unlocking it, scrolled through the messages before he held up the phone, showing the texts he had sent Raven years ago.

"Did you have anything to do with these not getting to Raven?" Liam asked calmly. My eyes snapped to Mr Jacobs, who swallowed, his heart racing ever so slightly, giving us the answer.

Damn…

"Why?" I asked quietly.

"I haven't seen those messages before," he denied, his face pale.

"Lie," Liam said coldly, flipping his leg onto the floor and spinning the knife in his fingers. "So, you stopped both Damon and me from seeing her on the excuse that she didn't want to see us when she had no clue that we even came. You deleted my fucking messages, too! You knew I was her mate!"

"I di-didn't!" Despite the fear that was coursing through him, Jacobs growled.

"Are you going to confess all your crimes, or shall I put you under Alpha command?" Liam asked coldly.

"I have done nothing wrong!"

"I don't think Alpha command would even work. If he doesn't truly believe he has done wrong, perhaps you need to ask him question by question," I said, frowning.

This was a side of Haru Jacobs I had never seen before. The hatred and anger on his face were as if I had never known the true person, just a mask put forward to hide his reality.

"Alright, let's do this; every time you piss me off you will get a little punishment... I just wish I had a bigger knife, though," Liam remarked, standing up and walking around Jacobs' chair.

"Why did you delete the texts?" He growled, his Alpha command clear in the air. The surge of power made me step back as I stared at my Alpha, someone I still considered my best friend.

"I..." Jacobs gripped the arm of his chair, his knuckles turning white as he fought Liam's Alpha command. Liam slammed his hand on the table and Jacobs flinched.

"She... she doesn't deserve... happiness! Okay?" He growled through gritted teeth.

It was almost as if we were in sync. Both mine and Liam's eyes flashed, letting out menacing growls. I grabbed his throat, and Liam slammed his knife into his hand. We glanced at each other before I shoved Jacobs back roughly into his seat and stepped back, clenching my jaw.

"Raven deserves happiness," I said icily.

"She does, and clearly you've ruined a lot for her. Care to fucking share why she doesn't deserve happiness?" Liam asked coldly, grabbing him by his hair and yanking his head back.

"Because she's the reason I don't have my son with me! From the start, she was a fucking failure!" Jacobs shouted, the hatred and anger in his eyes so fucking clear that it actually shocked me. How the fuck hadn't we ever seen it? I knew the answer, even when my wolf whimpered inside.

Raven hid it all. She always smiled and acted normal. Back when we were young, even when it came to going home at the end of a long day, she used to delay it... *Fuck... why had we never seen the signs?*

A scream of pain made me look towards the table where Liam had shoved the knife into his hand once again.

"First of all, your son died as a fucking kid!" Liam hissed.

Wait, son? Both Jacob's and Liam's words resonated in my head. Fuck, I never knew Raven had a sibling.

"We only produced her for her bone marrow! And even then, she failed!" He shouted.

"Oh yeah? Well, guess what, you're not fucking god," Liam shot back, punching him across the face, snapping his head to the right as blood squirted everywhere. "The chances for your son to survive were slim, Raven had nothing to do with that. If you want to fucking blame someone, then maybe you should look to yourself. Why were your pups born with illnesses or lacking something? If you ask me, the fault was in you."

"She deserved it all! The hatred, the contempt! You all should be happy that I didn't dump her in a river somewhere!"

Liam slammed his head into the table, his anger blazing around him. His eyes darkened strangely - more than normal.

"Mr Jacobs…" I began, wanting to ask a question that was bothering me. I crouched down, staring up into his bloody face. "Have you always treated Raven like this? Like, did you abuse her like this as a child or just when she grew up?" My stomach twisted when he sneered coldly.

"I have always treated her, exactly the way she deserved to be treated!"

Rage

LIAM

MY EYES BLAZED AS those words left his fucking mouth. I grabbed his hair, slamming his head into the table.

How could she not have mentioned it? Fuck, didn't she even think to tell us? Clearly, we weren't real friends. But I couldn't go fucking blaming her for shit when I should have picked up the damn signs.

"Have you hurt her physically?" I asked dangerously. *"Answer me!"*

"And if I have?" He spat.

The anger that was blazing through me suddenly snapped inside of me, ravelling out of my control. All I could see was the darkness closing around us and Haru's face; it twisted in contempt for my mate, looming before me.

"Liam… don't!"

Someone was shouting, but it didn't matter, all I wanted was to kill the man before me.

Was that the smell of blood?

Who was screaming?

I felt a jarring pain in my back, and I was slammed to the ground. Someone was trying to pin me down. I glared up at the man who was on top of me, and it took me a few moments to realise it was Damon. Another flare of anger and hatred rushed through me, but the look of concern on his face made me falter. Why was he worried?

Kill him, and get back to punishing Raven's dad…

I tried to push him off, but he fucking refused to let go. What I hated most about Damon was that he was strong, and he knew how I fought.

Apart from my extra training at the Alpha training, he was the one who would always spar with me.

"Liam, listen to me! Raven wouldn't want this. For her... calm down, man. Think about Raven!"

I shoved him off with one push. This time I succeeded, and he slammed into the far wall. I stood up, searching for Jacobs, but all I saw was a bloody body with several deep wounds and a slowing heartbeat lying on the ground. One of his arms lay a few feet away... I looked down at my own hands, which were covered with blood. *Fuck...*

I looked at Damon, who was standing up, a concerned look on his face – something I didn't want to see. He had a few slashes across his chest and a heavily bleeding wound on his hip... fuck...

"Should I get someone to come see him and throw him in the cells?" He asked as if he hadn't just seen me fucking lose self-control.

"Yeah," I said coldly. I walked over to the man, grabbing him by his fucking collar. "That's what happens when you hurt anything that is mine," I hissed, slamming his head into the ground. I didn't really give a fuck if he was dead.

I knew Damon was mind-linking someone. I heard the sound of running footsteps, and soon three men came in to handle the dickhead.

"Get him fixed up, chuck the arm in the bin, and throw him in the cells," I growled.

"Alpha... the arm can be re-attached," one of the men dared to suggest.

"Oh yeah?" I asked, menacingly going towards him. "I know that our fast regeneration means we can replace limbs... but if I say bin it... it means bin it!" He flinched before bowing his head to me.

"Yes, Alpha!" He said.

"Liam..." Damon murmured.

I glared coldly at him. Something told me he knew about the fucking curse. He was acting way too fucking calm when I had just lost my shit. Before I could even reply, Raven's voice came through the link,

Liam, Damon, I think someone was here in the house. Aunty is okay, but I heard something. Both Damon and I glanced at each other before we ran for the door.

We got to the Nicholson house in under three minutes, rushing inside to see Raven pacing the hallway. She turned, about to speak, when she looked at both of us, her heart thundering when she saw Damon's injuries. A pang of jealousy and anger flitted through me.

"Did you two fight?" She asked, looking hurt.

"No," we both said in unison. We looked at each other and Raven smiled slightly.

"It's uh… most of this blood is your dad's," Damon said quietly.

She frowned but said nothing, looking between us again before she walked over, bunching her sleeve in her hand and wiping the blood off my face, worry clear in those unique eyes of hers. It calmed me, knowing she came to me first. She caressed my jaw for a moment, sending off those rivets of sparks before she moved away, staring at Damon's hip, the only injury that hadn't healed.

"You need to be careful," she scolded, examining the wound. She brushed her hand along his waist just above the damn injury. "This needs to be bandaged."

I was surprised he didn't just tell her I did that…

"You said you heard something?" I asked, trying not to pay attention to her legs that peeked out from under her oversized top. Her over-the-knee boots covered most of them up, but, fuck, did she look good even when she covered those curves of hers.

"I did… it was weird," she murmured, staring towards the kitchen. "Look, you two should go shower and get dressed. How about I make hot drinks and then we'll talk? About everything."

"Sounds good," Damon said, then turned to me. "I'll give you some clothes."

I frowned but nodded, and we both headed upstairs, stairs that I remembered climbing so many times growing up…

I didn't even get why he still fucking considered me a friend… I mean, sure, when his dad died, I was there, but once shit went down with Raven, I left them. Dreading, afraid, and waiting for the day I'd get the call or something telling me they had mated and marked one another…

Damon tossed me a clean shirt and sweatpants before motioning for me to use the bathroom on the first floor. He, himself, grabbed his clothes and made his way down the stairs. I frowned before taking a quick shower. I didn't want any favours from him, but if Raven wanted us to fucking try to get on, I was going to.

I wouldn't fucking lie, the fact that I may only have a few months to live kind of threw me off. My insistence that Raven should be mine didn't seem strong anymore. What if the curse was not broken and I did die? Then what would happen to her? I mean, a part of me wanted to just ask her to be mine for the next few months and shower her with all the fucking love I could, but that was just fucking selfish. That would break her even more once I was gone. I knew she had told Damon. If I'd had any doubts, seeing the book on his bed had been enough proof of that...

I walked down the stairs, only to see Damon standing in the kitchen, his top lifted up and Raven bandaging his hip. She had changed her top, which had gotten blood on it thanks to wiping my face earlier. She was wearing something that probably belonged to Aunty Monica. It was a plain lilac top that outlined her bra slightly. It skimmed over her waist and fit snugly around her hips. Fuck, she was gorgeous. The top went well with her tiny shorts, which stuck to her sexy ass so fucking perfectly. Just looking at her made my dick fucking hard.

That same anger flared through me at the sight of them as I walked into the kitchen, where three mugs of hot chocolate stood on the table. I clenched my jaw, watching Raven pat the bandage gently.

"There. Honestly, you should be careful," she scolded.

I hated how she could be close to him without even her getting all nervous, and then when I was around her... I looked away, feeling my anger rising, and took a seat.

"I'm glad you're not injured," she said, placing her hand on my shoulder. Our eyes met, and I frowned, looking away.

"What did you hear?" I asked coldly, tensing when she ran her hand through my wet locks before taking the seat next to me.

"I was about to head upstairs with Sparks -" Damon and I looked at her questioningly, and she sighed, pointing to a torn-up teddy. "Sparks." I frowned. I remembered him.

"I remember that ugly thing. Didn't you get the wool from a cushion Mom was going to chuck out?" I asked. Her eyes snapped to mine, her heart thudding, and I saw the glitter of what looked a lot like tears in them. She pressed her lips together and nodded with a small, shaky smile.

"Yeah... that's where I got it from," she whispered.

I always noticed you, Raven. I just wish I had noticed there was so much more going on...

She looked away, as if just realising where we were. She placed one mug in front of Damon, who sat across from us, before placing the other two in front of me and her.

"I was heading up and that's when I heard the door shut ever so quietly. That back door always made that slight crunching sound where it scuffed the tiles, so I knew it was the back door... but when I came in here, there was no one."

I looked around sharply, a sudden chilling thought coming to me. Just as Raven was about to take a sip, I placed my hand over the top of the mug, stopping her, her lips meeting my hand instead.

"Don't drink anything. From the autopsies, we found that the poison that shuts down the body is first administered. If someone was here... for all we know, it could have been the killer."

Realisation

RAVEN

"Let's have a look around, just in case," Liam said quietly. The moment he took my mug off me, all three of us stood up. Damon scanned the kitchen before looking at the back door.

"How did they even get in?" He murmured more to himself than us.

"The door was unlocked," I said, scanning the ground to see if there were any footprints or anything.

"The door was definitely locked. I always check and hide the keys so Momma doesn't wander out."

"You check the kitchen, see if anything looks out of place. Although you are so fucking messy, I doubt you'd even realise if anything is out of place," Liam remarked.

"I cleaned the kitchen today..." Damon almost sounded like he was complaining.

"Hard to believe," Liam replied, looking around the fairly clean kitchen. "I'll take a look outside." It was almost like old times with their friendly banter. I just hoped that this could become permanent.

"How is the drug administered?" Damon asked. "Did Esteban say?"

"Nah, he said it could be in any way. The thing is, even if it's injected or taken orally, we wouldn't know as we heal pretty fast. Before the organs start shutting down, whatever way it's administered would be healed over."

"So it depends. If it was the killer, they would choose something tha-" I was cut off when Damon swore.

"Wait... for anyone to get in without a break-in means there has to be a copy of a key, right?" He murmured as if a sudden thought had come to him. "I'll be right back." Liam frowned as Damon rushed into the hall, pulling on some sneakers before leaving the house quickly. Liam and I exchanged looks.

"Guess someone else had a key, too?" Liam remarked, turning his back as he opened one of the cupboards. Robyn... wow...

Don't go there, Raven.

But I couldn't deny that it really hurt to know that they had been so close. Maybe it was to keep an eye on Aunty M... it wasn't like I was there, neither as a mate nor as a friend.

Liam left for a bit to search the back garden, but he came back frowning.

"Nothing?" I asked, looking around the kitchen for anything out of the ordinary.

"Nothing. So far, those who have been killed were not warriors. Either Omegas or just standard wolves. If that was the case here, then maybe if it is the killer, they would've only targeted Aunty Monica... I wonder if there is anything here specifically that only she uses..." Liam murmured, crouching down as he looked around, his eyes glowing. "No fucking scent either..."

"A spray or something?" I asked. He shrugged, standing up and scanning the kitchen. I continued looking in the food containers, sniffing for anything odd. "What happened with Dad?" I asked. His piercing eyes turned to me, and he frowned.

"How long has he been treating you like that, bitesize?" He asked me, his eyes darkening with anger, only making his scar stand out more.

Shit, maybe I shouldn't have asked. He walked towards me, and my heart skipped a beat.

"Like what?"

"Don't play dumb, love," he warned. I moved back, cursing inwardly when I hit the worktop. He leaned down, placing his hands on either side of the worktop. "I'll ask you again. How long has he been an abusive dipshit towards you?" I looked up at him. I couldn't lie when he knew the truth, or some of it.

"He's always been weird towards me, but it's okay... I'm fine. It's not like -"

"Stop with your 'I'm okay' crap all the time, Raven. You always want to help others out, but what about yourself?"

"I was planning on having a final word with them. But, Liam, right now, we need to see if someone was actually here…" I whispered, placing my hand on his bare chest. That intense spark rushed through me, and my heart thundered under his gaze.

"When you have that word, I'm going to be by your fucking side. Your father will be punished for his crimes, and I'm not going to drop this or cut him any slack," he growled.

"Okay," I replied softly, thinking, *Nope, I will face them alone.*

Reaching up, I brushed his hair back. His hands went to my hips, and he pulled me against him. In my heels, the top of my head reached just above his shoulder. *Still tiny,* I frowned. Maybe I needed to keep a stool close by so I could look him straight in the eyes and not feel so small.

Our eyes met, and I couldn't deny the intense chemistry that was present between us. My entire body yielded to his touch, wanting so much more…

"So, you told Damon about the book?" He asked quietly. I nodded, trying to ignore how good his body felt.

"He's your friend, and if you want to give up and act stubborn without even finding a solution, then you have us to help you," I stated with a glare. "And don't tell me I was wrong to do so."

I was about to tug away when he yanked me back into him, making me gasp when our bodies slammed together, sending off rivets of pleasure. I almost moaned, feeling him throb, my core clenching. *Fuck…* I tensed in his hold, not trusting myself.

"What's wrong, love? You don't seem to get so nervous when you're around Damon," he whispered seductively, yet I didn't miss the flash of anger in his eyes. My heart thundered, and I gasped when he suddenly lifted me up, placing me on the worktop and forcing my legs apart so he could stand between them. Goddess…

My stomach fluttered with butterflies as I looked into those sexy, piercing cerulean eyes. His hands went to the back of my ass, and he pressed me against him, making me gasp and grab hold of his shoulders. *Why don't you get the difference between you and Damon? When I'm around you, I feel giddy and nervous. My heart feels all funny, and I can't think straight…*

But I couldn't say that out loud.

"Because you make me crazy…" I whispered quietly. His scent was filling my nose, and my core throbbed at our position. A smirk crossed his lips, and his gaze dipped to my own.

"I like crazy," he murmured, lowering his head slightly.

I licked my lips, arching my back as I pressed myself to him fully. My eyes fluttered shut, but this time instead of kissing me, his lips grazed my ear.

"You're fun to play with, darling… have I ever told you that it's a turn-on when you get all flustered?" He whispered, making my breath hitch.

Oh, Goddess, don't make me into a pile of mush.

His lips met my neck, and I gasped. A soft moan escaped me when he sucked on my skin gently, sending explosive sparks rushing through me. His hand ran down my back, and no matter how much I tried to focus, I couldn't. My mind was going blank. All I could think about was him.

"Liam…" I whispered, running my fingers through his hair.

Suddenly, the answer to why I always stopped or pushed him away hit me like a tonne of bricks – with Liam, I felt like I lost control. My body yearned for nothing more than to melt into his touch. The way he pushed my boundaries… I knew all he needed to do was push me hard enough, and I wouldn't be able to resist the intense desire that ate me up inside every time he was in the same room with me. He consumed me completely.

He placed a second kiss just beneath my ear before moving away with a smirk on his face. I wasn't able to respond, my heart thundering at the thought that had just crossed my mind.

"Should we get back to looking?" He mocked softly. "Or do you want me to continue?"

"N-no, we should carry on," I said, feeling my cheeks burn.

"Sounds good," he smirked, leaning in.

"Liam, I meant looking!" I said, glaring at him despite the blush on my cheeks.

He chuckled, and for a moment, I remembered the old Liam. Somewhere deep down, he was still there. I found myself giggling weakly, too.

"Let's find answers," I mumbled, trying to get down, only for Liam to lift me off and place me on the ground. Our eyes met, and his brows furrowed.

"I'll be waiting for the full story on your old man soon enough," he said quietly, "and he's going to pay."

His eyes burned with anger, yet when he leaned down to place a soft kiss on my lips, his touch was tender, leaving me a mess of nerves.

DAMON

I left the house, mind-linking Robyn to ask where she was.

At the packhouse. Is everything okay, Damon? She sounded worried, and I felt a little bad. I had totally shut her out since Raven got back, and I ended things. Yeah, what I did wasn't right, but Robyn was the one who got hurt in this equation, along with Raven.

Yeah, all's good, I just need to ask you something, I assured her, breaking into a run.

She had a key to our house. Back when she used to house-sit and watch Mom, I gave her both the front and back doors. I just needed to make sure she still had them or ask if she had come around today, although I doubted that...

Okay. She sounded hesitant.

I entered the packhouse, going straight up to Robyn's room. I knocked on it lightly, and she opened it pretty quickly. I guessed she was watching out the window.

"What is it?" She asked, crossing her arms.

I didn't miss the fact that she was wearing a fluffy gown over her pyjamas, which were usually pretty skimpy. I liked how Robyn was taking all this and the respect she was showing Raven, although it just made me feel worse. She had told me she loved me, but I hadn't said those words back to her. I knew she felt it, but I had my reasons that I could never return her love.

"Damon?" I blinked and nodded.

"Sorry... it's just... you still have the keys to my place, right?" Her eyes widened before she nodded.

"Shit, I'm sorry, I didn't realise, I totally forgot -"

"Hey... it's okay..." I said, seeing the panic on her face. She nodded, forcing a fake smile before she rushed to her drawer and began rummaging in it.

"I'll give it to you right now."

"Robyn... Relax, I'm only asking because Raven thought she heard the back door, and it was unlocked." She looked at me, and I didn't miss the flicker of sadness in her dark eyes at the mention of Raven.

This was my fucking fault.

"Oh, no, I haven't visited again. I only see Monica on her walks. I haven't been to yours, and I swear I wouldn't have gone without your permission," she rambled. I walked over to her, placing my hands on her shoulder.

"Hey, it's cool. I'm not accusing you, I'm just wondering if maybe you did or if someone else was there or something," I said softly.

"Oh, okay," she said, shrugging my hands off her and turning back to the drawer. "It was in here with the SpongeBob keyring..."

I frowned. Had someone stolen it? But just when I thought she wouldn't find it, she pulled it out with a smile that lit up her face.

"Told you. Here. I no longer have anything that belongs to you," she said softly as I took them from her. Her heart was thudding. Although I wanted to give her a hug, I knew I couldn't.

"I'm sorry, Robyn, for being -"

"Don't. I don't regret the time we had together, even though it was just a distraction for you. I'm just sorry that you got involved when you had a mate. Now, goodbye, Damon. Leave." She turned her back to me, and I nodded. She was a brave one. Although she was nineteen, she was so damn mature...

"There's one more thing. There's something that we... that I need your help with, and there's no one else I can really ask. We just need a little insight into what a text might mean," I said hesitantly.

"First of all, make up your damn mind. Is it I or we?" She asked, turning back towards me with a frown on her pretty face.

Damn, I forgot how feisty she could get if you crossed her. I ran a hand down my face.

"We. Raven and I."

"Does she know you're asking for my help?"

"Yeah, we just want your intake on it."

"Fine, then just pass her whatever you need help with. She lives here at the packhouse. I'd rather talk to her than you," she replied in a clipped manner. I smiled slightly.

"Thanks."

She didn't reply. I left the room, staring down at the keys in my hand. *Do I give the keyring back?*

Deciding against it, I headed back home slowly. If Robyn still had her key, then who could it have been? Had Raven imagined it?

I unlocked the front door and saw both Liam and Raven still looking around the kitchen. Raven glanced at me when I walked into the kitchen, but Liam, who had just taken out Mom's pillbox, was frowning thoughtfully. He opened it up, looking down at the pills.

"Does anything look different in here?" He asked, holding it out to me. I walked over and looked inside.

"They all look fine," I said, shaking my head.

"Still, take them to get checked. We can't risk it," Liam said, frowning.

"Maybe I did imagine it," Raven murmured, looking worried. "Maybe there was nothing here, but I swear I felt watched at one point..."

"I doubt that you imagined it. If you heard the door, someone was here. Maybe it wasn't the killer, but we can't really take chances," Liam said, frowning. Opening the back door, he stepped outside, scanning the garden once more.

"I agree, we can't take chances," I added, sighing.

"I think we should get cameras installed within the pack grounds, too," Liam muttered, running a hand through his hair before he turned back to me. "Assign guards to watch this house. You're often not around; Aunty Monica can't be left alone." I nodded as Liam stepped inside again, locking the door. "Get the damn locks changed, too."

"I will. It's nice to see you care," I said with a smirk. He raised his brow, his scar catching my attention.

"I care for Aunty Monica. Don't get the wrong fucking idea," he growled.

Nah, you still love me deep down, bro.

Raven smiled as she watched us, and I couldn't resist smiling too. Things were looking a little better.

Once again, we became serious. We were no closer to knowing who could be behind this than we were an hour ago.

"I'm going to go grab my stuff," Raven said, leaving the room and leaving Liam and me alone. Suddenly, the kitchen seemed a tad fucking too small for both of us.

"She told you about the curse, right? I hope you're not pitying me right now because I don't need that," he said coldly.

"Nothing to pity because we will get to the bottom of it and break it," I said, shrugging.

"Delusional. You should be happy, though, right? I mean, if I die... Raven's all yours." My eyes flashed, and it took all of my fucking self-control not to punch him across that goddamn face of his to knock some sense into him.

"The fact that you think I'd even think that... I guess you really have forgotten what kind of person I am. You know I'd die for you if I had to," I said quietly.

"Yet you can't reject her for me." I felt a sharp stab of pain, staring at him. Would rejecting Raven help him? Because I would do anything for him. I wished he'd fucking see that. "Thought not," he said, smirking coldly before walking out of the kitchen, his aura rolling off him. It was different; I could feel the darkness swirling around him this time. Raven paused on the bottom step, looking between us as she clutched her bag.

"Shall we? Or do you wish to stay, darling?" Liam said coldly. I knew Raven could sense the change, too.

"Coming," she said, giving me a smile. "Goodnight, Damon."

"Night, guys," I replied.

The door shut behind them, but that question lingered in my head. Would rejecting Raven be the answer for us?

Burning Hot

RAVEN

W E REACHED THE PACKHOUSE, and Liam was quiet, but I could tell he was mind-linking from the way he nodded once or twice. I had a pretty good idea that he was discussing security or something. We entered the packhouse, and Liam went into the kitchen. I headed upstairs, wanting a shower and to actually just get a good night's sleep.

The lingering thought that time was running out for Liam niggled at the back of my mind. How did we break this damn curse? How would we know the curse was broken? We needed to do this ourselves; I would get to the bottom of this. *The boys can work on finding the killer, and I will work on this.*

Damon? I called through the link.

Yes, gorgeous?

Did you ask Robyn?

I did, she said you can show her since you're at the packhouse. I don't think she wants anything to do with me.

As much as I feel a little bad for you, I like her.

Yeah?

Yes, I replied. *She was there for you when I wasn't.* **Night night, Damon.**

Night, gorgeous.

I smiled, cutting the link. I grabbed some clothes and my toiletries, then went to have a shower, mulling over everything once again. I had felt someone watching me when Dad was there, but when I had looked back, no one was there. It couldn't have been Aunty Monica because I would have heard her come down or go up; it was down the hall towards the kitchen.

The bathroom was steaming up, and the warm water was soothing, making me drowsy as I pondered over everything. I had just shampooed my hair, massaging my scalp slowly, when suddenly, the water became scalding hot.

A scream escaped my lips as the water seared my skin, and I jerked away from the downpour, but it was a full overhead shower, not giving me much space to escape. The shampoo stung my eyes as I frantically felt for the sliding door. Tumbling out of the burning shower, I caught my foot on the edge and tumbled to the floor just as the bathroom door was ripped off its hinges.

"Raven!" Liam's voice called.

I quickly crossed my legs and arms over my chest. It felt as if my entire body was on fire, especially my left side.

"What the…" I heard him mutter before I felt a jug of cold water being tossed over me. I gasped, welcoming the soothing coolness. "Raven! Raven, baby, look at me." Liam's worried voice came before a towel wiped my face gently.

I opened my eyes, grateful for the towel he threw around my shoulders. Worry was clear in his magnetic blue eyes.

"I'm okay… the water just turned extremely hot," I said, looking down at my leg. My skin was already very red, but I could see it was healing already. Liam frowned, staring at the water and helping me to my feet. I turned and saw a few of the other young men and women who lived here at the door watching curiously.

"Are you okay, Raven?" One of them asked.

I nodded. Owen stood there. I glared at him when I saw him smirking and looking me over. I looked down, glad that the towel was covering the important bits, but I still felt bare.

"Get the fuck out of here," Liam growled, and they all scattered.

"I'm okay… I just… I need to wash my hair," I said, feeling a little dazed. Liam nodded, placing his hand under the water.

"It's okay again. Maybe there's a fault with the boiler. I'll have it sorted," he muttered.

"Hmm, I'll just wash my hair in the sink," I mumbled, feeling a little shocked still. Liam nodded as I wrapped the towel tightly around me and tucked it in over my breasts. "You broke the door," I said, staring at the door that lay flat on the ground.

"You screamed," he countered, unmasked worry on his face. "That fucking scared me."

"I'm sorry," I said, turning the cold tap on. "You can leave."

To my surprise, he picked up the jug and began filling it with water.

"Liam, I'm fine…" I protested, feeling bare. "I can hold a jug."

"I didn't say you couldn't."

With that, he gently pushed my head down in the sink and began pouring the water over my head, his fingers running through my hair as he washed the shampoo out. My heart was racing, and my stomach fluttered at the sweet gesture. I didn't say anything, clutching my towel, glad it fell to mid-thigh. Closing my eyes, I gave in, enjoying the feel of his fingers running through my hair.

"You do know the water's coloured."

I laughed, "Obviously, vibrant hair dyes always wash out."

"Yeah, I remember giving Mom a white towel once after she'd showered. She got annoyed. I actually never knew her hair wasn't naturally red until I was like ten."

"Really?" I asked when he finally turned the tap off and rubbed a towel in my hair. I slowly stood up straight, my heart pounding as I stared up at him.

"Yeah, she's always had red…" he said, tossing the towel aside.

"So how did you find out?" I asked, not missing the way his eyes trailed over my collar bones and cleavage.

"I asked who my hair took after." He shrugged. I smiled.

"You really were too innocent," I said, reaching up and pulling his cheek.

"That hurt," he growled, lunging at me. I giggled, ducking under his arm and darting to my clothes.

"Get my toiletries, please!" I got a few curious looks as I made my way to my room.

Whoring around with the Alpha, huh? Owen's voice flitted into my head. I looked around, seeing him standing down the hall.

Piss off, Owen. Remember I'm your trainer, I growled back, my eyes flashing. *And I don't think Liam will appreciate your crap.*

Whatever. He turned and walked off.

I entered my bedroom, closing the door and pulling on my Brazilian briefs. I slipped on an oversized black nightshirt and went to blow-dry my hair, remembering Delsanra's magic. How lucky was Rayhan's kitty to have magic? I know our kind was still not fully accepting of magic, but things were looking up since the treaty had been signed between both species. And I, for one, thought it was totally badass.

A knock on the door made me look up, turning the hairdryer off.

"Enter!" I knew it was Liam before the door even opened. He stepped inside, his eyes running over my bare legs.

"How are the burns?"

"I'm okay, it's literally gone. I think it was more the shock," I said, my stomach fluttering with nerves when he shut and locked the door.

"Good. The boiler is completely fine, no idea what that was about." He sighed, running his fingers through his hair.

"Don't worry about it," I said. Standing up, my oversized top fell to mid-thigh. Was he really going to spend the night? "Are you really going to sleep here?"

"I told you yesterday I am."

"Well, you didn't ask," I said, crossing my arms.

Liam smirked, slowly pulling his shirt off and tossing it to the ground. My heart thudded as I stared at his sexy, inked body, licking my lips at the way his muscles flexed with such a simple move. Goddess, he was so sexy...

"Well, I'm asking now. Want me to stay, love?"

LIAM

I ran my eyes over her, dressed in that clingy, black, oversized nightshirt that slipped off one of her slender shoulders, draping over her perky, round breasts. Her sexy legs were perfectly on display for me, making me fucking hard. Her gorgeous eyes stared at me, that slender nose and plump, pouty lips that were begging to be kissed... fuck, she was fucking beautiful. There was an innocence beyond that mischievous look of hers, one I was ready to destroy and show her exactly what she was missing out on, but I needed her to be ready for that...

I walked towards her, waiting for her answer.

"I'm waiting, darling," I murmured, taking hold of her chin. Her breath hitched, her lips parting slightly as she stared into my eyes.

"If you want to," she said softly. I smirked.

"Is that a yes?" I pushed seductively.

"Yes." She poked her eyes out at me, and I tugged her into my arms.

"Good," I murmured.

Leaning down, I placed a soft kiss on her lips, letting the sparks course through me. She whimpered against my lips, and I lifted her up, grabbing the back of her ass and deepening the kiss.

Fuck… her panties didn't cover her ass fully. The image of her in the steamy bathroom flashed in my mind. Although I had covered her quickly, far too concerned, the glimpse I did get of her naked made my dick twitch.

Fuck, she was going to be the death of me…

She wrapped her arms around my neck, deepening the kiss and sensually running her tongue along my lips, seeking entrance. She moaned when I squeezed her ass.

"Liam…" she whimpered, her cheeks flushing when I pushed her up against the wall, kissing her harder.

"Raven," I whispered, giving her a moment to breathe before I began kissing her neck hungrily.

Her heart was thundering. The addictive, tantalising scent of her arousal hit my nose, making me bite back a growl. My eyes blazed as I ran my fingers through her hair, yanking her head back and claiming her lips once more in a bruising kiss. Her nails dug into my back as she kissed me back with equal passion.

This was fucking heaven; this was all I wanted. If I could just kiss her forever, I'd be happy. She moaned loudly, her legs wrapped around my waist, struggling for a control I wouldn't give.

"Goddess!" She moaned, breaking away from my lips and gasping for air.

I ran my hands up and down her thighs before squeezing her ass just as she pulled me closer, placing soft, sensual kisses down my neck. Her tongue flicked out, running down my neck and making me groan. I pulled her back, kissing her over her neck and collarbones and down her bare shoulder, making her shiver in delight. Her nipples were taut against her shirt, her heart pounding, and I couldn't focus on anything but her.

I grabbed her breast, loving the way it fit in my hand, firm yet soft. She was fucking perfect in every damn way. The hottest, fucking sexiest girl I'd ever seen. I groaned, twisting her nipple and making her whimper. *I just wish this shirt wasn't between us…*

"Fuck, Liam…" she whimpered. Her back arched, her head tilted back, and her pouty plump lips parted slightly.

I took a deep breath. As much as I wanted to fuck her senseless, I needed to take it slow. I wondered how far she'd let me go, but I knew I needed to stop before I ended up losing control. I was good at controlling myself, yet… around her, it was getting fucking harder.

I carried her to the bed, holding her with one arm as I pulled the duvet back and placed her down. She looked up at me, sitting there with her legs tucked under her; her hand on the bed between her knees, the other to her lips and her cheeks flushed. I groaned.

"Raven, can you fucking stop?"

"Stop what? I'm not even doing anything." She frowned, despite the fact that her heart was still racing and her chest was heaving. That had always been the case; Raven never realised what she did, but she always looked so fucking sexy.

I got onto the bed on my knees, leaning over her. I tugged her back by the hair and gave her a sexy smirk.

"Exactly that, love," I whispered, flicking my tongue out and tracing it over her lips, only satisfied when she whimpered, her heartbeat thudding even louder. Smirking, I moved back and laid down, placing one hand under my head, giving her a moment to recover as I tried to control my raging emotions.

"Liam… when did you get this tattoo?" She asked after a moment, placing a hand on my chest.

"A few months after I left…" I replied, trying to ignore the sparks.

"Does the raven represent me?" She asked softly. I cocked a brow.

"I knew you were never a bright student, love, but isn't that a bit obvious?" I remarked. She glared at me, smacking my arm hard. "Fuck, what was that for?"

"For being a mean jerk! I wasn't that bad at studies; I just didn't bother…"

"Exactly," I smirked. She rolled her eyes.

"Well, we can't always be an A-star Westwood kid," she said, batting her lashes before laughing. "School… damn, I remember how all the girls would be googly-eyed over you, but you never paid them attention."

"Because my eyes were on someone else," I said huskily, placing my hand on her thigh. I loved how the blush coated her cheeks. The things she did to me…

I didn't get how I could love someone so fucking deeply, wanting to respect them and care for them, yet at the same time, I kept thinking explicitly about her and all the dirty things I wanted to do to her. Guess it went hand in hand, right?

"Eyes up here, blue-eyes," she said, and I realised I was staring at her thighs.

"Have I ever told you that I love your thighs?" *And that I want to kiss every inch of them before I devour you?*

She blushed, getting all nervous again, before pressing her legs together and tugging on her nightshirt, only resulting in straining it against her breasts. *Yeah, love, I love that, too; carry on.*

"Umm, I always found them kind of chunky compared to the rest of me," she admitted, unable to look into my eyes. She sure was amusing.

"Perfect legs to have wrapped around me," I remarked, ghosting my fingers up her thigh. She bit her lip, trying to not let it get to her and failing as she sighed softly. She slowly looked up and stared at me.

"Liam... there's something I need to tell you."

"Go for it," I said, not stopping my teasing until she swatted my hand away.

"This is serious," she pouted.

"Go on."

She took a deep breath, making me frown in concern. What was it?

"A year after the blood moon, remember you said you got drunk and you ended up kissing a girl, thinking it was me?" A flash of guilt rushed through me, and I clenched my jaw, feeling fucking terrible.

"Yeah..." Where was this going? She tilted her head, looking at me with a sad look in her eyes.

"It was me. You kissed me that night," she whispered, making my eyes fly open in shock. *What?*

I tilted my head, sitting up slowly. A hundred thoughts were rushing through my mind. That made sense... fuck, it wasn't just the drugs messing with me. It had actually been Raven...

"Why were you there?" I asked, staring into her alluring eyes.

"Aunty had some pack work to attend to, so I went, but the blood moon was always a painful reminder of that night, so I got away and got drunk," she whispered.

"Thank the goddess," I murmured, pulling her into my arms, feeling a huge weight lifted off of me.

I didn't fucking betray her.

She curled into my lap, her hand on my heart as she tilted her head up to look at me.

"Liam… why did you just leave if you cared so much?"

"I thought… if I stayed, I'd just cause more issues. I thought you didn't want to talk, so maybe if I was gone, you two would get it over with and mate. When I learnt you left, I was fucking tempted to try again, but my ego and anger were stronger… so I refused, instead focusing on my training," I said quietly. She looked up at me, her eyes saddening.

"I wouldn't be complete without you, Liam," she said softly, her eyes strong with emotions.

"And Damon?"

She fell silent, confusion riddling her. My heart clenched. Just when I was about to feel like I wasn't enough, she looked at me with sadness and longing in her eyes.

"You are and always will be my first love," she whispered, a single tear trickling down her cheek.

I could sense her confusion and turmoil. *I guess it must be fucking hard having a pull towards two people. Selene really must hate us to put us through this.* Why couldn't shit have been simple?

"And you are mine," I whispered, enclosing her in my arms tightly and burying my head in her neck.

In a perfect world, we could have been together and happy without any extra baggage. But we all know this world of ours is far from fucking perfect.

Fuck you, Selene.

An Outburst

RAVEN

*T*HE FOLLOWING DAY, THE conversation with Liam remained at the front of my mind. It almost felt like a cloud of doom looming over my head. I could tell that sharing me wasn't an option for him. Even though he was trying to at least tolerate Damon, it was obvious that there was no aspect of making it work. What did that mean?

Damon's kindness, patience and selflessness were things I loved, too. He was someone who was dear to me, with or without this bond, but ultimately, if I had to really choose one to have a relationship with…

A sudden wave of guilt washed over me, and I pushed the thoughts away.

"In sets!" I shouted, trying to focus on the training session. Everyone obeyed except Taylor, who seemed to be distracted.

Taylor? I called through the link. He blinked and looked at me.

"Sorry," he muttered, stepping up beside the guy next to him, ready to spar.

Everything okay?

Yeah, he replied, giving me a small smile that did nothing to hide his pain. I knew it was Zack's fault…

I frowned, thinking of how I could help them. *Should I talk to Zack?* He was still above me in rank, so I wasn't sure how it would go, but I would do it. I had run into Robyn earlier, too, when we were both heading out here, and she said she'd check the text out later.

"Why don't you spar?" Owen remarked. "Or are you saving your energy for something else?"

"Excuse me?" I frowned. He gave me a cocky smirk.

"We all know about you and the Alpha -"

"Owen, cut it out! She is our trainer," Taylor growled. I saw Robyn frowning as she stared at me, too.

"Whether or not she spends the night with the Alpha is none of your business, man," another of the men growled.

"You know, if you keep this up, Owen, you will be punished," I said, trying to ignore the whispers that were crossing through the group.

"Or you could call the Alpha," Owen added mockingly.

"Respect, Owen," I growled. My eyes flashed, and I clenched my jaw, trying to calm my anger.

"Respect is earned, not given," he taunted. "Did you really get this position fairly or…?" A few men snickered. I knew exactly what he was insinuating.

"Hey!" Taylor growled.

"Shut the fuck up, loser," Owen shot back contemptuously.

"I know respect is earned, and right now, you don't deserve any. Now, I think it's high time I show you how to overpower someone bigger than you. Owen, care to step over here?" I asked, ignoring his remarks. He scoffed and walked to the front.

Raven. He's strong. And fucking fast… Taylor warned through the link.

I don't care, I replied coldly.

I didn't get here for no fucking reason.

"It seems some of you think me being your trainer is a joke, or that my personal life somehow has anything to do with you all," I said coldly, glaring at the few men who had snickered along with Owen. "I'll show you exactly how I got this position."

Owen and I circled each other. I really wanted to knock that cocky smirk off his face. I motioned for him to come at me, my eyes flashing. Before he had even made two steps towards me, I spun around, slamming my palm flat in his chest. He staggered back, startled.

"What the… you said to -"

"Come at me, and you did, just too damn slow," I said, aiming hit after hit.

The Blood Moon Pack women were not weak. We would never be weak, and we would never let anyone think so – a legacy that I promised would continue no matter what.

"This pack stands for so much more than you think. Alpha Elijah and Luna Scarlett took this pack to new heights. They have a reputation that is known throughout the entire country. Yet there are people like you who mock that reputation!" I said, spinning around and kicking him in the ribs. I felt something crack. The jarring pain of the impact sent a shooting spasm up my knee, but right then, I didn't care about the pain. "Alpha Elijah has always stood for respecting others and treating everyone equally, yet we are still getting assholes like you tarnishing our pack's reputation."

I blocked his every attack. I got this position through my hard work. There was no way someone like Owen could defeat me, and with each hit of mine that connected, he was getting angrier and more frustrated, making his attacks sloppier.

"You want me to show you how I got this position?" I asked as he grabbed my top. That was something everyone went for.

I slipped out of it in a flash; the perks of oversized tops, I guess. I wrapped it around his hands, yanking him forward and aiming a kick to the side of his head. Spinning around, I kicked him in the back, wrapping my legs around his neck just as I slammed him face forward into the ground. Everyone flinched, knowing that if I didn't break his fall with my legs, he would have had his neck broken.

"This is how I got my position, proving that I'm capable," I said coldly. "I have tolerated enough crap from everyone. From here on out, if I get any attitude or disrespect, you will be punished! Now, I want everyone to run thirty laps around the entire perimeter of the pack grounds! As for you…" I crouched down next to Owen, who spat some blood out as he tried to get to his feet. "Fifty laps," I finished.

"I…"

"Now," I said icily.

He had a few broken bones, but they'd heal, just like my damn knee. Everyone was silent, but I could see a few smirks on some faces as they looked at Owen. I pulled my hair tie out, as half my hair had come out, and was retying it when Zack came over.

"Everything okay…?" He trailed off, seeing the team running off.

"Taylor called you?" I asked, raising an eyebrow.

"Yeah…"

"Hmm, and you came."

"He said you were being given a hard time," Zack said, running his fingers through his hair.

"And why do you care?" I retorted. He raised an eyebrow.

"Have I done something to upset you?"

"Yes," I hissed, looking around.

You're hurting Taylor! I added through the link. He sighed, looking away.

You don't understand, Raven.

Then make me understand! I cried back in frustration.

Don't get into my business, he growled.

Then stop hurting one of the sweetest men I have ever come across!

Me accepting him would hurt him way fucking more!

Oh, I highly doubt that! I shouted back, frustrated.

It sure would… because I've been in a fucking relationship with his brother's mate! Zack snapped, his eyes blazing grey.

A Reluctant Decision

ZACK

I GLARED AT HER. GODDESS! She was so damn stubborn. That got her to shut up. She blinked at me as if I had just spoken a foreign language.

Taylor's sister-in-law? She's like thirty-three... She looked confused.

Don't I know it? I was just a few months younger than Raven. I knew she was doing the math.

But... she's been mated for, like, twelve years... she replied. I could hear the realisation settle into her voice. Guilt flitted through me as she turned her blazing eyes on me.

Look, I'm not proud of it, but it happened just before I found out he was my mate. I was eighteen and an older woman hitting on you... it wasn't that hard to fall for it. It was just sex, I sighed in frustration. **So, just... stay out of it.**

No... I don't get it. She cheated on her mate? Goddess! Her mate is such a good person, too... Channing has always been so nice, he was injured... Although Kiara was able to save his life, there wasn't much she could do about something that had been completely destroyed.

Yeah, he lost his legs in the battle of Hecate's Betrayal, so his mate just -

She suddenly slapped me across the face, leaving a stinging pain behind.

So, you became her fucking whore! I hate people who cheat on their mates! And I hate when those they cheat with know they have a partner! She growled

I know... she was just fucking hot.

Men really do stick their dicks in every damn hole they see!

She stood there; her lips pursed, fists clenched, and I knew if someone saw us, they'd be fucking confused as to what the hell we were doing standing here silently glaring at each other.

I ended it when I found my mate. When I told her that we were done, she got angry and said she'd tell my mate and the damn pack that I assaulted her. I wouldn't have cared if it was anyone else, but the fact that she's Taylor's brother's mate could have destroyed him. I don't know... his family would never have accepted me. She stared at me as if I had grown two heads, but she had visibly calmed down a little.

I thought you didn't want to admit you're gay, she mumbled sheepishly. I cocked a brow.

I've known I'm bi for years and I have no issue with that. I glared at her. **Don't be so nosy.**

Hey, I'm not nosy! If I was nosy, I would have peeped around the tree that night to see what you two were doing! She protested, blushing. Fuck. I felt my cheeks burn and she grinned in triumph. **Look Zack, you can't let that stop you from coming clean to Taylor. You're hurting him more by not telling him. He probably feels like he isn't enough,** she said softly.

Taylor's brother is like his fucking hero, if I told him... I don't know what he'd think of me.

You won't know until you do, Zack... continuing on like this isn't helping anyone either.

I fucking know.

Now you know my issue... so why don't you tell me what crap's going on between you, Liam and Damon? It was only fair she shared. She looked down, before looking up at me after a moment.

They are both mated to me, she said quietly. I almost fucking gasped like a damn woman. Whoa...

Mated to you, or each other, too?

Me! She said, glaring at me, blushing again.

Where's your mind going? I narrowed my eyes at her.

Nowhere, kid! She shot back huffing. I cocked a brow.

"Whatever, midget."

"You didn't just call me that!"

"I think I just did," I replied. She glared at me before staring at her hands.

You know, Zack, don't make the same mistake I did... you never know

what might be if you give it a shot, rather than living unhappily with a 'what if he rejects me'. Her words were true. I was scared of him rejecting me, or me hurting him.

Her situation was more fucked up than mine and if I kept this up, I might just lose my mate to someone else before even giving it a shot. Maybe I did need to talk to Taylor about this.

❧

It was evening, and I had actually taken the damn plunge and asked Taylor to meet me outside the pack grounds. It was my night off and I thought if we were going to talk, we needed to do it away from the pack. Maybe I was reckless and jumped the gun, but apart from Raven's slap, she hadn't acted as appalled as I thought she might. It was getting fucking hard without Taylor, but the fear of rejection overrode that need.

I strummed my fingers on the steering wheel until I saw him walk out in his puffer jacket, fitted jeans that hugged his legs perfectly, and those damn fucking gorgeous eyes. He was fucking hot.

He opened the door and got in, and I swallowed, keeping my gaze ahead.

"Hey, Zack." Even the way he said my name was a fucking turn on in itself.

"Hey, Tay."

Our eyes met, and when he fucking looked at my lips, I licked them, looking away quickly. We needed to fucking talk. Twenty minutes later, I parked up outside a restaurant and Taylor cocked a brow.

"Never knew this was a date," he said, smiling.

"It's not a date," I replied, frowning. *I doubt he'll stick around when he knows my fucking truth.*

We entered, and I gave my name, having made a reservation in one of the private rooms. Taylor whistled.

"You sure this isn't a date?"

"Yeah, I'm sure," I said, frowning.

"Damn, someone's pretty uptight. You need to loosen up," he whispered. His hot breath brushed my ear, sending blood to my dick.

"You'll be the one loosening up, not me," I shot back, smirking when I saw his neck redden. *Yeah, thought so.*

The waitress showed us to our room and gave us both a smile.

"I'll leave you with the menu and I'll bring -"

"Just give us two of your premium grill share platters and make sure the meat is well done," I said, "and two bottles of coke." The waitress nodded and left us to it.

"At least you could have asked me what I wanted," Taylor said when we both sat down. I cocked a brow.

"You would have ordered exactly that," I said, stretching my arm across the back of the booth. He smiled and nodded.

"Yeah, true." Our eyes met, and that same fucking sexual tension between us settled in again. I looked away. I needed to tell him...

"Tay... there's a reason I brought you here..."

His eyes softened and worry filled them.

"It seemed too good to be true," he muttered, looking away.

Fuck, I didn't mean it like that. Reaching over, I took his hand in mine, not missing the way his heart raced or the tingles that coursed through me at our contact.

"After I tell you, you may not even want to see my face again," I said quietly. He gave me that smile that made my heart feel funny and shook his head.

"I don't think anything you do could ever make me not want to see you again," he replied softly.

I don't fucking deserve you, Tay...

I blew out a breath. Alright, I was ready to tell him...

TAYLOR

My heart was racing as I stared over at my sexy as hell mate, in his leather jacket, fitted shirt, and that pout that's always set on his sexy face. Goddess, I'd let him do me all the fucking time. Just the thought was turning me on, but the worry and guilt in his eyes had me on edge.

When the waitress returned, Zack retracted his hands, much to my disappointment. She left us with our drinks and food, closing the door behind her. Soft music was playing in the background, and I honestly could have just pretended we were on a surprise date if it wasn't for how apprehensive Zack was acting.

"Zack, what is it?"

"When I was eighteen… I kind of got into a sexual relationship with this she-wolf… but when I met you, I wanted to break it off. The thing is…" He ran his hand through his messy hair, his heart thudding. I knew Zack had had a few relationships, but I also knew our connection was strong.

"Zack, why are you nervous?"

"She was mated, alright? She had a mate and I still let it happen," he said. The guilt on his face tugged at my heart. That didn't sit right with me, but he was young when it happened.

"Zack, you were eighteen. It's okay. We make mistakes, I don't think any less of you."

"I'm not done yet," he said quietly. I frowned, waiting, watching him fight the conflict of whatever was bothering him. "Her mate was injured in the battle of Hecate's Betrayal. She just…"

His pain was so fucking strong that my stomach twisted. What the hell was it? I get that it was fucked up…it was really fucking messed up… but it was a -

"It was Anna. Channing's mate."

His words hit me like a fucking kick in the gut. My stomach somersaulted, and not in a good way. The pain I was feeling was so fucking strong. Guilt, anger, sadness, betrayal, anguish…

Of all people why his mate? Channing… Channing who fucking….

"Do you want to know how Channing was hurt, Zack? How he got into the state he's in, just so his future Delta could screw his mate?" I asked hoarsely. Zack looked up at me, his eyes pained.

"Tay -"

"He saved my life! If it wasn't for Channing sacrificing himself, I wouldn't be here today," I said, standing up. He had been right. After hearing that, I couldn't look at him.

"Tay, I'm fucking sorry," he said, those gorgeous hazel eyes of his full of regret.

I shook my head, unable to look him in the eye. It was crushing, dammit, this hurt.

"Tay!" He grabbed my arm when I reached the door, those damn sparks coursing through us both. Our hearts raced, but I couldn't do this, not right now.

"Let go of me, Zack," I said, shoving him off. Even that hurt. I left the room, just needing some damn space.

"Taylor!"

The moment I was out of sight and out of that place that had suddenly felt too small, I shifted, not caring that I left behind my phone or anything. I broke into a run, rushing into the woods. I howled into the darkness, wanting to get rid of that crushing pain in my chest. It felt like I was suffocating…

All I could think of was Channing, the man who had destroyed his life for me, had been betrayed by my mate…

I had already felt guilty for that night, but now…

I couldn't stop the tears from streaming down my face. It hurt so fucking bad. *I'm fucking sorry, Channing, I should have died that night. You should have let me fucking die.* Whimpering I curled up, wanting the pain to go away, but it didn't. Why didn't it?

After a short while, I felt someone pushing through the link.

Taylor! Where are you? Please be okay, Raven's voice came through the link.

I'm okay, Raven, I said, trying to sound normal.

No, babe, you're not. Please tell me. I'm so sorry, she whispered, and I could tell she was near tears.

Why are you sorry? What had Zack told her and why?

Please tell me where you are? She pleaded. She was stubborn, and I had no energy to argue.

I'm just outside the pack walls, down by rocky edge near the river, I said, **Do not tell anyone else where I am or I will run.** I could use someone to talk to, and she knew he was my mate.

I won't, I'm coming, she whispered.

All I could think about was Channing's smile. Despite the fact that he was in a wheelchair, he still tried to remain positive. For a werewolf, a life like that… it was fucking awful…

I don't know how much time passed, but it wasn't that long before I saw Raven's dark and light grey wolf come running, her two unique coloured eyes glowing as she dropped a bundle of clothes next to me and nuzzled my head.

I'm so sorry, Taylor, I told Zack to tell you, this is my fault, she whispered tearfully.

Don't blame yourself. Guess it was better he told me sooner than later, I mumbled back. She nudged my wolf, settling down next to me and staring into my eyes.

I could see the guilt she was feeling, but I looked away, burying my head in my paws. I heard her shift back, grabbing the oversized hoodie and pulling it on. She sat next to me, pulling my head into her lap, and hugged me tightly.

She didn't ask me anything, and I was grateful. I wondered what happened between her and Zack, what he had told her, but right then I didn't want to think about him. All I could think of was the fact that my mate had messed around with my brother's mate, and it was all my damn fault.

After a good while, when the moon was up and it was very quiet, the steady sound of the rushing river like a blissful song, she spoke.

"Do you want to talk about it?"

Her fresh floral scent was calming. I could probably stay there for a lot longer, but I did not want anyone like the Alpha coming for my head. Although that didn't sound bad right now; Channing had risked his life for me, so I wouldn't do myself harm.

No, I said quietly. **Let's go home.** She stood up and shifted into a wolf before we both trudged back towards the pack grounds.

Zack is worried about you. He does care for you. He feels so guilty, he didn't want to hurt you.

He hurt me the moment he agreed to that relationship, I said, my voice harsher than it was meant to be.

I know… I know how bad decisions can result in something worse, she said softly.

Don't be sorry, Raven, I'm glad it's come out. We were almost at the packhouse when I stopped. **I have somewhere to go.**

Where are you going? She asked.

I want to visit Channing.

Are you going to tell him? She asked worriedly.

I honestly don't know… I replied. That crushing guilt was consuming me once more. She looked worried, but after giving me a gentle nuzzle, she headed towards the packhouse entrance.

Take care, Taylor. Don't be so hard on yourself.

Thanks for tonight, I simply said before I turned away…

Helping Out

RAVEN

I FELT AWFUL. ZACK HAD told me what had happened, and I felt like shit. I didn't mean to make matters worse, but I had. I padded up the stairs in wolf form before entering the bathroom and grabbing a towel. Reaching beneath the cabinet, I slid my bedroom key out and trudged down the hall to my bedroom. Unlocking the door, I entered, feeling exhausted; however, I had asked Robyn for help tonight, and I needed to go visit her too.

I quickly told Zack that Taylor was okay. He seemed relieved and thanked me. I hoped they managed to sort their problem out.

I groaned, getting dressed quickly in underwear, sweatpants, and a ribbed vest top. I grabbed the book, shoved it into a bag, and headed to Robyn's room.

I knocked on her door, hearing music from inside the room. Despite the soundproof walls, you could still faintly make out the sounds. She opened it pretty quickly, dressed in yoga pants and a crop top. She really was gorgeous. I couldn't really blame Damon when he was stuck with a wallflower like me for a mate, one who hadn't even been there for him. Once again, the difference between what I felt for them both niggled at me, and I pushed the thought away.

I knew I was beginning to self-hate again, as I did years ago, but I couldn't help it. I felt guilty about my feelings, for being the cause of the rift between both of them.

"Hey, Raven."

"Hi, I hope I'm not too late. I got caught up," I said apologetically.

"Not at all, I was just finishing off some assignments. Take a seat." She closed the door behind me. I placed the bag down and sat on the edge of her bed.

"Damon said we could trust you," I said nervously. She nodded and crossed her arms, but I felt as if something was slightly off.

"Of course, what did you guys need me to check?" She asked, her tone sounding slightly clipped.

"Umm, it's a prophecy..." I said, taking the book out and flipping the book open for her. She came over and took the book from me, sitting down.

"What is this?"

"It's about the Deimos bloodline, the Westwood heritage," I explained. "There's a curse, and it's about Liam." I frowned when she tensed at the mention of Liam. "Is everything okay, Robyn?"

"Hmm? Of course," she replied, staring at me with those gorgeous brown eyes of hers.

"You got a little... you seem a bit tense." She looked down at the book before glancing at me and sighing.

"I won't lie or hide it... everyone knows you and Liam spent the last two nights together. Isn't Damon your mate?" She asked, almost protectively. *Oh, shit...*

"Oh... he is..." I said, nibbling on my bottom lip. This was no longer a secret; the number of people who were beginning to find out was growing... "It's... both Liam and Damon. They're both my mates."

Her eyes widened, and she stared at me, stunned. I waited for her to say something, but she just blinked, looking shocked.

"Oh, damn... I didn't see that coming. That's why you two aren't together. That's why he and Liam are at odds..."

"Yeah," I said, glad she understood it. She gave me a small smile.

"Sorry if I came off a little funny... it's just..." She looked sad and shook her head, changing her mind. "I'm sorry."

"It's okay. I'm glad you at least care for him," I said gently. She simply nodded. Although I knew she had more questions, she didn't voice them. "Okay... I'll tell you about the Deimos curse, and then you can read the prophecy," I said before I began to explain everything to her. She listened carefully, looking through my notes before skimming through the book as I talked. I filled her in on the card as well. Turning the page, she looked at the paragraph that contained the prophecy itself.

"So the promise of the sun is Helios's curse, and the wish they speak of is Selene's, so the birth of Kiara and Liam weakened the curse?" My eyes widened. I missed that part! That surely means there's hope!

"Oh, damn… yes, and then it says from light and darkness itself. The blessed wolf and the royal prince are born. Only then giveth the gift of breaking the curse…" I mused.

"Wait… the royal prince is born. There has to be more here. Kiara is a blessed wolf, but what makes Alpha Liam a royal prince? Would all the Westwoods be considered princes?" Robyn asked. My heart thundered.

"I don't know…"

"That's what we need to find out first. Why is he called the royal prince?" She said, tapping the book with her long nails. "Giveth the gift… so there's something that's been given in some form to break this curse…"

"Interesting, how do we find more answers?" I asked feeling so dumb right then. She seemed to understand it a lot better…

"Let's see, this book must have something… when the light gives birth to a… it's a three-letter word… son maybe?" She squinted, holding the book up to the light. I nodded.

"That's what we assumed too, so Liam has a lot less time," I said, feeling that worry settle into the pit of my stomach.

"The darkness will reign through the veins of the Deimos prince. Find the key within the darkness to break the curse. It keeps saying within and given, it's going to be something obvious, but I think there's definitely something that makes Alpha Liam a prince," Robyn said, looking at me. I nodded slowly, mulling over what she said.

"I'll have a think. Is it okay for me to hold on to this book and see if there's anything else I can pick up if I actually look through it?" She asked.

"Sure, but please keep it hidden away," I said. "And thanks for your time, Robyn, I appreciate it."

"No problem," she said, and I stood up, taking up the card and my notebook. Slipping them back into my bag, I exited her room.

Feeling a little peckish, I decided to go check the kitchen for any food. I quickly put the bag in my room before heading downstairs. When I entered the kitchen, the fresh scent of citrus detergent filled my nose and I inhaled it. I was going over to the fridge when Damon's voice came into my head.

Liam, Raven, the hot chocolate was fine, there was no poison in it or the milk, he said quietly. I frowned. He didn't sound normal…

And the pills? Liam asked.

There was wolfsbane, silver, and ricin in one of her pills, he said, his voice sounding strained.

The glass juice bottle that I had just taken out of the fridge slipped from my grasp, shattering as it hit the tiled floor, splashing orange all over. My heart was hammering as I stood there frozen. Goddess…

Fuck… Liam cursed.

If you two didn't… I… thanks, guys, Damon murmured.

The same thing was going through all our minds.

What if I hadn't heard the back door?

What if Liam hadn't said to search?

After last night's events, and the fact that Aunty Monica almost got poisoned, I felt down. Through training, although Owen behaved despite the unmasked hatred in his eyes, I was in a morbidly gloomy frame of mind.

Liam had been out all night. I knew they were trying to look for more leads. I had mind-linked Damon asking if he wanted me over; instead, he asked if I could spend the night as he was going to be out, and I had agreed. Damon had gotten back late at night and was sleeping when I left for training.

I had returned to the packhouse and showered, although the boiling water incident remained in my mind. I got dressed in a maroon halter dress, leaving my back on display, black lace tights, and heeled knee-high boots. I applied some smoky eye make-up, paying more attention to my brother's eye. I had never thought much of it but loved the fact that my eyes were different. It often made for a good conversation starter when people looked at me. I appreciated it so much more after learning where it came from.

I left the packhouse, wandering towards the playground, and sat on the grounds under a large oak tree, smiling at the few children that were playing, their parents watching close by. Once upon a time, there wouldn't have been any need for an adult around, but everyone was told to be vigilant. I opened the small bag I was carrying, ready to fix Sparks, when my phone beeped and I took it out, seeing it was a message from Kiara.

She had texted to say they were delaying their wedding that was meant to happen in a few months. After losing Alpha Rafael, no one was in the mood for a celebration. It just didn't feel right to have the wedding right then. I understood that, texting her that I totally agreed with it, and it would be better with the girls being a little older, too. I just hoped that the curse was gone, and we could all enjoy a royal wedding without any stress!

Although I would have loved to get Kiara's insight on it, I knew she'd feel dreadful if she realised Dante's birth was the triggering point of this curse. She had enough stuff going on in her life.

I sighed as I threaded my needle and began to patch Sparks' body back up. I wanted to visit Renji again, but I wasn't sure if it was the smart thing to do. I didn't want Dad to get angry. I had been expecting him to blast me after what the boys did, but oddly, nothing. No hateful words or anything. I guess he learned his lesson. I planned to visit them today; I just needed to get everything off my chest and end it. I also wanted to ask Aunty Red if there were any pictures of Renji that I could perhaps have. I just wanted something to remember him by.

I sighed inwardly, carrying on fixing Sparks when I heard the sound of Liam and Damon talking from not far off. My ears instantly perked up as I tried to listen to their conversation. Okay, I was a bit nosy… but I couldn't help it. I mean, if it was a secret then they wouldn't be talking openly, right?

"…to Mom, it's final," Liam was saying coldly.

"I appreciate it, but I don't know if she can handle the change."

I could smell their intoxicating scents now.

"Then stay there with her. When I told Mom and Dad that I put security in place, Dad said it's not enough. He wants her safe," Liam said icily.

I frowned. Were they talking about Aunty M? They had gone silent. I tilted my head trying to listen.

"It's rude to eavesdrop, love," Liam's husky voice whispered in my ear, sending my stomach into a fluttering frenzy.

I gasped and jumped in alarm. I spun around to see him crouching down just behind where I had been moments earlier, while Damon was standing there smiling in amusement. They both wore only sweat pants, displaying half their glory. I could tell from the thin layer of sweat that covered their god-like bodies that they had just had an intense run or workout.

"I wasn't eavesdropping," I denied, looking around for Sparks.

Liam reached over, picking him up and dusted him off before holding him out to me, a move that moved me greatly. Our eyes met and I tried to calm my palpating heart. I took it, our fingers brushing before I quickly got back to my stitching, trying to calm my emotions down as Damon sat down by the tree and leaned back against it.

"So will you two not tell me what you were talking about?" I asked. Damon chuckled, glancing at Liam before winking at me.

"So, you admit you were curious?" He teased.

"No, I'm just asking," I replied.

"Uncle Elijah wants Momma to move in with them until this killer is found."

"That's a great idea!" I said approvingly.

"I don't know, I'm not sure…" Damon said. He at least looked better than last night when I had gone by.

"It's not up for fucking discussion," Liam said firmly.

"It's a good idea. Also…" I said, glancing around and leaning closer. "Robyn had a good insight on the you know what." I emphasised towards Liam with my eyes pointedly.

"Really, what did she say?" Damon asked, looking curious. Liam frowned as he glared at both of us.

"Why don't we just make an announcement and tell the entire fucking pack?" He growled, his eyes flashing.

"Look, we're trying to find an answer," I pouted. Reaching out, I placed a hand on his arm, trying to ignore the way my stomach knotted and that need for him that consumed me, hoping it calmed him. "We can't lose you."

"Make sure you don't tell anyone else. I do not want this to get to Mom and Dad," Liam said warningly.

"It won't," Damon said nodding.

"So where were you two?" I asked.

"You sound like an old suspicious wife with all the questions," Damon teased. I snorted.

"Hah more like a mother waiting with a broomstick, or in my case, a needle," I said, holding it up before settling down against the tree next to Damon. I smiled when Liam sat on my other side. For a moment, it felt like old times. I stared up at the sun through the branches, letting the warmth bask on my skin.

Helios... surely you can't hold a grudge against one person over an entire line...

None of us spoke, each one of us enjoying the calm.

One of the pups threw a ball, which Damon caught and tossed back. I carried on stitching Sparks up until he was done. His head wasn't quite straight anymore... and his body was a lot smaller now, thanks to it needing to be stitched in so many places... I brushed my fingers over it, smiling softly.

"You did a neat job," Damon said, not sounding very convincing as I prodded Sparks' head, trying to make it stay upright, but sadly, it just lolled to the side again.

"It's as ugly as ever too," Liam added.

I gave them both a glare, nudging them in the ribs, feeling the sparks shoot through me, each one so different. I never knew the bond could feel different for everyone. Damon's were like strong tingles swirling through me, whilst Liam's was like a strong bolt of electricity coursing through me.

Damon put an arm around me, giving me an apologetic kiss on the forehead before Liam pulled me out of his hold possessively, his fingers running down my back as his lips brushed the top of my head.

"Eww! You two need a shower! I am clean, I don't need sweat on me!" I said before jumping away. Damon chuckled, and Liam cocked a brow.

"Really? I don't think you'll mind," he said, his eyes boring into mine. Goddess it suddenly felt hot out there...

"Umm, I... I got to go! I have somewhere to be!" I grabbed my bag and, blowing them a kiss, ran off. I heard Damon laugh and could feel both of them watching me.

Last night, I had expected Liam to get pissed when he saw me leave for Damon's, but he only scolded me for going out alone. I knew the only reason he even let me go there was because there were guards posted outside, but I was glad he wasn't getting angry over it.

Pushing the thoughts away, I decided to go check up on Taylor and then I was going to visit my parents...

Speaking Up

RAVEN

I HAD JUST ENTERED TAYLOR'S bedroom; the creams and browns of the décor and walls made the room look warm and welcoming. I saw him laying on his bed, staring at the ceiling.

"Hey. We missed you at training," I said softly, walking over to his bed. He sat up slowly and I hugged him tightly.

"I'm not feeling up to training," he muttered, laying down again and grabbing a square cushion. He hugged it to his chest as he sighed deeply.

"I know, but you can't stay cooped up," I said, stroking his hand. Our eyes met, and the pain in his tugged at my heart. "I'm sorry," I whispered. He gave me a pointed look.

"Really Raven, you need to stop with the self-blaming. I'm glad I know what a... jerk Zack's been. As for Anna, I don't know what the hell to do." He groaned in frustration. So that was his dilemma, but right then, I didn't trust myself to give him any advice.

"I don't even know what to do with my life, so I really can't advise you," I said with a gloomy pout. "Will you talk to Zack?"

"Sooner or later," he muttered, turning on his side and hugging the cushion tightly.

"Good, life's short," I murmured, thinking with each passing day, Liam's time was running out.

"Yeah. I know I'll forgive him sooner or later. He did that when he was a stupid eighteen-year-old, and we both know that crap happens," Taylor said.

"Tell me about it. I've been a dumb eighteen-year-old," I mumbled, tugging at the hem of my dress. "But I'm glad you are going to work on it."

"Yeah… when I'm ready. Right now… I'm pissed," Taylor said, sounding adorably cute. Taylor was just one of those people who couldn't stay mad at anyone for long.

"And you should be," I said, giving him a small smile.

"What about you? What's happening? I know people at the packhouse are being assholes," Taylor said sympathetically.

"So, you've heard, huh?" I said, making folds in my dress. Taylor reached over and gave my arm a squeeze.

"Hey… I'm here if you want to talk about it. I don't know why you aren't telling people, but he's your mate, isn't he?"

I gave him a small smile. How do I tell him I didn't know what to do? How the fact that I have two mates was hard? How do I explain that I didn't know how to balance this when both my mates were so different? Our relationships were so different? I just felt like I was lost in the middle of conflict with everyone giving me different advice.

I felt guilty for favouring Liam. How I forgot Damon when I was with Liam. Yet when I was with Damon, I felt guilty towards Liam. Then there was Damon telling me to make it work with Liam first, then Aunty Red saying to be equal or decide what I wanted. Not to mention Al's ultimatum that this would not work and I would have to pick one.

I really wanted to go bang my head against a wall.

"I know you are… I just don't even know what I need to do. Anyway, I'm glad you're okay. Do you want me to come over tonight? We can binge watch some comedy movies or whatever you want and get some takeout?" I suggested. His face lit up with a beautiful smile, and he nodded.

"I'd like that."

"Then it's a date!" I said, getting up. I hadn't really told Taylor the full deal between Liam, Damon, and me but I think tonight I will.

"Anything new with your dad?" Taylor asked, his smile vanishing. I looked at him and shook my head, wondering if people realised something happened after Damon took him away.

"No. I haven't spoken to him," I murmured, looking at the picture of Cher on his wall.

"Yeah… well, whenever you're ready," he said sympathetically. I nodded, thinking I was ready now.

"Well, I'm going to go face the music," I said, giving him a wave. He followed me out of his room and down the steps. I could see his mum was mixing something in the kitchen through the open archway. "Bye, Mama Dee!"

"Bye, Raven!" She called back.

I smiled at Taylor before I walked across the garden and jumped over the fence. Taylor watched me, giving me a final thumbs-up before closing the door when I rang the doorbell of my parents' house – a place that used to fill me with dread when I had to return here at the end of a long day.

The door opened and Mom stood there; to my surprise she looked a mess. Her eyes were puffy, and her hair had not been combed.

"So, you finally show your face?" She said to me bitterly. I frowned, stepping inside and shutting the door behind me.

"After Dad kicked me out, did you expect me to just come back?" I asked. She shook her head, turning away and clutching the wall as if she had no energy. I sighed, tugging at the skirt of my dress again. "Look, I haven't come to argue. Where's Dad? There are a few things I need to talk about with both of you." I wanted to get this off my chest and then get out of there.

"You got your dad thrown into the cells! Are you mocking us by coming here and pretending you don't know?" She shouted, her eyes flashing yellow as she glared at me. My heart skipped a beat as her words echoed in my head. *Cells?*

"I... I didn't know. That night -"

"You have only ever hurt your dad, Raven. I know you don't mean to, but look where you have got him! He never wanted you near Renji, yet you went and visited his grave! What did you expect? That he wouldn't get angry?" Mom cried, breaking into sobs.

My heart clenched in pain. The urge to simply stay quiet was there, but no, not this time. I came here to give my input, and I was not going to stay quiet like normal.

"So, you're saying I'm the reason Dad is in the cells? Actually, Mom, I'm not. He's there because he deserves to be there. I have done nothing to him. All I ever wanted was for him to notice me, to be proud of me, and to love me, but he never did," I said, desperation seeping into my voice. Was I really the crazy one that was in the wrong?

"I can't even mind-link him! They are probably injecting him with silver or wolfsbane! I feel his pain! You don't know what he's going through. Above all, losing Renji -"

"Hurt! I know! I didn't even know he existed, and it hurts me, too! I visited his grave because I wanted to know my brother! What did I do so wrong that dad hates me so much? I am his daughter too! Is it just because I was too weak to give my brother a bone marrow match?" I said, feeling defeated.

"You were never a daughter he could be proud of," she said, simply brushing away her tears. I looked into those blue eyes of hers, the very same shade as my blue one.

"I know. I've been told all my life that I am nothing but a failure," I said, looking around the hallway. Something told me it was the last time I'd be visiting. "I wasn't the child Dad wanted. Well, that's his loss, then. I have always tried my best to be the best I can be without losing my identity, but if it's not enough, then I don't care anymore. "

"You don't care? When have you ever cared, Raven?"

Somehow, her words just didn't hurt anymore. I was so used to her standing by and not caring that I didn't expect anything from her.

"Goodbye, Mom. I won't be stopping by anymore… I didn't know Dad was in the cells, but whatever reason the Alpha or Beta deemed sufficient, Dad must deserve it. I don't really care, and I don't feel bad for admitting that. I'm done," I said, casting one last look around my childhood house.

"Maybe we will be better off," Mom whispered, hugging herself. "They hurt him a lot… I felt it. I don't know what they've done, and I can't mind-link him either. I'm told I have to stay under house arrest until the Alpha questions me."

I frowned and felt a sliver of irritation. Once again, I wasn't told about this. Why did everyone keep me in the goddess-damned dark?

"Yeah, I think we'll all be better off. I'm done being stuck around parents who love to throw mental abuse in one form or another at me," I said bitterly. For the first time, I let my anger, pain, and sadness show in my voice. I turned away, ready to open the door again when I paused. "When I was a baby… you wanted the doctor to give me Renji's eye… you must have loved me, right? Before I became a useless disappointment to you both?" My voice was soft, my eyes stuck on the door before me. Maybe just one kind word… that at one point at least Mom cared…

"Hmm, a long time ago… I wanted to see a part of Renji live on too… but things changed," Mom's hesitant reply came. My lips quivered, and the urge to just run away and cry threatened to consume me, but I didn't move, keeping my heartbeat steady.

"Changed?"

"I should never have given Renji's eye to you. Perhaps if we hadn't, that constant reminder of his loss wouldn't be here! Maybe things would have been different!" I looked over my shoulder at her, trying to blink away the tears, and nodded.

"Maybe… but it's done. Goodbye…" I said, not even knowing if I should even address her as 'Mom'.

She didn't reply as I left the house, trying to hold that smile in place, although inside I felt as if everything was crumbling to pieces…

✿✿✿

I felt so angry. I hated that I didn't even know about Renji, and now the fact that Dad had been thrown into the cells! Both Damon and Liam had a chance to tell me, but they hadn't.

I wanted to talk to Dad, tell him how he makes me feel and end it, but did I really want to go and see him in prison? I couldn't let this drag on. I wanted to get it over with. I guess I had no other choice. I made my way to the Blood Moon headquarters and waited for the security team to let me in.

"Do you have a pass?" Ben asked. He was part of the security, but I knew him from around.

"No, I'm only here to speak to my father. You can escort me down," I said curtly.

"I'm not sure if he's allowed visitors…" he replied hesitantly. My eyes flashed, and I glared at him coldly.

"I can speak to my father. He's here because of me. Please, Ben." I could tell he was struggling.

"I… fine. As head warrior, I'm sure it should be okay. But I will escort you there, and I will remain with you for the duration of your meeting. Keep it short."

I nodded and let him lead the way down towards the cells. I had only been there once or twice before, and that was a long time ago. We had gotten in trouble, but a lot was different now. Even the cells had changed a lot compared to how they had been back then.

We walked past the cells that contained small beds, and I realised that the further we got, the emptier, darker, and colder the cells became. My heart skipped a beat as we went down a few steps to the lower cells. They were like those from a movie from long ago; creepy, dirty, and dark.

"Go. I will wait here. I'm not able to mind-link the Alpha, and I do hope this isn't breaking protocol," he muttered.

"I won't be long," I said, walking forward.

Dad's scent hit my nose, and I headed down towards the bottom, stopping when I caught sight of him. He was sitting, leaning against the far wall in the corner of a cell.

"Have you come to have a laugh?" Dad spat, turning his head towards me. Dry blood and dirt covered his face. His clothes weren't much different. I could see they were the same ones he'd had on when Damon dragged him away from me.

"No," I said quietly. "I came to talk to you."

"I am not interested in talking to you. Leave," he said resentfully, but he also sounded tired.

"You don't need to reply. I'm here to speak, and all I want is for you to listen. I'm always the one listening, the one trying to be okay. I'm done with staying quiet. I'm done with pretending that it's okay because it really isn't. I have never been scared of you, but for the sake of not arguing, I would stay quiet. I'm twenty-one now. I can't go on like this," I said, my voice breaking with frustration and sadness. I hated life right then, but I was going to move forward. I was totally done with staying quiet. Taking a deep breath, I continued,

"All I wanted growing up was to be accepted, to be told that you are proud of me, but I never got that from you or Mom. Even when you would throw something at me in anger or push me around… I told myself you were just upset because I was too loud and annoying. But you know, Dad, it hurt. It really hurt not knowing what I was doing wrong. All my life, I pretended I was okay, I always placed this big smile on my face and carried on hoping things changed, but even then, nothing became better. I know you wish Renji was the one alive, and I wish he was, too… maybe then you could all have been happy. If I had the choice, I would be okay with being the one who died if it meant -"

"Don't act like you fucking care! Don't even utter his name! Get out!" Dad growled.

In a flash, he was in front of the bars, rattling them hard with one hand, not caring about the silver that burned his skin. I stepped back, my heart thundering at his sudden move, but what alarmed me the most was the fact he was missing an arm. He saw my gaze on his arm and sneered at me.

"What? Happy to see what your Alpha's done to me?"

"Hey! Calm down, or I'll tell the Alpha," Ben warned.

My heart was racing as I stepped further back. His arm...

The boys' words rang in my head,

"This blood is your dad's..."

Why hadn't they told me?

"See? All you do is bring trouble to us all; Renji... me... your mother... I hope you are happy, Raven, because well done. You got what you wanted. You got me locked up," he spat.

I shook my head slowly. I didn't know why Liam had ripped his arm off, but...

"I didn't know you'd be locked up... But you must have triggered him off -"

"Don't fucking act like there's a reason! You are the reason!" He shouted, slamming his good hand against the bar. "You are useless. There's nothing special about you! As for your mates, no wonder the goddess gave you two because she knew exactly what kind of whore you are!" I flinched at those words, my heart thundering.

"Raven..." Ben muttered, trying to pull me back. "Let's leave."

"Useless!" Dad hissed

Don't let his words get to you.

"I wish I had gotten rid of you when you were a child! I wish I didn't have to see that disgusting face of yours before me! I wish -"

A sinister, menacing growl ripped through the air, echoing from every corner of the place and making me spin around. The heavy, dark aura surged around me. My heart was thumping as I stared at the man who had stepped out of the shadows. Ben flinched, moving back and cowering under his Alpha's power. Liam's aura was stronger than ever. The chilling darkness that emanated from him was spreading to every corner of the cold cells and making my stomach churn unpleasantly.

"I told you… that you will *not* talk to him without me," Liam's ominous voice came. His voice was deeper and harsher than ever. His dark navy eyes, which looked almost black, stared into mine. The anger and rage that burned within them were so intense that I felt my knees go weak.

"Finish me off. It's what you both want," Dad muttered.

Don't trigger him off, Dad.

"Good idea," Liam said icily. "Especially after you just talked to her like that."

"No!" I said just as Liam moved forward incredibly fast. I blocked his way, my back hitting the bars, and bit my lip as the silver burnt me. I spread my arms and shook my head. "Liam. No."

"Don't play the innocent party, Raven, we all know you want this," Dad spat.

"Move aside, love," Liam warned me quietly.

"No," I said, shaking my head.

Liam's eyes darkened, and his chest was heaving with suppressed rage, but even then, I could tell he was getting angrier.

My chest was heaving. I knew if I moved then, he would kill dad. Even if I was ending things with him, Liam couldn't go around and kill people.

"Move. Aside." His eyes blazed, and before my very eyes, the whites of his eyes began to turn black.

I gasped in horror as I stared into his completely black pits. A cold smirk crossed his face as he tilted his head to the side, looking at me, but before I could even say anything, his hand darted out and wrapped around my throat in a death grip, cutting off my airway. The sparks of the mate bond rippled through me, but Liam was unmoved. The darkness around him was only growing. My heart was thundering as a shiver ran down my spine. What was happening to him?

Shattering Control

RAVEN

"*L*IAM," I CHOKED OUT as his hand became tighter.

"A-Alpha!" Ben stuttered, clearly not expecting the change in Liam.

Liam's eyes snapped towards him, his Alpha command surging forth. With just one look, the man lowered his head and moved away. My eyes widened. That… Liam didn't even say anything…

"Liam!" I said, my nails digging into his hands as I tried to get him to let go of me. "Liam, please, let go."

My heart thundered as Liam threw me aside roughly. I hit the bars on the opposite side of the hall, groaning as pain jarred through me before I fell to the ground, just about breaking my fall. The burn of the silver searing my bare back made me pull away from them.

"A-Alpha…"

"No one can protect you, not even her," Liam hissed as Dad spluttered, backing away from the bars.

Run! I told Ben, praying he didn't have the keys just in case Liam tried to get them. He moved towards me, but I shook my head.

I…I'll call… He backed away silently, and I turned to Liam.

My eyes widened in fear, watching him take hold of two bars and stretch them apart. My heart was in my throat. That wasn't possible. Those bars were made to withstand a werewolf's limits…

My eyes snapped to his hands. Sure enough, they were burned, yet he clearly didn't care. He smiled, almost psychotically, as he stepped through the gap he had created.

"Alpha, s-stop! Y-You can't kill me!" Dad shouted.

I looked at Liam, stumbling to my feet as I ran into the cell. It wasn't Dad that I cared about right then, it was Liam. I couldn't let the darkness control him. Whatever this was, it was strong.

"Liam, please," I whispered, blocking his way. Reaching up, I cupped his face tightly, only for him to grab my wrists in a painful grip. I felt something crack in my left wrist, but I didn't let go.

"Stay out of this, darling. I told you… he will pay for the crap he's given you," he hissed, pushing me away roughly as he advanced on Dad. I saw his claws come out as he lunged at my father and slashed him across his chest. He didn't stop, picking him up and flinging him down to the ground.

"Stop!" I shouted as Dad howled in pain, not even able to defend himself. He needed to stop. I ran towards him, pushing him away from Dad with all my strength. "Liam, please listen to me!" I pleaded, feeling the sparks course through us as I grabbed his face, this time bracing myself. "Won't you listen to your bitesize?"

He sucked in a sharp breath, his heart thundering, and I saw his eyes lighten a little. The black that coated his whites was fading away slowly.

"Listen to me, blue eyes…" I whispered, trying to ignore the discomfort in my wrist as Liam tried to pull out of my grip, only crushing my already painful wrist further. I didn't let go, instead locking my arms around his neck. "Liam…"

His eyes flickered from cerulean to magnetic blue to midnight navy, his heart thundering loudly. I could feel his emotions as he fought against himself.

"You're okay," I whispered, locking my arms tightly around his neck. As I placed a soft kiss on his throat, I locked my legs around his waist, clinging onto him tightly. That seemed to work as he gasped for air, staggering back.

"Fuck," he whispered. I leaned back, staring into his bright cerulean eyes, relief flooding me. He looked around as if realising where we were for the first time. "Raven…" he said, looking at me and then at Dad's body that lay limp on the ground. He wrapped his arms around my waist tightly, and I could hear how fast his heart was beating as he buried his head in my neck as the realisation settled within him.

Just then, we heard the sound of running and saw Uncle El and Damon. Ben must have called them. Damon looked at us, worry clear in his eyes as Uncle El assessed the situation. I didn't miss the way his eyes flashed when he looked at the bent bars or the way his frown deepened as he hurried over to Dad. I unlocked my legs from around Liam's waist, but he refused to let me go. I didn't pull away. As much as he needed me, I was also worried for him.

"Will someone explain to me what the fuck is happening here?" Uncle El hissed, his eyes blazing cobalt blue as he looked at us. "Get him to the hospital!" Damon hesitated before frowning and walking over to Dad, only to stop again.

"I don't know if he deserves that, Uncle," he whispered, to everyone's surprise.

"I put him in here, he's staying here. He won't die, although he should," Liam added coldly.

"Liam -"

"I am the Alpha. My rules now, remember?"

Uncle El clenched his jaw, looking at me and then at Liam. I looked between Damon and Liam. Damon was tense; I knew he was angry with my father, and Liam's eyes kept flickering from magnetic blue to cerulean.

"Just let a doctor come see him… he isn't worth getting your hands dirty over," I whispered, looking up at Damon. I saw Uncle El glance between the three of us, and I had a feeling Aunty Red had probably told him our situation.

"What happened to Haru's arm?" He asked tersely.

"He lost it," Liam said coldly. I saw Uncle El pause for a moment and knew he was mind-linking someone. "I set an example of what happens when you abuse your child," Liam said icily as he glared down at Dad.

"Liam…" Uncle El said, concern clear in his eyes. Liam didn't reply, finally letting go of me and taking hold of my wrist.

"Ouch!" I yelled, unable to stop myself as pain shot up my broken wrist. All three men looked at me, and Liam let go quickly.

"What's wrong, love?" He asked as I clutched my wrist, my eyes stinging from the pain.

"I think it's bruised -"

"The angle is fucking off. That's broken. How did that happen?" Uncle El asked. Coming over, he took my hand in his. He examined my wrist before he snapped it back into place, making me gasp. Eye-watering pain shot through me before I felt my arm healing.

"Ow…" I said, pouting as I rubbed my wrist.

Uncle El gave me a sympathetic look before his brows furrowed once more. Damon was by my side, taking my hand as he massaged my forearm gently.

"How did you get hurt, Raven?" Uncle El repeated. My heart thumped. I couldn't, and I wouldn't say. Liam… He would only feel bad.

"I just got -"

"I did that, didn't I?" Liam asked quietly.

"No, it wasn't you," I said, firmly looking up at him. The guilt and pain in his eyes made my heart squeeze.

A tense silence fell. Even when a doctor and two guards came rushing in, I knew this conversation was not over. Liam turned away, yet I didn't miss the turmoil and shock in his eyes.

"Get him treated and put him in one of the cells on the top floor with a bed," Liam muttered, his irritation and contempt clear in his voice.

"And how about the four of us get back to my house? I think we need to have a talk," Uncle El said darkly.

I looked up at him. His jaw was clenched, his nostrils flaring. The way he was looking at Liam told me he was pissed off. Liam frowned, and as much as I didn't want to get him in trouble, I knew that if we told them about the curse, they could help.

"Let's go then," Liam said, coldly leading the way out. My thoughts were in vain when Liam's cold voice came through the link.

If either of you mentions the curse… He left his threat hanging. I stared at his back, my heart aching. I couldn't sense his emotions anymore; he had raised his walls once again. I prayed he didn't shut me out again because he needed us…

What happened? Damon asked through the link.

He heard Dad and me talking… he lost it… I'm scared, Damon. His eyes turned completely black… it was terrifying… he wasn't himself.

Yeah… I saw him rip your Dad's arm off, and he didn't seem like himself then, either…

Hmm, and I thought after talking to him, I was going to unleash my wrath upon the two of you. Neither of you told me he was in the cells, I said, trying to keep the annoyance from my voice.

Sorry, gorgeous, Damon's apologetic voice came. I looked at him, and sadly, those blue eyes of his looked sorry. Still, when things calmed down, I was going to unleash my wrath upon them. They were not forgiven!

I'll deal with that after this talk, I mumbled through the link, staring at Liam's muscular back.

Worry and fear consumed me as we walked through the pack grounds towards his parents' home. The power that rolled off of him reminded me that this was not just an Alpha, but one of the strongest in the entire country…

Time was running out, and we still had no solid answers.

✺◈✺

"Is anyone going to speak?" Aunty Red asked, placing a tray of snacks and drinks on the coffee table, her eyes full of concern as she saw Uncle El frowning. We were all seated in the living room of the Westwood home.

"Come here," he said, taking her hand and pulling her into his lap, trapping her in his arms as he kissed her neck.

I was sitting on the sofa opposite, with Liam on one side and Damon on the other. Azura was watching TV, and I was proud to see she was playing with the plushie I had gotten for her. From here, I could see she was enjoying eating her boogers. Aww, so cute!

"Care to explain how the fu-" Aunty Red placed her finger on Uncle El's lips, cutting him off. He smirked slightly, biting down on it. Hot couple goals! "How the hell did you bend those bars?" He continued once he let go of his mate's finger. I looked at Liam. *Okay, big boy, explain that.*

I crossed my arms as all eyes turned to Liam, who simply leaned forward, picking up a chocolate bar from the tray.

"Liam, your dad asked you a question," Aunty Red said pointedly. "What bars are we talking about anyway?"

"The ones in the lower cells. They are made to withstand our kind, and in no way are they able to bend… considering how thick they are," Uncle El said, frowning.

Liam shrugged, ripping open the chocolate wrapper with his teeth. My stomach fluttered, and I swallowed; I had to admit, he looked sexy… Goddess, why did something so simple make me feel all funny? Liam bit into the chocolate, but it was clear his parents saw his attitude as disobedient, no matter how hot he looked biting into it.

His eyes flicked to me. I felt my cheeks burn when he gave me the faintest hint of a smirk before glancing back at his parents.

"I guess I'm just stronger than your typical Alpha," he said.

"Inhumanly strong," Damon said quietly. My eyes snapped to him. Did he have a death wish?

We need them to know… and we can't tell them, he said through the link, his soft blue eyes staring into mine.

True…

"That's not fucking possible. Only Alejandro could possibly do that," Uncle El said icily.

"Guess he's not the only strong one around then," Liam remarked, shrugging as he licked his soft lips, taking another bite of the chocolate.

"And Raven's wrist, was it due to you not knowing your strength that you ended up hurting your own mate?" Uncle El hissed. Aunty Red snapped to him, poking her eyes out at him. I had a feeling he wasn't meant to have said that. I knew she had told him!

"Oo! Mate?" Azura jumped up as she stared at Liam and me. "Waven! Wiyam! You're mates?"

I gave her a small smile, but I didn't reply. I glanced at Damon, and he gave me that small smile he always did. I hated this…

"Okay, Azura, come on. Aunty Moni is in the other room. You can watch TV there," Aunty Red said before motioning for Azura to follow her. Uncle El glared at his son as Azura followed Aunty Red out, still giggling as she looked between Liam and me.

"We are going to have Waven and Wiyam babies…" Was the last thing she said before she disappeared. Goddess, that child!

"I… I didn't realise I was hurting her." His 'I don't care' attitude vanished, and he looked down at my wrist. "I'm… I'll make it up to you."

"Yeah, you will. But before that, how did you not realise? You ripped Haru's arm off Liam. That is no joke! You are Alpha. You can't do things without a trial. Without your Beta, your Delta, and your pack knowing why," Uncle El said as Aunty Red returned, motioning for Damon and me to take something from the tray. I reached forward, taking a packet of white chocolate buttons and a bar of chocolate. I passed the bar to Damon, giving him a smile before ripping open my packet and putting a button in my mouth.

"Your father is correct," Aunty Red said, sitting next to Uncle El and draping a leg over his thigh. He wrapped his arm around her shoulders, caressing her thigh as he leaned over and kissed her.

Mates… that is what a relationship is. One for one. How the fuck do you think anyone can be happy when the dynamics are so fucked up? Liam's cold voice came into my head.

I didn't reply. I got that, and even if somehow it worked, we weren't a trio of mates. It was the two of them for me, so I didn't get it either… I pushed the thoughts away.

"About Dad… he flipped when he found out I visited Renji's grave," I said, sighing as I ate another button and let it melt on my tongue.

"Care to elaborate? I am done with you kids hiding stuff. I want it all laid out on the table," Uncle El said, his eyes flashing. I swallowed. He was as scary as Liam at times… or even scarier… I looked at Liam, who nodded.

"Start from when you were little because there's a lot you keep skating around and hiding," he added.

"You got this," Damon added softly. Aunty Red sighed.

"Sometimes sharing isn't easy… I've been there… but it feels better when that burden of secrets is lifted from you," she said encouragingly. I frowned, staring down at my knees.

"Well… Dad has always never… liked me. I was always annoying and -"

"You were never fucking annoying," Liam cut in, his eyes flashing as he reached for my chin and turned my face towards him. "Stop saying that."

"Okay, he found me annoying. It was the small digs, pushes, and shoves here and there. In their eyes, I was useless and, apparently, the one whose fault it is that my brother is gone. He always referred to me as trash. There's not much to tell… he's just… I will no longer refer to him as Dad anymore. I am done with him. As for his mate, she would just stand by and didn't care. In her eyes, he was always right." It wasn't easy talking about it. I didn't want to go into it deeply. "It's done. I'm done with him, his mental abuse and sometimes physical. Although it was never anything big, just a shove or a push -"

"That is not something small, Raven," Uncle El said quietly.

"I can't believe we didn't pick up on it," Aunty Red said. I could see the guilt in her eyes.

"I don't want sympathy; some people have it so much worse. I'm okay. Besides, I was here so often you practically were forced to have me," I said, waving my hand. "So don't feel bad. If it wasn't for you guys, maybe things would have been different and far worse… he never left a mark or bruise, so I'm okay…"

"Why is there never an end to fucking dickheads?" Uncle El muttered.

"Because that's how humans are," Aunty Red said. "Killing him is not an option, Liam. Revise your punishment and hold a trial for them both, then set a punishment that they deserve."

"I don't need anyone to tell me what to do. If I say he's staying down there until the day he fucking dies, then he is," Liam said icily.

His eyes blazed, and I felt that dark aura surge around him once more. My heart thumped as I looked at the Alpha couple in front of me. Both had tensed, their eyes sharp and calculating as they stared at their son, who I didn't even need to turn to, to know that his eyes were probably a few shades darker…

Our Resolution

SCARLETT

MY HEART SKIPPED A beat. My nerves rippled through me as I stared at the man before me. I could barely recognise him, save his strawberry locks and his features that were a mix of both mine and Elijah's. The coldness and darkness that exuded from him made my gut twist, but it was the cold smile on his face that reminded me of someone long ago, someone that I still sometimes had to remind myself was dead. Someone who would still creep into my mind on an occasional rare night…

No. My son was not anything like him.

"Liam," I said, getting up. I walked towards him, cupping his face as I perched on the armrest of the sofa next to him. "Liam, look at me." My eyes flashed silver as I tried to get through to him, but he simply pulled away from my hold, something he had never done in his life.

"Liam… I think a trial sounds fair," Raven said, taking hold of his hand.

I felt him tense. The darkness seemed to flare up before it ebbed away. Raven caressed his hand, her eyes focused on Liam. Something was going on… something that I had a feeling the three of them knew of. *This was not just the mate issue here…*

Liam looked at Raven, who gave him a small smile, and I turned to Elijah, who was watching the entire scene with a thoughtful expression.

"Something's felt different about you since you returned, but now I know there's definitely more to it. Care to share what the fuck is going on?" He asked.

"There's nothing to say," Liam said, about to stand up when Raven took hold of his wrist.

"It's… there's a curse!" She blurted out. I raised an eyebrow, trying to make sense of what she'd just said.

"I told you it's no big deal, and that was something you shouldn't have mentioned!" Liam glared at her. His voice had never been harsher.

"Liam, do not speak to her like that," I said icily.

"She will tell us whatever is going on." Elijah added firmly, "and you will learn to speak to her properly." Liam ignored us, his gaze fixed on Raven.

"Do whatever the fuck you want, Raven. I trusted you with that and expected you to keep it confidential," he said. Despite his anger, I could feel the sadness and hurt in his voice.

"Liam, I -"

Raven closed her eyes when the door slammed shut behind Liam. I ran my hands through my hair and looked at the two that were left.

"Start from the top," I said quietly.

Raven's eyes were trained on the door before she looked back at me and then at Elijah.

"Damon can fill you guys in…" she murmured, getting up and rushing from the room.

I glanced at Damon, seeing the flicker of sadness in his eyes as he watched her leave. I frowned, remembering how Elijah had taken the news when I told him about both boys being mated to Raven…

"How… how can any man accept that?" Elijah asked, running his fingers through his hair.

"Baby… if the moon goddess paired them, surely she had something in mind," I replied softly, getting up and wrapping my arms around his waist.

"She creates a connection, not love," he replied quietly, looking down at me. "I don't blame Liam for acting the way he did, but I also don't like the way he's treating Damon. And is that boy crazy that he actually wants to make this work?"

"We can't question what they want. Regardless of their decision, we will support them," I murmured, kissing his neck.

"Yeah… but the bond alone isn't enough to make it work. If the bond was everything, people wouldn't cheat on their mates. There wouldn't be rejections, there wouldn't be anyone hurting their mates. The bond… it's a strong pull that ties us to people, but it's way fucking far from absolute."

I looked into his eyes. Elijah had never placed the same value in the bond as I did. Yes, we were fated, but he had been ready to throw away his fated mate for me, and that was the true extent of his love.

"I know it is, but I'm sure they will do what is best for them." Elijah shook his head.

"Yeah, maybe," he said. "I just don't think they should use the bond as an excuse to stay stuck without moving in any direction. I guess Liam is your son, so he places some value on the bond."

"He's your son, too, and loves unconditionally," I replied, my gaze lingering on his lips.

"That's the way it should be," he replied before claiming my lips in a sizzling kiss…

I pushed the thoughts away, looking at Damon as Elijah told him to start from the top. He took a deep breath. I knew he was worried about Liam as well.

"We need to know, Damon," I pushed, sitting on the sofa next to him as I took his hand in my own.

He looked at me, smiling softly. I reached over and kissed his cheek delicately. I had seen this boy grow up into the man he was today. Every time I thought of Aaron, all I remembered was Monica telling him she was going to be a mama and giving him that 'Daddy's Favourite BayBee' romper, a moment that would always remain in my mind, yet it hurt knowing Aaron was gone and Monica was not who she once used to be. Our little BayBee was brave. He was a selfless, loving young man who deserved the very best in life. I would never show him the sadness that I felt because he was staying strong, and so would I.

"Tell us," I said, not letting go of his hand.

He sighed in defeat and began telling us about this curse…

❧❧❧

"That's all we've got for now," Damon finished.

My heart was thundering, and I could feel Elijah's walls were up.

Goddess… Indigo, Dad, Mom, Grandma Amy, Liam, Aaron, Rafael, Daniel… how many people would you take from us? Now Liam?

Elijah was silent, running his fingers through his sandy brown locks.

"So, he practically has about two and a half months," Elijah said. "We break this curse, or he's gone." His voice was emotionless, yet I knew that wasn't the case inside.

Goddess, don't give my baby any more pain… please. He has been through so much… I looked away from Elijah, trying to contain my pain for him. I stood up, ruffling my hair.

"There is no 'or' or 'ifs' in this scenario. We are going to break this curse one way or another, or I'm up to facing Helios himself," I said, frowning. "No one is taking my son from me."

My eyes blazed at the very thought. I had lost far too much already. Then we had no choice. There was nothing we could do but this was different. There was a chance. I didn't care if he had drawn the same card as Zidane. I didn't care if we didn't have the answers. We *were* going to get through this.

Liam had always put himself second to everyone else. He was loving, tender and passionate in everything he did. My son was still inside there. He was battling this in his own way, and he will know that his family is with him. We are goddamn relentless, stubborn, and ambitious. We do not take shit from no one, whether that's a god or a curse. After all, we're the Westwoods, we don't bow down to anything or anyone.

His Touch

RAVEN

I KNEW THAT BY BLURTING that out, I was breaking his trust, but I couldn't just keep it secret when we needed all the help we could get.

"Liam!" I said, running after him. I grabbed the back of his shirt just as he exited the house.

His anger flared up and he spun around, the deep magnetic blue of his wolf's eyes piercing into my own. Thank the Goddess it wasn't those dark eyes...

"I trusted you. Don't you think I had my fucking reasons not to tell them?" He asked coldly, just as a strong wind blew around us.

"Liam, you need help -"

"Don't give me that fucking shit! I don't need help. You know what? I regret ever telling you about the fucking curse and card, then no one would have fucking ever known about it," he said. His voice was so full of anger and bitterness that I felt it inside. "I didn't want to tell Mom and Dad because they are already going through so fucking much."

"I know... but if they lose you, then -"

"Don't act like you know what you're going on about, Raven!" Liam snapped, making me internally flinch. He wasn't wrong... I felt like I always messed everything up.

"Okay... I'm sorry... I just wanted to help. I don't want to lose you. None of us do. They would never forgive themselves..." I said, staring up into his eyes.

He closed his eyes, exhaling sharply as he pinched the bridge of his nose in irritation. I looked down, feeling my stomach twist. *We've never argued before...*

"I'm sorry for shouting at you." His voice was a lot calmer. He cupped my face, and my heart skipped a beat as the electrifying sparks at our contact coursed through me, making my breath hitch.

I looked up slowly, trying to hide the hurt from my eyes, but it was hard to when it came to Liam. It felt like he was bearing into my soul. I felt bare and vulnerable. I gripped his wrists, brushing my thumb along the inside of his wrist.

"I don't mean to mess things up, although I know I always do. I just... we all love you. I love you," I said softly. "We only want to help, Liam. By shutting us out, what good will it do? I know you don't want to upset your parents... but don't you think they would be more hurt if you died?" I whispered, yearning for him to understand. I could see the struggle in his eyes before he looked down, his gaze flicking to my breasts, making my cheeks burn.

"A part of me wants to tell you to stay away from me. I don't want you to get so fucking invested in us when who knows what will happen in a few months' time... and then, another part of me wants to live every damn day as if it's my fucking last and to make the most of it with you..." he murmured, his thumb caressing my cheek.

"Liam... you will make it out of this, and we will be together," I said softly, my heart pounding at the intensity in those eyes of his.

"Will we?" He asked softly, his head tilted slightly as he looked at me.

"We will," I promised, and I meant it. "I love you, Lia-mmh!"

I was cut off when his lips crashed against mine in a sizzling kiss. My entire body was reacting to his touch; I felt giddy, my stomach fluttering and my core clenching as I began kissing him back. His luscious lips were so damn perfect. I whimpered as my emotions rushed through me. Goddess...

He plunged his tongue into my mouth, caressing mine before he sucked on it hard. One hand left my face and snaked around my waist, pulling me hard against his firm body. The other threaded into my hair and tilted my head back as he bent over me slightly. A wanton moan left my lips as I throbbed hard. There was something so intense about his kiss, fuelled by love, hunger, and desperation.

He turned us, pushing me up against the wall near the front door. His hard-on pressed against my stomach. Fuck…

His kiss was getting… hotter, dirtier, kinkier? I wasn't even sure how to explain it… but the way his hand ran up my thigh, the way he sucked and nibbled my lips and explored my mouth… the way his body pressed against mine… grinding against me ever so slightly… I wanted more, too. My core was aching, and I felt as if my entire body would explode from the intense emotions that were running through me.

Fuck… I muttered through the link.

Keep moaning and kissing me like that, and I might find it hard to stop, he groaned, breaking away from my lips as he nibbled on my ear, sucking on the lobe.

Maybe I don't want you to, I whispered back, moaning in pleasure and making him pause.

His lips were brushing my neck just below my ear. A certain part of him throbbed against me, making me sigh softly. He moved back slightly, a devilish smirk crossing his lips.

"You sure, beautiful?" He teased, his hand slipping under my skirt.

My eyes widened when his hand brushed between my thighs. I bit my lip, looking around. We were right outside the Westwoods' home! Although there were trees around, I knew there could be patrol passing around at any moment…

"Liam…mm…" I closed my eyes when his fingers rubbed against my panties, pleasure rushing through me, and the urge to part my legs or pull away were fighting against one another. "Someone might see us," I whispered, although I sounded completely flustered. I had never done this before… and out in the open?

My heart was pounding, yet the pleasure that just the brush of his finger was giving me was making my legs tremble and my stomach knot in anticipation. He looked around before taking hold of my wrist and pulling me around the side of the house, pushing me up against the wall.

"Better?" He asked, kissing my lips again.

"A little," I said in between his hot, hungry kisses.

"What's the fun in anything without the fear of being caught?" He teased, his hand going under the skirt of my dress once more. My cheeks burned when he pushed my underwear aside. "Fuck…" Liam murmured, sliding his finger between my folds.

I bit my lip, my eyes fluttering shut as a soft moan escaped my lips. The moment his finger touched my clit, I pressed my head back against the wall as pleasure rushed through me. *Goddess...* Yes, I had used a vibrator, it was as far as I dared go when it came to toys, but this... having his hands on me... it felt so good...

"Fuck, Liam..." I moaned. He massaged my pussy. His lips met mine in a passionate kiss, but he pulled away fast.

"I want to taste you, love," he whispered huskily, bending down before me. "Mind if I do?" His fingers ghosted down my inner thighs as he waited for an answer.

My cheeks were burning, and I knew they were probably pink as I gave him a small nod. The fact that we were outside now seemed like a distant worry. All I could do was stare into those deep, magnetic blue orbs of his. My eyes widened when he slipped my dress up slightly and slid my panties down to my ankles.

"Liam, what are... fuck!" I gasped when he lifted one of my legs to his shoulders, burying his face between my thighs.

If there was anything on my mind, it was completely gone the moment his tongue flicked out, running from the bottom of my pussy all the way up to my clit. I clamped a hand over my mouth to stop myself from crying out. Goddess....

Fuck, you taste better than I imagined, his voice came through the link.

So, you've imagined what I tasted like? I couldn't help but ask, despite my cheeks burning even more.

Countless times...

I have, too...

I whimpered, unable to reply as he ate me out like I was the tastiest thing on the planet. *Fuck...* My hand was tangled in his hair, and my entire body was reacting to his delicious assault. I moved my hips against him, unable to stop myself from wanting that tongue of his on my clit, but he had other ideas. I almost yelped when his moist tongue slipped into me.

"Oh, fuck, that's it!" I whimpered, struggling to keep my voice down as he tongue-fucked me.

It felt too fucking good... Goddess...

His hands stroked my thighs and squeezed my ass, but right then, I didn't care about anything but how much pleasure he was inflicting on me. His tongue slipped out of me, flicking my clit sensually.

"Fuck, Liam, right there! Oh, fuck, baby!" I moaned, quietly feeling that intense pressure building before my orgasm ripped through me, and I clamped my hands over my mouth as my entire body trembled. I gasped, my legs almost giving way. If Liam wasn't holding me, I would have buckled. "Fuck…" I breathed, my chest heaving. I could feel the hardness of my nipples as Liam moved back, and my dress slipped down after delivering a light spank to my ass.

"Fucking delicious," he said seductively, licking his lips. His eyes locked with mine.

My entire body was still tingling from the aftershock of my orgasm, my heart thumping when he kissed my inner leg before lowering it from his shoulder and sliding my panties back up. A smirk crossed those lush lips of his as he stood up, taking my chin and pressing his lips to mine. I could taste myself in his mouth, and it only made my heart thump even more. This side of Liam was reserved only for me… and there was something so fucking hot about that…

Don't you taste good, love? He asked huskily through the link. **Because I think I just found myself a new favourite thing to feast on…**

I didn't reply, blushing when he parted his lips and allowed me to roam his mouth with my tongue. My hand ran down his firm abs and over the bulge in his pants, but he stopped me, taking hold of my tiny wrist in his hands.

"Not today, love," he said quietly, his smirk vanishing as he stared up into my eyes. "When you're fully mine," he added, quietly answering my silent questions. The pang of pain that squeezed at my chest at the realisation that I had two mates returned to me like a slap in the face.

I didn't reply as he turned and left me standing there alone. I couldn't go on like this… it wasn't fair to any one of us.

I returned to the packhouse after that, not wanting anyone to know what we had just done. My mind kept replaying the moment with Liam, and I realised that, despite worrying about him, I was holding back from being myself completely with him because of my connection to Damon. It wasn't fair to anyone…

Damon had mind-linked asking if things were okay, and I told him that we didn't really talk, but he'd calmed down. He was glad things didn't escalate and filled me in on what happened inside. Yes, I felt dreadful…

Aunty Red had also mind-linked asking about Liam as well, but the thing is, we didn't really get to talk, so I told her the same thing I told Damon. Things had just gotten out of hand, but I didn't regret it. I just… I needed to sort myself out. Maybe talking to Taylor might help. I needed a friend's insight on this, and I think we both needed each other.

I pulled on some soft black loungewear, consisting of comfy bottoms, a crop top and a cardigan, before I grabbed some snacks from my stash; Doritos, a bag of mixed chocolates, and a share bag of candyfloss. Who doesn't love cotton candy? Of course, I brought one of my plushies, you can't have a movie night without a plushie, and of course, slippers! I looked down at my fluffy slippers proudly.

I was halfway down the hallways when Owen bumped into me on purpose, but I was kind of expecting it. I braced myself just in time, shoving him hard and knocking him into the wall on his other side. A young couple, Lee and Macy, snickered at that, and Owen shot them a glare.

"So, where are you off to tonight? Your other mate's for the night?" He asked, making me freeze.

"Excuse me?"

"Come on, we all know you have two mates. Wow, you're a little slut, huh?" He taunted.

"Owen cut it out," Lee warned him.

"I can handle this," I said, despite feeling shocked at the fact that the entire packhouse knew I had two mates. Was it the guard? Shit… "Actually, I'm going to Taylor's," I said icily.

"Oh, I never knew he rolled both ways. There might actually be a bit of a man in the fucking -" Owen was cut off when someone punched him across the face. Zack's scent hit me before I realised it was him as he knocked Owen to the ground, punching him across the face again.

"Who the fuck do you think you are insulting?" He growled venomously, punching him again. My eyes widened as I stared at them, but I wasn't going to stop them. Owen deserved it.

"What the fuck, man?" Owen growled.

"You don't fucking talk shit about him, or I swear I will fuck you up!"

Zack hissed, delivering a final punch to Owen's jaw, making the three of us watching flinch at the resounding crack.

He got off him, and Owen groaned, rolling onto his side. The smell of blood filled my nose as he spat a mouthful out whilst he watched Zack turn away. I stuck my tongue out at him before trudging down the stairs behind Zack.

"Someone got angry," I said, clutching my snacks tightly. He looked down at my plushie before shaking his head and giving me a look that clearly said, 'You know why.'

"And where were you headed to?" Zack asked, raising his eyebrow as he looked me over.

"Spending the night at Taylor's," I answered, tossing my hair. *Hehe, bet you want to be in my place right now, sucker.* I instantly felt bad when he swallowed and nodded, his eyes filled with guilt.

"How is he?"

"He needs time... but he'll be okay," I said softly as Nina and another Omega stepped out of the kitchen and passed Zack a large bag full of boxed food. I gave Nina a small wave, and she smiled back as Zack thanked them.

"What's with the food?" I asked, motioning to the Tupperware.

"Oh, I'm taking these for a few of the boys on patrol. With everything happening, they don't really get breaks often," he said, shrugging.

"Oh, okay! Well, have fun being a delivery boy," I said, strolling towards the front door.

"Hey, should you be going out alone? If Liam knew -"

"He won't know unless you open your mouth," I growled.

"I'll walk you." I raised an eyebrow.

"Are you worried about me, or do you just want to see a certain someone?"

"Both. He's avoiding me, not that I fucking blame him," Zack said quietly. I gave him a sympathetic smile.

"He'll come around," I assured him as we left the packhouse. Ah, the weather was good tonight...

We reached Taylor's house shortly after, and I paused, glancing at my own parent's home for a moment. It felt strange... I didn't know what to feel anymore...

"Raven...?" Zack asked, concerned. "You okay?" I nodded my head and smiled.

"Of course!" I said before I walked up to Taylor's front door and rang the doorbell. Zack stayed at the gate, but he didn't leave. His eyes were on the door.

Taylor opened it looking as handsome as ever in an oversized tank top and sweatpants. His eyes instantly snapped to Zack at the gates, and his heart skipped a beat. He clenched his jaw and looked at me.

"Hey, you got snacks! I got some too, and pizza is on the way," he said, smiling down at me.

"Mhmm," I said, giving him a hug despite having my hands full. I knew Zack had walked off. It hurt to see them like this.

We headed upstairs, and both of us plopped down on his bed. He put on a movie that he knew both of us would enjoy, although I knew we were both going to be watching less and talking more.

"So, how was your day?" Taylor asked as we both settled against the pillows. I placed my plushie next to me in the middle of us both, smiling proudly at it. He held out the bowl of popcorn he had already prepared, and I sighed heavily at his question.

"Okay, want me to tell you my problems? Because I have a lot to tell," I asked, pouting. Taylor propped himself up on his elbow, tilting his head.

"Okay... should I be worried? I mean, I have heard stuff..."

"Well... I guess you heard about the two mates, huh?" I said, throwing popcorn up in the air and catching it in my mouth.

"Yeah... I did, actually. Damn, girl..." He gave me a small smile. I sighed heavily.

"No, babe, not okay..."

I began to explain our entire situation. The pizza came halfway through, and we ate slowly. Taylor was more in shock than anything else as he processed the entire thing. I didn't hold back from how Dad deleted those texts to everything else. Telling him how I had chemistry with both and loved them both, but it was also so different. How I felt guilty and confused. The only thing I left out was the curse.

".... And there you have it. My life," I finished, biting into my third pizza slice. Taylor let out a low whistle as he gulped some of his fizzy drink down.

"So... that's why things between those two are weird as hell?" He asked, running his fingers through his hair.

"Yeah," I said, sighing heavily.

"Well, now I'm wondering who has it worse, you or me…" he muttered. I gave him a sympathetic smile.

"For what it's worth, I think things will get better," I offered.

"So, who will you pick?" He asked, picking up a few fries. My eyes widened as I stared up at him, my heart thundering at his words.

"Pick?" Taylor nodded, his warm eyes full of concern and curiosity.

"Yeah, because it's obvious from everything you just told me that you're going to have to pick one…" My heart skipped a beat, and I nodded.

"Yeah, that has been on my mind… but how am I supposed to do that without feeling guilty?" I asked the one question that haunted my thoughts.

Clarity

RAVEN

"YOU ARE GOING TO feel guilty, but we both know staying in this situation is hurting you all," he said softly. I could feel how bad he felt saying that, but it was the truth. "Putting aside everything... let's play a game. I ask a question, and you pick which one you would choose," he added, slapping his thigh as the idea popped into his head.

Putting aside everything... the curse included. Because that was what I used to make myself feel better every time I felt guilty for how I was treating Damon, but that was not an excuse.

"Okay..." I said, playing with the tab on my can.

"Now, picture them both standing right there... which one will you hug first?" I frowned as the answer came to me.

"Liam... because -"

"We're not justifying why here. Block that all out and just think about your instant answers, I don't want any breaks, you have to answer fast, okay? Whoever comes to mind first."

"Okay," I groaned.

"Both are hurt in a battle with rogues. Which one will you tend to first?"

"Liam," I said, feeling another flash of guilt through me. No matter the answer, I still felt guilty.

"If you did something that they told you not to, who will you confess to first?"

"Damon."

"Who do you want to fuck?"

"Li- hey!" Taylor chuckled.

"Soo... you done it yet? Details... now!"

"Stop it! We haven't!" I said, blushing as I remembered what had happened earlier.

Oh, my dear goddess, that was naughty! Liam was naughty... that side of him.... My heart skipped a beat, and I pushed it away.

"Okay, then, which one do you want to cuddle up to in bed?"

"Liam..."

"Cuddle with over a movie?"

"Both?" I pouted. "They both came to mind!"

"So, something you would do with a friend..." Taylor said. "Okay... out of curiosity, which one have you kissed?"

"Both, but Damon only once," I replied, pouting.

"Damn, girl! Dare I ask how many times you've kissed Liam?" He teased. I sighed.

"It's because Damon said -"

"Stop justifying it. We are talking about your feelings here," he said softly, giving my hand a squeeze before dipping his fries into the ketchup. I nodded, thinking about Damon once more. Deep down, I knew who I favoured, but I hated myself for it. "There's no guilt or shame in loving someone... it doesn't make you bad to feel stronger for one over the other. Can you imagine being with Damon and rejecting Liam?"

Life without Liam...

My heart clenched painfully, and my eyes stung. The fear of the curse and what if that became a reality. His words from earlier echoed in my mind,

"When you are mine..."

I knew he could sense my hesitation... it hurt so damn much. I was an awful mate to both. I placed my face in my hands as the tears came, no longer able to hold them back.

"Damn, I'm sorry, Raven!" Taylor's panicked voice came.

I shook my head, but I was unable to stop. I knew what I had to do, but just thinking about it broke me. I didn't want to hurt him... I couldn't hurt him. I sobbed loudly, clamping my hands over my mouth as I bent down, pressing my forehead to my knees as I tried to stop my tears.

Taylor's arms wrapped around me and held me tight.

"Shit, I'm sorry, Raven... I'm damn sorry..."

Don't be... you just made me realise I am doing more damage than good, I whispered through the link.

He stroked my back, and I felt ridiculous crying like this, but I realised all my life, I just stayed quiet because it was easier. We couldn't do this anymore. I couldn't do this anymore. I wanted all my firsts to be special, not constantly worrying about what the other might be thinking or the fact that I kept feeling guilty.

"I'm going to say this to myself as much as to you," Taylor said, kissing the top of my head. "Life isn't perfect or easy... the stories of soul mates and their eternal love are only sugar-coated versions of reality. Look at those power couples around us... Alpha Elijah and Luna Scarlett's. Sure we know them as this amazing couple who love each other deeply and have the chemistry to die for... but they did not have it easy — even on their journeys, there were difficulties. We need to create our own love stories and overcome our differences, issues, and hardships to make them perfect... but also remember that we need to get to that perfect part. To remember that the pain we're feeling right now is part of that journey, a part we need to overcome..." I nodded as I tried to steady my breathing and calm down.

"I know... you're right... I'm scared knowing I might hurt someone and knowing that I'm already hurting Damon, Liam... myself..."

"I know, baby girl, but that's life, and you are one badass queen who has got this." I wished I could tell him I was just an ordinary wallflower, not a badass queen... but he's being sweet, so I won't argue.

"I'm tired...tired of it all," I whispered.

"It's okay to be," he replied. I pulled away slightly and looked at him with a tilt of my head.

"So... what about you?" I asked, wiping my tears away. He looked down.

"I need to talk to Channing. He deserves to know... but I have been delaying it," he admitted, his eyes pained.

"I'm sorry," I whispered.

"Don't be. I'll figure it out," he comforted me. I nodded and took a deep breath.

"Okay, we are going to do what we need to do," I said with renewed determination, feeling a lot better after crying and talking to him. He gave me a small smile and nodded.

"Yeah... we will."

We had cleared up the takeaway boxes and settled down, nibbling at the cotton candy, when Liam's voice came through the link, making my cheeks burn at the memory of earlier.

Raven?

Yeah? I asked, my heart thumping.

Your father's trial is this coming Monday. Are you okay with testifying openly or privately…? My heart skipped a beat. So he was actually listening to Uncle El. I felt so happy about that. I smiled softly.

"I can do it openly," I said, my heart thumping, but I needed to be brave.

I knew the pack was probably already talking about me behind my back with the entire two-mate situation, but I would not let it put me down. If Liam was willing to do this by trial, something he didn't want to do, then I would also testify.

I'm willing to do so at the trial, I said softly.

Perfect. So, uh… what are you up to? He asked. I smiled at the awkwardness in his tone.

Thinking about you and playing with myself? I said as seriously as possible. His pause of silence made me unable to hold back my laughter. **Haha! Did I make you blush?**

I don't blush, came his reply, but I could tell he was pouting. **But I know how to make you blush.**

Oh, don't play that with me, blue eyes, I said, glad he wasn't there in person. **I'm at Taylor's! You are disturbing me!**

Cool, enjoy, but one last thing… I didn't expect you to have a Brazilian wax. It's really sexy… I like it. Scratch that; I fucking love it, and it's a damn turn-on.

My eyes flew open, my cheeks burning at his words, and I wasn't able to reply. His chuckle came through the link. **Have fun,** came his triumphant farewell, leaving me red-faced and completely speechless!

Taylor and I watched another movie after. We talked about our sucky situations as we ate all the snacks and even grabbed some beer from the fridge, comforting each other when we needed it and laughing at our lame attempts at singing. Yes, we were both tone-deaf and sounded horrifying, but we had fun and lots of giggles. Taylor was an amazing friend, and although we weren't close as children, it felt like I had known him forever. I mean, I did, but not like this.

The credits of the second movie had ended, and the TV had switched off, but Taylor and I were still awake, lying side by side on the bed and staring at the shadows that were cast across the ceiling thanks to the moonlight shining through the cracks in the curtains and tree branches.

"Raven…"

"Yeah?" I said, yawning as I rubbed my eyes sleepily.

"You know, when we were little… when I was weird and awkward, that shy kid no one wanted to know or play with, you used to always greet me and talk to me…"

"You were not weird; you were cute and adorable," I insisted, trying to keep my eyes open.

"Mmm, you'd think that… but you were this little, tiny girl, like the smallest one in the pack, and everyone used to say you had a growth issue… cause you were like six, wearing two-year-old clothes… " he said drowsily.

"Yeah… I remember… I'm sure it was three years clothing…." He chuckled sleepily.

"You were like a damn little doll… walking and talking yet so damn doll-sized… well… you always had this big smile on your face and always talked to me, complimenting me on what I was wearing, my hair… saying good morning… and although it was something small, it made my day… so, thank you…." He yawned, turning onto his side to face me. "I never even knew your name for many years…"

"Hmm? You didn't?" I asked, turning my head to look at him.

"No, I used to call you the girl who looks like a doll… until I heard Liam calling you once… I'm older than you, but I was timid, and back then, you were so brave… you still are. You're damn perfect, and no matter what you do, I'm going to support you, okay?" His eyes fluttered shut, and I yawned again.

"Mmm, thanks… I'll always support you, too…" I remembered saying before my eyes fluttered shut and sleep welcomed me into its folds…

My eyes flew open, my heart pounding. I sat up, looking around the room. It took me a moment to realise I had fallen asleep at Taylor's. His back was to me, and he was snoring lightly.

I looked around the dark room, brushing my hair off my face. How had I woken up? Something didn't feel right... I slowly got off the bed, not wanting to disturb Taylor. I walked across the floor, careful not to step on the chocolate wrappers and rubbish that we had littered all over the floor before I tip-toed to the window. Taylor had left the top one open to air the room that had smelt of take-out, but it was fairly silent outside. The distant sound of an animal and the rustle of the leaves in the trees were all that I could hear.

I peered out past the tree that stood in the corner of Taylor's garden, and my eyes fell on my old bedroom window that was just across from Taylor's. I was about to turn away when my wolf's uneasiness made me look back at my old house... almost as if urging me to pay attention to it. She wanted me to go there. Why? I could feel her restlessness, and I frowned, glancing back at Taylor, before I slowly unlocked the window and slid it up silently, flinching when it made a slight squeak. I paused as Taylor groaned and turned over, falling back to sleep.

I blew out a breath and slowly climbed onto the ledge, lowering the window as much as possible behind me before I jumped to the ground below, landing lithely. I stood up straight, ignoring the sharp poking of the stones beneath my feet, and padded towards my parents' home, jumping over the low fence. Mom lived alone now. Was she okay? My heart skipped a beat as a horrible thought came to my head. *No... don't think like that, Raven.*

I walked around the house, my heart pounding despite trying to push that thought away. Should I just do the doorbell and see if she was okay? Wait... it's night-time, she'll be asleep...

I stared at the dark house, hesitating before I turned away, but once again, my wolf's restlessness made me turn back. Since returning to the pack, she had been a little more active, and I didn't want to shut her out if she was trying to tell me something. I needed to respect that.

Okay, calm down. I'll mind-link her.

Mom?

No answer. She was probably asleep...

Mom? I tried pushing through that block, frowning at the fact that I was drawing a blank. What the heck? Had she shut me out? Could she do that so strongly whilst sleeping?

I turned, thinking to go ring the doorbell. I was beginning to feel worried. Maybe I was just overreacting. No, wait; a sudden thought came to me, and I padded around the house to the bathroom window, wondering if Dad ever got it fixed. I smiled when I saw the gap in it, something that Mom always asked Dad to fix. Seems like he never bothered! Perfect!

I scanned the ground. Finding a decent-sized branch, I used it to slip into the gap and pry up the dodgy handle. It was a small window, but I'd fit. Grabbing onto it, I pulled myself onto the ledge and squeezed in, frowning when my ass and thighs got a little stuck. Just great. Seems like the only place I had grown over the years was there. *Stupid fat thighs...* I pulled myself through, feeling the window scrape my ass and snag at my pants. Finally, I managed to get in and blew out a breath. Yay!

The cool bathroom tiles were pleasant beneath my feet as I made my way to the door, opening it ever so silently. I calmed my heartbeat to minimise the sound of it. One look at Mom, and then it was back out of there. She never needed to know I had been there! I made my way down the dark hall. The scent of pumpkin spice lingered in the hall, and I smiled sadly. It was Mom's favourite smell, year in and year out. She'd stock up on the festive scented candles in the winter and use them throughout the entire year.

I was careful, making sure to stay towards the wall. The floorboards didn't creak so much where they were hardly stepped on. Years of sneaking out really did help. I went up the stairs as silently as I could. Glancing down the hallway, I could see the door to Mom's room was open, and I frowned. Did she leave it open because Dad wasn't there? Wait, I refused to call him Dad...

The entire house was dark, and it was a little cold too. I felt my stomach twist. Wasn't she taking care of herself?

I silently made my way down the hall, frowning when I didn't hear a heartbeat. Wait, had she left the pack or something? Was that why my wolf was worried? After all, it had a link to family.

I rushed to the door, pushing it open, expecting to see a half-empty room. I froze at the smell of blood that filled my nose. My eyes snapped to the silhouette of someone under the sheets of the bed. My heart pounded as fear and panic settled within me, alarm bells going off.

No heartbeat... blood... was that...

"Mom?" I asked, my voice shaky as I edged closer to the bed.

Please be a prank. Please tell me I'm wrong.

"M-Mom?" I whimpered, sounding terrified.

Stay strong, Raven.

My entire body was shaking involuntarily. I couldn't breathe properly... I reached out with a trembling hand for the sheets. Mom's scent and the stench of fresh blood overrode my senses. I couldn't bring myself to lower the duvet...

My chest was heaving.

I'm scared...

Liam.... I whimpered through the link; he was probably asleep...

What is it, love? Are you okay? Worry and concern were clear in his voice, but the warmth of just hearing him made me feel an inch braver.

It was a struggle to reply as I yanked the bedding back. My mouth widened in a silent scream, and I stumbled back, my breathing ragged as I stared at the horrifying scene before me.

No, please, Goddess...no!

Fuck...

There lay Mom with blood-stained bedding under her, her empty mouth hanging wide open, slit from ear to ear. Her teeth were gone, and there were two gaping sockets where her eyes should have been.

Raven, where the fuck are you? Liam's voice snapped me out of my horror-struck state.

Liam... Mom... I trailed off when the sudden feeling of being watched overcame me. The hair at the back of my neck stood up and my heart thundered.

I whipped around, but I was too late. Something struck my head. A searing pain erupted through it, and before I could even recover or react, I felt a stinging pain in my neck. Then everything went dark...

A Team

LIAM

I WAS IN MY OFFICE with Damon. It was probably one of the fucking rare times we were completely alone, and the urge to get rid of him wasn't fucking overtaking me.

The entire table and part of the floor were littered with papers and photographs. I couldn't believe I was in this fucking situation where we were trying to rule out those who had full alibis around the time of the murders. Zack, Damon, and I were the only ones working on it, and it was fucking a lot. Maybe we needed to bring in a few more people. Dad offered; I might take him up on that. Mom had Aunty Monica and Azura to take care of. Maybe Raven…

I licked my lips, remembering what had happened earlier. Perfect was not even enough to describe it… she was fucking divine, and that pretty little pussy of hers was so bloody fine. Feeling myself twitch in my pants, I frowned, pushing the thought away. Fuck.

"It would have been easier to just put them all under Alpha command," I said coldly, trying to focus. I still intended to do that, but only with those who had blanks in their alibis. We were hoping to cut out at least eighty percent of the pack.

"It's about trust and respect," Damon murmured, organising the files into ranks. With a pack with over a thousand members, it wasn't fucking easy. At least we could rule out the pups.

"Still, they'd understand," I said. Looking at the warrior files in front of me, taking a few papers that were stapled together, I tilted my head. "I wouldn't be surprised if it's this fucking asshole…" Damon turned to look at the papers I held.

"Owen… yeah, he's a prick, but I don't know. I feel he's just too obvious," he murmured.

"And the job does feel too clean for him," I added, but still, we couldn't just cross anyone out.

The pile of those who were definitely ruled out thanks to full alibis was small… less than 200. That was far too fucking low…

"I'm covered," Damon said, holding up his pile, frowning when he saw the one under him. "You got yourself here? The fuck?" I cocked a brow, massaging my temples, feeling a headache coming on.

"With my psychotic tendencies right now, I could be a fucking prime suspect. I don't remember ripping Jacob's arm off, so…"

The only ones spared from the assessment were Mom and Dad. The rest were on it to make it fair, although deep down, I trusted Damon, Raven, and Zack. It was a guideline we were following. Zack did his search on Damon and me, and Damon did Zack's.

"Yeah, and made a mess. This job is too clean to even think it's you," Damon murmured. "Zack is totally covered."

"Great, at least two of the higher position ones are. The priority is the security team. Who do we have covered?"

"Esteban… Drew… Ben… Cassidy…" I nodded. That made me feel a lot fucking better. "Mom…"

I looked towards him as he picked up his mom's file and I felt a sliver of guilt. Putting Aunty Monica in this shit wasn't right. He simply flicked the file open, staring at the many blank sections. It was obvious there'd be blanks; she stayed home for the most part.

"I won't put her under Alpha command," I said quietly. He looked at me and shook his head.

"No, I get it," he said, his voice as calm and gentle as fucking ever, placing her file into the larger pile. I walked over, took the file, and put it in the other pile.

"I said, I won't," I said firmly, my eyes flashing warningly before I walked back to my desk. A silence fell between us before he called me,

"Liam…" I glanced at him, raising an eyebrow. "Thanks. I appreciate it," he said quietly.

I gave a curt nod, and we continued our work. It was weird yet calming, almost like old times before our fucked up mate situation. Hours had passed and we were still working on it. Even Zack had shown up and we scoured through the files together.

Damon had gone to get us some hot drinks and had just gotten back, shutting the door after him.

"Thanks," I said, grabbing a bar of chocolate from the tray as I massaged my forehead. My eyes fell on the tub of painkillers, and I glanced up at him, but he was back to his work. *Thanks…* but I wasn't able to say that to him. I took two pills, swallowing them down with some water.

"Shall we rule out the ten- to fourteen-year-olds?" Zack asked, looking at a wad of files.

"No, we know even kids can be killers…" I said, dropping back in my seat.

"I think it's a female," Zack said, suddenly making both Damon and I look at him sharply.

"What?" Damon asked.

"Look… don't you think the job is really clean? I don't know. I feel like a female would be this precise."

"I don't think so. Men can be too." I shook my head.

"Any reply about the handwriting analysis?" Damon asked.

"Yeah, both are inconsistent with one another. There's been some tracing, some changes between the slant, and the speed and pressure of the pen varied drastically," I muttered. "We only got that it is definitely the same person."

"So, they were careful there, too," Zack muttered.

"And no fucking scent," I said, frowning. "As if the messages were written and kept until nothing remained, or they wore gloves and somehow disguised their scents."

"Were the papers tested for any remnants of scent masking sprays or anything?" Zack asked.

"Yeah, nothing." I frowned.

"And our fucking werewolf abilities don't help with this shit," Damon murmured, grabbing a mug of hot chocolate for himself. Zack nodded, picking up his coffee and looking between the two of us before glancing away.

"Want to say something?" I asked, cocking a brow.

"No, just glad we are working together," he said, with a small smirk.

"Hmm," I said, ignoring Damon's grin.

"Raven didn't come home, did she?" Zack asked hesitantly.

"She went to Taylor's," I said, frowning when Zack looked disappointed. My eyes narrowed. "What's your problem with that?" I asked icily.

"No problem at all…" Zack said, but his tone said otherwise. He sounded fucking down. Did he have a fucking crush on her? My eyes flashed dangerously at the thought, but I don't know… I never got that vibe from him before.

We finished our drink and I glanced at the time: ten to three…

"Let's call it a night," I said, running my fingers through my hair, knowing it was probably a mess from the number of times I had run my fingers through it. I stood up, stretching. I needed to sleep. Maybe I'll take her room. Although I wished I could cuddle up to her, I'd have to deal with her scent…

Liam…. Raven's whimper came suddenly through the link, making my heart thud. Why did she sound… scared?

What is it, love? Are you okay? I asked, my heart beating way too fucking fast. A thousand worries and fear rushed through me. Zack and Damon looked at me, sensing the change. She didn't answer. I rushed to the door, both boys instantly following me.

Raven, where the fuck are you? I asked, fear enveloping me.

Liam… Mom…

Raven! Raven? Fuck!

Nothing. I felt as if I was hitting a wall, and I knew she had not fucking blocked me off.

"Something is wrong with Raven!" I said, running down the steps and out the door faster than the other two.

"I'll link Taylor, she was with him!" I heard Zack say as I rushed towards Taylor and Raven's parents' home. She had mentioned her mom…

Did she link you? Damon asked, worry clear in his voice.

Yeah, I said, speeding up.

I left them both behind. The moment I reached the houses, I saw Taylor banging on the Jacobs' front door.

"Alpha! Zack linked me -"

I pushed him aside, breaking the door down. Fuck, her scent was here… I ran up the steps, taking three at a time then ran down the hall. The smell of blood hung in the air. Panic and fear wrapped around me, and all I could think about was Raven. *Be fucking okay.*

My heart was in my mouth as I pushed open the door to the master bedroom. Coming to an abrupt halt, my eyes widened in shock at the sight before me...

❧❧

DAMON

I ran into the Jacobs' home a minute or so behind Liam, only to see him running down the stairs with Raven's body in his arms.

"What the..."

"I need to get her to the hospital. She's injured, and I think there's poison in her system. She isn't healing! Her mom's dead," he quickly explained, the fear and worry in his eyes tearing at my own heart.

I nodded, knowing he was the fastest to get her there... but to my surprise, he held her out to me, his cerulean eyes full of pain.

"Make sure she's okay," he said, his voice hoarse.

My heart thudded as I took her in my arms. She was tiny and didn't weigh much at all, her head falling against my chest. I nodded, not saying anything as I turned and ran from the house.

I knew he wanted to find whoever did it, and I could see the pain in his eyes as he let her go.

I could feel her blood coating my arm, which meant she wasn't healing. Was it the same poison that was killing the people around us? If it was, it meant we'd be able to save her. The fact that the killer let the body shut down itself by using a mix of ricin, silver, and wolfsbane was very intelligent.

I quickly mind-linked the head doctor and told him I was on my way, filling him in on the situation and carrying my little mate as I ran as fast as I could.

When a pack member is killed, or when they broke pack ties or joined another pack, the Alpha would feel the pack link break, but when an ill person passes away or if someone is dying slowly, it wasn't really noticeable to the Alpha. The tug was so subtle, you wouldn't realise it at all. The murders shut down the organs first, slowly yet surely. The fact that they seemed to have thought this entire thing out so fucking cleverly worried me. Time was running out and we were no closer to the truth.

I rushed to the room the nurse guided me too and placed Raven on the bed, placing a kiss on her forehead. She was pale and looked so fucking fragile...

"Please step outside, Beta Damon!" The doctor said before he began to shout orders. "She's been poisoned, get the antidote for silver and wolfs-bane. The Alpha said there may be ricin! We need to pump it from her body. Hook her up, check her blood pressure!"

I was pushed from the room, my heart thundering at the clear worry on the doctor's face. We couldn't lose her. I tried to contact Liam, but all I reached was a block. Fuck!

How is she? Taylor's strained voice came through the link.

I don't know yet. Where's Liam? I asked.

He's trying to search for clues. He's angry, and I feel so damn guilty. I'm sorry, I swear I feel like shit. I didn't hear her leave or I would have gone with her... I'm sorry, I know she's your two's mate, and I can't imagine how you must be feeling.

She'll be okay... I said softly.

I ended the link, pacing the hall feeling so damn frustrated, worried, and helpless. I ran my fingers through my hair dropping onto the bench. Please be fucking okay...

I was scared of losing her. We needed her. Heck I'd give anything for her to be okay. I'd happily take her place, too. Her smile, her unique eyes, her selflessness...

Come on, Raven, fight.

✺❧❧✺

A few hours had passed. Liam had mind-linked a few times asking how she was, but that was it. He didn't say much but I could sense his pain from his voice, although he was desperately trying to hide it.

Finally, the doctor said she was safe. The poison had been administered close to her neck, and if she had been brought in any later, things could have been worse. I entered the hospital room. A bandage was wrapped around her head. The doctor said she had been struck with a sledgehammer, but not with enough force to have done severe damage. Either the killer was in a rush to leave, or they were generally not fucking strong enough. My thought went back to what Zack had said. Was it a woman?

I brushed my knuckles down her cheek, a tingle of pleasure following. Her soft, plump lips were parted slightly as she breathed softly. Her long black lashes fluttered slightly at my touch. I bent down and placed my lips gently on hers. The sparks of the bond rushed through me, and the sweet taste of her mouth was something I wouldn't forget.

That ache in my heart was growing. I didn't know if I had a chance, or if I ever would. She was that special, rare gem that you wanted to protect forever and not hurt anymore.

I love you.

I took her delicate hand in mine, thinking how small and slender it was in comparison to mine before I kissed it softly. I heard the sound of running, and I knew it was Liam. I slowly placed her hand down, the pain in my chest heightening. She was meant to be mine, too, but I couldn't have her. I smiled gently, just hoping that no matter what, she got her happily ever after…

The door opened and Liam ran over. He was shirtless, the necklaces around his neck hitting against one another, the sound loud in this silent room. His eyes were fixed on Raven as he caressed her forehead, his other hand stroking her arm before he curled his fingers under her chin and pressed his lips to hers. His heart was racing; I knew he was as worried as I had been, if not more as he wasn't able to be here.

I looked away, feeling the painful tug at the scene before me. His love was so intense for her… was mine any less? Was there a difference between our love?

Don't think like that, Damon…

But no matter how much I told myself to stay positive, I did feel like I was losing all hope of the three of us making it work.

Liam pulled the armchair forward, sitting by her bed, holding her hand to his chest.

"Found anything?" I asked.

"A footprint, a partial one but it's there. The killer wasn't expecting Raven to show up, that was for certain," he answered coldly. "But we found no one that looked suspicious. Everyone seemed to have been asleep, but I did fucking order a search of the nearest places. I don't know… I feel like we are missing something big," he said, running his free hand through his hair.

I nodded, grabbing the other armchair and situating myself on the other side of the bed. I glanced at her hand and placed my hand over it, feeling Liam's intense gaze on me, but he didn't say anything.

"And was there a note?"

"Obviously."

"What did it say?"

"You deserved this."

Moments of Love

LIAM

I TRIED TO TELL MYSELF that he was just holding her hand out of concern, that he was her friend too... but I couldn't deny the irritation that was flaring up inside of me. That anger threatening to lash out. I tried to focus on Raven, letting the tingles that coursed through me at our touch calm me.

"You deserve this?" He repeated, frowning.

"Yeah, so, the three notes... the first said, 'Who's next?' The second, 'Two down, I wonder how many more to go?' And now this. There's nothing really in them," I said, pausing. "You deserved this is probably the most to go on."

"True, but who do they mean? Her mom? Raven? Do they have an issue with Raven?" Damon mused. I frowned, clenching my jaw.

"These murders started when Raven came back to town... there may be a connection there," I said, suddenly thinking he had a point. Damon looked surprised at that before becoming thoughtful.

"Good point. Do you think we should track down those who would have issues with Raven? I mean, her dad wouldn't kill his mate and he's in the cells, so he's ruled out as the killer."

"Hmm, yeah, I think we need to list anyone who may have any sort of link to Raven," I said quietly, just as the door opened and Dad stepped in.

He glanced at us. I didn't miss the way his gaze flickered to both Damon and me holding Raven's hands. I swear, if we weren't fucking mated no one would have ever even thought anything of us holding her hand. So fucking annoying.

"I think you need to make a list a lot broader than that," Dad said, checking the machine that Raven was hooked up to before frowning and sitting at the edge of the bed. She was so tiny, there was a good gap from the bottom and her feet.

"What do you mean? We're thinking of anyone who may have anything against her," Damon said. I think I understood what Dad meant.

"You mean, people who may have issues with Damon and me... her parents... anyone who is somehow even linked to Raven. An indirect grudge, right?" I said sharply

Dad smirked humourlessly and nodded.

"Yeah, exactly." He said, "You two boys look exhausted. Head to bed, I'll stay with her."

"No thanks., I said coldly. "If it was Mom, you wouldn't have left." He sighed. Once again, I had to try to fucking calm down.

"No, I wouldn't have, but you look a fucking mess."

"Don't really care. You two can leave, I'm staying." I said icily. I could feel my anger flaring up and that bitterness towards everything beginning to flare inside.

"Let's go, Uncle," Damon said, and I was glad at least one of them understood.

Dad shook his head but stood up. Damon placed a quick kiss on Raven's forehead before he walked to the door. Dad caressed her head before he turned. Pausing at the door, he glanced back at me, almost as if he wanted to say something but decided against it and closed the door behind him.

I didn't move. Even as the sun began to rise in the sky, I sat there waiting for her to wake up, but she remained asleep. The doctor came in around seven in the morning to do some checks, asking if I wanted to rest or have something to eat. I refused. All I wanted was for her to wake up.

Come on, love, wake up...

RAVEN

My eyes fluttered open, and I stared at the sun that was shining brightly through the blinds. Liam's scent filled my nose. I looked down to see his head of strawberry locks resting on the bed near my arm. His hand was holding mine. I frowned, seeing the catheter in my hand, and quickly pulled it out, irritated and confused.

What happened to me? Where am I?

I rubbed my head, feeling the bandages, and I froze. My heart began to race as Mom's face returned to me. No… was it a dream? Fuck, it wasn't… I was in a hospital room… I looked around.

Mom was dead. There was someone in that house…

My heart was banging against my ribs painfully and Liam sat up suddenly, instantly getting up from the chair and sitting down next to me on the bed.

"Hey, hey, baby girl, it's going to be okay," his voice, huskier with sleep, promised as he cupped my face and pressed his forehead to mine.

"Mom! She's dead. Someone was there, Liam, I felt it, but I didn't hear a heartbe-"

He pressed his lips to mine, sending a wave of calmness and pleasure through me. His lips grazed against mine sensually and I slowly calmed down. My rapid breathing eased and I slowly kissed him back. His hand moved from my face, tangling into my hair at the nape of my neck as his tongue slipped into my mouth. I sucked on it, letting him explore my mouth and moaning against him. His heart was beating fast and I could sense his emotions.

I'm okay, I said through the link, pushing the blanket off me and getting onto my knees. His arms locked around my waist, lifting me into his lap. I gripped his shoulders, blushing when I felt him throb against my core as I straddled him, and kissed him harder.

He broke away when I needed air, burying his head in my chest. I blushed even more, but wrapped my arms around his neck, brushing my fingers through his hair, feeling so safe there in his arms.

"I'm okay," I repeated, kissing the top of his head.

"I'm not letting you out of my sight from here on out," he said with such conviction that I was worried he meant it.

"You don't mean that, do you?" I asked suspiciously. He smiled, and my heart skipped a beat at the way the sun was shining on that handsome face of his.

"I do actually."

"Hell no," I said, pouting, before hugging him tightly.

"You must have felt the link with your mother, right?" He asked softly. I tensed before moving back and looking down at his glorious bare chest.

"I felt something, but I was asleep... my wolf was restless, and she must have felt the link break with Mom's," I whispered. He nodded.

"I'm sorry for your loss, even if she wasn't the best mother," he said quietly.

I nodded. Yeah, she wasn't, but I still loved her. I pressed my lips together and looked into his eyes, feeling that prickle in my own that I did not want to feel. He looked down at me, one hand going around my bare waist. I realised I was still in my clothes from last night, minus the cardigan. His other hand cupped the back of my head as he pulled me into his embrace once more. I clung to him, wrapping my legs around his waist like a monkey, feeling the sadness well up inside of me as I hugged him tightly.

I remembered my last words to her... wishing things had gone differently. Our relationship had been strange. Her passing was strange... but I would not cry...

After a good few moments, I moved back, my gaze falling to his bulky arms as I tried to change the topic.

"Your biceps are thicker than my waist," I said, running my hand over one of his arms slowly.

"Are we going to compare body sizes now?" He asked huskily. I stopped moving my hand up and down his arm.

"What else do you want to compare, our height?" I asked with a frown.

"No. If we're doing comparisons, I would say there's a certain part of me that is definitely thicker than your forearm," he smirked and I froze. It took me a second to realise what he meant as I stared at my arm. If sex seemed appealing a while ago... it was terrifying now. That would damage my insides!

"Raven..." I blinked and looked at him. "You okay?"

"Of course I'm okay!" I said, quickly climbing out of his lap and away from that very scary, forearm-sized thing. I couldn't help but stare at his crotch. Goddess....

Liam looked rather amused. I quickly looked away.

Just when Liam was about to speak, the door opened, and Aunty Red stepped inside, her hair up in a high bun with a few strands out. Even at this age, she looked like she was a model in her twenties. She had Azura in her arms, and the little girl was holding a gift bag and flowers.

"Raven, baby girl, thank the goddess you're okay," she said, coming over and giving me a tight hug. I hugged her back before giving Azura a kiss on the cheek. Aunty Red glanced at Liam when she moved back from me and cocked a brow. "Do I seriously need to have to see your morning wood every time?" She asked, feeling my forehead.

"Then don't come at the wrong time," Liam growled before getting up and walking off to the adjoining bathroom. Aunty Red shook her head before taking a seat on the bed.

"I heard about Kim," she said softly, placing her hand on my knee. I nodded, sighing deeply.

"What happened to your head, Waven?" Azura asked, looking at my bandages.

"I bumped it," I said.

"Oh no, let me kiss it better," she said, crawling off Aunty Red's lap and giving me a hug, then a big kiss on top of my forehead.

"Aww! I already feel better, Zuzu!" I said, hugging her tightly. She giggled and moved back.

"Mama! Gift!" She exclaimed, holding her hands out to Aunty Red, who smiled at her and passed her the gift bag and the flowers just as Liam stepped out of the bathroom. I couldn't resist smiling at the fact he no longer had a hard-on.

"Wiyam! Look, I got Waven bownies and a teddy!" She pulled out an adorable teddy bear and gave it to me. I took it and gave her a big smile.

"Thank you!"

"Have you two had breakfast?" Aunty Red asked. We shook our heads, and I realised Liam was frowning. Azura was busy wrestling open the lid to the tub of brownies before taking one out and holding it to my mouth.

"I got to go. They've done some analysis on the footprint and found another not far from it," he said, making my heart skip a beat. Aunty Red and I exchanged looks before looking back at him.

"Really?" I asked, trying to swallow the brownies.

"Yeah, we'll see if it's anything, but there was a scuff of blood, so it may be something," he said. Coming over, he kissed Aunty Red on the forehead before ruffling Azura's hair and kissing her cheek before turning to me. "Get the rest you need."

Oh, and I wouldn't trust anything from Azura's hands. She picks her nose... he added through the link, making me smile before he took hold of my chin and tilted my face up to his. His lips met mine in a deep, sizzling kiss that made everything fade away.

We parted after a few moments, and Liam moved back. My eyes fell on Damon, standing there with a bouquet of flowers and a brown bag that I could smell contained breakfast...

Guilt rushed through me as our eyes met, and I felt my heart completely crumble the moment that warm smile crossed his face...

His Ridiculous Lie

RAVEN

I HATED MYSELF FOR THIS. I hated how I was making him feel. He was no less a man than Liam. He did not deserve this.

Liam walked out, giving Damon a curt nod and shutting the door behind him.

"Hey, how are you feeling?" Damon asked, about to place the gorgeous bouquet of purple flowers down when I reached out and took them.

"I'm great, and these are beautiful!" I said, looking up at him.

I'm such a horrible person...

He bent down and wrapped his arms around me tightly. I hugged him back, his comforting scent and those tingles rushing through me. I could hear his racing heart and the guilt inside of me only grew. I glanced at Aunty Red and saw the sadness in her eyes, too, before she looked away, smoothly busying herself with Azura's hair. Damon moved back and jerked his thumb at the paper bag.

"I brought you breakfast," he said, turning to Azura and raising his eyebrows playfully before flashing her one of his dazzling smiles.

"What breakfast is it?" Azura asked, curiously staring at the bag that I had just picked up.

"You've eaten, baby," Aunty Red said, cuddling her.

"Of course, she can eat again. There's plenty," Damon said, and I nodded.

"You look tired," I said to him, concerned as I unboxed the food. Chicken sandwiches, yoghurts, and a box of freshly cut fruit. Azura took the box of fruit, and Aunty Red shook her head, settling back and helping her remove the lid.

"I'm not too bad," he said. "I asked someone to bring you a drink."

"Thanks, Damon," I said softly.

Aunty Red asked him something as I bit into a sandwich. Yes, I was a bitch, but I needed to do the right thing, and I would because the man before me deserved someone who would put him as number one…

I had been discharged from the hospital that afternoon, and Uncle El had come to tell me that he had told Dad what had happened. Needless to say, Dad didn't take it well. Although Uncle El didn't tell me exactly what he had said, I had a feeling he had nothing but hatred and blame towards me.

It seemed Liam was still going through with Dad's trial on Monday, something I was rather shocked about. I was even tempted to ask for an extension, but then I decided to leave it. I needed to let go of my past and remember how Dad treated me. He still had time before the trial anyway, although I knew losing a mate wasn't something you could just get over.

I had gotten back to the packhouse, managing to shower before a large number of the other members who lived there had come to ask how I was, several getting me flowers or cards. I found it so sweet. Mom's death still felt surreal, and I was glad that it wasn't common knowledge yet. I just needed some time.

It was a little awkward when two of the girls addressed me as Luna!

"I'm so sorry you had to go through that," Isla, one of the she-wolfs, said sympathetically as she arranged the bouquet of flowers for me. "I'll get someone to bring in more vases."

"Thanks," I said politely to her.

The bedroom door was open, and I felt a bit overwhelmed by the visitors. I just left the door open, which let me stay wrapped up in my blanket on the bed. I hadn't seen Liam or Damon again, although both had mind-linked to check up on me occasionally.

What sucked was that I couldn't really tell Kiara what was going on either, despite her texting earlier. I didn't mention my injury or that Mom was dead. Just then, someone I actually wanted to see walked through the door, and my eyes lit up.

"Taylor!" I exclaimed.

He flashed me a smile, his arms laden with a chocolate bouquet, drinks, and a hamper of more chocolates! Ah, that man was a keeper! Could I put him in my pocket and keep him forever? He placed the things down on the bedside cabinet next to me and the hamper on the bed.

"Hey, girl," he said, wrapping his arms around me and giving me a good squeeze. He moved back as Isla left the room, giving us some privacy and me a small wave.

"Thanks for everything!" I called out, appreciating her effort in sorting my room a little, which was beginning to resemble a greenhouse. Okay, maybe that was a bit of an exaggeration…

"How you holding up?" Taylor asked.

"I'm good," I said, even with Mom's eyeless face flashing in my mind.

"I'm so damn sorry. I should have taken care of you," he said with guilt in his eyes as he sat down opposite me. I shook my head, my hair falling in my face.

"No, you have nothing to apologise about. I went on my own, and I made sure I was quiet," I said, pulling a wrapped truffle off the bouquet and unwrapping it. I was about to eat it but paused to offer it to him. He smiled, taking my hand and biting half off before feeding it to me, a warm smile on his face.

"You need to eat all the chocolate you can, it will bring your energy back. I'm sure the Alpha or Beta would like you to be at your best." He winked teasingly, yet my smile vanished, Liam's traumatising revelation returning with full vengeance. "Sorry… bad joke." I shook my head, glancing at the open door.

"Oh, don't even talk about men. I think I'm put off for life!" I said, shuddering.

"Why?" Taylor asked curiously.

"I just…" I hesitated. Wait. Taylor was a guy… I should ask him… "Is it true…. that…" I glanced at the open door again, and Taylor frowned slightly. Getting up, he went and shut the door, looking at me curiously.

"What is it?" He asked. I huffed, embarrassed.

"Well, is it true that a man's penis girth can be thicker than my forearm?" I asked, cupping my arm just beneath my elbow. Taylor's eyebrows shot up as he stared at my arm.

"Damn, that's one hell of a picture… a terrifying picture," he said, sounding amused. I frowned. Oh, it was a terrifying thought too…

"It is… and now I'm scared…" He began laughing, and I glared at him. "Hey, what's to laugh about!"

"Sorry, it's just, like, seriously? I mean, maybe if we're talking huge, then about this thick at most, but even that would be super rare…" he said, cupping the middle of my arm between my elbow and wrist. To my dismay, he fell back onto the bed and began laughing. "Goddess, you are so innocent. Have you never watched porn? I mean, you must have seen an erect penis at some point, right?" He burst into more laughter, and I felt my face burn with humiliation. "How could you even think that big of a dick would exist? Like, how would it be possible to even make that fit?"

"Hey! Babies come out of a vagina! Things can fit!" I growled. *I swear I am going to kill Liam, the dickhead! How dare he over-brag about his dick when I swear it's probably going to be the size of a fun-size chocolate bar! The type you fill a party bag with- tiny! Miniscule and dysfunctional! Stupid, Alpha!* "Okay, stop laughing, it's not that funny!" I shouted, smacking his chest.

He simply rolled over, laughing more. I kicked him off the bed, grabbing one of my huge plushies and throwing them at him with as much force as possible! *Stupid, stupid men! Urgh, Liam is so bloody dead.*

"Okay, okay! I'm so damn sorry. Who told you that?" Taylor said, his face red as he tried to control his annoying laugh. *I swear if he laughs anymore, I will sabotage that Cher poster he cherishes so much!*

"Liam did," I said unhappily. Taylor grinned.

"Well… I would say he's boasting, but surely… you've probably seen him turned on, right? Like even if you haven't had sex, maybe when you kissed?" He questioned, making me frown even more.

"Of course I have!" I stated before my frown faded away, and I realised what he meant.

He nodded with a small smile. I had never seen a stupid forearm size shaft in there…. yes, he was big, but not that traumatizingly big… *Fuck, Liam, you're so dead!*

I was still fuming, and Taylor breaking into snickers every few minutes didn't help. *Goddess, I can't believe I fell for that. Urgh, I'm so angry right now.*

Liam had mind-linked not long ago to ask everyone to report to the packhouse meeting room. Taylor, Nina, who had come to my room with more vases, and I walked down the stairs together.

"I wonder what it's about…" Taylor murmured.

"Maybe they found something?" I suggested as we entered the large hall that was extremely full.

"Maybe." Taylor glanced around at the number of pack members that were gathered here. From my quick estimate, I thought two-thirds of the pack were there...

I saw Liam standing there at the head of the room, talking to Zack. Well, mind-linking... Liam was just nodding, his arms crossed with one hand on his chin. The frown on his face made me realise that he was still very much cold towards others, although, at times, I saw him bring those walls down.

More people crowded in. Taylor and I made our way through the throngs of people until we reached the front and I realised that there were no children there. Uncle El was there, but Aunty Red wasn't, and neither was Damon's mom.

"I know you all probably have a rough idea of why I've called you here. However, with one more murder taking place, I think we need to put down some more measures. Initially, I didn't want it to come to this, but my hand is being forced, and, as much as I hate this, if push comes to shove, I will put everyone under Alpha command to weed out the killer," Liam said, his eyes flashing dangerously. "Three people have been fucking killed already. This isn't a joke, so I'm going to put some drastic measures into place."

Everyone was silent as some exchanged looks. Others were worried, whilst some waited to hear what he meant.

He turned, and his cold cerulean eyes met mine. His gaze raked over me, making my stomach flutter before our eyes met for a fleeting moment, and he turned back to the gathered pack members.

"I won't hide the fact that every member of this pack, including myself, my Beta and my Delta, have been cross-checked. Those who have alibis that are absolute will be the ones I'm putting on guard duty from now on. I know some of those accounted for are not warriors, but they will be given charge of the surveillance." A ripple of murmurs and uncertainty rushed through the room, and I frowned. That would drastically cut patrols by a lot...

"I know this isn't ideal, however, it comes down to the fact that anyone could be the killer. They could be in this very room with us, finding this a fucking joke... if you're here then I'd like to say something. " Liam continued, "I will find you, and when I do, you're going to fucking pay. For every person you have killed and hurt, directly and indirectly, you will pay for your crimes."

A wave of unease crossed the room. I saw a few people glance at one another. Fear... un-trust against once another... that was beginning to seep into the pack...

"The rest will be put under strict curfew. I don't care if you have jobs, work, or whatever to do, at eight in the evening, everyone is to head home. If rules are broken, I will start putting fucking electronic tags on people, and I fucking mean it. Dismissed!" Liam said coldly, about to turn away.

A murmur of shock crossed the room and even Damon and Zack looked at Liam in surprise. It was clear they weren't expecting that part. Uncle El frowned deeply. I felt someone needed to give the people some hope. Liam was about to turn away when I quickly rushed forward.

"Wait! Li- Alpha, can I say something?" I asked. He turned back, frowning slightly as I stopped right in front of him. *Oh, I will bust you about the stupid forearm thing later, but right now these people need some light.*

"What is it?"

"It's about the last death," I said quietly.

He frowned and nodded. Those who had been about to turn away stopped. I looked at the group and gasped when Liam lifted me onto the table that stood behind them. A few people chuckled and I glared at him. I'm not that small! Well, now I was a foot or so taller than him and I had a good view of the room...

"I know everyone has things to do, I also know we are all feeling super scared and worried... I am too... but it's okay to feel that way. I won't take too much of your time." I began playing with my fingers. "The last victim was my mother, Kimberly, or as most of you knew her, Kim. I was the one who found her body."

Gasps and murmurs rippled through the room. I even saw a few suspicious looks but I didn't mind. It was human nature to look for something or someone to blame. It was our way of coping with things.

"I know things look rough now, but I promise things will get better. We will find the killer, and although the measures are harsh," I said, looking at Liam. I was not going to sugar-coat the truth. "They are there for a reason. To protect us and our people. That's all we can do right now, and I'm sure we will get to the bottom of this soon enough."

Many nodded, I felt the worry from them ease slightly. Damon gave me an approving smile and nod, Uncle El was smirking ever so slightly, and Zack nodded in agreement to my words. I looked at Liam, who was observing me with an emotion in his eyes that I couldn't read. He stepped closer to the table, but I jumped down before he could even lift me down.

"I need to talk to you about something," I said, narrowing my eyes at him. He cocked a brow and nodded.

I'll be stopping by tonight.

Okay, I said, my stomach fluttering.

I turned to Zack and Damon, looking at Damon. He deserved better... I would talk to him the next chance I had because he did not deserve this, at all.

"Nice speech, Luna," he said with a wink.

"Thanks," I said softly, unable to even come up with a comeback because it was like he already knew...

His arm wrapped around my shoulders and he kissed my forehead. I wrapped my arms around his waist, giving him a squeeze. No matter what, he'd still be important to me.

❧

Much later, I was pacing my room. *Do I kick him in the balls or do I just shout at him?*

I knew it was him the moment I heard the knock on the door and pulled it open; he immediately had me in his arms, kicking the door shut behind him and passionately kissing my lips. I kissed him back, trying not to drown in the pleasure that consumed me before I remembered that there was something I really needed to do! Tugging away, I frowned at him, making him raise a brow.

"Did I do something?"

"Yes! Your dick is not the side of my forearm!" I blurted out, instantly regretting how stupid that sounded. *Wait... what if Liam thought I knew it had been a joke?* It was too late for me to say anything when Liam crossed his arms, curling his lips in as he suppressed a smirk.

"Oh, yeah? Have you seen it?" He asked, and I could sense his amusement growing. "Or... has that been on your mind all day?" My cheeks burned, and I glared at him.

"Not at all! There are many better things to talk and think about than your disturbingly minuscule penis!" I growled.

"At least minuscule works. I mean from what I could see your fucking tiny -" I smacked his arm hard.

"Hey!" I scolded, feeling absolutely mortified. "Listen! This isn't funny; you scared me when you said your dick was that big!" He chuckled, and I mean full on laughed, not even caring that I was humiliated and terrified.

"Seriously Raven? I said your forearm; I could have meant from your wrist or any part of your arm," he teased, still laughing. The sound made my stomach flutter, but it was so awkward!

"You said forearm!" I said, staring down at my wrist. "That terrified me." He smirked, leaning down.

"Why were you imagining us having sex?" He teased, advancing towards me. My heart skipped a beat, and I did my best to poke my eyes out at him.

"Not at all. I don't want to have sex with you," I lied, my heart racing when he caged me between the walls and his arms.

"Really?" He whispered. Our eyes met, and I licked my lips.

"No, not really..." I said, my gaze falling to his moist lips. "I want a kiss though..."

A small smirk crossed his lips before his lips met mine in a delicious, sizzling kiss that ignited that flame of desire that coursed through me and made me whimper in pleasure. His body was pressed against mine and I became very aware of his hard wood that was pressing against my stomach.

Our kisses became hungrier. I wrapped my arms around his neck, pulling him down. Goddess, he was such a good kisser. I gasped for air and broke away, wishing I didn't need air... wanting to stay moulded against him. I stared into the magnetic blue eyes of his wolf, breathing hard.

Moving back slowly, I looked down at the visible tent in his grey sweatpants, although his boxers seemed to be restricting him somewhat. I swallowed, hard and a devilish smirk crossed his lips.

"What's the matter, love? Want to take a look?" He asked huskily.

My cheeks flushed. As much as I wanted to, I shook my head, tiptoeing and kissing him hard before running my hands along his shaft for a moment, trying to get a rough idea on the size. He groaned in pleasure before I pulled away and glared at him.

"You ain't getting anything more because you made a mockery of me!" I stated before getting into bed, trying to get rid of that ache between my legs.

"I've waited for years... I can wait a little longer," Liam said softly as he got into the bed behind me.

His words tugged at my chest, and I realised that he didn't really have long left. Time was ticking, and we still didn't know the answer to the curse...

Painful Revelations

TAYLOR

THE FOLLOWING DAY, I had decided to bite the bullet and go see Channing again. Shit. I wasn't ready, but I had to do it. Taking Mama's flapjack and shepherd's pie with me was not enough… but it was the time I needed to do this. Anna was going to be out, and I needed to do this when she wasn't around.

Goddesses and gods above, lend me your strength of courage and bravery because I need as much as I can get.

Reaching Channing's home, I rang the doorbell, before opening the door and entering.

"Channing?"

"Tay! In here!" He called out.

I quickly went to the kitchen, placing the food on the worktop and entered the living room. It was warm and cosy, decorated in browns and navy. Channing was on the sofa, remote in hand and holding a bottle of J2O orange.

"Grab yourself a drink and come join me. I was going to watch the replay of last night's boxing match."

"Right!" I said. Going to the kitchen and opening the fridge, I took a bottle for myself and returned to the living room.

I looked at Channing. That smile that he always had on his face was still there, his scruffy stubble, and his hair that reached his shoulders. My hero.

"What is it? I know something's on your mind," he said, his eyes crinkling as he smiled at me. I gave him a small smile, looking down.

"The kids out?" I asked, trying to stall a little.

"Yes, they are making the most of being out during the day, thanks to this curfew. I'm not complaining. I'd be happy if they came home on time every night. Would at least make me feel better and at ease."

"Remember how we used to sneak out after Mom and Dad went to bed?" I chuckled.

"Oh, don't remind me about the shit we got up to." He grinned.

I remembered how we used to always sneak out and go for a swim, or a run, or just spend some time alone, even leaving pack grounds. Unlike me, Channing was able to talk to everyone. I liked to be alone and was more of an introvert. I hated socialising, being super awkward and shy in large groups, so he never used to invite anyone extra on our brother time. Just the way I liked it.

"Fun times, huh?" I said quietly.

"Yeah, one hundred percent fun times!" He said, glancing at the screen as he took a swig of his drink.

"Yeah... they were..." I murmured.

Since the battle, I had taken Channing out a few times. I would shift and he'd hold on to me as we went for a run, but the pain in his eyes after killed me so I stopped asking to take him. I thought it would help, but it had only seemed to remind him of what he was missing out on. However, even then, not once did he refuse me... but slowly, slowly, our brothers' nights out stopped.

"Channing... there's something I need to tell you," I said, my voice soft as I stared up at him.

"Tell me, kid. I'm a big guy, and I know it's eating up at you," he said, placing a large hand on my shoulder. I nodded, looking at his tattoos that climbed up one arm as I took a deep breath.

"I found my mate...but he didn't seem to want to accept me," I began quietly. Channing's eyes flashed, and he growled.

"Tell me his name, and I'll show him what happens when someone messes with my brother!" I smiled slightly. Maybe he'd want to kill Zack after I told him the rest, too...

I didn't want to associate the two together because I wanted to tell him about Anna cheating as completely separate first. I didn't want him to accept everything because Zack was my mate. I knew Channing enough to know how selfless he could be.

"We'll see what happens. This is why I didn't tell you, you'd rip the guy to pieces," I joked. Channing chuckled.

"You bet I would. No one fucks around with my brother. That is unless you want them to," he said, making my cheeks heat up a little, only making him roar in laughter. "Ah, you are too easy to tease!"

"Yeah, I guess I am. There's something else I wanted to tell you, too," I said, biting off the metal cap to my bottle and taking a gulp.

"You can tell me anything, you know that, Tay," Channing said warmly. *Yeah... I know.*

"It's about Anna," I said quietly, looking up at him. I looked into his warm blue eyes determinedly. "Anna has been cheating on you over the last few years."

There, I said it... I watched him, preparing for the worst, my heart thundering loudly, but his reaction wasn't what I expected. He nodded, sighing heavily.

"Yeah, I know. I know," he said, making me stare at him in shock. He patted my shoulder and nodded.

"What? Then, how... like, why are you still..."

"For the kids... and the fact that I clearly am not enough anymore. I let it go... but I think she didn't realise that no matter how many showers you take, another man's scent stays behind," he said, staring unseeing at the TV. I felt so fucking bad, but the fact that he knew...

"Channing... you know, you don't need to stay like this. She does not deserve you..."

"It's not that easy, but I appreciate you telling me. How did you find out?" He asked, looking at me seriously. Another hard part... I stared at my hands, then looked at him, feeling a wave of guilt wash over me.

"My mate... he had a fling with her, but he cut it off when he found his mate - me - but she told him she'd ruin his reputation. He told me because he still felt guilty," I rambled. Damnit, why did this have to happen? I hated it! His moment of silence felt like flipping forever.

"He told you. That's a step in the right direction. As for Anna black-mailing him... that's not right." Channing frowned. "Do you like him?" I looked down.

"I love him, but -"

"No buts. Does he like you?"

"Yeah... but he was holding back because of all this," I mumbled. "Yeah... I think he does like me."

"Well, there's nothing not to like. You are one of the purest souls I know, Tay. I appreciate you telling me about him and Anna, but I feel like he's punished himself enough. Forgive him, Taylor. If he really wants to apologise to me, bring him around. I have a few things around here that need fixing, he can get those done for me," he said grinning. Only Channing could be so damn selfless. If he wanted Zack to clean the entire pack garden with his bare hands, I'd make sure it damn well happened!

"And Anna?" I asked, feeling so much lighter.

"Her messing around was one thing... her blackmailing your mate is another. I think I need to take that step and set us both free. It won't be easy, but I'll do it."

"I think that's the best decision," I said quietly.

"Yeah... I think I've had months to prepare. I knew it would inevitably happen, and now is the time. So, who's the lucky guy?" He asked. I felt my cheeks burn up again.

"Zack, our Delta," I said, taking him by surprise. He let out a whistle and slapped my back.

"Now that's a handsome fella." He chuckled.

"Yeah," I agreed. He was damn fine.

"Now don't waste any more time with me and go get that mate of yours," Channing said.

"There's no rush. I'm watching this show with you," I said, crossing my arms. Channing nodded, giving me a grin.

"Yeah, let's watch this first. I heard it was a good match."

I smiled and looked at the screen. Boxing was never my thing, but if Channing could sit through my RuPaul's Drag race, I could definitely sit through his, and I enjoyed it because I was there watching it with him.

After a good two hours, and when that bitch Anna returned, I took my leave, mostly because I really felt like slapping her a few. Stepping out of my brother's home, I mind-linked Zack, feeling so damn nervous.

Zack? Mind if we can meet up? There's something I want to discuss with you.

Tay... umm, can we do that another time? I'm pretty busy right now.

I felt like I had just been punched in the gut.

Yeah, sure, I replied, ending the link.

That really flipping hurt. I knew he was probably busy, but yeah, it still hurt. Maybe it was just me who thought he desperately wanted to talk to me.

ROBYN

It was mid-afternoon. The weather was cool, yet the sun was shining brightly, and the windows were wide open. The sounds of people shouting, some of the boys playing ball, and a few girls laughing in a room down the hall, filled my ears. If I didn't know better, I would never have thought such an environment would be shadowed by the eyes of a killer.

Right then, everything seems so normal. Raven and I were seated on my bed as I silently observed the girl in front of me. I didn't mean to be a bitch, but seeing Raven pay so much attention to Liam and literally just ignore Damon was fucking breaking my heart. At the same time, I wanted to go over to her and shout at her for doing that. Did she not see that he was fucking hurting? I wished I could just comfort him, but I knew that we couldn't just be friends, not in that situation. Me staying away was for the best.

I felt like I had been cheated too… I remembered the first time I told him out loud I wanted him as my mate and asked wouldn't that be great? He had smiled and agreed, but really, he had a mate already. On top of that, when the mating ball came, and I ran to see him, only to discover that we weren't fated, it broke me. But still, I held out hope that, somehow, we could be together. I lost the will to even want to find my mate.

Damon was just something special; someone sweet, giving, and so loving. He had a huge heart, and I knew he fucked up, but it didn't take away from the fact that he was a good person.

We were pondering on the curse once more. I swear I had done so much analysis into it that my head literally had memorised a lot of it. The book just delved into what we knew; there didn't seem to be any more clues. I wanted to break our Alpha free from this curse, because he meant a lot not just to our pack, but to Damon…

Raven was sat opposite, looking through the book once more. She wore an oversize net top that showed off her dark purple crop top underneath with leggings. She was a nice girl, I wouldn't deny that, but I was still mad at how unfairly Damon was getting treated. Even if she wasn't doing it on purpose, it was obvious!

"From your notes, it feels like you think the answer lies in Liam. Like he has to figure it out," she said, her eyes full of concern.

"That's what I feel like it's implying, and Amelia's message to him with the card. I feel like she believed he could do this."

"So, you're saying that there's nothing that we can do?" Raven asked, her eyes filled with hurt and worry. Damn, I felt bad about this entire curse thing, but I honestly thought that was somewhat what was being implied…

"I'm still looking and searching, I'm sure something will come up," I said comfortingly. *I won't give up, I'll keep trying.* She nodded, staring down at the book in her hands.

"Robyn… I know it may be out of line, but did you love Damon?" She asked quietly. Her question made my heart thud, and I swallowed hard. *Stay damn strong, Robyn.*

"Yeah, I do love him," I replied in a clipped tone. My voice came out colder than it was meant to, but can you blame me? It hurt, it really fucking hurt, and what sucked even more was that he was hurting too. Even if I had stepped back and sucked it up, hoping he'd feel no guilt and move on, I still saw him fucking hurting…

"You do…" she whispered, her voice holding sadness. I looked up at her, my eyes flashing green as I pressed my lips together for a second.

"You know, you need to stop hurting him., I said bluntly. She looked up at me, her eyes widening. I swear I felt awful. She was a nice girl, but she needed to get her shit together.

"I know… I know I'm hurting him," she whispered, clutching the book tightly.

"He's a really nice guy who has fucked up, I get that. But he doesn't deserve any less than the Alpha. They are both your mates, then treat them with equal respect and love. I just feel like Damon is being used, and he's a damn idiot for allowing it!" I said irritably. She looked at me, and to my surprise, she simply nodded.

"I know. He said to make it work with Liam, but it wasn't the right way, and I can't balance it… I'm hurting Damon every single day… I know that."

"Then reject him. Set Damon free so that he can at least be happy and find comfort elsewhere, comfort and love that you can't seem to give him,"

I said as gently as possible because I didn't want to hurt her feelings, but I was hella mad.

"If it came to that... would you be there for him? Would you... you know... " she trailed off, but I knew what she meant, making my heart squeeze in pain. I shook my head.

"No... I may find my mate... I don't want to hurt him the way I was hurt. I will just wait for my mate or stay single. I get dating, falling in love, and having fun is part of life... but I'm trying to hold myself together. It's not easy when you love someone so fucking deeply that when they suddenly cast you aside, you feel like you're nothing. I made myself a deal that I'd only fall for my mate from here on out because he won't cast me aside... but it seems like even mates get rejected," I finished off quietly.

I don't know why I said it all. I should have stayed quiet. She looked really upset, and I felt like shit, too, but if she thought that Damon and I could just pick stuff up, then no. It wasn't happening. It would probably make her feel better, but I was not going to think of anyone but me. I didn't want another heartbreak. He tossed me aside the moment she returned. Yes, I ended it, and I would not stay with a mated wolf, but it did hurt. *I'm human too. I have feelings, and I am going to guard this heart, now and forever.*

"I'm sorry, I didn't mean it like that. I was just wondering... Damon said he had a connection to you... so I just thought maybe you love -"

"I do love him, but that doesn't mean I'm going to go back to him," I corrected her. She nodded, sighing heavily as she looked down at her legs.

"You're amazing. You know what you want, how to do the hard thing even if it's painful... and you still hold yourself together," she said, frowning thoughtfully. I gave her a small smile.

"You're amazing too, Raven. You've been put in a shitty situation, and you're trying to do the right thing, even if it isn't fair for everyone. But... you need to make your choice, your decision. If you want Damon too, then you need to give your Alpha the ultimatum that he deals with it, or he walks. And if that isn't something you want to chance, then it's clear you need to reject Damon." Our eyes met and I saw the pain and sadness in them...

It wasn't an easy decision... but it was one she needed to make. Soon.

A Thoughtful Gesture

RAVEN

*W*HAT ROBYN SAID WAS so damn true, and I knew I needed to do this. I needed to talk to Damon. I couldn't keep hurting him like this. *I won't wait any longer, I'm going to go, and I'm going to talk to him right now. I can't carry on doing this...*

I was back in my room, pacing restlessly. I decided to mind-link Damon and ask if I could come to see him. I took a deep breath, my fists clenched. My heart was racing against my ribcage painfully fast.

Damon?

Hey, everything okay?

Can't I link you if there's not a reason? I asked, feeling guilty, thinking I didn't mind-link him as often. No wonder he thought that.

Course you can. But we both knew the truth.

Well, I wanted to meet up with you, like, to actually talk. Can I come around? I had to try my best to sound normal.

Sure, Zack and I are actually dealing with a potential clue, but as soon as it's done, I can let you know?

Perfect, thanks... I said, the guilt of what I was about to do eating up at me inside.

Take care, gorgeous, his soft, deep voice answered. I closed my eyes.

Not gorgeous, fucking evil and cruel. I sank onto my bed, wrapping my arms around my legs and resting my chin on top of my knees. Sadness washed over me, and the urge to wallow in self-pity threatened to overcome me, but before I could, Liam's voice came through the link.

Bitesize?

Hey, I said softly.

Are you okay? Concern was clear in his voice.

Of course I am.

You don't sound it... Ever the intuitive one.

I am, so why did you mind -ink? I asked brightly.

Two hours from now, I want you to meet me at the edge of the woods, by the park.

Okay... I said, wondering why. I needed to talk to Damon too. **Is it important? I had something I needed to do today.**

Yes, it is. Can you reschedule? I couldn't deny him.

Okay, see you then, I said, giving in. I guess I could talk to Damon after meeting Liam if he's not done before then. If he was done by then, that is.

I decided to clean up my room a little, thinking about Mom. She was gone. Would she be reunited with Renji? How was Dad coping? His trial was in the morning, too. I was not looking forward to it at all, but I knew I had to do it.

An hour later, my room was spotless and I still had time to kill. Damon hadn't mind-linked again and the sun was already settling outside. I decided to change into something a little more appealing. Going through my wardrobe, I pulled out a matte PU leather shirt, which was nice and loose, and paired it with a black fitted skirt that had a corset tie right down the front. I picked out some black six-inch heeled boots. *Perfect, now I'll be five-foot-six!* I touched up my make up out of boredom before I glanced at the time. *Guess I could head out and meet him early.* Was Damon still not done?

Damon? Are you still busy?

Hey Raven, yeah, I might be a while. Is it important? He asked worriedly.

No, I was just wondering. Liam wanted me to meet him, so I wasn't sure if you were done or -

Carry on. We'll talk tomorrow. I didn't mean that...

I'll come by later?

If you can. Liam won't want you out past curfew, he teased lightly, but I knew he meant it.

Okay... tomorrow then, I said, feeling down once again.

I walked through the pack grounds, the crunch of the gravel beneath my feet loud in my ears. I saw the guards glance at me; it was clear they were on edge. There was still an hour until curfew, but the streets were empty.

To my surprise, although I was ten minutes early, Liam was also there. His eyes ran over me appreciatively, and I felt suddenly very self-conscious.

"You look good," he said, closing the gap between us and placing his hand on the small of my back. Pulling me against him, he leaned down and kissed my lips softly. Sparks rippled through me, and I bit back my moan, only for Liam to deepen the kiss as a helpless sigh left my lips.

"Thanks," I said.

"Those heels are pretty neat; I may not get as much of a backache if you wear them more often," he said, placing a hand on his back and grimacing. I frowned.

"Hey, I'm not that short…" Okay, I was, but still! He didn't need to complain! "Besides, you aren't so old that you will get a backache!"

He smirked, "Oh yeah? Well, we both have got to admit you're tiny."

"Well, we all can't be gorillas like yourself," I huffed.

He put his arm around my shoulders, pulling me close as he planted a kiss on my forehead. I leaned into him, the comfort from his touch soothing the storm of emotions inside of me.

"So why are we going into the woods at dark…?" I asked.

"That's what the girl always asks the charming killer," he said, giving me a smirk, but it faded quickly and he slowed down. "With my unpredictable emotions, maybe we shouldn't do this…"

"Hey… I can handle myself, and you will be okay. We are doing this," I said firmly placing my hands on his hipbone as I stared up at him. He seemed to be struggling with himself, but finally agreed. Nodding, he carried on walking and took my hand. He threaded his fingers with mine and I smiled gently. The old Liam was in there… "So, will you not tell me where you're taking me?"

"Patience, love," he said, glancing down at me. I frowned, seeing some light up ahead. I realised he had brought me to Grandma Amelia's cottage.

"We're going in here?" I asked.

He reached into his pocket. I couldn't help but stare at the front of his jeans, looking away quickly before he spotted me. He unlocked the door, and I stopped dead in my tracks at the warm, welcoming scene before me.

The glow of the lights and the smell of freshly baked Victoria sponge cake filled the air as soft music played in the background. The place was spotless; a new fluffy beige throw was draped over the sofa with a few cushions in shades of purple on the couch, which were definitely not Grandma Amy's. The table had a dark purple tablecloth over it with a shimmery beige runner through the middle, set up with a few lanterns and an arrangement of fresh flowers in the centre. The fact that he had decorated in purple made it clear that it was for me.

There were a few things set out on the table; a thermos, two mugs, a can of spray cream, some sprinkles, and a Victoria sponge cake decorated with sliced strawberries - a cake that I knew Liam had baked.

Liam had set up a date for us.

The surge of emotions that consumed me made me look up at him. I pulled him close by the shirt, wrapping my arms around his neck tightly. My heart was thumping as I didn't know what to feel and hugged him tightly.

"It's not much, bitesize," he said, standing straight and lifting me off my feet in the process, his arms around my waist. I looked into his eyes. Despite everything we were going through, he still took the time to do this…

"I thought you would be busy with Zack and Damon. How did you find the time to do this?" He locked the door behind us and gave me a small smirk.

"Actually, I was working as I baked and cleaned this place up," he said, jerking his head towards a large pile of papers that sat on the kitchen worktop.

"Good boy," I said, patting his cheek. He gave me a look, prodding my cheek.

"It's only cake, though. I was thinking I should have gotten some food, but I was a bit stretched on time… and I remember you once joked about it, so…"

He remembered… Goddess…

FIVE YEARS AGO

"I don't get why you baked just one cake," I complained, looking at the cake he had sliced into four. "I'm a growing girl, I need a cake all to myself!"

"Growing from where? You're not even five feet," Damon teased, making me frown. Kiara giggled.

"It's a dessert, not a meal, Raven," she said, taking a bite of Liam's baked cake.

"Well, one day I want to have an entire cake for dinner, and I'm not sharing it! You owe me, Liam!"

"One day," he replied, pushing his slice towards me.

"No, no! You have it!" I said, feeling guilty as I tried to hide my pink cheeks.

"I don't actually want any," he assured me, clearly amused.

"Oh, perfect," I said, taking his share. All for me... My precious.

I stared at him. How was it that he remembered stuff like that?

"Thank you…" I said, staring at the table as he led me to it and pulled out a chair. "I love it."

"I hope it tastes as good. I haven't baked in a while," he admitted, bending down. He kissed my neck, sending a rivet of pleasure through me, tucking the chair in. My heart skipped a beat as I watched him take the seat opposite me; in his light grey shirt, blue fitted jeans, and those bracelets and chains he wore... he looked so fucking hot.

His intense gaze met mine as he picked up the knife and cut a small slice of cake, he placed it on his plate before placing the rest of the cake in front of me. My eyes widened as he held out a small spoon.

"Eat until you're sick," he replied, smirking.

"Right from the plate?" I asked, staring at the delicious, fluffy cake before me, that sprinkle of icing powder begging to meet my lips. Why was this so fun!

"Yeah," he said. As I took the spoon from him, our fingers brushed, and I bit my lip.

"Thanks. I'm going to eat like a pig, so don't judge."

"I've never judged before," Liam said, taking the cap off of the thermos and pouring us both a mug of hot chocolate. I narrowed my eyes as he shook the can of cream.

"Hey, are you saying I've always eaten like a pig?!" I said pouting.

"Have you?"

"Of course not. I just love food at times. Like all the time."

I watched him spray a generous amount of cream into both mugs before spraying some into his mouth. He licked his lips, raising his eyebrows at me as I found myself staring at him. Oh my...

Why was that so sexy?

My Everything

LIAM

WATCHING HER SIT THERE, licking her lips as she watched me, made me smile slightly. She was gorgeous and fucking perfect. The way her eyes sparkled when she looked at the cake in front of her... that hint of cleavage that I could see... her hair framed her face, her bangs fell into her eyes, and she had smoky black makeup. Her scent enveloped me welcomingly.

As much as I wished that we could be forever, I had to prepare myself that maybe, just maybe, the curse wouldn't break. I know I said I didn't give a shit, but I would give a lot just to get to spend more time with her. I remembered what the book held, I had a pretty good photographic memory, but there was nothing that seemed to hold the answer, no matter how many times I replayed it in my head. That was why, in this crappy time that surrounded us, I wanted to fulfil the promises I had made to her long ago... or at least some of them, no matter how fucking mundane they were.

Watching her eat that cake, the smile on her face, the way she seemed to forget I was there, it was worth it... because I also saw the conflict she felt when she was herself around me. Her guilt towards Damon was forever there, and it fucking hurt.

She licked her lips an,d, fuck, did I want them on me. It was clear she was a tad more innocent than she acted. I mean, she did snag a feel of my dick, but I was only half turned on. My poor little pint... how the hell were she and Kia friends? Raven talked naughtily, but clearly, she was all talk. That was cute. I'd corrupt her completely.

If I have time, that negative voice at the back of my head came. My mood darkened, but I pushed it away.

Not today…

"This cake is so good, it's even better than I remember," she said, looking at me, her eyes filled with happiness. I just hoped she wasn't hiding her true emotions from me. She discarded her spoon, breaking some cake with the knife and bit into it instead. "It's so much more fun to eat with your fingers."

She was about to lick the cream off her fingers, but I grabbed hold of her wrist, tugging it towards me. Her heart was thumping as I ran my tongue over both her fingers before I took them in my mouth, making her sigh as I sucked on them sensually. The sweet taste of cream and icing sugar filled my mouth. She bit her lip, her heart pounding, but she didn't tug away. I ran my tongue along the tips of her fingers before taking her pinky in my mouth and sucking gently. A small whimper left her lips, and she wriggled in her seat.

I tilted my head, slowly kissing her inner wrist before I let go of her. I'd let her eat her cake first…

❧

Half an hour later, Raven and I were cuddled up on the sofa. I couldn't stop teasing her. She had eaten the entire thing, although she gave me a few bites, and I knew her tummy was hurting.

"Don't laugh, it hurts," she pouted, a hand on her stomach.

"Really, why eat it all?"

"Hey, you gave it to me!" She said, sticking her tongue out. I leaned over, stroking her tongue with mine, making her eyes flutter shut and a soft sigh escape her.

"You weren't forced to have it all," I said with a smirk. She grabbed my T-shirt, stopping me from moving back as our eyes met, those irresistible sparks that coursed through me making my head fucking spin.

"Thanks… I loved it," she said softly.

"I'm glad," I said, lifting her onto my lap. I wrapped my arms around her, and she curled into me, resting her hand on my heart.

I knew, despite her being with me… her conscience always made her struggle... so I wouldn't push her. As much as I wanted to take it further... it needed to be for the right reasons and when she was ready...

"Liam?"

"Yeah, love?" I asked, kissing her neck. The urge to mark her was always there too. I brushed her fringe aside, looking at her arched brows that were always hidden by her hair. It made her look pretty different. Still fucking gorgeous, just a lot older.

"You know, I know this stupid prophecy keeps saying you are the dark... but you aren't. You will always be my light." Her eyes flashed, and the intensity of her emotions were clear in them. "You will get through this, blue eyes." She cupped my face, and I wasn't able to hold back my emotions. Fuck it...

I lifted her, shifting her so she was straddling my thigh. Her skirt was far too tight for her to straddle me completely, so I slipped it up, pulling her onto my lap and claiming her lips in a passionate kiss. One hand went to her ass, the other weaving into her hair. Kissing her hard and deep, I fucking appreciated her. The feel of her lips, this fucking fine feeling... Goddess... the sweetness of her mouth, her fresh floral scent... *This is my mate. My special someone, the one I always wanted...*

She kissed me back, and I groaned quietly against her lips. She was there... yet the fear that tomorrow she would be gone never left me. As if sensing my emotions, she wrapped her arms around my neck, kissing me deeper and pressing herself against me.

Pleasure fucking coursed through me, and I squeezed her ass. Fuck, did I love the tiny briefs she wore. A delicious moan left her lips as I squeezed her ass again. She grinded herself against my crotch, the smell of her arousal perfuming the air. Fuck...

Love... I couldn't even get the words out as she broke away, kissing my neck and sucking hard. **Baby, you need to stop.**

I don't want to, she whispered, her tongue flicking out and sending a shiver of pleasure through me.

My eyes flashed. I squeezed her ass before reaching down between us and massaging her between her legs. She got up on her knees, bracing her hands on my shoulders, granting me better access. I growled in approval at the damp spot that was already gathering there. Fuck... I ripped her underwear off, making her gasp, my other hand in her hair as I kissed her hard. She was soaking wet. She whimpered when my fingers slipped between her folds.

"Fuck, Liam!" She whined, throwing her head back.

I rubbed her clit, making her moan, and her legs shook slightly as I continued to tease her. She gasped, reaching between us and began to undo my belt. I gripped her wrist, stopping her.

"No," I said softly as I kissed her lips. Not until she was mine... heart and soul...

Our eyes met, her questioning gaze mixed with desire and need. I simply reached over, licking her lip as I pressed a finger to her entrance. She tensed, and any question she had vanished.

"Fuck, Liam..." she whimpered, her nails digging into my shoulders.

"Relax," I whispered, letting go of her hair. I quickly undid the button on her shirt, pushing it aside and staring at her strappy cut-out bra. Something told me that once I took away any innocence she had... I'd be opening the door to the little minx that was hidden inside of her. She gave me a sexy smile.

"Like what you see?" She asked in a very seductive voice, surprising me.

"Fuck yeah," I growled, grabbing one of her breasts just as I slipped a finger into her tight, hot pussy.

"Oh, fuck, Liam!" She cried out, moaning as I began to move my finger in and out slowly. "Fuck, that's it..."

"Good girl, just relax, love," I coaxed as I began thrusting in and out of her with my middle finger slightly faster.

She soon relaxed, her moans getting louder as I palmed her breast. The urge to flip her over onto the coach and take her right there was fucking hard to ignore. I yanked her bra down, staring at her creamy breasts with her hardened, dusky pink buds. I felt myself throb painfully. I was so fucking hard. She was fucking perfect.

"Faster, Liam," she whimpered.

As you fucking wish, darling.

I fucked her faster with my finger, feeling her juices trickling out of her. The sound of my finger against the wetness of her pussy mixed with her breathy moans was fucking music to my ears. Leaning forward, I sucked on her nipple just as her release hit her, making her let out one fucking sexy moan that almost made me come in my pants.

"Liam…" she whimpered as I kept going despite her struggle to move away, making sure she rode out her orgasm before I slipped my finger out. Her body collapsed against mine, her breasts brushing my face as she hugged me tightly, breathing hard.

"I love you, bitesize."

"I love you, too," she whispered back.

I held her tightly, laying back on the sofa with her on top of me, and pulled the throw I had brought over us both…

ZACK

I had just finished off what we had been working on with Damon, and after bidding him farewell, I decided to go to Taylor's. He had wanted to speak to me earlier, but I had been really caught up. We were getting somewhere with this killer. *Let's fucking hope so, anyway.*

The moment he had mind-linked, the urge to just drop everything and run to him had been so damn hard to ignore, especially since he had been ignoring me since that day.

Now, what the fuck do I take him? I can't just go fucking empty-handed… I was not good at this, but there wasn't anything I could really give him. I stopped at my room to shower. I was a mess, and I did not want to go over looking like this.

Once I was done, I pulled on some boxers, some jeans that I took a moment to pick out because, although I found them a tad fucking tight, I knew Taylor always checked me out in them. I smirked, pulling on a graphic tee and leaving the packhouse.

It was really quiet, although I could hear a few of the members in the pack lounge playing games. Guards who were in the clear flanked the entrance, giving me a nod. It really did feel like a fucking prison… I didn't miss the weapons they were holding.

Tonight, thanks to that footprint, we had been able to track back the killer's footsteps right towards one of the graveyards, but it ended there at the gates. We weren't able to gather any more information inside, but we had set up some cameras and sensors discreetly. Well, I hoped it was fucking discreet anyway.

I reached Taylor's house shortly after, my gaze lingering at the Jacobs' home, which felt eerie and ominous. The reminder of what had happened there returned to the front of my mind.

I turned away, ringing the bell, hoping it was Taylor who opened it and not his parents. The goddess didn't really hear my wish as his dad opened the door. It looked like they were both heading out…

"Hello, Mr and Mrs Olsten. Heading out?" I said.

"Hello, Delta Zack. Yes, we are… we will be staying at Channing's for the night. He's assigned for surveillance, so we are staying with the children," Mr Olsten said, smiling warmly.

Perfect, I get to talk to Taylor…

"We have an escort who will take us due to the curfew," Mrs Olsten added quickly.

"Yeah, of course," I said with a nod, spotting the two men who would guide them. Both were in the clear of being the killer. It was fucking strange to have to doubt your own pack members…

"Were you here for a reason?" Mr Olsten asked.

"Ah, yeah, I need to talk to Taylor," I replied.

"He's upstairs, go right up," Mrs Olsten said with a smile. "He's probably watching TV."

"Thanks," I said, squeezing past them.

They closed the door behind them, and I headed up the stairs, following Taylor's scent until I reached his room. The door was open, and I stepped inside. It was the first time I had gone there… I looked around, taking note of everything and wondering where he was. Maybe the bathroom…

I dropped onto his bed, looking at the poster on his wall. We really were pretty different. A perfect match…

I heard a door open and the sound of whistling mixed with the scent of bath products, something floral laced with Taylor's own delicious scent. He entered his room without a care in the world, and then he froze, his eyes on me, but I was too busy raking my eyes over that sexy body of his.

Damn, my mate was fucking fine. Water ran down his body and into his towel. I fucking wanted to yank off the towel and look at him properly. I mean, I'd seen him shift, but he was one of the more modest men when it came to walking around fucking nude, so I hadn't really seen the goods.

"Eyes up here," Taylor said. I clenched my jaw, my lips set in their usual thoughtful pout.

"You can't really control where I look. If I want to look lower… I can," I said cockily before leaning back on my hands, not missing his gaze falling to my crotch, something that made me fucking twitch. Was it wrong that I wanted him on his knees?

But I remembered what I had done…

"Right, I can't," he said, a small frown on that gorgeous face of his. "I'm surprised you came. Weren't you busy?" He walked over to his drawer, picked up some moisturiser, and applied it to his face. So, my mate was angry that I didn't come? Cute.

"I was, but I came as soon as I got free. You wanted to see me?" I asked, standing up and shoving my hands into my back pockets. Taylor turned, his heart racing. Our eyes met, and I swallowed. Fuck, how I wanted to pull him into my damn arms and ask him to fucking forgive me…

"I told Channing," Taylor said, those chocolate eyes of his softening. The pain in them fucking made me feel like a guilty fucker. It was my heart's turn to fucking race…. Shit… was it bad?

"And…" I said softly.

"Channing being Channing… he took it like a pro, and you know what? He knew that Anna was cheating on him. More than that, he's breaking up with her, not because of the cheating but because she blackmailed you, and he thinks it's high time he ended it…"

I closed my eyes, feeling a weight lift from me. *Thank the goddess… or, in this case, Channing… I will apologise to him in person, too…*

"I'm sorry… and I know I owe him."

"You do. He will make you work that ass off around the house and yard," Taylor said, sounding damn cute.

I tilted my head. I couldn't wait to work this man's fine ass… just the thought of fucking Taylor made me twitch. I had had a few one-night stands with men, but something told me Taylor was going to be a whole new level. I stepped closer, closing the gap between us.

"And what about you? Do you forgive me?" I ask, dragging my attention from his worship-worthy abs and into his eyes.

"I do."

Getting Closer

TAYLOR

I FORGAVE HIM. I HAD TO. I was too fucking in love with him not to.

Zack was standing so close to me that I could feel his breath on my neck. His fingertips ghosted up my bare arms, not touching, but close enough that I could sense the sparks of the bond rippling through the little air between us.

"Are you fucking sure?" He nibbled softly on his bottom lip. All that was standing between us was this barrier, and now that it was gone, there was nothing keeping us apart.

"I'm sure..." I replied quietly.

"I can give you more time if that's what you need." I knew he would. That was what made him so damn perfect for me. His patience.

"I forgive you, Zack."

I stepped in closer, my still damp chest lightly grazing against his own, those sparks rushing through us both. He closed his eyes for a moment, letting the feeling of it overpower him until his arm snaked around my waist, and he pulled me against his hard body firmly. His perfect hazel eyes snapped open, and our gazes met.

"Thank the goddess..." he exhaled. Before I had time to even smile, his lips were on mine.

Fuck, I loved kissing him. It seemed like every other one we'd had was in a stolen moment, but now that nothing was going to tear us away from each other... I finally felt like I could embrace every inch of his lips and enjoy the moment to the fullest.

His lips weren't soft like a few guys I'd kissed before; they were rough and firm. He knew how to use them, too, guiding mine with dominance before he took hold of my hips and guided me back until I slammed into the doors of my wardrobe.

This is my Delta.

He was only slightly taller, but it felt like so much more when he pressed himself firmly against me, threading one of his hands into the back of my hair and tugging my head up so he could force my mouth open and slip his tongue inside. The sparks that flew throughout my body were overwhelming. I'd kissed him before but never like this. It was like he was touching every inch of me; I could feel his nails digging into my back, his fingers pulling and tugging at my hair, and his tongue exploring every inch of my mouth.

He feels good. Being with him feels so damn good.

I didn't think it could feel any better until he slipped his hand down the back of my towel and grabbed hold of my ass. The towel started to slip away from my hips, but I grabbed it just in time. Apparently, that was the wrong move because Zack moved away, allowing me to breathe as his eyes ran down over my exposed body.

I suddenly felt naked, despite still clutching the towel to me. His eyes suddenly darted up to the vein pulsing in my neck as his fingers curled even deeper between my ass cheeks.

"Drop the towel."

My immediate instinct was to let go, but why should I listen? He couldn't just walk in here and think –

When he saw my fist tighten on the towel, he moved back from my body and took hold of my wrists. There was a part of me that wanted to tell him he won't get it this easy, that he could wait, but there was another part of me that just wanted to swallow his dick whole and watch him fucking tremble...

No, Taylor. No, you can't give him all he wants just because he's all your fantasies come to life. Bad Taylor.

But then he had to go and say the one damn word that immediately made me lose any grip I had on my self-restraint.

"Mine."

My towel hit the floor quicker than a drag queen's death drop. When he looked back at me, there was no trace of his stunning hazel eyes, instead replaced with the shimmering grey of his wolf. They were so beautiful, bordering on metallic, as they captured the moonlight like a hazy grey cloud surrounded by a silver lining. In many ways, that was what our relationship up until this moment had been. Tiny flickers of light being clouded by the dull darkness that wished to suppress our happiness.

The radiating glow within them only grew stronger as he let his eyes fall from mine and run down my body, taking in every curve and line of my muscles before settling on the part of me that most wanted his attention. We'd fooled around before, but nothing like this. He had never seen me exposed, completely his.

"You are fucking beautiful..." he whispers, his fingertips trailing up my abs. "And you're mine."

He grabbed hold of my waist with both hands, ripping me from the wardrobe and before I knew it, I was flat on my back on my bed. *He's so fucking fast...*

Oh, Goddess. The guy definitely had strength and, by the looks of it, stamina.

Before he even had the chance to climb on top of me, I had his shirt off, the sparks from my hands on his skin only growing that much more intense without the fabric between us. His lips move to my neck. Everything in my being cried out for him to sink his teeth into it, but I became slightly distracted when his jeans definitely didn't want to come off as easily as his fucking shirt.

"How tight are these? Did you paint them on?" I asked with a small smile. Zack pulled back from my neck, smirking down at me struggling to remove the denim pants.

"I thought you liked these jeans on me. You always seem to pay attention when I'm wearing them..."

He ignored my struggle, moving his lips back to my neck and grinding his denim-covered dick against my own. For a second, I lost all fucking thoughts of anything but how it felt to have him against me like this. Then I remembered how much better it would be if he was all I could feel.

"So, are you attached to them?" I asked as he sucked deep on my neck, ignoring my question completely and causing my back to arch up off the bed. My naked chest brushed against his, and he growled when his nipples stroked against my own.

Fuck... he likes that...

"Kind of, they're my favou-" he was cut off as I tore the jeans off of him, the sound loud in the room.

I thought he might be pissed, staring at the scraps of material that lay in tatters on my bed, but instead, it only seemed to fuel the growing fire within him. He straddled my hips and pressed his body down against my solid cock. I looked up at him, finally letting myself take in the sight of him above me like this. Almost every night since the day we found out we were mated... I'd imagined this so many times...

It's even better than I imagined.

He pressed his hands down on either side of my head on the pillow, lifting himself up just enough that I could slip his boxers down his legs and uncage the beast within.

Holy shit... a beast it is indeed. Yeah, I was definitely going to feel that in the morning.

Zack smirked as he watched my eyes grow wide at the sight of his solid monster, saliva filling my mouth when he slowly ran his hand down his abs and grazed his fingertips at his bobbing length.

"Scared?"

Me? Scared? No... nope... kind of. But I was not going to show him that.

I'd been with guys before, a few actually, but I'd never been with someone like him, someone who could make my heart race with a single look. Someone put on this planet just for me.

He was made for you, Taylor. He was fucking made for you.

So was that.

I slipped down between his legs, his body still hovering above me as I moved my hands around his back and pressed until I could suck his nipple into my mouth. If I wasn't hard before, then the sound of euphoria that left his lips the instant I flicked his bead with my tongue would have done it. He was so fucking sexy. Placing one hand in the middle of his shoulder blades, I began to twirl my fingers around his awaiting nipple, flicking and pinching it, making him moan in pleasure.

"Fuck..."

The spark of pleasure that ignited between his skin and my lips was enough to make my head dizzy, but it was the feeling of him leaking pre-cum onto my stomach that pushed me over the edge. He tried to move, but I didn't let him, keeping my grip on him firm as I ran my tongue down from his chest, slipping further and further between his legs as I kissed his stomach until I came face to face with his pleading cock.

"Tay... you..." he trailed off when I swirled my tongue along his tip. I loved that reaction…

His dick was so fucking big I could feel my lips stretching to their max just to wrap around him. It should have been uncomfortable, but honestly, it just felt so damn good. I'd always liked a man who could push my limits, and something told me that I was going to find a whole new level with Zack.

I only took his tip in to start, slowly rolling my tongue around it teasingly. My eyes stayed on him while his head tilted back as a string of swears and groans left his lips. I knew I should wind him up a bit more, I should tease every inch of him, but the moment he started to slide across my tongue, I knew what I wanted. Instead, I grabbed hold of his ass and slammed his entire length down into my throat.

"Taylor! Fuck!"

I knew he'd like it hard and fast. Everything about him screamed rough. Guiding him back by his hips slowly until only his tip sat in my mouth again, I waited before I pressed him forward fully into my throat, but I could sense his hesitation from him.

Why are you holding back? I asked through the link, feeling his thighs shake as I flicked my tongue against his tip.

I don't want to hurt you.

Cute, but does he really think I'm that fragile? *I'm gay, I'm not flipping China. Okay then, hard way it is.*

This time, when I grabbed his hips and forced him into me, I slipped my hands around until my fingers sat at his crack. I felt him tense, pausing with his dick firmly inside my throat as I slipped my finger between his cheeks and started to stroke over his little hole.

He practically jumped out of his fucking skin. If his cock wasn't in my mouth, I'd laugh. Pulling himself out, he stared down at me, the tip of him still sitting on my bottom lip.

"What the fuck are you doing?"

I honestly couldn't tell if he was turned on or dying of embarrassment right then. Either way, I was getting the reaction I wanted.

"What? You said you didn't want to hurt me. I assumed that meant that you wanted to be the one to..." He lets out a vicious growl, one that causes my eyes to flash a piercing blue at his show of strength, a damn hot turn-on…

"Taylor. I'm not… I mean, I haven't… you were practically born to be the…"

Bless his little forever-top heart. Can't even say the word.

I let him panic for a moment, just because it was so fucking cute to see him like that, but he quickly caught on, and all humour vanished from his face.

"You're fucking with me," he said, frowning.

I smirked at him and nodded, something that I thought might earn me a kiss but instead, I got something so much fucking better…

His hands came out to grab my throat, tilting my head back as his thumbs pulled my jaw open, and he placed his dick right back on my lips.

"I'm going to make you pay for that."

Yes, Daddy.

He immediately thrust his full length down my throat, catching me so off guard that I practically choked on his monster, but it didn't stop him. He pulled out just enough for me to catch my breath before forcing all the way back in again.

I'd never been against someone taking control of me, but having someone fuck my face like that was probably the most I'd ever been turned on. He didn't let my head move, holding it in place against the bed and thrusting his hips against me from above so that he controlled his speed and the depth at which he fucked me.

I'm in heaven.

My glorious mate hummed and groaned with satisfaction as I hollowed my cheeks and tightened my lips around his length until I could feel him swelling with his nearing completion. I prepared myself to swallow his load, but the moment he reached his climax, he pulled from my mouth and unloaded completely onto my face.

Best. Punishment. Ever.

His warm seed trickled down my cheeks, dripping from my lips as I became lost in the vision of him panting and groaning in pure pleasure. He took a moment to compose himself before he looked down at me, fire and lust burning in his eyes before he dropped his face to mine and began to nuzzle into the side of my neck.

"You look so fucking good covered in me… marked by me…"

Marked. I wanted to be marked by him in every fucking way.

His tongue slipped out between his lips, running up my neck and onto my face before I realised what he was doing, lapping up every drop of his essence from my skin and making me harder than I knew was possible in the process. Fuck… there was just something too fucking hot about that.

With his lips still glistening with his own seed, he looked down between our bodies at my raging hard-on. I shook with anticipation as he began clawing his nails down my stomach before reaching the bottom and grabbing hold of my hips. We stared at each other for just a moment, letting our building emotions flow through the bond. The tingling sparks on my skin flurried as he gripped my hipbones a little bit harder right before throwing his strength against mine to flip me onto my stomach. My shaft rubbing against the sheets alone made me moan, but pleasure like I didn't know was possible overtook me when he grabbed my ass firmly with two hands and started to massage my cheeks.

"Have you got any…?"

"Bottom drawer," I practically pant as he reached over my body and pulled open the drawer on the bedside table, taking out the bottle of lube and smirking at it. I twisted my head slightly, looking back at him over my shoulder as he let the cool, thick liquid pour out onto his fingers.

"You were prepared…" his husky response came just as he started to circle my awaiting bud.

"Well, it's not like this is my first time…" I let the words fizzle out when his wolf's raging grey eyes met mine. Shit, did this guy have some alpha in him or something? Because he was giving me some seriously dangerous possessive vibes right then.

I tried to think of the right words to settle him back down again, but apparently, they weren't needed as he immediately slipped not one but two fingers into me, stretching me and letting my mind float away on a cloud of fucking pleasure.

"F-fuck!"

His long, thick fingers reached deep inside me before pulling back and slamming in again. I knew he wasn't exactly a novice at this type of thing, but I didn't expect him to know exactly what he was fucking doing already.

A raw, animalistic growl poured out of his chest when he added a third digit, and I found myself thrusting back, trying to get him deeper. *Fuck, he feels so fucking good.*

"If you want me to lose control, you're going the right way about it," he moaned as I started to fuck myself with his fingers. *Does it say a lot about me that now that he's said that, I just want to do it more?*

I thanked the goddess that there was nobody else in the house when he tilted his wrist and thrust back in, hitting my pleasure point with such force that I screamed his name.

"Fuck, Zack!"

If Raven still lived next door, I would definitely be hearing about this in the morning. That girl had ears like a fucking bat.

The tingles that coated my body suddenly didn't feel like enough, the urge to be with him completely taking over completely.

"Zack... I need you... I want you to..."

My mate pulled his hand away, and I immediately felt empty. Nerves suddenly took over my body as it felt cold and alone, but that feeling disappeared completely when Zack forced my knees under my body and then laid his chest against my back, his tip brushing against my hole.

"Are you sure you want this, Tay? Because once you're mine, I'm never letting you go." His tip pressed into me just enough that I could feel the sparks starting to infest every fibre of my being. *When will he realise? I've always wanted this, always wanted him.*

I'm yours, Delta.

He smirked.

Then, without hesitation, he buried himself deep inside me with one harsh thrust.

Oh fuck, oh fuck, oh fuck.

Okay, Taylor, breathe... breathe.

He's big. Fuck, he's really big.

Zack didn't move, holding my body tight to his and kissing along my spine as the sparks seemed to grow with every passing second... until finally, I could feel the pain start to slip away.

His hand flattened against the mattress next to my head. I reached over and locked my fingers with his, telling him it was safe to move. He pulled out gently, focusing all his energy on me and sensing any hesitation before he pushed back in again.

Fuck, I know it's been a while, but I don't remember it feeling this fucking good.

"Fuck, Zack... harder, baby..."

The pleading groan of satisfaction that left my lips appeared to be all he needed before he pulled out and started to slam back into me. I knew he'd be dominant, but when he grabbed hold of my hips and arched my back so that he was hitting my prostate with each deep thrust, I found myself surrendering to him willingly.

"Tay, fuck, you are so fucking tight..."

It was hard for me to concentrate on anything but the overwhelming pleasure of having him inside me as he started to pummel me without mercy, just the way I liked it. His arms reached around my body as he delivered a round of short, sharp thrusts, pulling me up from the bed and slamming my back against his chest as he sat me in his lap and started to power up into my body deeper than before.

Everything overloaded my mind. The sparks from his naked skin erupted against mine. I could feel myself floating to the edge, tipping over it even further with each hard thrust that he used to worship my body with.

"I want you to come with me... fuck, Tay, you have me so fucking close."

Zack looped his arm around my waist firmly, keeping me on my knees against him as he reached around with his other hand and started to pump my dick. Tidal waves of pleasure began to drown me. I felt like I was suffocating in the best way possible as his movements grew ragged and his length swelled inside of me just as his lips came down to meet my neck.

I threw my head back against his shoulder, giving him the greatest access to my throat and shoulder as his teeth elongated and scratched against the skin. He hit into me hard repeatedly, then, finally, at the moment my eyes began to see stars from the overwhelming bliss, he buried his canines into my flesh.

Pleasure and pain become one perfectly balanced union. He unloaded deep inside me at the same moment streams of thick white come shot from my tip.

My head felt so fucking dizzy. I didn't know pleasure like that was even possible. I could smell the iron in the blood seeping from my open mark, but even that only added to my severely heightened senses... I felt the surge of the bond strengthening as his mark began to heal.

The moment he retracted his teeth, I collapsed. Zack hardly had enough energy to pull out of me and gently lay me on my back before giving in to exhaustion and resting his head down on my chest. I could hardly breathe; neither could he as he panted for air against me, exhaling onto my sweat-covered chest whilst our naked bodies intertwined.

The moonlight felt like it was glowing just for us. Zack eventually managed to pull his head up from my chest to look at my neck, his eyes widening with delight and casting back the glow of the moon in the sharp grey that took over them as he looked at his mark on my body.

"It's fucking beautiful." He reached up, slowly trailing his fingertips over the mark and unleashing a rush of pleasure through my body that I'd never felt before. "It's the silhouette of a wolf howling up at the moon…"

Fuck, I really want to see it, but I want to kiss him more.

Zack kept stroking at his mark, thoroughly enjoying the shiver that ran through my body each time, until I cupped the back of his head and brought his lips down onto mine. He moaned with pleasure as I slightly lowered myself under his body, our members brushing together as I moved my kisses to his jaw and had to bite back a growl at the sight of his bare neck.

Mine.

Zack's breath halted when I ran my tongue along with the place where my mark was going to sit. I got ready to ask for his consent, but when I moved my lips away from his skin, he only forced himself back against my mouth again. *Okay, Mr Delta, I know what you want.*

My wolf's instincts took over as my lips started to kiss his skin, my eyes glowing that bright, piercing blue at the moment I plunged my teeth into his muscle. The bond hit me like a fucking truck. The rich copper taste of his blood was like fine wine in my mouth. My eyes rolled back into my head at the moment our bond snapped completely into place. I could feel the power of just us against one another surge around us like a pleasant storm.

He practically collapsed onto my chest when I released him from my grip, forcing me to lean down so I could lick away the excess blood and look at my gorgeous mark on my even more gorgeous mate. It was still healing, but I could faintly see it taking on the form of two wolves embracing. A perfect representation of exactly how I felt about him, about us.

"I love you, Tay. I need you to know that. I know how fucking lucky I am to have you, after everything… I swear to you, I'm going to spend the rest of our lives proving to you that I was worth the fucking hassle." I couldn't help but laugh at his little confession. The truth was, he was already worth every minute of it.

Slowly, he gently drifted off into sleep, still lying against my body. I loved him, but he was practically crushing me, so I slowly moved him onto the bed next to me, gazing at my perfect man.

I felt perfectly content, perfectly happy. A small smile played on my lips as I stared at him before sleep overcame me, too…

For Someone We Love

RAVEN

*T*HE FOLLOWING DAY, I left the cottage early after showering and headed to training, feeling restless and nervous. My heart was breaking, and although I knew it was a decision I had decided on, it still hurt. I would talk to Damon, no matter what, right after. I couldn't keep delaying it.

After training and once I had showered, I quickly grabbed an over-sized hoodie that fell to my thighs and some over-the-knee boots. I left the packhouse, my hair still wet from the shower, and headed straight to Damon's like a woman on a mission.

Not today. Not today. Nothing is going to stop me.

I rang the doorbell, letting out a breath I didn't know I was even holding when I finally reached Damon's home.

Damon? I'm outside, I said through the link softly. My heart cracked a little more.

This must be important, huh? His deep, sexy voice came.

Hmm, I replied, feeling awful and waiting for him to open up. He did a few moments later. He had a shirt on, but the buttons were undone, showing off his perfect body. My stomach fluttered, and the pain in my chest reminded me of our connection.

"Hey," I said softly.

"Hey, gorgeous," he greeted, pulling me into his arms. I closed my eyes, hugging him tightly. His beating heart was like a soothing melody compared to the thundering of mine...

The decision I had made... was there really no other way? I knew the answer to that...

"Hey... what's wrong? Are you okay?" His soft voice brought me out of my reverie, my heart beating like a drum as I slowly moved back and nodded, forcing a smile. I was the selfish one, wanting them both... but I knew whom I was prioritising and what needed to be done was for the both of us.

"Yeah, kinda... can we talk?" I asked softly.

"Sure," he said. "Shall we go for a walk?"

"Okay," I agreed, thinking we could go towards the woods, somewhere alone...

Maybe being inside would just make it even more suffocating.

He stepped out and locked up behind himself, shoving the keys into his pocket. He gave me a small, sexy smile and began to button up his shirt, hiding those perfect abs from the world. We stayed silent, and he let me lead as we walked along. With every step I took, I felt as if my feet were dragging. *Goddess... please... give me strength...*

I slowed down when we were in a deserted area of the woods, the rustle of the leaves like a whisper of disapproval at what I was about to do. Walking down towards the river, I stopped and looked around. We were a good way away from the Alpha's home. I sat down, motioning for him to sit opposite me. He sat, his soft blue eyes meeting mine, and my heart clenched painfully. Why did I feel like he knew this was bad news...?

"It's okay, Raven. You can tell me whatever you need to. You know that," he said softly, taking hold of my hands, those sparks of pleasure wrapping me in warmth, and kissing my knuckles softly. I closed my eyes before staring down at our hands. He was special, too....

"I haven't been fair," I said softly, my eyes stinging already. No matter how hard I tried to keep the tears at bay, I knew I wouldn't be able to, not today. He frowned slightly, concern clear in his eyes, yet he waited for me to speak.

The sound of the river and the birds chirping in the trees were the only sounds around us, yet even then, our voices simply blended into our surroundings, promising that my words would remain a secret... or were they pleading for me not to do it?

"Raven... it's okay. Look, whatever it is, it's going to be okay." I blinked, coming out of my thoughts.

"I need to say this...please let me speak. Don't tell me it's okay, none of this is okay," I said, taking a deep breath. I licked my lips before biting down on my lower one.

Where do I start? How do you tell someone you are about to break their heart? Especially when they don't deserve it...

"I'm sorry you got a shitty mate like me," I whispered, my eyes stinging as I stared at his necklace, unable to look into his eyes. "I'm sorry that I treat you the way I do... that I haven't even treated you as mine... I'm sorry that I'm not the mate I should have been. I don't even get why the goddess paired someone like me with two mates when I have done nothing to treat you equally... I'm so fucking sorry, but it's not enough... Goddess, it's not enough..." My throat felt constricted. I couldn't breathe properly.

"Gorgeous... don't ever blame yourself. I haven't really stepped up either... but it's okay... maybe Liam -" I shook my head.

"Liam won't change his mindset... he won't, and we both know that," I whispered quietly, trying to fight back the storm that was threatening to break its dam. "If he doesn't agree, what will you do? Will you fight for someone who hasn't even been fair? Would you fight Liam?"

The sadness in his eyes tugged painfully at my chest. I knew the answer. No. Not because he didn't care enough, not because Liam was his Alpha, but because Damon had a heart of gold, and all he knew was giving, not taking... and that was what I was doing once again. Hurting him. His next words confirmed that...

"I'm so fucking sorry... I can't go against him. It's not just that he's my Alpha... he... he always put you as number one, Raven. When we were kids... he always looked out for you, always talked about you... always wanted you. I'm the one who was too busy looking elsewhere..." His voice held so much pain that he was trying to hide, but he was failing... failing so badly.

"Or perhaps you subconsciously told yourself I was off-limits because of Liam's love for me?" I asked softly. He looked at me and shook his head.

We didn't know... we never would know because we had already walked our chosen paths...

"No... if it comes down to one of us, he is the one that deserves you," he said softly, kissing my hands once again. "With this curse, pushing Liam would have been fucking catastrophic. I am not going to ever risk that."

I nodded. If Damon or I had tried to pursue anything, it would have caused Liam to go off the edge into the darkness. Love, bonds, and our situation weren't as easy as one might think… and regardless, I couldn't use the curse as an excuse. I clearly favoured Liam, so I couldn't hold Damon back any longer.

The moon goddess gave some werewolves second-chance mates… I prayed to Selene with everything I had inside to give Damon someone better. Someone who would treat him like a king…

A thought at the back of my head clawed its way to the forefront of my mind, asking me that what if Liam died? Would I break the bond with my surviving mate? But I knew the answer to that, too. Yes, because if that happened, I deserved to be alone. Damon was no one's backup. He deserved the best.

"Rejection… that's what you're implying," Damon said, smiling slightly, breaking the final grasp on my tears.

"I won't say this for the sake of it but because it's the truth. You deserve someone who treats you as the one and only king in her life. You deserve someone who doesn't favour another above you. For someone with two mates, I should be equal, but even if it's the circumstances or my own fault, I haven't treated you right… I can't string you along, Damon. It's hurting me, too," I sobbed, staring into his eyes.

I needed this, for me, for him, for Liam… no one was happy like this… but in the end, it was Damon who would get hurt the most by the rejection, but he was hurting like this too…

"I'm so fucking sorry…. I'm sorry…."

He let go of my hands, his heart pounding. I could sense his sadness, too, as he cupped my face and brushed away my tears. I gripped his wrists, the pain in my chest unbearable. It hurt so, so fucking much.

"The same thought came to my mind, too… that perhaps our parting is the right thing to do, even if it isn't the best thing. We can't let Liam turn to the darkness completely, and I can't go against him…" he said softly, brushing away more of my tears. My lips quivered, and I looked into the shimmering eyes of his wolf. "I love you, Raven, and even if we cannot be together as mates… will you promise me that you will always be my friend?" He asked, his eyes shining with unshed tears. My vision became blurred with the tears that were spilling down my cheeks.

Yes, that's a promise I'll always keep. Even if Liam didn't agree, I would always be there for Damon as a friend because he had lost so much in life. I knew it would never be enough… I wasn't doing him justice, and I'd carry that guilt with me for the rest of my life...

"You don't need to ask me that... Damon, you are always going to be someone special to me. I love you, too. I want you to know that…."

I also wish I could tell you that I had a connection to you, too. Before the mating ball, I had feelings for you both… Liam was my first love... but I loved you, too... but what's the point in saying all that when all I'm doing is hurting you?

I broke into wracking sobs, letting go of his wrists to clamp my hands over my mouth. It hurt. I couldn't breathe. My chest… my heart. *Breathe… breathe…*

His arms wrapped around me, pulling me into his chest. He stroked my hair, not caring that I was soaking his shirt with my tears. He rubbed my back as I took deep breaths, but for some reason, I was lacking oxygen.

"I love you, too... you're a pure soul, Raven…" he whispered, his voice thick, and I dared to look up to see his own eyes glinting with tears. I gasped, sobbing painfully. "It won't be goodbye…." His soothing words and gentle caress, why was he so selfless? Did he agree because he wanted to? Or was it because he didn't want to make my decision harder for me?

"This is for someone we both love," he added quietly, kissing the top of my head.

I nodded. For someone we both love…

LIAM

I frowned as I stared into the bathroom mirror, styling my hair, remembering Raven's rush in the morning to get going…

"You're in a hurry," I said.

"Yeah, training and then I have stuff to do," she said, towelling her hair after her morning shower.

"What stuff?" I asked casually, handing her a smoothie I had just made. She smiled and shrugged.

"Stuff," she repeated.

Damon. If she couldn't tell me, it meant it included him.

Since then, that irritating flare of anger wasn't subsiding. I wasn't fucking enough. First in my fucking arms… then in his. My chest heaved, my nostrils flaring as I combed my fingers through my hair, swiftly styling it with some hair wax, watching my eyes turn from cerulean to magnetic navy blue.

Breathe, Liam… maybe it's not Damon…

I stepped into my bedroom. I needed to get to my office. There was some crap I needed to…

My thoughts vanished when my eyes caught sight of the brown envelope that had clearly been shoved through the bottom of my door. It was thin and flat and, from what I could tell, blank. Frowning, I walked over to it and picked it up. Nothing was written on it either. I ripped it open, wondering what the fuck it was.

A photograph? I tilted the envelope, shaking it a little until the single photograph inside slipped out. I stared at it for a few seconds, my anger flaring up inside. My heart thundered in my ears, and the surge to destroy everything in my wake burned like the fires of hell needed to be released.

Lies…

It had all been a fucking lie…

Both of them were playing me…

I stared down at the image with burning hatred, a picture of Damon and Raven kissing. From her clothes, I could tell it was the day her father had been brought to me. So, they had been at it since the beginning.

All that fucking shit about waiting… he kissed what was mine…

As for my little mate… how could someone so innocent play such a fucking game…? Her smiles… fake… her struggle fucking made sense now…

How long were those two at it behind my back? It was worse than if they had done it fucking openly.

They had both mocked me…

If they wanted to see me fucking lose my shit, well, congratulations, they just fucking got it. It was high fucking time that I showed them exactly who was in charge.

I crushed the image in my hold, tossing it aside as I headed to the window, not even bothering to open it as I ran right through it. The shattered glass scattered everywhere as I jumped to the ground, feeling the pain rip through my knees at the impact, shards of glass cutting into me. I relished it. The smell of blood… I needed more.

"Alpha!"

I didn't stop to listen to anyone as I broke into a run. The anger enveloping me consumed me entirely. The urge to let it all out and tear every fucking living thing around me to shreds fucking consumed me. I wanted to destroy it all, to unleash carnage upon every single fucking person in the vicinity…

Liars… cheaters… and, above all else - perfect fucking actors. But I would save my wrath for the two who deserved it foremost…

DAMON

I held her tightly, the pain of what I knew was to come breaking me, but… I knew it was for the best.

I had been given an anonymous envelope of her and Liam kissing and making out just the other day outside of the Westwood home. Even one with Liam on his knees. Sure, you couldn't see anything, but it was clear what was happening…

It fucking hurt… so, so fucking much. It was like someone had ripped my heart out, scrubbed it over a field of broken glass, and then stabbed it with a thousand fucking knives.

I had told her to move on with Liam, but clearly, she wasn't able to forget me completely; I was just holding her back. She couldn't enjoy being with Liam if I was there, lingering in her mind and making her feel guilty for it. I had held hope that maybe there was just a glimmer of a chance… but there wasn't. Liam… he would never be happy until he had her completely. He wouldn't trust me…

This was something that we would both do for our Alpha, our friend… my brother… her mate.

There were many types of bonds in life, and each one was special. The bonds of family, of Alpha and Beta, of friendship… and of mates. Sometimes we had to sacrifice something for the betterment of something else. I looked down at her as she sobbed into my chest.

I love you so fucking much, but I'm not worth it… not worth you hurting yourself over…

I held her, telling myself it was not the last fucking time I'd see her or hold her, but whom was I kidding? It was the last time I'd hold her as my mate… my precious, perfect mate. For a fleeting moment, I saw us happy; mated… content… but that was all it was. A fleeting moment that was gone like a whisper in the night. We could never be. She was his… she would always be his.

We sat there for a while, the pain in our hearts fucking powerful. Her tears slowly came to a stop, and she moved back, wiping her eyes.

"Sh-shall we do it?" She whispered.

I nodded as she slowly moved back and sat on her knees before me. Fresh tears streamed down her cheeks, but she stayed brave.

"Want me to do it?" I asked, not wanting her to be in any more pain than she already was.

She reached for my face, wiping my tears away. I closed my eyes, letting myself relish in those sparks for the last time. I opened my eyes slowly. The sun shone down on her, a beautiful goddess with a heart as pure and dazzling as the first rays of the morning sun. I didn't want this… I didn't want to lose my mate. How many more people that I love would I lose? Fuck…

But I couldn't be selfish, for her and Liam. Seeing them happy, that would be my happiness…

"I'm so sorry," she whimpered, her hands trembling.

"Don't be…." I said, taking hold of her hands.

One last kiss… please?

I glanced at her lips, and she nodded, trying to smile as she understood my silent last wish. Her beautiful eyes were full of pain and sorrow. I leaned over, our eyes meeting, and she tilted her head slightly as I pressed my lips to hers.

The salty taste of her tears coated her soft, pouty lips, and I knew it was the last time that I would feel them. The tingles of the mate bond coursed through us, but there was nothing passionate about this kiss. It was deep, full of love and sweetness. I moved my lips slowly, trying to etch the memory of this moment in my mind.

I love you, Raven…

I moved back, taking a deep, shuddering breath. I would do it…

"I, Damon Nichol-"

A menacing animalistic growl ripped through the air, making every animal in the forest run. Birds erupted into the sky, alarmed from their resting places, and every hair on my body stood on edge. An enormous surge of darkness swirled in the air, covering the entire area with a feeling of pure blackness and foreboding, making us both jump to our feet and turn to the source. Our hearts thundered as one.

Shit... Liam had seen us kiss...

Fuck...

He stood there, his claws and canines out, but it wasn't that that chilled me. It was pure blackness that covered his entire eyeballs. His expression was one that was filled with so much hatred he was unrecognisable.

"Liam, this -" Raven began.

Another growl cut her off, and in a flash that was far too fast for even an Alpha, he was before us. Before I could even react, his claws ripped through my chest, followed by a bone-breaking fist that connected with my face, knocking me back with such force that I was thrown a few feet into the air. Before I hit the floor, pain lashed through my body as I tried to get up.

"Raven!" I shouted, worry for her safety filling every fucking nerve of my body. I got to my feet, the urge to protect her screaming at me to go to her. He had his hand twisted in her hair, and from there, everything felt like it was far away...

"You will only ever be mine, love," he hissed just as I began running towards them, but... I was too late...

I watched as if in slow motion as he yanked her head back, tilting her head upwards. She mouthed his name, trying to get through to him, but... it wasn't going to work. Fear had me in its grip as all I could do was helplessly watch him sink his teeth into her neck brutally.

The sound of Raven's scream of pain filled the air, a sound that I knew would haunt my dreams for years to come...

I pushed him away, but I knew I was too late. I shielded her body from him. My heart was pounding with an anger towards him that I had never felt before, and with worry and fear for the tiny precious woman in my arms, whose neck was bleeding far too deeply from his brutal assault that had ripped open half her neck. She was gargling up blood, clutching at her neck. Her eyes looked blank as she coughed up blood.

There was no fucking force on earth that could reverse what he had just done.

Not only had he marked her against her will, but he had ripped away what should have been one of the most sacred and special moments of her life. Blinded by his untameable anger, Liam had ruined everything.

Deja Vu

SCARLETT

I HAD JUST OPENED THE kitchen window when the sound of a vicious growl ripped through the air, making my heart thunder. Seeing the flock of birds erupt from the trees, unease seemed to swirl around me. It took me a split second to recognise the voice that was barely recognisable.

Liam. That was Liam!

I rushed out of the house, telling the guards to watch Azura and Monica as I raced in the direction of the commotion, faltering when the sound of Raven's scream pierced the air. No. Goddess, no! What has he done?

Elijah, it's Liam and Raven! I called through the link to Elijah.

I'm on my way, his soothing voice answered despite the worry that was consuming me.

Raven! Liam?

Nothing. I was hitting a wall. *Fuck*!

The wind rushed through my hair as I broke through the trees, the smell of blood seeping into my nose. The sheer blanket of something dark and evil that hung in the air made my blood run cold. I took in the horrifying scene before me; Damon was holding Raven, who was bleeding profusely, her heart beating far too fast as she choked on the blood that was pouring out of her neck and mouth. She was grasping at her neck, blood running down her fingers, making my stomach churn sickeningly. Worry and fear for her whirled around me, my heart beating fast.

My eyes snapped to Liam, who was advancing on Damon as he placed Raven down. That darkness... it was him. It was coming from him. His normal aura was completely gone... replaced by this horrible, sinister darkness...

"How could you?" Damon shouted, sounding angrier than I had ever heard him.

He blocked Liam, who had just lunged at him, his canines out and anger clear on his face. Damon jumped to his feet, meeting him mid-strike. It was clear both were ready to rip each other to pieces. I was about to intervene when Damon's next words made me freeze.

"You marked her!"

Reality came crashing down on me as the realisation settled in.

Her neck... her neck...

Fear washed over me like a bucket of ice-cold knives, piercing into every inch of my body.

Marked.

Fuck...

Memories from long ago flashed to the forefront of my mind, the pain with them making it hard to breathe. *History cannot repeat itself.*

"No... no!" I cried, staring at the blond male before me. His blond hair was matted with blood... so similar to his...

I walked towards them, willing every fibre of my shaking body to move, just as Elijah ran past me. A menacing growl ripped from his lips. In a flash, he was next to the two boys who were tearing into each other, ready to kill one another.

Elijah slammed Liam to the floor, pinning him down, only for Liam to flip them as both men growled with all they had. The surge of their Alpha power and that darkness enveloped the area like a blanket, their growls making it feel like the ground was vibrating at the intensity of the sound.

Raven's whimper made me come out of my thoughts, and I rushed closer, not even realising I was trembling excessively. *She needs a doctor!* Before I could even reach her, Damon got there first, tears in his eyes as he scooped her up as if she was the most fragile thing on the planet. She was...

Fuck, Liam had done this. Guilt and anguish enveloped me as our eyes met for a second. I had failed them... failed...

He turned, rushing from the scene, his only wish clear... to save his mate.

Suddenly, I felt something snap inside of me, and my mind seemed to become clear. This was not Zidane...

My eyes blazed as I spun around just as I felt a searing pain through the bond and turned to see Liam had ripped through Elijah's side, clearly winning the battle. *No one hurts my mate.*

I growled menacingly, rushing over in a flash and ripping Liam off Elijah. I pushed him to the ground, staring into those frightening black pits of the man before me. This was not my son. He had let his jealousy and anger fuel the darkness... let it take over him completely.

"Liam!" I growled, striking him across the face and letting my claws dig into his face. He hissed, attacking back, but I didn't care. "Liam, what are you doing?" I shouted as my back hit the ground, growling as I flipped us over, pinning him to the ground.

Nothing but blood, pain, and agony. It was all I could see, smell, and feel. My only thoughts were that I did not raise a monster... I did not raise a monster... *I did not raise a monster....*

"Scarlett!" Elijah's voice called, and I felt myself being pulled away.

I gasped, coming to. My heart was thundering as I stared at Liam, who lay on the ground breathing heavily, his eyes his usual cerulean blue. He was a bloody mess. I had wounded him badly. I could see the wounds that I had made weren't healing... they wouldn't because of my ability to slow down the healing of any wound I inflict upon anyone...

"He's back... calm down," Elijah murmured, rubbing my arms as he buried his face in my neck.

"He marked her! He marked her against her will!" I screamed, pulling out of Elijah's hold.

How dare he? Did he think this was okay? Yes, he was cursed, but... he had let his own emotions fuel that darkness. He had let the curse take over. Tears blurred my eyes, and I didn't even realise I was crying until then, the pain ripping me to pieces.

My son, my son had done this...

The pain of the entire fucking situation hurt. Zidane's blood would forever run through my veins... in the veins of my children. He was gone, but his shadow wasn't.

Elijah held my arms tightly, staring down into my eyes with sadness in his blue ones.

"I know, baby... he made a mistake, an-"

"Mistake? He ruined her life!" I screamed.

Was just marking someone a 'mistake?' It was so much more... I still awoke with the nightmares of that man...

"What hap..." Liam whispered, coughing up blood, rolling to his side as he tried to sit up. He was losing a lot of blood.

"Kitten... calm down. I know -"

"Don't tell me to calm down!" I shouted, hitting Elijah's chest.

History was repeating itself. History wa-

Elijah's lips crashed against me, kissing me hard. I struggled for a bit, but he held me in place, one hand in my hair and the other around my waist, until I finally began to calm down. The sparks of the bond coursed through me, soothing the storm within me slightly. Just a little...

"I'll handle this," Elijah said quietly when I stopped struggling.

I could see the pain in his eyes as he let go of me and walked over to Liam, who was getting to his feet. I was shocked he still could, considering the injuries, but he was a strong Alpha.

My son... I had hurt my son. He had committed an unforgivable crime... but it didn't stop a mother from feeling that pain. The pain of his injuries, but more than that, the pain of his sins... and the pain that he had no idea what he had just done...

"You marked Raven without her consent," Elijah said, his voice ice cold, laced with sadness, regret, and burning anger that he was doing his best to control.

The look of horror and shock that crossed Liam's face made my stomach twist and my heart break. He didn't know... this was going to break him...

"What? No... no..." He looked around as if trying to see where he was or what had happened. "Fuck... no. No. No!" He staggered back, staring at the blood on the ground, swallowing hard. Blood that belonged to all five of us...

He must have caught the scent, staring at the blood that belonged to Raven. Any colour he had left in him was gone, his ashen gaze turning to Elijah, who nodded gravely.

"I know the curse has given birth to this darkness, that you lost to it... allowed your emotions to let it consume you... I am your father, Liam, and I will help you. You are not alone, and you will never be alone, but you have committed a heinous crime, and for it, you will be punished. I love you, and I will be there for you, but you need to pay for what you have done."

I watched the anguish in Liam's eyes, watched his entire world come crashing down around him... and it was at that moment that I realised what the curse had cost. Not only had Liam become unhinged... he had committed a crime that was equal to rape in our community... one that Raven may one day forgive him for... but one he, himself, never would...

His gaze flicked to me, looking over my body before his gaze snapped to his father's bloody body. I watched my son crumble before me, that young boy who had nothing but love for others... who would hide his own pain and give away everything he loved for others... my smiling, little Liam...

"I understand, and I agree...." He swallowed; his breathing was ragged. "I, Liam Westwood, renounce my claim as Alpha of the Blood Moon Pack to my father, Alpha Elijah Westwood, and am ready to pay for the crimes I have committed under the laws of this pack and the council," Liam said, falling to his knees as the surge of power shifted. I felt the power of becoming the Luna once more course through my veins. Neither of us was expecting that. My heart pounded as I realised that he was giving up on himself and life.

"Liam..." Elijah said, shocked.

"I have one request..." Liam said, his chest heaving as he tried to breathe. He was losing too much blood...

My vision was blurred with tears. The urge to comfort him and the pain he had caused clashed against one another inside of me, but he still needed someone. Before I could even move, he tumbled sideways, losing consciousness. I rushed over, my heart pounding. Yes, I wanted him to pay for his crime, but he was still my son, cursed by the wretched gods for his ancestors' crimes.

"He needs a doctor," I said, my voice shaking. Elijah looked at me, his eyes pained before he sighed heavily.

"His final request, he mind-linked me it."

"What is it?" I asked, my heart thundering as I pressed my hands to the long gashes that I had made through his chest, trying to stem the blood loss.

"No one is to heal him. He made me take an oath upon you... I won't break it," Elijah said, pain and sadness in his eyes.

My heart squeezed in pain. He was punishing himself...

I pulled my shirt off and pressed it to the wounds.

"Then, at least get some bandages!" I screamed. I stared down at my son, my heart pounding. The image of Raven's neck flashed to the forefront of my mind... a brutal bite that had almost killed her. Was she okay? "And get someone to call Kiara, we need her!"

What have you done, Liam? There's no going back...

I kept my hand firmly on his stomach and chest, but my shirt was already drenched. I knew my son was deep down in there somewhere... and I knew that he would never be able to forgive himself. Ever.

༄༅

UNKNOWN POV

I smiled, staring at the old, stained passport-sized photograph in my hand. The smell of disinfectant was strong in the air, nice and clean.

"I did it. I have hurt them. She won't survive now..." I rocked back and forth, my grip on the photograph tight. "Everything has been destroyed... I'll avenge you... I'll make you proud... and I'll make him fall in love with me. He will be mine... all mine... all mine..." My breathing became ragged as the excitement within me grew.

"And as for her... I'll make sure I add her to my collection..."

I was almost there... *Soon, soon he'll notice that I am the one he needs. Soon!*

"Are you proud of me? Are you watching me?" I whispered heavily, my breathing ragged as I stared at the picture, unblinking. "Yes, you are, you are... you have to be proud! I will get revenge for you... for our family... for everything... but it's okay if I take him for myself... right? You won't be angry with me, will you?"

No...No, you won't. Because I will make you happy, too... I stroked my finger down the photo, smiling.

Oh... yes... He will be all mine...

Mine...

Mine...

I can taste it. That vengeance, that darkness in the air... the fear. Everyone is scared now... scared of who would be next... but they won't know, they'll never know, because I will kill them when they least expect it...

But I had my next targets already decided...

They'll never see me coming… no one ever does… and now that the Alpha has committed a crime… oh, this pack will be destroyed from the inside! Yes, from the inside! Now… who shall we kill next?

I hid the photograph away, sliding it in the gap between the wall and the skirting board, and stood up. I had two options; I didn't like either of them, and since Monica was kept far too safe, then I'd settle for either of these…

I smiled as I tapped my chin. Him or her? Which one…

Eenie, meenie, miney-

"Wait! Of course… it has to be him! Oh my… him and then his mate! Why didn't I do this sooner? Oh my, please don't be angry at me. I will avenge you… I will… I will!"

My eyes darted around my bedroom. I needed to clean it up once more… I didn't want any clues to be left behind. Grabbing the cloth and the disinfectant spray, I stared at the clean boards… they were clean, but I couldn't help but see the non-existent bloodstains.

It's always good to be safe… always….

I dropped to my knees, brushing my hair back as I began to hum softly, cleaning the floor.

"Scrub, scrub, scrub…."

DAMON

Watching the doctors shouting… being told that Kiara was on her way… the sound of Raven's heart rate picking up and dropping… Zack and Taylor trying to hold me back… someone trying to check me… I couldn't leave her! But the doctors didn't want me there. I hated it!

I should have been protecting her… I should have been fucking faster…

A blast of powerful magic and a rush of wind filled the hall, making every paper on the wall move. All three of us raised our arms, shielding our faces from the whipping wind, when two women appeared before me. My eyes widened in shock as I stared at them.

Kia? I looked at the other woman. Her head was pure white, her eyes blazing red, and something about her told me she was more than a human as I involuntarily noticed her beauty. I frowned, snapping my gaze to Kiara, who didn't even notice me as she pushed open the hospital door rushing into the room.

The woman before me blinked, and her eyes changed to a startling blue. She looked 'normal' again. I knew who she was. I had heard of her; Delsanra, Rayhan's Mate, and the Luna of the Black Storm Pack. She gave me a small nod before running into the room.

I got up, feeling relief flood me. Kiara could heal her. Raven will be okay! I went to the door, seeing Kiara's purple glow already surrounding her and Raven's heartbeat becoming steady.

"If we can take some skin, we can graft it before I heal her completely... Otherwise, it's going to leave a mark," Kiara's broken voice came.

"I'll do that with magic. Doctor, what section?"

"Ah... here..." Doctor Smith said, pointing at a section of her leg.

"Quick!" Kiara said, her voice filled with urgency.

Delsanra nodded, placing her hand above Raven's leg and whispering a spell as the doctors and nurses all moved back, clearly uncomfortable with the magic being used. I wrinkled my nose, flinching as a square of skin was removed from Raven's leg, leaving a horrible red patch behind and floating towards Raven's neck.

"Perfect!" Kiara said, moving her hand back as Delsanra placed the graft with her magic over Raven's neck. Kiara placed her hand on her neck. I saw both hers and Delsanra's auras merge as they wrapped around Raven's neck. My heart was thundering as I walked over to them, not wanting to get in the way but needing to be close to her. She needed someone...

"She's going to be okay..." Kiara said, quietly looking at me.

I nodded, unable to speak, as I walked around to the other side. Delsanra finally stopped whispering her spell and nodded as Kiara removed her hand. All three of us, the doctors, and nurses stared at Raven's neck, and I felt relief flood me.

"It's perfect," Delsanra said, smiling with approval.

"It's... she's marked?" Kiara asked, shocked, her eyes going to me. I clenched my jaw, looking down at the mark.

A crescent moon with a rose in front of it. Beautiful... yet the horror of how she got it would forever remain, a memory that would always be traumatic and painful. Marked by a monster...

There was no Liam at that moment. There had just been this his anger, hatred, and jealousy...

"It's not yours," Kiara said softly. I looked up at her, my eyes flashing.

"Do you think I would have ripped her fucking throat out?" I asked coldly, regretting it when her eyes widened at my tone.

"Oh, I'm sorry... I didn't realise... that mark was..." She looked horrified, putting the pieces together, and I looked away.

"Sorry, I didn't mean -"

"It's okay... I understand," Kiara replied, smiling gently as she bent down and kissed Raven's forehead, sadness clear in her eyes. "I'll give you two a moment."

She backed away, trying to control her emotions. Delsanra led her out, and I stared down at Raven. Her beautiful face was pale...

Collapsing to my knees by the bed, I kissed her hand, unable to stop the tears. She could have fucking died; she could have died...

My heart thumped when I felt the shift in power, a passing of power. What...

"I will get her cleaned up," a nurse said to me, gently placing a hand on my shoulder. It took me a moment to recognise her. An old friend of Mom's... "Go, son. She'll feel better soon. You need to get checked, too."

No, I didn't. I was fine.

I didn't argue, though, for Raven, but it took my fucking all to let go of that hand. She had lost far too much in life, yet all she did was smile and pretend to be happy. I walked out of the room, and the group fell silent, clearly having been discussing something.

"Care to share?" I asked quietly.

Kiara walked over to me, placing her hand on my chest as she healed my wounds. I frowned but said nothing. I didn't deserve to be healed...

"Alpha Elijah is the Alpha again." Zack said quietly, "Liam stepped down himself." I frowned. So he had come to his fucking senses...

"Who called you?" I asked Kiara as Zack placed his hand on my back, forcing me to sit down. I frowned at him, not missing the mark on his neck. I raised an eyebrow but didn't question it. It had not been there last night.

"Liana. Zack had told her to," Kiara answered. A flicker in her eyes made me wonder if there was something between them, but right then, the only thing that consumed my mind was what had happened inside that room.

"So, you're a witch?" Taylor asked Delsanra. "That's pretty cool."

"Thanks… yes, I am," she replied.

"We were at Rayhan's pack, and well, when I got the call, the two of us came quickly," Kiara explained.

"Ah. I see," I said quietly. Thank the goddess she had gotten there in time.

"Can anyone tell me why Liam did what he did?" Kiara asked, her voice strained. I knew she was trying to remain calm. "I'm unable to talk to Mom and Dad as well."

"You're going to have to talk to your parents," I said. It was up to them to tell her what they deemed fit.

"Go, I'll keep him company," Zack said quietly, as if I couldn't hear.

"I'll take them," Taylor said, looking at him. They exchanged looks, and to my surprise, Zack reached over, taking hold of his chin for a second before letting go. Remembering Zack's mark, I glanced at Taylor in surprise. Were they mates?

Kiara smiled slightly, although it didn't reach her eyes or do anything to hide her sadness before she turned to me.

"She's going to be okay," she said softly, placing a hand on my shoulder before Taylor led them away. I placed my head in my hands the moment they were gone. Zack sat down, patting my back and blowing out a breath.

"Things are going to be okay."

"You don't recover from that… being fucking forcefully marked."

"I know… Liam won't forgive himself either."

I didn't reply. My heart felt heavy.

No, he wouldn't, and neither would I.

The Bond of Twins

KIARA

*I*DIDN'T KNOW WHAT TO say… Dante's birth was the catalyst for Liam's darkness. Goddess, I felt devastated for my brother.

We had gone to find Mom and Dad, but only Mom was there. Dad was the Alpha of the pack again. Mom had filled us in on everything: the curse, the card, Liam, the killer, and the truth about Raven's past.

Alejandro had called to ask if everything was okay and if he was needed, but I told him we were okay. Right then, there was nothing more we could do.

"How could you not tell me? Raven lost her mom, and she wasn't allowed to tell me? She… how are we making a change if she's still being told to keep things on the low?"

I ran my fingers through my hair, trying to stay calm for Mom. I could tell she was distraught. Liam had marked Raven, and that had triggered Mom's trauma of what her biological father had done to her…

Raven… seeing the state she had been in… it broke my heart, and worse, my brother had done it. Seeing her small figure just lying there… it broke me. I wished I could take away more than her physical pain.

As for the card that Liam pulled, I remembered it, too…

I just couldn't believe they didn't tell me anything. Raven, too. I felt like a bad friend for not picking up on it, but she never shared anything with me, ever. Her dad was abusive… I remember how she used to joke about stuff often… "*Dad would throw a slipper at me if I did that… Dad is going to really kill me if I'm not home… I really don't want to go home.*" When she used to say it, I would put it down to her wanting to be a little rebellious... I never realised there was more to it.

I stared at the ground, my mind spinning. I'm a bad friend, to Raven, to Damon, and an awful sister to Liam...

"I'll try to see if I can find anything on the curse. Maybe I can try finding some answers," Delsanra said, frowning slightly. I nodded.

"Thanks," I replied appreciatively before turning to Mom. "What about the killer?"

"Still not caught. We have a few clues and have ruled out at least a third of the pack," Mom replied.

"Delsanra, is there anything that you can find out?" I asked.

"Do you have anything that belongs to the killer?" She asked, turning to Mom. Mom shook her head.

"They leave nothing behind," she said. Her eyes looked blank. I knew the entire situation with Raven and Liam was taking its toll upon her.

"Then, unless I probe the minds of everyone in this pack, I don't think I can," Delsanra said regretfully.

"Yes, and similar to the Alpha command, we don't want that. There's already a lot of tension and doubt going through the pack. Now, with Liam losing control, things will be even harder... people will feel even more worried. Doubt and fear from the inside can cause more damage," Mom said, running her hand through her hair.

Yeah, we knew that... I exchanged looks with Delsanra.

"I understand. Maybe I can take a look at the bodies, see if there's anything I can do."

"Sure. How long are you two here for? You've left the kids as well, Kia." Mom asked, looking up.

"The men know we might be a day," I replied with a small smile.

"I think they'll do perfectly well together. Rayhan and Dante get on like a house on fire," Delsanra added with a small smile. I looked at her, slightly amused despite the situation.

"Oh, they do indeed," I replied. Dante, due to his abilities, could see Delsanra's true form, and his infatuation with her was still there. "Where is Liam?" I asked, glancing at Mom as Azura came into the room, climbing into Mom's lap. Mom hugged her tightly, and I felt that Azura was that comfort and light Mom needed so often lately. As for Dad, how much more did he have to suffer?

"In the cells," Mom replied quietly. My eyes widened in shock.

"But you said he's injured!" I shot up.

"He is…but he marked her, Kiara… it's a crime," Mom said quietly. I could sense her anguish. Of course, she didn't want him there, but she had to be fair. I nodded.

"I get that, but he is injured, isn't he?"

"Yes, and I hurt him…."

Delsanra looked shocked but said nothing. I simply stared at Mom. We knew roughly what happened, but I didn't know that Mom had hurt him… I thought it was Damon! I turned and ran from the room, my heart ringing in my ears as I rushed from the house. The sun was setting. I heard someone shout for me to wait to be escorted, but I didn't care.

Liam. Didn't they get it? I knew what kind of person Liam was. He had always put others before himself. I knew that he had changed, but it was the darkness that made him do it! I knew it was still wrong but leaving Liam alone at this time was not the right thing to do! It would destroy him! That would only push him further into darkness.

Liam always loved with everything he had, gave willingly, and put himself last. I often saw so many qualities of Uncle Raf in him. Leaving him when he needed help was the worst thing possible. Fine, he made Dad take an oath to not heal him, but I didn't answer to Dad!

I reached the entrance to the pack headquarters, slowing down, and stared at the two guards.

"I demand to see my brother. Open the doors."

"Yes, Luna. We have to ask the Alpha -"

"Boys… I'm the queen. I answer to no one but my king. Step. Aside," I said icily, despite both men being in their late twenties at the least. My eyes flashed, and I let my aura roll off.

They exchanged looks and stepped aside, unable to refuse my command, and unlocked the entrance. I also knew they had probably mind-linked Dad, but I didn't really care. No one could stop me from healing him! I ran down the hall, my heart thudding loudly.

The bond we had was not something small, even if we were miles apart. Why didn't he tell me what he was going through? Why hadn't I felt it? Why was I such a horrible friend and sister? I tried, I tried to do my best, but it was never enough. My heart ached at that as I rushed past some pack members walking around, heading towards the cells.

"Open the door!" I growled. One of the men thumbed in the passcode. I rushed past them and towards the cells, slowing down when I saw a bloody mess lying on one of the beds in a cell.

Liam.

Dad stood outside. His eyes looked empty, like a man who had lost everything. I walked towards him, and he looked at me. I could smell the blood from him. My gaze dipped to his waist. I knew that, despite the leather jacket he wore, he was still sporting his own injuries.

"Kiara."

"Dad," I whispered, wrapping my arms around him tightly, letting my healing flow through us.

"Don't..." he muttered, pulling away. He was punishing himself too...

"Open the door. I need to see him," I said.

"You want to heal him, Kia. I took an oath."

Yeah, I'm not doing this... not now. I simply nodded.

"I do want to heal him."

"You can't," Dad said firmly. I looked down at him, placing my hand on his waist, but he jerked away. "No..."

So, you're really not letting yourself get healed because of your son... My heart ached for my family. They didn't deserve this.

"Okay, at least let me see him. I want to talk to him or at least hold him if I can't heal him," I whispered pleadingly, putting on the most innocent expression I could, making sure tears filled my eyes. It wasn't hard, considering the amount of pain I was feeling. I may have been mated and a mother, but I would always be daddy's little girl. He looked at me, his eyes softening, and he stroked my hair.

"Only to talk," he said quietly, placing a soft kiss on my forehead.

I nodded dejectedly, as if I was giving up, and Dad unlocked the door. I entered the cell, my heart thumping as I rushed to Liam. His familiar scent and the blood were mixed together, reminding me of what had happened. He was awake, but I wasn't sure if he was fully there. His usual cerulean eyes were washed out, his skin pale, covered in a layer of sweat...

"Liam?" I whispered, brushing his matted locks off his forehead. "Liam?" Genuine tears trickled down my cheeks as I felt the pain of seeing him in this condition. "Liam, can you hear me? It's me, Kia," I whispered, kissing his cheek.

His eyes fluttered slightly, and I closed my eyes, pressing my forehead to his, my hand still on his cheek as I let my healing flow through me. I felt it spread through him and sensed his pain.

"Kiara!" Dad called. My eyes blazed, and I allowed my aura to flare around me, raising a barrier of pure power as he ran inside. Unable to penetrate the barrier, he called out to me, but I was not going to listen to him.

He took an oath. I didn't.

Liam took a deep, shuddering breath, his eyes flying open as he shot up, backing away from me against the wall behind him.

"It's okay, Liam, I'm here," I said softly, cupping his face as he looked around the cell, his heart pounding. I sat on the small bed next to him, pulling him into my arms.

"Kia?" He whispered hoarsely.

"I'm here," I whimpered, trying to fight my tears that refused to stop falling. I heard Dad walk out and close the door behind him, walking off. I knew he was hurting, but as Alpha, he had to uphold his responsibilities, too.

"W-what are you doing here? Raven... fuck, I messed up. Raven. She needs you!" He said, struggling to escape me, but right then, I was stronger. He had lost far too much blood.

"I'm here for my best friend and my special friend," I whispered, referring to what I used to call him as a child. "For my brother, who always took care of me. Why didn't you share what was going on with me?" He moved back slowly, looking at me with eyes that were full of sorrow.

"I marked her, Kia... I fucking marked her," he said, his voice breaking. His eyes were full of anguish and glittering with unshed tears. "There's nothing that can fucking undo that."

I know. Goddess, I know... I cupped his face, tears streaming down my cheeks.

"I know... but we will get through this," I whispered. I didn't know how, but we would.

"You shouldn't have healed me. I didn't deserve it."

"Are you giving up on life, Liam?" I asked softly, my chest aching at the pain and turmoil that he was inflicted with. His eyes met mine, his heart thundering, and I realised I had just hit the nail on the head. Goddess, he was...

"I'm not safe to be around... you should go," he said quietly, his expression going blank.

"No. I'm staying right here," I said, my eyes flashing purple as I kicked my heels off and crossed my legs. An emotion filled his eyes, but before I could make sense of it, it was gone.

"She must be devastated or super angry," he whispered, looking at his hands.

I tensed; did he not realise that Raven had almost died? My heart thundered, and he looked at it sharply.

"What is it?"

"Nothing, she's... I guess a little angry," I said, not knowing what to say.

"You're lying. What are you hiding, Kia?" He asked, panic filling his eyes.

"I... she's still unconscious," I whispered.

"Unconscious... why? I... the blood... the..." The realisation hit him, and he looked at me, horrified. "What did I do, Kia? Why is she fucking unconscious?"

"Because you bit her so brutally, she lost a lot of blood. I came to heal her," I explained quietly, knowing I couldn't keep it from him forever. He needed to know. Although I couldn't bring myself to say he almost ripped her entire throat out, he still needed to know. A single tear escaped his eye as he slowly looked down, and, at that moment, I knew he would never forgive himself.

Faith Lost

TWO DAYS LATER
RAVEN

*I*HAD BEEN DISCHARGED FROM the hospital the following day, thanks
to Kia and Rayhan's Kitty. I still remembered the look in Kiara's eyes…
the moment she told me that I should have told her what I was going
through. The tears… the promises that we really won't hide anything any
longer, something I knew both of us would honour. I hated seeing her feel
like a disappointment when it was my own doing that I hid it all from
them when I had so many chances to tell them.

She had spent the night with Liam. I could smell his scent from her
when she had come to see me in the morning. I wasn't able to ask her
how he was. I didn't know what to think. She had spent the day with me.
It frustrated me that because of me, she was being torn like this between
him and me, but she had nothing but love and concern for me. Her parting
words still rang in my head, and despite the fact that I knew she meant
them, it still hurt.

*"I will always be here for you, hun, no matter what you decide, do, or want.
I will be by your side, okay?"*

Damon had brought me to his house, although I had no idea what we
were, remembering exactly what we were going to do before Liam had
arrived. I was just glad things were still good between us, and I knew that
would always remain. Damon hadn't left my side, only for short moments
to shower, check up on his mother, or if he had to do something, but for
the most part, he stayed.

Aunty Red and Uncle El had visited me. I could see the pain in Aunty
Red's eyes as she stared at my mark, the guilt and anguish that she was

trying to hide, the beating of her heart, and the way she hugged me tightly. Her whispered apology that she didn't give me a chance to refute.

She had asked if I wanted to go to theirs, but... I refused. I couldn't go there.

It hit me hard, knowing Liam had renounced his Alpha title and that he was in the cells. I could feel the pain Liam was going through through the bond, a bond that had become so strong that I felt restless. I could feel his regret, his agony, and his hopelessness. It hurt...

I was on Damon's sofa, a blanket over me and a mug of hot chocolate in my hands.

"Delsanra didn't find anything," Damon said as he sat down on the edge of the sofa.

"She didn't?" I sighed.

Delsanra and Kia had left last night, only after Delsanra had tried to see if she could find anything, with her final words, *"It seems even witches don't have the power to probe into the works of gods."* She felt guilty that she wasn't able to help, but we assured her we were grateful for it. I wished I could get to know her more, but we had exchanged numbers to keep in touch. Kia had started a group chat with Raihana, too, for the four of us called 'Queens', a title I didn't think really fit me.

"No," he said, frowning slightly.

"You're angry at him," I said softly. He clenched his jaw, staring at the coffee table.

"What do you want, me to go give him a pat on the back?" He asked, turning those blue eyes to me. "I saw him rip your throat out, Raven. He was so fucking blinded by his anger."

"I know... I'm not blaming you. What Liam did wasn't right..." I said, tracing my fingers over the mark on my neck, a mark that so suited the true Liam. My heart clenched painfully at the memory. It hurt me, too. The look of hatred as he bit into me was so painful... I knew I could have died. I had never thought he'd be able to hurt me... "I know that this curse hasn't made things easier. Probably seeing us kiss triggered his anger, and in turn, the darkness took over."

"Will you forgive him?" Damon asked quietly, his eyes flashing in anger. I looked up at him before staring at my mug of hot chocolate.

I was hurt, upset, angry, confused, and broken in a way, but my inner mind was clashing. A part of me wanted to scream and shout. Why was it that all my life, everyone took my decisions for me? I was choosing Liam, but what should have been a sweet moment of me telling him that I chose him has been taken from me by force. Then, a part of me wanted to comfort the broken man who remained in the cells, to tell him that it was okay. But… was it?

I loved him, so, so much. Every time I thought about him, I remembered the young man he used to be, the loving, caring, thoughtful Liam who always paid attention to me. Probably the only person who ever came close to knowing the truth about my life… he used to ask me if everything was okay, if I was happy, and I always assured him I was fine.

The Liam without the darkness, I loved him, too… the way he remembered stuff, the way he did things, the attention to detail, my favourite colour, the cake… even when we became intimate, he always gave, still waiting. He was always waiting… he never took advantage of us or pushed me further… he was considerate… but I also couldn't just pretend this didn't happen.

I wasn't something to be claimed. I had the right to make my own decision. What I didn't get was that Damon and I were willing to give up everything for him… but then… this…

"In time… I think I will…." I replied softly.

Time… he didn't have much time… My heart squeezed painfully.

"He doesn't deserve it," he said icily.

I reached out, taking his hand. He had always put Liam first. I knew witnessing that must have been hard for him, and right then, I knew both men needed me. Why did I feel like we were just making the curse stronger? Time was running out…

As for Damon, he had shown his love for me; the way his eyes filled with pain and love when I woke up in the hospital room, the way he whispered, *"Thank the goddess you're okay. I love you…."* The way his heart thundered in his chest as he held me against it. I wouldn't forget it.

"Have you talked to him? Have you seen him? He is probably regret-"

"Stop defending him, Raven! For goddess's sake, you need to stop letting everyone take advantage of you," he said, frustrated, pulling his hand from my hold. My chest tightened painfully; I wasn't doing that… I just… I wanted everything to be okay.

"I'm not letting anyone take advantage of me," I said quietly.

"I hope not," he said quietly. Standing up, he walked over to the window and stared out.

I looked down; no, this was an eye-opener. With everything that had happened, would I still choose Liam? This was enough to show me my true feelings. I knew the three of us would never work together, and I had given up on that a long time ago.

The ringing of the doorbell pulled me out of my reverie, and Damon gave me an apologetic smile.

"Sorry for getting irritated."

"It's okay, you're angry. Now, go get the door!"

"Going," he replied with a small smile. The look in Damon's eyes when he had held me as I bled… I still remembered it…

"Hey, beautiful girl," Taylor's voice called, his scent filling my nose as he came over and pulled me tightly into his arms.

"Taylor…" I whispered, hugging him back.

His scent had changed. I looked up at him sharply, noticing him looking at my mark. His eyes were filled with sadness, and I wished they weren't. I really… I didn't need sympathy. I knew the rumours had crossed through the pack, but there wasn't much I could do about it.

"Hey, Raven," Zack's voice came just as he entered, holding a large bouquet of flowers, a teddy bear, and a hamper. Totally from Taylor. "These are from Tay," he added as if he did not want to be seen holding such pretty things.

"Thanks, babe," Taylor said, flashing him a smile and making me gasp.

"Babe? You two are together!" I squealed, jumping up onto the sofa and hugging him tightly. Thanks to the sofa, our height was a lot more level. Taylor chuckled.

"We are," he said softly,

"Why didn't you tell me when you mind-linked me yesterday!" I shouted unhappily.

"I… you had just got out of the hospital…" he said. I moved back, wanting to see his mark.

"Show me it." The men exchanged looks, and I rolled my eyes.

"Just because I was marked against my will does not mean I'm going to become a crying puddle every time I see a mark," I said, annoyed. "Besides… my mark isn't dark or ugly. It's beautiful… like the real Liam that I know is in there."

Silence fell in the room. I realised that no one in the room held any faith in Liam anymore…

⁘⁙⁘

A week passed, and I finally decided to brave stepping outside. Everyone was being extra supportive, constantly keeping me company or mind-linking me to ask how I was feeling or what I was up to, but really, I just needed everyone to act normal. I didn't want their pity. Kiara was the only one who really understood that; when she texted, it was just pictures of the twins or Dante or talking about general things. I just wanted everything to return to normal, but could they?

My emotions were hot and cold. I went from happy to utterly defeated within moments of each other. Sometimes I'd remember flashes of the cottage and him telling me he would wait for me, and then I'd see him ripping through my neck. I kept waking up at night, those bottomless pits of his eyes flashing in my mind, his canines out as he bit me…

My last thoughts were always the same in my nightmares.

Liam won't hurt me.

I wrapped my arms around myself as I walked through the pack grounds, just wanting to think things through in the fresh air. I had wanted to return to training, but Damon had said it was better I didn't. I knew why: everyone was talking. I was going to have to face it sooner or later. I didn't want to be cocooned up.

Sighing, I tugged at the sleeve of my ribbed black shirt, which had three buttons at the top that I had left open. I was wearing some ripped jeans with net tights under, paired with some black heeled boots.

I looked at the small plushie in my hand. Sparks… I wanted to go back to the graveyard, but I hadn't been able to. Right then, I just need someone to talk to. He was the only real family I had. I was sure if he was there, he'd love me, right?

I heard snickering and looked up to see Owen smirking as he walked past me, smart enough not to push me. Guess he learned his lesson last time. I ignored him and headed to the graveyard. It was a dull day. I pushed open the small gate and made my way over to Renji's grave. I sat down on my knees before it and looked down at it. Like always, it was well-kept.

"Hello, Renji, I hope you're okay... a lot's happened since the last time I came here. I'm sorry it took me so long since I promised to meet you... but I wasn't allowed to come... I'm sorry. I wonder if Mom is with you now or not?" I asked softly, placing Sparks at the foot of the gravestone. "Look, Sparks is back... he's so happy to be here again." I smiled gently as a soft wind blew through my hair.

"I was going to reject Damon. We were going to do it. I chose Liam... but... he marked me forcefully... and I haven't seen him since..." I whispered, feeling my eyes prickle. "I don't know what to feel. At times I feel numb; at others, confused, upset, hurt... I know what he did wasn't right, but I also know that Helios' curse isn't something we can just ignore. I'm worried about him. He's in the cells, but I'm also... scared...." I covered my face as the tears began flowing, and I sobbed quietly.

"I mention him, and everyone gets angry. Is it wrong that I want to talk to him? But I haven't mind-linked him either... I... I'm scared... I just, I don't want him to shut me out," I whispered.

I loved him so, so much, but at the same time, I couldn't just forget what he did. The darkness in him was strong, but wasn't it the time to help him? The fear of what might happen was still there, but I was stronger than that.

Someone placed their hand on my shoulder, and I gasped, jerking away as I stared up at Nina. I had been so absorbed in my thoughts that I hadn't even noticed her.

"Are you okay?" She asked with concern clear in her eyes. I nodded, wiping my tears quickly.

"Yes, I am," I said, sniffling.

"You're a strong woman, Raven. It's all going to be okay," she said, her eyes filled with confidence as she patted my back. I hoped so. Right then, I didn't know what to do.

"I'm going to go. Thank you," I said softly.

I stood up, and she nodded. I glanced at Renji's grave, bidding him a silent farewell before I turned and left the graveyard. I walked along slowly, trying to make sense of my emotions, and remembered a conversation I had with Uncle El a few days ago when he had visited me at Damon's...

How do you feel? I mean, emotionally? He asked, shoving his hands into the pockets of his jeans as he stood in front of the fireplace.

It was just the two of us. Damon was out, and although I wanted to return to the packhouse, it would mean I would have to face everyone. I looked down at my knees. How did I feel?

"Lost... sometimes I feel like I got this, I can do this... how it's okay, I'm okay..."

"It's not okay, and it's all right to feel like that, Raven," he said quietly. "I think you need to stop trying to accept things and think deeply about what you want." I stayed quiet, and he continued, "Where's the confident Raven who was ready to own everything? I want her back. I want her to consider her happiness above all. This curse is not on you. If it's meant to be broken, it will be. We can do this, but it doesn't mean you need to be sacrificed or influenced to make decisions because of it. I want you to decide what you want without any external factors weighing on your decision. Without you feeling guilty about this or that. Until then, I want you to focus on yourself and nothing more. No what if I do this, or it's because of this." I nodded.

"I know, but we do know that the darkness of the curse played a factor."

"It did, but it's not an excuse. I love him, and I am there for him, but you need to stop justifying it. Think only about your feelings. Also... if Damon were to mark you, that mark could be removed."

My eyes widened in shock as I stared up at him. Remove the mark...

"I know that removing it won't undo the damage it has done mentally, but it can at least get it off you."

I looked down. Right then, I didn't know what I wanted. Although I knew that I would eventually come to terms with it, I wasn't sure what I wanted, but I had already planned to let Damon go... I wasn't going to use him to remove the mark. Right then, I felt like I didn't want anyone... I didn't want a man. I didn't need one...

"I'll keep that in mind," I said quietly.

I stared at the sky. Live for me... but to do that, I needed to get rid of the baggage from my life. All of it.

Alpha.

Raven? Uncle El replied.

I want Dad's trial to be soon. I know it's been delayed, but let's not postpone it anymore.

Are you sure you're ready?

I want to put this all behind me. I need this, I said quietly.

Very well. Your father's will be tomorrow, and Liam's, we will set it for two days after Haru's. I knew Liam would eventually be trialled, too... but so soon?

Okay, I said, quietly cutting the link.

I knew what I wanted to do before then, what I needed to do.

Visit Liam.

His Sins

RAVEN

*Q*UICKLY, I SWITCHED ROUTES, heading towards the pack headquarters before I changed my mind. I stopped at the entrance and looked at the guards.

"I wish to speak to Liam," I said quietly, not missing the way they looked at my mark. My stomach churned, and I realised that what someone wore with pride had become something awful for me. Something to be leered and gawked at like a spectacle in a zoo. I moved my hair forward, covering it.

They opened the door, allowing me inside. Another guard escorted me through the halls, unlocking the next door and leading me to the cells. My heart thudded when we slowed down.

"Do you wish to talk from outside, miss, or inside?"

I don't know...

"Outside is fine," I said quietly, my stomach twisting.

I can't do this... I can't...

Breathe...

I stopped when I saw him sitting in one of the cells on the bed. His eyes were closed, his back against the wall. He looked as handsome as ever, dressed in a plain white tee and grey sweatpants. His hair was falling in his eyes, and my chest squeezed. The memory of him biting into my neck sent a shudder down my spine. Was it the sane Liam or the dark Liam sitting there?

As if sensing me watching him, his eyes snapped open, and I stared at him, my heart racing. I balled my fists in an attempt to stop shaking.

I waited as the guards opened up a small narrow square window in the impenetrable glass walls of the room. I could hear his heart thundering through the opening. His eyes locked with mine, and I realised I felt scared, sick, tense, broken, and anguished.

The very realisation made me step back. I saw the guilt in his eyes before he looked away.

I came here. But what am I here to say? I couldn't do it... I thought I could...I...

He stood up and walked over to the window. His eyes, which were filled with a thousand emotions, met mine.

"I..." I couldn't speak.

"Nothing I say can undo what I did, what I let my anger do. I shouldn't have lost it... but I did, and look at the consequences," he said quietly.

Not once did his gaze go to my neck, and through the bond, I could feel his anguish and his pain. I knew that dark Liam was in there... ready to take over at any moment.

With sudden clarity, I realised what I needed to do. Even if it hurt him a little, I needed to tell him the truth. My heart skipped a beat, and I looked at him, needing to get my thoughts out there.

"A woman wears the mark of her mate with pride and happiness. We want the world to know we are claimed and happy... I have dreamt of you marking me countless times... but never had I ever thought it would be like this," I said quietly, trying to control the sadness in my voice. It hurt telling him that, knowing that right then, it wasn't the dark Liam I was talking to but the Liam who held no account of what he did. It didn't make this pain go away, though.

"I didn't either. I can't use the curse as an excuse... that's like saying I got drunk and assaulted someone but since I don't remember... I'm not at fault."

I get that. This wasn't just going to go away. It was going to take time.

"I let my anger and jealousy take over and jumped to assumptions the moment I saw that picture," Liam said quietly. Picture?

"What picture?"

"It doesn't matter, it was just something that was posted under my door. I don't deserve you, and I can't take back what I have done... but I can set you free."

"What are you -"

"I, Liam Westwood, reje-"

"Stop it!" I shouted, my eyes blazing in anger and pain as I felt the pull at my chest. How could he? He closed his eyes, and all I felt was his agony, his fists trembling slightly.

"Raven, it's for-"

"I said stop!" How dare he! "Don't make my decisions for me! Just... let me do what I want!" I shouted angrily. He frowned.

"You are better off without me," he said quietly. "What I did was unforgivable. If we reject one another, it's for the best."

"I'll reject you when I want to!" That was my decision to make, not his.

Yes, I'm hurting. Yes, I'm angry. Yes, I'm broken, but I still love him. Although I didn't know what the future held... I would do things for my happiness... and make my decisions for myself. I would also break his curse, not for my mate, but for one of my best friends. The Liam from my childhood.

"Open the door," I said to the guard.

He hesitated, but I didn't care, glaring at him until he obliged. I stepped inside, and he shut it, watching us apprehensively.

"I know you have been jealous and angry at the entire situation, but Damon and I weren't sneaking around that day. We were about to reject one another," I said quietly. His eyes widened in shock as he stared at me as if seeing me for the first time. The realisation of the truth sinking in was followed by a look of pure regret. "Yeah..." I turned away. I could tell from just looking at him that he would always regret those actions of his, and the guilt would always remain.

"I am sorry... although it can do nothing to help the pain I've put you through," he added quietly. I could hear him trying to stay strong, to make his voice sound emotionless, but I could hear it. Feel it...

I stared ahead, my heart squeezing painfully.

"Maybe someday I'll be able to accept it, and I know that I'll forgive you for it, but forgiveness and forgetting something are two different things." A part of me was telling me to stop, that I was hurting him, but I also knew I needed to do this for me, to share what I was feeling. "I love you, Liam, and as your friend... I'll be here for you, and we will work on this curse."

But more than that... I didn't know... I really didn't know. What I did know was that I needed to heal myself first. I needed to stop just tolerating and living with whatever I was given. I realised I wouldn't be able to make anyone else happy if I, myself, wasn't happy.

I looked back at him, at the man I loved. My chest squeezed painfully. I needed to stop thinking of him as the young Liam and see him for who he was, to see the goodness in him then and acknowledge his faults, too. Only then could I really make any kind of decision.

He didn't speak. I walked out of the cell, each footstep echoing in my ears, the sound of our beating hearts and breathing loud in my ear.

We could have done things differently… I could have been firmer. I should never have strung Damon along when I was only hurting him. I knew deep down that he was only getting hurt, and in the process, it only pushed Liam further.

I needed to stop behaving like a child and face every obstacle in life, no matter how painful they were. I needed to, for me.

༄❀࿐

I ended up asking Taylor if he was free, and the both of us left the pack grounds with him deciding we needed drinks. I actually agreed. I thought it would be a nice break away from everything.

There we were on our… I was not sure what number bottle, and with plenty more to come. It was too early to find a club, so we had gone to a pub, and I knew a few of the people there were quite surprised that we were still sane after all that alcohol.

"… So, I gave Sparks back to him," I finished, resting my cheek on my hand.

"Ah, baby girl, he is going to be happy. That's created with so much love from his sister!" Taylor said, downing another glass. I thought we were both done for the day. The sun was setting too… *How long have we been here?*

"Yeah, and then, Nina saw me and told me I had this in control and comforted me… I wonder whom she's lost there," I said sadly.

"Nina the Omega? That's weird. She doesn't have anyone there," Taylor mused, scrunching his nose thoughtfully.

"Really? Well, then, I'm surprised that she takes such good care of it."

"It's maybe assigned to her." Taylor shrugged, picking up an empty bottle.

"That's empty," I said with a small smile.

"I can't drive... there are three of you right now..." Taylor grumbled, pouting cutely.

"I'll tell someone to come to get us... shall I call Zack?" I teased. He blushed, his already flushed cheeks darkening.

"Call my sexy man..." He nodded. I smiled, mind-linking him, hoping we were still in range...

Twenty minutes later, we were in Taylor's car, with Zack and Taylor in the front, and I was staring up at the dark sky from the back, my mind pondering over Nina. I always saw her there. Surely there must be a reason... by any chance, did she have a child that passed away? She was an Omega — getting pregnant by a pack member wasn't unheard of. My stomach twisted. Was it maybe a mated werewolf, or was there something more to it?

I knew I was just coming out with assumptions, but I promised myself that the next time I saw her, I'd ask her. Maybe she was hurting in silence...

❧❧

Dad's trial.

The meeting hall in the packhouse was full. The Alphas, the Beta, and Delta were there, along with many other adult pack members who wanted to sit in.

Uncle El was seated at the table on the dais alongside Aunty Red, Damon, and Zack. As for Haru Jacobs... well, he was cuffed as he was placed in a seat, two guards flanking him. He was a lot thinner and looked like an empty shell. Losing Mom had indeed taken its toll on him. He didn't even bother looking at me, staring blankly at the ground as if he had already given up on life.

I was seated in the front row with Taylor next to me. Uncle El had just told everyone why we were there and listed Dad's crimes, from physical abuse, neglect, emotional abuse, manipulative behaviour, lying, and breaking every law that the pack stood for. I knew for many, it was hard to believe that the respectable Haru Jacobs could have committed such crimes.

"I have already heard evidence from a few others who have seen his behaviour and have seen him lose his temper with her. He also confessed this in the presence of the previous Alpha and Beta Damon. Without wasting further time, I will run a few questions past his daughter, the victim of his abuse, to affirm the facts. Both will be under Alpha command to attest the truth and only the truth." No one could argue with that as I stood up, and Uncle El looked down at me.

"Under my command, I expect you to speak nothing but the truth and not abstain or hold back anything." His command rolled over me, but unlike before, the power of his Alpha command wasn't as strong... was it because I held Liam's mark?

"I understand," I said. This was the start of my resolution to be whom I wanted to be, for me and no one else. "From as far back as I can remember, I was always told that I was useless, stupid, worthless, unwanted, and that I was the worst thing that could have happened to my parents. No matter what I did, I was put down, told that I was not good enough and that maybe it would be for the best that I died somehow. Growing up, I became so used to him getting abusive that I began to just deal with it... trying not to upset anyone. I just wanted to ride it out, and I became... numb to it. So familiar that it had become normal."

I was still doing that with everything, and I wanted that to change.

"I always did things wanting to make them proud, but I was never enough. Even when I became the head warrior, and I returned, I was told that I'm trash..." I took a shuddering breath and continued,

"Aside from the mental abuse, he'd hit me sometimes. Never enough to cause permanent damage, but a push or a thump. One time, he grabbed my hair and pushed me into the wall when I was thirteen. I broke my nose, but Mom just snapped it into place and told me to clean it up..." I felt a flare of anger, and I didn't need to look up to know whose anger it was. Aunty Red. "It was more emotional abuse than physical. Mom, she'd let it happen and just watch it."

"How can you talk ill of Kimberly when she's in her grave?" A woman behind me muttered.

"Silence!" Uncle El growled.

"She's stating facts, and it's mindsets like yours that make people think that behaviour is normal! Kim let this happen when she shouldn't have!" Aunty Red growled, glaring at the woman who had dared to speak. "I will deal with you afterwards."

"Yes... Luna..."

Uncle El nodded at me, and I slowly sat down before Dad was placed under Alpha command.

Do you want to wait outside whilst we question him? He mind-linked me.

No, I'm okay, I said. I would face this. I needed closure. He nodded curtly before asking Dad to attest to his sins.

"She's the reason my son isn't here... she shouldn't have been here..."

His voice was flat, as if he had no will to live. His eyes stared blankly at the ground. He carried on, repeating everything I had said. Each sentence that left his lips became more and more hateful. I could sense the anger, shock, and irritation from those in the room at his words, and I realised that if I had spoken out when I was younger, there would have been far more people on my side than I ever could have imagined. Taylor gave my shoulders a squeeze, and I felt a little comfort in him.

"Now that we have heard from both and we can all agree that he is guilty... it is time to hand out his punishment," Uncle El said.

"He should be thrown out of the pack!"

"Lash him and keep him locked up."

"Silence," Uncle El said loudly, and the room went quiet. "For his crimes, Haru Jacobs will get one hundred and fifty lashes with a silver whip... I would have him banished, however, that would only result in him turning feral due to the loss of his mate, and he may harm others. He will remain in this pack, stripped of his rank and, due to his deteriorating health... he will be placed under house arrest at his home rather than kept at the prison, but I will ultimately let Raven decide. If you want him in the cells, we can do that too."

"It's befitting. He can stay in his house," I said quietly. I never wanted to see that man again, to the end of his life... He can be alone... "I have one request," I said suddenly, swallowing hard as I stared at the man before me.

"Of course," Uncle El said.

"He is not to visit the grave of my brother Renji Jacobs. Ever," I said icily, my chest heaving as some light seemed to return to my father's eyes.

"What... no... no! I can! Don't you go there!"

"I will go there as much as I want. This is the last time I will ever see you. Goodbye." I stood up and turned away.

"Your request is accepted. He will be kept under house arrest anyway, and that means at all times, until his passing."

"Thank you," I said, not turning back to the man who was shouting at me and walking out towards the door. That first burden was lifted…

I felt like I was getting somewhere… *I've got this.* I felt my wolf stir, and I smiled gently. *No, we've got this…*

From the Heart

DAMON

*R*AVEN'S FATHER WAS COMMITTED, and although I knew the Alpha had set his punishment, I still wanted to tell Liam about it.

I was angry at him. So fucking mad at what he did. But past his split personality, there was that part of him that I knew. I wouldn't be able to forgive him easily... if ever. I didn't know if I could ever call him a friend again, either. Looking back, I thought that ended a few years ago. Maybe I was just stuck in a fucking illusion that things would work out. It did fucking hurt... but life was shit like that.

I entered the cells and, after unlocking the door, entered his cell. He was sitting there with his eyes closed. His hair, which he always had gelled and styled, was lying messily over his forehead. His eyes opened and met mine. They looked... broken.

I knew he'd feel it, but maybe this was the punch he needed to realise that he could be in fucking control. He needed to take control of his own shit. Neither of us spoke for a while, and Liam looked away first.

"What do you want?" He asked quietly.

"Raven's father was trialled today. He's been given one hundred and fifty silver lashes. He'll then be placed under house arrest and stripped of any rank or status he has. I thought, despite everything, you might want to know...." I said, clenching my jaw.

"Thanks..." he replied. Gone was the cold arrogance that had surrounded him since his return. All I saw was his emptiness. "Who will deliver the punishment?" He asked quietly.

"I thought I'd ask Alpha Elijah if I could," I answered. He nodded with the tiniest of smiles that didn't reach his eyes crossing his lips.

"Will you also deliver mine?" He asked, looking up at me. There was an emotion in his eyes that I couldn't read that unnerved me. My heart thumped, and I stepped back, narrowing my eyes.

"What?"

"My trial is in two days. I don't want Dad to suffer. What I did... I've caused him even more pain. My punishment won't be small, and it shouldn't be... but I don't want Dad to do it. You can tell her it was my wish that you do it."

"Don't want me to look like the bad guy?" I asked, unable to hide the bitterness from my voice.

"No, because you're all she has now..." he said. "What I did deserves capital punishment, and I expect no less, so... be there for her." I sighed heavily. He wasn't making it easier to hate him.

"I never wanted you to step aside. I was willing to make it work, all three of us. Raven is loving; she would have been able to treat us both well."

"That won't happen because I always believed that it's one-to -ne. There's no space for a third. There's no point in discussing it... I no longer deserve her, not after what I did," he said. "So, good luck."

"You're giving up because of what you did... but you still love her," I said quietly, hating that I couldn't just hate him fully even if I'd not forgiven him.

"I do, more than anything, but what I did was unforgivable, and it's a little fucking late. When we love someone... we do what's best for them," he said, running his hand down his face and massaging his jaw. His beard had grown, too.

"Yeah, we do," I said quietly.

"I just kept her stuck in the middle... in this constant tug of war. Not anymore." Our eyes met, and I nodded. "I heard from her that you two were going to reject one another..." he said quietly.

"Yeah... I realised that you would never accept it working between us, and she was hurting. You ruined it all." He nodded, staring down at his hands.

"Thanks... for telling me about the trial."

I nodded, looking at him. Something told me that with this clarity... maybe, just maybe, it was the push Liam needed to defeat the darkness inside of him. I turned away and paused. I needed to speak my thoughts, so I glanced back at him.

"Nothing is over until you let it be. There's goodness in you, Liam. Find it… embrace it and let go of all the negative crap," I said quietly.

We will always be here for you, to help you through it, I added through the link. **No matter how fucking hard it is or how angry we are at you.**

Our eyes met for a moment before I turned and left the cell…

⸎

RAVEN

Dad's punishment was carried out the following day in the cells at the hands of Damon, followed by being bandaged and returned to his home, where he would be kept under complete watch. From what I heard, he wouldn't last longer than a few months at most. Was it wrong that I didn't really care? There were some people who hurt you, but you could still love them, but Dad… there was no space for that when I felt nothing but bitterness towards him.

I returned to training, and it seemed that everyone had been warned to behave. Either that or the truth about Dad had made a few people feel guilty. Owen still acted like a prick, but that was his nature, and it wouldn't ever change.

After training, I showered, got dressed, and spent the afternoon pondering over everything. What I needed to do and what I wanted. I had taken the photographs of Robyn and Damon and headed out to his place in the late afternoon. I rang the doorbell, and he opened soon after, looking as handsome as ever. I would always appreciate him, but I didn't know what the goddess wanted. It was a mess.

"Hey," he said, pulling me tightly into his arms. I hugged him back, the tingles of sparks reminding me of our mate bond, but in life, there were a lot of bonds aside from the mate bond…

"Hey, how are you? Was the lashing okay? I didn't realise you would have to do it," I said quietly.

"I wanted to," he said, closing the door behind me.

"Ah… I see… Damon, I visited Liam the other day, and he mentioned that he received a picture of us kissing…." I said, taking a seat on the couch as I took out the envelope I had received, too. "That's what triggered him off before he came to find us…" The image of him marking me flashed through my mind, and that familiar squeeze in my chest returned. Our happy moments, sad moments, and painful memories all flashed before me.

"A picture of us kissing… I received something similar," Damon said, frowning.

Turning on his heels, he suddenly left the room before I could continue, and I heard him run up the stairs. My brows furrowed as I stared down at my envelope. Had we all received something similar? Oh, how I wished I had mentioned this sooner. Damon returned, holding an envelope, seeming to hesitate before he held it out to me.

"I got pictures, too," I said softly, holding out the envelope of him and Robyn.

We took each other's envelopes, and I slid the pictures out, my cheeks burning as I realised what it was. Shit! I quickly pushed the images back in. The day Liam went down on me outside the Alphas' home! I looked up at Damon, who looked utterly guilty as he looked down at his own pictures and pushed them back in, running his fingers through his curls.

"I'm sorry you had to see these… I, uh… guess it's good that Liam only got a kissing picture…."

"Yeah…" I said, shoving my pictures into my bag. A tense silence followed before he spoke,

"Someone's trying to cause issues…"

"Owen?" I suggested, frowning. There was no one else who hated me as much as he did.

"I don't know… maybe. It could be him. He is a piece of shit. Well, now that we know, we'll work on figuring it out."

"Yeah."

We both fell silent, and I realised that, somehow, things really had changed.

"I went to see Liam, too," Damon said quietly, making me look up at him sharply. "He wants me to deliver his punishment." My heart thudded, and I looked at him.

"Would you be able to?" He smiled sadly.

"He doesn't want Uncle El to do it, knowing it'll be hard for him. At the time, I didn't think of it, but… I think he knows how angry I am at him, too, and this is probably the only way I can vent my anger. He is my Alpha and there's not really a chance where I can vent my anger, so this is… it." He frowned as if he had just realised what he had said and closed his eyes.

I looked down, my chest squeezing. Yeah, that sounded like Liam…

"His punishment won't be light, will it?"

"No," Damon said quietly. I nodded. I thought as much. I turned to him.

"Thank you for being an amazing friend and mate," I said softly, reaching out and taking his hand in mine, my heart pounding in my chest at what I was about to do. He smiled, a glimmer of sadness in his eyes. We both knew he knew what was coming. "You're no one's second choice, and I won't treat you as such. I love you, and I always will. We will remain friends. We haven't done anything that could make it awkward," I joked. Damon nodded.

"I saw it coming. You… you've seemed different over the last few days. Smiling less, more lost in thought… but you seem to be… content." He brushed his fingers over my knuckles, sending a ripple of sparks through me.

"I seem to have gotten some clarity. How can I love anyone when I don't even love myself?" I said quietly. "When I'm so concerned about others' opinions and emotions? Since the start, I've felt like this thing, caged between the two of you, feeling guilty, torn, and upset. A king once told me that I need to stop trying to accept things, to think deeply about what I want - I want to be happy."

He smiled warmly, and there was no sadness in his eyes this time, just a look of understanding and pride.

"I'm proud of you, and I love you. I always will, and I'm still holding you to that chilling time as friends." I nodded vigorously, my hair falling in my eyes.

"Of course, you should!" I said.

The glow of the setting sun warmed the room, gracing his skin beautifully, only enhancing the handsome man before me.

A man who was selfless and loving.

A smile that was completely genuine crossed my lips. This time, there was no doubt or what-ifs. I knew what I was doing and why. For my happiness and for his.

I raised his hands to my lips and placed a gentle kiss on each hand.

"I, Raven Jacobs, reject you, my amazing friend, Damon Nicholson, as my mate," I said softly, holding his hands to my chest.

But I will always cherish you as a friend.

"I, Damon Nicholson, accept your rejection."

I will always love you.

We closed our eyes, feeling that painful pull that ripped through our chests. Our hands were still combined. I couldn't breathe for a few moments from the pain that jarred my body as I felt something snap and that emptiness settle somewhere deep inside. Yes, it was painful, but once it was done, I felt better.

We opened our eyes slowly, gazing into each other's, my eyes sparkling with so many emotions. Then, under that setting sun, we smiled at one another...

Redemption

RAVEN

WO DAYS HAD PASSED since the night of the rejection. I had spent it sitting next to Damon, refusing to leave him, because even if he was smiling, I knew he was hurting. We put a movie on, although I knew neither of us was watching it as we had soon fallen asleep on the sofa. I knew that it would take him time because he had held out hope. Somewhere along the line, I had given up, knowing that it wouldn't work, but he had held on.

I hoped somewhere in the future, we could look back and smile at this entire situation. Someday, one day.

It was the day of Liam's trial. It terrified me to know that that night he would be punished. He was the future Alpha of the pack, and although right then it felt like there was no hope, I was confident he would get there one day.

As for the curse, it was clear Liam, himself, had to do something to end it, but what? Even I didn't know. All we knew was that the answer lies within.

Moreover, the killer was still out there. The pack was still working on it, but since Liam had been the one leading it, they were set back. With him gone, they had to check over things he had already done, although from what Damon told me, they were in contact with him to help where he could. He was even reviewing files in his cell.

He had told me that Liam had ordered them to do a thorough check on the tracker and stealth wolves who had the ability to hide their heartbeats. As for no scent, sprays to hide them could easily be made or retrieved from the pack supplies, which were also checked, but none seemed to be unaccounted for. So, either someone was making their own or getting them from somewhere else. Since I hadn't felt anyone creep up behind me the night my mom was killed, we felt that a tracker wolf would be higher up on the list of suspects with a chance of being the killer.

I was in the hall, seated at the front once again. I wore a high-neck top, not wanting all eyes on my mark. Everyone was seated just as they had that day, but the room was far more uneasy, and there were more pack members than there had been for Dad's trial.

The doors opened, and Liam was brought in. His scent wafted into my nose, and I closed my eyes, trying to control my emotions. I watched him walk through the centre. Unlike Dad, who had had two guards holding him, Liam led the way. Despite his being stripped of rank, he was clearly still an Alpha. His eyes were trained ahead, and he took the seat that was awaiting him. The guards cuffed him to the chair just as Dad had been before stepping away.

Uncle El stood up, his face emotionless, a frown furrowing his brow. I felt dreadful that indirectly because of Liam's and my situation, they were going through this. No, because of this stupid curse, too.

"As you all know, we are here today to hold Liam Westwood accountable for the crime he has committed… one that deserves capital punishment for marking Raven Jacobs against her will and almost killing her in the process." Uncle El's eyes flashed dark cobalt and my gaze shifted to Liam.

The room remained quiet. I knew everyone was unsure of what to make of it. My heart was squeezing as I looked at him. He simply nodded slowly, his face emotionless despite his eyes clouded with emotions. What were we?

"Liam, do you have anything to say?" Uncle El asked. Aunty Red was frowning, the sadness in her eyes clear. Liam raised his eyes, staring ahead with those cerulean orbs of his, full of emotion.

"I allowed my anger to get the better of me and, in the process… committed a terrible crime. I don't deserve any leniency, and I don't think any punishment can make up for what I did," he said clearly. Uncle El nodded.

"I've thought long and hard. Considering you are an Alpha… you are meant to be an example to this pack. An Alpha is meant to be what he wants his people to be, a role model for the youth of his pack. If the Alpha commits a crime, it is far worse. With this title comes great responsibility, one we must always uphold. As your Alpha, I sentence you to five hundred lashes with silver in public."

My eyes flew open in shock. Five hundred? That was worse than Dad's! And in public? Why humiliate him? I looked at Uncle El, not missing the way his fist trembled by his side or the way Aunty Red gripped his arm. It was hurting them, too... yet they were doing the right thing for the pack.

A whisper of shock went through the room, and from the snippets I could hear, I knew people were shocked that the Alpha was subjecting his own son to something like that. But Alpha Elijah was always known for his fairness and equality.

"You will remain under house arrest at our home for the next six months. As for becoming Alpha... if the title is meant to be yours, then it shall be if and when the pack deems you worthy of it. Raven... do you want to add anything?"

"Yes." I stood up. For my happiness and what I felt was right... "I don't like the punishment," I said.

"It's befitting," Liam said, glancing at me. My heart skipped a beat, and I shook my head.

No, it wasn't. It wasn't just an external factor. Yes, marking someone against their will was bad, but was everyone forgetting the curse, too? Yes, he got angry, but the darkness was still there.

"Let him at least walk around the pack and carry on as usual. The killer is still out there, and Liam is needed on that case. No, he doesn't need to have his Alpha title, but the pack needs him rather than keeping him inside where he can't be of any use," I said, looking at Uncle El. He frowned, pondering over my words.

"Very well. He will be allowed to take his place amongst the pack. However... due to his... temper, he will be on wolfsbane until it's under control. He will, however, reside in the Alpha home," Uncle El continued. I knew he meant the curse.

That was better, Liam needed support, and I knew they said the Alphas' home so he wouldn't be completely alone. It was still better, but he needed more than just two people there for him.

"If that -"

"The lashes. I want the punishment lessened," I said quietly, my heart thumping. I wasn't stupid, I wasn't going to let my emotions take over completely, but I didn't like it.

"I can't do that," Uncle El said quietly. "I'm bending the rules -"

"I know what he did was wrong. I know that I could have died. I also know of every factor that contributed to it; mistakes were made, and although it will take me time, I don't hate him. I'm angry at what happened, hurt, too, but as the one whom it happened to, I have a right to -"

"I also have a right to this. This punishment won't take away what I did, but I'll feel a little better," Liam said quietly.

Liam, don't do this, I pleaded through the link.

I fucked up big time, Raven. I can't ever forgive myself.

You want to know how you can make up for this? I asked, my heart pounding in time with his as we stared at each other from five metres apart.

There's nothing that can change the past.

I know, but if you want to do something for me, then do something that will actually make me happy, I said. I knew people could tell we were mind-linking.

Anything, he said quietly.

Fight this curse, fix the bonds you have destroyed, and let's make things right, Liam. I love you, but giving up and just accepting things, that's not the way to go. I want to see the true Liam shine through. I believe only then can we get rid of this darkness. Let's do it together.

Our eyes were locked. I wished he'd understand. His brows furrowed, and I knew he was thinking about what I said.

I understand, and I will do all that, but... for me... let me have this punishment, bitesize, he said, his eyes full of pain as he looked back up at me. Goddess.... My heart clenched, and I realised he needed it, too. **The people need to see this too. What I did was fucking messed up. Not only did I mark you, I fucking ripped your throat out.** I looked down before nodding and slowly sat down.

"If that's decided... tonight at seven pm, Liam Westwood will get his lashings," Uncle El said before dismissing the trial. I sighed heavily as everyone began leaving. Aunty Red came over to me, wrapping her arms around me tightly.

"He is a Westwood. He has the strength to take his punishment," she said softly. I nodded, wrapping my arms around her tightly.

I knew that, but it didn't mean I liked it. It wasn't only going to be hard for me but for his family, too. I watched him being taken away, staring at his back, my heart clenching in pain.

Seven o'clock couldn't have come sooner. My nerves were a mess. I was advised not to go see him receive his punishment, but I wasn't able to avoid it.

The bond wasn't completed because, as I was a werewolf as well, his mark alone didn't complete it; I would need to mark him, too, to complete our bond. That meant I wouldn't be able to feel the pain of his lashings, only his emotions and a sense of unease, but that was already happening. I was a restless mess with each passing moment.

I entered the lower hall, which I hadn't really been in before. I knew Dad's lashing had occurred in the cells. I looked around. It was like one of those illegal underground arenas, cold, gloomy, and with that deep sense of foreboding.

Damon was nodding at something Uncle El was saying, his gloved hand around a silver chain. Liam wasn't there yet. Uncle El patted his shoulder before giving me a nod and walking away. Aunty Red wasn't there, but as Alpha, Uncle El had to be. I walked over to Damon, knowing that it wasn't easy for him either.

"Hey…" I said. He looked up, surprised to see me, before placing the whip down. I hugged him tightly, and he hugged me back.

"Hey, why did you come?" He asked quietly.

"Moral support? I actually have no idea… I just… I need to be here," I whispered. He frowned and nodded. "And how are you feeling?" I looked around. It was so dark and dreary in there. I noticed Robyn, Zack, Taylor, and even Owen were there. That bastard…

"Okay, I guess," he replied quietly. No, he wasn't.

"You got this." I said, "Just don't think."

He nodded just as Liam's familiar scent hit my nose. I turned to see him being taken to the centre, my stomach twisting as they hooked his wrists to the chains that dangled from the ceiling – chains that would keep him upright even when his body could no longer take it.

The sound of heels echoing on the stone floor made me turn, and I saw Aunty Red enter. She looked around, her heart thudding as she broke into a quick run, rushing over to Liam, who was already chained up.

"Mom?" He sounded surprised. I could only see his chiselled back towards me as his shirt had been removed.

"Liam," she said, cupping his face as she pressed her forehead to his.

"I'm fine. This is nothing," he said quietly.

Everyone fell silent, and I knew this was hard for Aunty Red. She had been through so much, and what happened had brought back her own traumatic experience. They switched to mind-linking. Aunty Red nodded and placed a kiss on his forehead, although he had to bend his head for her to reach. She stepped back, taking a deep breath, and walked over to me. I smiled gently as she came over and hugged me tightly.

"I'd stay... but I can't see this. I'm sorry," she whispered.

I nodded. I understood. She turned and walked away, casting a final glance at Liam and Uncle El before she did.

Damon walked forward, and any murmurs that occurred died down. My heart was thumping with every step Damon took. His hand twisted around the whip. Uncle El sat down next to me.

"Why are you here?"

"I... I wanted to be..."

"People only come when they want the victim to be punished. You won't be able to do anything," he said quietly, making my heart thud. I dared not look at him.

"I... I wanted to... just..." I mumbled.

I knew deep down I was scared of what was happening, and I wanted to make sure things didn't go too far... but... I looked at the man next to me, not Uncle El but the Alpha of this pack, an Alpha who needed to uphold the laws...

He didn't say anything, holding out his hand. I looked down at it and placed my own in his. He gave it a gentle squeeze as we looked ahead.

A Punishment

RAVEN

*D*AMON RAISED THE WHIP. I flinched when it struck Liam's back. He didn't even move. Another followed. Each lash made my heart squeeze.

For his mistake… it's for his mistake…

I had to tell myself that, my heart thundering as each lash struck him, slicing through his skin and letting the blood drip to the ground. Not once did he even flinch, despite his breathing becoming harder. Each lash was biting into me, the pain of watching him face this…

Thirty…

"Raven…" Uncle El said, and I realised I was shaking. My heart was beating far too fast. "Step outside."

"No," I said as I saw Taylor coming over. No doubt Uncle El had mind-linked him. "I'm staying." I stared at Liam as Damon continued.

The emotionless mask on Damon's face was gone, pain and conflict on his face, too, as he frowned deeply, continuing the punishment.

"That's enough now," I said suddenly, flinching as the silver cut into Liam's back that was a mess of lashes, torn skin, and blood.

"Raven. I told you you can't change this," Uncle El said softly.

"No, I can because he marked me. I have the right to," I said, standing up. I saw Damon glance towards us, but he continued his dealing.

Each lash felt like I was the one being cut open. My heart was screaming in pain. The fear and anguish inside of me were messing me up. He made a terrifying mistake, and one that would take time to heal, but let him have the chance to redeem himself! Not do something so painful as this!

"Take her outside," Uncle El said quietly to Taylor and Zack, "Your emotions are clouding your judgement, Raven."

No, no... I love him...

Taylor wrapped his arm around my shoulders, leading me firmly towards the exit.

No!

I stared at Liam's mutilated back, his shoulders heaving and his head hanging, yet not once did a sound escape him.

I'm fine, Raven. Please leave, his voice came through the link. No matter how much he tried to hide it... I could hear it. My eyes stung with tears as I shook my head at his back.

How could I turn my back on him? The darkness inside of him was feeding on all negative emotions; fear, loneliness, and regret were part of that. This was not the right way!

"Fifty," Damon said, breathing hard as he lashed him again.

I couldn't breathe.... My heart was ringing in my ear... the smell of blood...

I spun around in a flash, but Zack was ready. His arm was wrapped around my waist as I struggled against him.

"Stop it!" I cried out. My heart was breaking as if someone was ripping it apart inch by inch.

"Raven, come on. It's compulsory," Zack said quietly.

"Please, stop it! If this is for marking me, I was going to let him mark me anyway!" I sobbed, not caring for once that I was crying out in the open.

Damon hesitated, turning to me. Our eyes met, and I realised his eyes glistened with unshed tears. This was hurting him, too.

"That doesn't make the way he did things right," Zack said quietly.

"I know! And I won't forgive him easily, but brutally whipping him like this? I don't like it! Two wrongs do not make a right!" I shouted. "Alpha Elijah! As the victim, I demand that you let him go!"

"That cannot be done. Take her away," Uncle El said, his eyes flashing.

"Liam!"

I'm fine, love, please go.

"Let go of me!" I shouted as Zack carried me out of the hall and into the corridor.

No. I will do what I feel is right! Twisting in his hold, I rammed my elbow into his face. *Sorry, Taylor.* His grip loosened as he grunted in pain. I took the chance to knock him back and ran back inside.

"I said stop it!" I cried out, running onto the stage and wrapping my arms around Liam from behind. The strong sparks of the bond rushed through me as I tried to shield his back, but I didn't even cover half of it. "Please stop it, this is only hurting me more," I whispered in the room that was completely silent.

"This isn't easy for anyone," Uncle El said softly. "But a punishment is -"

"He's had over fifty lashes. Please, stop!" I shouted. The pain in my chest was growing, my eyes blazing as I stared at the Alpha.

"Raven, I'm fine," Liam said. His voice was hoarse despite trying to sound as normal as possible.

"I'm not okay with this," I said, slowly letting go of him and flinching at how deep the wounds on his back were. "Please… I love him… please stop this…" I joined my hands together in front of my face, unable to stop the tears that streamed down my cheeks as I looked at Uncle El. "Please… I beg you… this is causing me more pain than good." My voice broke as I stared up at our Alpha. He stood there, the conflict clear on his face.

"We make mistakes in life… and some may be unforgivable, but this is between Liam and me, and we will work on it. We also know he has no memory of what he did… he wasn't just fuelled by rage alone," I said quietly. The pain in my chest was overpowering everything. "Give him one chance to redeem himself! If he messes up again, then you can punish him. Please." My hands were shaking as I pressed my joint fingers to my lips, closing my eyes as sobs wracked my body.

I heard the clang of the whip hitting the floor, opening my eyes to see Damon had dropped it. He pulled me into his arms, stroking my back.

"I agree with her, Alpha… I think it's enough," he said quietly. Uncle El sighed heavily.

"Alpha… I'm with Raven and Damon. Liam regrets his actions, and he will prove his worth," Zack said, quietly wiping blood from his nose.

A murmur of agreement passed through the people watching, and I hoped Liam saw that we were not giving up on him. We would defeat the darkness together.

LIAM

"Let him down!"

Her voice made my heart clench, her words ringing in my head. I didn't get how she could even consider forgiving me at a time when I couldn't forgive myself. I had almost killed her...

I was unlocked, and I staggered, holding my stance as I turned to look at her. Tears streamed down her beautiful face as Damon embraced her. How many times would I make her cry? Our eyes met, and she pulled out of Damon's hold as she looked at me, stepping closer. There were still bridges to build between us...

She should have let me receive my punishment...

"Get him cleaned up, and then I expect him at my place after being given a dose of wolfsbane," Dad said, his eyes meeting mine. I looked away, knowing I had disappointed him. I had never wanted to ever cause him pain, but I had...

I turned to Damon. I knew it hadn't been easy on him. The first few lashes had held anger in them, but after that, each one had been hard for him, too.

Raven's words from earlier were still clear in my mind. Fix the bonds I had destroyed. For her and for me. I had a lot of work to do, with myself, Raven, Damon, Mom...

My stomach twisted, and I felt sick. I knew what her father had done and, unknowingly, I had done the same thing. I could only imagine what she was going through.

Everyone was leaving, and I was led into a side room by Zack, who was sporting a bruised nose. I had a feeling it was courtesy of Raven.

"I'm sorry, Taylor," Raven was saying as Damon pushed me down onto the bed. I glanced up at her as she pouted at Taylor, who looked as sad as Raven. "I won't hit him again." Raven pleaded quietly, "Sorry, Zack." I raised an eyebrow, glancing at Zack, who simply nodded.

"It's fucking understandable, but don't fuck the nose up next time," he said.

"There won't be a next time!" Raven promised. "Do you forgive me, Taylor?"

"Since it was for your mate…" he said, giving her a hug.

If I wasn't in so much pain, I would have probably found their exchange a little amusing. There was a lot that Raven did that was just cute… a cuteness I didn't fucking deserve to even witness. I didn't deserve to have her in my life. I looked at my Beta and Delta, not mine anymore… but… they were still there.

"Arms up," Damon said. I held back the hiss of pain as he splashed something on my back.

"That burns," I muttered, making Raven turn to him.

Her face became serious as she came over. Her scent enveloped my senses, and as much as I wished I could just wrap her up in my fucking arms forever… I no longer held hopes for that. I didn't deserve her…

"I'll do it," she said, taking the bandage from Damon, who nodded.

We were halfway done, her fingers often grazing my skin, sending off a rush of pleasure as she wrapped the bandage around me firmly when Damon swore, staring at Zack.

"What is it?" Raven asked, her heart thumping.

"There's been another death," Damon said, frowning. "The body was discovered ten minutes ago."

"Fuck…" I said.

"Who is it?" Raven asked with worry in her eyes.

"One of the elder wolves, Arnold," Zack muttered. The room fell silent as the five of us stared at one another. This needed to end.

"We have to do something… maybe we need to search everyone's houses. The teeth and eyeballs have got to be stored somewhere," Raven said, reaching up and brushing my hair out of my eyes. Our eyes met, and my gaze dipped to her neck, my chest fucking squeezing as I looked at it… half-hidden. She moved away, a flash of pain in her eyes before she turned away.

"I agree… but isn't that what Liam kind of wanted? How do we do that without making the pack restless?" Zack asked.

We all fell into thought. *How do we get the pack homes empty?*

Taylor snapped his fingers.

"We party!" The rest of us frowned at the question, but Raven gasped as if understanding.

"A party for the entire pack… so the homes are empty?" She asked. Taylor nodded, a small smile on his lips.

"Exactly. The Alpha can say it's just due to everything going on, a party for everyone would be good… I mean, I'd say his birthday would be ideal, but we can't delay this until then. When everyone is at the party, those at the top of our list of suspects, well… we search," he explained.

"You're pretty smart., Zack said, wrapping his arms around Taylor's neck, pulling him against him and kissing his forehead. I sure missed a lot.

"You two together?" I asked.

"Mates, actually," Zack said before looking away. "I fucked up, so it took a little time."

"We all mess up at times… we just got to work on it," Taylor said, looking at Zack and then at me. I nodded. Yeah.

"Well then, I think it's time we started planning this party," Damon said, smacking his hands together.

"Can I help search?" I asked quietly.

"Sure," Damon said. "We can use whatever help we can get."

The killer had been on the loose for far too fucking long…

Moments of Pain

RAVEN

THE FOLLOWING DAY, DAMON and I had just arrived at the Westwood's home and were seated in the lounge. I wasn't sure how to feel knowing Liam was going to be there. I had gotten all emotional when he was in pain, but I felt a little embarrassed about my outburst. The fact that I had literally shouted at Uncle El... I needed to apologise for that, too...

I looked at Damon, who was raising his eyebrows questioningly at me.

"I shouted at the Alpha," I whispered. He raised an eyebrow.

"You've teased and played pranks on him all your life. Are you scared now?" He joked quietly as he stroked his mother's hair. She was fast asleep on the sofa when we entered, and neither of us wanted to disturb her.

"I know... but I shouted at him when I knew it wasn't easy for him," I whispered back.

"Well, gorgeous, it's too late to regret it," he said. Our eyes met, both of us realising what he had called me, before he gave a small smile. "I can still call you that, right?"

I nodded. We hadn't told anyone about our rejection, and I knew Damon probably felt the emptiness more than I did.

Uncle El and Aunty Red entered alone, making me wonder where Liam was. How were his wounds? Yesterday, when we were leaving the side room, I had seen the pain on his face as he stood up, even if he was trying not to let it show.

"To what do we owe the pleasure?" Uncle El asked. I saw him exchange looks with Damon and frown. Why did it feel like I was missing something?

"Well, we had a request," Damon said.

"And I wanted to apologise for being rude yesterday," I mumbled. Uncle El raised an eyebrow.

"I was not proud of what you did, but I understood it. We all do shit for our mates."

"I remember Elijah doing the same for me. He stood up to his father for me," Aunty Red said softly. She smiled, but I could tell she was upset.

"What's your request?" Uncle El asked Damon. Damon and I exchanged looks before he began relaying the party idea and plan forward.

"I can't deny that we do need to do something," he said, running his fingers through his hair. "But this goes against my rules."

"If we're caught, I'll take it on me," Damon said quietly.

"I think we need to agree, Elijah, although even I'm not happy with this," Aunty Red said. Her face was pale. I felt awful knowing she was going through a lot because of what happened between Liam and me. Uncle El gave a nod, exhaling sharply.

"Fine, I'll keep everyone at the party and make sure no one leaves. That will give you all a bit of time."

"Perfect. Thank you!" I said. "How's Liam been?" I frowned, hearing Damon's heart skip a beat and the way Uncle El's jaw ticked. What was it?

"He's resting," Aunty Red said quietly. Uncle El pulled her into his arms, kissing her neck softly.

"Can I see him?" I asked, feeling like something wasn't right.

"He's asleep, Raven," Aunty Red replied, giving me a small smile that didn't mask the pain in her eyes.

Yeah, very suspicious. They were hiding something from me. I sat for a while longer. Aunty Monica woke up, so I knew Damon would be stopping for longer, and I excused myself.

I left the Alphas' home through the front door, but rather than return home, I walked around the house looking for a way in. I was glad that the guards were posted a little away, protecting the house from anyone approaching, yet not close enough that I would be spotted climbing through a window. Noticing an open bathroom window on the second floor, I climbed up, swinging myself silently inside. If I said I wanted to see him, I was going to see him...

Slowly taking my boots off so I made no sound, I silently made my way through to the hall and down towards Liam's room.

Liam?

No answer... then again, he was on wolfsbane, so maybe he wouldn't hear me. I frowned.

I turned the door handle, stepping inside before I froze in my tracks. The smell of blood and Liam's scent mixed, hitting me hard. My eyes fell on the bed where Liam lay on his stomach, his eyes closed and his breathing heavy, but it was his bare back that filled me with horror. From his neck down to the band of his sweatpants, his back was a mess of deep, ruthless gashes. Wounds that hadn't been there last night, far more than what was on his back when I had bandaged him up. What....

My heart thundered, my eyes flashing as I stepped into his room. My boots slipped from my grasp onto the carpeted floor as I rushed to the bed, shaking. A thousand thoughts ran through my mind. Did his dad make him take the rest of the punishment? Did Liam ask for it himself? How dare they go behind my back! I said it was enough!

Brushing away my tears of frustration, I covered my mouth. The condition of his back was sickening. They were far too deep... his skin was torn up so horrifically. A thin layer of some sort of balm was covering his back, but... he wasn't healing! I dropped to my knees by his bed, looking at his face.

I shook my head; I knew the answer... he asked for his punishment to be completed because he felt guilty. I placed a hand on his cheek, the sparks rushing through me as his thick lashes fluttered, but his eyes didn't open. I knew that he'd always remember what he did... even in years to come. I leaned over and placed a gentle kiss on his forehead. *When will we stop hurting?* Why was he going to torture himself like this?

Hearing the sound of footsteps, I stood up quickly and slipped my boots on. I went to his window, opened, it and climbed onto the ledge. Before I jumped down, I cast a final look back at the man I loved. I couldn't do anything for him right then. Maybe time would heal all...

I'm sorry.

The following day, I had mind-linked Liam but had reached a blank again. Remembering his injuries, I wished they had at least let him heal first. I had then texted him instead, but he had kept the conversation short, saying he was fine. I promised myself the next time I saw him, I would ask him about those injuries.

Two nights later, I had still been unable to see Liam. I was put to work helping with the party, so I didn't get the time. I knew he was avoiding me, so I didn't push it. Tonight, he'd have to face me.

Uncle El had made it clear we were having a party and that everyone was to join, from the Omegas to the warriors. He had made it clear that no one was to leave the area whilst the party was ongoing for everyone's safety. The only ones who wouldn't be attending were the essential patrol which would change halfway through the party. As expected, many pack members were looking forward to an evening of relaxing and not having to be confined to their homes thanks to the curfew.

I had gotten ready, too, making sure I looked good. For me, sometimes putting a little effort in made me feel better about myself. I had put on a lace bodysuit and cropped leather pants with a black belt with a gold buckle strapped around my waist. I added several delicate gold necklaces, bracelets, and rings. My ears, as usual, had studs in all my piercings. I left it, not wanting to look overly done. My hair was up in a sexy, messy bun. I was wearing six-inch black heels, and my make-up was flawless. I had added black glitter to my usual smoky eye and done a full face, finishing off with deep, matte, wine-coloured lipstick and nails of the same colour.

The party was in full swing. The place was lit up with lanterns hanging from the branches and fairy lights strung around. The long tables were to the left, holding lanterns, dishes, and some clusters of flowers that were placed across them. To the right were some chairs, and drinks were being served and set up behind there. There was a huge dessert table full of mouth-watering goodies, and the pups were all running around. At the back were the huge pots and boxes with the food, which were being put on platters, ready to be served.

Music was blaring loudly, and the mood was surprisingly light. I noticed there were guards posted every two metres; no one would be able to leave without being noticed. I glanced around, trying to find the boys. I was not able to see any of them. Well, we were all to make an appearance first. My eyes went to the two large chocolate fountains that seemed to be calling to me.

"Oo, chocolate!" I whispered, weaving my way through the crowds towards it. "Cake pops…" I reached the table, fitting in nicely with the young boys who were helping themselves to dessert.

"Shouldn't you wait until after your main meal first?" I asked.

"Same to you, midget." One of them frowned at me as I pushed to the front.

Damn, I was sure they were, like, nine or ten, but some were already taller than me… *Thank you, goddess, for six-inch heels.*

"Hey, I'm double your age! Now, behave," I said, stealing a plate and quickly piling it with three cake pops, a stick that I slid some brownies onto, marshmallows, and strawberries, before dunking it into the melted chocolate. The boys complained, but I ignored them. You couldn't come between me and chocolate. I was about to turn away, paused, and picked up a small cheesecake shot before hurrying away, leaving a disapproving group of boys behind. Now, where to eat this before we had to leave?

I spotted a tree not too far off and walked over, biting into my chocolate-covered brownie and sliding it off the stick, licking my lips as I enjoyed it. So yummy… I picked up one of the cake pops and shoved it fully into my mouth.

"Here you are. I told Damon you'd be near the dessert table," Liam's husky voice came, making me freeze, my mouth full of chocolate and the sense of deja vu of the night we found out we were mates returned to me.

I slowly turned and looked at him, remembering his mutilated back. My heart thundered as I looked him over. Black ripped jeans, boots, and a white collar-less button-down shirt with the sleeves rolled up and a few buttons open. My stomach fluttered, and I stared into his cerulean eyes, noticing his hair was perfectly styled. I was glad he felt better, or at least looked better.

I didn't miss how his eyes raked over my body, his eyes flashing their beautiful magnetic deep blue as he swallowed hard. His thudding heart made my core throb, and if the bond was strong before… it was far stronger now. My body was craving him, yet when his gaze fell on my neck, and the familiar flash of guilt filled his eyes, reality came crashing down.

Well, I saw no one… I said through the link, only to reach a blank wall. Oh yeah, wolfsbane. I quickly tried to swallow the cake in my mouth.

"Take your time, little miss glutton."

I frowned as he reached over, taking a cake pop from my plate before I moved my plate out of his reach. I finally managed to swallow my mouthful down and lick my lips.

"That's my cake pop, I fought a pack of boys to get there first!" I complained, picking up the last cake pop before he stole it.

"Yeah… a bunch of pups, I saw," he said, his gaze flickering to my lips.

He stepped closer, raising his finger slowly and placing two fingers under my chin, sending off a rush of sparks that took my breath away. He brushed his thumb along the corner of my bottom lip. My chest heaved, my heart pounding as he slowly moved back, slipping his thumb into his mouth and licking off the fleck of chocolate. Our gaze met. My core throbbed, and I felt blank.

"Shall we go?" He asked softly.

Go?

It took me a moment to realise what he meant. I knew that we were paired due to Liam being on wolfsbane, meaning he didn't have the pack link. I nodded, not missing the few glances we received.

Drama queen… if you wanted him, why make him go through the punishment? One of the younger females asked through the link, jealousy clear in her eyes as I glanced at her.

I frowned, feeling a sting of pain. I didn't even know her by name… but obviously, there would be people hating me for what happened. Ignoring them, I followed Liam, my plate still in my hand. I could make out the outline of bandages faintly through his shirt. I looked down, sighing deeply.

We walked away from the commotion of the party, the music fading a little, yet it was still loud enough to hear. He slowed down, falling into step beside me as I quickly ate my dessert.

"So, we get the packhouse," he said quietly, sliding his hand out of his pocket and holding out the piece of paper which contained a list of door numbers. "The ones marked off are those members fully in the clear."

I nodded, taking the paper from him. We had a lot of rooms to search…

"Shall we split when we get there? There are a lot of rooms to cover. Maybe one of us can start from the bottom and the other from the top, although I doubt it would be an Omega, " I said. Liam shook his head.

"No one gets a pass. Everyone is capable. In fact, Omegas have access to a lot of places with ease," he said quietly as we entered the packhouse, and he slid out a bunch of keys. "The extra keys."

Keys that I knew were not meant to be used.

"Where are those usually kept?" I asked quietly, although we were alone in the very silent packhouse.

"Dad's house, in a safe."

"So, no one could have accessed them," I said, closing the front door behind us as we headed up the stairs.

"Let's do a room at a time. It'll be faster," Liam said. "As for the keys, imprints can be made with ease."

"I was telling Damon about the picture you got…" I said. I knew he didn't know about the rejection, and I wasn't planning on telling him.

He frowned. I saw the flash of guilt on his face as he took out two anti-scent sprays, handing me one. Quickly, we sprayed them over ourselves before Liam tried to find the correct key.

"Well, I got pictures of Robyn and him, and he got pictures of us two," I said quietly as he unlocked the first door, and we stepped inside. He looked at me sharply.

"What? When?"

"I got mine when I moved to the packhouse. I think I ordered some stuff for my room and there was a thin flat package…"

"And you never thought to fucking mention that?"

"It was of Damon. I didn't want to make matters worse…" He sighed.

"I get it," he said as we both walked to opposite sides of the rooms and began searching.

I know, I messed up. Not speaking up was the issue from the start.

"Someone who can walk around with ease… mine was posted under the door when I stepped out of the bathroom that day," he said quietly.

"Strange…"

"Yeah, so it's possible it's someone with ease of access to the packhouse."

"Yeah, like someone who lives here…" he said. "Mind-link the others and tell them to come help out here. I don't know, I feel the killer's at this packhouse."

I frowned, quickly linking the others to come as I removed the bottom drawer, checking behind it whilst Liam rolled the rug back, checking the floorboards. With wolfsbane in his system, he was far weaker than normal.

"How's… the darkness?" I asked quietly. He tensed before glancing at me.

"It's there… growing stronger… but I'm trying not to let it get to me," he answered.

"Great."

Fifteen minutes later, we moved to the next room, but I didn't think a three-hour party was going to give us enough time. We wouldn't even cover one floor at this rate. The other three had come; Damon was checking the Omegas rooms on the bottom floor at the back of the packhouse while Zack and Taylor had taken the top floor. We moved on to the next room, not talking much as we worked fast.

"There's less time, isn't there," Liam muttered, unlocking the door to Owen's room. I wrinkled my nose, hit with the sweaty smell of male musk and unwashed gym wear.

"Yeah, let's do what we can, I guess. Goddess, it stinks."

I went over to the drawer and looked around. His room was such a mess, I was sure even if we ripped it apart, he wouldn't notice. I kicked a discarded shirt to the side as I began opening the drawers. Nothing.

I sighed as I watched Liam move the bed slightly. It was a low wooden bed that was stuffed with boxes underneath. I frowned when I saw the slight pink patch on his shirt, realising it was blood.

"Liam, you're straining your injuries!" I said, rushing over. I couldn't smell the blood, but I knew that was due to the anti-scent spray.

"I'm fine."

"You're not. Care to explain why your back was ripped apart again two days ago?"

"I have no idea what you're talking about."

"Liam!" I said, frustrated, and forced him back by his shoulder. He looked up at me from where he was crouching. "Don't lie to me!" He looked down.

"It's nothing."

"Liam... did you ask for your punishment to be completed?"

"It isn't."

"What?" I asked, sitting on the bed as I tried to get better eye contact with him. "Liam, what do you mean?"

"It doesn't matter. I'm just saying I didn't get my full lashings. I haven't."

"Yet you want them?" I asked. My stomach clenched, and I felt sick as I tried to make sense of what he was saying. Suddenly the room felt very small.

"Raven... I need this for me. I can't be let off lightly. I'm fine. Dad's even broken it down. It's not like I'm getting five hundred at once," he said, his hands closing around my upper arms. The sparks of the bond made my heart calm a little, but it wasn't enough.

"I told them to stop, meaning to forget about it!"

"I know, but this isn't that easy, Raven. Why don't you get it? I can't live with myself knowing what I did... please," he said quietly, cupping my face. My chest was heaving as I tried to calm down.

"I told you how to make it up to me," I said softly.

"And I will, but let me do this for me, too. I need it, love," he said quietly, looking down. His eyes flashed as they fell on my breasts before they snapped back up to mine.

I tried to understand what he needed, to make sense of it. In the end, I nodded. If that was what he wanted...

"Thanks for understanding. You look beautiful, by the way..." he said quietly.

"Thanks," I whispered. Our eyes locked, his cerulean ones meeting my unique ones, but the moment didn't last long as he pulled away and began moving around the boxes and rubbish that littered the ground.

"He's a fucking disgusting dickhead," Liam growled in disgust.

My eyes fell on some porn magazines that looked pretty old. I scrunched my nose as I stood up and got down on my knees to look under the bed at the back.

"I'll get the rest of the stuff out. You need to be careful with your back."

He nodded, opening another box as I took out the rest of the stuff from under his bed. I sighed, leaving Liam with the boxes as I went to look in his wardrobe. I had just opened it when Liam swore.

"Fuck." I turned sharply, only to see him staring down at a dark, green-coloured large pouch.

"What is it?" I asked.

He didn't respond, simply spilling the contents to the ground. My eyes widened as I stared at a spoon, a thin sharp knife, pliers, and a jar of what appeared to be very clearly human teeth. I looked at Liam in shock as our eyes met, his blazing a brilliant magnetic blue.

"He's fucking dead," he growled.

Doubts

RAVEN

*A*N HOUR HAD PASSED. Owen had been captured and tossed into the cells. Uncle El was making sure everyone was getting home safely. Right then, we hadn't told anyone we caught the killer because he hadn't admitted to it, although there were rumours going around that someone had been taken in.

My mind flashed to what happened with Liam not long after we had made the discovery and Owen had been brought to the cells, my heart thudding at the memory.

"Liam…"

"I'm going to kill him." His eyes blazed, and I watched the black begin to creep over the whites of his eyes. He had given Owen a few punches for talking back, but he was getting angrier thanks to Owen not knowing when the hell to shut up. Fuck!

"Liam… Liam, calm down," I said quietly, approaching him. The bond is stronger now, please let it help.

Raven, move! *Damon's panicked voice came through the mind link.*

Don't come closer. Trust me, *I said quietly through the link.*

Raven, I swear I'm not going –

Damon, I am begging you, please let me do this!

I knew what I was doing… or I hoped I did. If Liam truly was remorseful… he'd fight it. I was going on complete blind faith, but I wasn't going to give up on him. I gave Damon a small smile, knowing that it was hardest for him when he had witnessed what had happened to me.

I cupped Liam's face, watching his chest heave and his claws coming out. "Fight it… let's do this calmly," I whispered soothingly.

His hands went to my waist, and I knew how panicked the men behind me were. Right then, I was in the grips of dark Liam, and if he wanted, he could rip me to shreds for standing in his way.

"Raven…" His eyes flickered, and his grip tightened, yet I could see the fear make them widen, and his cerulean orbs return as he suddenly let go of me, staggering back as if afraid to hurt me. "Don't come near me."

"Liam, you got this," I promised. I was about to move closer when he turned and rushed out of the cells, the darkness swirling around him.

I'll be okay, *His voice came through the link, and I frowned. It was clear he became extremely powerful when that darkness took over. How else was he able to mind-link?*

"That was… dangerous," Zack murmured as Damon shook his head at me…

I was standing there, arms crossed, watching as Damon and Zack questioned Owen, or should I say tried. Liam had been gone for about twenty minutes. I hoped he was okay.

"What did you do with the eyes?" Zack asked coldly.

There was only one set of teeth in the jar, and there were no eyeballs anywhere. Even when we had searched the entire bedroom, the thought that those might have been Mum's made me sick.

"I'm fucking telling you it's not me!" Owen roared, his eyes blazing with anger.

"Calm the fuck down. We'll ask the questions," Damon growled.

"Let's wait for Liam or Uncle El to ask him under Alpha command," I sighed. Something just felt… off.

"What, enjoying this, bitch?" Owen growled.

"No, now shut the hell up. Things were found in your room, Owen, so obviously, you will be questioned. No one's hurt you or -"

"Liam fucking broke my nose! Bitch! I was fucking thrown in a fucking cell! What more can they fucking do?"

"Keep it the hell down!" Damon growled, slamming his hands on the bar.

"Open the fucking door. I'll put him in his place," Zack growled, his eyes blazing.

"Piss off, you fucking wanker!" Owen swore, giving Zack the finger.

I closed my eyes as Zack snatched the keys from Damon, opening the door. I knew what was going to happen before I even heard the sound of his fist meeting Owen's face.

"Alright, Zack, back it up. We need him conscious for his questioning," Damon said, glaring at the asshole. Owen was just a cockroach, the type you just can't get rid of.

"Bastards!"

"You can stay here for the night. One of the Alphas will question you soon," Damon said as Zack came out of the cell, wiping his bloody hand on his jeans. Owen didn't say anything, clutching his bloody nose.

We exchanged looks as we walked away. He wasn't going to admit it. Asking him under Alpha command was going to be the only way.

"He's so fucking antagonising," Damon growled, pinching the bridge of his nose. I smiled slightly.

"For you to get mad, it takes a lot."

"Yeah, he's a fucking prick," Zack growled, pissed off.

"Okay, maybe we should all just call it a night, although I want to be there when they question him," I said, sighing.

"It's late, but how about we grab some food and wait for Alpha or Liam?" Zack suggested.

Even though both Zack and Taylor were fully clued in on the curse, I appreciated that they didn't make a big deal out of it, carrying on as normal. A true Delta couple. We nodded, walking back towards where the party had taken place not long ago. The Omegas were clearing up, and guards were still stationed around for everyone's safety.

We grabbed some food, despite it being cold, and I piled extra onto mine in case Liam returned. The other two raised an eyebrow at my huge, overloaded plate, but I simply glared at them. That was enough to get them to stop looking at my food. We headed back towards headquarters, eating along the way.

"There they are!" Damon said.

I turned to see Liam walking alongside his father. He was in jeans, a t-shirt, and a jacket. I frowned. Had he shifted, or did he just dirty his clothes somehow? Even though he was on wolfsbane… shifting shouldn't be possible, but he had mind-linked, and I couldn't put anything past the darkness. He looked at me, and my heart skipped a beat, thinking, *He had fought through it…*

I smiled slightly, holding the plate out to him.

"Hungry?"

"Ah, now it makes sense why she got so much food," Damon teased lightly. I glanced at him, and he smiled at me before looking away.

It was going to take time for him to heal and for me to stop feeling guilty, but at least I knew I wasn't stringing him along.

"Actually, that looks about normal for Raven," Uncle El said with a smirk, making me frown.

"Hey! Uncle, that isn't fair! I need to eat to grow!"

"It clearly didn't help," he replied. The two boys chuckled whilst Liam simply smirked slightly. It was definitely payback for answering him back... I knew it!

"Thanks," Liam said, taking a burger from my plate.

We headed inside, and the mood that settled over us dampened. The place was pretty quiet due to the time. I left my plate on the side as we walked towards the cells.

"You put him in the lower cells, huh?" Uncle El said, raising an eyebrow. "Personal issues?"

"Not at all. All criminals go there," Zack said, making the rest of us smirk. Okay, we may have shoved him there because he's an ass, but he was a killer. Right?

I frowned. I didn't know about that. Something felt off. Like we were missing something, but I didn't know what it was. Shaking the feeling off, we walked to the cells.

"Fuck! Open the door!" Uncle El shouted.

My heart skipped a beat as I tried to look past the four giants, my heart thudding, to see Owen on the floor, but what was most worrying was the frothing foam that was coming out of his mouth as he convulsed on the floor. I stepped back in shock as Damon unlocked the door, and both Liam and Uncle El rushed inside to check his pulse.

"Call a doctor!" Uncle El shouted, and I quickly mind-linked any doctors I could reach. What the hell...

"He must have poisoned himself," Damon said, frowning.

"He knew it was over for him." Zack agreed.

"I still needed to hear it..." Uncle El said as Liam frowned.

"Was he carrying poison on him? Check the cameras, Damon, to see if he took something," he said, standing up and assessing the situation.

Damon nodded, rushing off to check, and I stepped aside as two doctors hurried in.

My heart was thundering as I stared ahead. Owen poisoning himself? I didn't know. It didn't seem like something he'd do.

※◎◎※

Owen had been taken to the hospital. Uncle El almost called Kiara, but the doctors said the poison had already affected his organs, and some had stopped functioning entirely. We all knew Kiara's healing had limits, too. If something was gone, she couldn't bring it back. She could only heal wounds, injuries, or diseases. The memory of her healing Al and him not waking up still made my stomach twist. It had been a horrible time for her... I shivered at the thought.

My eyes widened when Liam placed his jacket around my shoulders, making my cheeks flush lightly. I remembered him doing that when we were younger. I wasn't actually cold, but his scent and the warmth were welcoming.

"Liam... did you shift?" I asked quietly. He frowned and nodded, shoving his hands into his pockets.

"I feel more in control in wolf form..."

"That's good. So, even though you're on wolfsbane, you can shift?"

"Yeah. I told Dad about that... I may not be safe walking around."

"I wasn't asking because of that. You controlled it today... I'm proud of you," I said quietly.

"Yeah?"

His eyes met mine. My heart thumped, and I nodded as we stepped into the packhouse. We could hear talking from the pack lounge; no doubt everyone was discussing what had happened. By then, they probably knew Owen was missing, and word had gotten out, it seemed. We walked up the stairs, and Liam glanced around.

"I don't like you here alone, not with everything going on," he murmured. I paused in the process of unlocking my door. Was I not the only one having doubts?

"He's caught, though."

"I don't know, I don't feel at ease about it." He frowned. I smiled slightly.

"Oh? Or is that just an excuse to stay? " I asked before I could stop myself. His eyes flashed, darkening with desire, and my stomach knotted. "I'm kidding…" I said guiltily. *Stupid, Raven, don't tease him!*

"Do you want me to stay?" He asked quietly.

I froze, slipping the jacket off from around my shoulders, my heart thundering. I turned slowly, looking up at him… *Follow your heart, not your mind…*

"Yes," I whispered. He hesitated.

"Do you trust me?" He asked, but I felt the question was, did he trust himself?

"I do," I said quietly.

I didn't need to say more as he stepped inside and shut the door behind him. *Be still,* I told my heart. Suddenly, my room felt far too small.

"I feel like we're missing something, too," I said, trying to lift the sexual tension that had settled between us. Trying to ignore the ache between my legs and focus on reality.

"Me too. The pouch was too… classy for Owen. Keeping teeth? Washing them and then placing them in a jar…. He can't even fucking put his dirty underwear in the wash," Liam said as I heard him lock the door.

"Good point," I agreed as I walked over to my dresser and began removing my jewellery.

Liam walked over to me, and my heart thundered as he reached up and began to remove my necklaces. His fingers brushed my neck, making my breath hitch. He slowly dropped the first necklace onto the dresser.

"And how fucking elusive it's been up to now for us to find evidence, then Owen being poisoned…"

"But no one knew our plan," I whispered breathlessly before swallowing hard and clearing my throat. *Goddess!*

"There are ways we could have been heard… I don't know, I fucking don't know… but I told Dad I don't think it's Owen. He's too fucking dumb." I smiled at that.

"Good point. So are you saying the killer's still out there?"

"I think so, but until Owen wakes up, we won't know for sure. Dad will lift the curfew, but we are still going to investigate everyone," Liam said, placing the third necklace down before he started to remove the pins from my hair.

I looked at him in the mirror, our eyes meeting as he ran his fingers through my hair, letting it down. He brushed it over one shoulder, leaving my mark uncovered as he looked down at it. I saw the flash of guilt in his eyes before he looked back up at me.

"I'm sorry... sorry for this," he said, his fingers brushing over his mark and leaving a whisper of sparks in his wake. He was sorry; I could feel his guilt through the bond before he put his walls up. Taking hold of my shoulders, he turned me to face him. "I can't fucking turn back time... but I promise, for as long as I live, I'll make it up to you."

I wrapped my arms around his neck, my heart pounding as I allowed myself to embrace him. He hesitated before he wrapped his arms around me tightly. Our bodies moulded together as one, and my core throbbed. Although I knew I wasn't ready to go back to how we used to be right then, something told me our understanding and connection would be so much better this time around...

Healing

LIAM

I WRAPPED MY ARMS AROUND her, my hands roaming her back. The feel of her skin through the thin lace of her top sent sparks running through me. Fuck, she felt so good. I throbbed against her, biting back a growl of approval as she leaned into me, her fingers grazing the back of my neck. I nuzzled my nose against her neck, her fresh floral scent clouding my senses as she sighed softly, her lips grazing my earlobe. My eyes flashed, and the urge to kiss her grew stronger, but I couldn't…

"Liam…" she moaned breathlessly, the tantalising scent of her arousal seeping into the air.

Fuck…

I squeezed her ass, kissing her neck sensually. The moment my lips trailed along her collarbones, she whimpered loudly, sighing in pure bliss the moment my lips touched her mark. Extra sensitive.

I'll change it. One day I'll make the memory less painful… somehow.

I wouldn't last long enough. The negative dark thoughts came to the forefront of my mind, and the doubts grew as the darkness tried to push forward.

Not this time.

I kissed her harder, sucking slightly on her slender neck, guilt wracking me at what I had done. I had no right to -

"Hey…" She pulled back suddenly, cupping my face as I looked away from her.

"I'm fine," I said, unable to look her in the eye.

"You're not…" she said softly. Reaching up, she placed a soft kiss on the corner of my lips.

Our eyes met before my gaze fell to her lips. The pull… I was torn. Torn by the animalistic side that wanted to consume her completely, to devour her and fuck her senseless, and the other side that felt guilt for what I had put her through.

Just then, my phone rang. I was pulled from my thoughts as I slid it out of my pocket.

"Shit, it's Dad…"

"You're meant to be under house arrest," she whispered, her gorgeous eyes widening as I answered the call.

"Yeah?"

"You're meant to be home, Liam," Dad's voice came. Before I could reply, Raven took the phone from me.

"I asked him to stay…" she said. Her cheeks were burning, and I fucking swear it felt like we were kids or something. I guess it was my own fucking fault. I heard Dad sigh.

"Raven, I understand you're mates, but I can't risk him losing control. Just come stay here with him."

"We'll be okay. Uncle, trust me," Raven said, despite her blush deepening at Dad's unbothered tone as he invited her to stay.

"No, Raven, rules are rules. Either you both get the hell over here, or Liam can come back alone. I am not going to change my mind on that." Raven pouted.

"Okay, just for today… I'm so tired," she pleaded, and I raised an eyebrow. She didn't seem tired a few moments ago. I smirked at that, pulling her close by her hot-as-hell hips. *Goddess, I love her body…*

"Raven," Dad growled.

"Uncle, please! Pretty please…"

"Okay, fine, first thing in the morning, I want him back here. That's an order." Dad's voice was firm, but Raven being Raven, simply smiled and nodded, totally unphased. She did know Dad couldn't see her nod, right? She hung up and frowned at me.

"You know, this is your fault!"

"Yeah, I know." Her frown vanished and she looked at me apologetically.

"I didn't mean -" I cut her off, placing a finger on her lips.

"I know…" I said, giving her a small smile. She looked up at me, wrapping her fingers around my wrist and kissing my fingertip.

"Let's get some rest. Now I feel like Uncle El's eyes are watching us," she grumbled.

"He ain't no fucking angel."

"I know! I've heard the stories!" She said, taking her heels off.

My eyes fell on her ass. I looked away smoothly, trying to ignore the hard-on in my jeans. I removed my boots and got into bed. I wasn't going to take my shirt off, not wanting her to see my back. Although shifting seemed to have helped the healing, that or the darkness… I wasn't sure.

I never thought she'd trust me to be anywhere alone around her anymore, not after what I had fucking done, but she did. The mate bond calmed the growing storm inside of me, but I knew my time was running out. There wasn't much left until the blood moon and with every passing day, I felt that darkness pushing to the surface, stronger and more powerful – one I would do my best not to let take over. It was hard because, although I was trying, it was consuming me completely. Earlier, when I wanted to rip Owen apart, I had felt my wolf stir and decided to shift.

It did help; that and touching Raven since that I had strengthened the bond, but I didn't want to tell her that she helped because her tolerating me to this extent was enough. After what I did, she should have fucking put a restraining order on me. I wasn't going to abuse that.

Dad had wanted me to stay away from her, but I knew he got that we just couldn't stay away from one another. She was the very oxygen I needed. I didn't blame him, though. Not after I had hurt her and had put him through a lot. Him and Mom. Even if it was the last thing I did, I would try to fix all this crap, or at least make it less painful for them all.

She was snuggled into my arms and had fallen asleep pretty fast. All night I didn't want to sleep, I actually wasn't able to when I had a fucking hard-on from just looking at her. Even after what I did, she was still there in my arms. She was fucking selfless. I hugged her tightly. I didn't deserve her… but I wanted her. I kissed the top of her head, the beat of her heart like music in my ears, her rhythmic breathing lulling me into a sense of security. My mind wanted to ponder on the killer, but I was far too sleepy…

The last thing I remembered before I fell asleep was that I was sure the killer was still out there, somewhere.

Ripples of pleasure flowed through me as I felt her run her finger through my hair. I didn't open my eyes for a while, enjoying her touch. My hold on her had loosened and I opened my eyes, looking straight at her breasts in that lacy top that she hadn't changed last night and noticing the stickers she had over her nipples... *Fuck...*

Her thigh brushed my dick, which was fucking hard as could be, and she suddenly moved back, realising I had woken up.

"Liam...

"Morning," I said quietly, my voice thick with sleep.

I was doing my best not to pull her close and rip that tempting top off. Instead, I slowly let go of her, looking up into her eyes. She gave me a small smile, her gaze dipping to my lips. My heart thudded when she slowly bent down, pressing her lips to mine. My mind went blank before reality hit me fucking hard... *Why does this feel too good to be true?*

I reached up, threading my fingers into her hair and pulling her closer, deepening the kiss. She seemed to have other plans though, her hand going down between us until it rested on my rock hard dick. Fuck...

She moaned as she stroked it over my jeans, her lips not leaving mine. Our kisses became hungrier, and I knew if I didn't stop her then, I wouldn't be able to at all.

"How's your back?" She asked softly, her fingers unzipping my pants.

"Pretty decent -"

I was pushed on my back as she climbed on top of me. I raised an eyebrow. Was this my Raven? Her cheeks were slightly flushed as she grinded her hips against my dick, her hands spread on my chest before she bent down and kissed me again.

"Fuck, Liam," she whimpered as I tugged her closer by her hair, kissing her harder, feeling myself fucking throbbing, but just then, my fucking phone had to ring.

I ignored it, unable to focus on anything but the doll on top of me. If only there was nothing between -

The phone rang again. Raven frowned, glancing towards where I had left it on the bedside table. To my surprise, she picked it up and switched it off before tossing it to the floor. My eyebrows shot up at her move.

"So annoying," she said, about to tear my top off when I grabbed her wrists.

"Baby, are you okay?" I asked. There was something… different about her.

"Yeah… I just… want you," she said, kissing my neck.

I fucking loved her confidence, but there was definitely something -

A bang on the door made me sigh as Raven seemed to come to her senses. The scent of her arousal filled the room, and she took a moment to look between us. She sighed, climbing off me.

"Guys… Alpha wants Liam back home. Now," Zack's voice came.

"Honestly, this is payback for all the times I walked in on Uncle El!" Raven said, pouting. I sat up slowly, looking at her, her cheeks still a little flushed.

"Ahuh…"

"What?" She asked, seeming to realise I was a bit thrown off.

"Nothing," I said with a small smirk. "That was pretty sexy." She blushed and pouted.

"Trust me, even I don't know what got into me," she said, yanking the door open, Zack and Taylor stood there smirking. She glared at Zack with her hands on her hips, and I wouldn't lie, she really did favour some over others… because she didn't seem to be giving her friend any disdainful looks…

"Naughty Alpha… you're meant to be on house arrest, not getting dessert first thing in the morning," Taylor teased.

"And your naughty mate disturbed me," Raven countered.

"Oh, babe, I think it's good we did. I don't want anyone taking advantage of you," Taylor said cheekily, giving her a hug. *Wasn't she taking advantage of me?* Zack raised an eyebrow before turning to me.

"Come on. Alpha was getting really fucking stressed out."

I stood up, pulling my shoes on before going over to Raven. I wrapped my arms around her from behind, placing a kiss on her neck.

"I'll see you later," I whispered in her ear, hearing her heart rate pick up.

"Okay," she agreed.

"After you," I said to Zack, knowing he had to escort me.

"I'll stay with Raven," Taylor said, planting a quick kiss on Zack's lips.

The last thing I heard before Raven shut the door was Taylor asking her if she was okay and that she looked a bit flushed, only for Raven to deny it vehemently.

"Your dad wants me to escort you back," Zack said, leading the way downstairs.

"I figured as much."

We continued in silence. There was something I needed to do anyway. Speak to Mom... I still remembered the pain I felt from her when I was chained up for my lashing as she whispered to me that I was stronger than that, that I was better than that. That I was not a monster...

Those words had fucking struck home. I had broken something inside of her that was already not fully mended. It was as if she was reliving a memory whilst telling both of us that I was not Zidane.

She had been through so much in life, yet she remained strong to a point that I thought people forgot that she was human after all, and no matter how much time had passed, she had suffered a lot and that didn't just go away. There were things in life that would always trigger trauma, and what I did, it was unforgivable. I had hurt the two women that I should always worship – my mother and my mate.

A Mother's Hope

SCARLETT

THE SMELL OF CHOCOLATE and brownies filled the air, mixed with Azura's shrieks of excitement. Sliding on an oven glove, I took the fresh tray of brownies from the oven. I felt calmer when I baked.

Elijah was playing with Azura, tossing her up in the air and catching her with ease, looking as handsome as he did when I first fell for him. My king, my mate, my world. That wouldn't change, ever, but when you become a mother, the space in your heart grows. I had three beautiful children that I loved more than life itself. I would die for them, and I would kill for them, but if they made a mistake, I would also be there to tell them that.

The front door opened. I knew it was Liam from the way he shut the door. He was always quiet, as if he did not want to disturb anyone. Kiara was a little louder, but she was with Raven the majority of the time and that girl was loud. I smiled, remembering their giggles as they thought they were succeeding in stealing snacks from the kitchen. I shook my head; we had been young at one point, and I knew all those tricks.

Language baby, I mind-linked Elijah, knowing he often forgot his mouth around Azura. I was not happy with that.

"You were under house arrest," he said the moment Liam stepped into the kitchen.

"I know," he said, "but I told you I don't think it's Owen, so I didn't really want to leave her alone."

"Hmm, I know but at least for the sake of rules, just stay here. If she wants, she can come here," Elijah said, frowning.

"Okay… hey, pumpkin," Liam said, ruffling Azura's hair.

"Wiyam! Daddy, catch me!"

"That's great," Liam said before he looked at me. Coming over, his gaze fell to the ground. "Hey, Mom." He hugged me tightly, and I wrapped my arms around his waist. *Goddess, please don't hurt my son anymore.* "Can we talk when you're free?" He asked quietly. I looked up at him as I moved back and nodded.

"Let me just cut these brownies…" He nodded.

"I'll go take a quick shower."

He left the kitchen, and Elijah, who had just finished pouring a glass of milk for Azura, who was all ready to have some gooey hot brownies, came over to me, wrapping his arms around me. Strong sparks coursed through me, sending my stomach into a familiar frenzy, one I was so used to, yet at the same time, still made me a jittery mess.

"Things will get better," he said huskily, kissing my neck.

"I know," I replied.

"You're fucking strong, Kitten, but it's okay to not be okay at times," he murmured, nibbling at my neck. I bit back a sigh and nodded, trying to ignore the burning need that was settling into my core. I turned my head, kissing his lips.

He was right. I just needed to tell Liam how I felt too, even if it meant putting my fears out there.

❧

Twenty minutes later, I had a plate of brownies, milk, and some toast on a tray. I took it to the back glass conservatory, waiting for Liam to come down and join me. He didn't take long. Dressed in some grey jeans and a teal-coloured T-shirt, he sat down next to me.

"Eat. I'm guessing you didn't get time for breakfast."

"I didn't get time for anything," he mumbled, picking up a slice of toast.

I smiled slightly at that; my innocent Liam wasn't as innocent as I once thought. I watched him eat the toast as he stared out at the garden; the sun was shining, warming the room nicely and a soft breeze was making the tree branches and grass sway. My smile faded away and I looked down at the tray.

"Is she... ready? I know you won't push her, but..." I asked gently.

"Yeah, I'm not pushing her," he said quietly. I placed my hand on his leg.

"I know, I don't want her to feel emotionally guilty. I think she seems to know what she wants now and is stepping up to that. As much as I'm worried for her, I'm worried about you, too. Talk to me, Liam. You're going through so much; this curse, the entire mate situation..."

"It is what it is," Liam said, drinking some of the milk before picking up a square of brownie.

"It is, but there's always a reason for everything the Moon Goddess does. Grandma Amy knew that Mom, Indy, and I were going to come to this pack. She had a dream but knew it was more. The fact that she left that note... maybe she foresaw that there is hope. Kiara told me that Alejandro was also given a choice when he was in a coma, that he met the Moon Goddess. The Moon Goddess loves us all, Liam. I believe, deep down, she isn't treating you as any less or that you are not enough. This curse... I believe she chose you to end this curse because she knew you were worth it, because you were the one most capable of doing so. This loophole or something that she put against Helios' curse, I truly believe that she has faith in you because you are one of the kindest souls I know. You always put others before yourself," I said quietly.

I believed that. I'd been thinking long and hard. There had to be a reason for the curse to choose Liam. There had to be a reason the Moon Goddess made him share a mate... I mean, why would she do that knowing it would cause him more conflict? There was more to it.

"I don't think I'm as kind as you think, Mom... I don't want to share her, I can't... I want her for myself. She's not just an object for us to 'share' for fuck's sake. I don't get why this happened. Sure, people in polyamorous relationships exist, but it's not for me. I can't share her, and this is me saying this calmly, but I'm leaving it to her... I'm the selfish one here. If she wants us both... and I'm the one who can't accept it, then..." He shrugged, and my stomach twisted.

"Liam, what are you -"

"Nothing," he said, smiling as he turned to me. "I'm sorry, Mom. I know I brought back those painful memories. What I did... it's not something I can forgive myself for. I hurt you and Raven... and I'm fucking sorry for that." He took my hands, my heart squeezing at the sadness in his eyes. "I don't deserve the love you give me, the love she gives me. Even if

I got lashed daily for the rest of my life… it wouldn't be enough. Marking someone is… sick, but I promise you, I won't become him. I won't hurt you anymore… I will try to be the son you can be proud of, not the one who causes you to cry endless tears," he said, softly cupping my face. "I'm sorry for the pain I've caused you, for re-opening those old wounds, but I swear on my life itself that I will not become Zidane, because I'm your son and I will never let you down." Tears stung in my eyes, I nodded.

"We love you, Liam, and we have faith in you." He wrapped his arms around me, rubbing my back gently as I cried silently. "It did scare me… when I saw you covered in blood…" I whispered, clutching his top. "I saw him… it just brought everything back."

"I know, but I will not let myself become him. I promise you."

I nodded as he rested his chin on top of my head. The resolution in his voice was so strong that I truly believed him.

Not Taking a No

LIAM

*I*T WAS LATER IN the evening, and I had worked with Damon before returning home to Dad's place. I still needed to talk to him, and I would do it soon. I mind-linked Raven asking her if she wanted to come over, and she had sounded pretty flustered, although she had replied that she was obviously going to come and to leave the window open for her. Typical Raven.

I was glad she was coming because I needed it. Throughout the day, I felt myself on the brink of losing control, and the amount of wolfsbane I had injected in myself was enough to kill, but I was fine. The moment that darkness grew, it was as if I was suddenly immune to it.

I had just showered and grabbed a towel when I felt the flare of darkness grow inside of me.

Focus...

There was nothing that triggered me, but the urge it had to release itself and wreak havoc made it fucking hard to control.

Let it all out and this struggle will stop. Don't fight it...

I pushed the thoughts away, remembering what I had done the last time I had let it out.

Raven. Think of Raven... I almost killed her.

It wasn't working. I felt my anger flare, my claws coming out, and I plunged it into my chest trying to contain it, digging my hand into my chest, letting the pain override the darkness. I was not going to let it out...
Focus... focus...

Destroy it all… Let it go… I groaned, falling to my knees. I needed to shift… I needed –

"Liam!" The door flew open, and Raven's scent filled my senses as she fell to her knees next to me, her hand going to my shoulder. "Liam, breathe." I growled lowly. "Baby, move…" Her hand wrapped around my wrist, firmly removing my claws from my chest. "I'm not leaving you, Liam." Her voice was firm yet soft, and her touch seemed to fight the storm growing inside of me.

"Can I hold you?" I whispered, finally looking up at her as I fought against it.

"Forever," she replied, wrapping her arms around my neck.

Her lips met my neck, placing soft kisses that sent delicious sparks through me. I pulled her close, sitting back against the counter, and wrapped my arms around her tiny body tightly, feeling the darkness fading away. Her lips never left my neck or shoulder, kissing me sensually until I was finally myself.

She slowly pulled away, staring at my bloody chest. Pain flashed in her eyes as she touched the raven tattoo that was over my heart.

"Don't hurt yourself, baby," she whispered, cupping my face as she knelt between my legs.

"I was trying to pull it back, I'm okay," I said, running my hand through her hair.

"I'm proud of you," she whispered, cupping my face. Our eyes met, and I saw the concern and pain in her eyes.

"I'm fucking losing it, Raven," I admitted quietly.

A part of me was telling me not to burden her with my fears, but another part of me needed to share the fear inside of me and with who else but my mate?

"I've hurt you, Mom, Dad… Damon. I don't recognise the person I've become anymore," I said, running my fingers through my wet locks. And I hated it.

She tugged my face up, staring into my eyes, and shook her head.

"You have got this, Liam. You want to fight this. Just think, a month ago you were like, whatever I don't care if I die," she said, softly kissing my lips. "You are going to get through this, and you will be the very best version of yourself, because we are all rooting for that."

I hope so.

"We all love you, Liam."

"I don't really deserve it, though, the amount of crap I've done."

"Love doesn't work that way; we love you for you and that won't change," she said firmly, blushing as she looked me over, clearly realising only then that I was only in a towel. She moved back, her heart thudding as she grabbed another towel, busying herself with wetting it before dabbing my chest gently and wiping up the blood as my wounds started to heal.

"Let's get to bed," she whispered.

"Sure. I'll just wash my hands," I said, standing up and tightening my towel. Her gaze dipped to my waist, and I smirked. "Want a peek?" I asked.

Her eyes widened, and she shook her head vigorously, rushing from the room. I smirked as I quickly rinsed my hands off. Entering the bedroom, I saw her sitting on the bed, one hand on her hip, and she looked like she was in pain.

"Are you okay, love?" I asked, worry filling me as I rushed over to her. She nodded, despite her heart beating faster than normal, and it wasn't because of me.

"Yeah, I just… felt a bit unwell." She shook her head, and I nodded, hoping she was okay. I went over to my wardrobe thinking I needed to do something…

Perhaps I needed to visit Rayhan and Delsanra. Maybe she could put some sort of seal on my abilities…

❧❦❧

The following day, I had told Dad I had somewhere to go. Only Raven knew where I was going, and although she wanted to go with me, I didn't trust her being alone with me, not with my unhinged behaviour. At least at home, I knew that there were others not far off. She hadn't been happy when I said that and huffed in annoyance before she headed out to training.

I had called Rayhan and we had scheduled a place to meet closer to his pack but not in pack territory because I didn't want anyone to know we had met or that I had gone there.

"Take care of yourself," Dad said as he stood by the car.

"I'll be okay," I said, crouching down and ruffling the little pumpkin's hair. "Be a good girl, okay? And no picking your boogers, it's gross."

"I no do that anymore, I big girl," she denied it, as if that was obvious. *Yeah, I saw her this morning…*

"Ahuh…"

She smiled, and I smiled back. Placing a quick kiss on her forehead, I got into my black Range Rover, waving them goodbye and slipping on my shades. I knew Dad was worried about me going alone, but I promised him I would be okay, and I wouldn't be far. I just hoped I was and that Delsanra could help. I put some music on as I drove out of the pack grounds.

It was a good hour later when I thought I heard a thud from the back. *Fuck, did something fall onto my car?* I pulled up on the side, putting my hazard lights on, and got out. Walking around, I inspected the smooth metal, shaking my head. *Strange, I had felt something hit…* I was about to get back into the car when I froze in my tracks, staring at the trunk. A sudden thought came to me, and I frowned. *Don't tell me…*

Stepping back, I popped the lid open and raised an eyebrow, staring down at none other than Raven, curled up inside. She smiled sheepishly at me.

"You said I couldn't come, but I want to meet Rayhan's kitty!" She said, pouting as she sat up. Swinging her legs out, she stared up at me with those fucking gorgeous eyes that really made me unable to refuse her.

"How the… I didn't even smell you…" I still couldn't. She smiled proudly, then raised an eyebrow as if that was obvious.

"Anti-scent spray, smart guy." She jumped down, her breasts bouncing in that black corset top she was wearing. A jacket and pants completed her look. As always, she looked sexy.

"So, for the last hour, you were in there…"

"No, I think it's almost three," she sighed. My eyes widened in surprise as I slammed the trunk shut.

"Three? Seriously?"

"Yeah, I needed to get in there before you saw me," she pouted. I pulled her close, unable to resist her charm. *I can't believe I actually thought she'd listen when I told her no.*

"You know, it's dangerous around me," I reminded her quietly as she wrapped her arms around my waist.

"I also know it's dangerous for you alone, and your dad doesn't know you're going this far out, does he?"

"Yeah, he doesn't, or he would have definitely sent guards, but I have some wolfsbane, not that it works."

"Reckless move, blue eyes," she said, tapping my ass before sliding away swiftly and getting into the car from my side. *This girl...*

I got in to see her strapping herself in as if she was ready for a special trip or something. But could I deny that I enjoyed having her there? No. I leaned over, kissing her cheek softly before moving back.

"So, you've met Rayhan's kitty before. What was she like?" She asked when we were back on the road.

"Loud."

"Oh. And what else?"

"Short."

"Oh. Wait, shorter than me?"

"No, bitesize, I don't think anyone can be shorter than you," I smirked. Her mouth fell open before she frowned.

"Major burn, dude."

"Sorry, but I like your size. You are perfect," I said, looking her over. Her cheeks flushed, but she still gave me a narrowed-eyed look.

"You are not forgiven."

"I know," I said, thinking about all the things I really wasn't forgiven for. She placed her hand over mine, giving me a small soft smile.

"I wanted to tell yo- ouch!" She flinched, and I almost panicked until she rested her head back, closing her eyes, and motioned to me that she was fine. "Sorry, I just feel really... I'm okay."

"That's happened twice. Are you sure you're okay? Maybe we need to get that checked out."

"I'm seriously okay," she said, and I nodded, although I didn't believe her fully.

Was it... could it be heat? My stomach twisted and I really hoped not because I didn't want her to go through that...

༺♥༻

RAVEN

We had just reached the hotel suite where Rayhan had told us to meet him. It was one of the Rossi Hotels. *Dude, these guys were loaded.* I wondered how rich they were... *Remind me to check the Rossi Group of Enterprises' net worth later...*

There they were, Rayhan, as handsome as ever, and next to him, a woman who was as gorgeous as a winter queen! In person, her white hair looked even whiter, and her startling blue eyes were so... blue! She was slender yet she had curves that were in perfect portion, no extra wide hips like me or anything!

"Hey!" I said as the two men hugged before Liam gave Delsanra a nod.

"Hi, it's nice to meet you, Raven," Delsanra said with a small smile.

"Likewise."

She was taller than me... maybe about three inches. When you're my height, even an inch was vital...

"Long time no see, Raven," Rayhan greeted, and I didn't miss his gaze going to my neck, but it was only for a second and I had a feeling he knew what had happened.

"She hitchhiked..." Liam said, looking down at me.

"it's a big trunk," I said.

"I'm glad I got to meet you," Delsanra said. "In person, you're even tinier, like a little pear drop."

"Pear drop?"

"Yeah, like the sweets," she said, smiling slightly.

"She has a thing for naming people after food," Rayhan said, pulling her close as he planted a kiss on her lips. I smiled at that.

"Well, shall we get to this?" Liam asked, the mood instantly darkening.

"I don't know if it's going to work. We're talking gods," Delsanra said, running her fingers through her hair.

"If I didn't know that Selene existed, I'd find this entire God thing pretty weird," Rayhan remarked as he sat on the sofa, watching as Delsanra got to work drawing some symbols onto the ground.

"I know. Let's just try to see if we can suppress it, even if it's only partially. Wolfsbane isn't working on me, and neither is silver. I took four doses of wolfsbane this morning, and nothing. I feel normal, and I can mind-link," Liam said, his eyes on the symbols on the ground.

"There are a few things I checked up," Delsanra said. "I'll do a suppression spell, and the other is to target you..."

"What do you mean?" I asked. She looked hesitant, glancing at Rayhan before staring down at her symbols on the floor.

"I can block your healing... but that's risky. If anything happens, you'll be like a human. It's -"

"Do it. We do both; if the darkness isn't controllable, then we target the real me. If I do lose control, someone can easily injure me and stop me from going out of control. Let's do it," Liam said with a nod.

"Liam, think about it. This could go really wrong," Rayhan said, brushing his hair back as he frowned thoughtfully.

"I'm a risk, Ray, to everyone around me."

No...

"Liam, imagine if someone attacks you, an-" I began

"I can still fight," he said, cupping my face. I looked up at him, not liking it at all. "I didn't only hurt you, I attacked Damon, Dad, and even hurt Mom," he said quietly. "I'm dangerous, and I need to do something about it." I nodded. I didn't like it, but I understood what he meant...

I pressed my lips together, nodding, and stepped away. Delsanra looked at me apologetically before turning to Liam.

"Step into the centre of the circle," she said.

My heart felt uneasy, but I couldn't do anything but watch Liam make this decision...

Once Like Brothers

DAMON

IGHT HAD FALLEN, AND I was in the packhouse in Liam's office, trying to look at the tracker families in the pack - those who had the ability to hide their heartbeats - when there was a knock on the door.

"Enter."

I had left the door unlocked since I was in there anyway. The door opened, and Robyn's familiar scent hit my nose before I glanced up. She seemed surprised to see me alone, glancing around the room as if it was a mistake. She was dressed in figure-hugging clothes consisting of a black vest top and high-waisted denim jeans.

"I won't bite," I said, smiling slightly.

That emptiness in my chest that she had once partially filled had only grown since the rejection. It hurt. It fucking hurt. I pushed the thought away. I didn't think I ever had a chance anyway; I would always be second, whether that was simply because Raven and Liam always had a stronger connection or because I couldn't bring myself to fight for it and make matters worse.

One good thing about the rejection was that there was no holding on to hope that it would never be. There was no what if, or just maybe it could work. It was done, and I could look forward from there… it would get easier…

I wasn't the only one who had shouldered a rejection. Only recently, Channing, Taylor's brother, had rejected his mate. It was different as their marks would remain until the end, but they had weakened the bond by a lot. However, if, say, Anna took a new mate and marked them, the mark could be lifted from Channing's neck. The mate bond… it wasn't something simple…

"I thought Zack was here. He asked me to check the anti-scent spray supplies," she said, holding the file over her breasts.

"Leave it with me. Thanks for your constant help, Robyn. You've always been really hands-on and organised," I said, glancing down at the desk in front of me, remembering a conversation from about six months ago that I had overheard her having with her brother Rick…

"You're damn organised…"

"Of course I am! Who knows, I may be a beta female. It could just be in my genes to be organised and handle stuff."

The sound of her laughter echoed in my mind, and I knew back then that was the point where I should have told her I had a mate. Was this karma?

"Yeah, sure. So, there's nothing missing from the actual sprays, but there have been slight misses in the actual ingredients used to make them. My bet is that someone has been sneaking a little here and there, then making their own," she explained, brushing a coiled tendril of her hair back as she placed the file down, pointing something out. Her heart was racing at our proximity. I looked at where she was pointing and frowned.

"That's minimal… things get spilt when creating the sprays, are you sure it's not just a miscalculation?" I questioned, raising an eyebrow. She frowned, cocking an eyebrow.

"I don't make mistakes when it comes to things like this. Damon, trust me, I'm the one who checked the stocks for Rick last time," she replied snappily.

"Calm down, I'm just saying," I said, smiling slightly. She almost said something, the beginning of a smile on her lips before it vanished, and she shook her head, closing her eyes for a second.

"Yeah… so… I was thinking, maybe someone who has access to the supplies…" she said, smoothly moving away from me. My chest squeezed slightly at her move, but I smiled softly as I stared down at the file.

I had lost everyone to the point where they walked away, and when it came to her, that was my fault, but I couldn't just delve into this fucking pain in my chest. It was my choice to let her go and to let Raven go. I had to deal with the aftermath.

I nodded, and she turned away, hesitating before looking at me.

"Damon, are you okay?" She asked, her voice sounding unsure. I looked up at her, nodding.

"Yeah." She frowned, pursing her lips.

"I know you better than that, Damon. You're hurting. Do you want to talk about it?" She asked, fiddling with one of her rings.

I looked at her. I knew she was the one person I could lay my soul bare to, but it would just hurt, just as it would hurt Raven if I had told her how I felt. Even though Raven talked to me daily, asking how I was and checking in on me, I couldn't tell her that the pain in my chest was crushing me. Because I loved her, and for her happiness, I let her go. As for Robyn... bond or not, she had loved me. I was not going to hurt her by abusing that.

"I'm fine, thanks," I said just as the door opened and Liam stepped inside. I frowned, instantly realising there was something different about him. What was it?

My eyes widened, realising there was no aura around him. Although I knew it was usually suppressed, you could still tell when an Alpha walked into the room, and right then, I felt nothing from him.

"Hi... I'm not disturbing, right?" He asked, glancing between Robyn and me.

"No, Alpha, not at all. I was just bringing the list for the supplies," Robyn said before she walked past him towards the door.

If you do want to talk, I'm here. I know the three of you have a complicated situation, and I'm not trying to butt in, but if you just need an ear to listen... one who won't ever judge... I'm here, her words came into my head. My heart thundered as I looked at her back.

Thanks... Raven and I... we rejected one another, I said quietly. Her heart raced. She looked down, but she didn't turn back.

Oh... I'm sorry. Then she was gone, shutting the door behind her. Liam raised an eyebrow.

"All okay?"

"Yeah," I said. I knew that he knew that we had been mind-linking.

"Cool."

I glanced at him as he came over, picking up the file that Robyn had brought in. He hadn't said anything about the rejection so far... I wouldn't either. I'd let him bring it up first.

"You were out all day, and your aura's different. Or more like, there just isn't one," I asked as he dropped onto his chair. He glanced up at me and frowned.

"I got a seal or two put on me... just in case..." he said quietly after a moment's pause...

I frowned. Didn't his dad say he was just going into town? That meant he probably went to see Rayhan...

"Does your Dad know?"

"No, only you and Raven," he said, frowning as he tossed the file down and looked up at me. "I owe you a lot more than an apology... but I'll start there. I'm not going to justify my shit because even now, I can't think of sharing my mate... but my behaviour... it was wrong. I fucked up a lot and, in the process, lost a lot." I watched him, sensing the guilt roll off him as he stared at his hands, his elbows resting on his legs, his head hanging. "What I'm trying to say is that I'm sorry for treating you like shit... that I saw and still see everything you did for me, Damon. I'm a total prick, but you bent over backwards to make me happy. You've always put yourself aside. You sacrificed everything for me, and I realise I broke the very first promise I made to you years ago." His voice was hoarse, and I could hear the guilt laced with pain in it.

Promise... yeah, I remembered it.

FOURTEEN YEARS AGO

"Liam, you won!" I gasped, catching my breath, looking at the boy who was a little younger than me but already slightly taller. He smiled.

"I'm sure you will win next time, Damon. Rematch?"

"Okay!" I said, "Three, two, one!"

We broke into a run, our feet barely hitting the earthy ground as we raced towards the line of trees. I glanced at him, realising he was falling behind.

"I'm winning, Liam! I'm going to win!"

I slammed my hand against the tree trunk, bursting into laughter as I stuck my tongue out at him when he reached me moments later.

"Yeah, you did!" He said, high-fiving me.

"Is it bad? You're the Alpha. You will always be number one. You should be number one!" He smiled at me, his eyes sparkling brightly.

"We are brothers. There won't be a first or second, we will always be a team. I promise." He held his hand out to me, and I took it happily, nodding.

"Yeah, we are brothers!"

I realised years later that he let me win here and there… I was never stronger or faster than he was, but he let me think that because that was Liam for you. Until that blood moon…

"I've treated you like shit, and even then, you have stuck by me. You haven't made a move on Raven… but I still hate you for it. I acted like I'd always share everything, and then I realised that she was the one thing I couldn't… I hurt you, and I know you're probably mad at me, which you should be, but I'll try to do better. I'll make it up to you… or I'll at least try to," he said, running his fingers over his head and messing up his perfectly styled hair.

His words resonated in my head, and I could hear the sorrow and vulnerability in his words, yet the strength and confidence of his determination to fix things shone through. I moved away from the table, taking a seat in the chair opposite.

"I didn't mind any of your crap until you marked her… that was my limit, and what was worse was I couldn't do anything. I just watched."

"I know… but it's not your fault. You couldn't do anything. That's something I won't ever be able to forget. Ever," he said, his brows furrowed.

"I know you let me lash you so I can vent my anger," I said quietly. "I'm not stupid. Deep down, I know my best friend and brother is in there… I'm seeing him coming out, little by little. I just hope that he fights this darkness and realises that his actions are hurting those around him." He nodded, looking across at me.

"I'm going to try. Thank you for being a friend, one I don't even deserve."

"That's what brothers are for… we deal with each other's shit and are there for one another. You were there for me when Dad died, Liam. I won't forget that… but I still want to punch you," I said, despite smiling at him.

"No one is stopping you," he replied, smirking. I shook my head.

"Who would have thought a girl would be the reason for our conflict?" I asked, feeling that stabbing pain inside of me.

"Yeah… I love her… and I know you do, too. So I'm not going to stand in her way. I'm not an angel who is going to say yeah, I'll share… because I really can't. I have fucking tried to get my head around it. Considered it even, but I can't. I won't expect her to choose me. I have to deal with the fact that I'm not the only one in the running. It's late… I know… it's really late, and I have a head start, but go for it. Fight for her if you want to. If she wants you… I won't lie and say that I will be happy for you. I'll fucking be jealous… but I'll accept it. You are my Beta and my brother, Damon. I don't want that to change. Even if I'm fucking too late to say it, or maybe I've destroyed any hopes of that, to the point of no redemption."

My heart was racing, his words echoed in my mind, but it was his remark about Raven that threw me off. Liam didn't know we had already rejected one another.

Her Inner Conflict

ROBYN

L AST NIGHT I WASN'T able to sleep. All I could think about was Damon's words. They had rejected one another... Goddess.

The flames of hope had leapt up in my chest, but I had squashed them. He had hurt me and then cast me aside. Sure, he was hurt by many, and he had lost a lot... but I was hurting, too. I couldn't hurt him more and myself, too.

Why was the connection still there? I hated it. I hated how we just couldn't fall out of love as easily as we fell in it.

I rolled over in bed, staring at the rising sun through the gap in my curtain. I would never open myself to anyone ever again. Not until I met my mate. Before that, I needed to get over Damon to be able to even consider a mate. It wasn't easy to get over someone as handsome, gorgeous, and loving as him. In the nicest way possible, I wondered why Raven would choose Liam over him... Damon was far mor-

Stop it.

I pushed the thoughts away and decided to get ready for the day. My morning ritual those days was training, showering, having breakfast, and then going and trying to find something to break this curse. Urgh, why was our pack suffering so much? Even the battle of Hecate's betrayal took place there.

Two hours later, I had showered and dropped onto the bed, staring at the book and listening to music as I looked over my notes. The only thing I could think of was an act that had to come from Liam himself. Genuine and something he had to give... Wait...

A sudden thought came to me, and I jolted upright, staring at the page. Did it mean he had to give up his mate? My heart thumped. *I may or may not be right… but I should tell Raven.*

In a way, I was glad she had rejected Damon. At least she wasn't stringing him along. He deserved better than to be treated like that.

Raven? I called through the link.

Hey, Robyn!

She sure had energy. I was aching after training and wouldn't mind going to sleep again… a nap sounded good right about then.

I had another theory about the curse. I'm sorry I've not been of much help, but -

Ooh! I'll come over. Is that okay?

Sure, I agreed.

Sighing, I leaned back and stared at the ceiling. Damon's words once again rang in my ears. Rejection… I shouldn't care.

Raven came soon after, and she held out a box of brownies.

"Luna Red made them," she said.

"Oh… wow, she makes amazing brownies…" I said, remembering Damon used to share them with me sometimes. "Thanks."

"You are most welcome…" she said, taking a seat on my bed comfortably. I resisted a smile; Raven would be a good Luna. She was the type of person who made you feel relaxed.

"So… I feel like this is going to be something Alpha Liam needs to figure out for himself… but… I came up with one theory." *I hate this.* I wished I had never mentioned it. What if I was wrong and I caused more issues?

"Ouch…" She flinched, doubling over, the brownie falling from her fingertips.

"Raven!" I panicked, my heart thudding as I rushed to her side.

"Aah!" She gasped, her heart racing as her face contorted with pain. I looked around, unsure of what to do. Just when I was about to mind-link Damon, she gasped, letting out a breath.

"Are you alright?" I felt her forehead. She nodded slowly, sitting up, but she was shaking slightly. "Raven… that's…" I looked at her sharply, my gaze falling to her neck.

"I'm okay!" She said apologetically. "I'm so sorry about your bed!" She quickly began to scoop the crumbs up.

"Raven… have you had that pain before?"

"Yeah, it's happened a few times recently," she admitted, brushing her hand through her hair and breathing hard.

"Babe… I think you may be going into heat," I said hesitantly.

I was sure she was. Something told me she and Liam hadn't gone to that extent. Her face dropped, her heart thudding as she looked at me.

"Heat… it could be. Please don't mention this to anyone… I'll make myself a plan," she whispered, her heart thumping.

"I don't think hiding stuff is going to be wise…"

"No, you don't get it, I… now isn't the time. If I go into heat, I need to be alone." She sounded worried.

"How about you link me if you do? Maybe we could have the ice packs ready and stay away from the packhouse."

"You'll help me?" She looked surprised.

"Nope, I'm just going to take you far away from the packhouse and kidnap you," I joked. Actually, not a smart joke, especially with the killer that may or may not still be out there. "Sorry for the bad joke. I'm not a jokey person," I said apologetically.

"That's okay. You're the smart one, I'm the jokey one." She grinned as if she hadn't just doubled over in pain moments earlier.

"You're smart, too," I said, standing up. "You should tell someone, though. Going into heat… it's not a joke. Maybe mate before then…" I said. "It might actually be wiser than just coping… but I know the mark wasn't planned. Whatever you decide, I'm here if you need me."

"Thanks, Robyn…" She looked conflicted. I saw the flash of guilt and sadness in her eyes, and I knew it was not because of her situation but because of Damon.

"Stop with the face. It's going to be okay."

She nodded, and we began to discuss the curse once more, but like always, there were no more answers…

❧❧❧

Night had fallen, and it was really late. I had fallen asleep at eight pm and woke up an hour ago, deciding to have a nice long bath. It was almost three in the morning, and I had just stepped out of the bathroom, a towel wrapped around me as I headed down the hall to my room. Despite there being several bathrooms, there were still far more people there. I really wished all the rooms had their own bathrooms. Was there a way to pitch the idea forward?

I turned the corner only to knock into a hard chest. I gasped, stumbling back, my wet feet skidding on the floor, but a pair of strong arms caught me before I fell backwards.

"Easy!"

My heart thudded as my brain registered the scent and touch of none other than Damon himself. His soft blue eyes were wide as his gaze dipped to my ridiculously small towel that had been pulled down slightly in my moment of stupidity, showing off more than a small amount of breast. He looked away, quickly pulling me upright.

"Sorry. You're up late," he said, moving back as if I burned.

"You know I'm a night owl," I said, fixing my towel, suddenly feeling very bare. My stomach was a mess of nerves, and my heart raced.

"Yeah… uh… night…" he said.

Our eyes met. I knew that it had thrown him off. It had confused me, too… I missed his hold… but it was a one-way thing. He didn't feel anything for me.

"Night…" I said as he quickly walked off towards the stairs, and I returned to my room, still feeling a little lightheaded…

RAVEN

I sighed, staring at the men's perfume set that I was holding in my hand. I had gone out to Stratford Upon Avon's largest shopping centre to buy a gift for Uncle El's upcoming birthday. It was the afternoon, but I still couldn't get Robyn's words from earlier out of my mind about how I needed to tell someone about my being on the verge of going into heat. But forgetting that, more than my heat, I needed to tell Liam about Damon's and my rejection.

I was going to tell him yesterday in the car, but then that stupid pain played up. Then last night, I waited for him, but he had come late, and I had fallen asleep. Damon had linked me earlier, asking me why I hadn't told Liam. Last night, Liam had talked to him, and it was clear he didn't know. I explained to him that I had been about to tell him twice, but stuff came up. I had booked a table in a restaurant in town, and I was going to tell him.

I wasn't sure what to do about my heat; I figured I'd talk to Liam, and we'd go from there. I loved him, but I didn't feel as if I was ready for that last step, not when he felt guilty. What if I said it, and he refused? I'd be hurt, but I needed to talk to him regardless of the outcome.

He had promised to meet me. Although he was supposedly on house arrest, I was glad he was allowed to get out. Staying indoors would only drive him crazier, although I didn't think Uncle El realised Liam's always broken more rules than he knows. I wasn't complaining. I had liked our road trip.

I paid for the fragrance and headed out, glancing at my watch; twenty-to-six. Perfect, enough time for me to get dressed and head to the restaurant for seven! I got into the backseat of my car, pulling out the outfit I had decided to wear for tonight. A black, long-sleeved, high-collared dress with a cut-out back. *What's not to love about black?* I glanced towards my tinted windows before I undressed and slipped it on, pairing it with some net tights and heels. Taking my makeup back out, I began working on my face.

When I was almost done, a sudden surge of pain coursed through me, but this time, it was accompanied by a raging fire. I felt as if my entire body was burning. A whimper left my lips as I dropped my lip liner. Screaming at the spasming pain, my lower region throbbed, and I bit my lip, Liam's face flashing in my head.

I wanted him.

Liam… I called through the link. My mind felt fuzzy, and my entire body felt hot and crazy.

Raven, what's wrong?

Liam, I need you to come get me, I whispered.

Where are you?

Outside Red Fort shoppi- ah! I whimpered as another pain rushed through me.

I needed this clothing off! I grabbed the collar of my dress, tearing it off completely.

I'm coming. His voice was soothing, yet he was clearly worried.

Fast, I moaned.

I wanted him. My mind was hazy as I ripped through my tights and pushed my underwear aside, parting my smooth lips and began rubbing my clit.

Liam…

I imagined it was him touching me, imagining him running his tongue down my stomach, pushing my thighs apart before he drove his tongue into me.

"Liam…" I whimpered, moaning as I felt my orgasm building, moving my finger faster. "Fuck…"

My eyes flew open, my back arching as my orgasm ripped through me. I dropped back onto the seat, feeling a little cooler and somewhat returning to my senses. My cheeks were hot, and the flames that were licking my body were still there, but it wasn't as tense. I was aching for so much more…

I gripped onto the seat in front, whimpering as another jarring burst of pain rushed through me.

Wait… was calling Liam the smart thing to- ouch!

I whimpered, clamping my hand over my mouth, not wanting anyone to hear me. A sudden tapping on the window made my eyes fly open, my heart thundering when I saw Liam.

Open the door, love.

I reached over, unlocking the door and pushing it open slightly. My entire body burned with a dangerous desire to jump him right then. His eyes instantly blazed magnetic blue the moment my scent hit him. His heart thundered as his eyes trailed over me. I was in my lingerie and torn net tights, and, even in my hazy state, I could tell he liked what he saw from the pure carnal hunger in those shimmering deep blue eyes…

"You're in heat…" He swallowed, slowly getting in the car. His nostrils flared as he shut the door behind him and cupped my neck, touching his knuckles to my cheek. I whimpered at his touch, the sparks that coursed through me making me throb.

"Fuck, Liam…" I whimpered. I needed his touch. I climbed into his lap, and he tensed, gripping my arms.

"Raven… look at me," he said through gritted teeth, trying to calm his racing heartbeat.

"I'm burning up, I…"

"Raven... love, listen to me. Let's get you somewhere cold, a bath, maybe... ice..."

"Kiss me," I whispered seductively, ripping his shirt halfway before he caught my wrists.

"You're not yourself. I'll kiss you, but we can't go further..." he whispered. I knew I was breaking his resolve when I took my bottom lip between my teeth and looked at him with hooded eyes.

"Then kiss me, blue eyes," I whispered, rolling my hips against his crotch. A horny moan left my lips, and he swore, suddenly lifting me off him and placing me down.

"Raven, let's get you out of here," he said, his voice hoarse and almost animalistic. It just made me want him even more. Getting out of the car, he got into the front, grabbing my keys as I glared at him. "I'll tell Mom you're in heat. She can tell us what to do. I don't trust myself around you."

"You're responsible for this! So, you should fix it!" I growled. I knew I was being unreasonable, but I needed him. I wanted him. He turned the air conditioning on full, but it did nothing to satiate the burning desire inside of me. "I don't want to go to the pack, Liam... not like this. The world already seems to know everything about me... just take me to a hotel room or something. I don't want anyone to know," I said, suddenly feeling upset. Another jarring pain rushed through me, and I whimpered, curling up on the back seat. Through my half-lidded eyes, I could see his knuckles were white on the steering wheel.

"What about Damon? Do you want him with you instead?" He asked, his voice low. Although he was trying to sound normal, I knew just asking me that question hurt. I frowned, feeling the throb deep inside of me return.

"We rejected one another, Liam... I meant to tell you... but... fuck... something came in the way..." I whispered, biting my lip as another jarring pain rushed through me. He didn't reply, but I could hear the beat of his heart, knowing it was a shock to his system.

"After what I did..." I thought I heard him whisper, but I was far too lost in my own pain, the heat, and the need for more licking painfully at my skin. The leather of the seats burned, too...

"I'm going to go get ice... I won't be long," I heard him whisper and realised the car had stopped. I stared through the window. A supermarket...

His Control

LIAM

THEY HAD REJECTED EACH other? When? How? Did Damon think I was rubbing it in when I talked to him yesterday? Fuck, I wasn't...

I was late apologising... and although I wouldn't deny it gave me hope, it also meant he had taken himself out of the running because of me. At that moment, I knew that even if things became better between us, they would never return fully to how they once used to be.

Once we parked outside a hotel, pulling an oversized hoodie over her, I helped her out of the car, holding two bags full of ice cube packs. There were more in the car, but I needed to get her some sort of relief from the pain quickly, pain that I had inflicted upon her. *When the fuck will I ever stop causing her pain?*

I could smell her arousal, a thousand fucking times stronger than ever, and I was hard. The urge to mate with her was fucking strong, but I refused to even think about that.

I lifted her onto my shoulder the moment I had our key card and entered the lift. Once we were in the room, I dropped the bags and placed her on the bed, pulling her hoodie off. My eyes trailed over her body, those perfect round breasts in that black lace bra... with her narrow waist, curvy hips, and sexy thighs, in only her heels and those net tights, it only added to how fucking hot she looked.

"I'm going to run you a bath," I said, trying not to look at her pussy as I licked my lips.

She looked up at me, her eyes full of desire, pain, and something else. She nodded, curling up. I rushed to the bathroom. I had asked for a room with a large tub. Relieved it was a decent size, I opened the cold tap. She screamed, and I froze before turning back to the bedroom and rushing over to her. Fuck...

"Liam... it hurts," she whimpered, her legs parted and her back arched.

"Okay, wait..." I ran my fingers through my hair.

This is torture. I deserved it, though.

Opening the top ice bag, I grabbed a handful. Walking to the bed, I climbed between her legs and dropped the ice onto the bed. Keeping one in my hand, I ran it over her lips, watching the water melt and trickle down her neck. She was burning hot...

I leaned in, claiming her lips in a deep kiss. Instantly, her hands grabbed the back of my neck, and she pulled me on top of her. One of her legs wrapped around my waist before she yanked my jacket off, ripping my shirt down the centre.

I want you, Liam, she begged.

No, baby, but I'll help, I promise. I can't take anything more from you, I whispered tenderly. I felt awful. I had ruined her marking; I was not going to ruin her first time.

I trailed the ice cube between her breasts, my lips still devouring hers. Fuck, she was delicious... she fought for dominance, kissing me hungrily and moaning in satisfaction when I plunged my tongue into her mouth. Her moans alone were enough to make me come. *Goddess... this is so good...*

I broke away, grabbing another two cubes and trailing them down her stomach before I reached her tights and tore them open from the middle. She stretched her luscious thighs for me, and I pushed her panties aside, rubbing the cube over her clit. She groaned in pleasure, her back relaxing as she whimpered in satisfaction.

"That feels good...." she whispered. I smirked, pleased that it was working. I slowly pressed the cube to her entrance, making her gasp in pleasure as I slowly pushed it further into her. "Oh, fuck!" She whined hornily.

Once it was completely inside her hot core, I flicked her clit with my tongue before flattening it to her base and running it up along her dripping core slowly, growling in approval at how fucking good she tasted. She whimpered, her hand tangling in my hair painfully perfect. I couldn't stop the groan of pleasure as I flicked and sucked her clit faster, slipping another ice cube into her molten hot core.

"Oh, *fuck!*" She cried out as she came hard.

I rubbed my nose against her clit, drinking up her scent before I moved back, kissing her lips softly.

"Thanks…" she whispered, clearly feeling calmer. I gave her a small smile, caressing her hair.

"You look beautiful… you always do. As much as I want to take this pain away, I know you're not fully there and when… if the time comes and you want to give yourself to me, I'll promise it will be perfect," I whispered, placing a single chaste kiss on her lips before moving away, hoping the tub was full. I grabbed two ice bags and left the room, swearing when I saw the water was dangerously high.

Shit.

Quickly, I unplugged it, draining some out before dumping the ice into it and re-plugging it. There. Perfect. I returned to the bedroom, freezing in my tracks when I looked at her.

Her bra strap was off her shoulder, her sexy legs were parted, and she was slipping another cube into herself with one of her delicate fingers. *Fuck…*

She looked up at me with those eyes coated with lust and desire.

"Like what you see, baby?" She asked.

"You know I fucking do…" I said. The hard-on in my pants was fucking painful.

She tilted her head, smiling slightly as I walked over to the bed. As much as she was fucking tempting me, I would not take advantage of her. Not again. I lifted her bridal style and carried her to the bathroom. Placing her on the floor, I stripped off her net tights and was about to place her in the bath when she reached behind and unhooked her bra.

Fuck.

"Raven… are you trying to torture me on purpose?" I asked, swallowing hard as I stared at her breasts. This was the most naked I had seen her in one go… *Fuck….* In nothing but her panties, she looked… so fucking good. There was something so hot about her, from her size to her curves…

She giggled weakly, spinning around and hooking her fingers in her underwear.

"The fabric is chaffing my skin," she whined, wriggling her ass.

I looked away as I saw her discard her panties from the corner of my eye, praying for fucking strength. I felt the darkness trying to surface and pushed it away. Not again.

I helped her into the bath without looking at her, satisfied when she let out a sigh of relief. She sank into the tub until all I could see above the surface was her face and her hair splayed around her.

"I'm going to get more ice from the car, okay?" There was still some in the bedroom, but we needed more...

"Okay... sorry for teasing you. I'm just..."

"In heat," I finished. Leaning over the tub, I kissed her lips softly. "I'll take care of you, but I do need to tell someone. What about Mom? Because when night falls, Dad will want to know where I am." She frowned and seemed to think before whimpering and nodding.

"Only your parents, then," she agreed. I nodded before leaving the room and linked Mom, hoping we were still in range...

Mom, can you hear me?

Liam? Of course, I can.

I have an issue, and I need you to relax, and maybe I need you here...

Of course, what is it? She asked with worry clear in her voice.

Raven went into heat. We're in town at the Holden Hill Hotel. I'm in control... I'm okay... but just in case... can you come here? I get that Dad needs to stay in the pack, but you are strong enough to keep me in control if need be, I said quietly. She would be strong enough without a doubt, because I was weaker and completely vulnerable to any attack thanks to the seal Delsanra had put on me. As for the darkness, I could feel it fighting her barriers, growing stronger. I knew it would soon break free from her seal, but until then... *I'll do my best.*

Got it. I'm assuming... you two are not going to-

Obviously, Mom, or I wouldn't have asked you to come! I groaned. Seriously so fucking cringy. She laughed.

I went through heat in the same way. Don't worry; I will explain stuff to your dad, and I'll be there.

She cut the link, and I sighed. This was going to be awkward, having Mom around when Raven was in heat, and I was fucking turned on... but I couldn't risk Raven's safety. Not again.

Three days. Raven had been in heat for three days, and I was a wreck. Resisting her was draining me. I could only imagine how exhausting it was for her. She begged me to take her several times, saying she loved me, but it was the pain and need for a release that was making her mind a haze.

Mom stayed in the hotel bedroom, bringing food and ice. She left during certain periods to spend time with Azura but at night she was around, and for most parts of the day. To my relief, and I was sure to Dad and Mom's, I didn't lose control, something I knew Dad was worried about. I had a feeling Mom had to fight for him to allow me near Raven. He had mind-linked once. His words were still clear in my mind.

You are my son, and I know you got this... be the man she deserves.
I will be. I will try.

Having Mom around wasn't as bad as I thought. She didn't say anything or make anything fucking weird, thank fuck.

I made Raven come countless times, but I refused to take her completely. My fingers or tongue did the job, but with each passing day, it wasn't enough. She needed more.

Despite how weak and exhausted she was, she couldn't sleep, not with the pain she was in. Sometimes she'd drift off for a few minutes until the heat forced her awake. I stayed by her side, staying awake myself and easing her pain as best I could.

"How is she?" Mom asked as I walked out of the bathroom, buttoning up my white shirt to hide the scratches made by Raven earlier still covering my torso since I wasn't healing anymore.

"I think it's at its worst..." I said, running a hand through my messy locks. Mom nodded sympathetically.

"It's the final day. It's going to be the hardest today, and the bath won't help. An Alpha's mark can make the heat a lot worse. You've done well, Liam, and I trust you will handle it from here on out. I will be downstairs in my car. If you need me to come up, if you feel you are losing control, just mind-link."

I nodded, feeling embarrassed, knowing exactly why she was leaving... giving us some privacy. But I get it, I-

Raven's whimper made me look back at the open door.

"I'll be leaving. Link, okay?" Mom said. I nodded before she walked out the door, and I rushed back into the bathroom.

Raven was standing in the tub, about to get out of the ice-filled bath.

"Babe, you got to-"

"No, Liam, please... just... it hurts," she said, my stomach twisting when I realised she was crying.

"I know, love, but it's almost over now," I whispered, gripping her hips as she broke into sobs, breaking my heart in the process.

"It hurts," she whispered, wrapping her arms around my neck. She was shaking, her arms weak as she hugged me, sobbing weakly into my shoulder. The stronger the Alpha... the worse the heat...

Guilt consumed me, and I held her tightly, stroking her back.

"You said you wanted me..." she sobbed.

"I do. I want you, every part of you; to kiss you, make love to you, and cherish you. But I can't take advantage of you, bitesize. You are worth so much more than that," I said pleadingly, kissing her shoulder.

"I love you, Liam. So, so much," she whispered. I cupped her face, kissing her tear-stained cheeks before planting a soft one on her lips.

"I love you, too, Raven. Before I even knew what a crush was... you were the little doll I fell in love with," I whispered, our eyes meeting. She smiled weakly before I gently moved back, stripping my top and pants off.

"I'll sit in the bath with you. Skin contact will help," I said, getting into the ice-cold water that made me hiss. How the hell was she surviving in this?

She nodded, and I pulled her into my lap. She straddled me, wrapping her arms around my neck as she kissed me hungrily. I kissed her back, but no matter how much I wanted to take her, I wouldn't. We were going to get through this the right way.

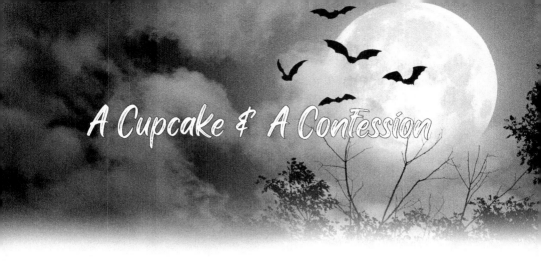

A Cupcake & A Confession

LIAM

HREE AND A HALF days. That's how long Raven's heat lasted. Three and a half intense days. I was close to breaking my resolution when I saw no end. Seeing her sobbing and begging me messed me up. Mom and Dad were shocked that it went over the three-day period, which was the common period for heat, but we assumed that maybe the curse made it worse. Or Mom thought perhaps I was just a stronger Alpha than Dad, but I didn't think so. When Dad and I sparred, I only managed to outdo him by a little, and I'd put that down to being younger.

The moment her heat was over, Raven fainted with exhaustion. I made sure her temperature was okay before I tucked her into bed, collapsing next to her and letting sleep consume me. We slept for almost an entire day, far too exhausted to do anything. That had been one hell of an experience. It had been more painful and draining than every lash I had taken. Seeing her in pain fucking hurt so badly, and I felt like I was being punished for messing up. I just wished she hadn't had to suffer again because of me, but there was something about this moment that helped.

There was something in her eyes when she looked at me, holding me tightly and completely vulnerable in my arms. I was meant to be her protector, but I had hurt her. In some ways, having her in my arms trying to fucking seduce me and rip my clothes off felt like a chance for me to prove I was better than what I had become.

My beautiful mate… she was perfect.

I had just gotten dressed, ready to head out to get all her favourite foods after running her a hot, warm bath with essential oils. I was surprised our toes didn't fall off after all that time spent in the icy bath.

I had requested someone to come to clean up the room and change the bedding. Once they left, I left, too, not wanting to be gone for too long. We hadn't really talked. When I had stepped out of the shower, I carried her to the bath. She had just woken up. Kissing her softly, I promised to be back soon.

Forty minutes later, I unlocked the hotel room door and pushed the handle down with my elbow, my hands laden with two paper bags, hot drinks, and a large cupcake in a box.

I saw Raven, looking breath-taking lying on top of the fresh white bedding, her hands tucked under her cheek, wearing nothing but one of my t-shirts that fell to her thighs. My heart thundered, and the thought of seeing her like that every morning, every day for the rest of my life, filled my mind. A guy could dream…

"Hey…" she said, sitting up and brushing her fingers through her hair. Her cheeks were painted a soft hue of pink, a pout on her plump, lush lips.

"Hey, feel better?" I asked, placing the bags on the bed.

She nodded as I bent down, kissing her lips. A soft sigh escaped her, and I moved back slowly, savouring the taste of her in my mouth, my lips tingling from where they touched hers.

I sat down as she reached for the first bag, my gaze going to her shoulder as my T-shirt slid down, revealing her smooth, creamy skin that I would never tire of.

"This smells great," she said as we both began to take everything out; egg and cheese muffins, bacon rasher sandwiches, pancakes, cinnamon rolls, buttered croissants, sugary doughnuts, brownies, hot chocolate, along with two bottles of orange juice.

"We're both fucking starved," I said, unwrapping a muffin for her.

"I know. When was the last time we ate?" She asked, biting into it. I watched her, my gaze dipping to her gorgeous lips.

"Around thirty hours ago, give or take," I said, our eyes connecting. The sexual tension between us was intense. Her gaze ran over me before she looked away, taking a bite.

"Thank you… for everything… I know it was probably hard. I mean, especially when I was begging…" she murmured, biting into the muffin again and pouting.

"Hard is an understatement, love. Have you seen yourself?" I asked, smirking slightly. She looked up slowly, her eyes softening, and she smiled slightly.

"It's weird that you loved me for so long... I'm nothing spe-"

"You fucking are. Now stop it. Stop thinking of yourself as any less. You are beautiful, kind-hearted, and everything a man could ever hope for," I said, reaching over and pulling her into my lap. She blushed despite having been in my lap, naked, many times over the last few days.

"Thanks," she said, caressing my face. I hugged her tight as we continued to eat.

Now that her heat was over, her telling me about her and Damon's rejection was on my mind again. She held the last bite of her muffin to my lips, and I took it, watching her unwrap another muffin as I bit into my sandwich, one arm around her slender waist. The sparks of the bond sizzled between us.

"You said you and Damon rejected one another..." I began. She paused from opening the bottle of orange juice and nodded.

"I realised what I wanted... I won't lie, when we were originally going to reject one another, it was emotional, and I wondered what if... but this time, I knew it was what I wanted. I could never treat him the way I did you. There was no point in stringing him along when I forget everything when I'm around you. It was for the best, for all of us." I kissed her shoulder softly.

"Thank you..." I said quietly. Yeah, I had been a jerk about it, but knowing she chose me...

"Nothing to thank me for. You're stuck with me for life," she said, biting into a croissant.

"Just the way I wanted it," I replied with a smile. I didn't know what it was, but something had changed between us. There was no longer any barrier...

"Oh, my goddess, a sponge cake!" She said, unboxing the little treat I had picked up at the bakery that had just been opening up when I had gotten our food. "This one I'm not sharing!" I smiled, amused.

"I knew you wouldn't. It's all yours," I promised, watching her scamper out of my lap as she quickly flattened the box open and took the giant cupcake out of it. I had to admit she looked fucking sexy sitting there on her knees in my shirt... "I need a picture." I quickly grabbed my phone.

She smiled like the little minx she was and parted her knees slightly. With one hand, she pulled her shirt between her thighs, making it strain against her breasts. I swallowed hard, noticing her nipples poking against it. She smiled coquettishly, raising the cupcake to her mouth. She stuck her tongue out sensually, licking the tip of the icing. Her eyes were looking straight at me, and I took a snap, feeling myself harden in my pants. Fuck...

"You know how to tease," I said.

"Do I?"

She knew exactly what she was doing to me. She simply smirked cheekily. It had been so damn hard to resist her as she tried to tempt me to take her. She giggled, biting into her cupcake.

"I can ..." she said, our eyes meeting as she licked her lips. "But you haven't seen anything yet."

"Looking forward to it..." I whispered, taking hold of her chin.

I leaned forward and she smiled, leaning into the kiss as our lips met. Sparks coursed through us as pleasure rushed through me and sent heat rushing right to my dick...

Fuck...

We parted and she looked up at me, her eyes solemn, and that glint of mischief was no longer there.

"I love you, Liam, and I'm ready to become yours in every way," she said quietly. Her fingers touched her mark, and she smiled softly.

My heart thundered, realising that, despite everything, I was getting a second chance. A second chance to make things right, but even though she had just confessed her love to me, what she said next threw me completely.

"I want to mark you, Liam. I want you to make me yours completely... I want to give you my first time, my every time, and my last time... I want only you. To be by your side through the good and the bad. You and only you."

My emotions swirled through me like a tidal wave that had just been unleashed.

She wanted me... me to make her mine completely...

A confession from her lips... a confession from the heart and one I would never ever forget.

"I love you, too. Always have and always will. You are mine. I promise I'll take care of you for as long as I can...." I whispered, my stomach clenching at the thought that perhaps I'll never get that.

"Yours," she said softly, placing the cupcake down. She climbed into my lap, straddling me, and wrapped her arms around me tightly. I hugged her tightly, feeling completely content despite the fear of losing it all eating up at me.

Just then, I felt something snap inside of me. The pain knocked all the air from me and something wrenched free from inside of me. My blood ran cold as the barrier on the darkness broke away. It rushed through me, stronger and more intense than ever, seeping into every corner of my mind and body, bleeding into my veins and heart.

The seal that Delsanra had put on it had been completely broken.

"Liam!" Raven said suddenly, cupping my face. The tingles of the sparks soothed the storm a little, but... it wasn't enough.

"I'm okay... the seal... it's broken," I said quietly.

I lifted her off my lap, feeling the darkness trying to take control, and I realised at that moment that no matter how much I didn't want it, I may still end up hurting those that I love...

There may still be a few weeks until the blood moon, but my time was over.

☙❧

RAVEN

The entire journey home, Liam had been quiet. His hand never left mine, but the storm inside of him, well, I could feel it. My heart hurt for him. I just... wanted us to be happy. I still believed we'd be okay, we'd be able to do this, but it still terrified me.

"How are you feeling?" Aunty Red asked me.

It was night, and we had just had dinner at the Alphas' home. I mean, I'd call it a small mansion, really... the kitchen was huge yet cosy. I had insisted on helping clean up.

"I'm okay," I said, smiling and flashing her a peace sign. "Thank you for everything."

"Anytime," she replied with a smile. "Heat is a bitch." I laughed.

"Oh, it definitely is," I agreed. "Aunty... I know what Liam did brought back painful memories, but he really regrets it..." She smiled sadly at me and came over, flicking my forehead lightly.

"Are you trying to speak in his defence?" She asked, amused.

"Maybe?" I said sheepishly. "He made a mistake, but there were factors and he's still working on redeeming himself. I love him, and I don't want you to be upset with him." Did I sound too bossy? I hoped not… but she just smirked slightly.

"I'm glad you both finally got there… I swear, it took you long enough!" She teased. "Don't worry. I'm okay, and I know he'll be okay, too. You better head to bed, it's late."

I nodded and dashed out of the kitchen, up the steps I'd climbed countless times throughout my childhood. However, unlike back then, I didn't stop at Kia's room; I walked right past it to my mate's room.

I opened it and saw him towel drying his hair. He was shirtless and I almost drooled at how delicious he looked. Water trickled down that muscular chest of his, down his chiselled abs, and into the band of his sweatpants that hung low on his hips, showing off his perfectly groomed V….

"Hey," I said, my stomach fluttering as I shut the door behind me.

"Hey…" he said, tossing the towel into the washing hamper.

My core ached and I knew, deep down, I wanted him completely. I had told him earlier; I just hoped he would lead the way. He pulled me closer, his hands closing around my waist.

"So… I was thinking… once I'm caught up with the work around -"

He grimaced, closing his eyes and stepping away. My heart thumped, feeling the darkness surge around him once again.

"Shit…"

"Hey, hey, look at me," I said, gripping his face.

"I'm okay," he said, looking up at me. His eyes were darkening to a deep navy. I could feel his struggle. I pressed my lips against his, kissing him deeply until I felt him calm down and finally kiss me back slowly. His heart was beating hard in his chest.

"We are going to get through this," I whispered.

But how? It was getting stronger, and I knew he was trying his best to fight it…

The door suddenly opened, and we both turned, moving apart to see Azura standing there in a fluffy unicorn onesie with her hood up, holding a large unicorn plushie in her hand.

"Waven, are you having a sleepover?"

"Umm, yes, I am Zuzu," I said as Liam smiled slightly.

"Then why I not invited?" She asked unhappily.

"Baby, what have I told you about knocking?" Aunty Red's voice came.

"I sleep with Waven," Azura stated firmly.

"No, baby, come, you can -"

"Let her. I don't mind," I said, glancing at Liam, who raised an eyebrow, looking unhappy. "We can all sleep here, right, Wiyam?" I cooed. He nodded, despite the fact that it looked like he was pouting. Aunty Red raised her own eyebrows.

"Are you sure…?"

I looked at Azura, who was staring at me with those large blue doe eyes. They were glistening with tears that threatened to fall should I refuse the little Chibi.

"Of course, I'm sure!" Bending down, I held my arms open to her, and she ran straight into them, planting a big kiss on my cheek.

"Yay! I sleep with Waven!"

"Great…" Liam said as Aunty Red gave us a wave and shut the door.

And that was how we spent the night, Liam's arm under my head, my back to his chest, and me facing Azura, who was hugging her unicorn as she told me endless stories.

"Oh, wow, that's amazing," I said, listening to another story.

"Yes, and then…." she carried on.

So, what were you saying earlier? I asked Liam through the link, very aware of his body heat behind me and his hand that rested on my hip.

I was saying I wanted to take you out…

I bit my lip the moment his lips touched my neck, his scent making my mind fuzzy and my core clench.

Out?

Yeah. I have some stuff I need to catch up on, but the day after Dad's birthday… you and me? Have a small getaway? He asked, his voice husky and seductive. I knew that if Azura wasn't here, I would have pushed him onto his back and kissed him hard.

I like the idea, I said, sounding breathless even through the mind link.

Perfect, he replied, and I smiled. I couldn't wait.

A sudden thought came back to me and my smile faded away. Robyn's words echoed in my made, her theory that Liam would have to give me up…

Was that the answer? But that didn't make sense. Damon and I had ended things, so how did that work? Something didn't feel right about it. I may not be smart, but deep down, I didn't think that was the answer. But a selfless act from himself... what if *that* was the answer?

৯৹৹৵

It was finally the day of Uncle El's forty-fifth birthday, and there was going to be a party in the packhouse.

There was still no sign of Owen waking up, but, to my relief, there had been no more killings. I wondered if I was just being too paranoid, and it was Owen. Hmm, I still didn't believe that, though.

As for Liam, he was losing control, and it broke me to see that. Seeing him fight to the extent that he was harming himself to keep himself weak - I hated it.

"Fuck, baby!" I whimpered, watching him stab the dagger into his stomach right in front of me.

We had just gotten ready for the party when it flared up again. We were kneeling on the floor in his bedroom, and I bit my lip, watching him yank the knife from his already bandaged abdomen, the blood spreading on the white bandages.

"You're killing yourself," I whispered, cupping his face and pressing my forehead to his.

"I'm fine," he said hoarsely.

He had lost his colour over the last few days, and I could see the constant pain he was in. Well, obviously, when he kept stabbing himself to control it. With his healing sealed away, he was badly injured.

I stood up, silently grabbed another roll of bandages, and returned to his side. He stood up, removing his teal shirt, and I began wrapping it up.

"You look beautiful," he said softly.

I looked up at him, fighting back my emotions. I could see the love and admiration in his eyes as he looked me over, trying his best to act normal when I was breaking at the pain that he was in.

"I like the colour on you," he whispered, caressing my cheek.

"Thanks," I whispered.

I wore a deep brown, strapless, knee-length, satin dress with a slit down the left thigh. My hair was up in a messy bun, and I had some sparkly beige fishnet ankle heels. My lips were painted a deep matte brown to match my dress.

"You look as handsome as ever, too. But you already know that," I said, tucking the bandage in.

I tip-toed, locking my arms around his neck and claiming his lips with my own. His arms wrapped around me, holding me tight. I lost myself in his kiss, loving the way he dominated me, the way he bent me backwards as he kissed me as if it were for the last time. *Please, Goddess, don't let anything happen to him.*

We broke apart and my gaze dipped to his neck. His scent intoxicated me. The sudden urge to mark him consumed me, and I pulled him closer, my canines elongating, but before I could sink them into his neck, he pulled away.

"What are you doing?" He asked, his heart thudding. I felt a sharp sting of pain rip through me.

"I want to mark you…" I said softly. I thought maybe, just maybe, it would help with the darkness.

"No, love… not now," he said, quietly looking down.

"What?" I knew I sounded upset, and I was, but I couldn't deny the hurt I felt. "Why can't I mark you?" He looked away; I could hear his thundering heart as he turned away, going to his wardrobe to take out a fresh shirt.

"It's just… let's not rush it. I mean, maybe at a better -" I closed the gap between us and grabbed his arm, turning him to face me.

"Liam. What is it?" He was never a good liar. My heart was hammered incredibly fast against my ribcage, my stomach twisting with unease. There was more to it.

"It's nothing, baby. Let's not do this right now."

"*No!* We need to do this right now. Why can't I mark you?"

He looked down for a few moments, but I didn't let go of him, waiting for my answer. He looked into my eyes, his cerulean orbs wracked with guilt, but the words that left his lips felt like a knife had just been plunged into my heart.

"Because if I do die… I don't want it to break you completely."

You Are My Dream

LIAM

RAVEN DIDN'T SAY A word. Her anger and pain were clear in her eyes. She had clenched her fists and stormed out. I had called after her, but she simply shook her head, not saying anything. Even when I had pulled her into my arms and apologised, she simply stayed stiff, a single tear escaping her eye. That hurt... but it was the truth. I was fucking scared.

We had walked to the packhouse in silence, but I held her hand tightly.

Raven...

She didn't reply, simply holding my hand tighter.

The hall was decorated in a rustic theme. The wooden tables were bare, with just a black runner down the middle. There were bottles of whiskey, ice, and drinks lining the table. It was definitely not a party for kids...

The double doors that led to the garden were wide open. The garden was decorated as well, and I could hear the music was louder out there.

"So, food's in here, dancing and drinking are outside," Taylor said, walking over, a bottle in hand and Zack by his side.

"Easy on the drinks. We just got here," Zack said, looking down at him with love clear in his eyes, despite the arrogant look on his face.

"Don't worry, I'll be fine. Damn, girl, you look good," Taylor said, smiling at Raven as she slowly let go of my hand, and he hugged her tight. "You okay?" I watched them, seeing the concern in Taylor's eyes for her. Even when she gave that dazzling smile and nodded, I knew she wasn't...

"Hey, guys..." Damon said, coming over. He was dressed similarly to me in black pants with a button-down shirt.

"Hi," I greeted as he turned to Raven.

"Hey!" She said, giving him a smile before hugging him.

I watched them as he hugged her back and looked away, giving them a moment. The sacrifice they made for me wasn't something I'd forget, and as much as I wanted to keep her in my arms, I couldn't be more selfish with her than I already have been.

"How are you feeling?" Damon asked her quietly.

"Perfect," she said, smiling.

I knew a few of the higher-ups probably knew she had gone into heat as both Zack and Damon needed to cover for me. I saw Damon's ex glance towards us, lowering her head to me before she walked out towards the back.

"Well, unless we are going to be like the old folks and stay inside, shall we head outside?" Zack asked.

"Oi! Who you calling old, pup?" One of the older men shouted, already downing beer like water.

"Or do you want to try us? We may be old, but we can assure you that we are strong and able!" Another called out.

"Oh, I can vouch for him! He is very able!" His mate said, blushing as the other old she-wolves all began to tease her.

Yeah, still young at heart. I smiled slightly as Zack raised his hand in surrender.

"Sorry."

"You deserved that, babe," Taylor said as they led the way out, Damon following them.

I turned to Raven, who looked at me just then. She looked breathtaking. It was a little different than her usual colour, but she suited it beautifully. The dress hugged her curves, emphasising that tiny waist and cleavage before draping over her sexy ass. She reached up, her eyes flashed, and her heart raced as she cupped my face, tugging me down.

Raven...

She didn't reply, simply placing a soft kiss on my lips. The sparks were dancing between us, yet beyond them, I felt her lips quiver slightly as she pulled away. A ripple of whispers spread through the old wolves, but I pretended not to hear them as Raven wrapped her arms around mine, resting her head against my shoulder. I was hurting her once again. I didn't like the silent treatment.

"I knew it!"

"That's our Luna!"

"I see Scarlett in her."

"They make a cute couple; I just hope she's not a magic lover…"

I frowned, feeling a flare of anger. I knew what they were insinuating; the birth of Azura…

"Ignore them," Raven whispered, but I was far too angry to do so.

I turned back towards them, staring at the granny who had spoken, about to speak. My eyes flashed when I felt a hand on my back.

"Patience, Liam. I'll handle it. Go outside," Dad said quietly, his eyes blazing cobalt. He didn't like anyone saying anything about Azura's birth as much as me. He had made it clear it was never to be talked about. I just wished people weren't so fucking backwards…

"Drink?" Mom asked, pushing two glasses into mine and Raven's hands.

"You look good, Mom," I said, giving her a hug.

"Thanks," she said, doing a small twirl in her cerulean dress that matched Dad's eyes. "Where's Elijah gone?"

"Handling something inside," Raven said, her attention going to the small kids' area that was all decked out with balloons, a bouncy castle, a ball pit, and some Omegas dressed up as cartoon characters. "Ooh, there's a kiddie area?"

"I don't think anyone is going to feel comfortable leaving their kids at home," Mom replied as Raven hurried over to go see the kids. "She sure loves kids."

"Hmm?" I raised an eyebrow, a little too distracted by Raven's ass.

"I'm not complaining," Mom said with a smirk as Dad stepped out, and she wrapped her arms around his neck. It took me a second to realise what she was hinting at. Pups…

I looked over at Raven, watching as she pulled faces, teasing the boys and complimenting the girls on their outfits. I felt a pang of pain inside. I doubted I'd live long enough to see that moment…

I swallowed hard; I wouldn't let the darkness get the better of me…

"Kiara won't be making it," Dad said as he stepped into the garden, phone in hand.

"Oh, no, why?" Mom said, playing with Dad's shirt.

"Because…" I looked away as Dad got a little too distracted checking Mom out. "Their Delta's mate has gone into labour early. It's high risk, the one having quads, so Kiara needs to be there."

"Oh, if we knew earlier, we could have sent someone to bring Dante at least," Mom said, sounding a little disappointed.

"Next time," Dad said quietly.

I watched Raven help a pup that had fallen off the bouncy castle to her feet, kissing the top of her head softly. She was beautiful, selfless, and so fucking perfect…

"Go have fun, or are you just going to stare at her from here?" Dad asked, smirking, bringing me out of my thoughts.

"Hmm," I murmured, slipping my hands into my pockets as I looked around.

The couples dancing, the teens teasing and messing around to the side, the children laughing and giggling with no care in the world. Taylor and Zack were standing to the side talking, or more like flirting quietly, before Channing rolled his wheelchair over, and they joined in talking together. Robyn was sitting with Aunty Monica, styling her hair. And Mom and Dad were making out like it was their bedroom… *Seriously*…

Damon was next to Raven, who was next to the dessert table, both smiling over something. She looked towards me, and her eyes softened, motioning me over. I gave a small nod, my emotions surging within me.

I was always in the background… I was sure if worst came to worst, they'd be okay because they had each other. They lived without me for three years, and they would live for many more…

I looked at her as she brushed her hair out of her face, nodding to something Damon said, but her gaze kept coming back to me. The only one I was scared about was her. Her reaction from earlier, her love for me…

I would fight for as long as I could. For her.

I walked over to her, and she excused herself, coming over to me.

"Want to dance?" I asked her.

Her eyes widened in surprise before she nodded vigorously and pulled me towards the dance floor. She wrapped her arms around my neck, and I gripped her waist, pulling her against me as we began moving slowly to the music. Her scent was like a wave of serenity.

"Please don't think like that," she whispered, her fingers brushing my neck, sending off sparks.

"With you in my arms… how can I?" I whispered huskily. Bending down, I kissed her with everything I had, pouring my soul and heart into it.

You are my dream.

You are my life.

You are my all.

RAVEN

It terrified me knowing that, deep down, he felt like he wouldn't make it. I saw him fighting. Even at night, he'd wake up and hold me tight, his heart thundering as the darkness surged. I felt him weaken as he repeatedly hurt himself to contain the threat he may become.

The emotions in his kiss terrified me. It told me how much he loved me, how much he wanted to be with me, yet the fear that he'll lose me…

"So… tell me, what colour should I wear tomorrow?" I asked, looking up into those gorgeous cerulean eyes that I loved as a new song began playing.

"Hmm…. I actually have something for you," he said, smiling softly. His eyes sparkled as he caressed my cheek before cupping my chin. "I hope you like it."

"Ooo, an outfit… I do like it! Even if I haven't seen it!" I said, kissing his thumb that was rubbing my bottom lip.

He smiled in amusement before his gaze fell to my lips as he licked his own lush ones. I wrapped my mouth around his thumb, taking it fully into my mouth and letting my tongue stroke it as I sucked on it for a moment, my eyes watching him seductively. My core throbbed with a need only he could satiate.

"Fuck, love," he growled huskily, pulling me close and kissing me hard.

This was the life.

LIAM

Much later, everyone had eaten and drunk a lot. I had gone easy on the drinks, having two, and that was it. With the darkness looking for any chance to seep out, I needed to be in my right fucking mind.

We were seated at a table; Zack, Taylor, Damon, Raven, and I were all playing spin the bottle, a game that Taylor insisted we play.

"Okay, okay, how old were you Zack when you lost your virginity?" Taylor asked, smiling goofily. The dude sure was drunk.

"Thirteen," Zack said, making Taylor pout.

"That's early!"

"You asked, babe," Zack replied, kissing him hard. Taylor pulled him close, although there wasn't much space left between them. The rest of us exchanged looks as Raven giggled, watching them.

"How old are you?" I asked her, standing up. Her reply was only to whistle and giggle again. Damon chuckled.

"Go home, guys," he teased.

The three of us went over to the side. The party was still going strong, and I knew it would continue for another few hours.

"Aunty seems happier lately," Raven said, looking over at Monica, who was sitting with Mom and Dad as Mom hugged her.

"Yeah, I think having more people around her has really helped..." Damon said guiltily. I knew he was probably feeling awful that he had to leave her often.

"You have work, don't feel bad. No one realised we could have done more... I'm sure we can make sure Aunty always has someone around her," I said, frowning thoughtfully.

"She's aware that Dad isn't here... but she's coping," Damon whispered, his eyes on his mother.

"Yeah, losing a mate isn't easy," Raven said quietly. All eyes were on Aunty Monica, but I wouldn't deny that we were all thinking of our situation.

I realised Damon only had his mother... and Raven... she only had us. Her family was gone.

"Ooo, they are cutting the cake!"

I smiled, watching her. Dad had cut the cake, and Mom had fed him a piece a while ago, but it hadn't been cut up for the rest until now. Trust Raven to want some, but in the process, she left Damon and me alone with that mate comment hanging in the air. I decided to ask him the question that was on my mind.

"Why didn't you tell me you two had rejected each other? I swear I didn't know, or I wouldn't have said -"

"I know you didn't. You're not a sly person, Liam. You're straight up. I knew you didn't know, and Raven confirmed that. We did what was best, for all of us…" he said quietly, looking up at the sky, sighing deeply.

"It takes a lot. Thank you," I said quietly, looking at him.

"It does, but that's the difference between us… you're an Alpha, and I'm a Beta." He smiled despite the pain in his voice, but his words hit home. "We won't ever be equal, no matter how much we say it."

I didn't say anything. I couldn't. I was an Alpha, and it was in my blood to be possessive, but in the process, I had made him feel inferior. That was never the intention.

"That's not true, Damon. My behaviour does not mean -"

"I love you, Liam. You are my Alpha, but don't use that line. We both know we aren't equal," he said quietly, his eyes full of hurt, hurt that he usually masked so well.

"Guys, come here!" Raven shouted.

"Come on," Damon said, patting my shoulder.

"Damon." He paused, glancing back at me.

"Yeah?"

"I may have wanted her all for myself, but never once did I think that I deserved her more than you because my rank was higher than yours. I've always loved her since I was young, that was all I could think of. That I loved her first… it was never because I was an Alpha, and you weren't," I said quietly. I needed him to know that.

"Isn't it the same thing?" He asked quietly. I didn't reply, unable to.

If anything were to happen to me… maybe they could be together. Maybe that was why she was given two mates? I watched him walk off, thinking he'd once said he'd die for me… *Didn't he realise I'd do the same for him, too?*

"Liam?" Raven asked, coming over and holding a plate piled high with two, no, three, large slices of cake.

"Yes, beautiful?" I asked softly as she caressed my face with her free hand.

"Are you okay?" I nodded.

"That's a lot of cake for one bite-sized she-wolf," I teased. She pouted.

"One was for you," she said. I raised an eyebrow.

"Was it? Or were you planning on taking my share?" I asked.

"Not at all… I mean, you should offer it to me because I need to eat lots to grow… but that wasn't the plan," she said, blinking up at me.

Oh, it was definitely the plan. When it came to sweet treats, Raven could eat lots. I chuckled.

"Depends on what I get in return?" I asked.

"And now you're bartering. Shouldn't mates be willing to give up everything for the other?" She complained, sounding cute.

"I still want something in return." I wrapped my arm around her as she did her best to keep her plate upright, and it was at that moment that I felt a wave of coldness wash over me.

Something wasn't right.

I may not have had the ability to foresee like Kiara... but I had always been very intuitive. It was the same when we had pinpointed where the witch Endora was trying to resurrect was buried. I just... felt it.

I looked around sharply, the sound of Raven's voice fading away, my eyes burning a magnetic blue. I could see the kids playing together... Azura in Mom's lap... *No, it's not...* I turned, scanning the crowd, watching Damon walk back towards the wall where we had been not long ago... and it was then that I saw it.

The flash of something out there, hiding in the trees, metres beyond the wall. My heart thundered in my chest as I saw the glint of metal, and I realised what it was...

Time seemed to slow down, my heart thundering in my ears as my eyes homed in on the man who was holding one of the deadly assault rifles we had designed only to use on the Wendigos years ago... weapons that were meant to be locked away.

A weapon that was pointed towards us, with Damon being in its first line of range, eating his cake, unsuspecting.

My instincts kicked in and I pushed Raven to the ground.

"Get down!" I shouted as I rushed towards Damon in a flash, spinning him around and shielding him with my body as I heard the shots go off. Screams erupted in the air, and pain ripped through me, knocking the breath from me.

Pain, suffocating pain...

My entire back was screaming in burning agony, spreading through my entire body.

I couldn't breathe, I couldn't....

The growls of wolves filled the air as Damon turned, his eyes wide in shock as he stared at me, catching me before I fell.

I said I'd die for you too...

My eyes stung as I realised this was it...

I never got to say goodbye to her...

Her piercing scream of despair ripped through my heart.

I had failed her. I wanted to see her... one last time to tell her I loved her... but I couldn't link...

I looked up at Damon's hazy face. He was saying something, panic and fear in his voice. I wanted to tell him... to take care of her...

I felt my heart palpitate before it seemed to slow. The agonising pain was fading... and darkness was surrounding me. Was this what death felt like? Was my time truly over?

≪◦◦◦≫

RAVEN

My heart shattered when I felt agony tear through me as I watched Liam pull Damon away from the wall... watching my love take the rain of bullets, the smell of his blood and wolfsbane hung in the air, his pain and sadness washing through the bond.

A scream left my lips as I ran towards him.

All I could think of was the seal on his healing.

Many wolves rushed past, heading to the attacker, but all I could think of was my mate...

"Liam!" I cried as Damon placed him on his side.

"Fuck!" He whispered. He was shaking. I was about to look when he shook his head, placing his hand on my shoulder. "Don't look."

"Liam, baby," I whimpered, cupping Liam's handsome face instead. His heartbeat was fading. I couldn't think straight...

This can't be happening...

He couldn't heal! *He can't...*

"He can't heal! His healing is sealed!" I sobbed as if someone could fix this.

"What do you mean, Raven?" Damon asked urgently.

"No... no, Liam, wake up!" I cried, cradling his head to my chest.

He can't die, or I don't want to live anymore. Goddess, take me instead!

"Liam!" Aunty Red called. "Raven, what do you mean he can't heal?" She looked ghostly as tears streamed down her cheeks.

"He got Delsanra to seal his abilities away so he wouldn't hurt anyone if he lost control!"

"No wonder… I couldn't sense his Alpha Aura…" Aunty Red murmured. "We need something to lift him onto! To get him to the hospital!"

I stared down at him…

This was a nightmare…

It's not real…

I couldn't breathe… *I can't…*

I don't want to live without him…

I need him!

The pain inside of me was ripping me apart, tearing into me like a thousand beasts ready to kill, each passing moment more painful than the last. My head was pounding, my heart was squeezing…

I felt someone dragging me away from Liam.

"Let go of me!" I struggled, tears blurring my vision. *I need him!*

"He'll be okay," Damon's soothing voice promised, but it was a lie! I could hear it in his voice, the broken tone of defeat.

The two doctors were shaking their heads and pointing at his back.

"…. can't move him…"

"He'll die…"

"It's too late…"

No. No! It's not too late!

"I need him! Let go of me!" I screamed.

I won't let him go!

I twisted in Damon's arms, slamming my elbow into his ribs as hard as I could, and broke free, rushing to Liam's side. Aunty Red was sitting there frozen, her face ghostly white. I pushed through, lifting Liam's head in my hands.

You are my world. I won't be able to live if my world is gone. I looked at his handsome face, tears streaming down my cheeks. *The fight isn't over until we take our last breath.*

I kissed his unmoving lips, and for a moment everything faded away…

The soft tingle of a dying bond remained…

There's nothing worth living for if he's gone.

I looked down at his neck, my heart pounding, my eyes flashing before I bent down, extracting my canines and sinking them into his neck, marking Him...

I felt the flicker of the spark flare through us as I felt the bond becoming complete. His heart skipped a beat, picking up for a moment, and my heart leapt with hope.

"Please, blue eyes, look at me," I begged.

"We need to get the bullets out. Just try!" Aunty Red was shouting. "Contact Kiara!"

"Luna, please, listen, he... there's no hope," one of the doctors was whispering. I stared down at him, begging him silently.

Wake up, baby... please, wake up...

His heart thumped, once... twice... and then...

It stopped.

I felt something being torn from my chest, agony slicing through me like a million lashes.

"No!" Aunty Red's scream filled the sky.

I closed my eyes as pain I had never felt before wrapped around me...

I couldn't breathe. The pain inside of me was crushing me...

Goddess... if you are to take him, then you will take me, too...

I opened my eyes as tears streamed down my cheeks, staring down into the face of the man I loved. Reality hit me brutally, wreaking havoc in my life in a way I never thought was possible, completely destroying me.

Only one reality rang clear in that raging storm.

Liam was gone.

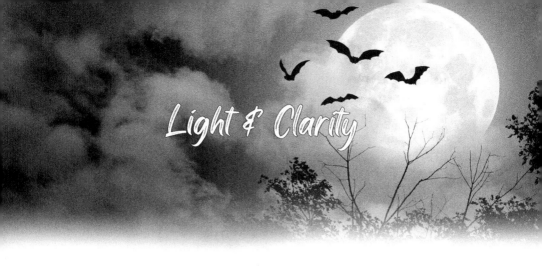

Light & Clarity

LIAM

RIGHT LIGHT. THAT WAS all I could see. I couldn't hear or feel anything…

I opened my eyes and looked around. There was nothing but light. It was dazzling, yet it didn't hurt the eyes. I was no longer in pain… I sat up slowly.

Where am I?

"You are nowhere, just in-between life and death," a majestic voice answered. It was strong and beautiful, but it didn't sound human.

A soft laugh filled the air, and I realised something was forming in front of me. A glowing outline of a tall woman with long hair… I had to look away. Looking at her directly made my eyes sting due to the intensity of the light. I didn't need her to introduce herself to know who she was. I lowered my head to her, not sure how to feel.

"Goddess…"

"Indeed, my child." I could tell from her voice that she was smiling. "I am proud of you; you sacrificed your life for your brother." I frowned, everything returning to me.

"I don't think he sees me as a brother anymore… I lost that right long ago," I said quietly.

She held her glowing hand out, her flowing white dress swaying in a non-existent breeze. I took it hesitantly, feeling a cooling smoothness wash over me.

"It is in your blood to want your mate for yourself. You are still brothers. You are one pack, one family," she said as I stood up, letting go of her hand.

That's true, we are…

"To err is part of life. You broke the centuries-old curse, child; one I knew you could." Surprise rushed through me, and although I couldn't hear it, my heart was thumping in my chest.

"The curse is broken?"

"You gave the gift of life, selflessly sacrificing your own for someone else, someone who has caused you great inner conflict. You cast aside your bitterness and fought this darkness…" I stayed silent, remembering the curse and prophecy. She laughed softly.

"The curse… ah… Helios is not one to forget the insult. His curse was strong. I knew I would need someone powerful to break it. I have waited centuries for the right wolf to be born. I have created many strong, powerful Alphas of the Deimos line, yet none as compassionate as you. Alphas are powerful, strong, and have the will to lead. It is their soulmates who are usually the more compassionate, loving ones. I couldn't simply evade the curse. When Helios foresaw your birth and the power that you would have, he came to me… I couldn't simply bend the rules to break the curse. We, gods, have rules and regulations, too, after all. Yours and the blessed wolf's births weakened the curse, but I had to seal away your abilities. In their place, he placed the darkness within you, the ultimate test to either break the curse or end the Deimos line for eternity. The burden was upon you before you even left your mother's womb."

I pondered on her words, taking them in slowly, and frowned slightly.

"Abilities?" I asked, trying to make sense of what she had said completely.

"Yes, you are the Deimos prince."

"Aren't all Deimos Alphas princes, since we come from the Deimos line, like Dad or Grandad?" I asked as we walked side by side with no destination in mind.

"Not at all. I placed within you the powers second only to the original Deimos wolf. You are far more pure-blooded than your predecessors, hence a Deimos prince. Far more powerful."

"Yet…"

"Speak your mind, child," she said, although I knew she knew what I was thinking.

"Raven... her having two mates... what was the reason behind it?" I asked quietly, unable to hide the sadness. I always felt that I wasn't enough.

"Oh, child, never think you are not enough."

"Then why?"

"To test you. I couldn't simply allow you to have a life of ease if I wished for you to break the curse. There were several outcomes that could have taken place, and even I did not know how it would go. I cannot foresee everything, after all, just the possible outcomes. When I made you, I created for you a mate whom I knew would be far too gentle to want to hurt either. It needed to be from you," she sighed, despite her voice sounding as light and powerful as ever. "You have broken the curse, yet you are neither alive nor dead." I knew that...

"However, your mate marked you."

I looked at her sharply, only to flinch due to the blinding light, and looked away, touching my neck. My heart thudded at the realisation.

"She's completed the bond between you two."

Raven... why...

"Because she loves you."

"But I'm on the brink of death, right?" I asked, my heart squeezing in pain.

"Yes, your heart stopped a moment ago. Here, time moves strangely... but she marked you. Even when your body could no longer fight, she still risked her life by sharing her strength with you, thus destroying this curse."

"But I was too late..." I didn't care... but Raven...

My heart squeezed thinking of her. She had lost everyone in life...

"If you die, wouldn't that mean the curse has won? You must live."

My heart soared with hope. I looked at her, fighting the bright light, knowing that the moment was about to end. I had one request.

"Damon... please give him a second chance. He doesn't deserve to be alone." He had given up Raven for me, and although I couldn't share her... I wanted him to find his happiness, too. He had lost far too much.

I couldn't see her properly, but I knew she was smiling.

"Fear not... I have a plan. I always have a plan. Fight for what you want, child... the Deimos line *must* live on..." Her voice faded away, and I looked around, realising she was gone.

Suddenly, I was plunged into darkness. What was this?

Then I was falling backwards at an incredible speed...

RAVEN

"No... no!"

"Raven..." Damon whispered, but I refused to let go of Liam. Even though it hadn't even been a minute since his heart stopped, it felt like an eternity...

"Do something! Bring him -"

A sudden darkness seeped out of him, sending a shiver down my spine, and then an enormous amount of dazzling blue energy emitted from Liam, throwing us all back. I gasped as Damon caught me, both of us getting thrown straight into the dessert table. The wave of pure blue aura burst outwards, shattering the windows of the packhouse in the process. The trees bent under the sheer force of the blue light that illuminated the entire sky, washing away the darkness.

"Liam!" I cried out, feeling the sizzling strong snap of the mate bond fall back into place, a surge of emotions and strength filling me.

He's alive!

I was the first to rush to his side, the glowing blue aura whirling around him. He took a deep breath, his eyes flying open, blazing a brilliant magnetic blue that stared directly into mine. He cupped the back of my neck, one arm pulling me into his lap.

"Baby..."

"Blue eyes..." I whispered, flinging my arms around his neck. His heart was thundering loudly, and that intense aura surrounded him.

"Fuck, I love you," he whispered. His heart was pounding, as was my own, his hands roaming my body as if to reassure himself that I was alive.

"I love you, too, so much," I whispered. His hand tangled in my hair, pulling me close and kissing me passionately.

I couldn't even kiss him back for a second, too shocked at the intense sparks that erupted inside of me. The pure intensity of the completed bond made my entire body sizzle with delicious tingles that sent my stomach into a knot of burning desire.

I can't lose you... I whispered through the link, kissing him back, our lips so perfectly moulded against the others.

You won't.

I whimpered softly the moment he broke away, kissing me down my jaw and neck, not leaving an inch of my bare skin empty from his touch as his arms wrapped around me tightly.

The muffled sob of Aunty Red reached me, and it took my all to pull away from his touch, my eyes full of tears. I looked at her, knowing she wanted to meet her son too. I motioned with my head, and she came over, smiling at us before flinging her arms around us both with her body shaking in silent sobs as she held us tightly. Liam's strong arms wrapped around us both, placing soft kisses on top of both of our heads.

"I'm okay," Liam said, my heart skipping a beat as I closed my eyes.

Thank the goddess…

Aunty Red moved back, and Uncle El pulled her into his arms, looking at Liam. He was in nothing but shorts since he had been one of the ones to go after the attacker in a blind rage.

"You gave us a scare there," he said quietly.

"Sorry," Liam said, standing up.

"No need to apologise. Guess you're just making up for being such a good pup when you were little," Uncle El said, his eyes full of emotions.

The man before me had truly been through so much in life, yet he still remained so strong. He hugged his son, and I smiled, watching them. Liam was taller and bulkier, and I realised that he was ready to let his father retire… to be the Alpha that Uncle El could rely on, too.

"Wiyam, are you okay?" Azura's little voice came, big tears splashing down her cheek.

"I am, pumpkin," Liam said, crouching down and pulling her into his arms. I smiled softly, staring at his back. Save the blood that remained, he was fully healed…

৩৩৩৩

Now that Liam was okay, the questions filled my mind. What the hell happened?

"Who was it?" I asked.

A silence fell, and my stomach twisted. Why weren't they telling me? I looked at Damon, who was still pale, watching Liam almost as if he couldn't believe he was okay.

"Damon?" He looked at me, his heart racing as he glanced at Uncle El. Even Aunty Red moved back questioningly.

"Haru Jacobs," Uncle El answered quietly, making my stomach plummet. My father... he...

"He's dead. I killed him. I'm sorry," Uncle El said, looking directly at me. I shook my head.

"No, I'm sorry that this happened because of me... I'm sorry."

"Hey. Stop apologising. You are not responsible for your father's crimes, Raven," Uncle El said firmly as I fought back the tears.

Liam stood up again, closing the gap between us. He pulled me tightly into his arms, making sparks erupt through me as he encased me in his embrace.

Please, never let me go.

"Yeah, you aren't responsible," he said quietly. I closed my eyes, clutching onto his ruined shirt as I sobbed quietly into it.

"It's been a long night. Everyone just head to bed for now...." Uncle El said. "The few who were injured, make sure your wounds are checked. Luckily, Liam took most of them..."

"The guards outside his home are all unconscious. Someone helped him," Zack said, making us all turn sharply.

"We'll figure this out," Uncle El said.

"The curse is broken," Liam said quietly.

Aunty Red gasped, her eyes lighting up. My heart skipped a beat as I stared up at him.

"You were willing to sacrifice yourself for me... a selfless sacrifice," Damon said quietly. "It broke the curse." He looked at Liam, who gave him a small smile.

"I always would," he replied quietly.

Their eyes met. I knew the conversation between them wasn't over. I gave Damon a small smile, and he smiled back.

"We'll get the area cleaned. You all should head home," Damon said quietly. Uncle El shook his head.

"No, we'll do this together. Red, take Azura and Monica home. Raven?"

"I'm staying to help," I said firmly.

"Okay." Uncle didn't argue, and I was relieved. Damon looked down, and I frowned, concerned.

You okay?

Yeah, I am, he replied through the link.

Our eyes met, and he gave me a wink. He was shaken by what happened… and something told me that would be the start of mending the rifts between them. I sure hoped so, anyway.

I looked at Liam, who was looking down at me with unmasked adoration in his eyes that were still shining magnetic blue. My heart skipped a beat, and I raised my eyebrows.

"What is it?" I asked.

"You look beautiful. Even with that cake in your hair," he teased, and just like that, I felt like everything was going to be completely fine.

༺☙☙☙༻

We returned to the Westwood home two hours later. We had helped clean up, including getting the glass from inside the bedrooms cleaned up too. I had caught a glimpse of Dad's body, but I didn't want to see him.

He hated me to such an extent that he was ready to kill those important to me. It baffled me that he went for Damon and not Liam… but that was a question for another day.

I locked his bedroom door just as Liam pulled his shirt off and tossed it in the bin. His body was perfection… every ridge and muscle so deliciously flawless…

He looked at me, and my heart skipped a beat. Even the scar down his eye added to his sex appeal. Oh, Goddess… why did he look even more distracting? Those eyes of his still blazed magnetic blue. My mate.

"Join me," he said huskily.

I blushed, nodding as I took his outstretched hand, and he led me to the bathroom. He had seen me naked when I was in heat, but… I realised that I was actually going to see him naked, too…completely.

"Nervous?" He asked huskily.

"Not at all…" I said, confidentially unzipping his pants as he slid the zip down my dress. "Your aura's stronger."

"Apparently, I have some special abilities, although we are yet to see what they are." I cocked a brow.

"Your eyes are still your wolf's, and your aura is so strong... can't you reign it in?" I asked as I shimmied out of my dress, turning away slightly, left in nothing but my underwear.

"It is reigned in, love," he said, taking off his pants.

My eyes fell to the front of his black fitted boxers. Goddess... I averted my gaze. The urge to take a good long look was strong, but...

I was about to step into the shower when Liam's hands gripped my hips from behind.

"Not forgetting these?" He whispered, hooking his fingers into my panties. I gasped, feeling his naked body behind me, making my core clench and my heart thump like crazy.

"Maybe I wanted you to take them off," I said softly. *No, I was planning on keeping them on!*

"With pleasure," he whispered before his lips attacked my neck with passionate, hot, hungry kisses. His hands roamed my waist and stomach, making me whimper.

"Liam...." I whispered as he began kissing me down my back, sending shivers of pleasure through me. I gasped when he tugged my underwear down with his teeth, making my core throb, and I knew he could smell my arousal... *Fuck...*

"You're mine, Raven," he growled possessively.

I gasped when his fingers brushed my inner thigh. His teeth grazed my hip as he peeled my underwear off, and I bit my lip as the fabric slid out from my ass cheeks ever so slowly.

"Yours," I whispered, unable to resist the way my body arched at his touch. My panties dropped to the floor, and Liam stood up.

"That's better," he whispered, his fingers skimming my hips. I bit back a whimper, feeling his erection prod my back.

My stomach fluttered nervously as he nudged me into the shower, reaching over and switching it on. Warm water poured down on us, and I gasped, not because of the downpour of water but because Liam's lips met my neck once more.

"You marked me," he said quietly. He reached for the body wash, squirting a generous amount onto his hands. I was about to take the bottle, but he put it back, rubbing his hands together before he cupped my breasts.

"I... I did. You marked me, too," I said, my cheeks burning at how turned on I was becoming. I could feel him rock hard behind me, the beating of his heart, the way he was controlling himself as he soaped my body, his hand running down my waist and stomach. My core clenched.

"I did... but you risked your life..." he said quietly. His husky voice sent a shiver through me.

"I didn't want to live without you," I whispered quietly; my eyes fluttered shut when his hand cupped my core, making me moan.

"Don't say that... but thank you for choosing me."

"I..." A moan left my lips when his fingers parted my folds, and he rubbed his soapy fingers along my clit. "Liam..." I reached behind me, tangling my hand into his hair, my heart thumping when he groaned.

"I wanted to take you out... make everything fucking special for you... but..."

His finger rubbed my clit faster, his other hand grabbing my breast. I moaned loudly. His lips met my neck in a slow, erotic kiss, his tongue flicking out and running up my neck, leaving behind a fire of illicit desire. His words, his touch, and the pleasure he was inflicting on me were making me go crazy, yet it was his next words and action that made me lose any control I had left.

"But I can't wait any longer. I want you. I fucking need you," he whispered seductively in my ear just as his finger penetrated me...

Taste of Heaven

RAVEN

I PRESSED MY HEAD BACK against his hard chest as I cried out in pleasure.
"Fuck, Liam…" I wanted him, too, completely.

He bit into my neck, an orgasm ripping through me. The mix of pain and pleasure tipped me over the edge, making me see dots. I groaned, riding it out.

"Fuck, that's it," Liam growled, licking my neck before he slipped his finger out and turned me around. He pinned my wrists above my head with one hand before he stepped back, letting his gaze rake over me like I was the most precious thing in the world to him. I was shaking slightly from my orgasm, but still, my core was clenching for more. "You're beautiful…"

My heart thundered, and I let my gaze trail over his delicious body, from his wet locks falling over his sexy magnetic blue eyes, his broad hard chest, abs that were carved to such precision… and his dick… Goddess… it was huge! My eyes widened, my heart thundering as I stared at it. That was not small! Taylor lied!

Taylor, you are so dead!

Goddess, that thing is terrifying!

Despite the thoughts that trampled across my mind, my pussy throbbed at the thought of having that inside of me. I licked my lips. The excitement within me was growing, overriding the fear, and with confidence, I reached over, wrapping my hand around his thick, large cock.

"I'm impressed," I whispered naughtily, looking up at him.

"Yeah? Not scared?" He winked, leaning in and kissing me hungrily. I moaned into his mouth, running my hand along his shaft.

"Scared? What's to be scared about? I can't wait to have you inside me," I whispered breathlessly.

He growled, letting go of my wrists and began kissing me down between my boobs, along my side, and under my arms, making me shiver. His hands were palming my breasts before he took one of my hardened nipples in his mouth. I whimpered in pleasure. His touch was hungry yet soft as he sucked on it gently, his thumb rubbing the other one. I cried out when he squeezed it slightly, gasping as he ran his tongue down my stomach and over my pubic bone. I gasped, spreading my legs.

"That's it, love. Spread these sexy thighs for me." He lifted one of my legs over his shoulder, at the same time plunging his tongue into my molten core.

"Liam!" I whimpered, feeling another wave of pleasure rip through me. I tangled my hand in his hair, pressing my back against the tiled wall behind me as he ate me out. "Liam… fuck, that's… don't stop," I whimpered, standing on the tip of my toes as I moved my hips against his face.

Biting my lip, I swung my other leg over his shoulder, making him growl in approval. His hands moved to my ass, and his tongue played with my clit. I cupped the back of his head, keeping my legs open as he devoured me. My moans only grew louder as a second orgasm built inside of me.

"Fuck, *Liam*!" I gasped, pleasure ricocheting through me, and I felt my juices mix with the water as his tongue worked its sinful magic. My entire body convulsed from the delicious pleasure.

He stood up, his hands on my ass as I slid back, keeping my knees hooked around his shoulders but enough space between us so I could look into his handsome face. A face that looked so fucking hot right then, with his plump lips slightly parted, his eyes full of pure want. Fuck…

"Nothing could ever taste better," he whispered, lifting me close and running his tongue slowly along my pussy once again, making me whimper before placing kisses over my stomach.

I bent down, claiming his lips in a passionate kiss as I slid my legs down and, instead, wrapped them around his waist. He pressed me back against the tiled wall, his tongue roaming every inch of my mouth possessively. His hand ran up and down my back, making me whimper in pleasure. Our tongues played with each other's sensually, fighting for control, which he wouldn't allow me to take.

The pleasure that rushed through me, the emotions from both of us running through the bond, the intensity of the sparks and the electrifying pleasure… it was heaven.

I broke away, gasping for air, and dropped to the ground, bending down before him.

"Raven…"

"I want to taste you, too," I whispered, cupping his balls.

"We can- fuck!"

He groaned the moment I twirled my tongue on his smooth tip, taking away whatever he was about to say. Even with the water pouring over us, the slightly salty taste of his pre-cum lingered, making me moan in satisfaction. I could get used to this…

He was huge. As I licked and sucked on his tip, running my fingers over his balls, I groaned in pleasure. My eyes fixed on his face. He was looking at me through those thick lashes of his, one hand flat against the shower wall, the other tangled in my hair.

"Fuck…that's it, love."

I leaned down, flattening my tongue to the base of his cock and running my tongue along it, feeling myself throbbing as he groaned. His aura was enhancing. His cock twitched as I made sure I didn't leave any part of it untouched before I licked and sucked his balls, making his legs tremble, my hand pumping his dick.

"Do you like that, baby?" I whispered. The confidence that flowed throw me was accompanied by the satisfaction in this indulgence of pleasure. This was the man I was going to experience my every fantasy with, the only one I wanted.

I took his tip into my mouth, feeling it stretch my lips completely, running my tongue along it. I knew how to do this, even if it was my first time. Kiara and I had practised enough on vegetables before we'd burst into fits of giggles, but… it seemed to have helped.

"Fuck, babe!" He growled when I sucked my cheeks in, wrapping my mouth completely around his cock as I began bobbing back and forth, letting him hit the back of my throat. He took over, thrusting into my mouth faster and harder.

That's it, baby, fuck my mouth, I whimpered hornily through the link.

One hand was still wrapped around the base of his cock, and the other gripped his thigh. I almost gagged at the speed and power he was moving at, although I could see the control he was trying to keep... but I liked it. I wanted him to lose control...

Don't hold back, baby... I may be small, but I'm strong, I murmured through the link, taking him more into my mouth and down my throat.

"Shit, you're driving me fucking crazy, baby." He groaned, "Fuck, Raven... You're damn good..."

For a few moments, all that filled the bathroom was the sound of me sucking his cock, his groans, and the pattering of the shower.

"I'm going to come, love," he warned.

I want you.

I was ready. I wanted him. He sped up, thrusting into my mouth and hitting the back of my throat as his hold on my hair became tighter. I looked up at him, thinking he looked so fucking good turned on. His cheeks were slightly flushed, and his lips parted; a sinful growl left his lips, and when I knew he was near, I moved back slightly so I was ready for his release.

"Fuck!" Liam growled and shot his load straight into my mouth.

I swallowed it, sucking and pumping his cock until I had milked him dry, enjoying every drop from my beautiful mate. I smiled when he swore in pleasure, sliding his cock out of my mouth with a pleasant 'pop'. I licked my lips, swallowing the last of his salty cum.

"You're delicious," I said, seductively sliding my hands up his thighs and squeezing those muscular buns of his. "And so fucking sexy."

"That's my line," he whispered huskily, breathing hard as his hand wrapped around my neck and tugged me up before curling around the back of my neck and kissing me hard.

You taste good, right, baby? I cooed through the link, knowing he could taste himself on my tongue.

Nowhere near as fucking good as you, came his husky reply, accompanied by the throb of his cock against me again as we kissed each other hungrily.

I didn't feel nervous or embarrassed. The only emotions that were coursing through me were pleasure, desire, love, hunger, and how horny I was feeling.

"Now to make you mine…" he whispered, switching the shower off. He lifted me, and I wrapped my legs around his waist, my heart pounding as he carried me out to his bedroom, exchanging kisses as we went.

It was our moment to finally complete the mating. There were no doubts, nothing but sincerity and love. Our journey hadn't been easy, but we got there… we did it.

He dropped me on the bed, and I bounced slightly. My stomach was a mess of nerves as I slowly lay back, parting my legs. His eyes seemed to shimmer as he climbed between my parted thighs, claiming my lips in a sizzling, dangerous kiss…

✿

LIAM

She was heaven and more, from her beautiful, gorgeous, alluring eyes to her pouty, sore lips and that perfect tiny body of hers. Was it wrong that the size of her petite tiny fucking body just made it all a whole lot fucking hotter?

This was my little doll, my hot plaything… my love, my mate, fuck, she was my all.

As I climbed between her legs and claimed those temptingly soft, pouty lips, I ran my hands down her waist and hips, memorising every dip and curve of her heavenly body, one I would worship forever. I caressed her ass, squeezing it before running my fingers between her pussy, massaging her there. Fuck, I wanted to taste her again. As much as I wanted to bury myself between her thighs, I also knew it was her first time, and I wanted to draw it out for as long as I could. To relish the moment and inflict so much pleasure on her.

I broke away from her lips, planting open-mouthed kisses down over her breasts before sliding onto the ground. I bent down as I yanked her by her legs to the edge of the bed and spread them open wide. She was very flexible… she always had been. I was looking forward to experimenting with her in every position possible. I had seen her when she was in heat, and it had been such a turn-on…

"Fuck... Liam..." she whispered the moment I plunged my tongue into her, making her cry out, probing deeper and further inside of her. "Baby... nh!"

She whimpered, twisting her hand into my hair as I brought my thumb to her clit, rubbing it harder and fast. Her moans became louder, her body moving against my face. I knew another orgasm was building within her. I looked up; her back was arched, her perky round breasts standing at attention with those tempting, hard nipples of hers.

"Liam!" She screamed as I felt her juices squirt from her.

She struggled to move, but I held her in place, eating her out and lapping up every drop of her sweetness until she had ridden out her orgasm. Her eyes were wide, a look of pure pleasure on her face before she collapsed backwards, trembling at the intensity of her release. I reached up, pulling her upright and claiming her lips in a hungry kiss, still crouching on the ground before her. With the other hand, I squeezed two fingers into her, making her whimper. She kissed me hungrily as I fucked her with my fingers hard and fast, feeling her core clench around me.

"Ready for me, love?" I whispered, breaking away from her lips that were swollen from my constant assault. Her eyes were blazing, lust and love screaming strongly in them.

"Without a doubt," she whispered.

Our eyes met, and I kissed her slower, deeper, pouring my emotions into it. Savouring her sweet taste and inhaling her scent. Wrapping my arms around her, I lifted her back onto the bed and laid over her, chest to chest, our hearts pounding as I rubbed myself against her tiny entrance. Yeah, I had wondered how it would fit... but she was made to cater to me, so...

"I'll go slow," I murmured, looking into her eyes. She smiled, closing her eyes. The look of pleasure on her face was enough proof that she wanted this as much as I did.

"I know. I trust you," she whispered, her arms wrapping around my shoulders. I reached down between our naked bodies, gripping my dick and rubbing it between her slick folds. "Fuck, Liam," she whimpered, her eyes fluttering open as she stared at me.

I gave her a soft smile, exhaling slowly, trying not to ram into her, and slowly penetrated her. Her eyes flew open, and I claimed her lips in a sensual kiss to relax her.

"Mmm…" she moaned against my lips as I thrust into her slowly. I had to bite back a loud groan of my own. Fuck, this felt so fucking good… "Keep going," she whimpered, her nails digging into my shoulders. Her pebbled nipples rubbed against my own chest, sending off fucking sparks.

I thrust into her, burying my face in her neck as I drove into her to the hilt, making her cry out before it changed into a sigh. I stayed inside of her, feeling her relax under me and began moving, thrusting into her at a steady pace. Pleasure consumed me. I made love to her nice and slow, our eyes locked.

My world… my dream… my all…

Her eyes glistened with unshed tears, but I knew it was more due to her intense emotions than the pain. Slowly, she cupped my face, pulling me down on top of her and kissing my neck. I was nearing; the pleasure of just being buried inside of her was something at a level I had never experienced before.

She had definitely ruined anything else for me, but that was okay because I wouldn't need to use my hand to get off from there on out, not when I had her. I smiled softly, claiming her lips once more.

"I love you, Raven. I always have," I whispered huskily.

I love you, too, so, so much, she moaned back breathlessly.

Feeling her body clench around me, I sped up, thrusting into her faster. It was taking my all to hold back, and when she cried out in pleasure, I let myself go, shooting my load into her. Pleasure rocked my body again, and for a moment, I went blank, simply enjoying the feeling of euphoria that ran through me.

"Fuck…" I groaned, about to pull out, when she locked her legs around my waist.

"You made love to me… and now… I want you to fuck me," she whispered commandingly. Despite her pounding heart and the look of contentment on her face, I could still see the burning hunger that I knew was mirrored on my own. I smirked.

"My kind of girl," I whispered, feeling myself pulsate inside of her.

Yeah, finally, I could unleash the beast of desire within me. My little doll had no idea what she had just asked for, for the rest of her life… but then again, I had a feeling she was my match. There was a minx hidden deep within that cute flirty front of hers.

Pulling out, I flipped her over, lifting her onto her knees, before I positioned myself behind her, admiring her ass. I squeezed it, appreciating her pussy that was leaking some of my white cum mixed with a bit of blood. *Mine.*

I gripped her hips, pushing into her once again, but this time I didn't take it slow, her moan of pleasure telling me she was completely ready. I sped up, slamming into her hard and fast. The slapping of our skin and our moans mixed perfectly as I fucked her harder and faster.

"Fuck, Liam, that's it!" She whimpered. Her ass jiggled from the sheer force of my pounding. "That feels so good." It sure fucking did…

Feeling her nearing, I pulled out, making her whimper,

"I-"

"I want to see your face when I make you cum," I said, flipping her onto her back and grabbing her hips. I lifted her off the bed, thrusting into her once again.

She cried out, placing her legs on my shoulders as I began fucking her again, my eyes fixed on her bouncing breasts and that gorgeous face of hers. No sound escaped her when her orgasm ripped through her, her flushed, glowing face a picture of pure bliss as her body arched, her plush lips forming a silent O as her body trembled from her release.

Fuck… My own pleasure was building with extreme intensity. I pulled out just as I came, stroking my dick a few times swiftly, letting my seed coat her abdomen and breasts. I watched the strings of pure white decorate her, and fuck did she look hot.

She was breathing hard, weakly running her fingers over her stomach, coating her tips in my cum before she slipped them into her mouth, licking it off. Her eyes locked with mine as she did, making pleasure rush south once again. *She'll be the fucking death of me.*

"Fuck, Liam…" she whispered, getting onto her knees. She wrapped her arms around my neck, and I pulled her close. Our bodies moulded as one, and she giggled when I throbbed against her stomach. "Not satiated, Alpha?"

"When it comes to you… never…" I murmured huskily, crashing my lips against hers before I dropped onto the bed, spooning behind her with my hard cock pressed against her ass.

We kissed hungrily, my fingers groping her breasts before I reached down, slamming into her pussy once again. She moaned, but she started moving herself. I knew she'd feel it in the morning, but right then, she was enjoying it just as much. I hooked my hand around her sexy thigh, lifting it as I sped up, fucking her harder and faster...

Her moans and cries of pleasure filled the room once more as I kissed her neck hard. Tonight was going to be long...

⁕⁕⁕

The first light of morning was peeping through the window when we finally collapsed onto the bed, totally wasted... her body a canvas of our night of lovemaking.

She had already fallen asleep, and I smiled, dragging my body onto my elbow, impressed at the stamina she actually had. I guessed the rigorous training built it up. I kissed her lips softly before peeling the top layer of my bedding off and pulling the blanket over us both. Tonight had been perfect...

I love you, my little bitesize doll...

Morning After

RAVEN

MY EYES FLUTTERED OPEN to the feel of sparks fluttering up my hip. I stared into Liam's dazzling magnetic blue eyes, his fingers the source of the sparks.

"Morning, beautiful," he said in his husky, sexy morning voice. He cupped the back of my neck as he leaned in, pressing his lips against mine. I kissed him back, moaning softly into his mouth.

Memories of last night sent a wave of pleasure through me, and I bit my lip, pressing myself against his naked body, almost groaning in pleasure at the feel of his cock against my stomach. The ache in my lower region was strong, and I could feel it in my lower back too. He was definitely a beast… not that I had complained…

"Morning," I whispered when he broke away, my gaze dipping to his neck. My mark upon him… it was gorgeous; a wolf's head with branches beneath it, and at the centre, right beneath the wolf, was a flower. "It's beautiful," I said, running my fingers over it.

"Yeah? Just like the one who gave it to me," he replied, pulling me close and nuzzling his nose against my neck. I blushed, a sudden thought coming to me.

"The walls are definitely soundproof, right?" I whispered.

"Definitely. Dad got this place made. We both know what that means," he murmured, sucking on my neck.

"You aren't an angel, either," I said, trying to ignore the urge to touch his manhood once more.

"I never said I was," he whispered, squeezing my ass before he sat up, got out of bed and walked to the mirror to look at his mark.

"Do you like it?" I asked, sitting up and grabbing a pillow to cover myself, although, after last night, I didn't think there was any reason for that.

"That's a huge understatement," he murmured. "It's perfection." He turned and gave me a smile. "I'll go run you a bath. You're going to need it."

"I'm okay, I'm not that weak," I stated, rolling my eyes as I stood up, only for my legs to give, and I plopped back onto the bed, making Liam snicker.

I huffed, blushing, but it didn't last long when I realised he was walking around in all his naked glory. He came over, placing his hands on either side of my thighs as he kissed me deeply, sending off rivets of pleasure before turning and walking off. My stomach knotted as I admired his ass and those strong, muscular legs… *My man…*

I was glad he didn't tease me, although I knew that he could tell I was watching him. I licked my lips, watching him disappear into the bathroom.

I stood up again, my legs feeling heavy. Stupid stumps! I knew my legs were too big. My poor body had to carry these fat tree trunks around. No wonder I was tired! It was only because they're big… I could handle sex with Liam any day!

I made my way to the bathroom slowly, almost falling a few times, but I got there, seeing Liam had run the bath for me. Walking over to me, he lifted me up and carried me to the shower.

"I'll rinse you off," he said, kissing my lips before he turned the shower on, and just like that, we were back under the very shower we were in last night. Our eyes met, and my gaze dipped to his hard dick. I bit my lip.

There was no suggestion, no question, just this sexual chemistry between us. Neither of us spoke as Liam pulled me into his arms, and I jumped up, wrapping my arms around his neck and my legs around his waist as we began making out once more…

❧❧❧

An hour later, I had showered and soaked in the bath before pulling on some lingerie and a black shirt of Liam's with a slogan written in gold foil. It slid off my shoulder, so I grabbed one of my belts, wrapping it around my waist.

By the time I had stepped out of the bathroom, Liam had stripped the sheets and had new ones on. The window was open, and if I didn't know better, I would never have known that the night before, we had fucked each other there countless times.

Liam was dressed in blue jeans and a fitted shirt that really did nothing to make him look any less hot, and he had his hair styled in his usual quiff. I was just applying my make-up when there was a light yet excited knock on the door. I smiled, knowing who it was before Liam even got to the door.

I felt my face burn up; it was already two in the afternoon… *Goddess, what is everyone going to think?*

"Wiyam, did you and Waven not wake up today?" Azura asked the moment the door opened. Liam crouched down to hug her, yet her large eyes scanned the room over his shoulder. For what? I had no idea. She was an adorable, curious chibi.

Aunty Red looked at me with a small smirk on her lips, holding a tray full of mouth-watering food. My cheeks burned, feeling completely mortified at knowing she probably knew what we had been up to.

"Nice to see you both awake," she said, carrying the tray over and placing it on the table beside the bed. The smell alone made my starving stomach squeeze.

"It's afternoon, Mama, why wouldn't they be awake?" Azura chipped in, placing two cans of Coca-Cola down before she hurried over to me. "Waven, I wear lipshit too?" She pouted her lips expectantly, and I couldn't resist a smile as Liam burst out laughing.

"That's a first. Lipshit," he snickered, getting a look from Aunty Red, despite the fact that she was smiling, too.

"Aww, Zuzu, you are so cute! Of course you can wear lipstick!" I said, quickly trying to find something that was light.

"This one, Waven," she said, picking up a tube of lipstick.

"That's not a nice one…" I said sheepishly. She furrowed her brows.

"I think I like this one." I gave in, tapping the deep plump lightly on her lips. She looked in the mirror expectantly, her pout only growing as she stared at herself before smiling happily. "Thank you!"

"Shall we go, baby?" Aunt Red asked her. She looked at Liam and me before shaking her head.

"I stay with Wiyam."

"Leave her, and thank you for the food," I said, smiling. My eyes fell on the steak fries and battered fish, and my stomach rumbled, reminding me now of how hungry I was.

"You are most welcome. Make sure you eat it all," she replied before smirking. "I'm sure you are both starving."

"Mom, seriously?" Liam grumbled as Azura skipped over to him.

"Well, I'd tease, but I think it was about high time," she mocked.

"Aunty!" I exclaimed. She laughed slightly.

"Well, enjoy the meal, and I'll leave you two to it. I hope you both were… careful, unless, of course, you want little Alpha babies running around."

The door shut with a small thud, and my blush vanished as I stared at Liam, both of our eyes wide. My heart thundered as realisation hit me like a tonne of bricks. We hadn't used anything…

Azura's dramatic gasp filled the room as she clapped her hands over her mouth, her huge eyes even wider as she stared between us.

"Are we having Wiyam and Waven babies?"

Neither of us responded, too shocked to even speak as we simply stared at each other, both of us trying to think how many times he'd come inside of me…

To the Future

DAMON

"ARE YOU OKAY?" ZACK asked, looking at me.

I frowned and nodded as we continued towards the hospital to check on Owen, a daily afternoon routine, although it didn't feel like there was any hope of him waking up.

"Yeah. I don't know, I'm good," I said, rubbing my forehead.

I was okay. In fact, I felt… great.

Last night… what Liam did, I knew he did it without thinking. The bullets shot would have killed me or anyone else. They were deadly. Luckily, Haru only had one arm. He didn't have the time to reload the damn gun for another round of shots. I didn't even want to think about the casualties if he was at his best…

But it wasn't that which was on my mind or of seeing Raven and Liam together. It hurt less than I thought it would. In a way… I felt free. Last night's dream returned to me again…

The sun was shining through the trees as I lay under it, the grass dancing in the wind.

Damon…

"Who's there?" I called, sitting up. I was alone in the field… strange.

The soothing touch of fingers running through my curls made me turn, but there was no one there.

You've been through so much… it's time to let it all go… *that same whispery, beautiful voice came.*

"Let what go?"

The pain, child… I am proud of you.

I felt those same fingers touch my chest, a soothing coolness spreading within me, and my heart thudded, feeling the gaping hole left at the breaking of the bond vanish from inside me. What was that?

"Who are you?"

You are so much more... so much more. Remember who you are... believe in yourself the way I believe in you.

I had woken up in bed, breathing hard, but the strangest thing was that the loss of Raven was still there in my mind, yet the gaping hole in my chest was... gone. I had a feeling who it may have been, but... she wouldn't visit me. I was no one imp-

I stopped mid-thought, remembering her parting words.

So much more...

I guess I had gotten into a habit of it...

Why me, though? I looked at the sky for a moment, knowing I would never get the answer to that before we stepped into the hospital.

Liam and Raven... *I'm glad they're happy.*

How did I feel...? Pretty neutral... I loved Raven, but seeing her with Liam changed a lot of stuff. It was going to take me a little time, but today... I didn't feel like I was just surviving. I felt like I was okay. That the future was going to be brighter.

We approached Owen's room only to see a few doctors around his bed.

"What the..." I muttered as Zack opened the door.

"What happened?" He asked.

"He woke up, but he... he won't make it," one of the doctors explained, using the defibrillator on him. "Again!" The blaring sound of the heart rate monitor remained flat.

Twice... thrice... nothing helped.

I stared at the man before me, thinking he was gone and, with him, any chance of finding answers...

"Did he say anything before he passed?" Zack asked.

"He did say something," one of the male nurses replied, frowning.

"What was it?" I asked, wondering who would be the one to tell Owen's parents he was gone. If he came out of this innocent... which we were pretty sure he was... then he had died with his reputation tarnished, even if he was a grade-A asshole.

"She isn't done." My stomach sank, and I turned away, running a hand through my hair.

"Fuck," Zack growled.

"He probably knew something… maybe that's why he was targeted," I muttered.

The killer was still out there, and they seemed to have bought themselves some more time. I left the hospital with my head spinning. Was it the killer who had helped Raven's dad? We all knew he'd had help.

I sighed heavily, the sun beating down on me as I continued walking, mulling over everything. We needed a plan to lure the killer out; we couldn't just let them do what they wanted.

The other thing was the graveyard. Although the suggestion to dig up some of the fresher soil and see if we could find anything was put forward, no one really wanted to do that, knowing it would upset the parents of those buried there.

A familiar scent hit my nose, and I glanced up, spotting Robyn sitting under a tree, a notebook and pen in hand. She was dressed for the weather in shorts and a fitted top. Still alone… like always. She looked up as if feeling watched.

"Hi," she said, looking back at her diary.

"Hey…" Our eyes met, and my heart skipped a beat, throwing me off.

"If you have nothing to say, Nicholson. Move on," she replied.

"Ouch, you got harsh," I joked, still not approaching her.

"I've always been straightforward, remember? The reason I have no friends," she said, returning to her diary. She was a good person. People needed to just look past her blunt personality, but even that was a good trait of hers, or so I thought anyway.

"Yeah, I guess so."

She really had shut me out. She stood up, her eyes softening, and she gave me a small apologetic smile as she walked over to me.

"I'm sorry, Damon, but I can't do this. Pretend that everything is okay. I'm not you," she whispered, the pain in her eyes unmasked for a moment.

"I'm not expecting anything. I'm sorry, I didn't mean -" She placed a finger to my lips and nodded in understanding.

"I know. It's just that you've been hurt enough, and I don't want to hurt you anymore," she said before turning and walking off.

I swallowed hard; I knew what she meant… when she found her mate…

She was right. I needed to stay away from her, and if that meant even a hi or bye… then that, too.

It was late in the afternoon. I knocked on Liam's office door before stepping inside. To my surprise, he was alone. I didn't know why, but I was expecting Raven to be there with him. His aura was stronger than ever, and his eyes still shone magnetic blue. Were they going to stay like that, like Dante's?

"Nice eyes," I said with a smirk.

"Thanks, I kind of like them," he joked back; they just made his scar look even more piercing. The atmosphere seemed to lighten, and he smiled slightly.

My gaze fell to his neck, seeing Raven's mark on him. I smiled. It was… bittersweet, I guess.

"Did you hear about Owen's final words?" I asked.

"Yeah, Zack mentioned it; a female, as we thought. I've sliced out half the females who were on the suspicion list, going back by their families. The tracker families and the Omegas remain since some of them have no known fathers," Liam said. *I'm surprised he was working, considering what happened yesterday…*

"Shouldn't you be resting?" I asked quietly. He cocked a brow.

"I'm good as new. We can't waste any more time. Now that the curse is gone, I can give it my all. Besides, I didn't get here that long ago," he said with a small smile.

The curse was gone… was this Liam the same as the one I once knew, or had three years still changed him?

"Thanks for saving my life," I said quietly.

"There's nothing to thank me for… you would have done the same for me." Yes, I would have, but I didn't expect him to do the same for me. His eyes softened with guilt, and he looked down.

"I know what I did was unforgivable… my attitude and my greed. I won't deny that I still wouldn't have changed my mind about her… but I went about it wrong. I promise I'll make it up to you, Damon. Maybe nothing can replace the loss of a mate, but I'm going to do my best," he said.

"It's in the past. Let it go," I said, sighing. "I'm okay. We just need to look to the future. Besides, she's still my friend, and you can't take that away from us."

He nodded with a small smile just as the door opened and Raven entered. Instantly her scent hit me; it had changed, meaning they had mated. I hadn't even realised that Liam's had changed... but I guessed his overpowering aura made you lose focus of everything else.

"Hey, Damon," Raven said, hugging me from behind my chair.

"Hey," I said, smiling at her before she walked over to Liam and hugged him.

She was wearing his shirt, too, styled as a dress, but it was obviously his. I saw their eyes meet, their gazes fall to the other's lips, but they didn't kiss. I knew it was because of me. Instead, Raven took a seat on the desk.

"So, what are you talking about?" She asked.

"Not that you need to know," Liam teased, making her pout, but he followed up quickly. "The killer."

"Hmm... oh, yeah, about that. Last night... I was thinking. Dad aimed for Damon when you were both at the wall for a while. Like, wouldn't it have been more vengeful to aim for Liam or me?" She mused. I sat forward. That was a good point.

"But there's no logic to why," Liam murmured.

"Then we best get through this pile and see what we can find," I said.

Raven nodded, and Liam handed us both a thick pile of files. I already had a headache coming on looking at it, and by the look of it, Raven was in the same boat.

"Damn... where's Zack?" I asked. Liam smirked.

"He has a day off since last night he was on duty, so it's just us three," he said.

"Oh, but these files are so big," Raven whined. Liam cocked a brow.

"Seriously, love?" He mind-linked something, and her cheeks burned up as she poked her eyes out at him.

"Can we get Robyn to help?" She pleaded. As much as I didn't want to see her, the files were depressing, and she was smart...

"You two are meant to be Beta and Luna. Are you really complaining about paperwork?"

"I didn't say anything," I protested.

"Exactly, meaning you agree," he said.

"Well... you did let Zack have a day off..." Liam smirked.

"Fine. I owe her a thank you anyway. I'll call her," he said, pausing, and I knew he was mind-linking her.

"So, what superhero powers have you got with that big aura?" I asked curiously.

"Nothing so far. Maybe a little stronger?" Liam suggested, shrugging.

"The Deimos' abilities were speed and strength, right?" Raven murmured. "Maybe you're just stronger and faster. Race Al!"

"I'd rather not…" Liam said, just as there was a knock on the door. "Come in." Robyn stepped inside.

"You called, Alpha?" She asked. Liam sat back as Raven waved at her.

"I did, and Liam's fine. I just wanted to thank you for all your help with the curse," Liam said to her.

"Not a problem. I didn't really do much. You are my Alpha, and I wanted to help," she said, glancing at me before looking back at Liam. He nodded.

"I still appreciated it," Liam said offering her a small smile. "Also… these two didn't want to use their short supply of brain cells; I was wondering if you were free to help look through some files?"

"Sure, I guess I can," she said, taking some files before going and situating herself on the couch.

"I guess I better be a good girl, too," Raven mumbled, getting off the table with a small wince. Liam pulled her into his lap, giving her a tight squeeze.

Their eyes locked, and I knew they were linking, so I turned my attention to the top file. I'd get used to it… I just needed a little time.

A good hour passed, and Raven had gone to get us drinks. I honestly wanted to go, but she beat me to it. I really wanted a break from spending my time studying with those two smartasses. Did they never tire of looking at books?

Geeks, Raven's voice came through the link as Robyn and Liam bent over a file.

I wish they'd let me vanish… I grumbled back. We exchanged a smirk. Just then, Raven's phone rang, making us all look up.

"Ooo, Tay!" She said, picking it up, only to frown. "Taylor? Hello?" She answered. We watched her frowning; did they leave pack grounds or something? Why did he call? "Taylor? Taylor?" Raven repeated, frowning.

Liam came over, motioning her to put it on speaker. Silence…

The sound of someone breathing hard could be heard. For a moment, I thought maybe they had called by accident.

"Oopsie, maybe they're doing it," Raven said, with emphasis on the 'it.'

"Taylor or Zack aren't answering the mind link," Liam said, his eyes full of concern. Worry began settling into me, and it looked like everyone had the same idea, yet as if to confirm our doubt, the groan of someone in pain came through the muffled speaker. "Fuck," Liam said, rushing to the door shockingly fast. The girls stared at each other, but Liam was gone.

"Talk about fast," I muttered.

"Taylor..." Raven murmured as we all broke into a run, the worry and panic for our pack mates settling in...

Two Birds with One Stone

ZACK

*H*AVING A DAY OFF was pretty good. Getting some alone time with Tay was even better and the best fucking way to spend the entire day. Right then, we were in Taylor's backyard, and although he was supposed to be showing me the treehouse at the bottom of the garden, I had something else in mind. Pinning him up against the tree, I grabbed his crotch, making him smile.

"Seems like this morning wasn't enough, and I can still feel it," he said, that playful smile on his lips. Wrapping his arms around my neck, our lips crashed against each other in a rough, passionate kiss. I throbbed against this fucking perfect human who really fucking drove me nuts. He groaned into my mouth, only making me crazier. I pulled away, trailing kisses down his jaw when he suddenly tensed.

"Babe…" I kissed his neck, but he pushed me back, a frown on his handsome face.

Zack, look, isn't that Nina, the Omega? What is she doing here? He asked through the link. I turned, watching her walk towards the back door of the Jacobs home…

I hadn't even sensed her…

Our eyes snapped back to each other's, my heart thundering as we both thought the same thing. She was one of the ones who were not in the clear…

I moved away and headed towards the wall between the two houses. Silently, we jumped over the wall and into the Jacobs' garden. Where was she? I saw movement through the window and frowned. So, she had access?

Fuck… an Omega who cleaned the entire pack… one who could have access to a lot…

Dammit, Raven even said she saw her at the graveyard a few times! She doesn't have family there, that should have been a big red warning sign, Taylor muttered.

It's done. She's so fragile looking. Who would have thought? I replied.

I didn't get it. Nina was a few years older than us, maybe around Taylor's age, in her mid-twenties.

I opened the door handle slowly, frowning. It was still unlocked. What was she doing here? Was she the one who had helped Haru? Probably, but why, though? Why the fuck would she do this? She always seemed so… normal. I stared into the dark kitchen. I needed to tell Lia-

I hissed when something was suddenly stabbed into my neck. Burning pain flowered through my body, and I felt myself losing control. My head snapped up as I stared at Nina, who was clinging to the wall above the door. Her eyes were unblinking as she stared at me emotionlessly. *Fucking psycho.*

I heard Taylor grunt, falling to the ground. Fuck it!

Liam! Liam… I couldn't link… shit…

I fell to the ground next to Taylor, and my body began to shake involuntarily.

"You're next," she said softly, getting down. She pushed us away from the door and locked it before turning to us. "One moment…"

My heart was thumping. Taylor's hand slowly touched mine, calming me a little, but then I fucking panicked. I couldn't let anything happen to him. *Shit, I shouldn't have brought him here…* My mind raced as I thought about what I should do.

Wait! He always kept his phone in his back pocket. I had to do something. Using all my willpower, I forced my body to work. Inch by fucking inch, it felt like forever as I reached behind me, willing and forcing myself to move, and slid my hand into his pocket. Removing the phone was going to be a completely different story. Shit….

I could hear her doing something, the sound of plastic rustling, and realised she was putting something on the floor. Fuck, what did she give us?

I managed to get the phone out, my heart thundering and the pain that was burning up my body getting stronger.

"You first," she said softly, looking down at Taylor.

She was wearing gloves, her face as emotionless as ever, but I couldn't even talk when she began to drag my fucking man away from me. My eyes flickered, but my damn wolf was suppressed. She gave me a small smile.

"Sorry, but I made the dose stronger… it'll work faster. Two birdies with one stone," she said, dragging Taylor onto the plastic sheet she had put on the floor.

Fuck! Fuck!

I rolled slightly, my body screaming against me as I inched the phone closer, trying to see what I was doing. She didn't seem to notice, and I grunted, finally getting it into my view. I kept it in my hand, unmoving. She was too busy, and I really didn't want to think about what she might do to Taylor. I needed to get us help.

"My spoon…" she murmured.

How the fuck was she so calm?

I wished I could talk, but whatever she had given me was making everything harder. Unlocking his phone, I called the top number; it was Raven's. I prayed she was with Liam…

Lowering the volume, I pressed call. Grunting in pain, I hoped my pounding heart and my grunts would drown out any sound from the phone, but the moment Raven called out Taylor's name, I heard Nina's heart skip a beat. *Take that, bitch.*

She was next to me in a flash, her eyes blazing with rage.

"You ruined everything!" She shrieked, her hands trembling as she looked at the spoon in her hand. A slow smile crossed her face as she knelt down next to me. "Be still, Delta Zack."

Fuck, she was a fucking psychotic bitch… but as long as Tay was okay. A low growl escaped him, but it was futile. The drugs in our system were far too strong. Her gaze shot to him, and she glared at him. *Dammit, Tay! Stay quiet!*

I struggled to move, but I couldn't, only managing to roll a little. However, it got her attention enough. I wanted to ask her why, why she was fucking doing this.

The spoon inched closer, and I forced my eyes shut, knowing what she wanted to do. *Fuck, this is sick! Stab me or something… not my eyes. You weird-as-fuck woman!*

Her fingers forced my eyelid open with one hand as the spoon came closer. Suddenly she dipped the spoon into the corner of my socket, the burning pain adding to my already agonising body, but I remained calm, hoping Tay couldn't see. Excruciating pain ripped through my eye and head when she forced the spoon in as if she was fucking picking out a fucking pickle from a jar.

Just then, the door was ripped off its hinges to reveal none other than Liam himself. His blue aura swirled around him. Nina gasped, dropping the spoon, and I prayed that somehow my eye would fucking heal. I could feel the blood trickling onto the floor as he looked at Nina.

"A-Alpha…" she whimpered.

"So… it's been you," Liam said coldly as he advanced towards her. Her heart was thundering as Liam's anger swirled around the room, weighing down on me.

"I…I did it for you," she whispered.

"How so?" Liam growled, grabbing her by the neck and slamming her up against the wall. *"Answer me!"*

～◎◎◎～

LIAM

She was smiling. Her hand that grasped mine as I held her in a chokehold caressed my fingers.

"You're holding me," she whispered, making me instantly drop her.

What the fuck was her problem?

Damon, Raven, Robyn - it's Nina. Get the antidotes. My guess is it's a mix of silver, wolfsbane, and ricin again. Taylor and Zack can't move. Bring a doctor immediately, I mind-linked.

Where are you? Raven asked, worry clear in her voice.

Your parents' house, I replied, thinking the place was just bad fucking luck.

I'm coming!

I'll get the antidote, Damon added.

I'll get help and call the Alpha! Robyn said.

"Why did you do this?" I asked, looking back at the fragile blonde on the floor. From the first man she killed to now, what was her fucking purpose? I demanded an answer. "I said… answer me!" I growled, letting my Alpha command pour out of me. She instantly lowered her head, sobbing erratically.

"I love you! But you never cared for me! I always wanted your attention. I wouldn't mind just being your Omega, but you never even looked at me," she said, tears trickling down her cheek. "I made your lunches, your breakfast, all your favourite food. You never cared."

Don't tell me she was some deranged creep with an infatuation with me... I'd never flirted or led anyone on.

"Why did you kill each of them, though? What did they do to you?"

"Because I wanted to! And then I wanted to hurt her! So I hurt her family!" She said, glaring up at me and twisting her head to the side. Her eyes were red from unshed tears and anger.

"Raven," I said just as her scent hit me.

"Zack..." she whispered, rushing to Zack's side. "Fuck!"

"How did you find me here? There was no scent!" Nina cried in irritation. "You ruined it all!"

"Let's just say my sniffing abilities have hiked," I growled. "Is that your only reason for killing all those people? Because you wanted to?"

"I didn't want anything linked! I had to make it look different!" She said, still clutching the spoon in one hand.

"All over what, a ridiculous infatuation? I should end you right here," I said icily. She froze, then looked up at me sharply.

"Ridiculous? You're just like them..." she said, her eyes full of hurt. I didn't turn even when Dad and Damon entered. Damon ran to the boys, administering the antidote.

"Like who?" I asked, my alpha command rolling off of me. She could try, but she could never resist it. She knew that, and it was clear she hated it as anger and rage filled her eyes.

"Your parents! They are the reason my dad was killed!" She screeched.

"Who was your father?" I asked coldly. Dad stepped forward, a frown on his face as he assessed the situation.

"Who do you think?" She spat with hatred in her eyes. She looked at Dad with a cold smile on her face. "Do you know who my dad was, Alpha?" She asked in a creepy, soft voice.

"You can hide your heartbeat and presence..." Dad began. I knew he was putting the pieces together, his heart thundering. "A tracker in stealth... by any chance, could you be the daughter of Hank Williamson?" He asked, his face pale.

Hank Williamson… I knew that name, or more like the story of the old Delta family. Who would have thought their shadow still lingered in this very pack? A slow smile spread on her face as she nodded slowly.

My mind was reeling, but it fucking made sense. Her being so quiet and able to sneak up on people… her strength and abilities, it had to be a high-ranking wolf that she was linked to. Fuck, the thing was, Omega births were never really questioned if there was a parent missing on the birth certificate. That was actually pretty normal.

"Yes… yes, I am. I found out. I learned it all by myself. I know that you and Luna Scarlett killed him and his sister. Fiona… what a pretty name," she said. Her eyes widened, and she looked fucking deranged.

"They deserved it," Dad said, swallowing hard. "Your so-called father tried to rape Scarlett! Not once, but twice. Do not fucking act like he was innocent!" I could feel Dad's anger and rage, so I placed a hand on his arm. I felt relieved when Taylor was helped to sit up. Despite looking pale, he could at least move with the antidote in his system.

"You killed several innocent people, tried to kill a few more, and framed Owen. Quite the plan," I asked quietly.

"He saw me at the grave one day, but he didn't like her anyway, so he didn't care, but I couldn't risk it," she hissed, glaring at Raven with pure hatred on her face.

"The graveyard, is that where you bury the teeth and eyes?" Raven asked sharply.

My eyes didn't leave the Omega, not trusting her. If she was the daughter of a Delta and had managed to kill several people, she may have something up her sleeve.

"Yes. I bury them all there… do you want to know exactly where?" She shuffled closer, her eyes fixed on Raven. "In that precious little coffin that you love to visit!" She laughed maniacally.

I felt the flash of pain through the bond as my gaze snapped to Raven, seeing the hurt in her eyes.

"What?"

Nina cackled, "Your so-called brother? I threw his remains in the river. His coffin is just full of teeth and eyeballs." She burst into another fit of deranged giggles, and Raven sprang up. Her eyes flashed as she rushed forward, punching Nina across the face as a vicious growl left her lips.

"How dare you!" She shouted, the hurt in her voice tugging at my heart. I pulled her back into my arms. She struggled, but I didn't let her go, kissing her neck.

I could feel her pain, sadness, and hurt. Once again, she had lost something, the last she had of her brother.

"It's going to be okay," I whispered to Raven, holding her tight.

The flash of anger and jealousy in Nina's eyes was strong, so I instantly moved Raven behind me protectively.

"The pictures… that was your doing, wasn't it?" She frowned and nodded, wiping the blood from her cut lip.

"I went to the mating ball, hoping you'd be my mate. But you weren't… you weren't…" she said. Her eyes looked haunted. "So, I needed to break you apart, and with her father already not wanting you two together, it helped."

"So, the attack last night, I'm assuming you bargained with him to target Damon because of your infatuation with Liam," Dad said in realisation.

"He has to be mine! Only mine. I've done so much for you, Liam…."

"You're deranged…"

"If I die, you die, too!" She spat, lurching to her feet. She growled, lunging at me, something flashing in her hand. My eyes blazed with anger, but I didn't even move. A wave of my aura threw her against the wall hard.

"Hatred… bitterness… resentment… it just gives birth to more… the circle never ends…" I didn't know if I was talking to her or in general, but there was never an end to the pain and darkness… "You committed more than one crime, and for it, you will be tried. Your father was scum, but it didn't mean you had to be the same. You were treated well in this pack, yet that didn't matter to you, did it?"

"If they knew who my father was, they would have killed me!" She screamed.

"No, I wouldn't have," Dad said quietly.

"Exactly," I said icily.

"Don't act noble, you are not perfect, either!" She screeched hysterically, her eyes full of burning hatred.

"No, I'm not, and I'm not the Alpha of this pack right now, but it's still my pack, my family, and my people. I'll always stand for what's right, and when I'm wrong, I know those around me will show me the right way." I stepped closer to her and struck her neck, knocking her unconscious. I'd had enough of her. "I'll throw her into the cells. I think we are done here." I turned away from her, looking at Zack and Taylor. Zack's eye was bloody, but it would heal. "Dad... could you take Raven home? Damon, could you get Zack and Taylor to the hospital?"

They nodded, and I looked at Raven, who approached me, her eyes still simmering with rage and pain. I was about to cup her face when Nina jumped up, but before she could even do anything or I could react, Raven plunged her hand into her chest, ripping her heart out. It was a reflex, and her eyes widened as she stared at the heart in her hand before dropping it and looking up at me, realising what she had done.

"I... I didn't mean -"

"It's fine," I sighed.

It was over... but to think someone so seemingly innocent had sowed discord into our pack...

I wrapped my arms around her tightly, kissing the top of her head.

"That was fucking weird," Zack said.

"You tried to distract her! I'd rather she carved my face up, I need your handsome face intact," Taylor scolded him, despite still sounding weak himself.

"Likewise," Zack said, tangling his fingers in his mate's hair and yanking him close. He kissed him hard. I looked down at my own just as Robyn returned with a few of the warriors.

"Get this place cleaned up," I said before pulling away from Raven. "Go with Dad. I'll be home soon."

She hesitated but nodded as Dad placed his arm around her. I walked past Robyn, not missing the relief on her face as she glanced at Damon. I smiled slightly. *Who knows...*

I walked through the dark pack grounds, heading to the children's graveyard. Renji's remains may no longer be in that coffin, but I was not going to let the grave stay like that. I had felt her pain, and it had fucking torn me apart.

I entered the graveyard, taking a moment to find his grave. I smiled slightly, seeing the plushie I recognised at the foot of the tombstone. Crouching down, I began to dig it up completely, my heart squeezing once more. I wouldn't let this area become a bad memory for her. It was the last thing she had of him. *I'll clean it out for her...*

An hour later, I sat back, brushing some dirt off my hands. I had removed the coffin; Nina had left a lot of disturbing messages on it, written in what was clearly blood and scratched into the wood of the coffin. It was again just soil, yet it had been the place he had once lay. Once I was done, I went to the Jacobs' home once again, a place that was still being cleaned out. Heading to the attic, I began searching for anything of Renji's. I wanted to return to Raven, but I couldn't go empty-handed, not after seeing that broken look in her eyes.

I finally found it; a small old metal carry case with a blue R painted on it in the farthest corner of the attic. I brushed the dust off it, opening it up, and hoped my gut instincts were correct. I smiled in relief, looking at the box, which contained some children's clothing, photos, a toy, a pacifier, a bottle, and a blanket. She'd be happy with these....

I stood up, glancing around the attic. I was sure when she was ready, she would come and see if there was anything she wanted, and then I was going to burn this place to the ground. I just hoped with it... all of its bad memories would fade away too...

A New Day

RAVEN

TWO HOURS HAD PASSED, and Liam still wasn't back...

After showering, we filled Aunty Red in on everything over some hot drinks. Although she was keeping me company, the mention of Hank Williamson had made her go into deep thought, so I gave the couple some privacy, calling it a night.

I had pondered on everything, mind-linking Damon and Taylor to ask how he and Zack were doing. I had texted Kiara for a bit as well, but I knew it was late and having three little chibis to look after wasn't easy. I sighed, staring up at the night sky through the open curtains, smiling sadly. We had caught the killer, but Renji's grave... what she had done made me sick.

I wrapped my arms around my legs, burying my head in my knees. She had thrown his remains away... the last I had of him. No sound escaped me, yet tears trickled down my cheeks.

A short while later, the door opened, and Liam's scent mixed with earth and dust hit me. I quickly wiped my tears away, looked up, and our eyes met. He came over, placed the case he was carrying on the bed and was about to pull me into his arms when he hesitated, glancing at himself before quickly pulling his dirty top off and scooping me up into his arms.

"Why did you take so long?" I asked, unable to stop myself.

"I needed to make things better," he said quietly.

His fingers weaved into my hair as he stared down at me, kissing me softly. I looked at him, resting my head on his chest and closing my eyes as I clung to him, enjoying the warmth of his embrace and those pleasant sparks of the bond.

"I brought you something," he said softly.

"Hmm?"

"I cleared Renji's grave out. That place is no longer tainted... I know that she got rid of... his remains... but always remember that he's always been a part of you," he said, softly caressing my cheek as he stared into my eyes. "He lives on as a part of you, bitesize, and no one could take that away from you; not your parents, not Nina, no one."

My heart thudded at his words, and I realised how true that was. Renji's eye was still a part of me. I still had him by my side.

"But I still thought you might want something more of him, so I did a little digging and found this." He unwrapped one arm from around me and reached for the case, opening it up with one hand.

My stomach did a flip as I stared at the blue baby shawl. I knew what this was: Renji's things... a case of his memories! I moved forward, taking the blanket out. The smell of old mothballs lingered, but my heart soared. Renji's belongings...

Liam kissed my forehead softly, running his fingers through my hair as I stared at the box of treasure before me.

"I'll go shower," he said softly.

I glanced up at him and nodded, knowing he was giving me a moment alone. His lips pressed against mine, softly sending sparks coursing through me before he moved away, leaving me a little lightheaded. I turned back to the case, slowly taking each item out.

Photographs...

I looked through them, my heart thudding loudly. He looked like me... there were so many similarities. Although I knew he had been a couple years old, it was clear he was a lot smaller than he should have been for his age, and he was extremely thin. There were a few pictures where he had a head full of black hair, but there were many where he was bald. I smiled sadly at the picture. Was it selfish to wish he was alive? I just hoped he was in a good place. Did heaven exist?

I hugged the picture to my chest, tears spilling down my cheeks as I rocked myself gently. Renji...

I had almost finished looking at the pictures when I stared at the last one. Mom and Dad were sitting on either side of Renji, who was holding a baby in his arms, with Mom supporting him, all smiling at the camera...

Me. That was me. Before our family fell apart...

One by one, I took the things out of the case, some items of clothing, a small teddy bear... it felt bittersweet, the moment. I would always cherish these items. I slowly replaced them, keeping one photo aside to keep close to me and looked down at the case.

Liam must have gone to the attic at my parents' house. My heart warmed at his thoughtful gesture.

He came out of the bathroom in a pair of grey sweatpants, which made him look far too sexy. My core clenched, my eyes dipping to those abs and the bulge in his pants. Remembering how he made me feel... the ache between my legs was only just fading...

His hair was dried; clearly, he had delayed to give me time alone. I placed the case on the floor near the bed, my eyes raking over him, wanting him to come over so I could snuggle into his arms or pounce him.

"Want to say something?" He asked, running his fingers through his hair.

Damn, a guy with messy hair is so sexy... not to mention the volume in it...

"Nothing at all..." I said, trying not to stare at how hot he looked.

He smirked, coming over. My heart fluttered when he climbed onto the bed, my chest rising and falling heavily as his scent made me giddy.

"You don't need to say anything..." he whispered, leaning over me. His magnetic deep blue eyes bore into mine. "For me to know what you want, love."

His lips crashed against mine in a hot, passionate kiss. I pulled him down, rolling us over until I was on top and kissing him harder. His hands roamed my body as he dominated the kiss, his hand threading into my hair.

Thank you for doing this for me... I whispered through the link.

Always... he replied as his tongue slipped into my mouth, wanting to taste every inch of it, making me moan softly...

Mine.

Three days had passed, and everyone had been made aware of Nina's truth. Her mother had passed away when she was a child; it had actually been after that that Nina had wanted to learn if she had any other family in the pack. Her grandmother, who was still alive, told them that she knew who her father was, but in fear of Nina being treated horribly, she had kept it a secret. She had no idea what Nina had been up to or how she found out. Apparently, Hank himself had made it clear he wanted nothing to do with the child. Nina's grandmother had been asked a few questions under Alpha command, as Uncle El did not want to risk anything. However, she was indeed innocent and knew nothing.

It was nice to put the entire thing behind us. With spring blessing us with the blooming of flowers and the leaves beginning to return to the trees, everything seemed so much better.

I stared down at Renji's grave, the soil was completely fresh, and a line of pebbled stones lined it, Liam's doing. I smiled gently, placing my hand on the soft earth. I looked at Sparks, smiling at the plastic covering Liam had covered him with. Trust him to worry about him getting dirty... Liam was one of the rare men who was so thoughtful and clean.

He's adorable.

I was lucky that I had people who loved me; Uncle El and Aunty Red, both of whom were really, in a way, like parents to me. It was Aunty Red who helped me when I first got my periods and I had been acting like I was dying. I knew what they were, but, hey, I liked being dramatic. She was the one who got me a few bras for my thirteenth birthday and joked that I needed them. She was the one who was there if I ever had a question. Aunty Angela was great, too. Even when she moved, she kept in touch, but Aunty Red was the true mother figure for me - our Luna, our Queen.

Uncle El shouldered every burden and never let his life spiral out of control. He was strong and caring towards us all, leading the pack fairly.

Then there was Liam; my life, my mate, my love. I didn't have any doubts. I knew we were meant to be together. It was just so right. I only wished that Damon hadn't gotten hurt in the process of our love story.

Damon... he was the true hero who sacrificed everything for everyone; for his loved ones and for the man he considered his brother, despite his ill-treatment... the most loving and selfless person I knew. Damon would always be special to me. Our friendship, that bond, was intact. Although I knew things between Liam and him might never be the same again... I hoped that they'd be okay when time healed those wounds.

I looked down at Renji's tombstone and smiled gently, a soft breeze whispering through my hair. I just hoped that the moon goddess could heal his heart and give him the happiness he deserved. He was a pawn in this game, used by the gods. Sadly, in all of this, he suffered as much as Liam and ultimately more than Liam.

Liam's curse was broken, he had me, his family, and soon I knew he would have his title. But Damon, in the end, was alone. I stood up and stared up at the dazzling sun, shielding my eyes.

We broke your curse Helios, with kindness, compassion, and love. Those are the things that will conquer all...

We are a pack, a family, and we will always be one. We will always be here for each other no matter what comes our way because, united, we are at our strongest.

Equal

DAMON

*I*T WAS A FEW days since everything had gone down. Liam and I were in Nina's room which had been cleared out. We hadn't found anything more from her room, which was so damn clean you could smell it. The room had been emptied, and her stuff given to her grandmother if she wanted them. She refused and said to get rid of them, although I knew that was more her respect towards the pack because she was devastated at her granddaughter's truth and death. *To think she was living here with so much hatred in her life...*

I walked over to the window. It looked out towards the training grounds, and I wondered how much time she spent here watching us, or Liam. Even in such a place, behind such an innocent mask, there was a killer, burning from within with hatred and vengeance...

There are all types of masks that those around us wear; masked by our fake smiles and passive expressions, the lies hidden inside, the pain we hide to pretend we are normal... the jealousy, the bitterness, the sadness... we all wear them. I did, too. Lately, though, I've talked about how I felt. Maybe it took Liam marking Raven to make me snap, but it worked. It had been a turning point that perhaps I needed. I just wished it hadn't been something so horrible as that to finally make me step up.

Liam crouched down by the skirting board, and I glanced over at him.

"What is it?" He stood up again, holding a small photograph.

"Who would have thought that piece of scum had a child..."

"I know…" I said, glancing at the picture for a moment. "If only she actually asked someone the truth rather than just wrapping herself up in lies and her assumptions."

"I've assumed stuff, so I can see it happening," he sighed as he opened his hand, his aura surging around it. I watched in shock as the photograph began to shrivel up as if it was burned by the blue flame-like aura.

"Whoa…" He gave me a small smile.

"I guess I have some similarities to Kiara."

"How did you hone it on just your hand?" He shrugged, dropping the burned paper to the ground.

"I've always been more in control than Kia. Besides, she carries the Asheton power whilst I think I'm definitely more Deimos."

"You are the Deimos prince," I said, crossing my arms.

"I don't like that title; I think I've used titles enough to last me a fucking lifetime," he said, sighing again as he crushed the remnants of the picture beneath his boot. "You are an incredible Beta, Damon. One who has stepped up to the job the moment your father passed away, but I know if I just say I don't think of you as anything less than me, it's worth nothing. So… I want to show you something."

He jerked his head towards the door, and I raised an eyebrow as we both left the room and packhouse, heading towards the north side of the pack into the trees. It was nice to see the children playing around the pack again.

"Is this like a surprise set up in the middle of a forest where you are going to confess your undying love?" I joked.

"Not exactly," he smirked as he headed towards the river. I frowned when he crossed the bridge and kept walking.

"Okay, are you planning on killing me in the middle of nowhere?" I asked.

"Definitely not," he replied as we walked through the trees, not stopping for a good ten minutes until he suddenly slowed down. I raised an eyebrow, looking around. We were on pack grounds that were only really used for running.

"What are we looking at?" I asked, glancing around.

"We are looking at the future home of the Blue Moon Pack." I frowned; this was Blood Moon territory…

"Are you changing the pack name?" I asked, looking around.

This location was big, but I was sure our current location was larger. Why would he move this way? He chuckled.

"No, the Blue Moon is going to be the Blood Moon's sub-pack, led by its own Alpha… Alpha Damon Nicholson, my brother," Liam said quietly.

My eyes snapped up to his. His words resonated in my head, and I was shocked to see the glitter of emotions in his eyes. My heart raced as I stared at him. There was no guilt in his eyes, simply sadness and sincerity.

"I wish I could keep being selfish and keep you by my side forever, to have you as my Beta, but you are worth far more… and the pack's growing too large. To start with, it was two packs combined. With what happened, it's clear a pack of this size is far too great to be run by one Alpha, and so I thought, who more fitting than you? You have always been loyal to me, come whatever, but I don't want you bound by my side when you are worth so much more. So… this is going to be our sub-pack. We will break the far wall, and you will take two-fifths of the territory. I've talked with Dad about buying the land around to the west, so we can spread both packs over more ground. You can start planning what you want and how you want the pack arranged. Once we decide how we split the pack, with the members' approval, of course, we will get two-fifths of the pack moved here under your command."

It was too much to take in. Me as an Alpha? I never considered that… I ran my hand through my hair, staring at the land. The vision of a pack-house and how I'd set it out already filled my mind.

I looked at Liam, who was watching me with a small smile on his face. I knew he probably knew it was hard for me to see them together, but I also knew he was doing this for me and not to get rid of me. He'd made mistakes, but it was like everyone kept telling me that I was more than I felt, Liam included. I had always been second to him, and there he was giving me the rank of Alpha, telling me we were equal… brothers…

We made mistakes, we hurt each other, but was one woman enough to destroy it all? I knew the answer to that. No, and I knew with time, things would get better.

"I don't know what to say…"

"You don't need to say anything. Maybe this way, the packhouse rooms can have their own bathrooms. Do you know there's one pack member who has anonymously left a long essay explaining why the packhouse needed renovating? Damn, it was long…"

"Robyn, guaranteed. Only she would take the time to write an essay to argue her point..." He chuckled.

"When I saw how neat and professional the letter was, I had a feeling it might be her."

"That's Robyn for you. I guess I have a lot of work to do then." *And something to keep my mind busy. Perfect.*

"Yeah, you do." Liam said, "So, tell me, Alpha Damon, what's the first step?"

"Getting an assessment and some building plans in place. Man, you know I hate paperwork. Wait, as Alpha, that means a shit-tonne of paper-work. "

"Yeah, it does, but I'm here to help you each step of the way. If you don't like the legal work, I can help with that," he said, shrugging.

"Thanks... but who will you have as Beta then? "I asked, frowning. Damn, that was my title...

Liam shrugged.

"I was thinking Zack, and then maybe make Robyn as Delta? The girl's smart, unless you want her..." he trailed off, sounding awkward as if he had just realised what he had said. "Shit, I didn't mean to take... forget me." I smiled at that.

"Didn't mean to take all my women?" I joked. "Well, Robyn and I are over. Raven was never really mine, I think I realise that now, but she's still my friend, so... you ain't taking anyone from me. Robyn is a good option. I guess that means I'll have to choose a Beta and Delta, too..."

"Yeah, we could do an assessment and see what everyone's stats are," Liam said as we both began walking along, taking in the terrain as we discussed it. I nodded.

"That's an idea," I said, giving him a genuine smile. "Thanks, Liam."

"No need to thank me," he replied, smiling. The Liam I knew.

"Race you to the bridge?" I suggested.

"Game on!" He said, readying himself.

"Oh, and one more thing. Don't let me win," I said, making his dazzling blue eyes widen in shock.

"You..."

"Yeah, I knew. You let me win, Liam, all those times..." I said quietly. He looked up at the shining sun and smiled.

"Actually, Damon… I don't need to let you win because, with everything we've been through, it shows as a person, you are the true winner." His words were sincere, and this time I didn't deny them or shake them off.

You are so much more… Those words echoed in my mind as I looked at Liam.

"We both are," I said. "Go!"

We broke into a run, and although I told him not to let me win… it was okay to play dirty, right? I elbowed him hard, barrelling past him as he stumbled, both of us laughing as we ran towards the bridge.

I was right. Things were definitely going to get better.

A New Home

SIX WEEKS LATER…

RAVEN

"*L*IAM, BE CAREFUL!" I shouted in alarm as he almost knocked over the tub of paint that stood on the ladder.

"Oops, that was close…" he said.

I looked at him in his ripped jeans and shirtless state, with splashes of paint all over him… he was making my stomach knot. Goddess… I wanted him… I had just come off my period, and after the scare from weeks ago, I was on contraception, which I was taking religiously! But getting my period also meant I had gone without sex for a few days, and I craved it.

"Like the view, love?" He asked, running his fingers through his hair.

"Oh, I'm definitely loving the view…." I agreed, licking my lips as I climbed down from the ladder and walked over to him.

We had decided to get Grandma Amy's place completely renovated before we moved in until, of course, we had pups, and then we'd need more space, but for the moment, we were both happy to wait and just enjoy each other's company with some privacy.

The place was completely changed; we had gotten the walls re-plastered, and the floors and ceilings were completely new. However, we had kept some of the furniture in the lounge, simply sanding them down and repainting them. The place was looking great; the kitchen had black worktops with dark grey units, a black cooker, fridge, and other electrical items. A touch of purple and teal decorated the kitchen. The living area was changed to grey floorboards and walls, with purple and teal décor. The sofa was Grandma Amy's, but we had covered it with a throw and bought two armchairs which sat in front of the huge TV. The small table was also painted black and had a runner down the middle, but we had replaced the chairs.

The shelves were re-organised, and many held crystals, candles, books, comics, and games for Liam's PlayStation, along with some ornaments. The bathroom was something we had to completely redo, decorating it in shades of dark brown and black, adding a warm touch to it.

I jumped into Liam's arms, locking my legs around his waist. His arms were tight around me as he peppered my neck with kisses, making me sigh in pleasure. We had just finished painting the small corners that were left, so we were officially finished!

"So, what's the plan for tonight?" Liam asked, his fingers grazing up the side of my bare waist, making me sigh.

"Tonight... I think although we got shopping in, I don't want to cook tonight. I mean, it would be you who would be cooking... how about you go get some pizza? I really want a veg one," I pouted, batting my lids. I wanted him gone so I could dress up in some kinky lingerie I had brought online... *Oh, this is going to be fun.*

"Sure, love, I'll do that." He glanced around the room in approval before kissing me passionately.

Once he put me down, he went into the bedroom to grab a shirt and his wallet. We had pretty much unpacked everything. A few boxes were stacked to the side, but apart from that, we were done.

I had visited my parent's house one last time and taken anything I wanted. There wasn't much, just a few photographs of me, some old toys from the attic, and a few items of my grandmother's.

When we finally told Aunty Angela about everything, she was shocked and had come down for a week. She was the one who packed Mom and Dad's stuff and had it donated to the human shelter. Nobody wanted their hand-me-downs. Liam was planning to destroy the house, but he had asked me first. To be honest, I needed it gone. The place had too many dark memories attached to it.

When I found out about the Blue Moon Pack, I was happy for Damon and for Liam and him mending their bond. It was nice to see them tease each other and discuss stuff like they once used to. They had already started working on the blueprints for the new buildings, and everything was going smoothly. The splitting of the pack was being discussed, too; everyone was given a say and was not compelled to move. Yet luckily, everyone was cooperating perfectly, and we were working on who would shift to where. We were going to be sub-packs, meaning we were still one in a way yet under two leaders. I knew they were going to smash it. When Rayhan had called Liam, he had joked that Liam was worried that the Black Storm was getting ahead and wanted to expand his own pack. Many of the young adults were excited about new rooms at the Blue Moon packhouse with en-suite bathrooms, whilst the packhouse here would be renovated as well. There was a lot to do, but we were moving at a good steady pace. We would get there.

The Blood Moon had come and gone. Although deep down, I wished Damon was given someone, I knew he didn't really have hope, and second-chance mates were so rare people didn't really go to mating balls to find them. All the single werewolves of age had gone to the mating ball being hosted at Kiara's pack, but there was someone else who refused to go as well; Robyn. She said she had exams, but I knew there was more to it - I didn't think she was ready to move on so soon.

I entered our bedroom, one that Liam allowed me to decorate completely by myself, saying the only thing in here he wanted to see was me! So, I had grey walls with one feature wall of black and silver. The curtains and bedding were black, and the décor was deep red, from the pillows to the throw at the edge of the bed to the light shade. It was a dark room. Cosy, sexy, and romantic.

Sitting in front of my vanity table, I began putting more makeup on, applying a deep maroon lipstick and adding some more highlighter before putting on the strappy black bandage lingerie, one that had a slit along the thong. I pinned my fringe back in a small quiff and loosely curled the bottom before I grabbed some of my strappy thigh-high heels. Putting them on, I looked around and began to set up some candles.

It was our first official night here. We had crashed on the sofa several times over the past few weeks, but it was our first night since the house was properly completed. I thought we needed to make it memorable...

I took out the basket of fresh rose petals I had cut from the garden earlier and spread them over the bed before sprinkling some over the black carpet from the door to the bed. Satisfied with how the room looked, I quickly grabbed my nightgown and put it on, then returned to the open lounge. Taking some drinks from the kitchen and plates, I placed them on the table, put some music on the TV, and draped a blanket over my legs to hide my heels. *There, now we can at least eat first!*

I heard the lock in the door and turned as Liam stepped inside, my eyes widening when I saw he wasn't alone…

"Aunty! Uncle!" I exclaimed, my heart thudding,

"We were out with Azura, and she wanted to see the house when we saw Liam. I hope you don't mind us popping over," Aunty Red said, looking around before giving me a small smile.

"No! Not at all…" I said.

They wanted to see the house, the house! Goddess…

Liam placed the pizzas down then I saw his gaze fall over my gown and linger on my cleavage before he looked into my eyes.

You look fucking gorgeous… he murmured through the link, taking my chin and kissing me hard. I wanted to get up, but I refused to, knowing my heels and nightgown might just give a lot more away! *Goddess, what do I do?*

I kissed him back before moving away.

"I eat pizza, Waven?" Azura asked me, her eyes staring at the large boxes.

"Of course! Come sit down here," I said, relieved that I didn't need to get up.

"I love pizza," she stated, brushing her black hair from in front of her face.

"Wash your hands first, pumpkin," Liam ordered her.

"Why, Wiyam? I wash my hands before," Azura asked innocently whilst pouting.

"Yeah, still. Wash your hands," Liam persisted, making Elijah smirk.

"You're such a clean freak."

"I don't trust kid's hands… or adults at that…" Liam remarked, frowning. Aunty Red raised an eyebrow as Azura skipped over to her to get her hands washed.

"I don't even want to know what goes through that mind of yours," she said, smiling slightly before looking around. "I love what you've done with the place, Raven. You have good taste."

"Thanks," I replied, smiling proudly.

"Is everything done now?" Uncle El asked, popping his head into the bathroom. "Nice tiles."

"Yeah, all done. Take a look," Liam motioned towards the two bedrooms.

Oh no, oh no…

"That's the spare room now, didn't really feel like taking Grandma Amy's room as ours," Liam added as Aunty Red opened the door.

Liam… I mumbled through the link. He glanced at me as Azura bit into her pizza, watching us with interest. **Our room… uh, not in there, I, uh…** I felt so flustered. Liam looked at me, concerned and confused, but at the same time, he opened the door to our bedroom, his parents standing right there as he pushed it wide open for them, his eyes on me as he raised his eyebrows questioningly.

Goddess! Kill me now!

I watched with a burning face as Aunty Red and Uncle El stared into the bedroom whilst Liam was staring at me in confusion. Goddess, that man may have brains when it came to other stuff, but he was so clueless at times!

Aunty Red chuckled, turning with a vixen-like smile on her face.

"Nice décor…" Uncle El remarked, smirking.

My face was burning, humiliation seeping into me as Liam finally glanced into the room, his eyes widening before he quickly slammed the door shut.

"So, yeah, uh, that's it, all done," he mumbled, running his fingers through his hair. Aunty Red smirked, crossing her arms under her breasts.

"So, I think we came at a bad time. Really, Elijah… you shouldn't have just asked to come here. Come on, Azura, we should get going," she said smoothly, despite the smirk that still lingered on her beautiful face.

"I eat pizza, Mama," Azura protested.

"Yeah, um, do you guys want to eat pizza?" I asked lamely. Uncle El smirked.

"I think Liam would rather eat something else, so we should just get going. Come on, Azura," he said cockily.

"Uncle, it's not that funny. We all know how you and Aunty Red are," I pouted unhappily as he smirked at me arrogantly.

"Well, we never deny that," he replied as Azura grabbed the packet of fries.

"Thank you, Wiyam, Waven, for the food. I come for sleepover tomorrow!" She stated.

"Of course," I said, wishing my cheeks would return to normal.

"Actually, maybe next month." Aunty Red said, "Let's let Liam and Raven christen the entire house first."

I pouted unhappily, my cheeks flushed darker as they went to the door, and Aunty Red gave me a wink before she stepped out. Liam stood there, completely silent until the door shut behind the trio.

"That was, uh… interesting," he said, dropping onto the couch as I glared at him.

"You are so clueless! I was telling you!" I complained.

"You actually didn't say anything," he said, wrapping his arms around my frame and pulling me into his lap, along with the blanket.

"I was trying," I replied unhappily, grabbing a pizza slice and kicking off the blanket that was tangled around my legs. "It was supposed to be a surprise."

"A surprise…" he said huskily, his voice almost a growl.

My eyes snapped to him, my heart thudding as I realised that when he had pulled me, my gown had tugged open, partially revealing what I was wearing underneath. His hand ran up my thigh, leaving a trail of fiery sparks in its wake, his magnetic blue eyes shimmering with hunger. Fuck…

"I think we can skip dinner and get straight to dessert." His hand ran between my clenched thighs, getting closer to my hot core and sending off rivets of pleasure. I gasped when his finger rubbed against the slit in my thong. "Fuck, love," he whispered hoarsely and with one pull, he yanked my gown off me, his blazing eyes trailing over my body like a predator ready to devour his prey…

And I wanted to be that prey.

Little Minx

LIAM

I PICKED HER UP, SLINGING her over my shoulder and stroking her ass in that tiny thong. Damn…

As the days went by, she had become more and more confident. She was normally a tease, but in the bedroom… fuck, she was on a whole new level. She knew what she wanted, and she wasn't afraid to ask for it.

I kicked the bedroom door shut behind me before walking over to the bed. I tapped her ass lightly, dropping her onto the bed and making her bounce a little. My eyes went to her breasts in that sexy, strappy bra that was teasing me way too fucking much. Her eyes stayed on me as she got on all fours, swinging her legs in those heels slowly as she wriggled her hips, making me swallow hard as I stared at her ass.

"What's wrong, Alpha? Not going to join me?" She teased, smirking as she stared at my hardened shaft in my jeans before crawling towards me while I pulled my top off.

"I fucking am," I growled as she began to unbuckle my belt, kneeling on the bed. My eyes were stuck on her breasts. Fuck…

She pulled my pants down and I helped her, stripping them off, leaving me in my fitted boxers. Her hands gripped my hips as she kissed my dick over the thin fabric, making me groan before her tongue pressed against the base of my naval making sparks fucking rage through me. Her eyes were locked with mine as she traced it up between my abs, making me suck my stomach in as pleasure coursed through me and my dick throbbed. I reached down, squeezing her ass as she finally reached my chest, flicking my left nipple and her nail scraping the right one.

"Hey, little minx," I whispered, tangling my hand into her hair and pressing my lips against hers in a bruising kiss that sent my world into a storm of emotions. The sweet taste of her mouth made me slip my tongue past those plush lips, caressing her tongue with my own.

My arm snaked around her waist and yanked her against me. She moaned softly, her hand raking down my back. The other wrapped around my neck as we kissed each other hungrily. I sat down on the bed and pulled her on top of me, grabbing her breasts and squeezing them as I attacked her lips once more. She gyrated her hips against me, her hot core rubbing against my cock. *Fuck.*

I squeezed her ass cheeks with both hands before tugging at her thong, making her whimper in pleasure. My hand slid between her ass cheeks before I reached the small slit in her panties, making her cry out when I slipped my fingers into her. Her slick hot folds made me hiss in approval.

"You're so fucking hot, love," I growled, kissing her neck hard.

She whimpered, her hand twisting into my hair before she nibbled on my ear. I lifted her off my lap, pushed her down onto the bed, and yanked her bra down, letting her boobs spill out. I grabbed them as I kissed her lips, then trailing hungry passionate kisses down her taut stomach before I spread her legs.

Damn... the way she looked...

I bent down, running my tongue along the slit and making her cry out in pleasure. I pushed the underwear aside completely, ready to go down on her, but before I realised what was happening, she had her legs around my neck and flipped me onto my back. Her hand tangled into my hair as she straddled my face. It took my all not to come right fucking there at her hot as hell move.

Fuck, love, you're a sexy little doll, I growled, plunging my tongue into her. She cried out in pleasure as she rolled her hips against my mouth.

"Fuck..." she moaned.

I looked up at her. If I could, I'd love to stay there forever... just seeing her moaning in pleasure, the way she was grinding against me, her hand tangled in my hair and the delicious, sweet taste of her juice on my lips. Heaven... she was my heaven.

"That's it, Liam…" she whined, cupping her breasts as I sped up, alternating between eating her out and playing with her clit. She was getting closer; I could feel her orgasm building. Her cries and moans of pleasure got louder. "Fuck, Liam, that's it, eat my pussy…" she whimpered. Her words became incoherent, the look of ecstasy on her face making me fucking crazy.

Come for me, love.

I squeezed her ass, palming it as she gasped, tensing as her orgasm tore through her body and she cried out. Her entire body shuddered from her release, her sweet juices trickling into my mouth. Fuck, did she taste good.

She slowly pulled away, still breathing hard. Her eyes met mine as she wiped her juices from my face with one hand. My heart thudded as I stared into her eyes, the passion, the love, and the hunger in them mirrored my own. She was all I needed… all I wanted…

"That was fucking hot," I whispered, yanking her down and kissing her hard.

Yes… she whispered breathlessly through the bond.

She kissed me back with passion and love wrapping around us in pure bliss before she moved back, going lower and yanking my boxers off.

"Like me sucking your cock baby?" She asked, winking at me as she stroked my hard shaft with her tiny hands that knew how to work magic. My gorgeous mate. I swore as the sparks mixing with the pleasure made me throb, her tongue lapping up the beads of pre-cum from my tip.

"I sure fucking do, love," I whispered in approval.

She was so fucking good at this, and I wouldn't deny I was curious to ask if she had done it -

Fuck! I groaned as she wrapped her mouth around me, her hand fondling my balls as she began sucking me off. She had talent, fucking talent!

I sat up slightly, resting on my elbows as I watched her bob her head on my dick, sucking and squeezing it as she took it all in. I grabbed her by the hair, holding it back so I could see her as she throated my dick. The pleasure… Goddess… I groaned in satisfaction, shoving my dick further.

"Do you like that, baby?" I asked huskily. She nodded, moaning. "Well, you look fucking divine with those plush little lips wrapped around my dick."

Her eyes flashed as she sped up and any other words left my mind, all I could think of was the pleasure. Fuck!

I yanked her back just as I shot my load. Pleasure erupted inside me, spreading to every inch of my body, and my entire body spasmed with the rush from the orgasm, and for a moment, my mind was blank, save for the pleasure she had just showered on me. I could feel her wrap her hand around my dick, stroking it and milking it for all its worth as I tried to fucking focus, hearing the groans of pleasure fall from my lips.

She licked my tip, and I opened my eyes, admiring the way my cum coated her breasts and neck. Sitting up, I pulled her against me and kissed her hard as I unhooked her bra and tossed it aside. We kissed hungrily, our hands roaming the other's body. I would never get enough of her, my doll...

I grabbed her neck, making her gasp, while the other hand grabbed her ass. I rammed into her, making her cry out. *Got to love my stamina.*

She groaned hornily as I stretched her out, taking a moment to adjust before she began riding me. I thrust into her harder and faster, meeting her every thrust with a more powerful one of my own. She moaned out in ecstasy as I slammed into her roughly, feeling her sides clench around me. I let my gaze travel over her, my hand around her neck, her bouncing breasts looked so fucking good, and the way I was pounding into that tiny pussy of hers... I yanked her close, my lips crashing against hers in a bruising kiss.

She gasped against me as I kissed her before lifting her off my dick. I delivered a sharp tap to her ass before turning her around so her back was to me. She whimpered, grabbing my dick as she pushed it into herself, moaning as she did before she began riding me again. Her cries and moans of pleasure grew louder, and her ass slapped against me. I reached around, playing with her breasts with one hand, whilst the other began rubbing her clit hard and fast.

"Fuck, Liam! Fuck... oh...nh..." she whined hornily, breathing heavily as I did my best not to come. I bit into her neck, sucking hard just as she came, making her sides clamp down on me, triggering my own orgasm. I groaned, breathing hard. "Liam!"

I didn't stop kissing her until she was a trembling mess in my arms...

An hour later, we had just showered and gotten ready for bed. I had heated the pizza up and we had eaten because we were fucking ravenous.

Raven had just put something away in her wardrobe, pausing as she ran her fingers over the two-toned wrap dress that I had gotten for her for our first date, one that we hadn't actually gone on until a few weeks after everything had happened. She looked good in tiny fluffy shorts and a matching crop top. Her ass distracted me - I loved watching it move...

"I'm going to wear this at our housewarming dinner next month," she said, her eyes meeting mine. I nodded, remembering how gorgeous she looked in it. Then again, it was Raven. She looked perfect in everything. She came over to the bed after shutting her wardrobe and climbed onto my lap, the tingles of the bond dancing across my skin.

"You looked good in it," I remarked, remembering our little cinema and dinner trip.

"Thanks, baby," she whispered, kissing my neck, and I twitched in my pants.

"Keep going, and we won't be sleeping," I groaned. She giggled.

"Well, we need to sleep. I have training to head in the morning," she reminded me.

"Although I'd prefer you just train with me here in the bedroom." I squeezed her ass.

"Hmm, that would consist of how many rounds I can go?" She joked.

"You're strong, and I know you can go a long way."

"I know I am," she said, locking her arms around my neck and kissing my lips. "I love you, blue eyes."

"I love you always," I replied, pulling her close and simply holding her tightly, feeling content...

Broken Hopes

OVER TEN MONTHS LATER…

RAVEN

"*Z*UZU, CAREFUL MY DARLING!" I exclaimed, grabbing her as she almost tumbled to the ground.

"Waven, I'm a big girl now," she stated firmly.

"Still, I don't need you getting hurt," I said, looking down at the stacks of supplies that had arrived.

We were all over at the Blue Moon territory; the buildings were up, and the furniture was partially in. Things had been great, and we all knew how the pack was going to be divided.

Originally Liam was going to take leadership again a month ago as he had proven himself, but he had refused his father, saying he wanted Uncle El to make him and Damon Alphas together. It was perfect; that way, it wasn't Liam giving him something but two brothers taking their titles together. The official Alpha ceremony would take place in a few days' time.

As for the three of us, we were doing great. The more weeks and months passed, the more we were back to how we used to be. Damon had to leave for six months for a shorter version of the Alpha training, but it was something Uncle El said he needed to do. I also thought he wanted him to get a break away from the pack.

Uncle El kept Aunty Monica at their home until he returned, and she was doing so much better. She spent a lot of time around people. Channing, Taylor's brother, and she had become fast friends. She visited Uncle Aaron's grave often now that she was in her senses. Damon would video call her daily; she was proud of him and what he had accomplished, saying Uncle

Aaron would be, too. She was back at her own house, yet she had a carer with her constantly and wasn't left alone. However, we were all positive that soon she wouldn't need even that.

Damon came back a few months ago and was impressed at the amount of work that had been done in his absence with the new pack. Liam had put in a lot to get it done and I knew he was still trying to redeem himself - to both Damon and me - although we had both forgiven him.

Zack was going to be Liam's new Beta, and although Liam had been set on having Robyn as his Delta, last week he suddenly announced she can't be his Delta but had no reason as to why. Well, that threw us back in a loop, but after thinking things through he settled on a young warrior, Bronson, who was twenty-four.

Damon had chosen his Beta, who, to Taylor's surprise, was his brother, Channing. Although he wasn't able to fight, he was still a smart man and that move of Damon's alone made us all proud. Channing had lost the ability to walk and his mate, but with his new position, it gave him purpose, something that truly warmed us all. Damon was going to be an amazing Alpha, I was sure of it.

He had then chosen Rick, Robyn's brother as his Delta. Although I teased him it was due to favouritism, he had assured me it wasn't. He no longer looked away if I and Liam had a moment. He actually called us out before he left, saying he was fed up with us walking on eggshells.

Things were perfect, and Kiara had *finally* set a new wedding date!!! It was happening in three months' time! The little ones would be eighteen months by then and probably walking. They were going to look so adorable in their little flower girl dresses! The delay had been long, yet it was time that their family had needed to heal.

"Raven, take a break," Damon called, throwing me a bottle of water. I caught it, flashing him a smile.

"Are we done for the day?" I asked, placing Azura carefully away from the boxes she was trying to climb dangerously.

"I think we are," Liam said. His strong arms wrapped around me from behind, sending off those sparks that made me lightheaded, and buried his head in my neck. I closed my eyes, enjoying his hold. My core throbbed when his lips met my neck.

"We are. I need food," Damon remarked, running his fingers through his hair. "I think we did good getting this much done before winter came."

"Yeah, I agree," Liam said looking at the huge packhouse.

"So, pizza and drinks at our place?" I suggested as Taylor and Zack came over.

"Yes!" Azura chimed in

"That didn't include you, pumpkin," Liam remarked with a smirk.

"I like the idea of that," Taylor added, smiling.

I looked up at Liam. He still needed to tell Robyn about his change of mind, something I was feeling really dreadful about.

"I'm going to invite Robyn." The group fell silent and Zack shook his head.

"Liam you need to tell her. I swear, I feel dreadful, and I don't often care about others."

"Course you do, babe," Taylor said, kissing him.

"I don't." Damon glanced at Liam.

"You know she's been working super hard, and since you told her about that rank, she's put even more in…" he murmured, crossing his arms and frowning slightly. I resisted a smile. I loved how he gave it to Liam as it was. Well, to all of us.

"I know… and I don't feel like letting her go… but I need to do it," Liam sighed.

We all remained silent. Liam's intuitive skills had been enhanced since the curse had been broken and we all knew there must be a reason.

"I'll talk to her tonight."

✺◉◉✺

Night had fallen; we had just got the food and the movie was chosen whilst Taylor and Zack had grabbed the drinks.

"Really, this movie?" Damon asked, raising an eyebrow as he checked the movie I had put on and paused.

"Yes, I love horror movies." I really did!

"Weird." He shook his head, and I stuck my tongue out. Liam came over, his phone in front of him as he spoke to a sobbing Azura.

"I don't like you anymore, Wiyam, I don't!"

"I'm sorry, pumpkin, but today's a big people day."

"Don't call me punkin! I'm not your stupid punkin!"

Her talking had improved over the last year but she still called us Wiyam and Waven. I had heard her say Liam once, so I thought she just didn't want to change it. She had also gotten a tad feistier. I loved the girl. Liam promised her a sleepover tomorrow before ending the call. I felt bad for her. *Poor Zuzu.*

"Tay, baby, grab me the plates?" I called out.

"Sure, girl. By the way, have I already told you I love the new hair?" He asked as he walked past to get the large plates from the top shelf. No, I couldn't reach with my height.

"Thank you! I like it, but I'm not keeping it pink-tipped. I'm changing it for Kia's wedding," I explained.

"I love that, coordinating with the dress. I'm coming with you when we go to check the fitting, okay?" I nodded happily.

"And you've let the bangs grow out." Damon added, "You look older."

"The height doesn't help," Liam added before they both smirked at each other.

"That's an insult! Hey, I assure you, I don't look like a kid!" I glared at them both whilst taking the drinks to the coffee table.

"I never said you did. I definitely know you're not a kid, love," Liam murmured, his eyes dipping to my body. My stomach knotted, and Damon snickered.

"Okay, guys, we get the picture. Flirt after the movie."

"Or during," Zack suggested just as there was a light knock on the door, and I knew it was Robyn.

"You can't flirt during a horror movie. I don't even like horror movies," Taylor pouted.

"Don't worry, I'll keep you busy," Zack added, pulling the door open.

"Not at my place man!" Liam added, before we fell silent as Robyn stepped inside.

✿

ROBYN

"Hey, I brought dessert," I said, holding up the tray of Tres Leches cake that I'd made. I glanced at them all, my heart skipping a beat when my eyes met a certain blue pair.

A year… we had split just over a year ago… but the feelings I had for him… they never left. I hated it, but what was I supposed to do? Well, I avoided the blood moons, for one; I was not ready to meet my mate yet. I didn't deserve him when I was hung up over another.

"Aww, thank you! You shouldn't have!" Raven exclaimed as she came over, taking the tray from me.

"I'd rather have the cake than beer," Liam added, flashing me a smile despite a flash of guilt in his eyes. Why did he look guilty?

I gave a small nod. I worked alongside the others for months, but since Damon had come back, I suddenly felt awkward around them. Like he was meant to be there, not me.

"Shall we get to the movie?" Damon suggested, turning around.

"Yes, I guess…" Taylor said, gulping.

"Why are you making him suffer?" I asked. His sad brown puppy dog eyes… I didn't feel sympathy often, but Taylor was one person I did feel bad for.

"He'll be fine," Raven said, giving him a hug.

"I don't think I'm going to be fine," Taylor said.

Damon took one armchair and I had to take the other since the two couples sat on the sofa. Great, now I was a mere twenty centimetres from him. I tried not to focus on his tempting scent but on the delicious smell of pizza instead.

❧

The movie was finished, so I offered to make hot drinks and cut the cake. Taylor was a drunk mess and telling Raven how hard it was to watch that movie. She was apologising profusely whilst he was being very dramatic. Liam offered to help me, so there I was in the kitchen with him.

"What is it?" I asked. I could sense that he wanted to speak to me from the few looks he had cast my way.

"That obvious?"

"Very." Liam sighed, "I… I can't make you my Delta, Robyn."

My heart skipped a beat, my stomach twisting. It felt like I had just been slapped. The excitement I had felt when he had first told me… I was ready to make my pack proud…

It's cool. Things happen.

Although I told myself that… there was also that little voice at the back of my head that whispered its doubts. *Everything you ever have or want, is always taken away from you…*

Don't go there, Robyn. I nodded, not even looking up from slicing the milk cake.

"Yeah, that's fine," I replied.

"I'm sorry, it's not on you. I just have this feeling that -"

"It's okay, Liam, you don't need to explain it to me. I'm fine." And I will be in a few days or weeks. I sighed inwardly. *Yeah, I'll be okay.*

"I'm sorry," Liam said quietly. "I just feel like there's more for you."

"Sure, thank you," I said, giving a small polite smile.

I ain't got time for emotional drama, I just… crap, Rick was going to be so gutted. Oh well, at least the entire pack didn't know.

I picked up the plated milk cake slices and walked off to the sitting area, feeling Liam's eyes boring into me. Zack was getting ready to leave but I held out a plate.

"At least try it. I'm sure he'll be okay asleep for a little while," I offered, glancing at Taylor, who was hugging Raven but seemed to be fast asleep.

He looked at me, and from the look in his eyes, I realised they all knew. They all knew he was going to drop me. Shit. I brushed my hands over my thighs after passing Damon the other plate and gave a small smile.

"Well, it's late and I'm super tired. Thanks for the invite, Raven. I'm heading out," I replied.

"Won't you have cake?" She asked. I shook my head. I wanted to puke as it was. I felt majorly queasy.

"No, I'm stuffed. Night guys." I looked around before grabbing my jacket, daring not to even look at Liam and Damon.

"Robyn… night…" Raven murmured.

"Goodnight," I said, forcing a final smile before I reached the door and left the warmth of the cottage.

I'm sorry, Robyn, Liam's voice came.

It's cool.

My lips trembled and I stared ahead. No, it was not cool, but I wasn't going to let anyone see my real feelings. I hugged my jacket to my chest, walking through the light drizzle of rain. Disappointment after disappointment…

Was I that horrible?

My eyes prickled, and I bit my lip, my heart thumping loudly. The rustle of the leaves whipping in the wind and the distant sound of the woodland animals seemed to just get louder in my ears. I gasped when someone grabbed my arm, spinning me around.

"Robyn." I stared up into Damon's soft blue eyes, concern clear in them. I glanced away, not wanting him to see the unshed tears.

"Can I help you?" I asked, pulling out of his hold. His scent enveloped my senses.

"He didn't want to give you up, but you know with his intuition, he sometimes gets feeling-"

"Oh, Damon, shut up." He blinked and I frowned at him. "Firstly, stop defending him. Secondly, I said it's fine. Now give me some space."

"No." My heart clenched at that; he really had changed. The Damon I knew listened...

"No?"

"Yeah, I'm not giving you space. You're upset... look, you once told me that if I ever wanted to talk, you're there for me. Talk to me. Just vent for once, Robyn," he said quietly. His deep voice, like always, affected me.

"That was different," I countered, irritated.

Because you didn't love me.

"It's not. I care for you, Robyn. Let me be that confidant. Just let it out. I promise I won't tell Liam if you speak shit about him," he said, placing a hand on his heart.

A confidant... yeah... he probably doesn't realise that I still cared for him in a different way... Shit... if I walked off, he might realise. Defeated, I sighed. I wouldn't tell him everything, but...

"Yes, I'm upset because I had actually thought I was capable of something, and it had never been my intention to aim high," I said, crossing my arms as I turned my back on him. "He just took that away, and you all knew... you all knew he was going to; I would have preferred he just told me through the link or something," I finished bitterly, feeling the pain in my chest squeeze and the first dreaded tear trickle down my cheek. Before I could wipe it away, Damon was in front of me, brushing it away before he cupped my face.

"You are worth so much more," he said softly, giving me a gentle warm smile that only hurt more.

"I'm not." Unable to hold the tears back, I looked away, trying to will them away. "Because… if I was… I wouldn't have everything taken away from me."

I pulled away from his touch. I had already said far too much. His eyes were filled with sadness, but I didn't give him a chance to speak as I ran towards the packhouse, to my space where no one could bother me. Where no one could come and take something from me…

Passage of the Alpha

RAVEN

ZACK AND TAYLOR HAD just left, so I was clearing up. I pursed my lips, glancing at Liam who had been silent since Robyn had left, deep in thought.

"You could have handled that a little better... in the kitchen, really, Liam?" I asked, frowning slightly.

He'd told me earlier that he'd tell her before she left, but I didn't think he'd do it in there! I'd expected him to take it outside. My words seemed to snap him out of his thoughts, and he looked at me.

"I'd kept my voice down. Only Damon heard. You and Zack were too busy with Taylor."

"That's still not nice, Liam," I persisted softly, walking over to him. He smiled slightly, and that knowing look that I often saw in his eyes lately was there again.

"It made Damon go after her. If I took it outside, she would have left alone." I raised an eyebrow questionably as Liam began washing the plates.

"Are you playing cupid? Liam, don't -"

"I'm not... I'm just... I had to do it then. I needed Damon to go after her," he sighed, and I felt my chest squeeze.

I know what he meant; he often had these instincts to do or say something, and, well, let's just say it saved someone from a broken arm once. Another time he had urged Aunty Red to go check on one of the she-wolves suddenly; she did, and she had found her in labour in her apartment and in need of an emergency C-section. Another time he had bluntly hurt Uncle El's feelings, pushing him, only for Uncle El to say he was fucking tired and then storm out. Yet the following day, Aunty Red had told us he talked about his losses; about Uncle Aaron, Alpha Raf, his father... his mother... how he just felt tired. It had helped Uncle El. Speaking about it had somewhat brought him the closure he needed. He promised Liam that once he handed the title to him, he would leave on a six-week holiday with Aunty Red, and we promised we'd take care of Azura.

If Liam had needed Damon to go after her, there had to be a reason, even if it made no sense or didn't feel right. I sighed as I began drying the dishes.

"At least give me the heads up when you are going to do something random like that," I requested gently.

"I'll try. When it overcomes me, I kind of go blank apart from having to do what I need to." He stared at the moon outside. "This coming Blood Moon is vital," he added quietly.

I didn't question it, having a feeling there was more to those words. I stared at the moon, wondering what was to come. *Please, Goddess, let things stay peaceful.* Something told me they would be. I just had a good feeling that things would continue to go perfectly well.

ꙮ

A few days passed, and the night of the Alpha ceremony arrived. The last two days had been spent with those who would be leaving the pack, being removed from the pack, and some cutting ties with the pack, so it wasn't a complete burden on Uncle El doing the removing of the members. It was going well, yet we didn't want to delay. After tonight, Damon would initiate them under him.

I was dressed in a black, sequined, net mermaid cut gown with a nude bodysuit beneath it. It had one puffy feather sleeve with a slit between my breasts. My hair was curled and left open, and my make-up was smoky with deep pink lipstick. Kiara was finishing off the last touches.

Becoming Luna, the responsibility that came with it... I was ready for it.

One thing was clear: when I came back to this pack, I'd thought I was ready to take everything on and be this fearless badass girl who knew what I wanted. I didn't. I had been confused, unable to move on from my doubts and just thinking the best way to deal with stuff was simply taking it in my stride. Everything that had happened, from the curse to the mate situation, had been an eye-opener and a learning experience for all three of us. We had made mistakes, but we learned from them to get to where we were today. I felt like we were finally adults, ready to take the titles we were destined to hold.

The day after our movie night, I had visited Robyn to check up on her. I was not going to be the Luna who stood by and let my Alpha do whatever. I would make sure everyone was doing okay, and if he had offended her, I would fix it. He had, of course, apologised, too. I made him bake her a Victoria's sponge cake and go say sorry!

Liam's words still rang in my mind, and I wondered… was Robyn going to somehow be Damon's second chance? I hoped so because even when I left the pack, he was able to have a relationship with her, meaning he had felt strongly enough to override the guilt of the mate bond. I had faith in it happening!

"Ready, Raven?" Aunty Red asked, popping her head in as the make-up artist finished off with some setting spray.

"Yeah, all done," I said, standing up.

"Damn, you look beautiful," she said, hugging me tightly. She looked breathtaking, too, in a maroon dress with a slit down the side.

"She looks like a goddess, doesn't she, Mom?" Kiara added, smiling at me proudly. She wore a deep plum-purple gown herself and looked as beautiful as her mother.

"Not like you two! But I think I'm a pass," I said in approval. Aunty Red chuckled as we headed downstairs.

"You really need to see what we all see, or at least Liam," she teased.

"Yes, a beautiful little sexy doll," Kiara giggled. I pouted; she had heard Liam… I knew it!

Liam… my heart began thundering as I realised what an important night it was going to be for us both.

"You'll be fine; we all feel like this when our time comes," Kia said, giving my hand a gentle squeeze.

I looked at our intertwined hands, just like long ago… but this time, it wasn't me supporting her. It was her holding mine to support me. Our eyes met, and I knew she had a similar thought.

"Thank you for being an amazing friend and the best sister-in-law I could ever have hoped to have," she said, stopping at the bottom of the steps. Aunty Red walked away, giving us a moment as I looked at Kiara.

"No matter where life takes us," I whispered. She nodded, and we hugged. Sisters. Forever.

"Shall we do this?" She asked softly.

I nodded, my heart hammering as we stepped out into the clearing. Everything was decorated in ivory, with lights glittering above and all around. It was brighter than most of the ceremonies, but I knew it was because of Kiara's eyes.

I scanned the crowds as all eyes turned on me, my eyes landing on Liam standing there looking incredible in a black tux. His eyes were on me, burning brightly with love and approval, before he walked over to me, pulling me into his arms and kissing me deeply. I kissed him back, tightening my arms around his neck, savouring the taste of his mouth as I bit back a sigh with my core clenching.

"You look beautiful, love," he murmured, squeezing my ass.

Yes, with the passing months, he was no longer able to control himself in front of his parents, and I was shocked to admit that he was probably as bad as his father!

"Thanks," I said, caressing his chest, my heart racing under his gaze.

My Luna... I blushed, biting my lip as I felt him throb against me.

My Alpha.

I stepped away as Damon stepped closer, and I smiled, giving him a tight hug. He wrapped his arms around my shoulders, planting a kiss on the top of my head.

"You look great. So, ready to become the pintsize Luna?"

"I'm not that small," I huffed.

"You kinda are, brat," Al's cold deep voice came.

"Nice to see you too." I frowned. I looked at the king himself as his hand pulled Kiara against him, kissing her lips before he turned to me.

"Be nice," Kiara scolded him lightly, her hand resting on his chest.

I'm sure she used that line a lot!

"I don't fucking do nice," Al replied coldly.

"Yeah, we know," Uncle El replied arrogantly as he smirked at Alejandro, someone that I would say was his friend... or at least more than just his soon-to-be son-in-law.

"You're looking a little better since the last time I fucking saw you, but still getting old, Dad," Al smirked tauntingly as Uncle El frowned at him.

"Do not call me that," he growled.

"Make me fucking stop then."

Ah, ever the blunt king he was. Well, a few months ago, I had asked him to race Liam… they had refused. However, they had gone in for a match and, well… Liam lost, but it wasn't by much. Impressively, the Deimos was almost as strong. He had even broken the king's nose in the process, not realising his own strength. I giggled, and all eyes turned to me.

"What are you giggling about?" Damon asked curiously.

"Al's broken nose," I whispered loudly, feeling his powerful aura and displeasure roll off him. Kia giggled, and I flashed the glowering king a peace sign before excusing myself and pulling Liam along with me.

"Sorry, I got to go get a drink!"

"Brat…" I heard the king mutter.

"Did you forget that he won that match?"

"Only by a bit," I giggled.

He had been shocked when he'd seen Liam's aura and ended by saying, *"Well, he is Kiara's twin."*

"You really do like to rile him up," Liam smirked, shaking his head.

"Maybe," I said, wrapping my arms around his neck and pulling him down. "And I like to do far more to you."

"I fucking know," he replied huskily, his lips meeting mine in a passionate kiss once again…

KIARA

The evening had passed in merriment, with the hustle and bustle of children playing and laughing, adults teasing and chatting, and the warmth of a pleasant night hung in the air. It was finally time for them to take their oaths.

Mum and Dad were on the stage with Liam, Raven and Damon making their way onto the stage. Looking at them on either side of Raven, I wondered, *What if things had been different?* Damon would have still been an Alpha… but it seemed he didn't need a mate to get that title. He was meant to be one…

Can't stand the fucker, Alejandro's voice came through the link. I raised an eyebrow.

I thought you'd be over that by now, my sexy beast, I questioned, caressing the back of his neck as I kissed his cheek.

Once a fucker, always a fucker, but I guess he deserves the title. He was a good Beta when Liam was in his training. I smiled slightly and nodded. Yes, he was.

I'm glad you see that, I replied, turning my attention back to the trio.

Of course I do, Amore Mio, but that doesn't mean I have to fucking like him.

He wrapped his arms around me, and I leaned into him. Life with Alejandro was perfect. I glanced over at the far side where the children were playing with the Omegas minding them and their own set of guards standing around. My little angels.

He kissed my shoulder before we looked towards Dad, who was beginning the oath. Damon would become Alpha first, as Dad would be handing him the honorary title of Alpha before Liam could take over from him. Dad looked a lot better; he, like the rest of us, was becoming accustomed to Rafael's passing. Gone but never ever forgotten. I placed my hand on top of Alejandro's, my heart racing as he kissed my neck.

You okay?

"Yes," I whispered, turning and kissing his lips.

"I, Alpha Elijah Westwood, honour you, Damon Nicholson, with the title of Alpha of the Blue Moon Pack under the full moon and by Selene's blessings. Do you accept this position?" Dad asked, authority clear in his voice, with his piercing eyes on Damon.

"I, Damon Nicholson, accept the title of Alpha of the Blue Moon Pack, giving my oath that it will always be united with the Blood Moon Pack and respect and honour this oath," Damon replied.

"Do you vow to protect, serve, and lead the pack to the best of your abilities?"

"I do."

Both men sliced their hands before shaking hands and sealing the pact. I felt the slight shift of power. Liam was actually sharing the Alpha power that he would have inherited from Dad with Damon, and I had to say I was proud of him. He had made mistakes, but he had redeemed himself.

"I present to you, Alpha Damon of the Blue Moon Pack!" Dad said as he hugged Damon, and everyone clapped and cheered...

❧☙

LIAM

Damon turned and hugged me, and I slapped his back. It was going to be hard, no longer able to link him anymore...

"Phones, bro," Damon said as if guessing what was on my mind. I raised an eyebrow.

"Yeah, phones," I agreed. He looked at me with his smile fading.

"Thank you."

"Don't." I shook my head, giving him a small smile and stepping back, allowing Raven to hug him.

"Congratulations! I am going to still call you Damon," she stated, making Damon chuckle.

"Of course, tiny Luna," he teased before we turned to Dad once more.

"Ready?" He asked me. I nodded. This time... I won't fuck up. "I, Elijah Westwood, relinquish my position as Alpha of the Blood Moon Pack to you, my son, Liam Westwood, to be bound by oath to serve, protect and lead this pack from here onwards to the best of your capabilities," Dad said. His eyes met mine, and I saw the confidence in them, one that had been slightly amiss the last time I took the oath.

"I, Liam Westwood, accept the position of Alpha of the Blood Moon Pack to honour, serve, and protect this pack to the best of my abilities."

Dad sliced his hand before passing me the knife. I cut a deep gash, shaking quickly as it healed incredibly fast. I felt the power of the Alpha title course through me, the murmur of the pack congratulating me through the link and the position of Alpha falling back into place. *By the goddess herself, I promise to always protect my people.*

I looked down at my little bite-sized Luna, knowing that the power of her title had shifted to her already. I took her hands, kissing her knuckles softly.

"Do you, Raven Jacobs, accept the position of my Luna, to always stand by my side as my mate and Luna of the Blood Moon Pack?" I asked, my eyes staring into her unique ones.

"I do," she replied softly. Everyone clapped and cheered before Dad looked at the crowds.

"I give to you the Alpha and Luna of the Blood Moon Pack!"

Everyone cheered and clapped. I scanned the crowd, seeing Kia and Alejandro… Zack, Taylor, Aunty Monica, Robyn, Azura, Damon… Mom and Dad…

I made it with the help of all those around me. They brought me out of the darkness…

I looked back down at my beautiful mate, my heart racing as I cupped her face, the sparks whispering along my skin. And, of course, her.

"Long live the Deimos line!" Someone called out as I pulled Raven close, kissing her passionately, igniting a storm of never-ending love and need for the woman in my arms.

My world.

My dream.

My all.

Mine.

৩৩৩৩

I pulled Raven away from the dance floor. It had been far too long, and I wanted to go for a run.

"Is it okay for the Alpha and Luna to leave?" She giggled as we stripped our clothes when we reached the thickest of the woods, far away from the party.

"Yeah, perfectly fine. I'm Alpha, so my rules." I winked at her, my eyes on her sexy body. Under the moonlight, she was fucking glowing. My dick twitched and I shifted before I ended up pinning her against the tree right there. I knew for a fact that Alejandro would hear us.

She shifted into her dark grey and black wolf. It was beautiful with her unique glowing eyes. She trotted over to me, nudging me with her snout. I was a lot bigger than her, and my light grey fur complimented perfectly with hers…

You are beautiful, regardless of what form you are in.

Thanks, you, too! She giggled as she ran off, and I fell into a run beside her.

Beautiful? I growled, nudging her playfully.

Yes, or do you prefer pretty?

At least I'm not tiny, I teased, licking her. Her giggle came through the mind link as we kept running faster and faster away from the pack.

Definitely not tiny. Our eyes met, and I nuzzled against her. **Besides, I may be tiny… but I'm strong!** She said before she pounced, knocking me off my feet. She was definitely fast and nimble. I chuckled as we went rolling down the slope, her on top of me. **See?** She remarked, staring down at me.

Shift, I commanded, my heart thudding… I fucking wanted her…

Her eyes widened as she shifted back, breathing heavily. Just the way she looked…

I shifted, too, sitting up and wrapping my arms around a naked Raven. She bit her lip, realising my hard-on was rubbing against her. My eyes feasted on her smooth skin, and I ran my hands down her breasts slowly. Her breath hitched when my fingers grazed her hardened buds. A work of art…

"Perfection…" I growled.

I grabbed her breast, biting down gently on her nipple and making her whimper in pleasure. The scent of her arousal clung to the air, a fragrance that I was fucking addicted to.

"Out here?" She whispered, despite her nails scraping down my chest.

"No one's around," I replied huskily before I pulled her close.

My lips crashed against hers hungrily and I entered her at the same time. She cried out before she began bouncing on my lap as she rode me. I grabbed her hips, slamming her down onto my dick, fucking her hard and fast. She yanked my hair, twisting her fingers into it as her lips met mine again. Her chest pressed to mine as I fucked her, pleasure drowning me, and I embraced it.

We came simultaneously, our release throwing us off the edge into pure bliss, our moans of pleasure synching, the perfect music to my ears…

I love you, she whispered through the link, breathing hard.

"I love you always," I replied, "you are my world."

Under the moonlight I kissed her once more, letting my emotions flow through the bond. I could feel hers... her love... her happiness, her contentment...

Another Night, Another Chance

DAMON

*I*T HAD BEEN A few weeks since I had become Alpha, and although we were two packs, we were still all over the place as there was still some stuff left to set up in my pack.

My pack... It still felt surreal to say that.

It was the night of the Blood Moon, and we were all over at the West-woods'. Aunty and Uncle were leaving the next day for their six-week holiday and would be back just before Kiara's wedding – a holiday Liam had really pushed them into agreeing to. Aunty Red had been a little worried about Azura, but with everyone reassuring them, they were doing this, and they really damn needed it.

"Careful with the glasses, Zuzu," Raven was saying, looking at Azura, who was balancing four glasses in her arms.

She looked as beautiful as ever, yet there was no ache in my chest when I looked at her. It kind of felt weird that I ever had feelings for her. Yes, I still loved her, but definitely just as a friend.

"Did she wash her hands?" Liam asked.

"Wiyam, I don't pick my boogers anymore!" She frowned.

"Still…"

I smiled. I was sure by the time Uncle and Aunty returned, Liam was going to have her completely changed into a hygiene freak.

"They're only glasses, Liam." Uncle El frowned at him.

"I fear for Azura when you leave," Momma said, smiling slightly.

"Don't worry, I'll take good care of her and spank Liam's butt if he is mean to her," Raven chimed in.

"Or I'll spank yours," Liam shot back with a smirk and a wink at Raven. Momma and Aunty Red chuckled.

"I'd say something, but I don't want to make him cringe," Aunty Red teased.

"Zuzu already told us about Uncle El's kink, or is it yours? Remember at that dinner ages ago?" Raven giggled, making Momma and Aunty Red laugh, despite the light blush on their cheeks. I exchanged looks with Liam. We so didn't need to know that.

As for Momma, she had done a complete turnaround. She was herself, and despite the pain in her eyes that often surfaced, she had been able to accept it. To be honest, I couldn't be thanked for it; Aunty Red, Robyn, Raven, and Channing were the reason...

Speaking of Channing, I saw him and Momma spending a lot of time together. I saw how they texted, laughed, and even flirted. Although Mom was ten years his senior, if they were happy, what more could I ask for? And when she had told me he would be joining us tonight... well, that was all the confirmation I needed.

The doorbell rang, and Momma looked up.

"I'll get it."

I saw Aunty Red smile and nod before she looked at me. I gave her a smile. Things had changed over the last year, but for the better. She came over and wrapped her arms around me.

"You are incredible," she said, kissing me on the cheek.

"Thank you, Aunty. So are you. It's thanks to you Mom got to where she is now," I replied quietly.

"No, everyone contributed, but above all, it was her own strength and the fact that she had a son as amazing as you by her side."

"If you two are done, shall we get to the dining room?" Uncle El remarked, a small frown on his face. I smiled. Damn, the man got jealous so fast. I wrapped my arms around Aunty tighter.

"I don't want to let go," I teased. He shook his head, leaving the room as Aunty Red smirked.

"Typical Elijah," she said, letting go of me. We both picked up the last two trays, leaving the kitchen and entering the dining room.

"Hey, Damon," Channing gave me a wave.

"Hey," I replied. He was my Beta, but he may just be my momma's boyfriend soon, too. That was a tad awkward, but, hey, this entire room was an interesting bunch.

"Sit down," Liam told me, motioning to the seat next to him. I nodded, dropping down onto my seat. Yeah, things were back to normal between us, and it felt great.

We all began eating as everyone chatted, and I turned to the window, staring at the moon. Tonight I felt a little restless whenever I glanced at it.

"The food is amazing, Luna Scarlett," Channing complimented.

"Thank you, but please call me Scarlett," Aunty Red said, glancing at Azura, who sat by Raven.

I really wanted those two to have pups of their own because as much as I'll enjoy being that cool uncle, I would also enjoy seeing Liam getting stressed out.

"So, when are you having pups?" I asked quietly.

"Let me enjoy a few years with my mate," he replied, glancing over at Azura. "Besides, we have Azura. She's enough." I smirked.

"Ah, I can't wait for you to be a stressed-out dad."

"Evil much?"

"I will enjoy your suffering."

We smiled at each other before returning to our food, Liam pulling Raven close and kissing her.

My mind wandered into its own thoughts. Would I ever find someone to call my own? I did want someone by my side, but as much as a certain someone came to my mind, I knew she had a mate out there, and I needed to get rid of any feelings as I did with Raven.

Dinner was over, and Mom had said she would head home a little later, so I left. With the passing of the night and the moon rising to its fullest in the sky, my restlessness was far too much for me to shake off.

Liam and Raven had vanished for a bit during dinner; I swear those two were as bad as the previous Alpha couple. We all knew what they were probably doing. When Azura kept insisting on going to find them, Aunty Scarlett tried to keep her occupied. All I could say was good luck to the two of them for the next six weeks.

I myself decided to go for a walk, or maybe I'd go for a run if need be. I just needed this feeling to go away, or I wouldn't get any sleep at night. I entered the woods, walking into the thickest parts of it, away from both pack grounds and followed the sound of the gushing river soothing me slightly. I was just going where my wolf was pushing me; he was far too on edge. Was everything okay?

I walked further in, the moon almost masked by the thick trees above, when I smelled it... a deep, deliciously tempting scent that made my heart pound. My eyes flashed brightly, and my wolf's excitement grew within me.

I didn't need to be told to know what it was... it rivalled Raven's up until we rejected one another.

I broke into a run, the thundering of my heart loud in my ears and my feet barely hitting the ground as I sped up. It was then I saw a flash of movement; a wolf running in the trees, but... it was running away from me.

No. Come back!

ROBYN

Another blood moon and I had stayed holed away in my room until Mikayla, one of the girls, asked me if I could drop something off to her parents because she wasn't feeling great herself. She looked like death, to be honest, so I agreed. It was when I had been heading back to the pack when the most intoxicating scent that I had ever smelled hit my nose, familiar yet so different... spiced cinnamon, fresh rain, and something so tantalising that my stomach knotted. It was so intense that I couldn't even focus on pinpointing it.

Mate.

My mate was there.

My heart thundered, fear consuming me, so I turned and ran as fast as I could. I wasn't ready. Goddess, I wasn't ready. *Why now? I'm not ready for a mate. I'm still in love with someone else...*

I shifted, although my mind was screaming that my torn clothes would give away my identity, but I wasn't able to think. The only thing I could think was to get away from it, all despite my wolf howling at me to stop.

"Stop!" A voice growled, and I skidded to a stop as someone jumped in front of me, his eyes blazing pale green. Our eyes met, the mate bond pulling taut between us, but it was who the man before me was that shook me to my core...

My mate was...

"Robyn?" He whispered hoarsely. I inched backwards, my heart thundering. How was that possible... how...

My eyes stung, and I frowned. If the Goddess was playing a joke on me -

"Robyn... shift," he said softly, peeling his white tee from his chiselled body. He had gotten even bulkier...

He stepped closer, and his scent wrapped around me. My heart was thundering, but I did as he said. His eyes locked with mine as he pulled his shirt over my head. His knuckles brushed my cheek, and the strong current of sparks made my stomach flutter. My eyes met his; they were still pale green, and I could hear his heart racing.

"Why did you run?" He whispered, stepping closer. I stepped back, trying not to look at those gorgeous lips of his.

"Because I... I didn't want to find my mate," I said defiantly, staring into his eyes. His eyes returned to the powdery blue I love so much, despite his heart still beating fast.

"Why not?" He asked softly, cupping my face, and those sparks that I dreamt of coursed through me, making me gasp.

"Because..." Our eyes met, and I knew he knew why. The guilt in his eyes spoke loud enough.

"I told you I still cared for you. We had a connection, Robyn... even though I had a mate, I was able to be with you in her absence," he whispered softly. "Surely that stands for something."

I tensed, realising what he had just said. Even if I wasn't proud of it... he had been able to have a relationship with me, meaning there was something between us without the bond. I knew for me it was a dream come true to be with the man that I loved... but what did he want? What if he just...

"What do you want to do?" I asked, trying to remain strong, despite how intense my emotions were right then.

"To kiss you," he replied quietly, his gaze dipping to my lips and his eyes darkening.

My eyes widened, my stomach knotting at those words, and I licked my lips just before his were on mine. I gasped, my entire body tingling as my stomach somersaulted. The feel of his plush lips against mine, caressing my own, kissing me with a hunger that was a thousand times more intense than ever, was even better than I remembered. His arms wrapped around my waist, the other tangling into my hair, and I couldn't help but wrap my arms around his neck, kissing him back. Was this really happening, or would a wake-up call tomorrow take it all away?

He tensed, moving back, his hands going to my face as I realised there was already a stray tear trickling down my cheek.

"Ryn…"

That name… fuck, that name…

"I don't trust this," I whispered, pulling away. "Tomorrow, you might realise that I'm not who you want."

I stepped back, shaking my head, about to run off, when he grabbed my wrist and pulled me back into his arms. My back hit his chest, and he wrapped his arms around me tightly.

"Then, explain to me why, more than a year on… you're the only woman I see as more than just a woman."

DAMON

Robyn was my mate.

I felt as if the moon goddess truly wanted me to be happy. The one woman who treated me as her number one. The one woman that I still thought of yet didn't dare approach, knowing that she still loved me. I figured that out the night Liam had told her she couldn't be Delta… and as much as I had felt something for her, I didn't want to hurt her, knowing her mate was out there and I didn't deserve her.

But… I was her mate. She was my second chance, and I was not going to let it slip away.

"I don't trust this." Her vulnerable whisper made my heart ache.

"Then, explain to me why, more than a year on… you're the only woman I see as more than just a woman," I murmured, kissing her neck. Her tempting, fresh citrus scent made my head go light. "Let me show you what you mean to me…."

Her heart was racing, her breasts, straining against my T-shirt, were heaving, and the shape of her nipples made my dick twitch. Damn…

"How?" She asked curtly, despite how her body was reacting to my touch. I let go of her, turning her in my hold, and looked into those gorgeous orbs of hers.

"Claim me as yours. Mark me. Let me mark you. I swear I won't ever let you be unhappy again. I'll never let you go," I whispered, cupping her gorgeous face.

Her heart thundered, and I knew she was considering it. I arched my neck to her, waiting for her move, but after a moment, she shook her head. She cupped my face, her deep chocolate eyes filled with raw emotion.

"Just promise to always be mine."

"I promise, I'm yours, only yours."

And I meant it. I meant every word of it. When she nodded, a soft smile crossing her lips, I knew we were going to be okay.

As one, we moved closer, our lips meeting once more. I pulled her body fully against mine, not caring that she could probably feel my hard-on. I wanted her, and I wasn't going to hide that. She was mine, and I was going to cherish her forever.

We somehow made it back to Blue Moon territory and into my apartment, where the smell of new furniture and paint still clung to the air. I kicked the door shut behind me, pushing her up against it. Our hearts thudded as one as her hands instantly went to the band of my pants. I bit back a groan when her fingers slipped inside before she unbuckled my belt and unzipped them. Our lips didn't leave the others.

My hands roamed her body, squeezing her large breasts. Her sigh of pleasure made me crazier. I ripped my top off her and pulled her against my bare chest. Our eyes met, and I brushed a tendril of her hair back. My beautiful, sexy treasure…

She moaned in pleasure when I went lower, kissing her neck and chest. She gasped when I took her nipple in my mouth, sucking hard just as she pulled my pants down.

"Fuck…" I whispered as her hand wrapped around my dick, familiar, yet so much fucking more intense.

I claimed her lips in a kiss once more as she stroked my wood before I pulled her to the bed and gently laid her back, peppering her beautiful body with soft, sensual kisses. My hands began playing with her boobs before I went lower, parting her smooth lips and beginning to devour her.

Perfection… she was perfection. I kneaded her ass as I ate her out, her moans of pleasure only driving me further. I slipped two fingers into her, making her cry out in pure ecstasy.

"Fuck, Damon…"

"Who do you belong to, beautiful?" I whispered, speeding up as I began to flick her clit faster with my tongue.

"Ah… you… you!" She whined just as her climax hit her. I didn't stop until she came down from her high, admiring her before I crawled between her legs, kissing her lips as I entered her.

"I love you," I murmured huskily as I began making love to her, savouring each thrust, the way she felt wrapped around me, her body moving underneath me, the way she leant into me…

"I've always loved you," she whispered, pulling me down into her embrace.

I kissed her neck tenderly as I slammed into her to the hilt, making her moan loudly as I sped up, knowing exactly how she liked it.

"Fuck!" She gasped, her hold on me tightening.

Pleasure I had never felt before coursed through me as I fucked her harder. The sound of our skin hitting against one another's and the scent of her arousal along with sex filled the air, and the urge to mark her overcame me. My canines elongated, and I pulled my head back, my heart racing as I stared into her eyes. I needed her permission.

She tilted her head, giving me the access that I so craved, and I bit into her smooth neck tenderly. She moaned loudly as her climax hit her, and her entire body trembled in pleasure. I extracted my teeth, gently licking the wound before I kissed her lips tenderly. She kissed me back before she pulled away, her gaze flickering to my neck.

I sped up, thrusting into her as I felt myself getting closer to the edge. My moves grew faster and jerkier just as my orgasm tore through me. She pulled me close, sinking her teeth into my neck, sending pleasure and a touch of pain through me as she completed the bond. Our emotions were surging as one as I shot my load into her, making her moan in satisfaction.

Our eyes met, both of us breathing hard before I rolled onto the bed, pulling away from her as I enclosed her in my arms. I wasn't expecting to find my mate tonight… but I was glad I did, and I was lucky it was her. I looked down at her. She was staring at my chest, a hand pressed against it before she kissed me there softly and looked up at me.

"My Luna," I said quietly. Her skin was glowing. I caressed her jaw, and I didn't need any foretelling to tell me that life was going to be great.

"My gentle Alpha," she smiled.

She kissed me once more, and I knew tonight was going to be a night neither of us was going to forget…

Bitesized Luna

LIAM

"*I* SLEEP WITH WAVEN, OKAY, Wiyam?" Azura proclaimed as she held Raven's hand, and we made our way home.

Although I was hoping for one more night of wild sex with Raven before we had to kind of behave for the next six weeks, Azura had begged to come, and although Mom said no, Raven hadn't been able to say no to those big blue eyes of my little sister.

I loved the little pumpkin, but she was a damn cockblocker.

"You're sleeping in the spare room, kiddo," I said, picking her up. She pouted, giving me a sad look.

"Wiyam make Azuwa sleep alone?"

"You sleep alone at the mansion… it's way bigger, pumpkin." She pouted at that, then rested her head on my shoulder.

"Okay, I sleep all alone," she said sadly, making me feel bad, but Mom had said she needed to stay in her routine.

"Don't worry, Zuzu, I'll read you a bedtime story, and I'll stay with you until you fall asleep, okay?" Raven suggested soothingly. I wrapped my free arm around her slender shoulders. She was a fucking sexy doll…

"Sounds like a plan, right?" I questioned Azura, who seemed happy with that.

"Yes," she said happily as she yawned. "Tomowow, we go back to say goodbye to Mama and Daddy?"

"Yes, we will," I promised, gazing up at the moon before I smiled, feeling another pack link break. I knew that this one was different. Damon had found his mate.

"What are you smiling about?" Raven asked curiously. I looked down at my tiny Luna, as she was often called.

"Just that an Alpha has found his mate tonight," I whispered, smiling. Her eyes widened, and she smiled.

"Wait, he has?"

"Yeah, and he's marked her," I replied, smirking. "The dude sure didn't waste time."

"Wait, did you- how did you know that?" My ability wasn't as strong as Dante's, but it was more like Kiara's.

"She's from this pack," I said. Although an Alpha usually can't tell which of his pack member's links were broken, I knew this one was her.

"Robyn?" Raven gasped.

Our eyes met, and we smiled. Damon had been thrown into this entire situation thanks to my curse, and deep down, I knew we both needed to see him happy for us to feel completely guilt-free.

I looked at my mate's beautiful mark. I knew that I'd always feel guilt for the way I had marked her, but we were at a place where I had accepted that I had done wrong. Rather than live with wishful thinking and regrets, I would always aim to be better for her.

"Do you ever think… what if you chose him?" I asked softly, careful of the girl who had fallen asleep in my arms. Raven became serious and shook her head.

"No, because I know that you are the one for me," she replied. "You know, before the mating ball, I did begin to question myself. I felt as if something was brewing between Damon and me, and I felt confused about my feelings. Then, the ball happened, but I think it was all the things getting ready to fall into place. I love him, but if it wasn't for the mate bond complicating things, it would have been the love that one has for a dear friend. He'll always be that selfless hero in my eyes, but we weren't meant to be. It's you." She tip-toed, puckering her lips for a kiss and looking so fucking cute and sexy. I leaned down, claiming her lips in a deep passionate kiss before she broke away, her heart racing.

"I swear…"

"Hmm?" She asked as I moved back, glancing down at her cleavage in that sexy corset of hers. Goddess, she dressed to tease, too.

"I swear my back's going to give with all this bending down." I laughed as her eyes narrowed in frustration.

"Liam!" She growled.

"It's worth it, though," I teased.

"That's it! You can sleep in the spare room today!" She stuck her tongue out as she stomped off ahead. I smirked, keeping up with her with ease and tapped her ass hard, making her jump. "Oi, big boy, you are so dead!"

I kept out of her reach as she tried to smack my ass all the way home, making her more and more annoyed as she missed. The moment I placed Azura in the spare room, tucking her in and shutting the door behind me, I spun around, grabbing Raven's wrist just as she was about to smack my behind.

"Not fair," she protested.

"Oh come on, it's fair. How about you go wait in the bedroom in that new leather outfit of yours and I'll give you a spanking you won't forget?" I growled huskily, pulling her close and kissing her hungrily.

She sighed against me, my hands on her ass, before she pulled away, and I knew she'd do just that. As naughty as she was, she loved to get kinky in the bedroom, or anywhere for that matter. I watched her walk off, my eyes on her ass in that sexy leather, and I smiled, locking the front door and closing the curtains in the meantime as I waited for my little doll to call me.

Come on in, she whispered through the link.

I walked towards the bedroom, opening the door and feeling a little suspicious. As expected, she wasn't on the bed. I turned in a flash just as she slapped my ass seconds before I grabbed her, lifting her off her feet and over my shoulder as she laughed hysterically.

"You played dirty."

"I like playing dirty. What are you going to do?"

"I'll show you," I said, tossing her onto the bed. My eyes raked over to the tiny leather outfit of hers that was wrapped around her body, the cuff around her neck right down to the leather strip across her boobs and squeezed them.

"Can't wait…"

Neither could I.

I pinned her to the bed, crashing my lips against hers, setting off fire-works within us. The sparks flourished into bursts of intense pleasure as we kissed like there was no tomorrow. This was our life, filled with a little teasing, a little fun, a few tears, and a few disagreements, all wrapped up in a lot of love, happiness, and joy.

Oh and sex. Lots and lots of mind-blowing, hot-as-hell sex. How the hell did I not mention that one first?

Well, either way, in the end, despite the emotional roller coaster, I got my girl.

My tiny, bite-sized Luna.

Minding Azura

LIAM

MOM AND DAD HAD been gone for over two weeks already, which meant Azura was here with us. Raven had gone early that morning to Kiara's pack as they had some shopping to do for the wedding. I didn't get how women's shopping never finished, but if they were happy shopping, what more could I ask for?

Anyway, since Raven was gone, I was stuck minding my adorable little sister. The only problem was that she was a four-year-old pup who had asked way too many questions and still picked her boogers, although she told me a few weeks ago she doesn't...

Lie.

She had been fairly good, to be fair, although she got a bit emotional every time she got off a video call with Mom.

"So, Wiyam, what we do now?" She asked, rubbing her nose. I raised my eyebrows. It was past five in the afternoon.

"Well, I'm thinking, how about we make a nice meal for when Raven gets back? It will be a nice surprise for her. What do you think, pumpkin?"

"Oo, Wiyam, I love the idea!" She said with her eyes wide with excitement. "We make cake, too?"

"Definitely make cake, Raven loves cake. But I'll make cake..."

Can't have her hands in the food. I felt guilty at the thought, staring at the bundle of cuteness.

"Waven loves Wiyam, too," she added, and I gave her a small smile, ruffling her hair.

"And she loves Azura, too."

She nodded, and I gave her a tight hug. She was an observant child, and I knew that as she got older, she'd begin to notice how some people treated her, their glances and their whispered remarks. I was going to protect her the best I could.

"Wiyam, do you miss Waven?" She asked, concerned as she stared up at me.

"I do, but can't I hug my little sister otherwise?" I questioned.

"You can. Okay, Wiyam, you cook, I go watch TV, then you give me the leftover cweam."

I watched her rush off before I got to work in the kitchen. She sure could be such a good girl.

৯৩.৩৵

I had just put the roast chicken in the oven and was stirring the custard when I realised Azura was no longer in front of the TV. Shit, I didn't even realise when she left!

I could hear her steady heartbeat and rushed to check up on her, pushing open our bedroom door to see her sitting on Raven's stool in front of the make-up table with several of her make-up palettes and lipsticks open.

"Look, Wiyam, I bootiful." I looked at her.

Wow, she sure turned into a Halloween horror pumpkin overnight...

Garish purple lipstick was smeared over her lips and all around them, her cheeks were a horrendous pink, and her eyes looked as if someone had punched her a few times, and, to make it worse, the liquid liner was spread all over her lids and around her eyes. Goddess...

"You were far more beautiful before, baby girl," I commented quickly, going over to her. Shit, would Raven get mad? She had totally wrecked half these powdery eyeshadows.

"No, I look nice now," she pouted at her reflection.

Did she really think she looked good? Shit, I needed to get this all cleaned up before Raven got back...

"Okay, look, let's get you washed up -"

"No, no, Wiyam! I keep it on! I show Waven I love her make-up."

"No, if Raven sees you like that, she might scream at how scary you look," I said, grabbing the wipes Raven used before showering.

Wrong fucking sentence.

Her large eyes pooled with tears, getting wider and wider by the second. Her lips quivered, and I closed my eyes just as she broke into sobs.

"Wiyam say I scawy, I no scawy! I want Mama!"

Tears. An entire fucking waterfall of them.

Damn.

I remembered the last time I triggered her off when Raven had first returned home.

"No, pumpkin, come on, no crying. You look beautiful. If you want to wear make-up, you wear make-up, okay?"

"Mama!"

Shit.

I picked her up only for her to scream louder, her sobs getting worse, and she began struggling in my arms. Whatever she had put on her eyes was spreading down her face, and I think even the joker would be put to shame.

"Okay, okay. Azura, listen."

"Mama!"

Shit.

I carried her from the bedroom, rocking her slightly to sooth her.

"Look, Azura! It's Peppa Pig."

"Wiyam watch stupid Peppa! I want Mama!"

Her face was bright red and, well, black, purple, and blue, too, but that wasn't the point right then. The smell of something burning made my gaze fall to the gas cooker.

Shit! The custard! Fuck, fuck, fuck!

"One second, pumpkin!"

I ran to the kitchen and switched it off. The smell of burned custard filled my nose, and I sighed. *There goes that…*

She writhed and kicked, wanting to be put down, so I took her to the sofa. I put her down and crouched before her.

"Okay, Azura, come on, baby girl, don't cry, please? How can I make it up to you?" She continued screaming and crying. "Please, Azura, come on, I'll do anything? Tell me, what do you want? Sweets? Coke? Chocolates?"

Her screaming suddenly stopped, and I narrowed my eyes. Wasn't that a bit too fast for tears to just stop? But... her cheeks were soaking wet... *I don't trust kids...* Our own mini Joker sat up, staring at me, and I could almost see the cogs in her brain working.

"Wiyam make me sad," she stated, her eyes blurring with tears all over again.

"And Liam is sorry. I just miss seeing my beautiful baby sister's face without this makeup," I said gently. The urge to wash her face was hard to fight.

"But Wiyam like Waven wearing make-up," she sobbed.

"But my sister is more beautiful. Look, Mom, Kiara, and Raven wear make-up because they are getting older and ugly."

Please don't kill me, ladies.

"But you don't need it because you are a beautiful princess. You don't need makeup," I said as she wiped her eyes, smearing the makeup over her hands.

"I tell Mama that," she promised, looking so sorrowful my heart squeezed. *Goddess, kids are hard.*

"It won't be our secret?"

"No, Mama say never keep secrets from Mama. If anyone make me sad or upset, no secrets. I tell Mama now. Phone Mama!"

I nodded, quickly taking my phone out and video-calling Mom. I'm sure it was still day over there. Sure enough, they answered, the sun shining down on them both, and I could see Mom and Dad were lounging on the beach.

"Baby girl!" Mom said, her smile vanishing when she saw Azura's face.

"Mama! Liam no like my make-up!"

"Fuck..." Dad commented, trying to suppress his smile.

"Oh my baby... why don't you take it off, and Raven can apply something pretty and pink?" Mom suggested.

"Raven is not here..." I reminded her.

"Then you can."

"Pink sparkly make-up?" Azura asked hopefully. "I no see any pink."

"Yes, Liam will put some pretty pink makeup on you, okay? I'm sure there's something there, okay?" Mom replied, smiling.

"Okay, Mama! Liam said you and Waven are ugly with no make-up," she added quickly. I narrowed my eyes. I was sure she just said 'Liam' correctly… that kid was shady.

"I will sort Liam out when I come home. Now go wash your face, and, Liam, put some glittery make-up on her, okay?"

"Right," I sighed in defeat.

This was going to be a long evening…

❧❧❧

An hour later, I had wiped her face clean, taken the roast out of the oven and put the sliced steak fries into the oil before I was once again in front of Raven's makeup table. I had salvaged what I could from her palettes that Azura had dug into, and I was currently putting make-up on her face.

Raven had mind-linked not long ago, telling me she was close and would be home soon.

"No Wiyam, you use this one," she said, pointing to a glittery royal blue.

"No, I think this pink is nicer…"

The tears were beginning, and I quickly dabbed the brush into the blue glitter and patted it lightly onto her eyes.

"Okay, now lipstick, Wiyam."

I nodded and added some lipstick lightly. Raven's make-up was dark… I realised Kiara used to have a lot of pinks and glitters in comparison to Raven's, which were so much darker. This girl… well, she had to go and touch Raven's stuff. I sighed and hoped Raven didn't get mad…

We finished with some gold polish, and I felt drained. This was worse than ten hours of extreme training…

We left the bedroom, and I looked at Azura, who was smiling contently.

"Okay, now you watch TV, and I'll go set the table. Raven will be back soon."

"You pomised me coke and sweets."

I looked down at the little gremlin. She sure knew how to get what she wanted. I poured a little coke into a glass alongside a small, fun size pack of chocolates. She needed to have dinner.

I returned to the kitchen, making sure I kept my eyes on her, not trusting her not to wander off again. When Raven finally opened the door, her scent hit me like a wave of calmness. I walked over to her before she even managed to put the bags down, pulling her into my arms and lifting her off the ground as I spun her around. Goddess, I fucking missed her.

"Liam!" She exclaimed, dropping the bags as she locked her arms around my neck.

"Thank goddess you're home."

Pulling her head down, I kissed her with everything I had. The tingles of the bond and the feel of her ever so soft lips against mine felt so fucking good that all I wanted to do was pin her up against the wall and never let her go.

"Waven!" Azura exclaimed, and I pulled away, thinking we only had a few weeks left... *We got this!*

"Wow, you look so beautiful!" Raven cooed as she gave me a final smile, her gaze lingering on my lips before she pulled Azura into her arms.

"Thank you, Waven." Her eyes turned to me, and I knew from the spark in those blue ones that she was ready to complain about me. "Liam was a meanie!"

The tears began flowing and I shut the door, wanting to bang my head against it.

Goddess, I know you want the Deimos line to live on, but let me live a few years or a decade in peace... without any kids. Please.

༺🌸༻

Dinner was over, and Raven had put Azura to bed. I had just washed up and dropped onto the sofa.

"Tired?" Raven asked sympathetically, stepping out of Azura's bedroom wearing a black silk cami and those tiny shorts with an open gown on top.

"Not that tired..." I said, my eyes trailing over her.

She smiled in amusement, coming over and walking behind the sofa. She placed her hands on my shoulders before she began massaging them. I closed my eyes, groaning in satisfaction.

"You're tense? It's hard to believe one toddler did this." She bent forward, kissing my lips as I stared up at her.

"That one is not just an ordinary pup," I said. "Oh, she kinda ruined some of your makeup... maybe you could buy replacements?"

"I saw. They're not that ruined; they're okay, still useable," she reassured me, kissing my neck. "But it seems my Alpha has been rather stressed. How about I take good care of you?"

I hardened in my pants, her hand running down my chest as she placed sensual kisses along my neck.

"I think I'd like that."

I tangled my hand into her hair, pulling her down just as her hand cupped my crotch, sending pleasure flowing through me. But before I could flip her over my shoulder into my lap, the guest room door opened with a creak and Raven jerked away as Azura appeared in the doorway, clearly sleepy, all dressed in her penguin onesie holding a matching penguin plushie in her hand.

"Waven, I'm scared."

"Aw, baby, don't worry. Come on," Raven cooed, hurrying over to her, leaving me with just a reminder of her scent and a view of her ass before she cast me an apologetic look and closed the door behind them.

I stretched my arms over the top of the sofa, resting my head back as I stared at the ceiling. *Yep, definitely no kids for a few years.* Twenty minutes later, I decided to go check if Azura was asleep. Opening the door, I stopped in the doorway, seeing both fast asleep and snuggled together. I smiled slightly. Okay, maybe kids weren't so bad. I walked over to the bed, slowly pulling the blanket over them, and planted a kiss on both of their foreheads before I left the room, closing the door behind me.

A Royal Wedding

RAVEN

THE WEDDING OF THE decade had arrived, and guests from all corners of the country were teeming into the king's territory for the occasion. Women in glamourous gowns from the latest designers and men in custom-tailored suits and tuxes were pouring into the grand open grounds below. My heart was racing as I stared out of the huge windows at the stunning, breath-taking view down below.

It was magical.

To the left was the table set for the reception dinner, decorated impressively. More guests would arrive later for the reception. Round tables were covered in blush-coloured tablecloths with matching chairs, garlands of ivory flowers, and ribbons of white fabric created a roof above. To the far side were the dance floor and the cake.

Right ahead to the right was the aisle with a carpet of the palest shades of pink and white roses leading from the entrance of the mansion all the way up to the dais, where they would take their vows. Above it, ribbons of white fabric were draped like a roof above the seats for the guest. Glass tables at the edge of the rows held vases of pale pink roses and garlands of green vines dangled from the ceiling similar to the eating area with chandeliers glittering in the centre. To the side was the string quartet that would be playing the music for the ceremony. Magical.

"It's perfect, Kia," I murmured in awe, turning to the queen herself. The beautician was finishing off her elegant bridal updo, making sure every wave of her hair was in the perfect position. A few strands framed her face, and she finished by adding the floral hair vine to Kiara's bun before pinning her veil in.

Kiara smiled at me, her face glowing radiantly. She wore an ivory, one-sleeved, embroidered dress that was decorated with pearls. It was a mermaid cut gown with a huge skirt that had a large trail with the same embroidered work as the top of the dress. She wore pearl earrings, but apart from that, her only jewellery was her engagement ring.

"You look beautiful," I complimented. She truly did.

"Thank you. It's really weird that I'm nervous since I'm already Luna, and we are already mated," she said when the beautician left, leaving us alone. I smiled softly as I walked over to her.

"It's still a new step," I said, taking her hand as I crouched down before her. Her acrylic nude nails looked as perfect as the rest of her with their glittery tips.

"Thanks." She smiled. "You look gorgeous."

"Thank you," I replied, my heart fluttering as I wondered what Liam would think. I had been with Kia since morning, and I missed him.

I was wearing an olive-green, metallic, halter-neck dress with a slit down the centre from the collar to my waist. It was fitted up to the knees and then flared out with crystal detailing around the bodice, neckline, and waist. My back was bare, save for the tattoo of Liam's name on the left side of my back, which I had gotten recently. My hair tips had been dyed a deep mauve pink and were up in an elegant updo with olive green flowers in it. My eye makeup was dramatic with nude lips, and I wore high pencil heels on my feet.

"It's time," Uncle El's voice came.

We both turned to see him, Aunty Red, Liam, and Azura standing there. My heart skipped a beat when my eyes landed on Liam in a stone-coloured suit with an open button olive green shirt underneath. His hair was styled to perfection, a single strand flicking over his forehead, and that scar of his made him look even sexier as his blazing cobalt eyes were set on me. Goddess, he was so handsome…

The urge to go over and run my hand down his chest that was teasing me from those open buttons was strong, and I had to fight it. I swallowed hard, my core clenching. The urge to move closer to him and kiss him tempted me, but it was Kia's day.

Fuck, love… Liam's voice came through the link.

Yeah… same… you look beyond sexy, blue eyes. His intense gaze was making me a little light-headed as he undressed me with his eyes, and I had to blink to remember where we were.

"She looks amazing, right?" I asked, looking down at my glowing queen, my heart thundering.

"She does," Uncle El agreed. "As do you."

They walked over to us as Azura stared at Kiara with pure awe on her face. She herself looked gorgeous, like Kiara's twins. She was in a blush-coloured gown with a trail and some lacework. Pearl buttons went up the back with a bow at the back.

"You look bootiful, Kiawa," she said, wrapping her arms around her.

"Thank you, sweetheart." Kiara kissed her forehead, smiling at her before I whistled.

"And you, Zuzu, are going to steal the hearts of all the little boys out there."

"I should hope not," Uncle El said, frowning slightly. "I keep forgetting that I'm going to have to give her away, too…"

"Oh, baby, not today," Aunty Red replied, kissing him.

She wore a duck egg-coloured, net embroidered gown with a tulle net skirt, a slit up to her thigh, and one ruched sleeve. Uncle El wore a grey pinstripe suit with a white shirt and black tie, looking almost as handsome as his son, yet was it bad that Liam took sexy to an entirely new level?

Liam walked over to us, pulling me into his arms and cupping the back of my neck as he kissed me deeply. His tongue slipped into my mouth, my core clenching as his hand grabbed my ass. Our lips caressed the others', and he nibbled on my bottom lip before he broke away, pressing his forehead to mine. His aura swirled around us. I closed my eyes, catching my breath, knowing if we continued, the entire room would smell my arousal and probably see his hard-on…

"Naughty Wiyam," Azura giggled as she twirled around in front of the floor-length mirror.

I smiled, pulling away and noticing how Uncle El was holding Kiara tightly in his arms. A father's love, something I didn't have from my own father, but I got enough from Uncle El. I didn't feel like I was missing out because I had people who loved me.

"You look beautiful, Kia," Liam said, making Kiara smile.

"Thanks, Liam," she said as he hugged her tightly.

"I'm sure Alejandro is going to love it," Aunty Red replied. "Well, we should get going. It's almost time."

"I'm ready!" Azura exclaimed. She was going to be the little flower girl, whilst Dante was the ring bearer. The twins were far too small for the job.

I was Kiara's maid of honour, but she had allowed me to choose my own clothing and hadn't set a theme for me. I loved that girl, as I couldn't really see myself wearing blush pink. Liam kissed me once more as we all headed downstairs. He and Aunty Red headed out first, and we waited until it was our time.

RAYHAN

I looked down at my kitten. She looked breathtaking in her strapless, pale blue sequined gown, with a silk layer clinging to her arms, her wintery makeup, and her gorgeous hair styled elegantly. She looked like a winter queen, and I was all for it. Her plush pink lips curled up in a small, tempting smile, cupping my face before I leaned down, claiming those lips in a deep kiss. The tingles of the spark spread through me, waking the desire that she always set ablaze within me.

"Del, we look great, right? Those women have nothing on us," Raihana murmured, scanning the crowds as Chris pulled her close, kissing her.

"You sure do. Wanna skip the occasion so I can admire you instead?" He whispered to her, and I cocked a brow.

"Really, Chris, we just got here," I remarked.

I was coordinated with Delsanra in a pale blue suit with a navy shirt underneath, which I had left a few buttons open, and my hair was down. Raihana was co-ordinated with Delsanra, yet at the same time, was the opposite, in a golden mirrored dress, and her silk top layer spread around her in a rather dramatic way. Yeah, she just needed a chance to dress up. Her bronzed skin glowed under the sun, and she reminded me of those golden trophies you won at some sports game or the Oscars or something. A little too much... but I wouldn't say that, or she'd skin me alive...

I smirked. Okay, she looked good in a very Raihana way, daring and just needing an excuse to show off, go all out, and be totally extra. Despite being a Luna, she was still known as the Rossi princess.

"Ooo, Uncle's there! Come on, Del, we need photos with him!" She pulled out of Chris' hold, much to his disappointment. He was wearing black pants and a waistcoat with a black and gold blazer. He and Raihana really were made for one another...

We walked over to Uncle Al, who was standing there talking to Marcel and Mom. Mom was carrying Skyla whilst Kataleya was being picked up by Serena, Uncle's Beta's mate. Uncle looked good, dressed in a black tux, his hands in his pockets as he nodded to something Mom was saying. More than a year and a half had passed since Dad had left us, gone but never forgotten…

Mom was doing okay. She had good days and bad days, but we were all trying to be there for her.

"Uncle, Photos!" Raihana said as she did a twirl. "How do I look?"

"Gorgeous. I'm glad you're fucking mated," he remarked, frowning as he glanced around as if making sure no one had their eyes on her. I smirked as Chris nodded in approval.

"Yeah, don't worry about that. I take good care of her." He winked at Raihana, and I had to admit it still frustrated me at times, one of your best friends totally flirting with your sister all the damn time. It was awkward, mate or not, and those two were always… handsy.

"Pictures," Uncle Al said with a nod as one of the photographers came over, "Looking good, spitfire. I can see you two have some theme or some shit going on."

"Thanks, King Burrito, I'm glad you noticed," Delsanra replied as Uncle put his hands on both women's waists, glancing at the camera.

"So, what are you both trying to fucking be, the moon and sun or some shit?"

"Ooo, I like that! I was thinking more winter and summer," Raihana said, pouting for the camera.

The photographer seemed a little nervous with the king's cold glare directed at her, but she did her job as Uncle just stood there perfectly stoic and effortlessly handsome whilst the girls posed. My eyes went to Delsanra, and I had to admit she was so fucking sexy…

She glanced at me, winking, and I was glad that little brat wasn't around. His addiction to Delsanra was ongoing. Speaking of kids… I glanced around, wondering where Leo was.

"Marcel, is Leo not here?" I asked.

"He is, but I'm not sure where. He hasn't even come to see Al." He spaced a little, and I knew he was mind-linking someone, probably to ask them to tell Leo to come over.

Leo… he had changed over the last year or so, and I knew it was because of me, yet no matter what I did, he refused to talk to me.

"Call him. I'll take some pictures with my nephews since I'm already doing this crap."

"Uncle, you know we look good," Raihana said with a pout.

"You fucking do." He hugged her, kissing her forehead. Since Dad had died, he had stepped in and been there for us all. He and Ri were really close, and I knew his being there had helped her as she had always been daddy's girl. For me, too…

I looked away before I got emotional. Delsanra wrapped her arms around me, kissing my lips softly. She understood me even when I said nothing. I held her close, brushing my nose into her neck, enjoying the feel of her body against mine…

Leo came over, and the tension between us was thick. I had tried to explain things to him over Christmas, but he flat-out refused to listen to me.

"What?" He asked, looking at his dad. His jaw clenched as he refused to look at me.

"Hey, kid, not going to fucking greet me?" Uncle Al asked, raising an eyebrow.

"Hi. Can I go now?" He was thirteen, yet as expected of an Alpha male, he was tall. Marcel was about to say something when Uncle shook his head at him slightly before he simply nodded.

"One picture with your uncle, then you can go."

Leo exhaled and walked over to him. Raihana and Delsanra exchanged a look as they moved away, and Uncle placed an arm around his shoulders. The photographer snapped a picture before Uncle jerked his head at me. I shook my head, and he raised an eyebrow.

"I want a fucking picture of the Rossi next generation. Now get the fuck over here."

"Only thing is, Dante isn't here," I remarked, walking over to him, noting the look of irritation in Leo's eyes, but Uncle's grip on his shoulder was firmly keeping him in place.

"The fucker already had an entire fucking photoshoot," Uncle smirked. We took a picture before Marcel and Chris joined in, and that was all Leo could take.

"You've grown, Leo," Mom told him the moment he pulled away from Uncle's hold. He gave a small nod before turning and walking off.

"It's not your fault," Marcel said quietly to me, but I didn't reply.

It wasn't intentional, but it had been my fault, and I couldn't just ignore that...

DAMON

The venue was huge, and there were so many guests out there. Guards lined the grounds, and although there were more guests who would be coming after the vows, there were still many people there.

We had all taken our seats, and Alejandro had taken his place on the small stage. Surprisingly, he didn't have a best man on stage. We were werewolves; we didn't really follow traditional weddings anyway. I looked at my gorgeous girl dressed in a sexy black dress that accentuated her curves to perfection as she sat, one leg crossed over the other, and I couldn't stop gazing at her breasts or lush, thick thighs.

Are you just going to stare at me or pay attention to the ceremony? She asked through the link, glancing at me.

Stare at you, I replied, **That's not even up for debate.** I kissed her deep red lips. She kissed me back, shaking her head.

"Seriously, babe, focus."

I will focus on what's most important to me. Her.

I wrapped my arm around her, kissing her forehead. I had never been happier.

She leaned against me as the musicians began to play, and we all turned to see Dante, in a tux, carrying the cushion bearing the rings as he walked down the aisle at a rather brisk pace. Robyn laced her fingers with mine, her heart skipping a beat as our eyes met. I pecked her lips as we turned to see our own little princess walk down the aisle, her large blue eyes wandering around, and I almost chuckled. Azura really did love to take things at her own pace.

Goddess, kids were damn cute. She seemed to pause, getting distracted by something before Aunty Red called her.

"Baby... sprinkle the petals," she whispered.

"Oh, yes, Mama!" Azura replied, making some of the guests chuckle.

She began to sprinkle the petals, walking along. She stumbled a little on the hem of her princess dress and paused. I realised her shoe had fallen off.

"Oh no," she said, confused, glancing at her shoe and then ahead at the stage. I knew she had been told to keep going forward.

I watched as Alejandro's nephew, Leo, got up from his seat, as it was on the edge of the row not far from where Azura was standing and grabbed her little heeled boot, holding it out to her. She blinked and lifted her dress, sticking her foot out and making me smile.

Cute. Damn, I need a picture of this.

Aunty Red was about to get up, but when Leo knelt down, she smiled and sat down again. He was frowning as he put the shoe on for Azura, glancing around and glaring at all of us who were watching. Damn, the kid had the Rossi fire in him. He needed a mate to tame that anger...

"What's your name?" Azura asked him, seemingly not bothered that she was being videoed right then or that we were in the middle of a wedding concession, ever the curious little princess.

"Leo," he answered moodily as he stood up.

"Thank you, Weo," she replied cutely before turning and walking to the front, forgetting to scatter the rest of the petals in her basket. Well, she did well enough, and the carpet was made of flowers anyway...

"That was so cute," Robyn whispered, smiling softly.

"Yeah, and that move coming from a Rossi," I said, feeling several eyes turn to me, including Rayhan's, Alejandro's, and Leo's. *Damn werewolf hearing.* I guess only a Westwood princess could make Rossi's do stuff like that. I smiled in amusement just as Raven came down the aisle, taking her place on the stage. Then it was time for the bride herself to enter.

We all turned as Kiara stepped out. She looked stunning in her gown, her eyes fixed on her king ahead...

ELIJAH

No matter how many times we did something like this, it was still hard giving your daughter away...

It wasn't the only role of mine in this wedding either. I looked at Kiara, thinking she had come so far from the little girl I used to worry so much over. I walked her down the aisle, but there was no regret or worry in me. The man who awaited her, the one who made her heart race and looked at her as if she was the most precious thing in the world, was the one man I could trust her with. The king, yet before that, he was hers. Her hand may be on my arm, but her eyes were locked with her mate's.

Life had been hard, but the light had returned, and talking about it all had helped. Liam may have pushed me, but it had worked. I was able to enjoy life and cherish what I still had…

We reached the small stage, and I placed Kiara's hand in Alejandro's, their eyes on each other's and unseeing of anything else. The intensity of their love for one another was clear as day. I smiled slightly, stepping onto the stage and taking the place of the best man, a position that Alejandro had asked me to take months ago…

"I had something I wanted to ask you," Alejandro said, taking a drag on his cigarette.

"Not like you to ask. Don't you usually state what you want?" I replied, cocking a brow.

"Yeah, well, we all know you don't fucking listen to shit."

"Yeah, I don't," I smirked arrogantly. He gave me a cold glare before frowning.

"I want you to be my best man at the wedding."

What? *I looked at him in shock, but he was dead serious, his eyes shadowed.*

"You were Raf's closest friend… and probably the next person in line who understands me the most…."

The pain of Rafael's loss would always remain, and at that moment, we both felt it. I could see it in his eyes, and I knew mine were probably similar. I looked at him and nodded. We may never ever fucking admit it because we were both too proud, but we were both there for the other if the need ever arose. I smirked despite the emotions that consumed me.

"So, guess you're bowing down and accepting that you appreciate me," I mocked cockily.

"Nah, what I appreciate is you making Kiara. She's fucking fine," he smirked arrogantly as I frowned.

Dickhead.

"But, yeah, admitting it or not, I've kinda lost my best man… so I need a fucking replacement."

Our eyes met, and no matter how cold or uncaring his voice sounded, I knew he was still hurting from Rafael's death…

I hadn't told anyone but Scarlett about it, and the surprise from many was to be expected, but the vibrant smile on Kiara's face made me give her a small smile.

"Dad…" she said, looking at Alejandro, her eyes filled with tears.

"Don't cry, or some fuckers may think I'm forcing you to do this shit," Alejandro murmured, making her laugh weakly before he kissed her.

"Alpha… you kiss the bride after the vows," Allen, one of the elder Alphas on the council, said.

"Are you fucking telling me I can't kiss my woman?"

"Ah, not at all, Your Highness…" Allen waved his hand.

"Good, so get a fucking move on. How the fuck am I supposed to not kiss her when she looks this fucking good?"

"Of course!" Allen replied.

"I have no idea who came up with this shit that we wait until the vows are done before a couple can kiss…"

I smirked as I heard Alejandro mutter that last line. Kiara smiled as Alejandro kissed her hands as they exchanged their vows and rings.

"I now pronounce you man and wife. You may kiss -"

Alejandro was already kissing Kiara, bending her backwards. I frowned, glancing at Azura, who was staring wide-eyed until Raven covered her eyes. I had a feeling she was going to be a handful.

A surge of petals rained down upon us, and everyone cheered. I glanced around, looking at all the familiar faces in the crowds. Kiara's kids… Liam and Raven, Azura, Damon…

My eyes finally fell to my own mate, looking like the goddess she was as she sat there, standing out from the crowd. My damn queen…

Our eyes met, and she gave me that sexy, teasing smirk of hers. Yes, there was still so much to live for…

KIARA

"So, how does it feel being Mrs Rossi?" Alejandro asked me.

"I like the sound of that," I replied, my gaze dipping to his sexy lips before I kissed him again. His arm was still around me as he motioned to Darien to bring the girls over. Dante ran over, wrapping his arms around my waist.

"Mama, you look amazing!" He exclaimed. I knelt down, pulling him into my arms, feeling so happy.

"So do you, my love."

I kissed his forehead before standing up as Darien passed the girls to Alejandro. I kissed them both, my little angels. Skyla was trying to tug Alejandro's earring whilst Kataleya simply rested her head on his shoulder. My eyes met Alejandro's, and I smiled warmly. My family, my loved ones, and my mate were right here, and I felt happy.

"Come on, guys, let's get some pictures!" Raven called.

I smiled and nodded. I would make the most of the day with them all because that night, we would leave for our honeymoon, just Al and I, and something told me it was going to be one that I was never going to forget…

A Nicholson Family Dinner

DAMON

*I*T HAD BEEN SIX months since Kiara and Alejandro's wedding, and whilst the king and queen had gone off on a four-week honeymoon, their children had resided at the Black Storm Pack. I heard from Liam that Rayhan had gotten stressed out with Dante just as much as Liam had with Azura when Uncle El and Aunty Red had gone on their trip.

Luckily for me, I got to spend time with my beautiful mate without any kids around, but I was still secretly praying Liam had a kid soon. I did love kids. They were damn cute, and when Robyn was ready, I didn't mind having one myself.

My mate, one who was so damn hardworking and organised. Speaking of…

She stepped out of the bathroom with a cloud of steam, wearing maroon lingerie and a black satin cap on her head.

"Don't look at me like that. I just showered," she replied, despite her heart racing. I tilted my head, winking at her.

"You need to keep your hair mask on for a while anyway…"

"I will get ready in the meantime." She smiled, coming over to me.

She climbed on top of me, claiming my lips in a passionate kiss. I grabbed her ass, pressing her against my hard bulge. I was in nothing but boxer shorts and she felt so fucking good. She smiled, pulling away despite feeling my hard shaft against her core.

"Not today, handsome." She smiled, kissing my neck tenderly. "Tonight we are having guests, remember? There's a lot to do."

"Oh, yeah…your brother and Momma and Channing… Momma and Channing have been, uh, staying over at each other's… I heard they may move in together…" I scrunched my nose; I got that there was something there… but to know they were taking the next step…

"They need each other," she replied softly as she began applying her make-up, giving me a fucking good view of her ass that swallowed up that G-string so fucking perfectly. That woman was blessed with curves that would make any woman envious.

"Yeah, I know. Momma's not been happier, and it's nice to see her becoming herself once more." I sat up. *I had so much work to do today.*

"Yes." She turned and looked at me; I didn't miss her eyes dipping to my hard shaft before roaming over the rest of my body. I winked at her, bending down and taking hold of her chin before I kissed her lips.

"What's wrong, beautiful?"

"Nothing… you going to be okay with that?" She asked, and I didn't miss the tell-tale sign of her pressing her legs together.

"Want to take care of it?" I asked huskily. The urge to fuck her right there was consuming me.

"With pleasure…" she whispered.

Although I had a quickie in mind, she had something different… and I was not complaining the moment she dropped to her knees, pulling my boxers down with one swift pull. She licked her lips as she ran her hands over my hard shaft, a groan escaping me the moment her fingers ran along the entire length before she wrapped her hand around it and licked the tip sensually.

Pleasure rushed through me like a fucking tidal wave. I placed my hand on the wall behind her just as her lips wrapped around my tip, and she moaned, swirling her tongue along my dick, sending shuddering rivets of pleasure through me. Fuck…

"That's it, baby girl," I whispered huskily with approval.

She used her hand to pump it as she began to take more and more into her mouth. Her moans and the scent of her arousal filled the air. My pleasure made me thrust into her harder. She looked so fucking sexy crouching before me, those lush thighs of hers parted, her nipples hard against the flimsy fabric of her bra. I leaned down slightly, grabbing her breast and making her whimper.

"Fuck, baby… that's it."

I couldn't stop myself from closing my eyes, revelling in the pleasure that she was inflicting upon me. She was so fucking good at this. I thrust into her mouth harder and faster. The sound of my dick fucking her mouth and our moans were the only things that I could hear as I felt myself nearing. My hands braced on the wall tightly behind her and she gripped my ass with one hand taking me in fully. I hit her throat a few times, fucking her mouth hard and fast, just as I fucking came.

Groaning in fucking euphoria, my thrusts became jerky, and she sucked me off completely, swallowing every drop of my seed as I came down from my high.

Delicious, her breathy voice came through the bond.

"Fucking perfect…" I replied huskily, pulling out and tugging her to her feet. My arms wrapped around her waist, my hand squeezing her ass as I kissed her hard. My orgasm was still sending waves through me, and all I wanted was to kiss her forever. The sweet taste of her mouth was mixed with my own seed, and I didn't really fucking care. It tasted perfect. She tasted perfect.

She moaned against my lips, and I slipped one hand between her thighs, devouring her mouth as I pushed her panties aside, finding her little pearl of pleasure. This girl was fucking heaven…

✨

Late in the evening, Rick was there, along with Momma and Channing. Both were definitely into each other. We had gotten food from out and were seated around the table.

"How you been, Momma?" I asked Mom, thinking I saw her less these days.

"Great. I started working with the team at the hospital and helping set everything up," she said, giving me a small smile. I nodded.

"I'm glad you're keeping yourself busy…." I glanced at Channing, who was smiling.

"We sure are. We're almost done with the final bits and our pack is complete," he said with a nod. Rick nodded as he forked some noodles up.

"We finished as planned on schedule. I think that calls for drinks." He raised his glass of juice.

"It does, only I have Uni tomorrow," Robyn reminded him. I smirked, pulling her close and kissing her.

"I'm sure missing one day won't hurt, right…?"

"I'm not missing Uni." She smiled, and I felt a sense of déjà vu.

"Understood." I smiled back at her, thinking she was passionate about everything she did.

As long as you stay up late tonight… that black dress looks fucking fine on you, baby girl, I remarked through the link.

I'll enjoy you tearing it off later… she replied, her hand smoothly reaching over and caressing my thigh. She paused as if realising something before tilting her head.

"Everything okay?" I asked her, lifting her hand to my lips and kissing it.

"Yeah… what's the date?"

"Twelfth?" I frowned in concern. She nodded.

"Hmm…"

"Is everything okay, Robyn?" Mom asked her.

I had to admit I loved their bond; Robyn had always taken care of Momma, and when she had found out we were mates, she had been in tears out of happiness.

"Yeah…" Robyn said, forcing a smile, but something was wrong. I could feel it through the bond.

"Baby, what is it?"

"Robyn?" Rick asked sharply.

"My period's late," Robyn said, abruptly standing up.

My heart skipped a beat as I realised what she had said. From the time we spent together, she was always on time… heck, twenty-eight-day cycle and then five days on.

"Oh…" Channing said before wriggling his eyebrows. "Do we see another Nicholson on the way?"

"Are you two using anything?" Mom asked worriedly.

"Momma, seriously?" I said as Rick choked on his drink.

"Can we not do this right now?" He cringed. "Robyn?" I looked at her. She was standing there frozen. I got up, pulling her into my arms.

"Hey… whatever it is, we'll deal with it. Maybe it's just a change…" I said, unsure of how to feel. Her reaction was worrying me. I knew she had Uni and plans ahead for so much more. "Excuse us."

I pulled her down the hall and into the bathroom, shutting the door behind us, my heart thudding as I stared at my gorgeous mate who was just… not reacting.

"Baby…" She blinked when I cupped her face and tilted her head up towards mine. "If you aren't ready…" Just the thought that filled my head made my heart sting. She placed her finger on my lips, shaking her head.

"Don't. I'm just… shocked… I mean, I don't know if I am… but if I am, then we'll be fine. I just, I don't want to get excited and then realise it was just a false alarm," she whispered the last part, and it took me a second to realise what she had just said.

"Wait… you don't mind having a baby?" She looked up at me, a smile spreading on that gorgeous face of hers.

"Not really."

I smiled at her, feeling a weight lift from my chest as I cupped her face and kissed her passionately, pulling her into my arms.

I fucking promise to take care of you, through it all, after it, and forever. She pulled away and raised an eyebrow.

"Don't get ahead of yourself, baby, I may not be."

"One way to find out…" I dropped to my knees, closing my eyes as I placed my ear to her stomach. I wasn't sure…

"Nothing?" She asked nervously.

"It's kinda early, I guess. Usually, people pick it up a bit later. We'll go to the doctor's tomorrow." She nodded, and despite how she was feeling, I knew she was trying to keep a level head.

"Well, you know… if you aren't and you want one…" To my surprise, she nodded and smiled shyly. That was a first for Robyn. "Yeah…"

"I never knew you liked kids…" I said, pulling her into my arms once more.

"I never said I didn't. Come on, let's return to the table." I smiled as she opened the door, hand in hand as we walked back to the table.

"Is everything okay?" Mom asked us worriedly.

"Yeah, Momma, we'll go to the hospital tomorrow."

"Or I'll get a pregnancy test… I don't want everyone to know," Robyn murmured, taking her seat again.

"Sounds like a plan. Either way, I'm sure you two will be amazing parents," Channing added. "Besides, I think Moni would really love some grandkids to play with." They smiled at each other, and I realised a child may just be what will keep Mom occupied when Channing, Robyn, and I were working.

"Then make sure you tell us if it's a yes or no," Rick added to his sister, who nodded.

"We sure will," I replied, sitting down and kissing her lips once more…

MONICA

Channing and I had returned to mine; well, it would soon be ours. His children and brother were as understanding of our relationship as my son was. It was just Anna who couldn't stomach it. She was strictly not allowed on Blue Moon territory. When she found out about Channing's new position, she wanted him back. Disgusting. I hoped I didn't have many run-ins with her, I was better off without it. She had cheated on Channing when he was an amazing, selfless man.

I would always love Aaron, and just the thought of him made my heart ache, but I was able to love Channing, too. Perhaps it would never reach the level of love I had for Aaron, but it was enough.

"Want to visit his grave tomorrow?" He asked, pulling me onto the sofa next to him. He was always so understanding. Despite both his legs being destroyed in the battle of Hecate's Betrayal years ago, he had not let it get to him. That man was strong, brave, and always happy. He'd use crutches when needed or his wheelchair, but either way, he never let it get to him. I placed my hand on the top part of his leg, looked into his eyes, and nodded.

"Yeah, tomorrow I will." I rested my head on his shoulder. The pain in my chest was often bearable but then there were moments when it returned with strong force. "Damon and Robyn, it would be amazing if they were going to be parents. I would happily mind the child." He chuckled.

"Oh, I know you would," he said, kissing my forehead.

"Do you think it's going to be a boy or girl?"

"Now that's a tough one. I'd like to say girl, but maybe a boy?"

"Oh, I'd love a girl. I always wanted a daughter. I have Robyn though." I smiled, kissing his cheek softly. "Thank you, Channing, for being you." He gave me a warm smile as I ran my fingers through his hair.

"And thank you for being so perfect." He claimed my lips with his, and although I was far from perfect, for him to look at me with such adoration and love made me feel like I was worth something. I hugged him tightly.

"Thank you."

"Okay, you need to stop thanking me," he remarked, wrapping his strong arms around me and tickling me. I laughed, trying to get away before he stopped and pulled me in front of him. "Moni…"

"Yes?" I asked, looking up at him. He looked serious, and I saw the conflict in his eyes. Whatever it was, it was serious.

"If Anna ever moves on and marks someone… would you allow me to mark you?" He asked quietly.

I looked at him sharply. The rule of marking… Anna was alive so there was no way I could mark Channing, and he couldn't mark me unless he was wearing my mark, or vice versa. Aaron was gone, so his mark could be removed by anyone bearing my mark, but Channing's mark would only be removed if Anna moved on.

I looked at him and smiled before nodding. A few months ago I wouldn't have been able to, but Aaron would always be a part of me, and as much as having his mark gone would hurt… It was something I knew he'd want me to do. I had Damon, my Aaron's son.

"Yes, I would," I whispered, knowing it would also ease the ache in my chest.

"Now I just pray that she goes, finds someone, and marks them." I laughed.

"Isn't that wishing bad on someone else?"

"That's true… maybe she'll find someone as awful as she is," he sighed heavily. "Sometimes it gets draining to be tied to her despite the rejection."

"I know, but I'm sure she will find someone and take a chosen mate."

"And I can't wait for it."

"Me too," I whispered, placing my arms on top of his as I leaned on his shoulder, inhaling his warm, comforting scent. Everything was no longer so dark…

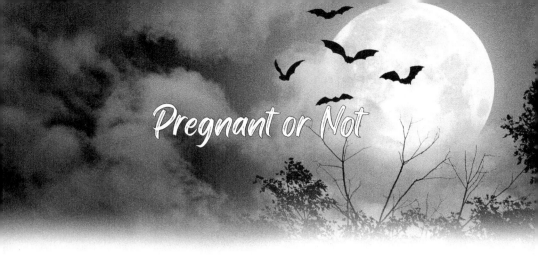

Pregnant or Not

ROBYN

*D*AMON HAD TOLD LIAM about my chance of being pregnant. Those two men could keep nothing from one another. So, he and Raven were there. I was going to pee on a stick and there was an audience to see the results. I wanted to kick Damon's ass, but he was just too cute and excited for me to do that. I stared at the stick that Raven had brought for me first thing in the morning.

"You should do one," I said suddenly as she giggled with excitement.

"Oh, I'm not pregnant." She waved me off. I raised an eyebrow. Well, I hadn't seen her for like two weeks, and I swore her stomach looked a little round…

"You might be." I shrugged, sighing as I unboxed the test, glaring at the two men.

The only good thing was they had brought an entire box of fresh dough-nuts, pastries, and rolls. Oh, and hot drinks…

"Okay! I'll do this for fun," Raven decided, taking the second packet.

"Love, you're on contraception, remember?" Liam reminded her, raising an eyebrow.

"I'm doing this for moral support for Robyn," Raven replied, hands on her hips as she stared at her mate. I smiled; *Well, I guess it's better than just one of us doing it.* "Want me to go first?" I nodded.

"Yes, please."

I could feel Damon's eyes on me as both men sat there, eating the sugary treats. Why did they still look so good even when they ate such high-calorie foods? Raven came out of the bathroom quite quickly, placing the stick flat on the paper towel I had placed ready on the cabinet.

"You got this," Damon said, coming over to me and kissing me softly. I nodded and took a deep breath, deciding to go do mine.

A few minutes later, it was time to take a look at my test. I took a deep breath, ready to look at the results, when my eyes fell on Raven's stick, the one that everyone seemed to have forgotten about. I smiled slightly at the two clear lines on the stick.

"What does it say?" Damon asked, coming over. My eyes snapped to my test and my heart skipped a beat.

Pregnant.

"Umm, you might want to sit down," I replied solemnly. "It's not what you guys were expecting." Damon's eyes softened and he smiled.

"It's okay." He was about to come over, but Raven was watching me with her eyes wide, and I knew she was trying to gauge my reaction.

"It sure is… because soon the both of you are going to be on daddy duties," I said, holding up both sticks. Damon froze, his eyes flying wide open before he rushed towards me and lifted me off my feet, spinning me around as he laughed in excitement.

"Damn girl, I… fuck, I don't even know what to say.…" I smiled, locking my arms around his neck.

"You don't need to say anything at all…" I whispered before kissing him. The excitement I felt inside was far too much to put into words. Oh, Goddess, we were going to be parents!

I was so thrilled, I kissed him with everything I had as he rocked me from side to side, his heart pounding, and even as he kissed me that smile never left his lips.

"Goddess, I can't wait to have a mini-you to hold," he whispered, kissing me again. I smiled, hugging him tightly before I glanced at the other couple, who were both standing there, staring at each other. Liam looked stunned, and perhaps a little pale.

"Guys?" I said, snapping them from their trance.

"I'm pregnant! Wow!" Raven suddenly exclaimed, blinking.

"Wow, indeed. You were on your pills…" a dazed Liam responded, shell-shocked.

"Hmm… religiously. The doctor gave them…" Raven murmured.

"Did you forget any?" Damon asked.

"No…"

"Yeah, she didn't…" Liam mused.

"I guess it didn't work since you are a Deimos prince," I replied thoughtfully. "Maybe just like a Lycan doesn't need to mark someone to get them pregnant, perhaps similarly the contraception wasn't enough…"

"Wait, what?" Liam asked, shocked. He was a smart man, but a little clueless.

"Just an assumption, but it could be that the medicine wasn't strong enough to stop your sperm," I said, making Raven's eyes widen as she nodded.

"That makes sense…" Damon murmured as Liam ran his hand through his hair that had seconds earlier been styled to perfection.

Oh, dear Alpha, you won't have time to style that head of yours once your child comes along.

"Shit, I had a dream and there were kids all around…" Liam shuddered as Raven walked over to him and cupped his face.

"We'll be okay."

He nodded, giving her a small nervous smile as he pulled her into his arms and kissed her forehead.

"Well, I think I'll book us in for a scan. It's best we know how far along we are," I remarked.

"It will have to be over at Blood Moon. Our maternity unit is still not finished," Damon remarked.

I nodded as Liam whistled. I glanced at him, thinking although his hearing wasn't as good as the Lycan king's, surely, he must have noticed Raven's tiny physique looking a little round around the stomach. Then again, Liam was a little clueless.

I wonder if there's two in there for her to be showing slightly…

RAVEN

The following day we were both at the hospital, Robyn had just had her scan, and I was so nervous and excited all at once! A little Liam! That was going to be so cute! Seeing Robyn's little bean had been incredible, and watching Damon smile as he held her hand made my heart melt. She deserved him. They were perfect together.

"Okay, Luna, come," Doctor Jenson motioned for me.

"Okay!"

I gave Liam a quick kiss, getting onto the bed once she had put a new paper sheet down. I tugged my top up and lowered my pants slightly.

"You got a belly," Damon remarked, making me stare at my tummy. Now that he mentioned it...

Liam frowned, tilting his head as he stared at my tummy.

"You may be further along than you think," Doctor Jenson replied with a smile as she applied the cold gel. "Let's see..." She began pressing around as I stared at the screen opposite. "My..." Doctor Jenson whispered in awe.

"Goddess..." Robyn gasped, clamping her hand over her mouth as Liam looked at her sharply. I stared at the doctor and then back at the screen, where there was clearly a womb that did not look normal. It looked....

"Doctor, why does that look so..." I began, my heart thudding.

"Fuck..." Damon whistled.

"Luna... Alpha, as you can see, you aren't having just one pup. Congratulations, you are having quintuplets! This is a miracle!" She exclaimed, a huge smile on her face.

My heart plummeted as I stared at the screen before me. Quintuplets....

"Five pups, Alpha," she said, staring at Liam, who was frozen, his hand holding mine, but he hadn't reacted.

"Liam?" I whispered, feeling far too stunned to wrap my head around it.

He still didn't reply, his face pale, his deep blue eyes wide as he stared ahead, completely still, far too shocked at the news that he was soon to be a father of five. And then, the next thing I knew, my six-foot-four handsome giant crashed to the floor.

My Alpha had fainted.

Goddess.

LIAM

Two hours had passed, and I was still stunned. I vaguely heard Damon tell the doctor not to pass the news on to anyone, that Raven and I would do that ourselves. I couldn't believe I fucking fainted... but it still couldn't be real, right? Five pups?

Goddess.

"Are you okay?" Raven asked me, cupping my face as I sat on the hospital bed. The sparks from her touch rippled through me. I closed my eyes, pulling her between my legs and resting my head against her breasts for a moment.

"Yeah… fuck, I mean, I should be asking you that." I looked up at her, concerned, my eyes skipping over her tiny frame; how the fuck was that even going to work?

I ran my hands down her waist. Despite the shock, there was a spark of excitement inside of me. Raven and I were actually having a pup together. Scratch that – *pups*. I looked up into her gorgeous eyes, raking my fingers through her hair.

"How the hell are you going to carry five?" I asked, tugging her close and kissing her softly.

"I'm sure I'm capable. I told you; I might be small, but I'm tough," Raven said, smiling at me. "I guess… we're going to be parents pretty soon, huh…?"

"Yeah… soon." I pulled her onto my lap, wrapping my arms around her tightly. "Are you really okay?" She raised an eyebrow.

"I am. I'm shocked… but I'm more worried about you," she replied, caressing my jaw. I sighed.

"One kid is hard, five…. but we'll manage somehow."

"We will!" She replied confidently. "So, how about we go and share the news with your family? And I want to tell Taylor, too."

I nodded, kissing her again. Although she seemed shocked, the excitement was there. Even though I was a mess of emotions about having children, I still could imagine having our pups in my arms. It didn't sound too bad…

୨୧

"What is it?" Mom asked, looking concerned.

Her gaze flitted between us both as she stood up from where she had been sitting, ruffling her hair. We had gone straight to their home from the hospital to break the news.

"We have a gift for you," Raven proclaimed, holding out the envelope with the scan image inside.

"A gift?" Mom asked, taking it and about to open it when Raven waved her hand, stopping her.

"Open it together."

"Yeah, a gift. Good luck," I added jokingly. I hoped they were ready for grandparents' duties…

They exchanged looks before Azura came running over.

"Is it a pwesent for me too, Waven?" She asked as Dad lifted her onto his lap, kissing her forehead.

"Yes, it is!"

Mom slid the image out, tilting her head. A frown creased her face as Dad's eyebrows shot up. *Yup… slowly processing it.…*

"Uncle, Aunty, congratulations! I'm pregnant with five pups," Raven announced, placing a hand on her stomach. Her words made my heart thud, and I tugged her into my arms, placing my hand over hers. My tiny bite-sized Luna…

"Holy…" Dad's eyes widened as Raven's words registered, whilst Mom's eyes blazed silver as she stared at Raven and then back at the image in her hands.

"Five babies! Five small Wiyam's and Waven's! I love it!" Azura screamed, making Mom and Dad both snap out of whatever shock they were in.

"Oh, my goddess!" Mom jumped up, pulling Raven from my arms and hugging her. "That's ju- that's amazing! I mean, oh my goddess. *Five?* How is that even possible? It's so rare! Oh, Goddess, what did the doctors say? It can't be safe, we need Kiara, or you need to go to Kiara. She needs to make sure all six of you are safe. Oh, my goddess, six of you! You are a family of seven now! Oh my…"

I smiled slightly at Mom's panic and excitement. Dad sat there stunned, not even bothered by Azura's jumping on the sofa whilst screaming and laughing like a crazy lunatic.

"Five… good luck," he now spoke, smiling slightly. "Congratulations."

He stood up, giving me a hug, and I couldn't resist smiling back as we stepped back. Mom was still smothering Raven with hugs and kisses.

"Let her breathe, kitten," Dad murmured, tugging Mom away from Raven before he smirked at us both. "I thought I had it bad with two, but we have an entire pack ready to help out, and, of course, Red and I won't mind helping. Liam wasn't a bad kid, so, hopefully, Karma won't come back to bite you two in the ass… but then again, Raven, on the other hand… all I'm going to say is may the goddess help you both."

"Uncle, that's not nice," Raven pouted as Dad hugged her, planting a kiss on her forehead.

"You were a little minion. An adorable little devilish one, though," he smirked, looking down at her as she stuck her tongue out. "See? You haven't changed." He didn't let go of her as Mom hugged me tightly, saying how excited she was.

"Azura, baby, are you excited to become an aunty?" She asked her.

"I a big girl. I take care of your babies, okay?" She said with such determination that I felt a little worried.

"You sure can," I said, although I thought she was just going to lead the little army to mischief.

She smiled up at me and I picked her up. Regardless of how naughty she was, I loved her, and I knew I was going to love these five, too. I glanced over at Mom asking Raven how she was feeling, what to avoid, and how she was going to be there for her every step of the way. We were going to be okay. Raven's and my eyes met, and she blushed, lightly smiling.

I love you, darling, and I know you are going to be an amazing bite-sized mama.

Love you, too… we will be okay, baby.

I nodded at her reply as Mom hugged her again, happiness and excitement clear in her eyes…

❧❦❧

It was evening and we were about to video call Kiara. We had already told Zack and Taylor; Taylor had been so shocked before it had turned to excitement, whilst Zack just looked stunned, saying he was glad Taylor wasn't a woman.

"I wonder how Kiara will take it," Raven whispered, her oversized jumper sliding off one of her shoulders. I kissed her neck softly just as the call was answered to reveal not only Kiara, but Alejandro, his arm around her shoulder as he smoked a cigarette. I would never have ever thought that the Lycan King would be my brother-in-law… it was still weird that he was mated to my sister.

"Hey, guys," Kiara said, smiling at us both whilst raising her eyebrows at Raven. "What is it?"

"Yeah, make it fast," Alejandro added coldly, wrapping his hand that was holding his cigarette around Kiara's neck before he kissed her ear.

"Well... I'm pregnant," Raven stated, looking at me. Goddess, she was beautiful. Kiara gasped, her eyes sparkling with excitement.

"Oh, my goddess! Aah!" She screamed, bouncing on her seat as she clamped her hand over her mouth. "I'm so happy!"

"Told you it's going to be that shit. Welcome to the world of no fucking privacy," Alejandro remarked with a smirk.

"Listen here, big boy, that's not even the main news," Raven pouted. Alejandro raised an eyebrow whilst Kiara couldn't stop smiling.

"Is it twins?" She asked suddenly, looking at me and smiling happily.

"No... it's quintuplets." Raven blurted out. Kiara's smile vanished, her eyes widening, and even Alejandro looked shocked, although he covered it up fast.

"Wow, guess you guys are actual fucking animals. That's a whole fucking litter," he snickered, and I frowned at him.

"Alejandro... be nice!" Kiara scolded. "Guys, that's amazing! But, hun, you need to take it easy; I'm going to visit and check up on how you're doing. I'm going to be there. Dustin, one of our Deltas, his mate had quads, and it was amazing! This is even more mind-blowing... babe, I need to see them! Do you have a picture?"

"Now, all night, she's going to be fucking gushing about these pups, although I'd rather you be gushing -" Kiara slammed her hand over his mouth, her cheeks flushing, and I sighed. Seriously that guy had no filter. I did not need to know that.

"We have a picture," I changed the subject smoothly, picking it up and holding it to the screen.

"And I'll send it to you, too," Raven chirped in.

"That looks fucking strange. Makes me wonder if I have trypophobia or some shit like that," Alejandro remarked as Kiara frowned at him before admiring the image.

"They are gorgeous!" She cooed.

"Aren't they?" Raven smiled happily.

"Um, they're just beans..." I added, confused as to what they were finding cute.

"Women are weird as fuck," Alejandro added, and for once, I kinda realised that I actually did agree that women could be a little strange. I nodded as the girls talked about some vitamins or something.

"Make sure you get Elijah to look after them. He ain't got nothing better to do anyway with his time," he snickered.

"Or are you just sad Uncle got to retire when you're only six years younger than him?" Raven piped in.

"Nah, I'm definitely not as fucking old as him."

"Well, we are definitely coming down because, girl, I need to see you in person," Kiara said before she smiled at me. "They are going to be perfect."

I nodded. Yeah, regardless of everything, I knew they were going to be fucking perfect.

The Struggle

FOUR MONTHS LATER…

RAVEN

*P*REGNANCY WAS HARD. I felt exhausted, and I could barely walk, sit up, or do anything. My back ached continuously, and I was actually going to be leaving for Kia's pack in a week or two as I was nearing the end of my pregnancy, and everyone agreed I needed her by my side. It was a lot harder for her to come here, so Liam and I would go there whilst Uncle El and Aunty Red would run the pack in our absence.

News had spread that the Blood Moon Pack's Luna was going to have quintuplets, and I knew it was more of a spectacle than anything else. I refused to go to events as I didn't want to see anyone. *Goddess! I'm not something to stare at!*

I looked over at Robyn with her normal-sized bump. She was due around the same time as me. She was further along than I was, but due to mine being a multiple-child pregnancy, I was probably going to have them first.

"You okay, babe?" She asked me.

I nodded, although I couldn't even see my lap… I had liked my belly when it was smaller, but it felt like all I was was this big round hot air balloon.

"Hey, ladies," Damon said, coming over with some ice cream cones. He passed Robyn one, kissing her lips before smiling at me and passing me the second cone. I frowned, taking it. Wasn't I already fat? "It's not poisoned, Raven," he said with a smile, caressing Robyn's stomach as he kissed her again.

"I didn't say it was," I replied, knowing I sounded snappy. "Sorry…"

"It's all good, I'm used to it." He winked at me until Robyn turned her head sharply to him.

"Excuse me? What do you mean used to it?"

"Oh, hey, I didn't mean it like that," he said, making her frown deeper.

"You insinuated that you are used to being snapped at," she replied icily. I nodded in agreement.

"She isn't wrong," I added before leaving them to their argument.

We were currently at our place, and Liam was cooking, but he was taking forever! A knock on the door made me turn.

"I'll get it," Liam called.

Well, obviously. I hated getting up.

My eyes followed him to the door, my eyes on that sexy ass of his. I hated how we weren't able to have sex as much anymore. I just felt horrible. No matter how doting Liam was towards me, I still felt so big and uncomfortable.

He opened the door to reveal Taylor and Azura.

"Hey, our princess wanted to come over, so I thought I'll pop in to see my favourite girls," Taylor said as Azura ran over to me, and I smiled.

"Waven, how are my babies?" Azura asked, hurrying over and kissing my belly five times. I smiled, giving her a hug.

"They are completely fine," I replied.

"And how are you, Waven?" She asked, her eyes full of concern. "Mama said not to bother you today, so I promise I won't."

"You never bother me, Zuzu. I'm great, and so are the babies." I gave her a cuddle as she turned to Robyn.

"Hello, Wobyn." She waved and quickly planted a kiss on Robyn's stomach, too.

"Hello, princess." Robyn smiled at her, and I didn't miss Damon's look of relief that Robyn was distracted. Taylor gave me a cuddle before sitting down next to me.

"Want me to massage your shoulders?" He asked. I knew seeing me pregnant made them all sympathise with me, but I was okay most of the time, and I didn't want them fussing over me.

"It's okay, Liam did that not long ago." I smiled at him. "Where's Zack?"

"Working," Taylor replied with a pout. "So, are you guys not going to find out the genders?"

"We already have," Damon said, caressing Robyn's thigh.

"But we are keeping it a surprise for now," Robyn replied. Taylor pouted.

"You won't even tell me?" Robyn smiled slightly.

"Nope, it's a surprise until the baby shower."

I had a feeling Liam knew because he and Damon didn't have secrets, but I had not asked Liam, knowing that he would tell me, and I wanted to respect Robyn's wish.

"That's unfair. I love babies." Taylor said, looking at me. "And I know you said you're keeping them a surprise. Still sticking to that?"

"Yes, we are," I replied, looking over at Liam, who was plating the food. Goddess, he looked so sexy working in the kitchen. He turned and gave me a sexy wink.

Looking beautiful, love. I gave a small smile; I didn't feel beautiful.

"Oh, no, Waven, why are you not wearing makeup?" Azura said suddenly.

"I'm too tired," I replied. She looked at Liam over in the kitchen before shaking her head, her eyes full of worry.

"But Wiyam said you need makeup because you look ugly with no makeup," he told me. The clang of something falling in the kitchen area made my eyes snap to Liam.

"Did he now?"

"I only said that to get her to stop wearing makeup," he said quickly, his eyes wide as he stared at me. I frowned unhappily.

"Yeah, nice," I said coldly. "Taylor, babe, help me up."

"Raven…" Liam came over as Azura simply shook her head, sighing.

"Don't." I suddenly felt really emotional. I already felt awful and unsexy, and that didn't help matters.

"I sorry, Waven," Azura said, realising I felt upset.

"Oh, Zuzu, don't be. You did and said nothing wrong. I just need to go lay down for a bit," I replied as Taylor helped me off the sofa.

"Love." Liam tugged me into his arms, glancing at Taylor, who refused to let go unless I said so. I smiled at him. Now, that was a good friend.

"I'm tired, Liam. I want to go lay down until dinner," I said quietly as Taylor let go of me.

"Not when you're angry at me," he said softly, lifting me up bridal style with ease and carrying me to the bedroom.

I didn't reply, knowing the tears would come if I spoke. He placed me down on the bed as if I was the most precious thing to him. No matter how huge or weird I looked, he still looked at me with adoration.

"Talk to me, love," he whispered. Kneeling down by the bed, he took my hands and kissed them tenderly.

"I'm fine, I just, how could you say I look ugly without make-up when I feel ugly as it is?" I pressed my lips together, refusing to cry.

"I really just wanted Azura to stop messing with your make-up. It happened months ago, before you were pregnant! I don't even know how the hell she still remembered that," he replied with annoyance.

"Hey, don't blame her, okay?" I scolded. He got up, claiming my lips in a passionate kiss, not giving me even a moment to breathe.

"I don't care what you think, but you are far from ugly, goddess. Baby girl, you are a miracle right now," he whispered huskily, moving back and caressing my hair. "You are carrying our little pups. Carrying one child isn't easy, and you're here with five. You are still the most breathtaking woman on this planet, and you're mine."

My heart melted at his words, and suddenly I hugged him, turning my body so that my stomach wasn't in the way. He was right. This moment was special. I just felt so emotional at times...

"Thanks, Liam," I whispered. He wrapped his arms around me and kissed the top of my head.

"Not long left, and then it's going to be a hell of a lot crazier, but I promise it'll be easier. I'll do my best to take the load off you because right now, I can't do that." He placed a hand on my stomach, and I felt a movement inside. Every time he touched my stomach, and the sparks of the bond coursed through me, the pups would react to his touch.

"I know you will, and you have been so amazing. Don't think I don't notice you massaging my back or legs when I'm asleep," I said, caressing his face before kissing him softly. "I do appreciate you, blue eyes. Even when I'm annoyed and irritated."

"I know. Now, how about we go back out there, and I give you an amazing foot massage after we eat?" He suggested.

I nodded and he gave me that gorgeous smile of his, lifting me up bridal style and carrying me back out to the living room...

A Miracle

LIAM

THE DAY HAD FINALLY arrived. Our pups were on the way.

"That's it, Raven, you got this, hun," Kiara encouraged, holding her hand. Her purple aura swirled around her as Raven breathed steadily, pain contorting her face as she pushed. "And again! Almost here, babe, you're doing amazingly."

My heart was racing, and seeing her in this much agony was tearing me to shreds inside. *She was going to have to do this five times? Fuck this wasn't fair.*

"I'm okay," Raven whispered to me, her face scrunched in pain before she pushed once more. I caressed her clammy forehead, my other hand holding hers tightly. Her nails dug into my skin, drawing blood, but I wished I could take away the pain she was in.

"Almost there, Luna," one of the midwives added.

We were in Kiara's pack, having spent the last ten days here. Raven let out a scream as she pushed with all her might, and the sound of a cry filled the room. I kissed her forehead as her head dropped back on the pillow, my attention turning to the first of our pups.

"It's a boy. Congratulations," the midwife said.

"A boy," Raven whispered, smiling weakly.

"He's beautiful," Kiara murmured softly. Her eyes, like Raven's, filled with tears of happiness.

The nurse brought our little pup over to Raven, despite her wincing as another contraction ripped through her. She kissed our son softly, and I quickly gave him a kiss; he was gorgeous, so tiny, and his head was full of black hair. He was taken away and wrapped up in a blanket. My gaze followed him until Kiara told Raven to push again.

"The next one is ready to come out, hun. You are doing amazing," she encouraged softly. Raven nodded as she began to push, stopping when Kiara told her to.

"I'm so fucking sorry you are going through this," I whispered, trying to push away the pain in my chest at her agony.

She didn't reply, trying to give me a smile, only to bite her lip as pain shot through her. Four more to go...

"Push, Luna, you got this," the midwife encouraged as Kiara held her hand. I knew she was waiting for any dip in Raven's stats to heal her.

Our hearts were pounding with nerves, and no matter how beautiful the moment was, it was also painful. I didn't like seeing her in such agony. *Goddess, please make it easy for her.*

"Liam... Liam!"

I snapped my gaze to Kiara only to realise my own aura was swirling around me dangerously.

"Sorry..." I said, reigning it in as I kissed Raven's forehead.

I brushed her hair back but was unable to ignore the tears that streamed out of the corner of her eyes. I brushed them away as she let out a half-scream, half-groan, and then, the sound of another baby crying. I heard Kiara laugh softly.

"Another gorgeous baby boy!"

I turned as she brought the baby to us, a head full of light hair. He instantly stopped crying when Raven pressed her lips to his cheek gently. I smiled, reaching over and caressing his cheek before he too was taken away.

Three more...

"You got this," I encouraged softly, pressing my lips to hers. She kissed me back weakly, but she still nodded with determination...

Another twenty minutes later, the cry of our fifth child filled the room.

"Another boy," Kiara announced, a huge smile on her face as she placed the boy in Raven's arms, kissing her forehead. "You did amazing, hun. I'm so proud of you." Raven smiled up at her, her eyes glistening with tears.

"Thank you... for being here with me for the last two days," she said softly.

I watched them, glad of the bond they had. My hand never left Raven's head, even when she took her hand from mine to hold our youngest son.

"Always." Kiara replied, "I'll get the others over here for you."

"How you feeling, love?" I asked her.

"Kia's healed me, I just feel exhausted," she replied.

"Thank the goddess," I whispered, pressing my forehead to hers for a moment.

"Two for you, Liam," Kiara said, passing me two wrapped-up babies.

I knew one was the firstborn, but I wasn't sure about the second. They all looked different from one another, yet there were some similarities.

"I think this one is going to have blue eyes..." Raven murmured, looking down at the youngest, his hair as dark as Raven's. "Can we name him Renji?" Her question took me by surprise, but I smiled softly.

"Yes." She returned my smile with a beautiful one of her own.

"Thank you," she whispered.

We'd had a few names of both genders, but we did not have five boy names. I don't think either of us thought we'd have five of one gender, and Raven had said she wanted Mom and Dad to choose one name each, too.

"No, thank you for being such an incredible woman and mate," I replied, sitting on the bed next to her as Kiara gave two more babies to her without their blankets so they could get some skin-to-skin. Seeing Raven with three kids was... crazy, and then there were the two in my arms...

"I can't believe I have five nephews!" Kiara exclaimed as she came over to me and wrapped her arms around my shoulders.

"Thanks, Kia," I whispered, kissing her cheek.

"Anytime, brother," she replied, smiling happily. "After a short while, we'll switch skin to skin for these two. Then you can get cleaned up. Mom and Dad are on their way." I nodded, knowing Raven needed her rest too. "I'll give you two some time alone, and I'll break the news to Alejandro," Kiara added as the midwife took away the bloody towels and sheets that had been placed under Raven.

We were soon left alone with our five pups as I sat on the bed next to Raven, and she kissed the top of the three boys' heads she was carrying.

"Can I see those two?" She asked. I placed them closer to her and she broke into tears, alarming me.

"Love..."

"They're so beautiful," she whispered. I wanted to reach over to wipe her tears away, but, damn, both my arms were full.

"Yeah, they are... is it weird that I can't even imagine having even one less right now?"

"No, I feel the exact same way…" I leaned over to kiss her lips.

"I think we're done, though, forever," I chuckled.

"Never say never! I want a girl, too," Raven murmured, her gaze on her pups as my eyes widened in shock.

What?

I hoped she'd change her mind in a few months.

❧

We were in a new room, which was a lot bigger and had five cribs. Mom and Dad had just popped in, and although Raven breastfed each one for a short while, they were all topped up on formula before Raven went to shower, leaving us with the five pups.

"Five boys… that's something," Dad said, smiling as he held two of our pups.

"Yeah…" I said, smiling down at Renji.

"Any names?" Mom asked.

"Just this one. He's Renji." Mom and Dad smiled.

"It's perfect," Mom murmured, softly kissing our first-born pup on his forehead. "Don't worry about how you will manage. Apart from the Omegas' help, you will have us there, too."

"I can't believe I'm admitting this, but I'm definitely happy to help," Dad added. "They're all Alphas… I can sense their auras."

"Well, they are Liam's boys."

"I think you forget that we made Liam and Kiara," Dad smirked.

"I actually haven't forgotten that. Making kids -"

"Mom, Dad, I really don't want to hear that," I groaned.

Mom laughed just as Raven re-entered, looking gorgeous as ever and, to my relief, a lot fresher. I got up, instantly placing our pup on the bed, and pulled her into my arms, hugging her tightly.

She hugged me back, and I bent down to kiss her passionately. She cupped my face, kissing me back. Pleasure coursed through me at her touch, and I wouldn't lie; being able to crush her completely against me without her tummy in the way felt great. I held her tighter, never wanting to let go, but when she needed air, I had to pull away.

"I love you," I whispered.

"Love you, too, blue eyes."

I pressed my forehead to hers, never wanting to let her go. My world.

"How are you feeling, Raven?" Mom asked.

"Just a little tired, but Kiara has fixed me up perfectly," Raven replied, brushing a strand of her wet locks out of her face.

"That's good," Mom replied as Dad smiled at Raven.

"You looked damn cute when you were pregnant, like this huge round thing with legs and a head, but I'm glad to see you back to your usual self."

"Thank you for that description, Uncle. I felt like I had been inflated," Raven pouted. Dad smirked,

"You kinda were."

Raven stuck her tongue out, and Dad did the same, displaying his pierced tongue that I often forgot he had. I smiled, looking between them. They had a good bond. Dad stood up and pulled her into his arms, giving her a tight hug.

"You did amazingly. I know how hard twins were for Red to carry and raise, yet here you are, beating that record with five," he said, giving her his trademark smirk. "So, any names for the other four?"

"Not yet... but we wanted you and Mom to choose one," Raven said, smiling up at him.

I glanced at Mom, seeing the smile on her face and hearing the beat of her heart. I knew it wasn't because she was getting to name one of her grandsons but because Raven called her mom. Something Mom had gently asked her months back, but she often still said Aunty. However, the times she'd slipped and said mom, she truly cherished those.

"Hmm, I'd actually like that." Dad nodded with approval. "Which one do I get to name?"

"Any you like." I smiled as Dad walked back to the bed whilst Mom stared down at the baby she was holding.

"Ares... Ares Westwood," she said, her voice thick with emotion. "If you like it of course."

"She already had that one picked out... in hopes she could suggest it to you guys," Dad smirked, making Mom glare at him.

"It's perfect," Raven smiled.

"Jayce," Dad stated, picking up our firstborn. "The future Alpha of the Blood Moon Pack." I smiled at Raven, who wrapped her arms around me, resting her head against my chest.

"It's perfect," she replied happily.

"So we have a Jayce Westwood, an Ares Westwood, a Renji Westwood. Two left," Mom smirked. "Goddess, five…"

"I think their daddy and Kiara should pick those two," Raven said, kissing my chest as she smiled up at me.

"Well, I like Theo," I mused. "This one's Theo." Just then, Kiara entered after a light knock.

"Right on time!" Raven smiled. "We want you to name the last one." She motioned towards our last unnamed pup and Kiara's eyes widened in shock.

"Me?"

"Yes, for everything you have done for us," Raven replied softly. I nodded in agreement as Kiara walked over to the little one, picking him up she kissed his forehead, her eyes full of emotion.

"Carter… if you like it?"

"Absolutely," Raven said, smiling at her before looking at me. I gave my nod of approval before kissing her softly.

And there we had it, the Westwood Alpha quintuplets.

Home & Family

ROBYN

THE WESTWOOD QUINTUPLETS WERE born eleven days before our little princess. Artemis Luna Nicholson. She was beautiful, with grey-blue eyes, black hair, and lashes that curled up perfectly. My beautiful little baby girl. She was a good baby who slept well, I often had to wake her up to feed her myself.

Damon was the perfect partner to have. He willingly took care of her and me, it never felt like he didn't want to do it or let on that he was tired. Even after a long day of work, he didn't let it affect his care for me or our baby.

Being a new Alpha, there were many on the council who didn't like it. He was the second non-alpha born to take the title of 'Alpha', and it was something he had to prove that he was good at. I knew the king didn't like him due to his previous involvement with Kiara; however, at the council, he was fair and just, not letting any of his personal opinions blind his judgement of seeing Damon's capabilities. In fact, he'd even questioned the council as to why Damon wasn't efficient and if they wanted to test his strength to battle it out. Plus, the king had stated that Damon was a better Alpha than half of them there.

Damon was strong and he had worked hard, plus he was given the title by a powerful Alpha, one whose position on the council remained. I knew he would have to constantly prove he was capable, but I had no worries because he was more than capable.

As for our little princess, despite her birth making us both so happy, it gave way to more questions and criticism. If Damon was a true Alpha, then he would have had a male born first. Of course, this was shut down by the first Alpha female herself, Luna Scarlett, stating she was a firstborn and if any Alpha wanted to battle it out on the field, she was willing to show them what an Alpha female was capable of. My little angel was going to be protected by her family and pack. We may be divided into two packs, but we were still one.

Azura, that little princess, doted on Artemis and was so happy she had a name starting with A. She also asked Liam why he didn't have any baby girls and finished by stating that next time Waven should bring five girls. Goddess, I hoped not. Raven had gone through so much. It had been so hard to see her with her huge belly- knowing I'd had it so much easier.

We were having a small get-together at the Westwoods' mansion. Raven and Liam had moved in with them; due to having five pups, it wasn't really ideal to remain at the cottage, and although they were getting their own place made, they wouldn't be moving there for a few years.

I had my little angel dressed in an ivory lace dress, a little matching hairband on her head, and she was good to go. I was in a matching ivory colour, although mine was a bandage dress with an under-boob cut out. Goddess, those things had grown since I was breastfeeding, something I realised Damon didn't mind at all.

"There are my beautiful girls," Damon's sexy deep voice came, coming over and wrapping his strong arms around me as he kissed my neck. "You look beautiful, Ryn."

"Thanks." I turned my head, kissing his lips as I tried not to press into his package.

Sex. That was something that we were surprisingly still finding time for despite having a baby. Artemis was three months old, and I would say we had it easy. I wondered if that would change when she got older, but I'd enjoy whatever I could get.

We had just arrived at the Westwood mansion. Luna Scarlett was wearing a thin-strapped satin red dress. I had often thought red hair and red clothes would clash, but she was just someone who could pull it off with perfection, right down to her red lipstick. Raven, on the other hand, looked gorgeous in a two-toned dress I had seen her wear ages ago at her housewarming dinner. It was the dress Liam had gotten for her for their first date. Looking at her, you wouldn't think she'd had five kids. Guess the werewolf gene helped get us back into shape fast.

"Hey, guys, come on in!" She said as she met us both.

Damon gave her a hug and kiss. I was proud to say I never felt jealous of their bond. He was mine regardless of the past.

The house was a bustle. Zack and Taylor were having a moment; they were a sexy couple, and, well, Taylor, who didn't love him? He actually admitted I scared him a little, to begin with, but we were good friends. Liam's new Delta was there, one I still held a teeny grudge against for taking my place, although I realised it was because I was meant to be Luna.

Monica and Channing were together, and I was happy that Anna left the Blood Moon Pack when she met someone, and then a few weeks later, Channing's mark vanished. Monica actually got a tattoo of Damon's dad's mark done on her collarbone before Channing marked her so her two mates' marks were not far from one another. I was happy for her because she deserved every ounce of happiness she could possibly get. She was great with Artemis, too.

After hugging Rick, I stepped away from everyone greeting each other and looked at the five little Westwood princes who were laid out on the floor on a large playmat with several thick blankets placed beneath them. They were absolutely adorable; Jayce, the eldest, had black hair and green eyes, whilst Theo, the second one, had blond hair with blue eyes. Next was Ares, who had a darker shade of blond hair with hazel eyes. Carter had hair the exact shade of Alpha Elijah's with green eyes, and then there was Renji, with his black hair and blue eyes. Each one looked different and each one had a different personality. Jayce was the most demanding and got angry quickly, whilst Renji was the gentlest and softest. Theo was the type to smile and baby talk when you called him. I planted a kiss on each of their foreheads just as Azura came rushing over.

"Wobyn! I wear the same colour as Artemis!"

"Yes, you are, and you look stunning," I said, giving her a hug.

"I want a picture with her."

"We will surely get a picture," I promised, stroking Theo's hair. Raven came over, holding my little princess, and knelt down next to me.

"Goddess, she is breathtaking," she complimented softly. I smiled as I looked around.

"Life's great, right?" I whispered to Raven. Her eyes sparkled as she nodded.

"It sure is," she replied, placing Artemis in the middle between Theo and Ares. The future of our packs... our legacies.

"Come on, let's get a mocktail," Raven offered, taking my hands as she tugged me up.

Once upon a time, I didn't really have friends or anything, and now I had family, friends, the love of my life and my baby girl...

"I don't trust her with them," Damon said, staring down at the five boys who were as innocent as babies could be.

"Damon!" I scolded while Raven giggled.

"Oh, you should be worried. She's too adorable to be ignored," she teased as Liam shook his head, frowning deeply.

"I hope they're nothing like their granddad..." he mumbled.

Ah... the original Alpha was known for his playboy ways. Well, I would make sure my girl was a badass queen who took no crap from anyone. Liam quickly picked her up as if worried his boys would attack her, making the rest of us burst out laughing.

"Don't worry little one, Uncle Liam's got your back..."

Epilogue

LIAM

"*D*AMON, WATCH IT!" I growled as he kicked the thermos over. Yes, it was closed, but it fell, making a loud sound that made Theo, who had just fallen asleep, wake up with a start.

"Fuck, guys, can you two not even mind six pups?" Zack asked, raising an eyebrow as he stepped into Damon's lounge from the kitchen area eating a fucking sandwich.

"Make yourself useful and feed Carter." He raised an eyebrow.

"I don't know how." Damon, who was currently rocking Artemis and Ares, raised an eyebrow.

"Seriously, Zack?" Zack simply smirked, dropping onto the sofa.

"I'm only here because Tay said to help you two, but I have no clue about kids." He switched the TV on, only for the volume to disturb the two pups who were sleeping on the sofa. Jayce became completely fresh as he stared around him.

Our mates had gone for a spa day out, and there we were with these six, plus Azura... *Help me, Goddess.*

"Fuck, man, just go. I feel like kicking your ass," Damon growled. Zack smirked. I knew he could see we were damn stressed out.

"Just think, this is what your mates deal with."

"Hey, we help a lot. Just not used to doing this alone...." I shot back.

"Has Raven been with them alone?" He asked me as I tried to reign in my Alpha aura.

"Yeah..."

"My point exactly," Zack replied.

Cocky shit.

"Taylor loves kids." Damon said suddenly, "What will you do, because I'm sure he'll want one?" Zack shrugged, munching on his sandwich as I finally managed to make Theo fall back to sleep.

"That's for when the time comes… not right now, and we'll probably adopt, I guess."

"Not planning to use your own sperm and a surrogate?" I asked surprised.

"Nah, I'm good without. I think there are plenty of orphan kids who could use a good home," Zack said, and I almost forgot about his cocky attitude from moments earlier.

"That's true," I said quietly.

"Something stinks." Zack scrunched his nose as Damon and I exchanged looks.

For fuck's sake, don't tell me one of these lot has done a shit. I swear, the amount of diapers they go through is so fucking much. It's diapers day in and day fucking out…

"It's not these two," Damon replied with relief.

"Oh, fucking hell." I glanced around, realising the smell was coming from Jayce. He stared back at me with a look that I swore was saying, 'Serves you right, Dad'.

"Diaper duties, huh?" Zack smirked. "Where the hell are the Omegas?"

"Well, they would be here if Damon didn't say that minding kids wasn't too fucking hard, and then your damn mate suggested we mind them," I growled.

"So Damon should change the diaper," Zack offered.

"Hell no. Your pup," Damon replied. "Besides, I've only changed Artemis. Aren't boys like, harder?"

"What the fuck, man? You're a guy with a damn dick," Zack replied.

"Yeah, well, his shit's going to be all over."

I sighed, listening to them both. Fuck. Azura came over, holding out a diaper and wipes.

"Here, Wiyam, now change Jaycy Waycy's nappy," she commanded.

Was I really the fucking Alpha? I was not so fucking sure anymore. Changing a diaper didn't make me any less of one, but fuck, I hated that job. We sat down on the ground, and I placed Jayce on the changing mat and then undid the nappy. *Fuck, Raven, I need you... or Mom... why isn't Mom here?*

"Wiyam, what's that?" Azura asked, pointing at Jayce's bits.

I narrowed my eyes. I was sure she asked Raven and Mom the same question... what they replied, though, I had no fucking clue.

"It's just something wrong with him," I said, making Zack and Damon look at me like I was a fool. But what the fuck did they expect me to explain to Azura about guy bits?

"Oh, no, Jayce has something wrong with him?"

"Don't be so dramatic. Didn't you ask Mom and Raven? What did they say?" I asked, flinching as I grabbed several wipes, wiping the brat's ass.

"Mama said it's because he's a boy. Boys are so strange. Why do they have an extra toe there?"

"Toe. I'm dead," Zack snickered.

"They just do. The goddess made them like that," I replied. Why was I having this conversation with my sister?

"Oh, dear, the goddess made boys so ugly. Wiyam, do you have an extra toe there?" The boys cackled like fucking hags, and I glared at them.

"No, I don't," I have way more than a fucking thumb. "But Damon and Zack do."

"Oh, so are you a girl then, Liam?"

Fuck, that backfired...

The boys couldn't stop their fucking snickering as I glared at Azura before looking away, not wanting to fucking make her cry.

"I'm not a girl."

"Then you have a toe?" Azura persisted. I swear she knew she was messing with me...

"Yes, I have a damn toe," I gave in, displeased. "Now, did Mama not teach you not to talk about things like that?"

"Oh no, Mama said it's good to talk about everything." Azura nodded fervently.

"Yeah, Liam, it's good to talk about everything," Damon smirked.

"Jayce has an ugly toe." She shook her head as I closed the damn diaper.

Next time: No fucking changing diapers in front of her. Why the hell did Mom entertain her?

"Chill out, dude, you're so fucking old school," Zack smirked as I dunked Jayce in his arms and went to soap my hands. Kids sure were gross.

"Wiyam is very old school," Azura agreed.

"Do you even know what that means, pumpkin?" I asked, drying my hands and returning to the lounge area. *It's a fucking tip... how the fuck did it get messy when these kids can't even walk yet?*

"I don't know." Azura shrugged, raising her hands before kissing Theo, who was meant to stay asleep!

"Azura, let him sleep. Come on, pumpkin," I almost begged.

"He's awake now, Wiyam."

Obviously, you just woke him up...

"Zack, why the hell did you leave that empty can there...?" I growled, spotting the one on the table.

"He's worse than a fucking woman," Zack remarked as Damon snickered, slowly trying to lower Artemis into her Moses basket.

"Fuck, she just puked..." he groaned.

"Shit, didn't you burp her?" Zack asked, grabbing a wipe. I looked at them, frowning as Damon just wiped her up. It was a lot...

"She needs changing."

"I can't fucking change her, man," Damon complained. I sighed, *You can't leave a kid with sick on their clothes... that's gross.*

"I'll do it."

And that was how I ended up having to change the little doll. She seemed more fragile than the boys, but she sure was a fat little thing with leg and arm rolls. She was damn cute. She had been bigger at birth, but the boys were definitely bigger.

Once she was all dressed, I began cleaning the lounge, putting both Damon and Zack on feeding duties. I swear if this place stayed a mess and Robyn saw it, she'd cry.

Two hours, six diapers, and three vomit projectiles later, the pups were all asleep whilst Azura was watching *Ben and Holly* on TV. I dropped onto the sofa with a mug of coffee.

"You're pretty good at this..." Damon remarked.

"He is. I guess three months of minding five helps," Zack agreed.

"I don't think we'll ever become pros... but our mates went through hell and back to birth them. They gave up a lot and carried them for the entire pregnancy. The least we can do is let them have a getaway and know that the house won't be a fucking mess and that the pups are clean, fed, and safe in their absence," I said, gulping down my coffee and placing my mug down before closing my eyes.

"Good point..." Damon agreed.

I think it's okay if I shut my eyes for a few moments...

The moment I was about to doze off, Jayce's loud cry erupted in the air, and like a domino effect, every single pup began crying. I opened my eyes, exhaling deeply as both Zack and Damon got up, grabbing two pups each. I got up, picking up the last two.

Here we go again... just an hour left...

❧

RAVEN

"We need to do this again," I commented, feeling so good after that massage.

"Oh, definitely. Those facials were the best," Taylor said, brushing his finger along his cheek.

"I just hope we can... the men didn't even complain..." Robyn added, uncertain, as she passed me the pizzas.

"I'm sure that's because they didn't want to worry us," I replied as Robyn unlocked her apartment door.

I was a little scared, too. What were we going to see inside? Was it going to be a mess? I peered around the pizza boxes as Taylor held the drinks and paper bags. Robyn took a few boxes from me as we all stared inside...

To our shock, the place was sparkling. The light aroma of oils from the diffuser scented the air. The place was spotless, and each man held one baby whilst three were playing on the carpet with Azura sat colouring.

"Wow," Robyn said. She was the first to speak, and I felt sorry for her, knowing that she had been the most worried.

"Babe." Damon was up and came over, pulling her into his arms and kissing her hard as she tried to balance the boxes she was holding.

I placed the pizza boxes on the kitchen worktop as Liam slowly placed Renji down and came over to me, lifting me off my feet and kissing me passionately.

Baby! I exclaimed through the link, my core throbbing as his tongue slipped into my mouth, his hand squeezing my ass. I moaned against his lips, trying to suppress it and failing as I tangled my hand into my handsome man's hair, and I kissed him back harder. *Oh, goddess...*

I fucking missed you, love.

"I missed you, too," I whispered when we broke apart, praying no one could smell how turned on I was right then.

"So, we got pizzas, and it seems you boys managed the kids perfectly," Taylor remarked as he broke away from Zack. "By the way, babe, you looked gorgeous holding a kid."

Zack simply raised an eyebrow; I didn't think he was ready to be a dad yet, but when they were ready, I was sure they were going to be amazing parents!

"Well, as the kids are settled, shall we eat?" Robyn suggested. "But I'm surprised the place is clean..."

"Thank Liam for that. He is a clean freak."

"It's a good thing," both Liam and Robyn said at the same time. They smiled at each other as I walked over to greet the kiddies.

Our perfect life...

Liam Westwood

Raven Jacobs

Damon Nicholson

Robyn Mclay

OTHER WORKS

THE ALPHA SERIES
Book 1 – Her Forbidden Alpha
Book 2 – Her Cold-Hearted Alpha
Book 3 – Her Destined Alpha
Book 4 – Caged between the Beta & Alpha
Book 5 – King Alejandro: The Return of Her Cold-Hearted Alpha

THE ROSSI LEGACIES
Book 1 – Alpha Leo and the Heart of Fire
Book 2 Leo Rossi, The Rise of a True Alpha
Book 3 – The Lycan Princess and the Temptation of Sin

THE UNTOLD TALES OF THE ALPHA AND LEGACIES SERIES
A collection of short novellas.
Book 1 – Beautiful Bond
Book 2 – Precious Bond

MAGIC OF KAELADIA SERIES
Book 1 – My Alpha's Betrayal: Burning in the Flames of his Vengeance
Book 2 – My Alpha's Retribution: Rising from the Ashes of his Vengeance

STANDALONES
His Caged Princess
Mr. CEO, Please Marry My Mommy
His Dark Obsession

THE RUTHLESS KING'S TRILOGY
Book 1 – The Alpha King's Possession
Book 2 – The Dragon King's Seduction (Coming 2023)

SOCIAL MEDIA PLATFORMS
Instagram: Author.Muse
Facebook: Author Muse

AUTHORS SUPPORTING AUTHORS
Jessica Hall – Fated to the Alpha (Kindle)

Printed in Great Britain
by Amazon

39194647R00324